Clare Dowling was born in I   1968. She trained
as an actress and has worked   tre, film and radio.
She has had drama and children s fiction published and
she writes scripts for Ireland's top soap, *Fair City*. She
lives in Dublin and is married with one son and one
daughter.

Praise for Clare Dowling's novels:

'Commercial fiction at its most entertaining . . . a very
satisfying read' Marian Keyes

'Very funny and original' Cathy Kelly

'Will leave you with a positive and uplifting feeling at
the end' *Irish Tatler*

'Very warm, very funny . . . witty and refreshingly honest'
Irish World

'For Sheila O'Flanagan and Cathy Kelly fans, a warm,
Irish, poignant read' *Bookseller*

'What sets this apart is the quality of the writing. It is
great fun, a great read' RTÉ

Also by Clare Dowling

Fast Forward

Expecting Emily

and

Amazing Grace

Clare Dowling

headline

EXPECTING EMILY first published by
Poolbeg Press Ltd Dublin in 2001
First published in the UK excluding Northern Ireland in 2002
by HEADLINE BOOK PUBLISHING

AMAZING GRACE first published
by Poolbeg Press Ltd Dublin in 2003
First published in the UK excluding Northern Ireland in 2003
by HEADLINE BOOK PUBLISHING

First published in this omnibus edition in 2005
by HEADLINE BOOK PUBLISHING

A HEADLINE paperback

10 9 8 7 6 5 4 3 2 1

ISBN 0 7553 2670 9

Typeset in Palatino

Printed and bound in Great Britain by
Clays Ltd, St Ives plc

HEADLINE BOOK PUBLISHING
A division of Hodder Headline
338 Euston Road
London NW1 3BH

www.headline.co.uk

Expecting Emily

For my parents

Acknowledgements

Thanks to Gaye Shortland, Paula Campbell and all at Poolbeg. Thanks to Betty Moore for sharing her medical knowledge. Thanks to Margaret, Pamela and my mother for those Sunday morning brainstorming sessions. Thanks again to Siân and Caroline for reading it. Thanks to Stewart for all his overtime at the weekends and to Sean for helping me with the research.

Part One

The day started well enough for Emily except that she was late.

'Excuse me, excuse me, thank you, excuse me. Oh! You're very kind!'

She beamed at two men who whipped open the double doors of the clinic for her and rushed past, not seeing the look of fear on their faces. It was the huge, tent-like denim maternity trousers that did it, and the way her belly swung wildly from side to side like an uncontrolled missile.

Now. Floor three. Emily paused by the lift. It said 400kgs only. She hadn't been weighed since last week but just to be on the safe side she headed for the stairs. It would be unfair to put the other lift occupants at risk.

'You're late,' Mr Chapman's receptionist said with a little sigh. Her hair looked nailed on. Emily admired it. She'd left half of hers on the pillow that morning. Conor said that soon they would have enough to stuff a duvet.

'Sorry,' Emily said. The thirty-mile drive from

Paulstown to Cork City always took longer than she anticipated.

'I'll see if Mr Chapman can squeeze you in.'

'He did the last time I was late. Squeezed me in. Or should that be squez?'

The receptionist didn't crack a smile. She never did. Oh well. She was probably only on 15k a year and couldn't afford to smile.

'Are you feeling all right?' she asked instead, looking at Emily.

'Fine. Well, maybe a little dizzy.' Big black dots were bouncing before Emily's eyes. Next time she would definitely take the lift.

'Dizziness tends to happen.' The receptionist nodded sagely. 'You know, when you're pregnant.'

This was rich from a girl who Emily guessed had been on the pill since she was twelve and still double-bagged everything. Emily stealthily reached behind and unzipped her 'roomy' maternity pants. The relief was instant and enormous, and the black dots disappeared.

'Why don't you take a seat,' the receptionist said. 'But as you've missed your appointment, I should warn you that you could have a bit of a wait.'

'That's fine,' Emily said quickly, inching away, but the receptionist had long experience of dealing with the likes of Emily. A long, pale hand shot out over the reception desk.

'Your sample.'

'I forgot it,' Emily admitted.

Behind her, she could feel the rest of the women in the waiting-room startle into awareness. Imagine forgetting to bring a sample! When they had probably been up since dawn drinking gallons of mineral water and decaff tea to generate that perfect, precious 10 ml. Some of them had probably used a tea-strainer in an effort at quality control.

The receptionist gave another little sigh.

'Mr Chapman needs a sample from you every week.'

Emily looked at her. 'Why, can't he produce his own?'

'No, no, he needs yours for the tests, you see . . . oh! You're joking. Um, aren't you?'

'I am,' Emily said patiently. Sometimes she wondered why she bothered. But then a tiny snigger escaped the receptionist, before she guiltily covered her mouth with her hand. Nobody laughed at Mr Chapman, the most eminent obstetrician in the whole of the southwest. Some women planned their pregnancies around his holidays.

The receptionist produced a spare plastic sample jar and leaned in. They were co-conspirators now. 'The bathroom's down to your right, Emily.'

'Thanks, ah . . .?'

'Sandra.'

The tiny plastic container defied all reason. Emily did her best but her efforts were as usual more miss than hit. She dried up the bathroom floor with wads of toilet paper and hoped that nobody would notice her damp shoe.

'My God!' A bloated, pasty face suddenly confronted her. 'Oh, it's only me,' she noted sadly, looking quickly away from the bathroom mirror. Once upon a time she had been quite nice-looking.

She carefully washed her hands. Her wedding ring wouldn't budge, she noticed, the skin around it pinched and red. She should have taken it off before it was too late. Now they'd probably have to cut it off.

Still, Conor would buy her an eternity ring, wouldn't he? Wasn't that what men bought their wives on production of the first heir? A little well-done-love, smashing-job – mind you, I'd have done it ten times better myself if I'd had a pair of ovaries.

'Excuse me . . . sorry . . . excuse me.' It was extraordinary how much of her life Emily seemed to spend excusing herself. She squeezed into a corner in the waiting-room and picked through the same tired selection of magazines. All the good ones were gone of course; *Gardener's Monthly* and 1998's copy of *Newsweek* had already been snapped up. Emily opened up *House & Home* and immediately wished she hadn't. The baby's room was only half-painted. She and Conor had spent an hour last night trying to assemble the easy-to-assemble cot. Conor had given up in a near tantrum, vowing to write to the manufacturers. Emily didn't know what that would achieve apart from causing a fuss. Conor had retorted that there would be a greater fuss if the baby fell through the bottom and broke its neck. 'Jesus, Conor!' Emily's knees had snapped together in case the baby might fall through her own bottom. Conor had lugged the cot into the garage. There were sounds of sawing. He'd reappeared, triumphant. 'It's assembled.'

The waiting-room was silent save for the sounds of magazine pages furiously turning. Not that anybody was reading, Emily included. She was watching the woman in the red trouser suit out of the corner of her eye. The woman in the red trouser suit was watching your woman in the baggy jumper. *She* was watching Emily and Trouser Suit simultaneously. And the one in the flowery frock was watching them all, or at least their midriffs. The air of competition was intense. Who had the biggest belly? Who wore the nicest maternity clothes? Whose ankles were the least swollen? And occasionally a smug sense of reassurance – thank God *my* baby won't have a hooter like that.

It had been the same in antenatal classes. Everyone watching each other in a kind of guarded way. And the men were worse! Strutting about, giving each other I've-got-a-functioning-willy looks. It was nonsense really. Surely they were all in this together?

Emily lowered her magazine and leaned in to the woman in the trouser suit. The woman started a bit, her hands flying protectively to her belly.

'How many weeks are you?' Emily enquired politely.
'Thirty-two.'
'Me too.' Emily smiled. 'I'm due the tenth of May.'
'I'm the eleventh!' Trouser Suit was delighted now.

'No!'

'Have you had any Braxton Hicks yet?' Trouser Suit asked eagerly.

Emily looked at her blankly. 'What?'

'You know, the preparatory contractions?'

'Um, no.'

'Oh.'

Emily was losing Trouser Suit – it was happening before her very eyes. 'But I'm hoping for one any minute now.'

'I'm getting quite a few of them,' the girl in the baggy jumper offered shyly.

Trouser Suit's defection was complete. She turned her back on Emily. 'Thank God! I thought I was the only one!'

'They woke me up the other night,' Baggy Jumper confided. 'I thought I was going into labour!'

The woman in the flowery frock just couldn't keep out of it. 'You've a lovely little bump,' she told Baggy Jumper.

'Oh stop! I'm like an elephant!'

'*I'm* like an elephant!' Flowery Frock cried. 'And I'm only twenty-eight weeks!'

'God, I thought you were nearly full-term,' Trouser Suit said.

Flowery Frock was sorry she'd opened her mouth now. Emily saw her chance to get back into the fray, but Baggy Jumper beat her to it.

'Mr Chapman thinks I'm not putting on enough

weight,' she murmured nervously even though everyone could see she was delighted. 'I've to eat more.'

'I ate a whole sliced pan last night,' Trouser Suit sighed.

Emily leaned forward eagerly. 'That's nothing! I had three Aeros and a Galaxy ice cream!'

Baggy Jumper, Trouser Suit and Flowery Frock looked at her in silence.

'Um, all that sugar and additives . . . it mightn't be good for the baby . . .' Baggy Jumper eventually offered.

Emily felt like she had been slapped across the face. She retreated behind her magazine, raging with herself. Why hadn't she said something about the sliced pan? All that gluten! Not to mention the pound of butter that had probably gone with it. But the moment was gone. The women had moved on to various discharges now, discussing colours and textures with glee. And she after starting the bloody conversation too!

She gave her bump a quick, loving pat. At least you won't have ears like hers, she reassured it.

The baby kicked her roundly in the kidneys. You little shit, she thought dispassionately.

Here came the husbands now into the packed waiting-room, having been despatched to park cars, buy mineral water and phone the office. There was much confusion as each tried to get as close as possible to the mother of their child without upsetting the mother of anybody else's child.

'I can scoot over . . .'

'No, no, you're the one who's pregnant.' A nervous laugh.

'I'm not that big.' More laughter.

'Jerry, there's a space over here.'

'Oh right. Excuse me . . . sorry . . .'

Jerry slid in beside Baggy Jumper, relieved, and took her hand as though she were made of bone china. He was no sooner settled before the glass plate at reception flew back.

'Michelle? Jerry? Mr Chapman's ready for you now.'

Baggy Jumper and Jerry exchanged a secret smile before walking down the corridor and into the inner sanctum, him steering her with a firm hand on the small of her back, as though by being pregnant she had also lost her sense of direction.

There was no more chatter in the waiting-room. It was all very well to confide in your womenfolk about eating sliced pans, but not in front of the men. It would have been as tasteless and embarrassing as discussing period pains.

The door opened again and Conor breezed in. Sensibly, he had bought a copy of the *Irish Times* in the shop next door.

He didn't try to squeeze in anywhere. He simply stood by the door, looked at Emily and nodded around easily at everybody.

Emily felt she should speak to him, claim him or something. 'Did you manage to get parking?'

'Yes,' he said. Of course he had. Everybody else had

driven around the clinic in circles for half an hour but car parks seemed to swell and open up for Conor.

They had driven down separately. Conor would be working in Cork tonight and figured he would pass the afternoon shopping, rather than making the sixty-mile round trip home and back again.

'Did you?' he asked. 'Get parking?' He had a great interest in these things.

'Oh yes,' Emily said breezily. She had ended up parking in the consultants' car park. She had stuck a note to the windscreen saying 'On a delivery'. She had been quite pleased with that.

'We're going to have a bit of a wait,' she told him. 'Sandra told me.'

Conor's eyebrows jumped up at the cosy reference to Sandra. So, Emily had finally broken down the hard-faced bitch. Conor himself didn't waste his energy on people like that.

'Well, we'll see about that,' he said, throwing a grim look towards reception.

'Conor, please don't make a fuss.' Emily was embarrassed. She hoped he wouldn't trot out his argument in front of everyone – that they paid handsomely for Mr Chapman's time and that it wasn't right to make pregnant women wait around like this.

Thankfully, he didn't. He merely shrugged and opened his paper.

Emily sat back, closed her eyes, and concentrated on the movement in her tummy. The baby was turning over. She still wasn't quite used to it after all these months. In fact, it was very odd sometimes when she was lying quite still to see her belly bulge and flop over entirely of its own accord. She thought she knew exactly how Sigourney Weaver had felt in *Alien*. Or was it *Alien 2*?

She had confided this to her sister Liz once. Liz had five boys and liked to be consulted for advice.

'My God, Emily, you're not very maternal, are you? Robbie! Get out of that puddle this instant or I'll murder you!'

Emily had felt guilty afterwards. Maybe there was something wrong with her. Surely her maternal instincts, whatever they were supposed to be, would come to the fore once the baby was born? Or was it possible that she was one of those freak mothers who took one look at their new infant and demanded that it be taken away and reared by apes or something?

The baby had gone very still now. Probably frightened out of its wits. Or else, of course, it had just gone to sleep.

Mr Chapman, as usual, wanted to palpate her.

'Conor, there's no reason why you shouldn't see this,' he said generously.

Emily found herself lying on the examining table with Mr Chapman on one side and Conor on the other. They looked at her as though waiting for her to perform a trick. Emily vaguely resented them; she was growing a baby inside her, wasn't that enough?

'If you could just ease up your top,' Mr Chapman prompted clinically. 'Great. And loosen your trousers . . . oh, they're already loose.'

Telling herself there was nothing to be embarrassed about, Emily peeled down her trousers, embarrassed. Her underwear came into view.

Conor winked at her. Emily shot him a stony glance.

They had discussed knickers the night before (just before the cot incident). Emily had been hand-washing a roomy white pair with a pink trim especially for today. She had three pairs that she rotated for this weekly visit, all new and white and granny-like with different coloured trims. The trims were important – that way Mr Chapman would know that she had actually changed them.

Emily had tried to explain to Conor why she could never wear her black lacy ones in here, for example. Well, the mere idea of sex at these examinations seemed obscene or something. But sex had led to her condition in the first place, Conor said reasonably. Of course it had, Emily said, wanting him to understand. But she didn't want Mr Chapman . . . well, to get a fright. Supposing he thought she was coming on to him?

Conor laughed. Chapman's a professional, he said. He's sick of the sight of women's bums. He probably turns his back on his wife in bed at night with the words, 'Sorry, darling, but if I see another one today . . .'

Emily, perversely, took umbrage. What was wrong

with her bum anyway? No, no, she understood perfectly! It's all very well to say that pregnant women are gloriously sexy, but when push comes to shove, it's only lip-service!

Conor said that she sweated the small stuff. It had sounded like an insult. Emily opened the first of the three Aeros in a dignified silence. Conor enquired carefully whether they were having a row over knickers. The way he said it made her laugh. She dropped the subject. She hadn't thought it was a row. She had thought it was a lively discussion. Still, no sense in letting it spoil the cot assembly. Conor had already studied the instructions for ages in anticipation.

Mr Chapman, of course, never once looked in the direction of her knickers. He just palpated, pressed and pinged her naked stomach, a detached smile on his face.

'The head's starting to engage,' he announced.

Having maintained a respectful distance thus far, Conor now stepped up close to Emily's belly proprietarily.

'Is that good?'

'It just means that the baby's head is working down towards the birth canal.'

'So he's in the vertex position?'

'Exactly!' Mr Chapman was delighted to be speaking to a man, having spent most of his life dealing with women. And a man with knowledge to boot. 'He's head-down which saves us a lot of bother when it comes time to get him out.'

Conor nodded vigorously. He had read *The Pregnant Father*. It's a manual, he had patiently explained when Emily had roared laughing; you wouldn't take a new computer out of its packaging without first reading the manual, would you? Emily would and had. Conor had persisted with his reading and could now fling around words like 'haemolytic jaundice' and 'tainted meconium' as though he were a chronic sufferer himself. He wasn't so hot on the practical aspects; when the book had gone on about voice recognition, he had laid his head on Emily's naked tummy that night and directed a rather stiff monologue at her belly-button, starting with 'Um, this is your father here.' Emily had said that if the baby didn't recognise his voice when it got out, at least it would know all about how the lawnmower was acting up. She had only been joking. But he hadn't done it again after that.

'He's lying side-on at the moment,' Mr Chapman said, digging his fingers into Emily's pelvis. It hurt.

'Or she,' Emily said, as loudly as she dared. Mr Chapman could be very intimidating. He reminded her of Magnus Magnusson in his three-piece suit. His chosen subject was pregnancy, naturally. But today Emily felt brave with Conor beside her.

Mr Chapman smiled in a detached way. 'Are you hoping for a girl?'

'We don't mind so long as it's healthy,' Conor said strongly.

'Sensible attitude,' Mr Chapman said just as strongly.

Any minute now Emily expected them to excuse themselves and go off for a round of golf together.

'Are we done here?' she asked, wondering how she had managed to become superfluous to the entire proceedings.

'Not quite.' Mr Chapman was indulgent now as he picked up a stethoscope. 'Let's listen to the heartbeat, shall we?'

It was the part of the visit that everybody liked best. Emily shivered a little as Mr Chapman applied cold gel to her belly. Then he laid the stethoscope gently on her skin, moving it around, his brow furrowed as he listened.

'Ah!' He reached over and dramatically flicked a switch over Emily's head. Immediately, the baby's muffled heartbeat filled the room. Mr Chapman stood back to watch Emily and Conor's faces. This was his moment, the time when he modestly felt like the giver of life.

'It's so fast!' Emily said, more because it was expected than anything else. She lived with this baby twenty-four hours a day, felt its every hiccup and kick. That was enough.

No, let Conor have this one, she magnanimously thought, peeking at him. His wonder was there for all the world to see – well, for Emily anyway, who over the years had learned to spot those subtle signs of emotion. He blinked more than usual, for example, and his chin would occasionally dip in a violent bob.

She knew that he would go into Mothercare that afternoon, arriving home with baby ski boots or a car-seat neck-support or some high-tech toy that would confound adults, never mind a newborn. Emily would put it away in the baby's room along with all the other ridiculous stuff he'd bought. She never said anything. She could afford to indulge him. And it made her feel a bit superior in a way.

Back at his desk, Mr Chapman made cryptic notes on Emily's chart. He caught Emily looking and shielded the notes with his hand; lest she discover something about her own condition.

'It's a fine big baby,' he pronounced eventually, as though it were all his own doing.

Emily felt a nervous twinge in her nether regions. Conor sat a little taller.

'And doing quite well from what I can see,' Mr Chapman concluded.

'Great,' Emily said with feeling.

There didn't seem to be a lot else to say. Emily decided that she would take the initiative and dismiss herself.

She stood airily. 'Cheerio then! Same time next week I suppose?'

'Not so fast,' Mr Chapman said.

Emily sat down again clumsily. He peered at her over his bifocals.

'We need to talk about your blood pressure.'

'What about it?'

'It's up a little.'

'How much?'

'Nothing to be too worried about,' Mr Chapman assured her. He hadn't answered her question. 'High blood pressure is a common complaint in late pregnancy. We just need to keep an eye on it.'

Emily's eyes flew to Conor. He gave her a measured look that said 'don't panic'.

'I'm also a bit concerned about your weight gain,' Mr Chapman added.

Jesus Christ, why did everything come back to weight in this world?

'It's due to water retention,' Mr Chapman clarified. 'Surely you've noticed a bit of puffiness?'

'Yes,' she admitted. She had been hoping he would not mention it.

'Nothing to be too worried about,' Mr Chapman said again, tactlessly. 'But I'd like to see you the day after tomorrow all the same. Sandra will fit you in.'

It rained all the way back from Cork. Conor was forced to drive in the end because Emily's car had been towed. When they'd rescued it from the car pound, the battery went flat because she'd left the lights on and the jump leads had mysteriously gone missing from the boot of the car. They'd left it on the side of the road. Conor would have to get Billy Middlemiss to help out tonight.

She felt him looking at her from time to time. But

mostly he kept his eyes on the road. At least he hadn't given out about the car. That was some indication that he knew how upset she was. And his index finger was twitching for a cigarette, an indication of how upset he was. Any minute now he would say something momentous, something so sweet and comforting and insightful that all Emily's worries would be blown away.

'Look at that joker! No brake lights! It's a good thing I'm not a plain-clothes garda.'

Conor had missed his calling. Every single trip he wished he were a plain-clothes garda. And he would have been very good at it too, Emily often thought. She could just imagine him whipping out his notebook and leaning in a car window, stern yet compassionate. 'Do you realise you're doing forty in a thirty-mile zone, madam?' And he would write a ticket in his clear, strong handwriting. If the driver were elderly or infirm, he would let them off with a caution.

Conor had a robust appetite for law and order in all areas of life. Which made it all the odder that he was, in fact, a professional pianist. But that too had its own order, Emily supposed, as she thought of him doing his scales on the piano on Saturday mornings, his long brown fingers belting methodically up and down the keys, head cocked slightly towards the piano as though he suspected it were trying to catch him out. But then, when she had left the room, she would hear him launch into Chopin's Revolutionary Study. Peeking in the door, she would see his head flying backwards, his body coiled with a peculiar, passionate energy. His eyes would squint up and become very far away. Emily would sometimes have the sensation that he was a total stranger. Which was ridiculous. When the piece was over, he would straighten up and he was just Conor again, and he would go and put the rubbish out.

Emily's hands smoothed her belly. The baby hadn't moved since they'd left the clinic. Typical. It would probably torture her all day with its stillness, and then break into a samba just when she was trying to go to sleep. But she wouldn't mind, not this time.

The weight of this new worry settled down on her shoulders, adding to all the other worries Emily seemed to pick up so effortlessly. Please God, she prayed, let nothing go wrong. Oh, and sorry I haven't been to Mass since 1996.

'Look, Emily, it's a bit of high blood pressure, that's all.' Finally, he said something.

'And water retention,' she pointed out.

'It's a common complaint in late pregnancy. Chapman said so. There's nothing to worry about.'

He roundly pipped the driver in front as they overtook. 'Conor?'

He knew what she was going to say and he swiftly headed her off at the pass. 'Nothing is going to happen to this baby.'

'How do you know?'

'Nothing is going to happen.' He just didn't want to hear it.

'Do you think I'm doing something wrong?' Emily asked. She knew this was ridiculous, but you had to be clever with Conor, you had to find little ways of drawing him out. Sometimes she thought a lot of their conversations only came about because of her increasingly imaginative ploys to get him to talk.

'Maybe,' he said, flooring her.

'What?' She twisted in her seat, hotly defensive. 'What a stupid thing to say!'

'But you asked!' He was confused.

She hadn't meant for him to agree. Didn't he know anything?

'And what exactly am I doing wrong, Mr Expert?'

'I don't know . . .'

'Don't try and backtrack!'

He shrugged. 'Maybe you're working too hard.'

'Well!' It was difficult to argue with him. Crawley Dunne & O'Reilly, solicitors, demanded forty-eight hours a week of her time, plus the odd weekend. But everybody worked the same hours. It wasn't just her!

'What am I supposed to do, take it a bit easier because I'm pregnant?'

'That would be an option,' he said mildly.

'I can't do that! They've been very understanding so far,' she said loyally. 'Letting me off for appointments and hospital visits and everything!'

'They're obliged to by law. Being solicitors, I'm sure they're well clued up on their obligations.'

She detected that familiar faint note of contempt in

his voice and was insulted on Crawley Dunne & O'Reilly's behalf. They had given Emily her first big break! They gave her a pay rise without fail on June 1st of every year, and regular bonuses too. Crawley Dunne & O'Reilly knew how to reward their workers. And now Conor expected her to turn around and admit that she couldn't hack it just because she was pregnant? Five other women in the office had had babies in the past two years, and not a single one of them had taken so much as a day off before their official leave. So what if Emily didn't feel so hot some mornings? There were standards to be upheld, expectations to be met. She was well aware of them.

'I don't know what you have against them,' she said stoutly. 'They pay our mortgage.'

'I contribute too.'

'Yes, yes, of course you do, I didn't mean . . .' She moved on swiftly. 'And then there's the partnership.'

He looked at her blankly – as if she hadn't been talking about it for weeks now!

'Oh yes,' he eventually said. Doubtfully?

'The meeting's today.' She checked her watch. 'In five minutes to be exact. I was hoping to make it back to talk to Mr Crawley.'

They were only in Fermoy. Another eleven miles to go.

'What difference would it make?' Conor enquired carefully. 'They're either going to give it to you or they're not.'

'Well, yes, but there's no harm in stating my case.'

He impatiently slowed at a roundabout. 'Surely you've proved your case, Emily? After giving those guys six years of your life? I'd think the bloody least they could do is give you a partnership.'

'Yes, well, it'll happen today,' she said, sitting back.

He had taken the good out of it somehow. She had put a bottle of champagne and everything in the fridge for a little celebration later. One glass only, mind. But not now. And especially not after Mr Chapman's news.

Emily suddenly wondered how they had ended up talking about work, instead of her worries. Conor had that knack, though. Last week she had been putting baby things into a box that would go in the attic. Conor had come upstairs and somehow or other they had ended up discussing Mrs Conlon-next-door's application for planning permission to extend her kitchen. Right into Emily and Conor's back garden, as it transpired. They had hurried to the back window to assess the potential damage, the box forgotten.

He surprised her now by reaching over and squeezing her hand.

'This baby is thirty-four weeks old. Fully formed. If it were born this minute it'd have a good chance. Look at the statistics.'

He was in his plain-clothes garda mode again, breaking her down with facts and figures. And it was working because she wanted it to.

'You're right, I suppose.'

'Of course I am.'

They drove in silence for a while, Emily looking out the window. The landscape grew more and more familiar. And here now was Paulstown, population two thousand.

Conor checked his watch. 'That meeting will have started. Why don't we just go home?'

She thought of the stack of work waiting for her in the office. They might cheerfully let her off for her appointments but it was sort of on the understanding that she caught up in her own time. She should delegate, really, but those law-student ninnies on work experience never got it right, which meant more work for her in the end. Besides, she wanted to have her desk cleared before she went on maternity leave in two weeks' time. That too was sort of expected of her.

But this business of the high blood pressure was bothering her. If she took it easy today, then that might sort things out. She owed it to the baby. Anyway, she could always work at home.

'You know, I think I'll take the rest of the day off,' she said loudly. 'They can ring me if they want me.'

Conor's eyebrows disappeared into his hairline. 'Good God, are you sure about this, Emily? Let's not do anything rash here.'

'Shut up,' she snapped. It was easy for him to laugh, with no commitments all day long except for three hours' work tonight.

He was repentant now. 'I'll make you a cup of my special cappuccino.'

Emily was pleased. Conor hardly ever made cappuccinos these days. It seemed to take too long. When they married six years ago, making cappuccinos was an altogether quicker business and they had drunk it morning, noon and night.

Still, there were other compensations, Emily was sure, for the froth of cappuccinos.

She looked over at Conor now, fondly. He reminded her of that Beamish ad – consistency in a world gone mad. And there was a lot to be said for that, wasn't there?

Crawley Dunne & O'Reilly was the biggest solicitors' firm in Paulstown. In fact, it was the only one. It did a brisk trade in farm auctions, period house sales and occasionally drew up wills for the more well-heeled locals. Business was so good that they had recently refurbished the entire reception area in glass and chrome. This deterred some of the more undesirable elements in the town who took their minor legal worries elsewhere, leaving Crawley Dunne & O'Reilly to the business of selling vast tracts of farmland for a hefty two percent of the sale price. The last time they had set foot in an actual court of law was to defend Mr Crawley's nephew who had been up on drunk-and-disorderly charges two years ago. It had been a distasteful and unprofitable experience for everyone concerned and they had gratefully returned to selling land. They were auctioneers by any other name but would have been highly insulted at the accusation.

Crawley Dunne & O'Reilly were not only rich but also shrewd; they watched *Ally McBeal* and knew that bright young things helped to shift properties much faster than ponderous old farts, and so they actively headhunted solicitors from the bigger firms in Cork City. One of the brightest of these bright young things was Neasa Martin who right now was studiously applying herself to her computer in the open-plan office. She heard the squeak of new leather shoes approaching. Here came Creepy Crawley. She quickly closed the poker game on her computer screen and brought up a contract instead.

'Neasa?'

He stood as close to her as he dared. She smelled mouthwash and Joop! He was a man desperately fighting Old Spice and middle age.

'Yes, Mr Crawley?'

'Is Emily back yet?'

'No, she must have been delayed. You know she had an appointment with her obstetrician?'

'Yes, yes,' he said quickly. For all his put-on panache, Charles Crawley had led a sheltered life. Pregnancy to him was still that horrid picture in that book his father had forced on him at the age of twelve; after all his talk of graceful white storks, too. It had been a desperate betrayal. For seven months now, Charles Crawley had been unable to look Emily Collins in the stomach.

Neasa smiled innocently. 'Or maybe she's dropping it

right this minute.' She enjoyed his blush.

'Oh! Well! Let's hope not!'

'Absolutely,' Neasa agreed. 'With the partners' meeting and everything. I know she was anxious to talk to you before it starts.'

'Yes, I was hoping to talk to her too,' Crawley said with a regretful nod.

He was lying. Neasa just knew it.

'Still, I suppose she'll be in later this afternoon. To hear all the news, you know . . .?'

She offered him one of her wide-eyed, inquisitive looks. Usually this induced an erection and he would babble on in an effort to distract her while it subsided. But Crawley's trousers remained resolutely flat today and his lip buttoned.

'We won't be finished before the close of business,' he said, clipped. 'By the way, Gary is waiting for that contract on The Paddocks sale. He's meeting with their people this afternoon.'

'He's about to get it now,' Neasa told him sweetly.

'Good.' Crawley's eyes lingered on her shiny black, clean, clean hair. Sometimes at night he dreamed that she was waiting for him when he got out of the shower and she would offer him her mane of black hair to dry himself with. He had fantasies of telling her about this some day and her nodding understandingly.

'Carry on,' he said, thickly.

His shoes squeaked across the plush carpet and down the corridor into the boardroom where the other partners, Daphne Dunne and Ewan O'Reilly, waited. The door shut firmly as they went into session.

Neasa picked up the phone and dialled. At the other end of the open-plan office, she saw Gary look over before picking up.

'What!'

'I have that contract you need.'

'About bloody time.'

'Yes, I'm sorry. Would you like to go over it?'

'I think I should. The last one was littered with mistakes.'

'Will I come down to your desk?'

'I can't concentrate with all the noise in here!'

'I think Emily's office is free . . .'

'Fine. Now.'

He hung up on her. Regina looked over, her eyebrows jumping up. That pig Gary seemed to have it in for Neasa. Neasa rolled her eyes in silent agreement, picked up the contract, and walked into Emily's office.

The smell of Emily's citrus air freshener hit her. The desk was completely bare except for a neatly folded document. Oops. Emily was slipping up on her filing again.

Gary was lolling in Emily's swivel-chair. He had his penis out.

'Oh goody,' Neasa sighed, locking the door, hitching up her skirt and leaping on him. The swivel-chair went flying backwards, violently colliding with Emily's cheese plant. The leaves bobbled merrily for five minutes as they went at it hard.

Neasa eventually flung herself away. 'My thighs. They're killing me.'

'No problem,' said Gary, flipping her over in a daring manoeuvre. There was nothing wrong with his thighs, honed and fine-tuned by ten years of amateur rugby. The cheese plant wilted under a fresh assault.

'How are you doing?' Gary eventually enquired, his eyes glazed.

'Just keep going,' Neasa panted.

'Are you sure you don't want me to slap you or anything?'

He was so sweet.

'No, I think I'll be all right.'

Through the wall, they heard Mr Crawley's voice as the partner's meeting began. It was enough for both of them.

'Ohohoh,' Gary said.

Neasa simply broke a fingernail on his back.

Then they were tidying up quickly, straightening Emily's chair, sellotaping the cheese plant. They gave each other little aren't-we-so-daring looks, thrilled with themselves and each other.

'I am so in love with you, Neasa Martin,' Gary said sincerely. He was big and butch enough looking to carry this off.

'I know,' Neasa agreed smugly. 'Me too.'

She had washed her hair every single day since she'd got it together with Gary. If that wasn't love, she didn't know what was.

'Better get back,' he said.

'Absolutely. I think Regina might be starting to twig.'

Not that it mattered really. Office romances weren't forbidden here – only heavily frowned upon and greatly discouraged. But Neasa and Gary had talked seriously about it and felt that what they had was so precious that they didn't want to expose it to tawdry office intrigue and, well, gossip. Besides, they would no longer be able to nip into empty offices for quick sex. They found it desperately exciting. Also, it was the sort of thing you only read about in very trendy magazines and both of them were rapidly pushing thirty.

Gary's penis was growing big again.

'Wow!' he said cheerfully. 'Are you wearing new perfume or something?'

'No,' Neasa said, fascinated. She would love a new spring coat in just that shade of purple.

'Oh, well! I'll put it away now,' Gary said efficiently.

'Don't! Let's just watch for a minute.' It was enormous now. How could he manage it again so soon?

'Maybe it's that kinky underwear of yours,' Gary said, embarrassed.

'You've seen it before,' Neasa reminded him, suspicious now. He was trying to stuff the penis back into his pants. He bent it this way and that, but it escaped and waved its bulbous head merrily.

'What the hell is going on?' Neasa said accusingly. 'I've never had this effect before!'

'Oh all right!' Gary shouted. 'I've got the partnership, okay!'

Neasa blinked. 'What?'

'Creepy Crawley came up to me before the meeting. He more or less said I had it in the bag.'

'Fantastic!' Neasa spat sarcastically.

'It's not my fault, Neasa! I didn't go canvassing!'

'Turn it down!'

'I can't turn it down! Jesus Christ, I've waited six years for this! Six years of selling boggy bits of fucking land!'

'Don't curse.'

'Sorry.'

'I mean, fucking hell, Gary!'

'I deserve it! Come on, Neasa, I feel just terrible about all this!' His erection pointed gloriously towards the ceiling.

'For God's sake put it away!' she snapped.

He did so in silence. She found that she was trembling. She couldn't believe that they were having their First Fight. And it was only this morning that Gary had told her that he actually thought she looked better without make-up.

The silence stretched. They were on dangerous territory now. Neasa knew she would have to handle this one very carefully.

'They're pigging bastards,' she said eventually.

Gary looked up warily. 'I suppose.'

'They suck the blood out of you.'

'Shamelessly,' Gary agreed more robustly.

'It just makes me sick to have to work here!'

'Me too! God, I hate this place! If it wasn't for my two mortgages, I'd . . . I'd . . .'

'Quit!'

'Well. That's a bit drastic.'

They smiled crookedly at each other. Whew. That was a close one. Neasa didn't feel she had given in by deflecting the anger onto Crawley Dunne & O'Reilly. It was just that if they were going to have a Big Row, then she would at least like to be a main player in it, as opposed to an interested third party.

'Emily's my best friend,' she said. 'What kind of person would I be if I didn't feel bad for her?'

'I know,' Gary groaned. 'I feel bloody awful too. I mean, I wouldn't have minded beating Phil or Tony.'

He'd have had an erection for a week.

'But Emily . . . she works so hard.' He added hurriedly, 'not that I don't work hard too.'

'You're a total dosser.'

'Well, yes . . .'

'And you fiddle your expenses.'

'Naturally, I . . .'

'You're always calling in sick.'

'Can we stick to the important things here? I close the sales, Neasa.'

And that was it, really. He was known around the office as Jaws. He was sent in by Crawley Dunne & O'Reilly to all the biggest sales, where he would bite lumps out of potential vendors until, bleeding and legless, they coughed up the asking price plus twenty grand more.

What hope had Emily against him, ploughing away at her desk behind the scenes, running the entire office with unseen strokes?

'When are they going to announce it?'

'In the morning.'

At least she would get a chance to tell Emily tonight. She would bring a bottle of wine and they would eff and blind Crawley Dunne & O'Reilly out of it. Neasa would even threaten to hand in her notice at this latest piece of debauchery from them. She would be half-serious too. She had no intention of hanging around six years to be made partner in this backwater firm. But they had offered so much money when they had poached her from a proper solicitors' office in Cork, and Neasa had her priorities right. Still, she had an itch to practise real law again, and figured she would soon move back to a young, exciting firm in Cork. She too watched *Ally McBeal*.

'Aren't you pleased for me at all?' Gary asked in a small voice.

'Of course, Gary, amn't I mad about you!' Oh, the treachery.

'This could be a future for us,' Gary said meaningfully.

Cork suddenly receded at a dizzying pace. The 'future' had not been discussed thus far. They were too busy having sex in any case.

'Let's not jump the gun,' she said with admirable coolness. She flicked her long black dyed hair over her shoulder and left, secure in the knowledge that Gary was watching with his tongue hanging out.

'Yoo-hoo! Anybody home?'

'Isn't the car parked outside and the key in the door?' Conor said mildly, as he reached for milk to make the two cappuccinos into three.

'She's probably just passing.' Emily always felt she had to make excuses for her family, even though she no more wanted to see Liz than Conor did. She had a pain in her back and the start of a headache. Also, there was a nasty, buzzing sensation down there somewhere, as though she were sitting on an electric fence. *The Pregnant Father* had nothing to offer about this. Conor had already checked it.

The kitchen door burst open and Liz barged in, dragging Tommy, Robbie, Mikey and Bobby by various bits of their clothing. Willy was strapped to her front in a baby carrier. At least Emily assumed it was Willy. His face was sandwiched between Liz's breasts and he didn't appear to be breathing.

'Not disturbing you or anything?' Liz's colour was a bit high. But then again she was always rushing somewhere.

'Not at all,' Emily said.

Conor grunted something.

'And you've brought all the boys!' she added, feeling

she had to compensate for him.

'Say hello to your Auntie Emily and your Uncle Conor,' Liz commanded automatically.

'Hello,' they chorused glumly.

'Hi there!' Emily said, smiling her big, bright Auntie Smile. 'How's everyone?'

Tommy looked at the floor. Robbie and Mikey sniggered as though she had made a joke. Bobby was looking at her tummy in fascination.

'You're getting very fat,' he said happily.

'Bobby!' Liz was mortified.

'No, really, Liz, it's all right . . .'

Bobby knew he had said something wrong but he wasn't sure what.

'Apologise right now,' Liz ordered.

'Honestly, Liz . . .'

'Sorry,' Bobby said miserably. 'You're not fat at all.'

Conor miraculously produced a plate of biscuits. Not mean old fig rolls or boring digestives, but lovely big Chocolate Kimberlys in their own individual wrappings. Tommy, Robbie, Mikey and Bobby fell on them like a pack of starving dogs, before belatedly looking up at their mother for permission.

'Oh, go on then!' Liz looked at Emily rather accusingly. 'They won't eat their dinner, you know.'

'Why don't I give them a run around in the back?' Conor offered. 'They can burn it off.'

Liz looked suspicious that anybody would want to spend time with her sons. 'They can be very rough.'

'I'm sure I can handle them.'

'I suppose it'll be a bit of practice for you,' Liz said, with a nudge-nudge look at Emily.

'Yes,' Conor said evenly. 'Boys, would you like to go and feed the dogs?'

This sounded safe enough. The boys, though not exactly thrilled, were glad of the opportunity to get away from their mother. 'Yes.'

'Yes, please,' Liz said automatically.

The boys traipsed out.

Conor deposited two cappuccinos on the table. 'You two relax and have a chat.'

He dutifully followed the boys out the door.

'Isn't he lovely?' Liz said, sitting down with a sigh. She always sighed when she sat down, but today it seemed to have more resonance than usual.

'Lovely,' Emily agreed. Conor always found some reason to get out of the room when Liz arrived. He was so good at it that nobody ever suspected anything, including Emily herself until recently.

'Anyway,' Liz said, 'I just called in to see how you got on with your consultant.'

'Oh, right. We're just back actually.'

'That drive must kill you,' Liz said. 'All the way to Cork and back every week!'

'It's only thirty miles away, Liz.'

'I couldn't have done it,' Liz declared. 'Not with the rest of them in the back of the car. They'd have murdered each other by Fermoy.'

'Well, of course, you couldn't—'

'No, I was just as glad to go to Martha's. It's only down the road, so handy, and the Outpatients' there is terrific.'

St Martha's General Hospital was five miles away in Mitchelstown.

'You see the same consultants, you know. Whether you go private or public,' Liz added.

'Yes, I know that.'

'Not that we could have afforded a "private consultant".' She put this in rather scornful inverted commas, before nodding violently after the boys. 'That lot go through five packets of cornflakes a week. And Robbie's shoulder popped out again yesterday. Another twenty quid to the doctor. Eamon says that next time he'll try and bang it back in himself.'

Eamon would, too. He was the local builder. He had laid the patio for Conor and Emily last year, because they hadn't the nerve to go to anybody else. He had done them a special price because they were family.

'Threw in a dead body and everything,' he'd winked.

'Money down the drain, on private consultants,' Liz finished.

'Yes, well, we just decided to go private,' Emily said, gritting her teeth. 'It's probably silly, but we just felt safer.'

She could see Conor through the window. He was still standing, which was a good sign.

'Safer! Shur what could possibly happen to you down

in that big hospital in Cork? With all their new equipment and private rooms and Indian doctors coming out of the woodwork? Tommy! If I have to come out to you . . .'

Emily carefully lifted her cappuccino. It was easier to have something to do with her hands when talking to Liz. Sometimes she came perilously close to belting her.

'We didn't actually get to choose the hospital, Liz, believe it or not. I'd have had the baby in St Martha's except that it's closing down.'

Liz was sent scurrying in another direction. 'It's a disgrace, that's what it is. The memories I have of that place! All five born there, right down to little Willie.'

She gave the bundle on her chest a vague pat. Emily had forgotten all about Willy. He still hadn't moved. But she didn't dare ask if he were okay. The last time she had expressed concern about Robbie, whose nose was bleeding violently, Liz had got terribly defensive.

'It's the politicians, of course,' Liz said. 'They don't care so long as they have Blackrock Clinic.'

'They don't actually deliver babies there,' Emily felt she had to point out.

'Well, Vincent's Private then.'

'They don't deliver babies there either.'

'You're so difficult, Emily. Anyway, they've got a petition going and everything to stop the hospital closing. I've signed it. I don't suppose you have.'

Oh just leave, Emily wanted to shout. But Liz would be appalled, uncomprehending. Their mother would be informed, their mother with the weak heart. She would be on the phone asking Emily why she couldn't see fit to be nice to poor Liz who had five children swinging out of her, six if you included Eamon; Liz who had only called around out of the goodness of her heart to find out how Emily was getting on. A huge family rift would develop and it would be all over the place. That was because Eamon knew everybody right down to the outskirts of Cork and possibly into Cork City itself. Emily might as well move country.

'I haven't signed the petition yet because I haven't actually seen it,' she said with great care, 'but you can rest assured that I will.'

'Not that it'll do any good,' Liz said. 'Those politicians will close it down anyway. And we'll all have to drive thirty miles to Cork in the throes of labour.'

'Thinking of going again?' Emily enquired.

'Jesus Christ, are you mad? No, we were going to hold out for the girl but, to be honest, I don't think Eamon's sperm has got what it takes. The sex is determined by the father, you know. We were thinking of having it tested or something, but he's not keen on the idea of going into one of those cubicles with a magazine.'

She was joking, surely. Eamon, who went around with a copy of the *Sun* glued to his armpit?

'Oh well,' Emily said, because there wasn't really anything else to say to that.

'I suppose you'll have a girl,' Liz said.

'It's a fifty-fifty chance, isn't it?'

'Oh, you will.' She sounded very depressed.

'Don't you want to know how I got on with Mr Chapman?' Emily enquired coolly.

'Of course. How did it go?'

'He said my blood pressure is up.'

'By much?'

'He didn't say.'

'They never do. It's like some kind of state secret, isn't it?'

'And he thinks I'm a bit puffy.'

'Well, maybe a bit. But I was puffy too. With all of them. Like a balloon.' Liz threw her eyes to heaven and smiled. She was great when she was like this. Not exactly sisterly, but definitely friendly. But then things seemed to rub her up the wrong way again. Or maybe it was just Emily.

'I'm kind of worried, Liz. You know, after everything.'

Liz was sympathetic. 'I know. But Emily, you're thirty-four weeks gone, you're nearly there.'

'That's what Conor said.'

'Of course he did,' Liz said, as though any words that came from Conor's mouth should be set in doctrine.

'I'm thinking of giving up work sooner than planned.' She wasn't really, but she wanted to sound Liz out on it. She immediately regretted it.

'Didn't I work until the day I dropped Tommy? And on my feet, too, not like you. Standing behind that counter handing out Lemsips and Vicks Cough Syrup to people who don't even know what it's like to be sick!'

Liz had wanted to study pharmacy. She had believed that it would be glamorous and rewarding, and had been impressed by the white coat. What she'd really wanted to do was get a job in Boots in London, where medicine and make-up seemed to blend seamlessly. But then Eamon Clancy set his sights on her and college was somehow put on the back burner for a year. Then they got married, and Liz had taken a part-time job as an assistant in Roche's pharmacy in Paulstown to keep her hand in, where the only make-up was a cheap line of American cosmetics on a white plastic stand inside the door. Not that the customers were interested in make-up. Mostly they came in to confide in Liz about their irregular bowel movements, and peculiar patches of hair that had sprung up in odd places overnight. After having Tommy, Liz's maternity leave from Roche's was up the week she discovered she was pregnant again. She hadn't worked since. In the meantime, Eamon had expanded his business and was apparently doing well.

Emily sometimes wondered if Liz minded giving up her ambitions, but Liz never said anything, contenting herself with the odd dig about Emily's job, which she and Eamon regarded as a very cushy number. 'Fallen on your feet there,' Eamon was fond of saying, as though it were merely a matter of luck. 'Oh, who knows what way it might all have turned out,' Conor would nod vigorously in agreement and Eamon would look at him suspiciously. But then again, Conor was one of those arty types, playing pianos for a living. A nice enough fellow but not the sort you'd play darts with in the pub on a Saturday night.

'You're lucky being able to work,' Liz said glumly. 'Try staying at home all day with five children.'

'Go back to work so,' Emily asked impatiently. 'What's stopping you?'

'If you need to ask that . . . childcare, of course! I'd be paying out more than I'd be earning! And those children—'

'They go through five packets of cornflakes a week, yes, I know.'

Liz was hurt at her tone. 'Honestly, Emily, I don't know what's got into you today.'

Emily took a long, deep breath. Her headache was there in all its glory now, throbbing nicely just behind her eyes. 'I'm tired, Liz, okay? I'm as big as a whale, my back is killing me and I want to put my feet up.'

Anybody else might have offered a smidgen of sympathy. Liz merely sprang up from the table. 'Oh, well, sorry! I'll just get the boys and go.'

'Stop, Liz! Just sit down and drink your coffee.'

'I'm not that keen on cappuccino. Well, I usually only have it when I'm out.'

'You are out.' Jesus, Mary and Holy Saint Joseph. 'But never mind, because guess what! We have Maxwell House as well, the good old pulpy stuff that we keep especially for visitors!' She got up noisily to refill the kettle. Behind her, Liz started to cry.

'Liz?' Emily swung around, her heart beating fast.

Liz was hunched over in her chair, her head in her hands. She didn't seem to notice the baby strapped to her front. Emily could see only two tiny blue-tinged feet sticking out either side of Liz's heaving ribcage.

'Liz, please, what's the matter?' Emily was frightened. Liz never cried. She shouted and roared and cursed, but she didn't cry. It was alarming. Surely to God she wasn't that upset about the coffee dig? Suffused with guilt, Emily leaned over. She put out her hand to touch Liz, but drew back. They weren't a touchy family.

Liz eventually straightened, her nose streaming. Emily ran for a tissue, wondering whether she should call Conor. But no. That would mean Tommy, Robbie, Mikey and Bobby too, and they might be too traumatised by the sight of their mother in this state. But Emily was worried about Willy. His feet were definitely blue. She wanted to offer to take him from Liz but didn't want to upset her further.

'The bank is foreclosing on the mortgage,' Liz said, her voice thick with tears.

'What?'

'I know, it was news to me too. Eamon's been hiding the post. But he went out early on a job this morning and I opened the letter. Apparently we've made no repayments since last August.'

'But that's six months.'

'Seven,' Liz said grimly. 'He's been hiding it from me for seven months!'

Emily felt dread. 'Maybe it was a clerical error . . .'

'No. I went through all the files, the ones he keeps hidden away. And the business is gone to the wall, Emily. He's been borrowing like mad, hasn't made a tax return in three years and the Revenue are looking for twenty thousand.'

'Oh my God,' Emily said.

'And now we're going to be thrown out onto the street with five kids!'

'How could this have happened, Liz?' This time Emily actually did touch Liz. Liz drew away jerkily and sat up a bit straighter.

'Oh, he lost the Gannon contract last year. Or his mother's nursing home fees have gone up. Or the kids are bleeding him dry. Or I'm bleeding him dry, who knows? But he'll find someone to blame, you can be sure of that.'

'Oh, Liz,' Emily said again. She was raging – that big stupid lump of an Eamon! And sad, too, for her belligerent, harassed sister with her work-worn hands and her flabby stomach that wasn't back into shape after Willy yet. She kept the whole shebang together. And this was the thanks she got?

'Can I use your bathroom?' Liz asked. She always asked, like she was in a hotel or something. In anyone else's house, it was just, 'I'm running to the loo.'

'Of course.'

'Hold Willy for me, will you?'

She popped the baby out of the sling with a speed born of long practice and Emily found him thrust onto her lap. Or more precisely, onto her big belly.

'Liz . . .'

Emily was terrified that the child was dead and that, when Liz got back from the toilet, she would get the blame for that too. But Liz was gone down the hall, her thin, angular body held with an awkward kind of pride. The bathroom door slammed.

Willy lay precariously on Emily's bump, quite still, his eyes closed. He was so small that Emily was afraid she would break him. She had held him before, of course, but always under Liz's eagle eye and constant instruction; 'You have to support his neck, Emily!' or 'Don't bounce him like that, he'll puke.'

Now Emily gingerly lifted Willy up so that his head was nestled comfortably on her arm and he was more or less balancing on her bump. She looked worriedly at his chest for signs of motion, but there was none. On the plus side, he was quite warm, but that could just have come from Liz.

'Willy?' Emily said gently. Nothing. His blue-veined lids seemed glued together. And why were his feet now so white? Conor, she decided. Conor would know what to do.

Willy's eyes opened and looked directly into hers.

'Oh!'

Unfortunately he had Eamon's eyes, but Emily ignored that. She smiled tentatively at him. 'I'm your Auntie Emily.' She always introduced herself. Just because three-month-old babies had the memory span of a goldfish was no reason to dispense with courtesy.

Willy looked steadfastly at her. It was gratifying. And oh, how lovely it was to have him all to herself, with no one watching and judging. Emily lifted him higher and gave him a little kiss. Yummy smooth white skin. And he still had that newborn baby smell, although Liz maintained that she only threw him into the sink in the kitchen for a wash once a fortnight. She managed to get the dishes done at the same time.

Emily pressed her finger into his palm now, and watched his little fingers curl around hers strongly. She cocked an ear and heard water running. Good. Liz was still busy.

'Buh buh buh buh,' she said to the baby, feeling a bit ridiculous. But in Liz's presence, she'd always had to suppress her urge to talk nonsense to Willy. Liz said it was unhealthy to indulge in 'baby-speak' and that one should just talk normally to children.

But Willy was mad for it. His little fists pounded the air and his feet kicked out robustly. What with his four brothers, he hadn't had so much attention since he was born.

'You're lying on your cousin,' Emily whispered.

She cuddled Willy's floppy form into her. Might as well take advantage of the opportunity for a dry run.

Imagine, in two months' time, she could be holding her own baby. All going well. Which it would, please God, I'll do anything. She didn't mention about Mass again. Best not to remind him.

'A smile!' He was definitely smiling at her.

'Wind,' Liz said, having arrived back in the kitchen. Her hair was freshly scraped back. 'But I think he likes you,' she conceded. Well, that was something. None of the others seemed to.

'I'd better get going,' she said, efficiently scooping up Willy and stuffing him back into the carrier.

'Look, why don't you stay here for the evening? We could all have dinner together or something. The boys would love it.'

'I can still manage to feed them, you know,' Liz said stiffly.

Emily tried again. 'Maybe Conor could have a word with Eamon or something.'

Liz gave a high-pitched half-laugh. 'And what would that achieve?'

'I don't know,' Emily said unhappily. 'But Conor's quite good about all that tax stuff.'

'I don't think so,' Liz said, tight-lipped.

'You're right,' Emily said. 'It's up to you two. Maybe you can work something out with the bank or something.'

Liz's eyes flashed a bit. 'Emily, I know you're trying to wave your magic wand and make everything all right.'

Emily was annoyed. 'You're my sister. I'm just trying to help.'

'Just be thankful that Conor hasn't taken the roof from over your head.'

Well. There was no arguing with that.

Liz looked a bit bitter now. 'Conor would never let you down. You're very lucky, you know.'

There was that luck thing again, as though Emily and Liz had been dealt their entire lives in a random hand of cards. Emily didn't tell Liz that she felt exhausted and depressed sometimes too, that she was riddled with worry over this baby, that she felt her entire life was out of control on her most of the time, that Conor was great but increasingly silent. It would look like childish griping compared to the demands of raising five boys, and Eamon Clancy's gargantuan capacity for financial folly.

'Maybe I should cancel,' Conor said.

Emily was irritated. She was lying on the sofa with her feet on a cushion. Her headache had developed into a migraine. But she had risked taking one aspirin and expected it to work very soon. The box had promised as much.

'I'm fine.' Creepy Crawley hadn't rung. The meeting was over by now. At the very least, would he not be wondering where she had been the entire afternoon? It was all very ominous.

'I know, but all the same . . .' He looked at her. She

knew he was waiting for her to make the decision for him. He was playing in the Cork Opera House tonight with the orchestra, a performance of *The Nutcracker Suite*, and needed to be there for a warm-up at six o'clock. But he had to rescue her car from the side of the road first.

'How can you cancel, Conor?'

'I could pick up the phone and just cancel!' he said stalwartly.

He couldn't, that was the thing. It wasn't as though the double-bassist could cover for him.

'Neasa's coming round after work.'

'Is she?'

'Yes.'

'Well, in that case . . .' He was already reaching for his sheet music.

Emily smiled fondly, remembering Liz's words. 'At least you'd never let me down.'

He went a bit still. 'Sorry?'

'Eamon, Conor?'

'Oh. Yeh. Eamon.'

I give up, Emily thought. She had told him the whole sorry saga the minute Liz was out the door and now he was acting like he'd forgotten all about it. Something as big as that! Or, more likely, it just wasn't important to him. His reaction had been predictably downbeat. He'd contented himself with a few murmurings of 'Bad situation, that,' and had refused to get involved in any bitching about Eamon.

'Haven't we enough problems of our own?' he'd said rather ominously.

Sometimes Emily wished that she'd married a right little gossip, someone who would indulge in all kinds of bad-mouthing and speculation with her. It wasn't half as satisfying doing it on one's own, and she just ended up feeling mean.

'Are you sure?' Conor asked again, edging towards the door.

'Go, Conor. You're off the hook!' If he stayed, he would just be watching her all the time and looking up that book of his and asking her all kinds of stupid questions about her perineum.

'Just say the word and I'll stay,' he said coolly. 'It's my baby too.'

It was hardly Eamon Clancy's.

'Yes yes yes,' Emily said, trying to smile nicely. She didn't want to row with him before he left. If he got killed on the drive down she would never forgive herself. Mind you, when Conor was annoyed he tended to drive slower.

'I'll be home at midnight,' he promised. 'But don't wait up if you're tired.'

'Good luck tonight.'

He kissed her and left. Emily plumped up the cushions under her feet. The headache was receding. She would do a bit of work before Neasa arrived.

She reached for a file and patted her bump. 'And I don't want to hear another word out of you.'

★ ★ ★

'I'm really sorry, Emily.'

'No, don't be, Neasa, no, no, that's ridiculous, no . . .'

'I feel terrible.'

'No, no, it's nothing to do with you, no, no, no . . .'
She was trapped in a vicious cycle of no's. She had to
break it.

'Yes,' she said.

'Yes what?'

'Yes, they've passed me over, yes, they're pigging
bastards, yes, yes, yes . . .' It was happening again. She
decided to stop speaking altogether.

Neasa was watching her carefully for signs of
unhingement. 'Would you like a drink?'

This required a yes or a no answer. She wasn't going
down that road again.

'Maybe.'

'I've brought a bottle of wine. And some snacky
things. Are you hungry?'

Another trick question. 'Possibly.'

Neasa efficiently unpeeled a miniature bottle opener
from her heavy, jangling key-ring. Her key-ring also
held a miniature pair of scissors and nail-clippers.
Nothing remotely useful such as an actual key, which
she always put in her pocket. She got two tumblers
from the sideboard, poured wine, then dumped a
packet of salt and vinegar crisps into a clean ashtray.

'There *are* bowls in the kitchen, Neasa. And proper
wine glasses.'

'You can't be left alone at a time like this. And if you can't think of yourself, at least think of the baby. Cheers.'

Neasa drank her wine. Emily looked at the crisps. Ten years of friendship and not a word to say. That's what happened when boyfriends complicated the picture.

What Emily really wanted to do was ring Conor's mobile just as he was tuning up with the orchestra and cry lustily down the phone to him.

'Gary didn't want to take it from you, Emily.'

Like this was somehow to his credit.

'But he did,' Emily said a bit spitefully. God Almighty, she was allowed a bit of spite at a time like this, surely? Neasa seemed to think so too. She bowed her head in acknowledgement.

'You deserved it. Everyone knows that. Gary does too.'

He had probably heard the news in Emily's office. Emily knew very well that the pair of them went at it like knives the minute she vacated her swivel-chair. She had found a pubic hair there once the exact shade of blond as Gary's large head. And the cheese plant was haemorrhaging leaves. How the partners would love to know that their most recent addition was lifting his leg all over the office furniture!

'Are you over the shock?' Neasa asked eventually.

'I can't seem to feel anything below my hips.'

'That's par for the course,' Neasa said knowledge-ably. 'Remember when my grandmother died?'

'God yes,' Emily said. 'Your legs gave way at the graveside.'

'They didn't even ring you, did they?'

'No.'

'The pigging bastards.' Neasa thought this might be a good time to threaten to hand in her notice. Emily was so white. And she hadn't even given out about Gary, which was very nice of her. Neasa had even been prepared to join in, a little bit.

'You could sue,' she suggested instead. 'Discrimination against pregnant women.'

'Or just sexual discrimination.'

'Get them on both counts. And Crawley on sexual harassment.'

'He doesn't sexually harass me.'

'Oh, of course, you're pregnant.'

Emily didn't seem that enthusiastic about suing. Neasa was relieved. Gary would have a fit.

'I mean, it's not as though he said to me "You're going to get the partnership",' Emily gulped. Crawley's words were 'you could be in line for it', if her memory was correct. And the year before, it had been 'you never know', or something equally vague. In fact, he had never really promised her anything at all. Everything was just a distant possibility. If she put in the required work, of course.

Her face felt a little hot. 'Why do you think I didn't get it, Neasa?'

'They're a law unto themselves, those bastards,'

Neasa spat. 'You wouldn't know.'

'But why do *you* think I didn't get it?'

Neasa shifted indignantly. 'Well, this is the thing, isn't it! You work so hard! In at nine every morning, you drag the secretaries out of the bathroom, set up the Internet server for everyone, chase up the bad payers – my God, you even re-organised the entire filing system last year!' She gave a delicate shudder. 'Nobody else could have done that! You even make the coffee!'

'I also sell land,' Emily said quietly.

Neasa realised what she'd implied. 'Of course you do! Acres and acres of it! That goes without saying! I just meant that you do that on top of everything else. In addition.'

'Has Gary ever made the coffee? No, no, it's not an accusation. I'm just wondering.'

'To my knowledge,' Neasa said slowly, 'he has not. He certainly might have at some time in the past but I've, ah, never actually witnessed it.'

They were speaking like solicitors. It was terrible, like they were on different sides of a courtroom – not that either of them had ever been in a courtroom. But they had got their law degrees together, meeting that very first day in college, Emily sick with nerves and Neasa sick with a hangover. It was unthinkable that a man should come between them now.

'Oh fuck them all anyway,' Neasa said in a rush.

It unleashed something in Emily. Two fat tears slid

down her face. 'I really wanted this!'

'I know,' said Neasa, crying now too. She could never watch anybody crying, even on the telly, without joining in. 'It's very unfair, isn't it?'

'It's the lack of respect, Neasa. They didn't even bother to let me know!'

'I know, I know!' Neasa bawled. 'They're so spineless!'

'There's lawnmower petrol in the garage – will we go and burn Crawley's house down?'

'We could,' Neasa gulped, doubtfully.

'I know. I wouldn't normally. It's my hormones. They're all over the place. Did you know that my hair is falling out?'

Neasa's hands flew protectively to check that her own was still in situ. If it ever fell out she might as well commit suicide.

'You'd never notice, the way you comb it over like that,' she said loyally.

Emily cried harder. 'Thank you. And have you seen my ankles?'

Neasa tried to lie again but her natural brutality got the better of her. 'I know. They're huge,' she sobbed.

'Thank you! And Eamon's after bankrupting himself and Liz too.'

Neasa had to think for a minute. Oh yes, that horrible, jolly builder married to shrewish Liz. Neasa stopped crying. Otherwise she'd be puffy for two days.

'More wine,' she pressed.

'I can't. I've already had one glass and I'm not really supposed to be drinking at all according to Conor's book.'

'Shut your face, Emily, and have a half glass. The baby won't die.' She saw Emily's expression. 'Jesus Christ, sorry. I've an awfully big mouth.'

'You haven't. It's all right. Don't be silly.'

'Emily, why do you always say everything is all right when it's bloody not?'

Emily blinked. Somehow this conversation had sneakily mutated into an entirely different conversation. This always seemed to happen to her. Well, this time she would retaliate. She would fight her corner fair and square.

'Oh, leave me alone. I'm pregnant!'

Neasa didn't push it. There was a fine line with Emily, not that you'd think it to look at her. Anyway, Neasa was a bit drunk. Her natural honesty tended to flourish under the influence of alcohol and there was no telling what she might say. All her deepest thoughts and feelings about herself and, unfortunately, others tended to come out.

'I might get pregnant,' she said airily. This took her as much by surprise as Emily. Obviously the thought had been festering all day.

'You?'

'What's so odd about that?'

'No, it's just that, well, you don't particularly like children.'

'Other people's children,' Neasa said haughtily. 'It'll be different with our own.'

'Our?'

'Me and Gary, of course. He's talking about a future.'

She looked at Emily fiercely, defying her to say something mean and nasty about Gary.

'Well, if that's what you want,' Emily said.

'Why wouldn't I want it?' Neasa challenged.

'Then I say good luck to you,' Emily said sincerely.

Neasa deflated a bit. You'd think that Emily might at least be a little bit anti-Gary after the partnership and all that. She was just so fair and nice. It wasn't natural.

'Can I have a feel?' Neasa asked politely.

Emily had a strict policy about people feeling her bump. It was amazing the liberties friends and even total strangers took. Once, a woman had planted her hand on Emily's midriff in the supermarket, clucking and benign, as though Emily were public property.

'Just to see what I might be in for,' Neasa added.

'Of course you can.' Emily generously hitched up her baggy t-shirt. Neasa bent over to have a good look.

'Your belly-button's gone sideways.'

'I know. It's weird, isn't it?'

'And look at all those veins!'

'Conor said if you look closely, you can actually see a map of Munster.'

Neasa was rapidly having second thoughts. She didn't say anything about the stretch marks. It was like an army of slugs had marched drunkenly across Emily's belly.

'My hands might be cold,' she said, trying to get out of it now.

'Oh go on.'

Neasa put her hand down squeamishly. Emily's belly was as hard as a rock, not at all nice and squishy and soft. Then Neasa felt something poking through the hardness right under her hand.

'That's the baby's bum,' Emily told her.

That was enough for Neasa. She snatched back her hand. 'Obviously, it's something Gary and I will have to talk about.'

He would be at home now, maybe even cooking a nice romantic dinner. Neasa, in the throes of drink, had a wild urge to be with him. Still. She mustn't let on. She was here for Emily.

'Oh go home, Neasa. You're dying to.'

'I am not! Well, if you're sure you'll be all right.'

'Yes.' There was no lawnmower petrol left anyway, now that Emily thought about it. Not that burning Crawley's house down had been a remote possibility. She had only said it really to sound dangerous and exciting. Because surely a blow like this demanded some kind of drastic action? Instead of just crying and bitching around the house, which was all she would end up doing. Before going meekly in to work tomorrow, of course.

'Well, I just won't!'

'Won't what?' Neasa was looking anxiously at the door.

'I won't go in to work tomorrow. That'll show them!'

'It would,' Neasa said dubiously.

'Decided then,' Emily said, wondering how long she would be able to stick it out in the morning, looking at the clock every ten minutes, before finally giving up and going in. She wished her parents had been members of any other cult but the good, loyal, hard-working Catholic Church. And Emily had never perfected the art of rebellion.

Emily's mother Pauline was very fond of saying that one should count one's blessings. She had applied this maxim to the instance when the chimney had caught fire one Christmas. 'At least it didn't spread to the roof.' Then it had. 'At least the whole house didn't go up.' Then it had. 'At least nobody was hurt!' she'd shouted, daring somebody to fall down dead.

The blessings thing went naturally hand in hand with the need to be grateful for what one had. This could be liberally applied to any situation, and was. The time Liz had decided to cut Emily's hair, for instance. By the time she was finished, Emily looked as though she had been through extensive chemotherapy. 'Be grateful she didn't cut off your ear,' Pauline had said, kindly.

Situations that defied blessings and gratitude generally fell into the 'expect not and you won't be disappointed' category, a kind of useful, catch-all phrase. Emily was very familiar with this from the time she had been studying for her Leaving Certificate.

In fairness, her Trojan work had been noted, encouraged and praised. But all the good had somehow been wiped away by the advice not to expect seven A's, that way she would be spared disappointment. In the event, she got only six.

Sometimes, harassed, Pauline would get confused and mix up the three. 'Be grateful that your blessings are not disappointed!' she would shout. 'At least your expectations won't be grateful for what they have!'

The household was routinely weighed down under blessings, gratitude and disappointment. Everybody else seemed happy enough with this state of affairs. But it seemed to Emily that it kind of quenched any hope, ambition or hand in one's own fate. Once she had voiced this.

'Can we not expect anything?'

'What?' Pauline was startled.

'This disappointment thing – I was just thinking that maybe a bit of disappointment is okay. It means that at least you've tried for something.'

'What are you talking about, Emily?' Pauline was busy dishing up dinner from seven different pots and pans and it required considerable concentration.

'She's off,' Liz said, as though Emily routinely upset dinnertime with philosophical discussions, which she didn't.

'I'm just wondering, that's all.'

A piece of pink, wet ham landed on her plate.

'It's just a saying, Emily.'

'But why do people say it?'

Pauline was impatient. 'I don't know! It wouldn't be a saying if it didn't have truth in it!'

And they had all looked at Emily as though she were being very unreasonable. She had kept any other thoughts on disappointment and ambition to herself.

She hadn't told her mother or Liz or indeed any of the family about the potential partnership. She was fiercely glad now. She would have proved the thesis that anybody who dared to aspire higher would be brutally and swiftly squashed. Proper order, too.

At least I know before Crawley tells everyone tomorrow, she thought – oh Christ. She was doing it. She had said At Least.

Furious, she dragged herself off the sofa before she started naming Conor and the baby amongst her blessings. Upstairs, she went through her wardrobe. It was divided neatly into 'Before Pregnancy' and 'Pregnancy'. She shunned the flowing, suitable, sensible maternity dresses and trousers she usually wore in to the office. From the other section, she took a skin-tight red lycra dress and laid it on the bed. She would go in to the office tomorrow (after making them sweat for a few hours first, of course) in all her red glory, her belly sticking into Crawley's face. She would wear matching violent lipstick and high heels. And she would refuse to make the coffee. She would do nothing except what was required of her and she would be sure that everyone saw her reading the 'Situations Vacant' at tea break.

She mightn't even wear a bra!

The phone by the bed rang. Ten past seven – Conor, checking to see how she was before he went on stage. He wouldn't expect her to put on a front for him. She snatched up the phone, already crying a bit in anticipation.

'I didn't get the fucking partnership!'

It was Mr Chapman.

'Oh! Sorry, I thought you were . . .' Just move on. 'You certainly work late!'

Mr Chapman hadn't time for chitchat. He'd been given two tickets to a performance of *The Nutcracker Suite* in the Cork Opera House that night by a grateful patient whose triplets he had delivered, and he was greatly looking forward to it. He informed Emily that he'd had her urine sample double-checked in the lab and that there were indications of uric acid in it. Protein, in other words. It was a cause for concern.

'How, exactly?'

He went on a bit about her raised blood pressure again, and her water retention and then he said the word 'pre-eclampsia'. Now, pre-eclampsia was a condition—

'I know what pre-eclampsia is,' Emily said, who wasn't all that sure. 'But I feel absolutely fine.'

Yes, par for the course, usually the sufferers didn't experience any physical discomfort—

'No, really, I'm about to start ironing.'

Mr Chapman advised her not to do that. Instead she

was to pack a small overnight bag and go to the hospital. No panic, just for observation. He would see her in the morning.

Emily could think of nothing except the obvious. 'I don't have any car. It was towed, you see.'

A small silence. Mr Chapman wasn't used to dealing with patients' travel problems.

Could she prevail upon a friend? A relative?

Neasa was probably under Gary at this very moment. And to ask Liz to come over with the five boys? Deirdre and Jackie lived in Cork. Michael and Brian, Emily's two brothers, lived in Australia.

Into the lengthening silence, Mr Chapman suggested a taxi.

'They'll never take me to Cork,' Emily said. 'They don't even like going too far out the Cork Road.'

Mr Chapman was nonplussed now. Short of coming to get her himself, the only thing he could suggest was an ambulance.

'An ambulance?' Emily had visions of being borne down the High Street of Paulstown, sirens wailing and lights flashing, drinkers in Milo's pub coming to the door to see what was happening. She would die of mortification.

Mr Chapman told her he would organise the ambulance and got off the phone before she complicated matters further.

Emily's brain went into a peculiar, very practical mode. Should she ring Conor? No, what was the point?

He was about to go on stage. It would only worry him. Best to pack and get there and ring him later. He would be in the same city anyway; he could just nip by when the performance was over.

Emily's hospital bag and the bag for the baby were already packed in readiness for the big day. It would be easiest to just take those. But she wouldn't. It would be like admitting that everything was going wrong. And it wasn't. It wasn't. Chapman had said just to pack for overnight. She would do that.

Two nightdresses and a pair of pyjamas just in case. Her huge old bunny slippers, because the new ones were already packed away. Underwear, toothbrush, toothpaste. A towel. Even her anti-wrinkle cream.

The suitcase on top of the wardrobe was much too big. It would look like she was going on holidays. Should she just empty her hospital bag? Too much hassle. She dragged Conor's bag from under the bed and shook off the dust.

Unfortunately it had Manchester United emblazoned across it. It had been a freebie. Stickers for Germany, Italy and France were plastered on the sides, relics from his tour with the orchestra last year. They would probably think in the hospital that Emily was a football hooligan who followed the team all over the world.

She began to pack, removing a pair of Conor's forgotten socks first. Rancid. She threw them in the laundry bin. When she was finished, she zipped up the bag and went downstairs. She switched off the TV and all the lights, and took her house keys. Then she sat on the chair by the front door, the bag on her knees. It all seemed very unreal.

The doorbell rang, startling her. There had been no lights or sirens or anything. In the darkness, Emily felt her way up the door towards the latch. She had to put the bag down first. It took a while. The doorbell rang again.

'Could have a stiff in here, Joe,' one of the ambulance men said outside.

'Easier really,' Joe said.

Emily flung open the door and loomed out of the darkness, giving them a fright.

'Emily Collins?' Joe asked.

'Yes.'

'Hop in.'

Joe was very kind as it turned out.

'All right, love?'

'Great, thank you,' Emily said. She was perched on the little bench at the side. Far from screaming down the town, the ambulance chugged along at a leisurely thirty miles an hour. The driver was called Liam, she learned, and he was eating egg sandwiches in the front. She could smell them. Occasionally the radio crackled and she heard him mumble incomprehensibly into it.

'And how's the babby?' Joe wanted to know.

'Oh, kicking away.'

'Good, good,' Joe said, his brown eyes crinkling. 'That's the way to have him.'

'They think I have pre-eclampsia,' Emily found herself saying.

Joe clucked and shook his head. 'Do they now?'

'But I feel fine,' she insisted to him.

'Most people we pick up do,' Joe said sagely. 'They ring 999, all hysterical, saying they're having a heart attack or a brain haemorrhage or they can't breathe or they're unconscious. We rush to the scene and find them sitting up having a cup of tea, telling you that it was only wind. But we have to bring them in all the same.'

'I didn't ring,' Emily quickly clarified.

'Oh I know. Some consultant did. They think we're a taxi service.' He banged on the partition. 'Don't they, Liam?'

'What?'

'Taxi service.'

'Oh, yeh.'

Emily looked at the wires and tubes and masks hanging from the ambulance ceiling. It all looked very clinical and menacing and she felt frightened now.

'Don't mind that stuff, love,' Joe told her. 'That's only for the serious cases.'

'What'll they do to me down there?' she blurted.

Joe scratched his head. 'I don't honestly know. Our job stops at the front door."

'Of course, sorry,' Emily said. She thought that this was a shame. Joe seemed much more human than Mr Chapman.

'But the girls are very nice down there,' Joe assured her. 'Fiona, she's the Head Nurse in Maternity, she's a real cracker – isn't she, Liam?'

'Smashing,' Liam shouted.

'They're all very nice,' Joe repeated. 'Most of them have babbies themselves. They'll take good care of you. And the food's great, for a hospital. Chips and everything.'

Emily nodded vigorously. She fixed her gaze on a plastic mask dangling near her nose.

'My wife had one four weeks ago,' Joe said shyly.

'Sorry?'

'A baby.'

'Did she?'

'A girl. Eight pounds four ounces.'

'Oh! That's a great weight.'

'It is,' Joe said proudly. 'We named her Tamzin.'

'Tamzin?'

'I know, I wasn't that keen on it to be honest, but the wife is a terrible *EastEnders* fan. That blonde one in it, she's called Tamzin. In real life, mind – I can't remember what she's called on the telly.'

'Melanie,' Emily said faintly, vowing never to watch it again.

'That's it! Anyway, I couldn't get me tongue around this Tamzin business at all in the beginning, but funny, the baby, she seems to have grown into it.' He pondered this for a moment. 'But the point is that the wife had her in the same place you're going to now.'

'I'm not having it now, though,' Emily clarified quickly. 'I'm only in for observation. It's not due for weeks and weeks yet.'

'Sure,' Joe said easily. 'This your first?'

'Yes,' Emily said, eventually.

They sat in silence for a while. Emily thought of Conor who was probably ringing the house at this very minute before he went on stage. Would he be worried when he got no reply? Probably not, sensibly assuming that she had gone out to the dogs or something. Emily herself always got slightly panicked when Conor was unreachable by phone for any length of time. She always imagined that something nasty had happened or, if he was driving, that he'd been in a crash. Conor, home safe and sound, would listen to these fantasies with a faint amusement. He would ruffle her hair and tell her she was a dreadful worrier. Once, she told herself, just once, she would like to see him harried and hassled. It wasn't that she wished him discomfort; she would just like to share with him occasionally, that was all.

She jumped as the black glass partition separating the driver flew back. She was presented with the back of Liam's head. He was replacing the radio mike. He spoke over his shoulder.

'Car crash down by Finnerty's Cross. Three vehicles, one a truck.' He cast a look at Emily, and said carefully, 'Fairly bad. They're sending two units up from Cork, but they'll be at least forty minutes. We have to divert.'

Emily swallowed hard. She didn't know if she was up to a bad car crash at the moment. And what if there wasn't room enough in the ambulance for everybody? Emily's problems might look fairly tame compared to some poor soul who had lost limbs, or worse. Would she have to get out and walk? But what about her baby? If it were just Emily, she wouldn't mind. She was going to say something to Joe about it when he jumped to his feet.

'Are you strapped in properly there?' he said.

'I think so. Why?'

The siren exploded on the top of the ambulance. Strobe lighting flashed on the tinted windows. The ambulance shot off at speed and Emily bounced from side to side.

Joe – nice, slow Joe – mutated into a person of extreme efficiency. Balancing expertly in the careering ambulance, he checked tubes and wires and opened little cupboards that Emily hadn't noticed before. He took out big pouches of clear-coloured liquid, rolls of white gauze, syringes, more tubes. Things must be very bad down at Finnerty's Cross.

'Do you want me to do anything?' Emily asked loudly over the roar of the ambulance.

'What?'

'If it's bad. I did a first-aid course last year.'

Joe looked at her.

'It was quite advanced,' she added.

'Thanks, anyway, but sure you'll be getting out.'

'What?'

'We're here.'

Emily looked out and saw lights – shops, a petrol station. They were coming into Mitchelstown, just five miles from home. And now here was St Martha's coming up on the left. Joe was apologetic.

'Don't worry. They'll transfer you to Cork in the morning.'

The ambulance screeched to a halt, lights still flashing. Joe flung the doors open and held out a hand to Emily. She stepped out to see a porter and a nurse rushing out the front door at all the commotion. The nurse was pulling on plastic gloves.

The pair stopped just short of Emily, taken aback to find her on her feet and clutching a Manchester United bag. Suspiciously, they looked around her person for signs of blood or broken limbs or indeed any injury at all which would merit such a noisy and dramatic entrance.

'Diversion,' Joe explained. 'She was due to go to Cork. Pre-eclampsia.'

'Oh,' the nurse said, deflating. The porter sighed and went back in.

Emily looked around for Joe but he was springing back into the ambulance.

'Good luck,' he said to her, and the doors closed. The ambulance screeched off, leaving Emily feeling bereft.

The nurse looked at Emily. Her badge said V Mooney. 'Pre-eclampsia then?'

'I don't know,' Emily said unhappily. 'That's just what Mr Chapman thinks.'

'Mr Chapman. I see.' Her mouth went a bit tight. She reached over and took Emily's bag, her last object of safety and comfort in a world gone insane. 'Right, let's get you inside then.'

She was put in a ward with three other pregnant women. A television blared high in a corner. Despite this, one patient appeared to be soundly asleep, her hair all over her face. The woman in the bed next to Emily had so many visitors that they were perched on any available piece of furniture, including Emily's bed.

Nurse V Mooney shooed them off. 'Don't tire Maggie out now,' she said mildly. Maggie, the patient, was sitting up in the bed like a queen and eating oranges.

Emily nodded politely at her and got a big beam back but Nurse V Mooney whipped around the curtain, cutting Maggie off.

'You can get undressed and into bed,' she told Emily. 'I'll be back to take your blood pressure and all that.'

'This pre-eclampsia—'

'We don't know if it's that yet. I'll have to find out what instructions Mr Chapman left, which means I'll have to phone Cork.' She sighed as though she personally shouldered the phone bill.

Emily was left alone. She unzipped her bag and neatly stowed her belongings in the battered metal locker. The catch on it wouldn't close properly and the door kept swinging open to reveal her knickers and socks to anyone who cared to look. In the end she unfolded her towel and tucked it in around her things. Now it just looked as though she were hiding a stash of vodka.

She had forgotten to bring a book, of course, or a magazine. It hadn't been high on her list of priorities. But she couldn't face an evening of making small talk with the other women. She was too upset. And the thing on the telly was in Irish, of all languages. At the bottom of the Manchester United bag was a copy of Conor's concert programme from his tour last year. It was better than nothing.

It felt silly to be getting into her nightie at a quarter past eight in the evening. The bed was old-fashioned and high and she had to give a little hop to get into it. She tried to pull up the stiff sheets but, as in all hospitals, they seemed to be welded to the bed some-where around hip region. Short of stripping the bed and re-making it properly, which she suspected wouldn't go down too well with that nurse, she would just have to put up with it. Also she didn't want the other women to think she had some kind of fetish. When the lights went out later she would sort it out.

The din from the visitors in the next cubicle was deafening as more people arrived – Maggie's husband Tiernan, his two sisters and a brother, a couple of second cousins and someone from Boston. It was unclear whether they'd flown over especially to see

Maggie. Emily's curtain bulged as they squeezed in. It must be a special occasion. Probably Maggie's birthday or something.

'Okay.' Nurse V Mooney was back, carrying all kinds of equipment and a chart. She proceeded to fill in details with a pen that she had to give a good shake to every now and again.

'Everything in this blasted place is falling apart,' she said, to herself more than Emily. 'Now. If you could hold out your arm.'

Emily did so obediently and a pressure cuff was put on it. She felt it tighten unpleasantly. Nurse V Mooney didn't meet her eyes.

'Well,' she said, looking at the pressure gauge.

'Is it bad?'

'One eighty over one ten.' She glanced up. 'It's high but I've seen worse.'

Emily bet she had. Nurse V Mooney now sat down on the bed. Emily had to move her feet.

'Any nausea?'

'No.'

'Vomiting?'

'No.'

'Flashing lights?'

'Apart from the ambulance.' Joke, woman, joke!

The nurse didn't smile. 'Any pain in the abdomen?'

'No.'

'Any bleeding, irregular discharge, discomfort?'

'No, no, no.'

The nurse shot Emily a look as though she were making fun of her.

'Any headache?'

'Yes. Well, not now. But earlier. I took an aspirin.'

The nurse hadn't much interest in this. 'Right, good.' She flipped a page in the chart. 'Well, we've certainly caught it in time.'

'The pre-eclampsia?'

'We don't know if it's that yet,' the nurse insisted, as though it were all a fuss about nothing. 'But if it is, it hasn't developed into eclampsia.'

'That's bad, isn't it?' Emily remembered reading up on the condition, but there were so many things that could go wrong during pregnancy that she couldn't remember the exact details.

The nurse seemed to cheer up for the first time. 'Oh yes. Convulsions and a coma, usually.'

Oh, how Emily wished she were in Cork, in a nice bright hospital with low beds and lockers that worked, away from this mean, cheerless cow.

Nurse Mooney was nearly finished with the chart now.

'Have you any other children?'

'No.'

'Is this your first pregnancy?'

'No.'

The nurse looked up at her. 'What was the history of that, please?'

'I had a miscarriage at twelve weeks,' Emily said. She

had been due to come to Martha's for the first scan on that Thursday.

The nurse filled this in carefully. 'Any complications or problems after that?'

'No.' Just one of those things.

The nurse snapped the top back on her pen loudly and stood. 'I'll get one of the girls to bring you up a cup of tea.'

'That'd be nice.'

'Mr Chapman appears not to have left any notes for you in Cork, or at least the staff down there can't find them,' the nurse said, that tightening of her mouth back again. 'They're going to page him and ring me back.'

'Thank you.'

'He'll probably just prescribe bed-rest, which is usual in a case like this. In the meantime, if you'd do a sample for me' – she slapped a plastic container down on the table at the bottom of the bed – 'we'll check it for signs of uric acid. But a house doctor will be around later anyway to examine you.'

She looked at Emily's chart one last time then back at Emily.

'You're not by any chance Liz Clancy's sister? You look very alike.'

'I am!' Emily was delighted that they had finally found common ground. 'She had all her five boys here.'

'Yes. I was here for every single one,' the nurse said grimly and left.

Emily rang Conor's mobile three times from her own mobile, even though there were stern signs up all over the place not to use mobile phones. Maybe it wasn't so bad if it were mobile to mobile, she reasoned. Anyhow, the concert must be running over because all she got was the answering service. She didn't want to leave a message. No matter what way she worded it, it would sound like a panic situation.

The house doctor had been around and had told her more or less what the nurse had. Bed-rest, sleep, and monitoring of her blood pressure and urine. Mr Chapman apparently had ordered the same. They had found his notes. Emily would be transferred to Cork in the morning and she would see him then.

The curtains were still pulled over. Relatives kept coming and going in the next cubicle at a steady pace, paying no heed at all to the hours set for visiting time. The telly blared some American sitcom and canned laughter exploded into the ward from time to time, jarring Emily's nerves. She lay in bed on her left side, as the doctor had advised. Apparently it helped the flow of blood to the placenta.

Nobody knew she was here. Not a single soul. She was tempted to use her mobile again, but what was the point? It was nearly half past ten – what could Liz or Neasa or her mother do? Anyway, she didn't really want to see any of them.

She rubbed her tummy and wanted nobody but Conor. He always made her feel safe. He would stroke her hair and tell her that Chapman was only covering his ass in case she sued, that it was all a storm in a teacup. She'd be out tomorrow, just wait and see.

She turned over in the bed carefully and picked up Conor's concert programme. There would be a photo of him in it; they always printed little photos of the orchestra.

There he was, page seven, his hair a bit longer maybe, but otherwise looking exactly like a plain-clothes garda, stern but compassionate. Billy Middlemiss, the fat cellist, was on one side of him; Ffion Rivera, the first violinist, on the other. That was her stage name, of course. Everybody else just called her Mary Murphy.

Mary had her violin in the picture. And Billy Middlemiss was holding his cello. You could see the top of it. Conor had obviously been playing the piano when the photo was taken because his arms were held out from his body. But they hadn't been able to fit the piano in the picture so he looked like he was levitating.

Emily smiled fondly. Her eye travelled down to the tour dates. Italy. Then France, before going over to Germany for the final weekend, the 3rd and 4th of September it said here. She had driven up to Dublin airport to collect him when he'd arrived back from Germany on that Sunday night. It would have been the 5th. But no. The 3rd was a Thursday. It said so here. And the 4th was a Friday, the last concert date. She must have collected him on Saturday.

She hadn't. She'd had the whole weekend to herself, she remembered it. Indeed, she would never forget it. She'd gone for a pregnancy test in the Well Women Clinic in Cork on Friday and it was positive. She didn't want to tell Conor on the phone; the news was too precious, especially after the miscarriage. Saturday and Sunday had crawled by until six o'clock on Sunday evening when his flight came in.

The programme was wrong. Probably a misprint.

She had a sudden memory of Conor coming through arrivals on his own. No Billy Middlemiss dragging his cello, none of the other thirty members of the orchestra.

No one, in fact, except Ffion Rivera. She had waved quickly over at Emily and gone out another way. She hadn't waved at Conor, nor he at her. She hadn't looked at him at all.

Emily carefully put the programme down and lay quietly on her left side. Maggie's visitors eventually left. The woman across the way asked if anybody minded whether she turned the television off. Emily didn't reply. Her mind was in a different place.

Her mobile rang, startling her. It was Conor, sounding the same as always.

'Where are you? I've been phoning home all evening. Emily?'

'Yes, yes. You see, there's been a bit of a development.'

'Well, what?' He was a bit impatient. Emily knew that he expected her to say that Liz had called in the throes of some new crisis and that Emily had dutifully gone over.

'I'm actually in hospital.'

'What?'

She told him about Mr Chapman, the pre-eclampsia, St Martha's.

'Jesus Christ. Are you all right?'

'Fine, fine.'

'You sound a bit funny.'

'Do I? I'm in a ward. It's hard to talk.'

'I'll be there in forty-five minutes,' Conor promised.

'No, it's too late. And you'll be tired after the drive up.' Emily wanted to go to sleep too. She felt exhausted.

'I'm coming in.'

'They won't let you, Conor. It's a quarter to eleven.'

He was silent. 'In the morning then. First thing.'

'Sure, fine.'

'Emily?' She heard his concern over the phone, his love for her. 'Just . . . sleep well.'

'Yes,' she said. 'You too.'

Nurse V Mooney came by, pushing a drugs trolley. Emily wondered whether she ran the place single-handed.

'Everybody all right here?' she called.

'Have you got any sleeping tablets?' Emily asked. She wasn't able to drop off; it was the strangest bed and the worry about the baby.

'I'm sorry. You're not down for sleeping tablets. You'll have to consult Mr Chapman in the morning.'

'Oh.'

The nurse looked cannily at Emily and came over. Emily tensed for another invasion of some part of her. But the nurse just switched the light off over the bed and poured a glass of water from the jug on the locker.

'Listen,' she said quietly, 'it's perfectly natural to be worried about something like this. But you'll be absolutely fine. Bed-rest and sleep. That'll sort you out.'

She pulled up the covers over Emily as though she were a baby herself and tucked her in.

Hospital wards are the natural enemies of bed-rest and sleep. The whole night long people came and went in Emily's ward, toilets flushed, babies bawled in the distance, phones rang, nurses talked at the tops of their voices and at one point someone, somewhere, screamed. Emily had bolted up wildly in the bed, wondering if it had been her.

It had all taken on a rather surreal air sometime around half past four. Visions in white would appear at the bottom of Emily's bed and loom over her. They had Mary Murphy's face and one of them even started playing the violin. Quite well, too. Emily surfaced only to find yet another nurse checking her chart.

Emily got up quietly and negotiated the leap from the bed to the floor. The nurses at the station outside were eating Roses from five different boxes. 'He's such a fucking pisshead and he's not even a real DJ, did you know that? Oh, Emily, are you feeling all right?'

'Terrific, thanks.' She went on her way, moving through the dim warm corridors in her bare feet, aimless and dislocated. The wards were dark and quiet on either side of her, but she could see shapes moving around inside slowly: someone picking up a baby, someone else just drifting up and down. It was all like some kind of benign horror movie.

She moved on slowly, past doors that said Staff Only, Kitchen Staff Only, Private, No Entry. She looked in vain for one that said Okay, Come On In. But there was no refuge for Emily tonight.

'Make way, please!'

Emily whirled around to see a wheelchair coming towards her at speed out of the darkness. A woman lay prostrate in it, her huge belly heaving. Her eyes were closed and her skin white. She looked to Emily like she was dying.

A porter pushed the wheelchair. A midwife ran beside it.

'Breathe, Martina. That's it!' she shouted enthusiastically, as though she were an Olympic swimming coach. 'I didn't hear you breathe!'

Emily saw the whites of Martina's eyes as the wheelchair flashed past and through big double doors at the bottom of the corridor: Delivery Ward – Authorised Personnel Only.

Emily, stricken, hurried down and pressed her nose to the glass at the top of the door. It was bright inside, fluorescent lights everywhere. There was no sign of poor, pitiful Martina. Something had obviously gone terribly wrong for her. Emily made sure to stand to one side because surgeons, consultants and possibly resuscitation staff were bound to be on the scene in seconds.

But nobody came. And inside the delivery ward, midwives and doctors hung around in small, cheerful clumps. There was no panic. A doctor said something and everybody laughed.

Emily was confused. What about Martina? What right had they to go on laughing and behaving normally at a time like this? Didn't they realise that there was a woman not thirty yards from them on another planet with pain? Did they not care?

Emily, ludicrously, found that she was crying bitter tears for Martina. She wanted to march in there and take Martina's hand, protect her, curl up on the bed beside her and tell her that everything would be all right. God Almighty, what kind of a sick world was it when the woman didn't even have a friend or relative or anybody at all who understood her at a time like this? And where was the wretched husband or boyfriend? Probably conveniently fainted back in the ward.

The air in the delivery ward was thick and warm and quiet. Nobody was around now except for a nurse at the station and she was busy filling in notes. Emily drifted past as though she had every right to be there. The nurse didn't look up.

The first two cubicled delivery rooms were empty. In the third, a woman and a man walked up and down slowly, him rubbing her back. They looked very intense. Emily felt a bit like a voyeur as she stood on tiptoes to look over the glass at them. She moved on.

The door to the next delivery room was shut tight. The glass on this one was too high to see over. Voices came from inside, low and calm. Emily heard moans: Martina. Her heart constricted in sympathy. She put her hand on the door.

'Hello?' The nurse from the station was bearing down on Emily, curious and wary.

'I'm looking for Martina,' Emily told her politely.

'This is a restricted area.'

'Yes, but I'm looking for Martina.'

The nurse cocked her head to one side. 'Why?'

'I'm a friend of hers,' Emily informed her. 'And she's in there all on her own.'

'She's not, you know. There's plenty of people in there with her.'

'Will she be all right?'

'I'm afraid I can't discuss patient information.'

Emily was surer than ever now that something had gone terribly wrong for Martina. Fresh tears cascaded down her face.

'I'm very sorry,' she said.

'That's all right.' The nurse must think that Emily was a very close friend indeed of Martina's. They might even have planned their pregnancies together. 'I'll tell her you called by okay?' she assured Emily. 'Now I'm going to have to ask you to go back to your own ward.'

She kindly escorted Emily to the double doors and went back to her station. Emily half expected her to whip out a walkie-talkie and murmur, 'Psycho in Delivery, can we have security please?' But the nurse just took a chocolate from a box of Roses and went back to her notes. The wonder of it was that none of the staff was fat. It must be something to do with night shifts and botched-up metabolism. It would be interesting to see whether any of the day staff was fat. There could be a whole new diet book in this one, Emily thought. Eat all you like between the hours of midnight and 6am.

'You've certainly cheered up.' Nurse V Mooney swished by. 'Now, back to bed with you.'

'I'll go in my own good time,' Emily said pleasantly and turned a corner.

Back down the dim, warm corridors. Emily bit back more tears and felt very unsure about everything. She didn't even know how to get back to her own ward from here. She felt she was halfway between normality and utter insanity and feared that if her mind went down a particular road then the balance might just be tipped. Best not to think at all, just keep on walking. Eventually morning would be here.

At last she approached a door that was open. Bright, welcoming light spilled out, and spirited chatter, along with the unmistakable stench of cigarette smoke.

Emily went in and sat down. Two women in their dressing-gowns were perched on hard plastic seats, both puffing furiously.

'Couldn't sleep either?' the one in pink said sympathetically.

'No. It's very noisy.'

'It's desperate, isn't it?' the one in the blue said. She was heavily pregnant. 'Get your hubby to bring in some earplugs. Want a cigarette?'

'I don't smoke,' Emily said regretfully.

The woman tensed, expecting Emily to look at her judgmentally. Emily couldn't give a hoot if she jumped off the top of the building. Now they were wondering what the hell she was doing in the smokers' room. *Their* room. Emily sat there defiantly and tried not to breathe in.

'When are you due?' she politely asked the woman in pink, eyeing her big belly.

The woman looked at her. 'I had my baby yesterday.'

Just when Emily thought that nothing else could happen that day. But then the woman threw back her big head and guffawed. 'Jesus Christ! And there was me thinking that I was tiny!'

The woman in blue laughed too. So did Emily, after a moment. She laughed harder and harder. Then she was the only one laughing. She screeched to a silence, her mouth still open in a silent bray.

'Are you all right?'

'Oh yes,' Emily said vigorously. 'I'm in for preeclampsia. I was passed over for a partnership in work today and I've just discovered my husband might have been unfaithful. Maybe he still is, who knows.'

The woman in pink looked at the woman in blue.

'She's a ticket, isn't she?' And they both guffawed heartily again. They liked her now, her supposed humour had broken down that difficult barrier between smokers and non-smokers, and she was one of theirs.

'Cathy,' said the one in blue.

'Petra,' said the one in pink.

'I'm Emily,' Emily said, not at all sure.

'Seriously, girl, what are you in for? You're not due, are you?'

'No, no. Just observation.'

'Who is it, O'Mara? Dunphy?'

'Chapman,' Emily said, feeling a bit irreverent at dropping the 'Mr'.

'Chapman!' Cathy said. 'Don't get me started.' Before Emily could, she was off. 'He had my sister in and out to Cork three times on her last one! He won't come up and see you here, you know. Too far a journey for him in his big Mercedes.'

It felt very bad to be discussing Mr Chapman like this, and Emily leaned in eagerly for more. It was a kind of escape.

'He heads up the maternity unit down in Cork. Did you know that?' Petra hissed.

'I didn't.'

'Oh yes. He can't wait for this place to close so that he can get his hands on even more women. Some people say that he was one of those lobbying hard for the closure. For his private practice, you see. We'll all end up paying him instead of O'Mara or Dunphy.'

'No!' Emily was amazed at her capacity to still feel shock.

'I'll tell you, it beats the hell out of brown envelopes.' Petra stubbed out her cigarette authoritatively and reached for another. 'I have O'Mara this time. He's very good, except that his hands are always cold.'

'I've got Dunphy,' Cathy confided to Emily. 'He's great with a needle. Stitch you up good as new.'

Emily was feeling a bit light-headed. Either it was tiredness or the second-hand smoke. 'I think I might go back to bed, see if I can sleep.'

'Good idea,' Cathy said. 'Although you won't have much chance of that. The kitchen girls are setting up for breakfast now. They bang around a good bit, don't they, Petra?'

'They do,' Petra agreed. 'Did you order an egg?'

'What?' Emily was mystified.

'You'll only get Weetabix and brown bread so. Take my advice, fill in the menu forms as a matter of priority. Otherwise they'll just give you whatever's handy.'

'Okay, thanks.' Emily stood. 'I'll see you around.'

'You will, girl,' Cathy said. 'And come up and see the baby tomorrow. I'm in Elizabeth's Ward – I'll let you look after her for a few minutes.'

Who was looking after the baby now was unclear. Emily nodded and smiled some more and left.

Her own ward seemed oddly familiar and safe. She

got back into bed and pulled the covers up tight around her and listened to the snoring, the crashing of breakfast utensils, the nurses' chatter outside.

'Are you all right?' someone whispered.

It was Maggie, peering in the side of the curtain.

'Fine, thanks,' Emily whispered back.

'I've got half a sleeping tablet left – I could slip it to you and they'd never know.'

'You're very good, but I'm not allowed.'

Maggie nodded and smiled and let the curtain drop back. Emily fell asleep instantly and dreamlessly.

Neasa heard the news the next morning. Conor had phoned at the crack of dawn, after first trying Neasa's house. But Neasa had stayed in Gary's overnight, as she did every Monday, Wednesday and Friday night. Gary stayed at hers on Tuesday, Thursday and Saturday nights. It was only fair, they assured each other. Equal. Sunday was a day of rest, which they were both secretly grateful for.

'Isn't that just the worse luck?' Neasa said to Gary. 'She must be in bits. After losing the partnership too.'

Gary shifted uneasily. He wasn't used to this feeling of guilt. 'But it's just for observation.'

'All the same, I'll go in. Tell them in work that I'm taking the morning off,' Neasa ordered.

'Right . . . are you sure you can take off just like that, honey?'

Neasa observed that a new note of loyalty had crept

into Gary's voice when it came to Crawley Dunne & O'Reilly.

'You're a partner now. You can okay it,' she said, sweetly.

'Of course,' he said quickly. 'Not that you'll be taking any liberties now that I'm a partner.'

'Will I heck,' she said. 'You're as good as a sick note from the doctor.'

She left Gary at the breakfast table looking slightly worried. She wouldn't rush straight over to Martha's, of course. Eleven o'clock would be a perfectly acceptable hour to be by Emily's bedside. She had time to get her roots touched up at the hairdressers' first, and see if they had any decent make-up in the chemist. It was very high maintenance being in love, she had discovered over the years. You constantly had to be on your guard against underarm hair and wayward cuticles, not to mention bikini lines. Expensive too: all the new clothes and underwear, romantic meals out and little spur-of-the-moment presents. It would nearly be a relief to slide into domestic cosiness where chipped nail varnish was just that, not some indication of a slovenly and weak character. She might actually be able to save some money, too.

Immediately she regretted her thoughts. Imagine turning into Emily and Conor, for example! Lovely, lovely people, God knows. But like two old comfortable boots at the end of the day. Finishing each other's sentences and forgetting to kiss each other every time they left the room! How could they have let themselves slide like that? They had been married six years, true, but that was no excuse.

Neasa and Gary had made love on the kitchen table the night before. Then they had opened a third bottle of wine and taken it into the living-room where they had talked and talked. Neasa couldn't remember for the life of her now what they had talked about, but it had all been very deep and meaningful. Gary had actually cried at one point. Naturally, so had Neasa. Then he had puked. Neasa hadn't been a bit offended; in fact, she had felt very tender and maternal, unusual for her, and had cradled his smelly head as he bent over the toilet.

Neasa herself never puked. She had a very strong constitution that way, even if the head was falling off her this morning. They really must buy better wine next time – you couldn't drink three bottles of that Spanish stuff without some ill-effects. More expense.

'Do you think I should call by Conor on the way to work?' Gary enquired, having followed Neasa into the bathroom. He looked a bit green.

'What for?'

'I don't know, to offer a bit of support or something.'

'He's probably on his way to the hospital now,' Neasa said.

Gary was relieved. Conor didn't like him. He never gave the slightest indication of this, but Gary just knew. He seemed to irritate him or something. And all the effort Gary made too, just because Emily was Neasa's friend! He was just trying to be nice, for heaven's sake. Asking Conor what it was like being a pianist and all that and even asking to see Conor's piano. Conor had dutifully shown it to him and had pointed out the difference between the black and white keys. You'd think he was taking the mick except that he looked so serious. Gary had then tried to talk about football to him, a sure fire safe bet. But Conor had no interest in football. He wasn't normal in that respect. Gary secretly thought of Conor as a bit snotty and removed, content to stand on the sidelines and observe other people, and looking as though he were enjoying some private joke.

He sometimes wondered what Conor was like in bed. Oh, nothing sexual, you understand. Gary was a man's man only in the pub, nowhere else, and anybody who suggested otherwise would get a black eye, all right? No, Gary only wondered about Conor in bed because he'd love to see him out of control for once. Abandoned and lustful and roaring, 'Come get it, baby!' Gary tittered.

'What?' Neasa said.

'Nothing, sweetness.' He was applying Neasa's cover-stick to a spot on his chin. All this drinking with Neasa was taking its toll. But apparently copious amounts of red wine went hand in hand with romance. 'Just thinking how lucky we are, that's all.'

'I know, I've never met anyone like you,' Neasa said fervently.

'Would a touch of powder over this be too much?' Gary wondered.

'Not at all,' Neasa said tenderly. 'Although, really, you're gorgeous enough.'

'You're just saying that.'

'Am not!'

'Awww.' He kissed the back of her neck. Neasa sighed in bliss. She must not let this one slip through her fingers like all the others had. Not that it had been her fault, of course. None of them had turned out to be what she thought they were. Take Fintan, for example, the nicest, sweetest, most romantic man you could ever hope to meet. That had lasted four heady months, until Fintan had revealed himself to be a chat-room junkie on the Internet. Then there was Michael, the secret cross-dresser. Neasa had thought that she could live with it until he confided that he would like to walk down the street just once in one of her dresses. He'd swiftly been dumped on the refuse heap along with Darren the sexist and Neil the guy who didn't believe in washing. There had been others too, whose infractions had been less dramatic but none the less unpalatable. She always seemed to go for men who let her down in some fundamental or deeply embarrassing way.

Gary was blissfully normal. The others had started out normal too, but the cracks had appeared much sooner. Neasa had six months with Gary under her belt and it was looking good. In fact, it had never looked better. She hated to say it, because she had said it so often in the past, but this time she knew she was right: Gary was The One.

'Got to go, baby,' she said.

'All right, chicken. See you for lunch?'

'Great. Crawley's office?'

'I suppose. Although we could just go for something to eat.'

Something to eat? They always had sex in Crawley's office on a Wednesday because he took a half-day. 'We could,' she said slowly.

Gary saw that he had displeased her but wasn't sure why. 'Crawley's office it is,' he said easily. 'I'll buy two Mars bars.'

Neasa beamed at him. Everything was great.

Nurse V Mooney woke Emily at a quarter to eight.

'Do you work here all the time?' Emily asked. She wondered what the V stood for.

'Eight to eight, the night shift,' the nurse informed her crisply. 'Now, let's see how the blood pressure is this morning.'

It wasn't much better from the look on her face.

'The urine came back, by the way. It's clear.'

Some good news at last.

'So I won't have to go to Cork?'

'No use asking me. Nobody tells us anything.' She added notes to Emily's chart. 'Mr Chapman will make the final decision. But he's not a man to take risks with other people's health.' She made this sound like a bit of an insult. 'Now, up you get and have some breakfast. Oh, and there's a man out there who says he's your husband.'

'Right.'

'He's been here since seven.' The nurse didn't look at her. 'But I thought you needed your sleep.'

She was gone before Emily could thank her. Emily got out of bed and put on her dressing gown. Then she brushed her hair back rigidly and found herself hunting for her powder to take the vulnerable shine off her nose.

She leaned against the bed heavily. What was she doing, armouring herself against her own husband? Against Conor, her plain-clothes garda, the man who couldn't even bring himself to double-park? The very idea of Conor and Ffion, Conor and Mary, seemed ludicrous in the cold bright light of the morning.

Emily was embarrassed at her conjecture now, mortified by her emotion last night. She wouldn't even tell Conor about this. He would be outraged by her suspicion. She would be if he thought the same about her.

But the heavy feeling in the pit of her stomach wouldn't go away, like she had opened some Pandora's box and would be sorry ever after.

She stepped out past the curtain and into the ward. The two other women and Maggie were sitting at a small table under the television, munching their way through Weetabix and boiled eggs. Emily hadn't even introduced herself to them yet, and she didn't now either. She slipped out into the corridor and found Conor sitting stiffly on a hard chair by the nurses' station, his feet sharply drawn in for fear of tripping up anybody.

'Hi.'

'Hi yourself,' Emily said, trying out a smile.

He looked at her belly. 'How are you feeling?'

'Okay, I suppose. Tired. It's hard to sleep in here.'

He nodded. He hadn't had much sleep either from the look of him. And he hadn't shaved either. He came over and awkwardly embraced her. It was very public here – nurses were everywhere as the shift changed over.

'Can we go somewhere?'

Emily thought of the smokers' room. 'Not really. Just back to my bed, I suppose.'

The other women didn't even look up as Conor arrived in. Like Emily, they had been poked and prodded and palpated throughout their pregnancies and were past embarrassment at being seen in their nighties by strange men. They'd been seen in a lot less.

Emily pulled the curtain tight around them again. It gave some small illusion of privacy.

'You have the chair,' she said.

'No, no, you must be sick of the bed, you sit in the chair.'

'Conor, take the blasted chair!'

She didn't know who was more surprised, her or Conor.

'Sorry. This is all a bit odd. Being here, I mean.'

'I know. You should have rung me, left a message or something. Remember, we agreed that I'd check the answering service at the interval?'

'I know, I know.' Emily felt as though she had broken the rules.

'I'd have come straight up.'

'I didn't want to worry you.'

'Oh Emily. I don't know why you do this. Try and take everything on by yourself.'

'I know,' Emily agreed. 'I should be shot really.' Oops. There she went again. She breezed on quickly. 'How did the concert go?'

'What? Oh, fine, fine. Look, have you talked to Chapman?'

'No. They might be transferring me to Cork. I don't know yet. Nobody tells the nurses here anything.'

'Neasa will be in later.'

'Why did you have to go ringing her?'

'What? She's your friend. I thought you'd like some company, that's all.'

He was feeling under attack. This was pointless and silly, Emily knew. And very unfair.

'I didn't get the partnership, Conor,' she said.

'Ah.' This explained everything. He looked very sympathetic. 'I'm sorry, Emily.'

'Yes. Gary got it instead.'

'Gary?' Conor's face said it all. 'Well. They'll be sorry.'

'Maybe.' Emily was unable to shake the feeling that she was making conversation.

Conor produced a plastic bag that she hadn't noticed before.

'I brought you some supplies. You know, 7UP and stuff. And some magazines.'

He must have stopped by the Spar that stayed open all night. A bunch of flowers stuck out the top of the bag, the ones you see in buckets outside garages.

'It was all they had,' he said apologetically. 'But I wanted you to have something nice to look at in this place.'

'Oh, Conor.' She took the bag and held it tight to her chest as though it were some kind of shield, and looked at his square, handsome, confused face.

'I do love you, you know,' she said.

He looked a bit embarrassed. 'Ah, I know. And I love you too.'

He got up and sat on the bed beside her and stroked her tummy, their baby. Emily laid her head on his shoulder and they sat for a while like that.

'It's just a precaution, Emily. Chapman's covering his ass. They're all terrified of litigation these days.'

Emily tried to find solace in his predictability but couldn't.

'You'll be out today, I bet you anything. And I'll take you home and everything will be like normal.'

'I suppose.' Reluctantly, she lifted her head off his shoulder. 'Conor, I have to eat breakfast now. Then the house doctor will be around again and they'll have to see about transferring me to Cork and all that.' She didn't look at him. 'Maybe you should go on home and get some rest.'

'I'm staying here.'

'There's nothing you can do. I'll ring you as soon as I know anything. I promise.'

Conor wasn't happy at all about this. 'I can just sit quietly in that chair – I won't be in anybody's way.'

'You'll be more use at home.' Emily appealed to his practical side. 'I might need more clothes and things for Cork and I'll need you to get them for me. And people will be ringing. Someone should be at home to tell everybody that there's no panic.'

Conor looked at her for a moment. 'Okay. If that's what you want.'

'It is,' she quickly assured him, adding brightly, 'and who knows, I might be ringing in an hour's time to ask you to come and drive me home!'

She wasn't fooling him. She knew by the twitch of his left eyebrow, a dead giveaway.

'Ring me anyway,' he asked.

'Of course I will!'

He stood and bent to kiss her. She turned her head slightly so that he kissed her cheek.

'Take care,' he said.

'You too.'

It was all a bit awkward and formal. Part of Emily hated sending him away like this; it seemed very heartless when he was probably as worried as she. But she was afraid of what she might say if he stayed any longer.

She gave a little wave as he went out into the corridor, but he didn't look back and she let her hand fall.

Her stomach rumbled, surprising her. She'd had no dinner last night, she remembered. The thought of Weetabix revolted her, but the baby would start eating itself if she didn't feed it soon.

For the first time since she'd arrived, she pulled back the curtain around her bed all the way to the wall. The breakfasting women looked up in surprise; they'd been having a whispered argument as to whether Emily was very sick or just plain rude. Only Maggie smiled.

Emily was weary. She would have to be civilised because they would all turn out to be related in some distant way to her neighbours in Paulstown, don't you know, and she wouldn't give any of them another excuse to think that she was getting above herself.

Neasa didn't like hospitals. It was to do with her grandmother dying three years before. Mrs Martin had been in and out of hospitals for eighteen months before somebody had finally said the word 'terminal' to her. She had looked at them, upset. 'What do you mean, terminate?' For weeks afterwards, in her drugged haze, she had been convinced that there was some plot afoot to carry out euthanasia on her, and wasn't happy unless Neasa was there to protect her. 'She's a solicitor,' she would ominously remind the doctors every now and then.

Towards the end, Neasa had taken a week's compassionate leave from work and had spent it by her grandmother's bedside, leaving it only for a quick shower and a change of clothes. It had been a slow, miserable, painful death. Neasa had gone on a bender for three days. If there was one lesson to be learned from it all, it was to enjoy life while one could, because the odds were that there was no happy ending in store.

And so she strode down the corridors of Martha's carrying a big red helium balloon and a six-pack of Guinness. Emily wasn't sick, thank God, and there was no point in pretending she was.

Neasa found her chatting with three other women as though they had known each other all their lives.

'Oh, hi, Neasa! This is Trish. She's overdue by two weeks. They might have to induce. And this is Siobhan, a false alarm. She'll be out today. And Maggie, of course. Maggie was going to try for a water birth, but they don't do it here, apparently.'

'I'm going to ask for a birthing chair instead,' Maggie told Neasa earnestly.

'Oh, yeh, I saw one of those in Habitat,' Neasa said, and roared laughing.

Maggie and the rest looked at her blankly. Shit. They were serious.

Neasa looked around for a window to open. She wished now that she wasn't so hungover.

'You've had your roots done,' Emily observed.

Neasa was embarrassed. Nobody in the world knew that her hair wasn't naturally black except for Emily, and that was only because a pack of Clairol Midnight Black had fallen out of Neasa's bag one day.

'It's all right. We're all women here,' Emily said, seeing her face.

All pregnant women who didn't have to worry about their appearance. Neasa wasn't part of their club, thank you very much.

'This your bed?' Neasa asked. It was dressed differently to all the others: the covers were brought right up to the pillow and folded under neatly. She dumped the Guinness on the end of it and sat down.

'See you later,' Emily said cheerily to the others, and pulled the curtain around herself and Neasa. A bit unnecessary, Neasa thought.

'So,' she demanded, 'what's the diagnosis? They're not going to do a caesarean section or anything like that, are they?'

'No, no,' Emily said vaguely. 'I'm not even being moved to Cork. No beds available, apparently. I'll probably be out tomorrow.'

'Great! They were all asking for you in work, you know. Gary rang. And Creepy Crawley is mooching around the place looking sick as a parrot. He told the cleaner this morning that he thinks he might have brought it all on you. When I go in this afternoon, I'm going to tell him that his name is down on your chart as a possible cause.'

She had expected Emily to laugh. Come on. It was a little bit funny, wasn't it?

'I want you to do something for me,' Emily said. She looked very intense.

'What?' Neasa asked warily. She hoped that this wasn't something to do with delivery wards and birthing partners and all that. Maybe Conor had bottled out. Neasa would just die.

'I want you to ring a hotel in Germany. You'll have to look up the number in directory enquiries. That's the name of it.' She pressed a piece of paper into Neasa's hand. Or, rather, a square of hospital toilet roll, the stuff that looked like greaseproof paper. The pen had run out halfway, before starting again with a big blob of blue.

'You're not thinking of taking a holiday, surely?' Neasa asked, confused.

'I'm not.'

Neasa looked from the piece of paper to Emily's too-bright eyes. 'What then?'

'Well, you see, it's all very silly, really,' Emily said lightly, and stopped.

'How silly?' Neasa enquired.

'Probably extremely silly.' Emily bit her lip. 'But I need you to check some dates for me.'

'I see.'

'I need to know when the orchestra stayed there last

year when they were on tour. What nights.'

Neasa looked at the piece of paper again.

'The entire orchestra?' she asked eventually. 'The whole thirty-one of them?'

'Thirty-two,' Emily corrected. 'You see, I think most of them might have left at the one time. But some of them might have stayed on. Two of them.'

Neasa nodded slowly. 'Wouldn't that kind of information be . . . privileged, so to speak?'

'You might have to be clever about it,' Emily agreed.

Neasa said nothing for a little while, then, 'Is this urgent?'

'Not urgent, no.'

'Maybe you should wait until you're out of hospital.'

'Maybe. But I can't.'

'Emily,' Neasa said, 'of course I'll do it for you if you really want me to. And I'm a great one for rushing in there myself.' As her last nine boyfriends would testify. 'But you've got a baby to think about. And your own health. You've only two months to go, you know. Maybe you should just concentrate on that and tackle everything else afterwards.'

Emily looked at her, closed. 'Will you do this for me or not?'

Neasa folded the piece of toilet paper and put it efficiently into her bag.

'So, how's Gary getting on as a new partner?' Emily enquired, as though Germany had never been mentioned at all.

'Oh, terrible,' Neasa said cheerfully. 'Already he's been put in charge of the timesheets for everyone – you know, making sure people are there when they say they are. Which means, of course, that Gary has to be there himself, which is an awful pain.'

'Forgive me if I don't have much sympathy.'

'Neither do I,' Neasa agreed. 'And listen to this – Daphne Dunne has announced a crackdown on people fiddling expenses and has asked Gary to root out the perpetrators.'

'Which is himself.'

'And Phil,' Neasa felt she had to point out. 'He taught Gary how to do it in the first place. Gary's told me that I'm not allowed to put in a claim for make-up any more either. Imagine!'

'Terrible,' Emily said.

'If they expect us to wear make-up in to the office then they should pay for it,' Neasa complained. 'But Gary's said no. He doesn't want to show favouritism in case anyone suspects.'

'Why don't you just tell people you're an item?' Emily said impatiently. They all knew anyway.

'Because we have to keep it more of a secret now than ever! He's a partner – he can't be seen to be humping the staff!'

'I don't see why not,' Emily said. 'Unless he's going to stop humping you, is he?'

'Well, no.' Emily was being difficult today, which was very unlike her. Still, you couldn't expect too much of her, given the circumstances. 'Listen, Gary said that this isn't common knowledge, but Creepy Crawley and the rest are writing you a letter officially informing you that you didn't get the partnership. Apparently it's a very nice letter, full of praise for you and all that, and saying that they value you very much in the company. Plus giving you a big pay rise. Can you believe that?'

'I can,' Emily said, grimly.

'I'd write a letter straight back telling them they're right fuckers. And I'd threaten to go to the Revenue Commissioners on them too. Gary said that from what he saw of the accounts this morning, they're fiddling tax right left and centre. I'm sure I could get you details if you want.'

Emily just gave a tired shrug.

Maybe it wasn't a good idea to be going on too much about Crawley Dunne & O'Reilly in the present circumstances, Neasa thought. Certainly she wouldn't be telling her now or ever what Crawley had told Gary about Emily this morning in his office. The partners had considered Emily to be too soft for the top job, too malleable and eager to please. Didn't have that necessary aggression and elusive go-get-'em mentality. A fine, fine worker though. In fact, Crawley had confided, the best they'd ever had.

'How are you feeling? Really?' Neasa asked quietly.

'How do I look?'

'Like shite.'

'I don't know, Neasa. It's all a bit strange. Like

everything is happening to someone else. Do you ever get that feeling?'

'No,' Neasa admitted. She had never understood this thing of being 'outside' yourself, looking in. Except when she had smoked cannabis for the first time at college. That had been very odd, and she had stuck to drink ever since. At least you knew where you were with alcohol.

'But the doctors say there's no cause for alarm.' Emily seemed determined to stick to the practical. 'They just don't want it developing into eclampsia. That's when your placenta starts packing up.'

'How exactly?'

'Clots start forming and that kind of thing.'

'Oooh. Sounds nasty.' Neasa was all interest.

'The baby doesn't get vital nutrients and stuff, and maybe even oxygen.'

'Does it make a break for freedom?'

'Sometimes. Other times they do a section.' A caesarean section was now a 'section'. Emily was talking the talk after only twelve hours in hospital.

'But the baby's not ready for that yet,' Neasa said. 'It might still only have one ear or something.'

'No, no, the baby has been fully formed since it was twelve weeks, Neasa. Remember I showed you the picture of the scan?'

'You couldn't tell anything from that,' Neasa declared. 'It looked like a tadpole. And I certainly didn't see any ears.'

'Anyway, the point is, it's the lungs they'd be worried about. They're the last to mature.'

'Well, Conor's a smoker,' Neasa said, more to test the waters than anything.

But Emily didn't react. 'He doesn't smoke in the house, Neasa. And it's nothing to do with cigarettes. Every baby's lungs are the same.'

'The poor blighters,' Neasa said. 'If I were to be born prematurely, I'd rather have only one ear than one lung.'

'They're not actually missing a lung . . . oh, it doesn't matter. The thing is, it's not going to happen. Everything seems to be all right.'

'Apart from the high blood pressure, the water retention and the presence of uric acid in your wee,' Neasa said helpfully.

'Well, yes.'

'And what has Mr Chapman to say about any of it?'

'I haven't seen him. I would have if I were in Cork. Still, they're taking good care of me here.'

'But you're paying him.'

'He delivered four babies this morning in Cork, Neasa. I can pay him all I want but he can't be in two places at the one time.'

Neasa just shrugged. She had dragged a doctor from his holidays in Kerry to come look at her grandmother. And she hadn't even been paying him.

'I wish I'd paid more attention in antenatal classes when they were going on about this,' Emily said. 'But I suppose I always thought these things happened to someone else.'

'We always do.' Neasa paused slightly. 'I suppose Conor's been in?'

Emily nodded. 'Oh yes. This morning. Brought me flowers and all.'

'Good, good.'

Neasa was confused. From Emily's expression, there didn't seem anything too wrong in that department. What was with all this Germany business so? Neasa had a very strong urge to wrestle Emily to the bed and drag the information out of her. But Emily seemed too fragile this morning, everything about her too tenuous. Neasa was forced to go for the subtler approach instead, which she had no confidence in. She always ended up sounding like some tit from a B movie.

'Emily,' she said awkwardly, 'you would tell me if anything was wrong, wouldn't you?'

'Of course I would.'

'Because, you know, a problem halved and all that?'

'Yes, I know.'

'And I always tell you when things are going wrong for me, don't I? Remember when I caught Gary going through my underwear drawer a couple of months ago?'

'I do,' said Emily, quickly.

'And I was upset because I thought, oh fuck, here's another cross-dresser – I mean, what is it about me? But you said no, calm down, that you bet he was just checking for my size. And, hey presto, he comes home with a dinky little number from one of those basement shops in Cork and everything was fine!'

'Glad to be of service,' Emily murmured.

'So, like . . . I'm here, just so you know that.'

'Thanks, Neasa.' But she wasn't going to say anything more, that much was clear. Neasa, in a bit of a huff, collected her bits and pieces.

'I'd better get in to work. Gary's told me that my timesheets are particularly bad. I hope he's not going to be a pain in the arse about this.'

'Thanks for the Guinness.'

'No problem. And that Maggie woman has blackcurrant cordial on her locker – you might be able to score some if you give her a can.'

When Neasa's grandmother had been in hospital, the patients had swapped all kinds of things. The items most hotly coveted had been alcohol and cigarettes and Neasa had been able to procure for her grandmother the TV remote control in exchange for a hundred Major and a bottle of vodka.

Emily walked with her to the corridor. 'Neasa – let me know, won't you?'

'Yes.'

At Emily's pointed, anxious face, Neasa felt so moved that she gave her a quick, hard hug. It felt awkward. They weren't kissy-kissy friends.

'You'll be grand, girl.'

'Oh, I know. Out tomorrow.'

'Out tomorrow!'

Neasa went off down the corridor, the piece of toilet paper lying in her bag like a stick of dynamite. It must be big, she thought grimly, if Emily hadn't told her.

Mr Gerald Chapman was at that moment delivering his fifth baby of the morning.

'I can see the head, Maeve – why don't you give one more push,' he told the mother.

'I can't,' she sobbed. 'I'm dying.'

Mr Chapman smiled sympathetically. Out of the side of his mouth, he said to the midwife, 'Pain relief?'

'Insisted on a natural birth,' she murmured back. 'Until it was too late.'

Epidurals were not usually given once labour had passed a certain stage. It slowed things up.

Mr Chapman sighed inwardly. He had no truck with the way natural childbirth had become a sort of a badge with some women, something to boast about to their weaker sisters who had epidurals. 'I was in labour twenty-seven hours without so much as gas!' And the bloody hospitals were worse, promoting pain like it was some kind of lifestyle choice. Tell that to this poor young one here who was beside herself with anguish.

He looked at her frightened face and spoke in the trademark calm tones he prided himself on. To everyone else he sounded bored stiff. 'You are not dying, Maeve. Believe me. But I can't get this baby out unless you help me. Let's give another push, shall we?'

She didn't argue. She hadn't the breath in any case. Besides, he was the expert in the white coat. Nobody had argued with him in years.

'There's a contraction coming now,' a trainee midwife said, watching the monitor.

'Right. Have the vacuum ready just in case.' But Mr Chapman thought he'd be able to manage without vacuum suction, which usually temporarily distorted the soft bones of the baby's head. The parents always got a fright when their baby came out looking like an extra from Star Trek. 'Okay, let's give her some help.'

Everyone scurried around him. Maeve braced herself, holding on tight to her husband's hand. He hadn't said a word in ten minutes and his face was ashen. That was another thing that Mr Chapman had no truck with. Half the men didn't want to be in the delivery room in the first place and, in his experience, half the women didn't want them there either. They'd have been much more comfortable with another woman. But the men came because they had been told it was their rightful place, that their presence was necessary to make the event meaningful. Next thing, people would be encouraged to bring in any other children to witness the wonderful event, maybe even a couple of close relatives and the family dog.

It was all in danger of going too far, Mr Chapman sometimes thought. Not that he ever voiced these opinions. He would look like a dinosaur. Instead, he contented himself with banishing videocams from any of his deliveries, and only allowing photographs to be taken at the end. You wouldn't believe what some people tried to photograph for the album.

'Oh, Christ,' Maeve moaned as the contraction swept over her.

'Let's do it this time,' Mr Chapman said.

Helen, the chief midwife, went into action. She knew her stuff. She watched the monitor all the time as the contraction slowly peaked.

'Don't push don't push don't push, Maeve, wait wait wait wait wait . . . okay, here we go, push push push, come on Maeve girl, PUSH PUSH PUSH!'

Everyone was screaming push, even the husband.

It was merely background noise to Mr Chapman, who had the baby's head out. Now a shoulder, which popped out wetly. Mr Chapman eased the baby sideways and got the other shoulder free just as Maeve ran out of steam. But it was okay. A little gentle manoeuvring, a little pull, and the rest of the baby was in his hands. He held it up for Maeve to see. It started to cry – a thin, outraged wail at the brutality of it all, and Mr Chapman felt compassionate.

'A boy,' he said.

Maeve burst into tears. Her husband resisted, thank God.

Mr Chapman handed over the child to Helen, and quickly cut the cord. He never offered to let the father do this, as some doctors did. Ridiculous. They weren't opening supermarkets. And what if something went wrong? What if the father mis-aimed and inadvertently stabbed his wife? You see! Those doctors never thought about that, did they?

Mr Chapman did. Most of his more sensible colleagues did. Some of them had been on the receiving end of solicitors' letters for a lot less. Caution and accountability were the order of the day. It would strangle them all yet, Mr Chapman often thought sourly, this entire compensation culture. Oh, people expected them to work miracles, but they were not allowed to make a mistake. As if medicine were an exact science where nothing could ever go wrong.

Now he had the placenta out and had put two neat stitches into Maeve. She was oblivious to Mr Chapman, cradling her baby.

'Let's have a look at the little fellow,' Mr Chapman said, preparing to leave. Maeve shyly held out the bundle, all gratitude now. The father was bursting with pride.

'He's grand,' Mr Chapman said, looking at their shiny, smiling faces.

Little did they know what was ahead of them. Mr Chapman's own three teenage sons should have been drowned at birth. Drinking and taking drugs and crashing cars, then coming to him looking for money. After all their fine education too, and all their mother's hard work in trying to put manners on them. When they were twenty-one, he would buy each of them an apartment very far away and tell them to pack their bags.

It might have been different had they had girls, they often consoled themselves. But some said that girls were worse, far more devious than boys. They sucked up to you, smiled at you, gave you a hug before they went to bed. Next thing you know they've shinned down a drainpipe and are shagging the gardener. This had actually happened to a colleague of Mr Chapman's.

And even if by some miracle your children turned out to be a credit to you, what kind of a world awaited them? One ruled by greed and jealousy, internal squabbling and political back-stabbing, Mr Chapman thought gloomily. Life was an endurance test until you amassed enough for a very comfortable retirement split between West Cork and a villa in Spain. And then you were too old and fat to enjoy it.

Mr Chapman had had plans when he was young. He was going to dedicate his career to groundbreaking research into birth defects, holed up in a laboratory paid for by meagre grants. Somehow the plan had changed. He couldn't remember now how or when.

'Mr Chapman?'

'What?' he hurled over his shoulder as he briskly left the delivery ward. Nurses, doctors and interns reverentially stepped out of his way, like the Red Sea parting. Dr Doolan, a junior doctor, eventually caught up with him, a commendable feat given that he hadn't slept since Monday.

'Two of yours have been admitted,' he panted. 'One's just started; the other looks like a false alarm.'

'Right. Don't discharge the false alarm till I look at her.'

He hurried on. He had a lunch appointment with a member of the hospital board. He had issues about the closure of Martha's to discuss with her. Like, how to pile more people into an already overloaded public healthcare system; how to manufacture extra beds where there was no staff to administer them. His sinus headache began to throb nicely behind his eyes.

Dr Doolan caught up with Mr Chapman again, like a terrier on its last legs.

'What about Emily Collins?'

'Emily Collins Emily Collins . . .'

'In Martha's.'

'Oh. Yes. Emily Collins.' The threatened pre-eclampsia. He had meant to ring Martha's this morning but had been caught in delivery for the past three hours.

'How's she doing?'

'BP is still up.'

Mr Chapman sighed again. He had hoped to be able to tell them to discharge her.

'Haven't we any bed here for her?' he said impatiently.

'We did an hour ago, but now . . .'

'God almighty!' This didn't bode well. Everybody had assured each other for the past two years that Martha's could be seamlessly devoured by Cork. He would have to bring this up with the board. Again.

And he would have to drive up and see Emily Collins. He wouldn't be satisfied otherwise. This meant that everything this afternoon would be pushed back. Another late night. Hannah would go mad. There was a golf do on at the club. She would just have to go on her own.

'Tell them I'll be up around four.'

Dr Doolan looked very far away. He was in fact asleep.

'Dr Doolan,' Mr Chapman said sharply. 'Go home.'

'Did you put a birthing chair down on your birth plan?' Maggie wanted to know.

'Not yet,' Emily conceded. She didn't want to tell Maggie that she had yet to draw up a birth plan. Maggie's seemed very elaborate, running to five pages of dense handwriting with two diagrams thrown in lest anything be open to confusion or question. She was making a change now with Tipp-Ex and a red pen.

'I'm going to put down that if there's no birthing chair available, I want extra pillows,' she confided. 'Oh, hello, Auntie Paula!'

Auntie Paula was followed by several more relatives. Apparently the influx of Maggie's relatives happened all day every day, according to Trish, who now took out a pack of cards and started playing by herself, very concentrated. Siobhan packed to go home. Emily put on her dressing gown and took to the corridors again.

There was a visitors' room at the end of the floor; a dark, cheerless room with shabby chairs and a big poster on the wall that warned, Don't Wait! Vaccinate! Someone had added a moustache to the pink-faced baby on the poster, and two rotten teeth.

Emily wondered why people felt the need to destroy things, to ruin them on an impulse.

She closed the door behind her and sat down. It was the first time she had been truly alone since she'd arrived here.

'Hello, baby,' she said, patting her belly. She liked to have conversations with the baby every now and then but not in front of other people. 'It's all a bit mad in here, isn't it?'

The baby lay quietly, listening.

'Mr Chapman's on his way,' she said. 'He might let us out soon. Wouldn't that be nice?'

She heard her own voice, false and forced, and wondered how she had become such a sham.

There must have been some definable point at which she had made a decision not to notice what was going on in her marriage. But these things were subconscious, weren't they? Surely she didn't consciously ignore the signs that Conor was having an affair? What did that say about her, after all?

Either way she was not coming to this fresh. There wasn't the sharp, horrifying shock of a first discovery, no wordless trauma as though she had unexpectedly been hit a stunning blow. Hers was a feeling of dull realisation as the full impact of something coming for a while now hit her at last.

It was more painful in a way. She had colluded with it by her silence and her stark refusal to notice. In some ways she had gone along with her own betrayal, and in typical Emily fashion, had hoped that if she left well enough alone, it would all go away.

Not that Conor gave much away, in fairness to her. He was too careful, too considerate to leave any tawdry clues around that might hurt her. To come home with lipstick on his collar would be so ludicrous and crass. No credit-card receipts for Ann Summers in his pocket either. The mere notion!

No, what Emily had ignored was much subtler in some ways and more obvious in others. His increased preoccupation, for example, hard to spot in one so preoccupied anyway. His reluctance to just bloody talk about things that mattered. And her own vague unhappiness and loneliness, feelings that she assumed most married people took for granted once the first flush was over.

They had joked about these things in the beginning, those silly jokes that people make in their newly married smugness, and that lie there like time bombs to explode years later. 'Don't go kissing any boys now,' Conor would say when she left for a night on the tiles with Neasa. 'And don't you go filling Mrs Conlon's sugar cup while I'm gone,' she would deliver as a riposte. Mrs Conlon-next-door was always coming round to borrow something. She was sixty if she was a day, and they had both thought this great gas. It wasn't funny at all now.

Emily sat there in the dark visitors' room in her long-buried knowledge, frozen and numb. She was denied those initial hot feelings of disbelief and anger. It would be very false of her to shout and scream hysterically, and throw things across the room. There wasn't anything to throw anyway, except for the ancient television and she'd probably be billed for breaking that. She remembered now all those crappy late-night movies on the telly where the blissfully ignorant wife suddenly discovered a used condom in the back seat of the family saloon and had predictably gone ballistic, setting fire to the car before going after the wayward husband with a shotgun. Emily felt very jealous of these women now. But she suspected there were many more like her who, for a billion reasons, had known all along but had ruthlessly convinced themselves that there was nothing wrong.

Part of her wished fiercely that she hadn't seen that concert programme. She might even have got away with it. They both would have. And that was the honest-to-God truth.

But it was the first and last piece of stark evidence – how she hated that word – that she simply couldn't ignore. Not even her.

She thought about herself and her baby and her marriage, the safe existence she had painstakingly built for herself, the energy and commitment she had invested in everything, like a hard-working squirrel hoarding nuts for a comfortable winter. She even included the dogs in this scenario, and the house and the cappuccino-maker in the kitchen. She thought about all her hopes and dreams and expectations, and she felt the first stab of real rage at Conor for making her entire life seem so fake and contrived now, so worthless. As if he were God or something, free to dabble as he pleased. He had no consideration! That to Emily was a terrible sin.

She took a deep breath, looking at the grey walls of the visitors' room. She supposed that this was where it would all happen later – the confrontation, the angst, the anger. It was, she thought, a wearying prospect. And it wasn't as though there would be something nice at the end of it all, a little reward for putting them through the mill. No well done, let's move on now even better than before. She didn't know what was going to happen but none of it would be nice.

She supposed she should at least wait until Neasa rang with confirmation, and that's all it would be. Perhaps she shouldn't have involved Neasa in her sleuthing. Perhaps she should just have asked him straight out. But Emily was too precise, too hungry for order in her facts to do that. There was still that slim chance she was wrong and she would not accuse him in the wrong.

Also, she was terribly afraid that he would lie to her

face. And that would somehow be worse. That would be unforgivable.

No, she wouldn't play any cat-and-mouse games. They weren't that kind of people. She didn't even feel bad about snooping around behind his back, checking up on him. Honesty had already been a casualty in their marriage, long before any affair had reared its head.

He was at home on his own now, probably worrying and waiting for her to phone. She didn't want to talk to him. But neither did she want to worry him. After all, this baby was fifty percent his.

Cold dread crept over her at this thought of 'percentages', like she was already mentally dividing things up. He had become separate from her already.

The baby had hiccups. Emily crossed her arms over her belly as far as they would go and knew that she had to be very careful about everything. She could not afford to be self-indulgent, neither of them could. It wasn't just about them.

It was strange, she thought, how events had a way of outdoing each other. The loss of the partnership had paled into insignificance when the pre-eclampsia had reared its head. Now the affair had overridden that in a different way. What would it take to outdo the affair? Maybe if Conor dropped dead.

'Look at you! Sitting up grinning! I thought you were sick.' Liz had found her.

'Hello, Liz.' Emily tried to look welcoming. 'You

shouldn't have come in – I told Conor to tell everyone that there was no panic.'

Her voice sounded perfectly normal. And she hadn't even paused before she'd said Conor's name.

'Of course I had to come in! Mammy's very worried.' Oh, it was for their mother then.

'Tell her I'm fine.'

'Obviously.' Liz looked her up and down. 'I thought it was pre-eclampsia?'

'They're not really sure yet.' Emily felt like she had been repeating this piece of information all her life.

'Oh.' Liz looked even more like it was all a storm in a teacup.

'Where's the gang then?'

'I left them with Eamon except for Willy here,' Liz said stoutly. 'It'll serve him right. And I gave them all a can of Coke before I left so they'll be climbing the walls with caffeine.'

'And how's Mammy?' Emily said, when it became obvious that her own health wasn't going to be enquired after any time soon.

Liz sighed. 'She had more palpitations this morning.'

'I think it's that new postman.'

'You can be so facetious sometimes about really serious things, Emily. Poor Mammy might be on the way out for all we know.'

'We're all on the way out, Liz. Even little Willy there.'

Liz hugged Willy to her. 'That's a horrible thing to say!'

Emily didn't see why. 'He'll have seventy good years first.'

'Maybe ninety,' Liz declared. 'If he takes after Eamon's father.'

'Let's hope he doesn't take after ours.'

Their father had died of a sudden heart attack ten years ago at the age of fifty-two. 'It could have been worse,' their mother had said bravely.

Liz looked at Emily suspiciously. 'Have they put you on drugs?'

'No, no.'

'They should. You don't look well at all, now that I get a good look at you.'

'I'm afraid, Liz. After the last time,' Emily said.

Liz was a bit discomfited at this show of honesty. 'Well, of course. But lots of women have miscarriages. And go on to have a clatter of kids, thank God. Too many in some cases. Look at Myra Byrne. She could open her own crèche.'

It could have been their mother speaking, combating any hint of complaint with her mish-mash of religious clichés and good, old-fashioned Irish insistence that there were always others worse off than themselves.

It was just another aspect of the endless denial that Emily had bought into too. Emily didn't pursue it. There was no sense in forcing Liz to see the light. Emily was only starting to see it herself.

'Have you talked to Eamon?'

'I phoned the Revenue this morning from Mammy's,'

Liz confided. 'They were quite sympathetic, if you can believe that. I'm going to start paying off bits of the tax bill straightaway. I'll have to use the Children's Allowance.'

'So you didn't talk to him then?'

Liz sensed criticism. 'And when would I talk to him? He was working till midnight last night. And this morning I had to take Tommy to school, then Willy here to the doctor for his vaccinations, and now I'm visiting you.'

'Okay, Liz—'

'It's not like your house, Emily, nobody to worry about except yourselves, nothing to do any day except talk.'

They talked all right. Emily did most of it, with Conor chipping in occasionally. They discussed endless things in depth, such as Mrs Conlon's kitchen extension, the latest news from Crawley Dunne & O'Reilly, Conor's efforts to find a replacement key for the piano at home. Oh, there was plenty of communication in the Collins' household. And they went to bed at night secure in the knowledge that the TV had not been on while they ate dinner, like they had passed some kind of test.

Emily looked at Liz and for a brief moment considered confiding in her. Surely they might find some common bond in all this? Maybe even be some kind of support to each other?

But Emily would only be telling Liz so that Liz wouldn't feel that her own problems were so bad. Liz would sympathise but she would be thinking that whatever Eamon might be, at least he wasn't a cheat. If their situations were reversed, Liz would think that at least Eamon didn't plunge them into financial chaos.

'And I have to fill out some kind of form for the bank,' Liz said, rummaging in her bag. 'To change the joint savings account into just my name, so that Eamon can't go buying a new hydraulic drill or something stupid. Can you look at it for me, Emily? You're good at these things.'

Emily's expertise as a solicitor was often called upon by members of her family who routinely got confused by ESB demands, bank forms, insurance policies and other standard day-to-day documentation. Institutions had always been held in a kind of fear and awe in their household. It had irritated Emily, but the sight of a brown envelope through the door had always been greeted with great caution by her parents, and exam-ined at length before any decision was taken.

'You just fill in the details of your bank account number, Liz. That's all. And sign there where there's an X.'

'Thanks, Emily.' Liz gratefully signed her name.

'You need Eamon's signature too. You can't change the account into your own name without his consent.'

'I know. I have to trick him.'

'What?'

'I'll have to tell him it's something else and trick him.'

Emily was astounded and disbelieving, until she

thought of the trickery she had just put Neasa up to. Was this what relationships had come to, after all the movements and revolutions and the joyous dawning of an age where there was at last meaningful communication and understanding? Wives filling in bank forms and checking hotels behind their husband's backs, suspicious and conniving. Husbands reneging on mortgages and merrily chasing other women, while their wives gave birth and reared numerous children. Somewhere along the way the plot had been lost, she thought.

Liz saw her face. 'Look, he won't admit how bad it is, Emily. I was trying to tell him we should go and work something out with the mortgage people, but he won't hear of it. Do you know what his solution is? Borrow more! Throw good money after bad! Now, if it means I have to trick him in order to pay last month's ESB bill so that they don't cut us off too, then I will.'

Emily acknowledged this. 'Liz, don't be insulted, but if you need money—'

'No.'

'It would just be a loan – you could pay me back.'

'No. Thanks anyway, Emily,' Liz said stiffly. 'This is our mess. Oh, and you won't say anything about it, will you? To Mammy.'

'God, Liz. Of course I won't.'

There wasn't even any sisterhood any more.

'And she said for you to ring her, by the way. Put her mind at rest.'

There was no question of their mother ringing Emily. She always claimed that she didn't know how to work mobile phones. You're not working one; you're just ringing one from your own phone in the hall, Emily had tried to explain. But their mother cleverly refused to get the hang of the 'new technology', as she called it. Instead she sat at home, raging that nobody ever thought to ring her and put her mind at rest.

Liz rummaged some more in her bag. 'They dropped that petition into the chemist. You know, to stop this place closing. I brought it in.'

'Oh, right. Give me that pen.'

'No, I meant I was going to leave it with you. You could get loads of signatures in here.'

'Sorry?'

'You could go around a few wards, couldn't you? Haven't you plenty of free time?'

'After I ring Mammy and put her mind at rest, and do that form for you for the bank, of course. And see Mr Chapman about my condition.'

'Just whenever you have a minute,' Liz agreed.

She was perfectly serious. Never mind that Emily should probably be on the flat of her back. Never mind that her career and marriage had hit the rocks. But Liz didn't know that, Emily found herself rationalising. But still, she didn't want to do this, why should she?

'Oh, okay! But just my ward,' she said grudgingly.

Willy stirred and started to cry. Liz lowered the sling, hiked up her shirt and stuffed a breast into his mouth.

'At least I don't have to fork out for formula,' she said bravely.

Gary was a bit put out when Neasa abruptly changed their lunchtime plans.

'I have a condom on and all,' he complained.

'Well, take it off,' she said a bit snappily. 'I have work to do.'

'What work?' He peered over her shoulder at her computer screen.

'Creepy Crawley's asked me to touch up the contract for the sale of Tilbury House,' Neasa lied easily.

'That contract went out this morning.'

Gary, through no fault of his own, had done more work in three hours this morning than he'd managed all month. The pace was killing him and he had hoped to let off a little steam with Neasa in Crawley's office.

'I meant Tamworth House.'

'That's gone too,' Gary said self-righteously.

'Oh, all right! I'm doing some personal work, okay? It's not a crime. It's in my lunch break.'

'What personal work?'

'Just bits and pieces,' Neasa said vaguely.

Gary was hurt that she wasn't confiding in him. He told her absolutely everything. She even knew how much he had in his savings account, which was considerable.

'I'll leave you to it so,' he muttered, hoping that she would stop him. She didn't.

'Yeh.'

Out of spite, Gary went off to Milo's with the laddish element in the office and had three pints of Smithwicks. And actually, it turned out to be exactly the right thing to do, because he was able to reassure them that he was still a lad even though he was now a partner, and everybody had a great time.

Alone in the office, Neasa procured the number of the German hotel from the relevant directory enquiries. Now, how to worm the information out of them? What if they didn't speak English on the reception desk? The only German Neasa knew was from the old war films her father was fond of watching and most of it translated into 'Die, you English pig.'

In the end she plucked up the phone, dialled, and just went for it.

'Hello,' she said clearly and slowly. 'Do you speak English?'

'Very well, thank you,' she was told.

Well, if they were going to be *shirty* about it . . .

'This is Crawley Dunne & O'Reilly,' Neasa said in a very threatening tone. 'International solicitors.' Well, there were rumours that a branch would open in Kinnegad. 'We're acting on behalf of some clients who stayed in your establishment last year. There appears to be a discrepancy about the bill.'

A silence at the other end. Feel the fear, Neasa thought nastily.

'I need the details please.'

Neasa told the woman what she knew. 'That would be sometime in early September. We're concerned that a couple of members of the orchestra were billed for some extra nights after that.'

She heard rapid computer clicks on the other end of the phone. The Germans really were very efficient, she thought admiringly. If only Mandy at reception here could work a keyboard like that.

'There was a group booking for the 3rd and 4th of September. Two members of the party stayed on after that,' the receptionist eventually informed her.

'Two?' Neasa barked. 'I'm afraid I have no record of that.'

God, she was hot today.

'They paid for the room themselves.'

Ah-ha. Now they were getting to the crux of the matter.

'And these people, their names . . .?'

'May I ask whether you are acting on behalf of these two individuals also?'

Oooh. The receptionist was hot too. Time to change tack.

'You see, this is the thing,' Neasa murmured discreetly. 'Basically, this pair are trying to claim expenses to which they are not entitled. A little holiday paid for by someone else, you understand?'

The receptionist did, and warmed up immensely. Nobody of any nationality liked to see other people getting away with a fast one.

'I can fax you their account,' she offered immediately.

'That would be lovely,' Neasa gushed, giving her the work fax number. 'Au revoir.'

She hung up triumphantly, buzzing with adrenaline. Wow! How great for a change to actually put into practice everything she had learned in law school – lying, bending facts, bullying and threatening lawsuits at the drop of a hat. She had missed it more than she'd thought. Her New Year's Resolution this year would be to ditch this kip and go back to Cork.

But Crawley Dunne & O'Reilly were very clever. They didn't give bonuses before Christmas, knowing that half the employees wouldn't show up in January. No, they held off until the end of January, when any New Year's Resolutions had gone out the window. And in case there was still some ambition lingering amongst the hardened dissidents, Crawley Dunne & O'Reilly hit people with another bonus at Easter. 'Jesus Christ!' people would moan as they looked at their bank accounts, 'Another fucking bonus!' It was the same in summer. Everyone would gather in Milo's, grim-faced, and try to form a pressure group to stop the bonuses. But the bonuses kept coming and so people kept staying. Neasa personally knew two people who had been trying to leave for fifteen years but had given up and bought holiday homes instead.

Sometimes Neasa woke at night, wet with sweat and screaming, having dreamt that she was still selling boggy land at forty.

'It's all right,' Gary would murmur. 'I get those dreams too. Everybody in the office does. But it's pay day tomorrow.'

And Neasa would happily go back to sleep.

But lately the lack of mental stimulation was getting to her, and she was annoyed with herself. Most people were bored senseless in their jobs; what was wrong with her? And it wasn't as though she had chosen law for any reason other than the money and the fact that she got to wear her own clothes.

Now she had Gary complicating the picture too. It was unlikely he would be open to any suggestions about moving to Cork, now that he was part of the establishment. Was it possible that the 'future' he had talked about meant a detached home with a double garage out on the Cork Road?

It was all becoming very complicated, Neasa thought. Maybe she and Gary should have a chat. But then again, she didn't want him thinking she was putting pressure on him. Neither did she want him thinking that she was happy to put her career on the back burner and gaze adoringly at his star rising higher in Crawley Dunne & O'Reilly.

Neasa jumped as the fax machine over by Mandy's desk chugged, whirred, and spat a piece of paper onto the ground. It lay there, its corners curling incriminatingly.

Neasa walked over slowly and picked it up. Her eye caught Conor's name and she looked away in distaste.

Please God may the other name be Billy Middlemiss or someone. But hang on, wouldn't that be worse?

It was Ffion Rivera. They hadn't even bothered with the pretence of separate rooms. They'd shacked up in Room 134. Room service detailed a bottle of champagne, dinner for two, followed by breakfast the next morning. There was also an international phone call, to Emily and Conor's home number. He'd probably called Emily while Ffion was washing the smell of sex off herself in the shower.

Neasa was generally unshockable and was shocked to find that she was shocked. Wonders will never cease, she thought darkly, as she thought of Conor rolling buck naked on Mary Murphy, pages of sheet music scattered across the bed with abandon. Had they hummed little arias to each other as the pace hotted up?

She tried to do some work, but couldn't. Instead she sat at her desk for ages and ages, her eye constantly straying to the fax.

She heard footsteps on the corridor outside and quickly folded the fax and put it in her pocket. She would decide what to do with it later.

'Hi!' It was Gary, red-faced and slightly foolish with Smithwicks. 'You missed a great session in the pub. Did you get what you wanted to do done?'

'I did.' This came out as extremely bitter and twisted. 'I did!' she said again, happily.

Gary, pissed, nuzzled into her neck. 'I almost told Phil about you and me.'

'What?' Neasa was aghast.

'We have to come clean at some point.'

'Why?'

'I want to legitimise our union, Neasa.' This mightn't have sounded so pretentious if he hadn't slurred it.

'Why is it so important that Creepy Crawley and the rest give us the thumbs-up?'

Neasa knew that Creepy would be sniffing around her even more if he knew she was definitely having sex with someone.

Gary looked at her coolly. 'You know, I'm starting to think that you're a bit embarrassed to be seen with me.'

'I'm not going to dignify that with a reply.'

'She replied.'

Gary was going into Jaws mode, his chin jutting out and his eyes getting smaller. His incisors even seemed to come forward in his mouth. Neasa had never been on the receiving end of this before and wasn't about to start now.

'Gary, can we just leave this? I have other things on my mind.'

'In that case, don't let me intrude.'

He stomped off to his desk at the top of the office. They had offered him his own office years ago, of course, but he hadn't taken them up on it. Not in the interests of team spirit, he had declared sincerely. There'd be no crack at all to be had on his own, and he wouldn't get sent all those jokes and dirty pictures over the internal email. But now he thought that maybe he should reconsider their offer. There was one free room near the back of the building. Unfortunately it was right beside the toilets and some people didn't flush as often as they should. Hardly fitting for a man in his new position, he thought gloomily. Still, he supposed he could always use Emily's office – just while she was on maternity leave. He would mention it to Charles Crawley this afternoon. He had decided to dispense with the 'Creepy' business, it was very childish and immature. And, really, Charles was quite nice once you got to know him.

Vera Mooney should have been in bed hours ago with a cup of cocoa and watching last night's videotaped episode of *Horizon* on the telly in her bedroom. Lay people always thought that nurses watched nothing except *ER* and *Peak Practice*. Those kinds of programmes made Vera Mooney's blood boil. Collectively they were responsible for luring hundreds of naïve girls and boys into a world they believed to be full of glamour and intrigue and revealing pink uniforms, and where George Clooney would spring out at you from every corner. Oh, the hurt and bewilderment on their faces when they were confronted with the reality of bedpans and piles, bullying consultants and chronic staff shortages. Vera would take the worst cases under her wing, feed them sweetened tea in the canteen and advise them on how to sew little tucks into the waistline of their uniform so that it sat a bit better on the hips. She would murmur about the altruistic rewards of looking after sick folk, the wonder of delivering babies. She pointed up the subsidised canteen and played down the vicious hours. Then she would send them back out onto the firing line, looking a little less beaten. Occasionally she would come across a hopeless case and would quietly advise a change of career. The army, maybe. *Soldier Soldier* was a lot more realistic in the portrayal of its profession, in her view.

Anyhow: Vera Mooney should have been in bed, but was in fact still in the staff room along with the rest of the night shift who had given up their sleep to fight the cause. The cause, of course, had been irretrievably lost a year ago, but Vera Mooney wasn't the type to go quietly.

She took a sheaf of application forms from her satchel and slapped them on the table, which rocked violently due to its missing leg.

'Ennis General. Limerick. Athlone.' She looked around at them all. 'And there's always Dublin, of course, but if people are interested then maybe they would contact those hospitals themselves.'

Karen and Suzanne reached for Limerick. Vera nodded approvingly. She was going there herself, even though it would entail her changing her car. Her 93 Clio had a hundred and twenty thousand miles on the clock and the weekly journeys to Limerick and back would add three hundred and fifty more.

Darren took a form for Ennis General. 'My girl-friend's going there,' he mumbled.

'Aw. So sweet.'

'Ooooooh, lurve.'

'Thank you, girls,' Vera said crisply. 'Now. Christine. How about you?'

Nurse Christine Clarke looked up, her blonde curls bouncing. She had already changed out of her uniform and put on fresh make-up.

'I haven't decided yet.'

Vera looked at her. Christine had been one of her very worst cases and had taken a lot of counselling in the canteen. 'But on the telly all that blood is never real,' she had cried, traumatised. 'I know,' Vera had soothed. 'But maybe you could pretend here that it's just ketchup. How about that?' It had worked miracles. Christine now enjoyed blood so much that she was thinking of training to work in theatre.

'Why don't you take application forms for them all and think about it?' Vera said.

'Okay,' Christine said.

Karen shot her a filthy glance. 'Don't waste the paper.'

'Sorry?'

'You heard her, you two-faced little cow,' Suzanne muttered.

'What the hell are you talking about?'

'Don't bounce your curls at me!'

'What's going on here?' Vera enquired politely.

'She's after applying for a transfer to Cork,' Darren chimed in, disgusted.

'I have not!' Christine said indignantly.

'How come you've got an appointment down there next Tuesday?' Karen shot triumphantly.

'Were you eavesdropping on my telephone conversations?' Christine demanded, her curls about to take off.

'Yes!'

'I don't want to move to the back of beyond just because this place is closing! Why should I?'

'Solidarity, you thick eejit.'

Christine looked like she was going to cry. 'But they have Top Shop in Cork.'

'Forget it.'

'And Wallis. And Principles.'

'Big swing.'

'Wallis?' Suzanne said with a slight catch in her voice. She was five-foot nothing and Wallis did a lovely little line in petite wear.

'What the hell is going on here!' Karen said viciously. 'I thought we all agreed to boycott Cork! I thought we all said that they could offer us a million pounds a year and we still wouldn't take a transfer down there!'

'Half a million. We said half a million,' Christine pointed out quickly.

'What difference does it make? Nobody is going to Cork! That's what we agreed!'

Vera cleared her throat. As always, it had the effect of shutting everybody up. Vera had once cleared her throat during a delivery, entirely accidentally, and even the newborn baby had screeched to a silence and looked at her.

'What we agreed at that meeting was that if people felt strongly enough, then they should boycott Cork. But it wasn't an order. People can go where they want. Of course they can.' She looked at Christine without any judgement or malice. 'It's absolutely your prerogative to go to Cork. And nobody here will say another word about it. Isn't that right, girls?'

Karen and Suzanne shifted indignantly, but kept their mouths shut. Christine found herself unable to look Vera in the eye. Vera, who had brought her through her first difficult months as a trainee nurse, Vera who had subtly warned her off Doctor Keating with just one word, 'married'.

'Okay! I won't bloody go!' she shouted.

'Go if you want,' Vera encouraged her. 'You might like it in Cork.'

'I wouldn't! How could I spend a single pay cheque in Wallis knowing that I was a turncoat!' Christine was raging now at being forced by her own hand to do the right thing.

'Well, if that's how you feel, then we're all delighted,' Vera soothed, resolving to take her for a cup of tea in the canteen that night and point up the benefits of Limerick. They had Wallis there too, silly girl, and all kinds of wonderful places to spend pay cheques. She must also mention that some of the more attractive doctors from the general wards had already gone to Limerick.

'Okay, well, everyone should start applying immediately. Time is running out.'

St Martha's would close in exactly five weeks' time. Most of the general wards had already been closed. Martha's was really only open for business in Casualty and Maternity.

'I can't bear it,' Karen suddenly said, her lip quivering. 'I know this place is an awful kip, but I don't want to go.'

'I know,' Vera said. 'But we must be brave, girls.' She nodded at Darren. 'And boys.'

Vera herself was very unsentimental about the whole thing. It wasn't that she didn't like Martha's; she loved Martha's with a passion. She had worked there for fifteen years, she'd had her own two girls there; she personally knew nearly every patient who came through the door.

But what use was it to anybody to get all emotional and upset about it? Vera had taken the practical approach of making submissions to the Board of Management. She'd solicited meetings with the Health Board. Then there were the local TDs and Councillors, all of whom she had personally canvassed. She had even written to the Minister for Health and had all the staff do so too.

It had all been in vain. Martha's was caught up in the unstoppable forces of rationalisation and modernisation and, more crucially, staff shortages of crisis proportions. Martha's could no longer attract specialised theatre staff to carry out operations. What junior doctors were still coming into the system went to Dublin or Cork or Limerick or Galway. Nurses couldn't be found for love nor money.

They could have thrown resources and financial support at the place. They could have paid people better to come and work in it. But they didn't, of course. They decided to close it. Their main reason was that it was servicing a decreasing rural population that could be better facilitated by Cork.

Hogwash, Vera often thought. Still. She didn't get involved in the politics of it all. She was just angry for the sake of her job, and everybody else who worked in the hospital. But there are plenty of jobs, they had told her – God knows, aren't they crying out for nurses! Yes, if they relocated or else drove their cars and themselves into the ground.

Vera would commute for as long as she could. But she would no longer be home after a night shift to see the girls before they went to school. She would have to leave every evening before they'd even had dinner together, for God's sake. And what about driving them to ballet lessons and taking them to parties? She would be stuck in her car – albeit a new car – in a bloody traffic jam. For two pins now she would strangle Chapman and O'Reilly and every other goddamn consultant who had sunk this ship, either intentionally or by their silence.

'There's a petition going around again,' Karen said. 'I saw it in one of the wards earlier.'

'Is there?' Vera said, with no interest. There had been many such petitions over the past year.

'With plenty of signatures.'

'Karen, let the patients fight for themselves.'

This sounded a bit harsher than Vera Mooney actually felt. She was not unsympathetic to the cause of the locals, who now had to travel to Cork sick or in labour. People were very angry and upset about it, but it hadn't really translated into action. True, some of them had turned up at the meetings Vera had organised. But the problem was that most healthy people never thought that they would end up in hospital. Cancer, heart attacks and long-term illnesses always happened to someone else. They were emotionally removed from the fight, and that was no good at all. In fact, the people most upset about it were the pregnant women, the ones who knew that in three or four or six months' time they would definitely need the services of a hospital. Those, and elderly people to whom hospital was a future reality rather than an unlikely possibility.

Vera felt very tired and disillusioned now. It was difficult leading a revolt when the revolutionaries weren't that pushed in the first place. But then she saw the faces of Karen, Darren, Suzanne. They had come this far with her and she owed it to them to finish this thing.

'Right. Will we go pound the pavements?'

Today was the start of the next phase: marching up and down outside with placards. The day shift would take it in turns to join them for an hour.

'Can we have a cup of tea first?' Christine begged. She wanted to touch up her lipstick too.

'Of course we can,' Vera said. 'And a nice salad or something.'

They always had salads in the canteen. It was all the blasted Roses. They tried to give them away to porters, ambulance drivers, the cleaning staff. But those sly cows in Delivery always got there before them, and you couldn't even off-load the smallest box. Once someone had given them Quality Street because the shop next door had run out of Roses, and there had been great excitement for a week.

They all traipsed out, faces pasty from lack of sleep. Emily Collins drifted past them in the corridor, eyes very far away. With her huge belly, massive bunny slippers and thin little legs, she looked like a cartoon figure. The woman never seemed to be where she was supposed to be, which was in bed.

Vera was going to say something, then stopped herself. She was not on duty. If she said something, she felt like she would be getting involved. And one of the first things she had learned as a nurse fifteen years ago was never to get personally involved with the patients.

Emily couldn't bear the waiting game any longer. She had already brought up her lunch, what little she'd eaten. She rang Conor and told him that Mr Chapman was coming in in an hour.

'I'll be there,' he said, sounding glad that something was finally happening.

'Come in early,' she said.

'I'll set off now.'

She wanted to ask him to bring in her deodorant which she'd forgotten but the request seemed too cosy and domestic. But she needed it; she was sweating. When Maggie went to the loo, Emily helped herself to two quick blasts of the Sure on her locker, but felt no surer. Guiltily, she checked the contents on the canister. She had read a frightening article once on how breast milk can be poisoned with more than two hundred different chemicals from the products that mothers used, anything from hairspray to the can of Coke you treated yourself to. You might as well be feeding your baby a bottle of Domestos.

Then other articles rubbished this, maintaining that breast milk was the best food for your child until they were well into their teens. But who were you to believe any more? Sometimes Emily thought that there was a conspiracy out there to confuse, addle and bewilder those who simply tried to do their best. Those who didn't bother reading this stuff were able to enjoy guilt-free spraying and a much drier lifestyle. It made Emily feel gullible and annoyed.

'Anybody for a game of bridge?' Trish enquired across the way. She was now fifteen days in Martha's and had started an inter-ward bridge league. Elizabeth's Ward was currently winning and Trish was taking it all very badly.

'Count me in,' Maggie said happily, back in from the loo.

Trish wasn't a bit pleased. Maggie had only learned how to play bridge in the past week and was worse than useless. But she always wanted to play, damn her.

'Emily, will you be my partner?' Maggie pleaded.

Emily pretended not hear. She slipped out of the ward and wandered until she found herself outside the main doors of the hospital. As with every other health institution in the country, hordes of people were standing on the front steps smoking. Emily watched them as they collectively inhaled and exhaled fiercely and wondered who was in the hospital belonging to them. A wife? Sister? Father? Martina, even? Who knew what stories they all had? Who was to say that her own was any more interesting or tragic than theirs?

The elderly man with rheumy eyes and a stooped, beaten back particularly touched Emily. He held his cigarette as though it were the only thing keeping him going right now. He reminded Emily of her own father.

'They're very good in there,' she said, trying to give him some solace, 'the doctors and nurses.'

The man looked up, surprised. 'I'm sure they are.'

'Just, you know, if you were worried.'

He looked at her and put out his cigarette. 'You're a very kind girl.'

'No problem,' she said, embarrassed.

He pulled open the front door and poked his head in. 'Taxi for Tynan?'

She dived into the band of smokers, mortified. She never seemed to learn. Time and again she went right on in there, investing herself in situations and people that never gave her back a thing. Crawley Dunne & O'Reilly. Liz. Her mother. Martina, a woman she'd never even met, for heaven's sake! But she never, ever thought she'd be adding Conor to that list.

His red Peugeot drove into the car park. He didn't go and park in the empty spaces at the back, of course, but came right up towards the hospital. Lo and behold, another car conveniently vacated a position just thirty yards from the front doors, and Conor eased in.

Emily found that her heart was beating fast, and she was thrown back to those days when Conor used to come and pick her up for their dates. She'd hear his car crunching on the gravel outside and she would feel her cheeks reddening and her heart banging away and she would rush to the front door to open it. With previous boyfriends, she would pretend that she hadn't heard the car, and she would make them get out and ring the doorbell. Sometimes twice. She had never tried that with Conor – it simply hadn't occurred to her. He would have seen right through it anyway, and he would have thought less of her. He was always so straight, Conor. That was one of the biggest shocks of this whole thing. She felt that he had irredeemably diminished himself in her eyes.

'Excuse me . . . excuse me . . . oh, get out of my way.'

Emily elbowed her way through the smokers and went fast down the hospital steps. Conor was just taking off his seat belt when she slid into the passenger seat of his car.

'What are you doing?' he said.

'Getting in.'

'It's cold out here. Are you mad?'

'No. Just sick of the hospital.'

He didn't kiss her. The look on her face didn't invite him to.

'They're walking up and down on the road with placards,' he said eventually. 'I nearly knocked one of them down.'

She felt very sad as she turned to him. 'Conor. I know about Germany.'

His whole body seemed to sag a little. Emily had a funny feeling inside, like something was breaking.

'It's over,' he said.

This was no great news or consolation to Emily. She guessed that her pregnancy announcement had probably put paid to it.

'Did you love her?' she asked.

'No.'

It was hard to know whether this was more insulting.

'It was Mary, right? Correct me if I'm wrong.'

'It was Mary.'

His knuckles were white on the steering wheel, but

he didn't say anything more. He offered no bluster or excuses. And he didn't look relieved that it was finally out in the open, either. She'd have slapped his face for him if he had.

They sat like that for a while. Emily was dry-eyed, cold. Somehow she had thought that it would be different. She had anticipated some emotional release, a catharsis of sorts. Not this dry, barren silence that was more frightening.

'Conor, have you nothing at all to say?' she said at last. 'Am I to sit here and drag it out of you bit by bit? Like I always bloody do?'

'Sorry.' He seemed at a loss. 'I just figured the gory details wouldn't make you feel any better.'

She looked at him, askance. 'Don't you dare try to tell me how I feel.'

'What do you want me to do? Sit here and fling platitudes at you, Emily?'

'Platitudes would be something! Platitudes would be a start!'

He sat up a big straighter. 'I can tell you that it wasn't an important relationship, which it wasn't. I can tell you that I'm desperately sorry, which I am. I can assure you that it won't happen again, which it won't.' He looked at her. 'But I figured those were easy words to say right now, Emily.'

His rationale made Emily angrier than she had ever been in her life. 'So you just thought you'd say nothing at all?'

He buried his face in his hands. 'Look, I know how much I've hurt you.'

'You don't. By God, you don't.'

'I'm sorry, Emily. I'm so sorry.'

'So why did you do it?'

'I don't know.'

'You don't know? It just happened? One of those things?'

'No, of course not . . .'

'I'm sorry if this analysis is upsetting you, Conor. I know how much you hate unnecessary chatter, but I find it quite important.'

She stopped. It was just the same old pattern endlessly repeating itself, even with the topic and the emotions involved spiced up a bit. They might as well have been discussing Mrs Conlon-next-door's kitchen extension. 'But they won't pass it in planning permission, will they, Conor?' 'I don't know, Emily.' 'But she can't build in our garden, Conor!' 'Let's just wait and see.' And on and on and on.

The taxi driver got into the car next to theirs. He nodded and waved enthusiastically at Emily. She tried to ignore him.

'Who's he?' Conor asked.

'It doesn't matter.'

The taxi driver reversed out. Emily looked at Conor, her face detached. It wasn't a show. She felt right now that the two of them were so far from understanding each other that they might as well be on different planets.

'I'm worried about the baby,' she said.

'I am too. I'm sorry you had to find out now. It doesn't help.'

'Indeed.' She looked at the dashboard. Had Mary been in this car? Of course she had. She must have been. 'I'd like to keep the upset to a minimum. For my own sake too.'

'Of course.'

'So . . . there isn't anything more I should know, is there?'

'No.'

'Mary Murphy's not pregnant too, by any chance?'

'Emily. Please.'

'Well, let's be thankful for small mercies. It would just be too ironic if you had to visit two wards at the same time. Not to mention the maintenance payments.'

Conor shifted unhappily. Now that she had her pound of flesh, Emily decided to call it a day.

'I think you should go home now, Conor, before we both say things we'd regret. I'll ring you, of course, and let you know what Mr Chapman says.'

'Do you want me to move out?' he asked quietly.

'Why?'

She saw that she had surprised him, perhaps for the first time in years. Oh dear. Things were worse than she'd thought.

'Well, I suppose because you couldn't bear the sight of me,' he offered.

'Not right now,' she agreed. 'But I don't have to look at you, do I? I'm in here.'

'But you might be out today. What'll we do then?'

Emily felt pressure bearing down on her hard. This hadn't figured in her confrontation scenario either. Who would have thought it was all so practical and domestic, with decisions needing to be made immediately? Decisions that somehow seemed to come down to her? Didn't the offending party have to do *anything* except say they were sorry and look guilty?

'Whatever you want, I'll do it,' he said fervently, compounding the injustice of the situation.

'Oh, do what you like, Conor!'

A car eased into the space the taxi driver had vacated. She looked over and locked eyes with Mr Chapman. She rolled down her window.

'Be in in a minute!'

She rolled the window back up quickly before he could say anything.

'By the way, Neasa is on to you,' she told Conor.

'What? How . . .?'

'It doesn't matter,' she said quickly. 'But just be prepared.'

He gave a small sigh. 'Right. Thanks.'

'I'll try and keep her away from the house, but you know what she's like with drink on her.'

'I'll leave the dogs out.'

She adjusted her bunny slippers for the trip back into the hospital, and retrieved a packet of mints she had left in the glove compartment.

'Goodbye then,' she said formally.

He didn't want to leave it now. He wanted to talk. Wasn't that just typical?

'Emily, we've had six years together. We have a baby on the way. Don't write it all off.'

'Let's not paper over the cracks either.'

She saw that she had shaken him to the very core with this. Herself too. Neither of them had really entered into this discussion believing that parting was a real possibility.

Emily got out of the car quickly and walked fast towards the front doors. She bent her head so that the smokers didn't see her face, and slipped into the lift as Mr Chapman started to climb the stairs.

Conor sat in the car, staring at the grey pebbledash wall in front of him until the car fogged up so much that he was looking at his own breath. He wanted to smoke but wouldn't let himself.

Emily had left the glove compartment open. He reached over and shut it carefully, because he had to, because he wanted to finish off an action she had started.

She could not have meant it, could she? About it being over? Emily often threatened things in Conor's experience, but her innate good sense and conservatism usually won out. She sometimes threatened to drown the dogs, for instance, when they dug up one of her plants in the garden. Conor had never been unduly worried for their safety. Sure enough, ten minutes later she would be cuddling them and talking about buying them water bowls with their names on them.

But her face had been different this time. Emily was one of those people who wore their feelings on their face. You could nearly tell what she'd had for breakfast just by looking at her. There was something hard about her today, like an animal who had been kicked one time too many and had made its mind up to run away.

He wouldn't let her. He just wouldn't.

He shut his eyes tight now, trying to blank out the image of her face: that terrible, wounded look, the white pinched skin around her mouth. The shock and revulsion in her eyes. For a moment he thought he was going to be sick.

He did not know how she had found out. Not that it mattered. He had pictured this moment for months and months now; had lived in dread of it, even though he had done his best to cover his tracks. But that was the awful thing about betrayal – you can never be sure that it will not catch up on you. And you do not realise this until long after the affair is over, when the guilt and fear of discovery do not abate but only grow stronger with each passing week. Conor felt that he had been living with a terminal illness since the day he and Ffion had broken up.

He wondered how he had ever thought at the time that the affair was worth it, because he must have thought that. He must have weighed up the illicit excitement against the awful feelings of guilt and betrayal, and gone ahead anyway. At some point, he must have faced the possibility that Emily would find out. Or that he would tell her, which he very much wanted to do afterwards.

But that would only have been selfish. In the end, there was nothing he could do except bury it and hope that it went away. It hadn't and now she was talking about leaving.

Stupid. *Stupid*.

Conor did not fear being on his own. He had always been on his own anyway. He feared being on his own without Emily. He saw no contradiction in this. Without her he would be scratching about on the outskirts of civilisation with no one to help him step in.

He remembered that day all those years ago, the very first day they'd met at a mutual friend's wedding. He had misplaced his date for reasons he could not even remember now, and had ended up hanging around the bar on his own like the proverbial spare part. A big boisterous group had rolled in, the kind of people who always made Conor feel grey and dull. He had noticed Emily immediately, small and darkly pretty, and chatting animatedly to a big handsome fellow with a ruddy face – her own date. She hadn't noticed Conor at all, of course, until her date had collapsed with suspected food poisoning and was carted off. Conor had approached her with the help of seven pints of Guinness. She had invited him to join her group at the bar, and he had felt like he was coming home.

Even back then, she had talked and he had been content to listen, delighted and charmed by her, and quite unable to believe his luck. It wasn't that no other woman fancied him. They did, lots of them, because he was good-looking, and intelligent, and his career seemed very glamorous. But he felt he didn't have to try with Emily. There wasn't that awful forced falseness of early dates, all that careful questioning about background and family, as though each were attempting to eliminate a psycho or hopeless case from their enquiries. Emily took him to her heart straightaway like she did every other eejit, and it all felt so right. Or maybe so easy.

They were different, of course. They wore jokey badges: she was the expressive one, whereas he would intellectualise things. He had felt that it worked very well, in the beginning at least. They had been fond of saying that it was a classic case of opposites attracting.

But he often thought back to that wedding in Paulstown, and the big handsome fellow with the loud laugh. He wondered what would have happened had the egg mayonnaise not been off that day. Would Emily have ended up marrying him instead?

He wondered about these things because sometimes it seemed to him that Emily had come to him purely by virtue of luck. Luck, and his own perseverance. He was the one who had done the chasing; he was the one who had put himself on offer. She'd only had to say 'yes' or 'no'.

In his more insecure moments, he would wonder whether she regretted her decision. It was the way she would look at him sometimes. Oddly. With disappointment?

She never said anything. But as the years went by, those looks became more pointed and he became more defensive and guarded. She had become less bubbly anyway, and more critical in a sort of irritated way.

He listened to her chatter less. It was just married life.

He believed they would have trundled on like this, content enough, had not two things happened. Firstly, Emily had the miscarriage and everything fell apart at the seams.

Secondly, Ffion Rivera, with whom he had become friendly, was suddenly plunged into marital difficulties of her own. Everything that followed seemed inevitable.

The affair had not lasted long. A matter of weeks only. Conor had tried to treat it as a brief lapse, a minor fall from the straight and narrow. He blamed his own weakness rather than his own unhappiness. And with Emily pregnant again, he was gripped by a great need to make things work the second time around. He had to. He and Emily were going to be parents.

Well, Emily was, anyway. For all his determination to become involved, his function seemed to be almost entirely to support her, the person really having the baby, if everything he had read and learned in antenatal classes was to be believed. He was forced to laugh at 'hilarious' jokes about men being confounded by the sight of a dirty nappy, and endure that stupid Liz's remarks about him nipping to the pub while Emily gave birth. This wonderful opportunity to forge something new between them, to make amends to Emily for his behaviour, was whipped from him by doctors and nurses and medical books and hospitals, all of whom seemed to have a great deal more to contribute than him. Even Emily herself sought to exclude him, poking fun at his efforts to educate himself. As if he hadn't felt foolish enough talking to the baby through her belly button.

He went through her pregnancy feeling like this, resentful and jealous and inadequate. And the guilt was always there, poking and prodding away at him. These were not feelings he could admit to Emily. Or to anyone. He had tried once to talk to his brother Mark about impending fatherhood. Mark had two kids himself. But Mark had only seemed embarrassed. They did not talk about feelings in their family. They never had.

Conor reached for the key now and started the car. But why would he go home? His wife and baby were right here – if indeed either of them belonged to him in any sense any more.

He turned off the engine anyway and sat.

The whisper started at the general reception desk on the ground floor.

'He's here.'

'Where? Here?'

'No, he's going up to Brenda's Ward. Emily Whatser-name.'

'The bunny slippers?'

'Her. Tommy-the-porter saw him arrive. In a brand new car.'

'They always have brand new cars, don't they?'

'A convertible.'

'What, in this weather?'

'You know Tommy, it's probably just got a sunroof. But he swears it's new.'

'Well! What's he doing, a tour of the place before it closes?' This was said very bitterly.

'No, no. It's just to see her.'

'What is she, a blue-blood or something?'

'No bed for her in Cork apparently. Tommy saw them talking in the car park.'

'What was she doing in the car park?'

'Chatting away with him – her and the husband. Parked side-by-side, very friendly.'

'So he knows them?'

'I'd say she must be a relative or something. I'd better go see if the girls up in Bernadette's know.'

They didn't.

'A *cabriolet*. He must have had it imported. Probably from Japan or somewhere.'

'He asked Tommy to park it.'

'He didn't!'

'How else would Tommy know that it was a Japanese import with automatic gear stick and a sunroof?'

'Must have cost a fortune.'

'They can afford it, those consultants. I suppose she's loaded as well. Emily.'

'Of course she is. Look at those slippers and that tatty dressing-gown. Only the very rich dress like that. They don't need to bother, you see.'

'Is she from his wife's side?'

'I don't know. I think she looks a bit like Chapman himself.'

'What, have you seen him?'

'No, just his picture in the medical magazines. But she's the spit.'

'The girls in Brenda's say that she never sleeps. Just walks the corridors all the time.'

'Weird.'

'And as for the husband . . .'

'What about him?'

'Someone said that they saw him in the Cork Opera House last night.'

'He dropped her here and went off to a concert?'

'No, no, he was on stage.'

'He's an opera singer?'

'I suppose. Didn't bother his barney showing up last night at all. Highly strung.'

'Not as highly strung as her by the sounds of it.' A beat. 'Did anybody tell them in Brenda's that he's coming up to them?'

Nobody had. The girls in St Jude's Ward volunteered to pass on the information. By the time Mr Chapman arrived at his destination, he was the proud new owner of a stretch sports car with a retractable roof, bonnet and wheels, which did a hundred and ten miles to the gallon and which his Japanese chauffeur drove. Emily Collins was his rich eccentric niece who had ended up in Martha's after a fight with the ambulance men, Joe and Liam, and whose opera singer husband was recording an album and was too busy to visit.

Mr Chapman quickly poured cold water on most of the conjecture by going straight over to Trish and saying, 'Hello, Emily.'

'I'm over here,' Emily said.

Emily knew of white people who thought that all black people looked the same, and vice versa. It seemed that this could be extended to pregnant women. But then she saw that Trish was asleep with her hair all over her face and gave Mr Chapman the benefit of the doubt.

Also, she was secretly glad of the extra few seconds to prepare herself after her sprint down the corridor. She smoothed down her hair and wiped her nose with a tissue. She hoped that he wouldn't be able to tell that she had been crying.

But he didn't really look at her as he crossed the ward and stood at the foot of her bed. Two nurses, a doctor and an intern trooped after him like a gaggle of geishas. One of them reverently pressed Emily's chart into his hands like she was giving him Holy Communion.

'So! How are we this morning?' he asked the chart.

Nobody was looking at Emily. Not the nurses, the doctor or the intern. Emily knew that the world roughly divided into two kinds of people: those who looked, and those who were looked at. Emily had always fitted firmly into the first camp. She had never been the kind of person other people looked at. It was a charisma thing and she believed that there was nothing that could be done about it. But, bloody hell, did courtesy have to go out the window for her kind too? And respect?

'Why don't *you* tell me how I am?' she said, quite loudly.

Mr Chapman looked up, surprised. The nurses, doctor and intern stiffened a bit. Was she giving lip to Mr Chapman? Still, everyone knew that she was a bit off her rocker. Look at those eyes! Kind of sunken and burning, like something you'd read about in a Stephen King novel.

'Your blood pressure is still up,' Mr Chapman said, straight to her face this time.

'I know,' she agreed.

'Nothing too alarming, but we really do have to keep an eye on it.'

He looked again at her chart, peering over his bifocals. He never seemed to actually look through them. Was it possible that they were just for effect?

The thought made her braver still and she struggled to sit up a bit more in the bed. No one could sound forceful on the flat of their backs.

'Is it pre-eclampsia or not?' she enquired politely. 'Because nobody seems to know.'

Another small silence fell at the implied criticism. But thankfully Mr Chapman was used to dealing with all sorts and took this one on the chin.

'It can be difficult to identify,' he intoned pleasantly. 'A woman with high blood pressure alone may not have pre-eclampsia. Or, indeed, with fluid retention alone. It's the combination of factors that lead one to believe that the condition may be present.'

His voice was hypnotically boring and one of the nurses behind started to sway on her feet. Emily fought down her natural urge to smile and nod, her body and face contorted into an apology. Where had nodding and smiling ever got her?

'So it is pre-eclampsia then?'

Mr Chapman found himself forced into that position which every doctor tries to avoid – actually having to commit himself.

'Possibly,' he said, trying to work around it.

Emily was back in the car with Conor again, using all her wiles to extract information from him. Did people see her as some kind of fool who shouldn't be told things for her own good?

'When will you know for sure?' she asked, her voice distinctly frosty.

'That depends,' he said, again trying to shake her off.

'On what?'

Mr Chapman was very aware of the nurses, the doctor and the intern behind him, breathing down his neck.

'On four-hour monitoring of your blood pressure, daily urine checks, and the presence of swelling,' he said, sounding much less bored than usual. 'But from what we've seen so far, I believe it is pre-eclampsia.'

'Thank you,' Emily said quietly. 'I just wanted to know.'

The nurses, doctor and intern relaxed a bit. Mr Chapman took a moment to regroup behind Emily Collins' chart, rattled. The Emily Collins he remembered from the weekly visits at his clinic had been quiet and polite, sometimes forgot to bring in her sample but that was about the size of it. Nothing like this one in the bed here. Was it possible he was mixing her up with someone else? Still, he saw so many women – surely it was only natural that he got confused every now and then?

A small sliver of dread stabbed at Mr Chapman's insides. He was forty-eight next week. But his hands were rock steady still, he reassured himself fiercely. He had years in him yet. Years and years.

Emily was wondering whether it was wise to have ruffled Mr Chapman's feathers. He was looking after her baby, she didn't want to go annoying him. It could all backfire horribly at delivery. Did he have the power to deny her an epidural?

When Mr Chapman and Emily eventually looked at

each other again, it was with guarded eyes.

'I'm afraid I'm going to have to keep you in.'

'Keep me in?'

'Yes. For observation. I can't take any chances until your blood pressure is down. Also, I'd like to prescribe some diuretics, see if we can get rid of some of the fluid retention. Just a mild dose.'

The doctor behind furiously made a note of this.

'I'm going to hold off prescribing anything for the blood pressure. We'll see if it'll sort itself out.'

'Right,' Emily said carefully. 'And how long do you think I'll be kept in?'

Mr Chapman sighed inwardly. She would be difficult about this as well. Where were all the nice patients these days? 'Indefinitely, I'm afraid.'

Emily was relieved. At least one decision had been taken from her. She could stay in here safe and sound for the moment, away from Conor until she had sorted some things out.

'Great,' she said with feeling.

Mr Chapman looked at her even more warily. 'We could be talking a couple of weeks,' he said slowly, sure that she hadn't understood.

'Lovely,' Emily said, beaming at him.

Mr Chapman stopped worrying about his memory loss and started fretting about his ability to interpret patient-doctor situations. Suddenly he felt vulnerable and old and he wanted to leave Martha's very quickly.

'Right,' he said, thrusting the chart into the intern's

hand. 'I'll see you again in a couple of days.'

'But I'll be transferred to Cork, won't I?' Emily enquired.

Cork would be even better. She felt a huge need to put as much space between herself and Conor as possible.

'Yes,' Mr Chapman said gravely. 'I'm sorry.'

He waited for her disappointment.

'Great!' Emily said again.

Mr Chapman was astounded when she threw back the covers energetically, grabbed a Manchester United bag and started to pack. He had never seen a pregnant woman move so fast.

'Um, not right now,' he said, rattled.

'Oh. When then?'

Mr Chapman thought he saw one of the nurses smile. Things were getting out of hand.

'Soon,' he said loudly. 'You're fine here for the moment.'

Emily Collins was not good for his health, he decided. Best to keep her in Martha's for the moment – he could probably discharge her next week anyway. Besides, he had quite enjoyed the drive up here this morning. It had been a refreshing break from the bureaucracy in which he was currently mired.

'Right. Good.' He turned to leave, the nurses, the doctor and the intern trooping after him.

'Mr Chapman?'

He swung back suspiciously. 'Yes?'

'Just thanks for coming all the way up to see me,'

Emily said earnestly. 'I appreciate it.'

Mr Chapman felt colour flood his cheeks. Somehow this was shifting from the impersonal to the personal.

'Um, you're welcome,' he stuttered and strode out of the ward so fast that his entourage were hard-pressed to keep up.

'You were great with him,' Maggie said through the curtain. She'd been listening to every word. 'Mr Dunphy frightens the life out of me. I've put down on my birth plan, quite nicely, that I don't want him to intimidate me during labour if he can help it at all.'

'Oh, you just have to know how to handle them,' Emily bluffed.

Old Chapman wasn't so bad really, she thought. It was funny how she had been so put off by him. Why? Because he wore a suit and accessorised bifocals? But it was difficult to be bolshy with someone who held your health in his hands. And she just wasn't a confrontational person. Emily wondered whether it was a gene thing or the fact that she had been raised in a house where fear had its own place at the table.

She remembered her father now, who had had pains in his chest for weeks before his heart attack. Dr Leahy had prescribed large doses of Milk of Magnesia and told him to stop eating big meals at night. The poor man had watched everyone else tucking into egg and chips at teatime, and would then spend most of his evenings on the toilet. Emily had suggested going back to Dr Leahy. But there was no question of that. A man of medicine! He knew indigestion when he saw it.

After the funeral, Dr Leahy had tucked into ham sandwiches back at the house. Their mother had plied him with whiskey. She should have thrown him out into the rain and filed a lawsuit. The man shouldn't have been practising medicine at all. Emily had felt angry about it for years.

She was angry with her father now. For nodding and smiling, and for taking no responsibility for his own health. And at herself for not insisting at the time. But there was safety in numbers and she had let her dissent be swallowed up.

She was on her own now and it hit her like a slap. For six years she had enjoyed the security of being in a couple. There was always someone there to make the decisions with or, indeed, to take no action at all. Almost every aspect of life was approached with some-one else in mind. There was, of course, the odd defiant strike at independence. Going to London on the piss with Neasa, and let Conor cook for himself! Choosing a new car purely on the basis of its nice blue colour, and let Conor laugh! But these were feeble things, and always indulged by the other. No real difference of opinion had existed.

Everything had changed now. She felt the aloneness wrap itself around her like cold fingers, and found that she was shaking. It was like half of her had been brutally hacked off.

She curled up tightly on the bed and wondered how

Conor could have done this to her. How could he tell her he loved her and still do this to her? She thought of his square, handsome face, and she very badly wanted to damage him, to hurt him as much as he had hurt her. The dogs he had nurtured since they were puppies, she wanted to boil them in a pot on the cooker. She wanted to tamper with his car brakes so that he would have an horrific accident that would leave him wheelchair-bound, and she would enjoy the look on his face when she waltzed in on her own two legs with their child for his visitation rights. Or his fingers – she wanted to break them one by one so that he never played the piano again, unless he learned to play with his elbows.

She lay there and fiercely wished that the baby inside her would die. That would hurt him the most. I'm sorry, I'm sorry, she told the baby, weeping now.

The catering girls were very nice in Martha's. Maureen especially, who firmly believed that half the drugs the doctors prescribed to these women were totally unnecessary. In her experience, a nice cup of sweet tea usually did the trick.

'I don't want it,' Emily said thickly.

'Nonsense, of course you do,' Maureen said, expertly balancing the cup and saucer in one hand and fixing pillows, covers and the sliding tray with the other. 'Up you sit,' she said.

Emily had no choice but to do so.

'Thank you,' she said, taking a small sip of the tea. It was sickeningly sweet but strangely nice.

'No problem,' Maureen said, watching as the colour came back into Emily's face. Maybe this one would remember the kitchen staff when it came time to leave. It was always the blasted nurses and midwives who got all the Roses. It wasn't fair.

'Do you want to have sex?' Gary grudgingly asked. He was still in a bit of a snit from earlier but hadn't the energy to go around with a puss on him all night. He was exhausted after all his work today. And Creepy Crawley wanted him in for a meeting at nine in the morning. Nine! Gary had quickly reverted to 'Creepy' as the afternoon had progressed.

Neasa looked at him vaguely. 'No, but thanks anyway. I think I might go to the hospital.'

But she made no move to get her coat. How did you break this kind of news to your best friend? And she banged up in hospital? What Neasa really wanted to do was get tanked up and go over to Conor's. Alcohol would give her the verbosity to sort him out. She would buy two pork chops on the way. That bastard would leave the dogs out. They were well known for their propensity to attack anything that came through the front gate.

'Dinner, then,' Gary offered. He was anxious now to get things back on an even keel. Neasa wasn't paying any attention to his sulking and he was getting rattled.

'No, but you go ahead.' Neasa considered lying to Emily. This went against every fibre of her being, but she was trying to do the best thing. The fax in her pocket would send Emily's blood pressure through the ceiling. It could even bring on labour! Neasa did not want to spend the rest of her life apologising to a child who was born with only one lung.

'A drink? Wine? Gin and tonic?' Gary was getting desperate now.

'No,' Neasa said again, shocking him. Neasa never refused drink. There must be something awfully big bothering her. The blond hair on the back of Gary's thick neck rose slightly. Was it possible that she was going off him?

'Is it me?' he blurted.

'What?'

'Whatever's upsetting you.'

Neasa looked at his big, meaty, open face and felt terribly tender. 'Of course not, sweetness – sure don't I love you?'

Gary beamed back. 'Great.'

She went back to looking terribly vague. Now that he wasn't the problem, Gary's mind travelled in a different direction.

'Will I put the kettle on for a cup of tea?' he asked rather quietly.

'Yes, yes,' she murmured.

'And a biscuit?'

'Yes, fine.'

'Will we tell people in the office that we're seeing each other?'

'Yes, sure, whatever.'

'Great!'

Neasa shook herself. 'What?'

'Now that I'm a partner, it's unseemly to be sneaking around behind people's backs,' Gary said piously.

'No. It's none of their business.'

'But you just said yes.'

'I wasn't listening.'

'Doesn't matter. A verbal agreement is binding.'

'You're such a fucking solicitor,' Neasa said. This was the most vicious insult anybody at Crawley Dunne & O'Reilly could throw at each other.

'We could take a few of them out for a pint and break the news. I'll pay,' Gary offered. He still had some fiddled expenses in his post-office account. It was the same post-office account he had opened when he'd made his First Communion. Neasa didn't know about it. There were some savings accounts Gary didn't tell her about.

'No,' Neasa said.

Gary was annoyed now. What was her problem? Was it because they wouldn't get to have sex in empty offices any more? Secretly Gary wished they could do it in the bed once in a while. It mightn't be as exciting, but it would be a hell of a lot more comfortable – and safe. The last time they'd had sex in Crawley's office Gary had impaled himself on a thumb tack.

'Conor is having an affair,' Neasa said very fast. She hadn't wanted to tell Gary – it seemed disloyal to Emily somehow – but she needed to talk to him about what to do.

Gary laughed. 'You're a gas, woman.'

'I wouldn't joke about something like this. He's shagging someone else.'

'What?' Gary's pale eyes popped.

'And I have to tell Emily,' Neasa wailed.

'Well, well,' Gary said slowly, his mind still on Conor shagging. Who would have thought it? Mr Superior, Mr Cultural, getting down and dirty with the best of them.

'Who?' he asked.

'What?'

'Who is Conor having the affair with?'

Neasa didn't know why this mattered. 'Ffion Rivera. The first violinist.'

'Well, well,' Gary said again. Mary Murphy with the long legs and the short, shiny hair. Trust Conor to go for a classy bird. It would be beneath him to go for the barmaid in Milo's. Gary wondered where they had done it.

'How am I going to tell Emily?' Neasa said a bit tearfully.

'I know. Poor Emily,' Gary said quickly. 'Isn't he a right bastard?'

'Totally.'

Gary was cheering up immensely. 'For all his airs and graces. He's a right fucker.'

'Yes, yes,' Neasa said. 'But what about Emily?'

Gary shook his head in a great show of disgust. 'I know.'

'I think she knows already,' Neasa said. She was feeling better now. Gary was a great comfort. Well, the important thing was to share. 'But I found out that the pair of them stayed in a hotel in Germany and I'm supposed to confirm it to her.'

Well, well, Gary thought to himself, stuck in a groove now. No seedy B & Bs for Conor Collins. A hotel in Germany, no less. He must have been very anxious to keep it quiet.

'What do you think I should do?' Neasa prompted. 'She's seven months pregnant, Gary.'

Gary reluctantly stopped thinking about Conor and Mary and schnitzel, and moved on to the problem of Emily. He wondered why it was that Emily Collins, whom he'd blithely ignored for years, seemed to rouse all kinds of uncomfortable feelings in him these days.

'Can you lie?' he said bluntly.

'No!'

'Don't look at me like that. You know you've thought about it.'

'It doesn't mean I've entertained it!' Neasa looked disgusted.

'Then you're going to have to tell her.'

'What kind of a solution is that?'

Gary sat up a bit straighter, the way he did at meetings where sales were being closed. 'Look at it like this. If I were having an affair on you, and Emily found out, would you like to know?'

Neasa didn't like the way this argument was progressing. 'But you're not.'

'If I were.'

Neasa thought of the cross-dresser and the sexist and the chat-room junkie. This was a bit too close to the bone.

'I don't know . . .'

'Would you like to know the truth about me?' Gary insisted.

Jesus Christ, was he going to drop some kind of bomb on her? Was he going to reveal that not only was he having an affair, he had also been born a woman?

Not another wacko, please God, Neasa implored. She really liked this one. 'Yes! Yes, I would like to know!'

'Even if it meant that it was over?'

Her throat felt a bit tight. 'Even if it meant it was over. I would still like to know the truth about you.'

Gary nodded slowly. Then he slapped the table energetically. 'There you go. Tell her.'

Neasa took her first breath in minutes. Gary hadn't been about to reveal anything unsavoury about himself after all. It was just her imagination.

'Are you all right?' he asked.

'Yes, yes,' she said, relieved. 'I suppose something like this makes you think, that's all. About your own relationship.'

'It does,' Gary said, who hadn't been thinking anything of the sort.

'I mean, Conor and Emily . . . they seemed so stable

and happy, didn't they? You couldn't imagine anything going wrong between them.'

'You never know what goes on behind closed doors, do you,' he said sagely, putting his big, bear-like arm around her.

She nestled into him, hating this treacherous feeling of relief that everything was great with her own relationship. But sometimes it took someone else's unhappiness to make you appreciate what you had.

'Let's have that gin and tonic,' she said fervently. 'Make mine a double.'

'Can we not just hug for a minute?'

'Of course we can.' She laid her head on his shoulder sadly. 'I suppose it's over now. The marriage.'

'Well, you don't know that,' Gary said.

'He cheated on her, Gary. God Almighty! You don't expect her to take him back, do you?'

'Well, obviously it's something they'll have to talk about. And now with the baby . . .'

Neasa drew away a bit. 'I wouldn't forgive something like that.'

Gary laughed and kissed her hair. 'That's because you're a tough old bird, Neasa.'

'What?'

'Look, what Conor did was awful, I totally agree. But, come on, at the end of the day, it was probably a roll in the hay.'

'So it's not that serious?'

'It's an affair, Neasa. Unfortunately it happens quite a

lot. But people don't throw everything away because of it.'

'We'll have to agree to differ, won't we?' Neasa said lightly. What was she getting so uptight about? People were entitled to their opinions, weren't they? It wasn't as though Gary had had the affair. 'You'd never do something like that, would you?'

'On you?' Gary said. 'Never! I wouldn't dare.'

He had been joking. But Neasa looked terribly serious. 'You wouldn't want to.' Then she snuggled in again. 'Anyway, I believe you because you're perfect.'

The trouble was, Gary was not. And he knew it, and he was worried.

Emily rang Conor after tea. She kept the curtains pulled back so that everyone could see her. She did not want to risk getting angry. And she wanted to deny him the courtesy of talking to him in private.

'Emily.' He picked up on the second ring.

She did not say hello. She just told him what Mr Chapman had said in even, rehearsed tones.

'He's keeping me in indefinitely.'

'Right. Well, I suppose he's the doctor.' You couldn't tell anything from his voice either. He must be able to hear the television in the background and know that she was ringing from the ward.

'So, there you have it,' Emily said, trying to make her side sound normal to anyone who cared to listen.

'Can I come in and see you?' he asked.

'No.'

'Please, Emily.'

'No.' She hoped he wouldn't ask again, because it was difficult to keep saying 'no' in this high, breezy voice.

'Charles Crawley called around this evening,' he said eventually. 'To see how you are.'

Emily didn't reply. It would be dangerous to start discussing trivia. Before you knew it, you were involved in entire conversations. Conor had learned that much from her, the sneaky, sly bastard.

'I have to go now,' she said instead. 'Goodnight.'

He spoke fast. 'Emily. I've resigned from the orchestra. Just so you know that.'

He hung up without putting her through the charade of a public reaction.

Emily put her mobile away and tried to sort through the confusion of her emotions. He was making her a gesture. He would not be consorting with Mary Murphy even in a professional capacity. It was a clear and forth-right effort to lay the groundwork for trust again.

She could not fail to see what this had cost him. People were hardly crying out for professional pianists. He'd given up a steady job, some good colleagues, the buzz of performing in large venues. He'd probably have to go back to playing in restaurants where he would compete for attention with pan-fried trout.

It was too much. And too soon. Emily felt over-whelmed. She needed things to stand still for a while.

Conor had lived with this much longer than she; he was at a different stage. It wasn't fair of him to pressure her like this.

At the same time she was desperately glad that Mary Murphy had gone from their lives. Mary Murphy, that long streak of misery, with her peculiar, starey eyes and bleached moustache.

This wasn't really true. Some people found her eyes quite intense, and you'd have to look closely to see the moustache. Strangely, Emily found that she had no heart for denigrating Mary Murphy. And it seemed rather fruitless to compare Mary's physical attributes with her own – as though the affair had started purely on the basis that Mary had bigger breasts than Emily. Which she did. And longer legs. But Emily had a much better bottom and a neat little waist when she wasn't pregnant. No, all in all, Emily did not feel inferior to Mary Murphy in that way.

In fact she found that she did not care about Mary Murphy at all. Mary Murphy had not made Emily promises and broken them. It wasn't Mary Murphy, Ffion Rivera or whatever the hell she liked to call herself, who had let Emily down. Stand up, Conor, and take a bow.

Emily felt that she would never stop being angry with him. She couldn't imagine it fading, like other emotions did eventually. But then again, when they had married she had felt that she would never stop being totally engrossed in him to the point of grinning foolishly every time he walked into the room. She tried to think now how long that had lasted. A good while. But you couldn't keep that up, for heaven's sake – all the touching and kissing and having showers with each other. You could never get the shampoo out of your hair properly in any case. No, the time naturally came to pass when they took separate showers and did not eat off each other's forks.

Emily felt she had been realistic on the romance front. She had assumed that it would make way for something deeper, a greater knowledge and understanding of each other. And she had believed that it had in a way. She thought she knew Conor to his predictable core.

And now he had done this. Emily forgot about her hurt for a moment. She thought of those Saturday mornings when he played the piano, lost in some secret, passionate world from which she was excluded, and she wondered whether she had ever really known him at all.

Obviously not. Obviously there was some part of Conor not fulfilled by their marriage. By her. Otherwise why would he have turned to Ffion Rivera? To her shock and hurt, Emily added a layer of self-doubt and defensiveness.

Trish ambled in. She smelled of the takeaway curry her husband had brought in and which she'd just eaten in the visitors' room.

'Any joy?' Emily asked sympathetically.

'No. And it was a vindaloo and everything. It

brought on my youngest two.'

The vindaloo was a last resort. They were going to induce her in the morning.

'I suppose I'd better shave my legs,' she said, going to her locker. 'It'll take ages. They've not been done since the last one.'

'It'll all be worth it in the end,' Emily said consolingly.

'Oh, I don't know,' Trish said with a sigh. 'It was a mistake, you know. A burst condom. Blew out like a tyre.'

Emily was mildly shocked. She wouldn't dream of sharing such a personal detail with a stranger. Her heart always went out to those poor souls who were lured onto Jerry Springer-type shows and informed that their boyfriend was in fact their biological father. Emily fretted now as she thought about Conor's affair getting out. She could not bear to have her personal business dissected by the staff of Crawley Dunne & O'Reilly down in Milo's of a Friday night, or doing the rounds of the weekend dinner parties, every hushed sentence prefixed by the words 'Poor Emily'. But these things had a way of getting out. They always did.

She wanted to strangle Conor now for violating her privacy.

Trish went off as Maggie arrived in, her husband Tiernan in tow. Maggie handed Emily two sheets of grubby paper stapled together.

'I got some signatures for you,' she said.

'Me too,' Tiernan added fervently.

'What?'

'The petition,' Maggie explained. 'I saw it on the end of your bed. I went around Jude's Ward. They all signed.'

'And I got a few people as they were coming in,' Tiernan said. 'At least somebody's doing something.'

And they looked at her expectantly, confidently. This was because Maggie had discovered during conversation that Emily was a solicitor. Further probing had revealed that Emily had sold Maggie's brother's house for him last year. Apparently her brother spoke very highly of Emily. 'She didn't treat us like idiots,' he had declared warmly.

Emily looked at the petition. She didn't need this. 'It's not mine. I mean, it wasn't my idea.'

'I know, but you'll get things done,' Maggie said confidently. 'Right, I've to go practise my breathing. Well, it's for Tiernan, really. He always goes much too fast, don't you, Tiernan?'

'I do,' he said cheerfully, pulling the curtain around Maggie's bed.

Emily looked at the petition with its handful of signatures. Even total strangers had her marked down as the kind of person who would get the grunt work done. 'Conscientious', 'Hard-working', 'Disciplined' were words that had routinely appeared on her school reports. Once, her English teacher had run out of superlatives and had simply put down, 'Emily is a Good Girl.'

It sounded vaguely insulting now.

Emily lunged over in the bed and scrabbled in her locker. She took out a can of Neasa's Guinness and cracked it open. It tasted foul, warm and yeasty, but she took another slug anyway. And that was how her mother found her.

'Hello, Mam,' she said defiantly.

'Well, love,' Pauline Ryan said, plonking herself down on the chair, the three crucifixes around her neck rattling. 'I used to drink Guinness too when I was expecting. A can every night.'

Emily deflated and put down the Guinness.

'How are you, Mam?' she said before she could help it.

'All right,' Pauline said, doubtfully.

'Liz said you had palpitations yesterday morning.'

'I did,' Pauline confirmed. 'Liz told me that you thought it was the new postman.'

Thank you, Liz.

'What's this you have then?' Pauline enquired.

'Pre-eclampsia.'

'We didn't have that in my day,' Pauline declared. 'The big worry was high blood pressure and water retention. Oh, and protein or something in your waters.'

'That *is* pre-eclampsia.'

'Well, now, you learn something new every day,' Pauline said, delighted at being able to use another of her favourite phrases.

Emily looked at her mother, finding it hard to believe

that she was only sixty. She always thought of her as an old, old woman. Would Emily's own child look upon Emily the same way, with a mixture of curiosity and pity? The thought was so hurtful that she sat up straighter and tried to look at her mother with new eyes.

'What was it like for you, Mam? When you were pregnant?'

'What?'

'You know, did you feel tired and puffy and did the waiting kill you?'

'I suppose.' Pauline looked unsure. 'It's such a long time ago.'

'I know, but you must remember something. You remembered the Guinness for example.'

'That's true,' Pauline agreed with more spirit.

Emily was eager now. 'And what about childbirth? Don't people say you never forget the pain of that?'

'We didn't have epidurals in those days, that's for sure.'

'Did it last long? Each labour? Was it awful?'

Pauline looked adrift again. 'I honestly can't remember, Emily . . . I think Liz was the longest, but she was the first. You should ask her, you know. If you need to know anything. She'll be able to tell you.'

'I know, but I'm interested to know what it was like for you.'

But Pauline just looked hunted. 'Oh, Emily. Do you have to make such a song and dance about things?'

Emily was terribly hurt. 'Mam! When do I ever make a song and dance about things?'

'Such a chatterbox as a child,' Pauline said with relish. 'Now that I do remember. Always wanting to know things, to talk endlessly about things. Like, where did birds go to die!' She laughed.

Emily looked at her, wondering was she finally going senile.

'And what happened to snake's skins when they shed them? As if you'd ever seen a snake!'

Definitely there was something loose. Emily could not remember this person she was talking about.

'You had us driven demented,' Pauline finished.

'And did I ever find out?' Emily enquired. 'Where birds went to die?'

'Oh, we knocked sense into you in the end,' her mother said, smiling with the satisfaction of having squashed an annoying bug.

Emily vowed fiercely that if her child wanted to know where birds went to die, then Emily would take him or her to the woods where they would camp out in a tent for as long as it took for a bird to pop its clogs. They would go to the jungle in South America and wait for a boa constrictor to shed its skin and see what happened to it. She would, of course, organise all the necessary vaccinations first.

'Mam, I don't want you to stay too late, not if you're feeling a bit under the weather.'

She was finding Pauline hard work. She always

did. 'And you don't like driving in the dark,' she added.

Pauline drove at twenty miles an hour in the dark and pulled over to the side of the road for every oncoming car. If it were a truck, she would go halfway up the ditch.

'Better be safe than sorry,' she would mutter under her breath.

Emily knew now that there was no guarantee at all that if you practised safety you would not get sorrow.

'That's true,' Pauline said. 'And I want to catch eight o'clock Mass.'

This was unprecedented. Pauline went to Mass on Sundays, naturally, and every first Monday of the month. Then there were the Stations of the Cross, of course, and she usually went every morning during Advent. She never let a funeral pass either, and always turned up for the remembrance Masses. But on a Wednesday night?

'Has somebody died?' Emily enquired.

'No, no. I thought I'd go for you, Emily.'

This was Pauline's way of supporting her.

'I'm not that sick.'

'Still. Every little helps.'

'Oh, Mam, sign this for me before you go.' Emily reluctantly reached for the petition. Maggie was probably listening expectantly.

Pauline didn't like this. For no reason at all she didn't like it.

'It's just to stop the hospital closing,' Emily said impatiently.

'But it's going to close anyway,' Pauline said.

'Well, yes, but there's no harm in trying, is there? There's no bloody law against making the effort!'

Pauline fretted as she looked at the form. 'I won't get sent any unsolicited material, will I?'

'No, Mam. I can assure you of that,' Emily said grimly.

There had been a very embarrassing incident last year involving unsolicited material. A monthly magazine had got Pauline's name and address from somewhere and had sent her details of a prize draw. All she had to do was sign and send it back. Each month, more material would arrive from this crowd, breathlessly informing Pauline that she had been selected to go through to the next round, and the next. Pauline's natural antipathy of forms had been overcome by the promise of big money, and she had signed and sent them all back, telling no one. Then a sample cheque had arrived from the magazine people for a quarter of a million pounds, made out in Pauline's name. Pauline hadn't noticed the 'sample only' stamp on the top of the cheque and had tried to cash it in the bank in Paulstown, whispering to the bank manager that she was going to give some of it to Emily and Liz, and the rest to the church fund for a new roof. She had even generously urged him to keep a tenner for himself. The bank manager had discreetly called Emily in. Emily had sent a stiff solicitors' letter to the magazine crowd, warning them never to darken her mother's doorstep again.

Pauline had been very embarrassed and upset about it, and Emily had felt more sad than anything. For the first time in her life her mother had sensed real independence, only for it to be whipped from her because she wasn't sharp or cynical enough for this world.

Emily felt a greater connection with her now as Pauline laboriously signed and handed back the form.

'Thanks, Mam.'

'Who will you give it to?'

'What?'

'The petition?'

'Well, I don't know,' Emily said unhappily. She hadn't thought about this.

'I don't see why you bother half the time, Emily.' This was said with no rancour, just genuine puzzlement, and Emily felt annoyed again.

'It'd be a fine old world if nobody bothered, Mam.'

Pauline just shrugged and stood. 'I'll leave a shepherd's pie over to Conor in the morning.'

'He can cook. He has nothing else to do all day long,' Emily said sharply.

'It's no trouble,' Pauline said, gathering her bits and pieces. It seemed to take ages, as she took keys from her big bag, put her umbrella back in, changed her reading glasses to her driving glasses, checked her keys again.

Emily hadn't noticed her doing any of these things when she'd arrived.

Then she reached in and took Emily's hand. Emily was so touched that she felt tearful, but only until she realised that Pauline had pressed a wad of ten-pound notes into her fist.

'Mam? What's this?'

'For the baby. Best that you choose something yourselves. I wouldn't know what to be getting.'

You'd never think she'd had four children herself.

'But Mam . . . this is too much.' There was at least a couple of hundred pounds there.

Pauline stiffened with pride. 'It's not for you, Emily. It's for the baby. I did the same for all of Liz's.'

'Sorry, Mam . . . thanks. I'll buy something nice.'

Pauline nodded and left, buttoning up her thick coat and pulling on gloves as though she were stepping out into the Antarctic.

Emily put the money away carefully in the little zippered pocket inside her washbag. It was the first present she'd got for the baby. Most people had the tact to wait until the child was actually born alive and in one piece. But it hadn't occurred to Pauline that Emily had had a miscarriage and might be a bit sensitive. To Pauline it had been nature's way of dealing with defects, and had consoled Emily with the words that she could always have another one, and 'lightning never strikes twice'.

Emily wasn't at all sure about this. What about cleft

palates and heart defects, congenital abnormalities and haemolytic jaundice? This was in addition to the big worries of spina bifida and Down's syndrome, which Emily had spent many hours convincing herself the baby would have. Eventually she had stopped reading pregnancy books altogether, because they always seemed to fall open at some new disease or disorder that you'd never heard of before but would immediately start fretting about. It was the deodorant premise again; the more information you had, the more you worried. And the more you worried, the more likely you were to end up in hospital with stress-related pre-eclampsia. It was a vicious circle, Emily thought darkly, and she would very much like to meet the person who had started it all in the first place.

Conor's car was in the driveway, so Gary knew he was home. Gary was delighted with his suggestion to go over and talk to Conor. For one thing, it had earned him untold brownie points with Neasa. 'Oh Gary, would you? Because if I go I'll only wring his neck. You might be able to talk some sense into him.'

Also, Neasa had finally made up her mind to go in to the hospital, and it would be no fun without her at home. He supposed he could have rung up someone to go out for a few jars in Milo's, but then he realised that he didn't have any friends. Not any bosom buddies anyway, he quickly corrected. He had a very wide-ranging circle of laddish acquaintances all right, mostly the guys from work and the boyfriends of Neasa's friends. But he didn't have best friends like Neasa did. It seemed an awful lot of work, all the phone calls and the popping around to each other's houses, the dinner dates made weeks in advance. Sometimes Gary did make dinner dates, of course. He didn't want Neasa to think that he had no friends.

He stepped out of his BMW, grabbing six bottles of exotic beer he'd bought in the off-licence. They would need much more as the night progressed but Conor was bound to have some in the house.

He rang the doorbell with a confidence he'd never had on Conor's turf before, and fixed a suitably empathetic expression on his face.

The two dogs came galloping around the corner, barking viciously.

'Bollocks,' Gary said. Neasa had warned him. But he'd been so busy anticipating Conor's confession that he'd forgotten to buy two pork chops.

Conor came to the door in the nick of time.

'Get down,' he told the dogs quietly and they turned and slunk away.

Conor didn't look unshaven or drunk or red-eyed, as Gary had expected, and he faltered a bit.

'Ah, hello. I was in the neighbourhood.'

Conor looked at him, and Gary had the same uncomfortable feeling he'd had back in school when his science teacher had found him pulling the legs off a live bluebottle.

'I suppose you'd better come in,' Conor said.

The living-room was devoid of leftover TV dinners, whiskey bottles or damp tissues. Was the man human at all? Then Gary got the whiff of cigarette smoke. Ah-ha. Conor had been smoking inside the house. A crack in the armour.

'Neasa not with you?' Conor enquired, looking over Gary's shoulder just to be certain.

'No. She's gone to the hospital,' Gary said softly, as though he were talking to the recently bereaved.

Conor didn't react. Instead he offered tea or coffee.

'I brought some beer,' Gary said unnecessarily.

'You go ahead,' Conor said. 'I'll stick with tea.'

Gary was starting to regret ever coming around. You couldn't have any kind of a bonding session on tea.

In the kitchen, Conor emptied the kettle of hot water and refilled it with cold. It would take longer to boil. He wondered had Neasa sent Gary around in one of her ham-fisted attempts to get even on Emily's behalf. Conor was aware of Gary's reputation as Jaws in the office and wearily anticipated that at some point it would get physical.

When he eventually went back into the living-room, Gary was plonked comfortably on the sofa as though he intended to stay there for the night.

'Would you like a glass with that beer?' Conor asked politely.

'No, no, I drink it by the neck.' And he demonstrated this by twisting off the top and throwing half of it into his big mouth.

Conor sat down in the armchair opposite and tried to think of something to say. Gary didn't seem bothered at all by the silence; he just leaned back and lifted one ankle to rest on the other knee. Conor had tried to sit like that once, it looked so casual and relaxed, but he had just had this awful feeling that he was exposing his genitals. Which, actually, Gary was doing, if you looked closely enough. Those jeans were welded to him. It was almost obscene, and the sort of thing only very confident men could carry off. Conor wondered what it took to become that confident in your own skin.

'What's the beer like?'

'Oh, lovely. Mexican, you know? Lovely little bite to it. Go on, have one.'

'No, really—'

'One won't kill you.'

Conor took the bottle Gary held out. It was quite pleasant actually. Conor felt it was his turn again to say something.

'Manchester United won 2–1. I saw it on the news.'

Gary looked very surprised at this. 'Did they now? Well, well.'

Conor hoped that he wouldn't ask him who had scored, because he didn't have a clue. The appeal of football had always eluded Conor. Everybody else seemed to love it, women too. It was a kind of social grace now to have a favourite team. Conor, rudely, had never had one. He did have a Manchester United bag, though.

'2–1,' Gary repeated, his brow furrowing furiously. Conor was taking the mick again. Just when you thought he was loosening up, just when he'd lowered himself to have a beer. 'I'm not a Manchester United fan,' Gary said loudly, just to let him know that he was on to him.

'Oh,' Conor said. He had even picked the wrong fucking team to talk about. He had thought that Manchester United were perennial favourites. If Emily could hear him now, she would laugh her head off. Talking about football and beer, giving himself airs and graces.

He grappled around for something else acceptable to say. That was the trouble with him, none of it came easily.

'Mind you, they're the cup favourites. Again,' Gary said.

You see, Conor thought, Gary was in the know. Gary had his finger on the pulse of what was normal social interaction. No situation confounded him or left him lost for words. Most of what he said was absolute shite, in Conor's opinion, but that didn't matter. People loved it. Emily too. She'd laughed all night long the last time they'd had Gary and Neasa over for dinner. When they had finally left, the house had seemed empty and devoid of energy and Conor had felt very defensive.

Gary threw more beer into his mouth and decided to cut to the chase. 'So, Neasa was telling me. You know, about yourself and Emily having a bit of trouble. I was just wondering if there was anything I could do at all.' Gary had rehearsed this on the way over and had thought it perfect. But on reflection it sounded like he was offering to take over the shagging of Mary Murphy or something.

Conor was very surprised. Gary sounded sympathetic and Conor had not expected this. Sympathy was something usually reserved for the hurt spouse. The most the offending party could expect was a dose of vilification and the possible destruction of personal property.

'Thanks,' he muttered. He had not talked about the affair to anybody. Who would he talk to? Mark would wilt with embarrassment. Certainly he couldn't confide in any of his friends in the orchestra. Billy Middlemiss would look at him with such utter disappointment that Conor would die. Most of his other friends were shared with Emily and all would be very firmly on her side. How could they not be?

'Ffion, wasn't it?' Gary prompted, leaning forward. Best to call her by her proper name. It sounded much more sexy and mistress-like than Mary.

'Ah, yes,' Conor agreed.

Both of them had known it wouldn't go anywhere, and neither of them had wanted it to. It wasn't some great passion that had been bubbling for years and years under the surface. It was more a recognition that the other found life wanting. Ffion's husband had been made redundant and was suffocating her with his listless presence in the house all day. Conor was suffocating under Emily's disappointed looks at home. It started with Ffion joking about Conor being the strong, silent type. He had found it reassuring at first. Then he had found it necessary. It was like the beginning of his relationship with Emily, when everything was perfect, before he had been found out.

The sex wasn't particularly great. Ffion loved the secrecy and the excitement and the stolen moments. That was her kick. He hated all that – he lived in mortal dread of letting something slip and Emily finding out. But in those evenings and nights with Ffion, he told himself he felt worthwhile and desirable again. She wasn't demanding that he be things he wasn't. There was a curious release in that.

Gary was itching to ask about the details. Like most folk, he had an intense curiosity about other people's lives. If some salacious and forbidden act had taken place, all the better. Gary's desire was all the more acute because of his intense preoccupation with comparing and contrasting his life with that of others, and making sure that he was doing and experiencing all the right things.

'So, ah, is it over?'

'Of course it is,' Conor said testily. Jesus Christ, did he think that Mary was up in the bedroom at this very moment?

Emily's announcement that she was pregnant again had been like a bucket of cold water over the affair.

Conor and Mary had looked at each other as though stepping out of a dream. There had been no discussion about the matter really. Mary, mildly embarrassed, had taken an unscheduled holiday with her husband, who was delighted.

Conor had returned to Emily, whom he had never really left. In his more optimistic moments, he thought that perhaps his self-esteem might be in better shape now and that he might have more to contribute to the marriage. The naiveté of this still astounded him.

Gary had the tops twisted off two more bottles of beer.

'No, one is enough for me, thanks,' Conor said. It had already gone to his head.

'You've had two,' Gary pointed out.

Conor saw that he had. Gary pressed the third into his hand.

'Get that down you,' He said with the authority of a man who dealt with broken marriages all the time.

Conor obediently took it. He found that he was glad now that Gary was here. He really was all right, if you looked past all the shite.

'She won't let me go in and see her,' he blurted.

'I know,' Gary said sympathetically.

'You know?' Emily must be giving Neasa a blow-by-blow account on the mobile.

'No, I mean I don't know, I *didn't* know, I'm just . . .' Jesus, even with alcohol on him, Conor was sharp. 'I suppose you're going to have to play by her ball.' Shit.

Play by her rules? Play ball? This Mexican beer was strong.

'What would you do, Gary?'

Gary was astounded. Conor had never once asked his advice on anything. Not even legal stuff. The only time Gary's 'friends' seemed to ring him up was to get free legal advice.

'Talk to her, Conor,' he said in his most serious voice. This was what everybody recommended. Communication. Openness.

'How can I talk to her if she won't let me in to see her?'

Gary was at a loss. He'd only come around to find out if Mary Murphy had any kinky little tricks involving foodstuffs.

He pictured himself at his desk in the office and he immediately felt better. 'That seems to me to be very unfair, Conor. Especially as she's carrying your baby.'

'Well, it's hers too,' Conor felt he had to point out.

'Yes, but even if she doesn't want to see you, does that give her the right to deny you access to your unborn child?'

Conor blinked rapidly a few times. He wasn't at all sure what Gary was on about. But Gary sounded very confident and certain about things, which was more than Conor was right now.

'I love her, you know. Desperately,' he announced without any embarrassment. 'I've always loved her. I could never love anybody else.'

Gary wasn't embarrassed either. He was half-shot. Neither of them had eaten.

'Yes, yes,' he said soothingly. 'But let's get back to the visitation rights. I'm not sure where the law stands in this when it comes to unborn children, but I could find out.'

'I just want to see her, ' Conor said. 'I want to talk to her. I can talk too, you know. Look at me, I'm talking now!'

'Of course you are!' Gary said staunchly. He was damned sure that there was no law existing regarding visitation rights over unborn children. Was it possible that he could set a precedent here? Get his name in the history books?

'That's what went wrong, you see,' Conor admitted, peering over at Gary. 'I let her down after the miscarriage.'

Gary blinked. 'The miscarriage?'

'Didn't Neasa tell you?'

'Of course she did,' Gary lied, surprised at how hurt he felt. Why hadn't Neasa told him? 'Anyway, go on.'

Conor looked at Gary's fleshy, avid face and sobered instantly. This wasn't the kind of thing you talked about with total strangers, tanked up on beer. It had been the most vulnerable, hurtful time of their marriage and it was intensely private.

Conor had never encountered death before at close hand and it had terrified him. He was hurled into a pit of black thoughts about mortality and had ceased to see the point in any of it. He saw the dangers of becoming too dependent on someone who might so easily die. Look at the newspapers! It happened every day! Women and men were killed in car crashes, in fires, in domestic accidents. They were drowned, murdered, or they died of illness. Women even died in that most natural of human activities, childbirth. Not many, it was true. But women still died. It was in the pregnancy book in the chapter on complications.

Conor felt so overwhelmed by morbidity that on some days he could hardly speak to Emily at all, much less connect with her.

Her feelings seemed a much simpler affair to him. She grieved openly and copiously and wanted to talk endlessly. Insisted upon it, in fact, as though her way was the only way of dealing with things. But she'd already had experience of the process with her father's death, and seemed to know instinctively what to do, which was to seek support. And so her need for him was suddenly huge and desperate, a need that she had never really had before. He was unprepared and unpractised and, anyhow, was in denial. He felt like he was choking. He reacted in a knee-jerk way by rationalising, by offering her logic.

She believed that he was not as affected as her and there were accusations that he had not wanted the baby in the first place. At the same time the understanding was very clearly there that this event had happened primarily to Emily. Which it had, of course, in a physical sense.

Conor was very confused. He needed to talk but couldn't, and anyway, it seemed that Emily's feelings were more valid and that he was merely there to support her, as always.

He couldn't. He did not know how to deal with her pain. He had not seen this side to bubbly, optimistic Emily before and it was disconcerting. Certainly, his old ways of bucking her up didn't work now. He felt that he was abandoning her at her most vulnerable time. They were on wholly new territory and both of them were treading on minefields. Conor felt that every time he opened his mouth, or kept it closed, he let her down.

He knew he had. He saw it every time he looked in her eyes, and he couldn't bear it. But she did not end it, as he feared she might.

Instead she moved on. She started to enjoy her work again, and to smile, and to make friends with total strangers. Conor took his cue from her and pretended that he had moved on too.

It was around that time that Ffion Rivera made her little joke. And two months later, Emily got pregnant again.

'Will we go to Milo's?' Gary asked, without any heart. He really was very upset with Neasa. Oh, he was all right for sex, but could not be trusted with confidences. Hell, she'd only told him about Emily and Conor *after* she'd made that phone call to Germany. It was like his opinion didn't really count for much.

Sometimes, he felt a bit like . . . well, like a toy!

'No, I'm a bit tired,' Conor said.

'Me too. Knackered.'

Both of them stood awkwardly and quickly. Gary was glad to leave and Conor was glad to see him go.

Emily was not in her bed.

'She never is,' Nurse V Mooney said with a disapproving sniff.

Neasa had come up against bigger and better than Nurse V Mooney. 'Where is she so?'

'I couldn't tell you.'

'You do try and keep tabs on the patients?'

Nurse V Mooney's eyes narrowed a little. 'We stopped chaining them to their beds a while ago now.'

Neasa gave a frosty, I'm-going-to-sue look. 'I hope for your sake she hasn't done anything stupid.'

After combing all the wards on the floor, Neasa was getting worried. But Emily wouldn't do anything rash. She was pregnant, right? Neasa suddenly remembered the picket line outside the hospital. Surely to God she hadn't got dragged into that?

'Oh, hi, Neasa!'

Neasa whirled around to find Emily cradling a tiny baby, cooing and smiling beatifically.

'Isn't she just the most beautiful little thing you've ever seen?'

Neasa peered at the baby suspiciously. 'It's not yours, is it?'

'God, no. It's Cathy's. She let me hold her for a while. Isn't she just lovely?'

'Lovely.' It wasn't true that all newborn babies looked exactly alike. This one was particularly ugly, with a big thatch of coarse hair and a face that was all bent sideways.

'Forceps delivery,' Emily murmured, and Neasa swallowed hard.

'Let's go and talk,' she said firmly,

'But I've only just got her,' Emily said.

'Now.'

Neasa watched as Emily reluctantly turned and handed the baby back to a big, rough-looking woman, the kind who wouldn't mind giving birth in a cowshed. The woman tucked the baby under one oxter and pressed a crinkled sheet of paper into Emily's hand.

'Good on you, girl.'

Neasa wondered if Emily had got involved in running some kind of underground tuck-shop or something.

She waited until they were in the murky visitors' room before asking.

'Oh, it's just a petition,' Emily said, offhanded. 'To stop the hospital closing. I've been getting a few signatures.'

Neasa sighed. Only Emily could get dragged into revolutionary activity during a personal crisis.

'Look, Emily, I rang that place like you wanted me to.'

Emily looked at her with those big, trusting eyes and Neasa's heart broke. But she told Emily about the hotel, the receptionist, the fax, Room 134 and Mary Murphy.

'I just hate being the one to tell you this, Emily,' she finished, illustrating this by letting two big fat tears slide down her face.

'Oh, Neasa.'

'No, really, I wasn't going to tell you at all. I didn't know what to do,' Neasa cried.

'It's all right, I already knew,' Emily said.

'Did you?' Neasa said hopefully.

'Yes.'

Neasa was greatly relieved not to be the bearer of horrible news. Belatedly, she remembered that she was supposed to be consoling Emily.

'Anyway,' she said quickly, rooting in her bag and taking out a draft separation agreement. 'I'll act for you, of course. For free. By the time we're finished with that bastard he won't have money for condoms, never mind hotel rooms.'

Emily looked at the separation agreement for a moment. 'Neasa, I'm not filing for separation.'

Neasa understood. 'Sure, you probably want to wait until you get out of hospital. But I'll have him out of the house by then. Don't you worry about that. I've already made arrangements to have the locks changed first thing in the morning. And maybe we should go for a barring order too?'

'He's not going to be leaving the house, Neasa.'

'Okay,' Neasa said more slowly. 'A mistake, in my opinion. You know the rule – never, ever give up the marital home. I mean, where are you going to live?'

'I'm not going to be leaving the house either.'

'Right . . .' Neasa said eventually. 'This could bugger up visitation rights – you know, for the baby. If you're both living in the same house.' Her face cleared. 'Unless, of course, you took one floor each. Now, that might work.'

'It's a bungalow,' Emily reminded her.

Neasa lost patience. 'What the hell are we going to do then? As your solicitor, you've left me with very few options here!'

Emily knew that Neasa would think her terribly weak. 'I know. But the fact is, I'm not going to do anything.'

'You have to do something!'

'Why?'

'Why? Why? Because that big shitty bastardy cheat of a two-timing fucker did the dirt on you! Betrayed you! Humiliated you! Let you down!'

'There's no need to rub it in.'

'And you're just going to let him get away with it?'

'Neasa, I know you're on my side here—'

'Too bloody right I am!' Neasa was very upset. 'Are we just going to let these kind of men make fools of us time and again?'

'No, of course not—'

'Should they not be punished in any way?'

'I suppose—'

'So what's all this "he's not moving out" shit? Emily, have you no dignity?'

Emily had known that this would be difficult. 'It's not about dignity. Look, I have things to think about. A lot of things. And I'm not going to do anything rash.'

Neasa looked at her. 'You're going to stay because you feel you ought to. Aren't you? You're going to stay because of the baby.'

'The baby is a consideration. Of course it is – I wouldn't be much of a person if I didn't think about the baby!' But Emily did her best not to get angry, because she knew this whole thing was more about Neasa than herself. 'But the baby isn't everything, Neasa.'

'Don't tell me you still love him?' Neasa asked in disgust.

'I don't know what I feel about him right now.'

Neasa stood, looking on the verge of more tears. 'I really think you're letting yourself down, Emily. If I were in your shoes, I wouldn't put up with it. I'd have too much self-respect.'

And she jerkily left the visitors' room, taking the separation agreement with her. Emily took a deep breath and let it out slowly. She had expected much of what Neasa said, but not all of it. Something must have happened with Gary. From the smell of Neasa's breath, she'd had more than one gin and tonic.

But Emily had once had the same ideals as Neasa, hadn't she? They all had, Jackie and Deirdre too, on those drink-fuelled nights down in Milo's. They were very young back then, of course, and single, and had had very high expectations of men in general, and potential husbands in particular. There had been an unofficial list of Necessary Qualities which had included intelligence, a sense of humour, earning power, sexual prowess, middling-to-good looks, a hairless back, some cooking ability (though Neasa pointed out that this wasn't absolutely vital if he had the earning power to take them out for meals instead) and a car. Most important, he had to be desperately, desperately in love with them. Crazily. Suicidally, even!

Because what could possibly go wrong if he was mad about them? And as for infidelity? Ooooh! Out the door! This very instant, without even a coat on his back! Whatever else happened, they wouldn't stand for that kind of thing, they would hiss venomously. If he even looked too hard at another woman, he was in grave danger.

At this point, Neasa would go to the bar to refuel with four pints of Heineken.

But as they got older, and the men they went out with were invariably and heart-breakingly lacking in most of the above-mentioned qualities, the girls had come to expect less. Not that they ever admitted this in their nights in Milo's. No, they made excuses for their men instead. 'But he's very good with the garden,' they would sincerely explain to each other. 'And he's mad about me.' At this, the girls would shrug, nod grimly, and agree, 'Well, I suppose if he's *mad* about you . . .', whilst pulling faces behind their hands.

In the end, only Neasa had shouted 'No compromise!' and would view the others' relationships as though they were odd, unnameable matter in a Petri dish. Emily hadn't been offended. It was all subjective. At the end of the day, love was a peculiar thing and there was no accounting for taste.

They had all held firm on the infidelity issue though, and Emily acutely felt the pressure now To Do The Right Thing and kick him out, if only to show the girls and everybody else that she was no pushover this time. She hated herself for always caring so much what other people thought of her.

Not that she had ruled out a separation agreement by any means. In fact she was giving it a lot of thought. But there were long-term implications of any action and Emily knew that she must continue to resist the temptation to do something in the heat of the moment.

Everything had been thrown to the four winds. How she would piece things back together she did not know. And Conor was only a part of this.

She stood and tidied up the visitors' room. As an afterthought, she ripped down the defaced vaccination poster of the baby and put it in the bin. Then she opened a window and let some fresh air in.

Her little ministrations didn't make a whit of difference. It was still a nasty, grim room. What this room needed, she thought, was to be blown sky-high and rebuilt again.

The vindaloo appeared to work. Trish went into labour that evening, very fast, and was carted off to Delivery immediately, smiling between the pains.

'I'm delighted,' she kept saying. 'Delighted.'

'Good girl, Trish,' Nurse V Mooney said in satisfaction. Not that there was anything wrong with being induced; it was just always nicer to get off the starting blocks by yourself. 'I'll ring Aidan,' she promised.

'Oh, no need,' Trish panted. 'I'll have had it by the time he gets his mother over to look after the rest of them.'

After she was gone, Maggie came over and huddled on Emily's bed.

'Do you think she'll get to the epidural in time?'

'I don't know,' Emily admitted.

'I tried to book one, you know,' Maggie said. 'But they told me that you can't book epidurals in advance.'

Maggie was very fearful about the whole thing. She was a severe asthmatic and had been hospitalised after a particularly frightening episode. She would not be going home until she had had her baby, due nearly three weeks before Emily's.

'Put it down on your birth plan that you want one,' Emily advised.

'I have, in big red letters,' Maggie said, chewing her

lower lip nervously. 'I've put it down on Tiernan's as well.'

'Tiernan has his own birth plan?' Emily enquired, after a bit.

'Oh no, just a copy of mine. In case it gets lost,' Maggie explained. 'We want to be absolutely sure that everything goes the way we want.'

It seemed a bit rigid to Emily but she said nothing.

'How long will Trish be in, do you think?' Maggie asked now.

'I don't know,' Emily said. She wished that Maggie didn't think that she was the font of all wisdom. If she only knew.

'I got all my relatives to sign the petition for you, by the way,' Maggie said.

'It's not my petition,' Emily explained again.

'I don't want to go to Cork.'

'Of course it would be nice to have our babies here, but I don't suppose we've much choice,' Emily said.

'Tiernan can't drive,' Maggie blurted. 'Well, he can, but he's been banned.' She didn't elaborate on why. 'I'll never see him when they move me to Cork!'

'There are buses and trains, Maggie – he hasn't been banned from those too, has he?'

'We don't think so,' Maggie said doubtfully, leaving Emily to wonder further what Tiernan had done. 'When I get an attack, he's the only one who can calm me down.' And she started breathing very fast.

'Now relax, Maggie,' Emily said sternly. 'You've

rakes of relatives. Can't one of them drive him down?'

'Oh, they're always visiting all right, but they're not dependable,' Maggie said darkly.

Cathy and Petra arrived later, having heard the news about Trish. Cathy brought a two-litre bottle of Coke and a family bar of Cadbury's chocolate.

'Tuck in, girls,' she encouraged. 'Once you start breast-feeding, the fat will fall off you.'

Petra glowered. Lies, damned lies. She'd put on a stone for every child she'd had, despite breast-feeding every last one of them until they were a year old.

'I suppose that's the end of the bridge tournament,' Cathy said. No one was sorry.

Cathy and Petra were much more sanguine about Trish's labour than Emily and Maggie, the first-time mothers. They dispensed advice liberally.

'You see, nobody tells you what labour is really like,' Cathy said candidly, and proceeded to do so in gory and bloody detail. Maggie's face got whiter and whiter as Cathy talked about membranes tearing and placentas that wouldn't come out, but most about the excruciating, horrifying pain of it all.

'They don't want to frighten you, you see,' she finished up cheerfully. 'They fill you with shite about how it's just like bad period pains. Well, if I had periods like that I'd shoot myself. No, girls, don't be fooled by that kind of talk. I was fooled on my first one. And do you know something? I was raging that nobody had told me what it was really going to be like.'

Emily tried to lighten the mood for the sake of poor Maggie. 'Maybe it's a conspiracy.'

'I'm inclined to think so,' Cathy said seriously. 'Because if girls and women were told how bad it really was, then there's no way they'd get pregnant. And the human race would die out.'

She had obviously given this a lot of thought.

'So I've decided that I'm not colluding in the conspiracy any more,' she declared. 'I'm not telling other women that labour is grand, that it'll all be worth it when you look at the little fecker's face. Well, girls, don't be fooled by that either.' She looked at them darkly. 'I often think that children aren't worth the bother at all. And I don't mind saying it either.'

'So why did you have two of them so?' Emily felt she had to ask.

'My husband wanted four, and two was the compromise,' Cathy said evenly. 'I've done my bit now and that's that.'

'You might soften and have another in a year's time,' Emily joked her.

'I don't think so. I'm sending him for the snip next month,' Cathy said, and roared with laughter. Everyone else laughed too. But nobody doubted that she was serious about this as well.

'You'd have thought we'd have had news by now,' Maggie said, desperate to get onto less bloody ground. She must review her birth plan at the first opportunity. 'She's been gone nearly two hours.'

'All in good time,' Petra said, and she and Cathy exchanged knowing looks.

There was still no news after another hour. Cathy and Petra gave up and went back to Elizabeth's Ward. Maggie stayed perched on Emily's bed, her little pixie face anxious.

'Maybe her placenta got stuck,' she said.

'Don't believe everything Cathy tells you,' Emily advised.

'It wasn't fair to frighten us like that!' Maggie said. 'Now I won't be able to sleep a wink!'

'It probably won't be as bad as she says,' Emily said, trying to sound authoritative. 'Anyway, it's different for every woman.'

'I don't know,' Maggie said doubtfully.

'Look on the bright side,' Emily cajoled. 'At least we've been warned. And now we can prepare ourselves better for the big day, right?'

'You're right,' Maggie said, looking greatly cheered. She reached over and rummaged in her locker. She took out her birth plan, her red pen and went to work, her brow furrowed in concentration.

'What are you doing, Maggie?'

'I'm asking for more drugs during the labour. You know, in case the epidural doesn't work.'

'Oh, Maggie.'

'I heard a story once about a woman who had an epidural,' Maggie said darkly. 'And only her left leg went numb. She didn't get back the use of it for six months.'

210

'Who tells you these things, Maggie?' Emily said impatiently.

'Supposing that happens to me? What use is a numb leg to anybody in labour?'

'It won't happen,' Emily said with a sigh.

'I just don't want to leave anything up to chance, that's all,' Maggie insisted, turning a page in the crumpled birth plan. 'You know, I think I might get Tiernan to type this up.'

Nurse V Mooney came in later and went to Trish's bed. She took Trish's washbag from her locker.

Maggie bounced up in excitement. 'Did she have her baby?'

'She did,' Nurse Mooney said without looking at them. Emily watched as the nurse pulled out Trish's suitcase from under the bed and started to pack her things into it quickly.

'Is she all right?' she asked.

'She is,' Nurse Mooney said. 'We're just moving her to a post-natal ward.'

'Can we go down to see her?' Maggie asked. 'Just for a minute?'

'No, she's exhausted, and her husband is in with her.'

Maggie was indefatigable. 'Is it a boy or a girl?'

Nurse Mooney looked tired. 'A boy. Look, the baby died, girls. So don't be sneaking off down to see her. She's very upset.'

She saw their faces and came over. 'It's very rare these days, but it does happen. There was nothing anybody could do. Now don't be worrying that anything is going to go wrong with your own. It won't.'

Later, Emily and Maggie dragged Maggie's locker into the middle of the ward and pushed their beds together. Maggie said she didn't want to sleep on her own. Then they pulled the curtains around on Trish's bed because they couldn't bear to see it empty. They got into bed side-by-side. They did not pay any heed to Nurse Mooney's advice not to worry. They were only in this place because something had already gone wrong.

Emily lay awake in the dark and knew that Trish too was lying awake in the dark, in the room they'd put her on her own, where there would be no other pregnant women or babies to upset her further. She would be fretting because the baby had been a mistake, convinced that it had sensed that it was not wanted in the first place. She would be going over and over possible things she had done wrong. She would be searching for someone to blame but there would be no one. She would be in shock, that numb half-awareness that the thing you dread most has actually happened. 'Emily?' Maggie turned over in the dark. 'Are you crying?'

'No, no,' Emily said. How could she explain that she was not crying for Trish but for herself?

'It's all right,' Maggie said. 'I'm crying too.'

And she curled into Emily's back for protection.

They hadn't even told anybody that Emily was pregnant that first time. Bad luck, they'd declared. They would wait until they'd passed the three-month mark;

they would hold off until they got the first scan. When Emily lost the baby, there was no sympathy or support because nobody knew. Emily and Conor only had each other.

Conor had not really accepted that the baby had existed in the first place, Emily believed. There was no little scan picture, and Emily hadn't even had a bulge. His sorrow was a private and closed affair.

Emily in turn had felt that her depression and sadness was unwarranted, that she was being over-emotional and dramatic. Eventually she learned to hide her grief. Eventually she learned to deny her own feelings.

Maggie had fallen asleep. Emily lay there letting the honest tears fall and she felt very high up on the hospital bed, like she was floating, free.

Part Two

'Morning, Emily.'

'Oh, hi, Maureen. Don't tell me that rasher is for me.'

'It is. And I done you a sausage as well.'

'You're an angel!'

'Only don't let Maggie see. She'd be foaming at the mouth.'

'Of course I won't,' Emily assured her. Maggie was on a strict diet supervised by a nutritionist. Apparently animal fats exacerbated her asthma.

'Slip it into a butty,' Maureen advised. 'And tell her the smell is in her imagination. Most things are anyway.'

Maureen didn't have much truck with Maggie's breathlessness and wheezing. But then Maureen managed to smoke forty cigarettes a day without a bother in the world.

'Any luck on that job?' Emily asked.

'No, but I've got an interview with that other crowd you were telling me about. Are you sure it's all right to use your name?'

'Absolutely. I did some work for them last year. They owe me one.'

'I'll get some severance pay from here. I suppose that'll keep me going for a while,' Maureen said optimistically.

Emily ate her rasher as she watched Maureen plonk down a big pot of tea and some toast onto the table under the television. There was only Maggie and Emily left in Brenda's Ward now. They were officially the longest serving patients in the hospital and the catering girls had taken them to their hearts – well, Emily anyway – slipping her chocolate biscuits and extra cups of sweetened tea when the nurses weren't looking. Emily reciprocated by helping them set up for breakfast at six every morning. Now that the baby had dropped in readiness for the birth, it was lying firmly against her bladder and she was up most of the night running to the loo. That's when she wasn't sitting up fighting heartburn. Who would have thought, looking at those glossy pictures of smiling, placid women with tanned, swelling bumps, that the reality was so uncomfortable and distinctly lacking in dignity?

'Right. I'd better go feed the other animals in the zoo,' Maureen said, and off she went, cackling as though she'd made a great joke.

Maureen did such a useful job, Emily often thought, keeping everybody in the hospital alive with Weetabix and fish pies. Not that her fish pies were anything to write home about – Emily had once found a whole fish head on the end of her fork, complete with staring eyes – but what Maureen did was essential. Not like selling hilly farmland and crumbling old houses, and passing them off on the public as 'prime grazing lands' and 'stunning period havens'. In the office, Emily had been particularly good at overlooking a property's bad points and finding superlatives for its few miserable assets. But there was nothing surprising about that really.

There was Vera now, bustling up to the nurses' station and taking out her pen. She would record the night's happenings, who had been poorly and who had not. In a minute she would come around to do blood-pressure readings and take temperatures in her calm, unflappable way. Vera Mooney and Maureen would be able to look their Maker in the eye and say that they had used the talents he had given them to the best of their abilities.

The most Emily would be able to stand over was a handful of glossy sales brochures, and say that she had used her talents to fill the coffers of Crawley Dunne & O'Reilly. And not one of the partners had made the five-mile drive from Paulstown to visit her in three long weeks. Except for Gary, of course. For the entire visit, he had held himself as though he were an official ambassador.

'Place isn't the same without you, Emily. In fact, it's a shambles.'

Big, fat lies. Neasa had told her that Creepy Crawley

had calmly divided out Emily's unfinished files to everyone else. They took it in turns to make the coffee. Nobody had yet discovered the wire in the photocopier that only Emily knew how to jiggle to make the damned thing work, but someone had found that if you kicked it, it worked just as well.

Emily found it chilling how dispensable she really was. And so very hurtful. She had never viewed her place in the world before with such clear eyes, and found it so wanting.

Not that she had ambitions towards brain surgery or running soup kitchens. And someone had to sell land, after all. It was a well-paid job and many envied it.

But, oh, those migraines she would get on Friday nights. That ache she would have in her cheeks from smiling like an idiot all day long. And that heavy feeling on Sunday evenings, knowing that another week was starting where she would beaver away in her office, patting herself on the back for working through lunch. As if anybody cared. As if anybody even noticed.

She had thought herself so full of possibilities once. It was a long time ago, admittedly, and much of it could be attributed to teenage hormones. But sitting in a steamed-up classroom while a teacher droned on, Emily would stare out the window at the hockey pitch and wish that she could be done with school and get out there and start her life. She could do anything she wanted, be anybody she cared to be. And she would go home that evening and diligently do her homework, as if this were her passage, her entrance ticket to all the world held.

Even then she had not broken the rules.

'Do you ever wonder sometimes what she's thinking?' Karen said out at the nurses' station.

Vera Mooney said nothing but she watched Emily Collins through the door very carefully. She wanted to be sure that Emily was not becoming institutionalised. Oh, laugh if you like, but Vera had seen it happen to others, and in a very short time too. They frantically did crosswords and watched Sky News, but eventually the boredom got them down, and the sheer frustration of having no control over their own lives. The outside world receded on them very quickly and visitors would suffer through an exact account of what they'd eaten for tea, and what they had chosen for tomorrow's tea, and the snoring patterns of the other occupants of the ward. It was worse for pregnant women. The endless waiting often drove them mad.

Emily Collins was waiting all right. For what, Vera wasn't sure. It was like she was doing a gigantic multiplication sum in her head, one that occupied her wholly and endlessly. Vera rather hoped that she solved it before the baby arrived.

Vera, like Emily, was running out of time. St Jude's Ward had closed yesterday. It meant that Bernie and Yvonne and the rest were free to do picket duty, but it was another nail in the coffin. They had no hope now. All they could do was give one last dying kick.

'Have you written up the notes for Mr Dunphy?' she enquired of Karen.

'Um, no.'

'Well, do it then.' Just because the hospital was closing on Monday week did not mean they should slack off.

Vera went into Brenda's Ward and sat on the end of Emily's bed. Emily was cleaning out her make-up bag, running a cotton bud around the rims of tubes and powders.

'I don't know why I'm doing this,' she told Vera cheerfully. 'It's not as though I ever put any on in here.'

'It's the nesting instinct,' Vera said wisely. 'If you were at home, you'd be defrosting the fridge or spring-cleaning cupboards that you hadn't opened in years. Most women go mad cleaning just before they're about to give birth.'

'And you did it twice,' Emily said, marvelling.

Emily already knew that Vera had two girls. She knew a lot of things about Vera that Vera had never intended to tell her. She had a way about her that had you spilling your guts.

'Any more pains?' Vera asked, strapping a pressure cuff on Emily.

'They were pretty bad earlier,' Emily admitted. She was getting preparatory contractions thick and fast now. Some of them really hurt, and Emily wished that Cathy had not told her that they were child's play compared to the real thing. Emily had been practising her breathing techniques recently, and then remembered that Cathy had told her that she'd be lucky if she were able to breathe at all.

'Well, only three weeks to go now,' Vera said. She looked at the dial on the pressure cuff. 'You'd want to think about getting that baby bag sent in.'

The words were carefully chosen. The husband's absence had been noted up and down the floor. There had been only two visits in three weeks. Something was up there all right, but it was not Vera Mooney's place to speculate.

'I will,' Emily said.

'Mr Chapman will be here this afternoon,' Vera said.

'Oh, right.' Emily was unfazed. Mr Chapman came up every week, sometimes twice, to see her.

'He wants to do a scan, Emily. What with the pains and the bit of blood you had yesterday, he needs to check the condition of the placenta.'

'It was only a little bit of blood,' Emily said.

'All the same.'

'And what if he finds something?'

'Look, I can't really say. I'm not a doctor.'

'Ah come on, Vera. You know more than most of them.'

'I don't want to go pre-empting Mr Chapman,' Vera insisted primly.

'He'll do a section, won't he? If my placenta is malfunctioning.'

'That might be a course of action he would consider.'

'Oh, Jesus.'

'Now don't go upsetting yourself,' Vera said sternly. 'You're into your thirty-eighth week. All that baby is doing now is putting on fat, and it can do that just as well on the outside.' She stood. 'And it'll be lovely to see the baby on the scan. You should be looking forward to it.'

Vera left. Emily had to fight the urge to scuttle down in the bed and pull the covers up high over her head. She deeply resented her little bubble being so rudely burst with talk of caesareans and scans and placentas. Could she not be left in peace until she reached her fortieth week, or even longer if the baby decided it was happy where it was?

It had been funny, these past few weeks. They reminded Emily of the retreat she'd been dragged to by her mother years ago, to some holy house in the West. It was a proper retreat, with loads of suffering and praying and starvation, not one of those namby-pamby ones where everyone took it in turns to cook gourmet dinners before massaging each other's inner child. No, this was the genuine article, involving barefoot hikes up Croagh Patrick on nothing more than a cup of tea and a slice of Brennan's bread. Talking was forbidden, the better to help you focus on what a sinner you really were. Then four hours' sleep before a dawn Mass and a couple of rounds of Hail Mary's. Emily had thought it a total waste of time, except for the fact that she lost two pounds. But then she had looked at the faces of the other survivors. Past the paleness and exhaustion, there was a kind of hard-won peace and she was almost sorry that she hadn't made more of an effort.

Martha's had been a retreat of sorts too. There were rashers and sausages in Martha's, of course, and talking was not forbidden. But there was plenty of suffering and lots of time for contemplation. At the end of the day, Emily hadn't climbed any mountains, literal or metaphorical, and come down the other side shouting, 'I've solved it all, yippee!' She hadn't solved much at all. There had been no epiphany, worse luck, just endless grappling and searching and questioning, with the occasional foray into steam-filled classrooms for a little light relief.

The truth was that Emily did not know where she was going. But she had seen very clearly where she was coming from, and that was something. And it wasn't good enough any more. It had never been good enough to begin with, but she had nobody to blame for that except herself. For accepting, endlessly accepting.

Conor had been restrained. He seemed to sense that if he pushed things any further with her, it would backfire badly. He had left her alone, only to ring up once and anxiously ask whether Gary had been on to her in any legal capacity. Emily, mystified, assured him that he hadn't. Conor had seemed very relieved. Emily had always thought Conor despised Gary and was surprised to learn that they were obviously pally. Another side to Conor that she had never seen before.

She had phoned him a few times herself, to keep him in the picture about her health. And she had asked him to come in twice. This was out of necessity. She'd needed clean underwear and pyjamas, and the charger for her mobile. They'd managed by talking about the baby and her medication and the dogs. He had stayed less than twenty minutes both times and she had been grateful.

She rang him now and told him about the scan. He said he would come in.

She got out of bed and went to take her morning shower. Today, she found that her anger was less. Today she would talk to him.

Creepy Crawley came up behind Neasa in his usual stealthy way. God, that *hair*. She had it in a French plait today, which showed off her very fine, long white neck. Creepy imagined himself taking off that little bow at the bottom and unravelling the plait, twist by twist, inch by inch, and he was nearly undone.

Rumour had reached his ears last week that Neasa Martin and Gary O'Reilly had something going. Apparently it was common knowledge. The depth of his upset had surprised Creepy. *Gary*, who always reminded Creepy of a side of beef. Neasa had gravely disappointed him. Surely she deserved a man of intelligence and culture, a man whose knowledge of wine extended beyond red and white? It must be a momentary lapse, Creepy decided. Gary had just not taken no for an answer. The partners had already discovered that Gary did not understand the meaning of a lot of words, including 'paperwork', 'desk-bound' and 'middle-management'. He still thought he could drop everything to go off and close an exciting sale, not realising that it was now his job to select the person who would close the exciting sale. Still, he would learn. There was plenty of time yet before he started getting a slice of the profits. A rather small slice.

Neasa would most probably be at the partners' dinner on Friday. Creepy would see to it that she was sitting by his side, and at the far end of the table to Gary. A woman of her taste would quite easily spot the difference.

'Neasa?'

'What! I mean, can I help you, Mr Crawley?'

Neasa was working on a particularly difficult sales contract for a farm, and was bogged down in meaningless phrases such as 'heretofore assign' and 'decree unto the vendor'. She had a huge urge to draw a red line through the whole lot and write at the bottom, 'I'll give you my land if you give me your money'. They shouldn't have opened that second bottle of wine last night.

Gary had noticed her discontent of late, especially when she went around the house shouting, 'It's all a load of bollocks.' Sweetly, he had bought her a box of chocolates and some new silky underwear, and told her that her feelings would pass. At least he'd noticed, she reassured herself.

Creepy Crawley held out a letter as though it contaminated him. 'This arrived this morning. I was wondering whether you knew anything about it?'

Neasa saw that it was addressed to Emily.

'I didn't realise we were opening her post,' Neasa said. The letter had 'Private & Confidential' written on the top. The envelope would have had the same.

'Well, we have to, now that she's gone.'

'She *is* coming back,' Neasa pointed out mildly.

'Of course she is,' Creepy said quickly. 'How is she, by the way?'

'As well as anybody can be after three weeks in hospital.'

'Yes, yes,' Creepy said quickly. He didn't want to get into any talk about babies or labour. He was about to have his lunch.

The letter was from the Health Board. It was regarding the petition Emily had sent in.

'I have no idea what they're on about,' Neasa said primly. This was perfectly true.

'We don't want to get involved in that kind of thing,' Creepy said dismissively. He had private health insurance and a very good car to take him to Dublin should anything ever go wrong.

'Of course we don't,' Neasa soothed. 'To be honest, I think that hospital is getting to Emily. All that time on her hands. Anyone would go a bit cracked and start up petitions. Why don't you leave it with me?'

'All right,' he said reluctantly. 'And maybe you'd tell her that she can't be using our headed notepaper and name to back this petition thing.'

'I'm sure she didn't mean it like that,' Neasa assured him.

He went off. Neasa scrutinised the letter. How Emily had sent the thing off to them in the first place was a mystery. It wasn't as though there was a post office on the ground floor of the hospital, or indeed any typing facilities.

Emily was running away, Neasa knew. She didn't want to deal with the real issues and so she had latched onto this petition thing as a distraction. Hadn't Neasa's grandmother got very obsessive about her pension book as death stared her in face? It was pure escapism, as clear to Neasa as the spots on Gary's chin. Oops. Where had that come from?

On cue, the door to Emily's office opened and Gary came out. His tie was loosened and his shirtsleeves rolled up. This was purely for effect, of course, to give the impression that he was working so hard that he was actually letting off steam. He came over.

'I'm going out for a sandwich – want to get one and go back to Emily's office?'

Gary was annoyed that he'd said 'Emily's office'. It was his now. But everybody else persisted in calling it Emily's office too. It was most irritating.

'I'll pass,' Neasa said regretfully. 'I'm taking a late

lunch – I want to pop over and see Emily this afternoon.'

Gary was secretly relieved. He'd been working like a dog all morning and was totally knackered.

'Why don't you go to Milo's with the lads?' Neasa suggested.

Gary didn't really want to go to the pub. It was impossible to do any work after three pints of Smithwicks. The bottles of red wine every night were killing him too. But Neasa never seemed affected at all, and he just looked wimpish in comparison. He felt that any attempt to cut down on his consumption would be noted and chalked up against him as some kind of black mark.

'I don't think any of them are going,' he hedged.

'They are. Annabel told me.'

'I don't think I could be bothered,' he said quickly. He didn't want her thinking that he would be flirting with Annabel, the new temp in the secretarial division. He had looked at her once. Just once, when she had handed over a file. It seemed the polite thing to do. But Neasa had noticed, and he had never looked at Annabel since, to the point of directing any enquiry to a point two feet above her head. He seemed to be watching his Ps and Qs all the time recently.

'Go and have a few pints. I'm busy here,' Neasa said in a voice that brooked no argument. She wanted to read the letter from the Health Board.

'What's that?' Gary enquired.

'Oh, nothing,' Neasa said quickly. For some reason, she didn't want to tell him about the letter. It wasn't that she didn't trust him. She was just afraid that he might, well, sneer. Unless letters contained very large cheques Gary didn't have an awful lot of interest. She had a suspicion that he might find Emily's petition funny.

There she went again, Gary thought, holding things back on him! Oh, she could talk for Ireland over those bloody bottles of red wine, leaving no stone unturned when it came to stories of her childhood, her adolescence, her whole bloody life. When she was drunk she tended to repeat herself, which became terribly tedious, but he still listened! But he had noticed that she didn't discuss things like Conor's affair with him any more, and had been very unenthusiastic when he'd told her about his idea to secure Conor visitation rights to his unborn child. Had nipped it in the bud, actually. And he only trying to help!

Neasa saw that Gary looked a bit down. Probably because she hadn't agreed to sex and a sandwich in Emily's office. But it just wasn't that exciting any more now that it was actually Gary's office.

'Creepy wants to know whether I'm bringing someone on Friday night,' Gary said.

They were having a sort of official swearing-in dinner for Gary and all the partners and their other halves would attend.

'Oh, Gary, I don't know.' The thought of it made her

ill. She would have to get very drunk.

'Something better to do?' he asked lightly, but there was an underlying edge.

'Sweetness! Don't be ridiculous. It's just that it'll be full of stuffed shirts.' She hurried on, 'Except for you, of course. Let me think about it.'

Gary wasn't happy, she saw. She smiled brightly. 'Tell you what. Why don't we have a big romantic dinner tonight? With loads of wine and candles and I'll fill a big bubble bath for us later and we'll use that new thing you bought in that sex shop?'

'Great,' Gary said.

'Great,' Neasa echoed.

Mr Gerald Chapman set off from Cork at twenty past one. He would have to drive hard and fast if he were to make his two o'clock appointment in Martha's. The traffic was terrible out of Cork, which only added to his black mood.

Killian, his seventeen-year-old son, had arrived home last night sober. This had immediately made Mr Chapman suspicious. The boy had stood in the living room, head hanging, and told them that his girlfriend was pregnant.

'Oh my God,' Hannah had moaned. 'How could you do that to poor Deirdre?'

It wasn't Deirdre. It was a new one, apparently. Andrea. She was sixteen.

'I'm very sorry,' the little sod had said to Mr Chapman

beseechingly. Because somehow, his father would sort it out. He always did.

'Don't worry, son,' Mr Chapman said calmly. 'I'll deliver it for you.'

The boy was aghast. 'But we can't have it. I mean . . .'

'You mean you don't want it,' Mr Chapman said. 'Why didn't you think of that before you went sticking your little willy into a schoolgirl?'

'Gerry!' Hannah was horrified.

'No, Hannah.' Mr Chapman had never been angrier. 'You make a mistake and so you think you can have an abortion just like that? Like you were buying a fucking CD in a record shop?'

'Gerry, stop it now!'

He didn't even want to think of the irony of it. An obstetrician who couldn't teach his own son the basics of birth control! And now a young girl's whole life ruined. Children, bearing and rearing children. It was obscene. Mr Chapman felt as responsible as if he'd impregnated the girl himself.

Killian was looking at the floor, as though waiting for Mr Chapman to tell him that he was going to indefinitely suspend his pocket money. What was the point in talking to him about courage and responsibility and the value of human life?

'This is your mess, Killian,' was all he said. 'I wash my hands of it.'

It wasn't that easy. Andrea, it transpired, was the daughter of Cork Councillor Henry Maher. Councillor

Maher rang Mr Chapman later that night and left him in no doubt about his feelings on the matter. Andrea was sitting her Leaving Certificate next year, and she hoped to go on to veterinary college, and what was Mr Chapman going to do about *that*?

'It isn't a decision for us to make,' Mr Chapman said strongly.

'Bollocks it isn't,' Henry Maher said. 'She only turned sixteen a week ago. You *are* aware of the law on statutory rape?'

There was a meeting of the clans scheduled for Thursday evening. The outcome was inevitable.

And now there were more problems with Cork. They had just taken receipt of an extremely expensive piece of equipment for the paediatric intensive care unit, afforded by the cost-cutting measures of closing Martha's. Wonderful, except that nobody was trained in the use of the damned thing. It was sitting there in its packaging while staff they couldn't afford to lose went off to find out how it worked. It looked like his fault, of course.

The pickets were out in force outside Martha's, forcing him to slow to five miles an hour. Not that anybody dared to stick a placard against his front window. They contented themselves with stony glances, as though the hospital closure had been entirely his decision.

And there was Emily Collins going around gathering signatures for a petition. His one and only patient in Martha's. That had raised a few sniggers in the staff canteen.

Let them keep Martha's. He didn't bloody want it.

Full of self-pity, he marched from his car and inside.

Emily had her scan at five past two.

'Oh, look! A hand!' she said. She couldn't help herself counting the fingers, and was grateful that her baby had the correct number, plus the requisite thumb.

Mr Chapman saw her doing this. 'Obviously the baby is so big now that you'll only see bits and pieces of it on the scan,' he murmured, lest she accuse him of mislaying most of her baby. He had gone over her file and discovered she was a solicitor. Of all things.

'And the nose!' Emily marvelled. It was very cute and button-like, at least as far as she could tell. The picture was fuzzy and close-up.

She turned her head. 'Conor – why don't you come over and have a look?'

But Conor was no longer hanging back there by the wall. He was right behind Emily, looking at the scan. Emily found herself a bit taken aback that he had not waited for her permission.

'I take it you don't want to know the sex?' Mr Chapman enquired.

Emily was a bit torn. Part of her would love to know. She felt very strongly recently that it was a girl, even though they'd bought all yellow Babygros in case she was wrong. But she wasn't. A mother knew these things.

'I don't want to know,' Conor said quite definitely.

'I suppose not,' Emily said.

'Best to keep it a surprise,' Mr Chapman agreed, manoeuvring carefully over Emily's greased belly. It would be just his luck to inadvertently reveal the baby's genitals. It was a boy in any case.

Now he was concentrating on the placenta. As far as he could see, everything was intact. Good. They would be able to leave the baby alone for a while longer.

He snapped off the monitor and checked his watch. If he left now he would make it back in time to talk to Marion Spencer in Cork. She would know all there was to know about adoption. He wanted to be able to offer as many options as he could to Henry Maher and his daughter Andrea. But he knew that he might as well be talking to the wall.

His disillusionment wrapped itself around him now familiarly.

'What do you think?'

'What? Oh, sorry.' There was Emily Collins, eager for information about her baby. He gave himself a little shake and put on his professional face.

'We're not looking at a section right now,' he declared. 'If there's more bleeding, I'll have to reconsider.' He busied himself with her chart, adding as an afterthought, 'The medical term for the bleeding is antepartum haemorrhage.'

'Yes, I know,' Emily said.

'Oh. Right.'

He had been prepared to leave it at that. That was all

most people wanted to know anyway. The minute you started to get into unpronounceable names, they backed off. But she was waiting.

'Well, you see, there are three reasons why there might be blood.'

'Yes,' Emily agreed again. 'But they're quite rare, aren't they? When the placenta starts peeling away and that kind of thing?'

Those nurses must have been filling her in. Half of them believed they knew more than the doctors. 'Ah, yes, but that's only one reason. The other reason is when the placenta is positioned low. Which yours isn't.'

'That's right,' Emily said encouragingly, and Mr Chapman had the bizarre feeling that he was a medical student again and that she was putting him through his paces.

'The third reason is that the blood mightn't be placental at all, but has come from a urinary tract infection. Which you don't have.' He went on fast before she could get her spoke in again. 'So I'm inclined to think it's none of these things, and that in fact it was simply the loss of the mucus plug that often happens after the thirty-sixth week and which is perfectly normal.'

'That's what I thought,' Emily said with relief. When Conor had brought in her clean clothes, she'd had him bring all the medical books in too and had read them cover to cover, even the boring technical bits. And it was very interesting really, all that was happening to her body. She felt much less afraid now that she knew exactly what to expect. She wished she had read much more after the miscarriage. It would have helped to know that there were medical explanations, and she would have felt less like it was all her own fault.

'Anything else you'd like to know?' Mr Chapman asked warily.

'No, no, that's fine, thanks.'

He was relieved. Some of these people read so much that they became self-styled experts in their own condition. Not that Mr Chapman was against information. He was just against too much information in the hands of lay people.

He put away his bifocals. 'So we'll leave the baby where he is,' Damn. 'Or *she*, of course. I always call babies him.' Shit. Now he was a sexist. He cleared his throat loudly. 'We'll be moving you to Cork at some point today or tomorrow.'

Best to have Emily Collins where he could see her, for a number of reasons.

'Oh,' Emily said. For some reason she thought that Cork would never happen. She felt safe here in Martha's. She knew all the staff. She trusted them.

'Martha's is closing on Monday week anyway,' Mr Chapman said crisply. He shot her a look to let her know that he was on to her and her petitions.

'Will you be there for the caesarean?' Conor finally spoke and Mr Chapman jumped. He'd forgotten all about the husband. Jesus, was he a solicitor too?

'I never said there would definitely be a section,' Mr

Chapman said quickly. 'It's just a possibility. There is no reason why this shouldn't be a natural birth.'

'The delivery then, whatever. Will you be there?'

Mr Chapman was neither contractually nor legally obliged to be there for Emily Collins' labour, even though she was paying him as a private patient. Most times he did attend the labour of his private patients, of course, but there were some instances where he could not. If he were sick, for example; if he were delivering another baby; if he had family circumstances or if he were on holiday. There was any number of reasons why he did not attend births.

But he knew that if Emily Collins were to go into labour at four o'clock in the morning on the top of a mountain, he would feel obliged to be there.

'Yes,' he said heavily.

Emily and Conor did not go back to Brenda's Ward. Instead, Emily led the way to the visitors' room. She switched on lights and the heater, and closed the door. She wished now that she had not been so excited and vocal during the scan. She felt as though she had given something away. She resented him again, for robbing her of some of the joy of their baby.

Choosing a seat was a minefield. If she sat opposite, it would look like she was going to attack him. Side-by-side was out. In the end she chose a chair at a right angle to him, with a large, shabby armchair between them as a buffer.

She resisted the urge to fill the silence with words. It

was such an effort that she had a pain in her throat.

'So, Cork today,' Conor said, as a fairly harmless opener.

'Yes,' she agreed. 'I need the baby's bag. And my own bag.'

'Of course.' He nodded vigorously. 'I'll bring them in straightaway.'

'Tomorrow or the next day will do. If you want to come and see me in Cork.' She didn't want to encourage a flood of visits until they knew where they stood.

'If that's what you want.'

He didn't go on any more about practicalities. Instead he looked at her directly.

'How have you been?'

'All right, I suppose.'

Conor himself didn't look too rough at all, she suddenly noted. Not thinner or older or paler. In fact, he looked a bit too healthy and bright-eyed for someone who should have been sitting at home applying a rod to his own back. His fingers were tapping his knees in some silent tune, and she felt obliged to say, 'How's the job search going?'

'Oh, I've got some weekend work in Baccaro's.' Baccaro's was a restaurant two streets away from St Martha's. It was a very upmarket restaurant, but still a restaurant, where his music would compete for attention with *penne napoletana*. He must hate it. She found that she didn't feel too sorry for him.

He stopped tapping his fingers on his knee. It was a

nervous thing, she realised. 'Emily, I wish I'd never done what I did. It was awful and I'm truly sorry.'

She said nothing.

'But I can't keep saying sorry.'

'You've hardly said it at all,' she pointed out. 'Twice, actually.'

'Is that all?' He seemed genuinely puzzled. 'I keep having these conversations with myself, you see. Well, with you. Well, not *actually* with you, because you're in here . . .'

'I know.' She'd had many imaginary conversations too. Most of them had been blue.

He looked at her. 'Do you think there's any way we can move on?'

'We haven't discussed the affair yet, Conor.'

He seemed a bit puzzled. 'What do you want to know?'

'I don't know . . . why you did it, I suppose.'

'Emily, it was the most stupid thing I've ever done in my life. I was a fool. That's the only excuse I can give you.' He seemed to think that this was a satisfactory response.

'Come on. Surely there was more to it than that, Conor?'

'Look, do we really need to go backwards here? It's history.'

He was making her feel unreasonable. But she persisted anyway. 'I really feel I need to know what happened.'

He shrugged. 'We were going through a rough patch. You and me. I gave into temptation. It was stupid. Simple as that.'

She saw that she was not going to get anywhere. Perhaps he hadn't figured it out for himself yet.

'I want to put all that stuff behind us and make a fresh start here, Emily.' At least he'd declared his intentions. 'What do you say?'

She looked at her slippers. The bunny ears were sagging sadly from all the wear and tear.

'I don't know. I feel now that I wasn't getting what I wanted from us. I wasn't happy, Conor.' She felt she'd hurt him more with this statement than she'd been hurt by the affair. It wasn't intended for that purpose.

'Well, at least you're being honest,' he said, after clearing his throat.

'We have to be, Conor.'

'It's the talking thing, isn't it,' he said. 'I can go to lessons, you know.'

She realised that he was having a little joke, and was amazed at his audacity. Then she found herself smiling. His dry humour had always appealed to her. She didn't go so far as to joke back, though.

'We don't seem to connect any more,' she said. 'Not really.'

A small silence followed this. Conor eventually looked up.

'We did once.'

'I suppose we did. But everybody makes the effort when they're dating.'

'The whole thing didn't collapse the moment we walked up the aisle,' he said.

'Well, no, of course it didn't. It was more like a dry rot.'

'It was the miscarriage, Emily.'

'No, it was earlier than that.'

He seemed quite annoyed. 'You can't negate our whole past because I had an affair.'

'I'm not negating it.'

'You are. You make it sound like you were suffering in silence for years.'

'Conor!'

'What, can I not have an opinion because I'm the one who had the affair? And martyred you even more?'

Emily was furious. 'I am not a martyr!'

'If you were so unhappy, why didn't you say something?' Conor was red in the face now. She couldn't remember ever seeing him like that. 'Why are you telling me now that you were unhappy, making me feel like a fool?'

He felt like a fool? Emily was so angry that she could hardly speak.

'I didn't know I was unhappy!'

'What do you mean, you didn't *know*?'

She was momentarily blind-sided. 'I *did* know, I . . .'

'But you just didn't want to say anything about it? You expect me to understand your unhappiness by osmosis?'

This was shockingly unfair. 'You're my husband! If you'd bothered to open your eyes every once in a while, you might have seen!'

'No, Emily,' he blurted. 'Take some responsibility for once in your life.'

'*What*?' She stared at him, round-eyed. 'I'm sick of taking responsibility! I take responsibility for every bloody thing that ever happens within a ten-mile radius of me!'

'But not for your own happiness! You blame me instead!'

She stood up and left. Just like that. She slammed the door behind her – she, who had never slammed a door in her life.

Her slippers slapped loudly and violently against the polished floors of Martha's. She didn't ever want to see him again, ever ever ever! Who was he to sit there and dissect her, to batter her already ailing self-esteem? But that was typical of men who had affairs, wasn't it? To blame the wife. 'Oh, the pressure she put me under! Couldn't keep that one happy. I might as well go off and shag someone else. Someone easier.' He could talk about responsibility? He couldn't even take responsibility for his own actions!

She slowed down. She had to: she was out of breath. The baby's weight pressed heavily down on her, dragging her, and she wished fiercely that all of this was over.

'You're looking well,' Neasa said.

'You're not. Sorry, sorry, sorry. I just meant you look tired.'

'Oh.' Neasa wasn't a bit pleased. She and Gary hadn't even had sex last night. She watched as Emily turned over in the bed.

'God, you're huge now,' she observed. She might look tired, but she would never let herself get into *that* state. 'Mind you, I've seen your ankles worse.'

Emily seemed to be looking at some point over Neasa's head. She wasn't herself, Neasa knew.

'Has someone been saying bad things to you?' she enquired suspiciously. That Conor yoke had been in. Neasa knew, because she'd seen his car in the car park. Since this whole thing began, Neasa had only met him once. They'd run into each other in the chemist's, where Neasa had been buying a bumper pack of condoms. Conor had been buying maternity pads. She had contented herself with a 'Ha!' before walking out.

'No, no,' Emily said.

Things had been a bit tense since Neasa had accused Emily of letting Conor walk all over her. Neasa had regretted her words afterwards. She'd meant them, of course, but that didn't mean she couldn't regret them.

'How's Gary?' Emily enquired, not giving a thing away.

'Oh, great! Fine. Not a bother.' Two could play at that game.

'What's wrong, Neasa.'

'There's nothing wrong. Oh, how do you always know when something is wrong!'

'Except in my own case,' Emily pointed out.

'That's true,' Neasa said. Her lower lip quivered. 'It's horrible! It's not that Gary and I aren't in love – we are. But somehow it's gone a bit funny and forced.'

Emily listened sympathetically. She'd been down this road many times before with Neasa.

'Has he done something?' she asked, bracing herself. Still, nothing could be worse than the cross-dresser.

'That's the whole point – he hasn't. He's being as good as gold. He even came back from the pub at lunchtime after one pint. One pint! He said it was because he missed me.'

'So what's the problem?'

'I don't know!' Neasa wailed.

Emily sort of did, by looking at Neasa's hair. It was in an elaborate French plait. It looked terrifically sexy and must have taken her a good hour this morning to do. This was on top of the immaculate make-up job, the buffed nails, the polished shoes and the matching underwear. Neasa was the only woman Emily knew whose bra and knickers always matched. Things must be bad if she was resorting to French plaits.

'Maybe you need to relax a bit more with each other,' she suggested.

Neasa thought this was a bit rich coming from someone whose husband had recently strayed. There was relaxing, and there was letting things go to the dogs altogether.

'I refuse to let romance die,' she declared proudly.

'Indeed, and we could all take lessons from that,' Emily said. 'But maybe you're afraid of looking past that in case . . .' Well, in case she discovered that Gary was horrible. 'In case you mightn't be all that suited.'

Neasa sat up straighter. 'We are. He's exactly what I want in a man.'

Not 'I love him', or 'I'd die without him'.

'I don't want to state the obvious, Neasa, but none of them are perfect. Neither are any of us.'

'Speak for yourself.' She sighed deeply. 'And now there's this dinner thing on Friday.'

'Oh, yes.' Once upon a time, Emily would have gnashed her teeth in anguish at the thought of Gary O'Reilly sitting at the partners' dinner when it should have been her. Now she just felt sorry for him.

'Gary's afraid that if he doesn't produce someone, they'll think he's gay. He'd be very upset.'

Emily imagined that gay people would be more upset.

'Why don't you want to go?'

'My private life is my own.' Well, it was. She didn't understand why Gary had such a bee in his bonnet about making it 'official'. It was like some kind of rite of passage for him. The car, the two mortgages, the partnership, the public girlfriend.

Which was ridiculous, Neasa assured herself. Gary loved her for herself, just as she loved him for himself. She supposed she would have to go. Maybe Gary would be less tense if they were out in the open.

Emily winced and clutched her belly.

'Jesus Christ!' Neasa stood, flapping. 'Will I call a nurse?'

'No, no, it's just a preparatory contraction. There. It's gone now.'

How could Emily be so calm? When a big lump of a baby was going to force its way out through a very small place in the near future?

'Are you not nervous at all?'

'Yes.'

'Take whatever they'll give you,' Neasa advised.

'It's not so much about the labour.' Emily looked at her. 'I don't think I'm going to be a very good mother.'

'Oh, Emily.'

'No, I'm not just saying it.'

'But they sleep all the time,' Neasa said reassuringly. 'And then you just have to feed them and change their nappies occasionally. It's a piece of cake.'

Emily didn't look convinced.

'I'll even help,' Neasa offered generously. Just so long as she wasn't left alone with it. She wouldn't know what to do if it started crying or something.

'I just don't feel ready,' Emily said.

Neasa resisted the urge to point out that it was a bit late in the day for that.

'I feel like the baby's going to look at me and expect me to be brilliant and capable and know everything and I don't know *anything*.'

'Um, yes, I can see how you might feel that way,' Neasa said, who didn't. 'But the baby will love you anyway, Emily.'

'Why?'

'Why? Because you're its mother! It won't be able to help loving you, even if you're a totally crap mother!'

'And that's supposed to be good enough?'

Neasa was raging. That Conor again! Imagine having an affair on Emily, and then turning around and putting notions in her head that she was going to be a terrible mother!

'Emily, you are going to be fine. Trust me. You have loads and loads to give a baby.'

'We'll see,' Emily said.

Neasa clearly didn't understand. Emily wasn't sure she did either. But she had this sudden fear that she was not yet a grown-up. Not really. How could she be entrusted with a helpless infant when she wasn't a proper adult herself?

She felt that Conor, this afternoon, had inadvertently shone a spotlight into her soul and illuminated some nasty, mould-covered part of her that had been left festering for years. This mouldy thing, far from lying forgotten and benign, had actually been very busy undermining all her efforts, and laughing in the face of her hard work. It played jokes on her when it came to partnerships and promotions, and would occasionally tease her when she lay in bed at night wondering why things weren't as great as they looked on the surface.

She had thought it was merely her capacity to accept. It was much more sinister than that. It was putting her own needs last. And it had spread its tentacles into every single aspect of her life, blighting it.

Her stomach churned and jarred, mixing with her heartburn, and she burped.

'Excuse me.'

She felt a bit better now.

'That's disgusting,' Neasa said.

'One of the joys of being pregnant,' Emily said. 'You'll know all about it some day.'

'I will in my swiss. Oh, here,' she said, rummaging in her bag and taking out the Health Board letter. 'This came today. I didn't know you were writing to Health Boards.' This was said a bit accusingly.

'Yes, well, I just sent it in. No point in it lying around here.'

The letter thanked Emily for her concern, assured her that it was aware of the community's upset, but regretfully informed her that there was no other course of action open to them at this time.

'They don't even mention the petition,' Emily said.

'Actually, they do. Up there under "subject matter",' Neasa pointed out helpfully. 'They've probably filed it away in a deep dark drawer.' She might as well have added, 'Under Earnest but Useless Efforts'.

She tossed the letter into the bin by Emily's bed as though it were not worth the paper it was written on. The action annoyed Emily.

'At least I tried.'

'Well, yes, of course you did,' Neasa said, with no great conviction.

'What do you expect me to do? Go out there in my dressing gown and march up and down with the nurses?'

'I don't know what you're getting all defensive for,' Neasa huffed. 'You've done your bit. Leave it at that. I would.'

'You wouldn't have bothered doing a petition in the first place,' Emily pointed out.

'Of course I wouldn't. Those kinds of things never get results,' Neasa said, inadvertently annoying Emily more. Emily knew now that Neasa had not really been surprised that Emily had been passed over for the partnership at work. She'd been outraged all right, but only because Emily was her friend, not because she'd believed there had been a miscarriage of justice.

Emily felt very small and insignificant and powerless now. She did not particularly like herself.

'You know, Neasa, I'm tired. I might go for a bit of a sleep.'

'Me too. Oh, not here. I'm going home. I've a bit of a head on me. They can take half a day's holiday off me if they want.'

'Things that bad at the office?'

'Worse. Everybody's working so hard, there's no crack at all,' Neasa complained. And she had promised Gary a romantic dinner tonight. She would have to wax and shave everything, paint her nails and touch up her false tan. She sighed. Men had it so easy.

Nurse Christine Clarke came in as Emily was nodding off. She was covering for the day girls who were marching outside, and hadn't slept in thirty-six hours. Her blonde curls drooped sadly.

'Emily, are you not packed?'

'What?'

'The ambulance is waiting to take you to Cork. I thought somebody would have told you.'

'No,' Emily said, sighing as she sat up.

'They don't actually have a bed for you in an antenatal ward,' Christine said apologetically. 'But you'll be moved at the first opportunity.'

'And where exactly are they putting me in the meantime?'

'I don't know. You'll have to check when you get down there. Probably in a general ward or something. You don't mind, do you?'

It was the last straw. The very final straw, in fact.

'Yes, I do bloody mind!' she exploded. 'I'm a pregnant woman. I'm not going to be stashed in a corridor while they wait for someone to die before a bed becomes free!'

Christine burst into tears, her fatigue getting the better of her.

'I'm sorry,' Emily said miserably.

Christine turned and left, still sobbing. Emily buried

her head in her hands. The nurses here were so kind and nice; they didn't deserve to be shouted at. Well, Christine was a bit of a tit, but it wasn't her fault Cork had no beds free in the antenatal wards. Neasa always said that it was a sign of a very weak person when they were nasty to people who couldn't be nasty back. Not that that had ever stopped her.

Vera Mooney arrived in, in her civvies. Her nose was pink from walking up and down outside.

Emily sank down further into her dressing gown. 'Vera, I'm very sorry – is Christine all right?'

'Oh, fine. What's the problem? You don't want to go to a general ward?'

It seemed very small and mean now, and Emily felt like she was disrupting everybody's plans. But she was going to stick to her guns this time.

'I'd just rather not be moved around all the time, that's all,' she said apologetically. 'Especially in a strange place.'

'Quite right too,' Vera said. 'So will I send Liam and Joe away?'

It *would* be Liam and Joe. They were probably eating egg sandwiches and bitching about her right now.

'It's up to you, Emily. I'm sure they'll have an appropriate bed free tomorrow.'

Emily was relieved. A day wouldn't make any difference to anybody, would it?

'I'll wait if that's okay,' she decided.

Vera went and Emily snuggled down in her safe,

familiar bed and slept for four hours solid.

Conor was still sitting in the visitors' room. He saw little touches here and there that had Emily written all over them: fresh flowers in a vase, for example, left behind by some patient. The out-dated and crumpled magazines on the three-legged coffee table were arranged attractively, and two mismatched cushions had found their way onto the threadbare chairs. Give her another couple of weeks and she'd have repainted the entire hospital in a nice warm peach and added dado rails.

The house was wilting without her. Oh, everything was clean and tidy – he made sure of that. But the place had a stale, unlived-in feeling, like the heart of it was missing. Even the dogs – his dogs – looked at him accusingly, wondering how he had managed to mislay Emily. They'd been lucky to get any dinner at all that day.

He could not believe he had lost control like that, and said all those things. He could not remember the last time he had raised his voice. It always seemed to him such a weak thing to do, to go spilling feelings and emotions, giving away some percentage and diminishing your own position in the process.

It had been the shock of the discovery that she had never really been happy. Well, maybe not never. But from early on, much earlier than the miscarriage which he'd thought was the root of all their problems.

Or liked to think, anyway. It was such a neat thing to pin it all on, like those disappointed looks in the years before had counted for nothing. But nobody likes to admit that their deepest, unspoken fears were true all along – that really, he wasn't enough for her and never had been.

He thought again about that big handsome man at the wedding. He remembered his laugh, a booming, merry noise that had rang out across the bar. He remembered the look on Emily's face as she had watched the man.

He remembered also the look on Pauline's face when, meeting her for the first time as Emily's new boyfriend, Conor had tried to explain that he was a musician. Further intense questioning had forced him to admit that he was a pianist, to be precise. It seemed futile to explain to her that his real interest lay in the area of composition. He might as well have told her that he hoped to land on the moon.

Emily had assured him afterwards that Pauline's reaction didn't matter to her. And Conor had thought that it didn't matter to him either, but he remembered his sense of pleasure, of victory, the day he won a position with the orchestra. Emily was not now engaged to some hippy musician, but to a concert pianist. Take that, Pauline. Emily had been pleased too. Pleased and proud, and he had basked in it.

He promised himself back then that he would not lose sight of his ambition; that he would continue to write his own music. And he did, initially. But gradually his time and belief was whittled away until he stopped altogether. And he didn't want to do anything to rock the boat. He didn't want to do a single thing that might put Emily off him.

He wondered now whether he had tried too hard at the beginning. Had she got the whiff of a desperate soul, a man so in need of her that he would do anything to keep her? And he had thought he'd masked his feelings so well behind his veneer of cool reserve.

And he was still doing it to this day. He was much better at it now, of course, after years of practice. You'd be hard pushed to know whether a heart was beating at all underneath the urbane exterior. And he got away with this kind of behaviour, this kind of withdrawal, because he could. Emily's niggling and nagging and disappointed looks were quite easy to ignore. She wasn't one to push herself forward, and he had taken advantage of that. Preyed on it, even. All that shit she took from Crawley & Co. The liberties Liz and Pious Pauline took. Emily swallowed it all because she was good and kind and she always thought of others before herself. It had been easy to offer her less than the best.

Conor had never thought of himself as innately self-ish but realised with a shock that he was sounding perilously like it.

And now there was a baby on the way. It would not be so easy to offer it less than the best. As the time grew closer and closer when he would hold his baby daughter or son in his arms, Conor felt more panicked. He had up to now vaguely thought that Emily would cope for both of them. She was so warm and so giving; she would be able to do it for him too, wouldn't she?

But the grim reality of visitation weekends was rearing its head. Conor might find himself quite alone with a baby, a child. And no Emily to help him, except to say to the child when she collected it on a Sunday night, 'Don't mind your Da. He loves you really. He's just not great at showing it.'

Nurse Christine Clarke went out onto the picket-line in a foul mood. To make matters worse, it was raining and she had no umbrella. Her mascara streaked down her cheeks sadly. Nobody bothered to tell her.

'That high and mighty cow won't go,' she said venomously to Karen.

'What high and mighty cow?'

'Emily Collins. Gave me loads of grief just because there was no bed free in antenatal in Cork. Refuses to go until they find her a proper bed.'

How Christine wished that St Martha's would close and be bloody done with it! She was going on two weeks' holiday to Ibiza before she started in Limerick, and had bought several little string bikinis in anticipation. She fully intended to give nurses an even worse reputation than they already had.

'Those private patients, they think the health service belongs to them.' Karen said in commiseration. 'Here,

Darren, did you hear that Emily Collins is refusing to go to Cork?'

Darren told Alice from Jude's Ward. He got a bit mixed up about the bed situation.

'What, she wants to bring her own bed with her?' Alice asked. This was a new one.

Darren wasn't really sure, but he didn't let on. Some of the girls could act very superior, like he wasn't a proper nurse just because he was a man. Oh, the sexist stories *he* could tell. 'It's nothing to do with beds,' he said loftily. 'She just won't go.'

When Alice told Bernie, she didn't mention anything about beds.

'She was behind that petition, you know,' Bernie said, excited. 'She must be upping the anti.'

Alice was still a bit doubtful. 'You'd never think it to look at her.'

'Isn't she Liz Clancy's sister?'

'*What*?' Alice hadn't known this.

'Oh yes,' Bernie said grimly. 'Hard as nails, that lot. I wouldn't mess with any of them.'

Tanya from Casualty had been biding her time. 'She's a solicitor too. Did you know that?'

'What?' The girls didn't.

'Crawley Dunne & O'Reilly. They'd buy and sell your mother. She'd know all the tricks.'

Bernie was nearly tearful. 'Isn't she great? We always said this campaign would go nowhere until the patients got off their arses and did something.'

The bed issue was by now totally forgotten, and Christine Clarke, the only one who knew exactly what had happened, left the picket-lines and went home. Vera Mooney had already gone ages.

'What has the board of management said?' Geraldine from catering wondered.

It transpired that they didn't know and a great wave of excitement swept through the picket-lines.

'This'll rock the boat,' Alice declared, delighted, as someone went off to make an anonymous call to the local radio station.

Emily heard them before she saw them.

'*Robbie!* Where did you get that syringe? Give it to me this *instant*.'

In they trooped, Tommy, Robbie, Mikey and Bobby, with Liz bringing up the rear in case one of them tried to escape. Willy was strapped to Liz's front as usual. He didn't seem to have grown or progressed at all in a month and Emily wondered whether that sling might be constricting him.

'Hi, Emily.'

'Hello,' Emily said. She felt better after her sleep.

'Not disturbing you or anything?'

'Not really,' Emily said, watching as her beans on toast went cold. 'Hi, boys!'

They stood in a semicircle at the bottom of her bed and looked at her with a mixture of fascination and horror.

'Are you going to die?' Bobby eventually asked.

'Bobby! Honestly, Emily, I don't know where he gets these things.'

'It's all right, Liz.' Emily remembered asking her mother about birds and snake skins, and she gave Bobby a special smile.

'I'm not going to die, Bobby.'

'Oh.' He looked very disappointed and turned his attention to her locker instead. 'Can I have a grape?'

'Ah, yes, of course you can.'

The rest of them took this as their cue, and descended on her locker like a swarm of locusts. Emily watched as grapes, chocolates and bottles of 7UP were devoured at speed.

'Those grapes, they have seeds in them,' she warned Liz.

'It'd take more than a few seeds to kill them,' Liz said rather gloomily. 'Boys! Take them over to the table.' She sat in the chair by Emily's bed. She didn't sigh today. 'I've tried to explain to them that you're having a baby. Poor Mikey and Bobby are too young, of course. But Tommy! Do you know what he said to me, Emily?'

'What did he say to you.'

'He said, I suppose Auntie Emily and Uncle Conor had sex then. Sex! He's six years old, Emily!'

Emily laughed. Well, it *was* funny, a little bit. But Liz was annoyed that she wasn't taking it seriously. She puffed up further. 'And do you know what Myra Byrne heard some lads talking about in the school yard last week?'

'What?'

'Blow-jobs!' Liz hissed. 'She didn't know what they were on about at first – they were just talking about BJs. BJs, Emily! But she put two and two together. She's very sharp, is Myra.'

Indeed. She'd given a few of them in her time, according to local lore.

'I'm going in to talk to Mr Harrington. First thing tomorrow,' Liz declared. 'I'm not having that kind of filth coming into my house.'

'They're going to pick it up anyway, Liz. You can't really stop them.'

'Quite the expert now,' Liz said a bit loftily.

Emily threw her eyes to heaven. 'No, I'm not an expert, but I'm going to have to contend with the same thing myself in a couple of years' time, and I'm entitled to an opinion, aren't I?'

'Well, yes, of course you are,' Liz conceded. 'So, how are you?'

'All right. They're trying to find a bed for me in Cork.'

'Oh, that place is a right mess,' Liz said, as though she'd just come from there herself. 'Can't cope with the amalgamation at all, for all their guff. Poor old Larry Power was sitting in Casualty for three hours yesterday.'

That was pretty par for the course in any hospital, Emily thought. The noise level from the other side of the room dropped dramatically. The boys had put the television on and had found a cartoon.

'How are things at home?' Emily asked.

'Grand, why wouldn't they be?' Liz said.

'Well, you know – Eamon, the bank situation.'

'I don't know why you have to keep bringing that up, Emily.'

'What? I wasn't—'

'We're sorting it out,' Liz announced.

'Good,' Emily said tightly.

'He's made an appointment to go in and see the bank manager and the accountant and work out a system of repayments.' She looked at Emily. 'If you could believe a word out of the mouths of any of them.'

So, she knew about the affair. Emily was only surprised that word hadn't got around sooner. Liz shook her head vigorously from side to side now. 'I don't know. I just don't know.'

'Neither do I,' Emily agreed.

'At least it wasn't with some local one,' Liz said in commiseration. 'That was the only good thing about Eamon's mess – he doesn't owe money to anybody in the town. At least we know there'll be no gossip about either of them on the church steps on Sundays.'

Eamon and Conor had finally found common ground, unbeknownst to themselves.

And so had Emily and Liz, sitting there counting their blessings and telling each other that it could have been worse.

'I don't really want to talk about it, Liz,' Emily said.

Liz was hurt. And she after confiding in Emily and all! But that was typical of Emily. She'd encourage you to go on about yourself, and then tell you nothing at all about her own situation. She could be very selfish that way.

'Mammy's heard. She's worried,' she said, a bit superior. Liz had kept her own problems within the four walls of her house, and not bothered Mammy with them.

'Yes, well, Mammy's not married to him', Emily said and she didn't care if she sounded heartless.

'Anyway, I told her to stop dropping around shepherd's pies to that fellow.'

'Conor,' Emily said in a voice that invited no further comment on the subject.

The boys were bored with the television now and were jumping up and down on the two spare beds. Bobby was making a tent with the sheets and pillows. Vera would go mad.

'You did great work on that petition,' Liz said eventually.

'It wasn't too hard. People were in and out of here all the time.'

'Oh, can't you just take a compliment, Emily?' Liz said irritably.

'You're absolutely right,' Emily said. 'We don't pat ourselves on the back enough, you and me. We should blow our own trumpets every now and again.'

'I suppose.' Liz looked doubtful at this.

'No, really, we're brilliant.'

Liz threw back her head and laughed. She looked younger. 'I wouldn't go that far, Emily.'

'I would. Why not?' Emily smiled too.

'Despite the odds,' Liz added.

'Despite terrible odds. We should look at ourselves in the mirror every morning, like they tell you to do in those self-help books, and tell ourselves that we're magnificent.'

'Eamon would think I was mad if he found me talking to mirrors.'

'Eamon hasn't a leg to stand on.'

The nice moment was broken by a wail from the corner. Tommy was suffocating Bobby with a pillow.

Liz sighed and stood. 'I don't suppose I'll see you again. Not if you're down in Cork. I could try . . .'

'No, really, Liz. Maybe when I have the baby.'

Liz fidgeted with her bag. 'If you want to come and stay in our house when you get out, you're welcome – if we still have a house, that is. You could have Tommy's room. He can sleep in with Bobby and Mikey. It wouldn't be the quietest place on earth, but just until things settle for you . . .'

'That's very good of you, Liz. I'll keep it in mind.' Emily was touched. She wouldn't in her wildest dreams go and stay with Liz, but that wasn't the point.

'Right, well, good luck with everything.' Liz rounded the boys up with a bellow, and went off.

Emily thought about getting out of bed and packing her things for tomorrow. But the effort was too great, and she was having those pains again. Her breasts were also leaking; her pyjamas felt damp. She'd never heard of that happening to anyone she knew and she was mildly embarrassed. But her books informed her that it was perfectly normal.

At least something was. She felt that she and Conor were at a crossroads, and that things could go either way now. And it wasn't just on her part, either. She had not seen him like that before, like he had lost control. It was that stranger in him again. What had he been like with Ffion Rivera? Had he shown her hidden depths that he had withheld from Emily? Emily felt robbed, cheated.

Too much had happened for them to go on in any previous capacity. They would have to rebuild from the ground up.

Emily wondered now whether it was really possible to change. For *anybody* to truly change. All the magazine articles and self-help books assured you that it was. A simple quiz first to diagnose how hopeless you really were, then ten revelatory tips which could be applied in any order, followed by a paragraph on how great you should feel now that you were actually somebody else.

But what about things that were so ingrained, that underpin your entire life, things that form the essence of yourself? Even if you did manage to change those parts of yourself, was it a constant battle to maintain it?

Would you live your life as though it were one long, miserable calorie-controlled diet?

And if it were hard enough for one person to change, how did two people in a flawed relationship change in perfect synchronisation? Especially if they didn't know what it was about them that the other person *wanted* changed? Would it require endless, heartbreaking effort? Would the relationship become not one of spontaneity and joy and love, but gruelling hard work?

People in so-called happy relationships were very fond of saying 'oh, you have to work at it', as though it were yet another chore to do at the end of a long, hard day. Emily did not live in never-never land like Neasa, but neither did she want to become one half of those tight-faced couples who were together for all they were worth, but would really be much happier on their own. Or possibly with a small dog.

Neither was she afraid of hard work. Indeed, she loved hard work, was too fond of it really, as though it were an end in itself. But not this time. She would not waste her precious energy unless her conviction was there. And that's what it came down to at the end of the day.

She wondered whether Conor was thinking these things right now. It was odd, the way they'd always had of thinking exactly the same thing at the same time. Emily used to laugh and think it meant some kind of spiritual bond. Now she was inclined to think it was just coincidence.

Maggie came in, pink-cheeked and breathless.

'Are you having an attack?' Emily asked warily. Maggie's asthma attacks always frightened the life out of Emily. All that wheezing and gulping, and Maggie's hands would claw at the air as though she were trying to gather it up. The attacks had become more frequent recently as Maggie's due date approached fast.

'No, no.'

'Pains, then?' Maggie had been having a lot of pains. Everyone expected her to have her baby any day now.

'The girls were telling me!' she said in a rush. 'About you not going to Cork!'

'Oh, yes.' Had they nothing better to be talking about?

'Well, I think it's great,' Maggie declared.

Emily wasn't sure why. 'I'm going in the morning, Maggie. They just haven't got an appropriate bed.'

'Oh, they're desperately trying to find one. That's what the girls said. They'd nearly chuck someone out onto the streets to get you a bed!' Maggie was triumphant.

'I don't want them to chuck anybody out onto the streets.' Jesus, hadn't she enough on her conscience?

'I've decided that I'm not going either,' Maggie declared.

Emily roused herself from her cosy cocoon of sheets and blankets. 'What are you on about?'

'Well, the more the merrier,' Maggie said. 'They won't be able to ignore a sit-in.'

Emily thought about this for a minute. Then she laughed. Maggie was a desperate eejit sometimes.

'What?' Maggie asked, understandably hurt. 'I know I'll probably go into labour any minute, but I could sit-in until then, couldn't I?'

'Maggie, I'm not starting a sit-in,' Emily explained patiently. 'I just didn't want to go to a general ward, that's all.'

'But it's on the radio and everything.'

'What?'

'On LKR fm. Everybody heard it.'

'Everybody' was the thousand or so citizens who tuned into LKR fm on a regular basis. Emily imagined Conor listening to this, slack-jawed, and she laughed again.

'They didn't actually name you,' Maggie said stiffly.

Emily found she was a bit disappointed. Anyway, Conor didn't listen to LKR fm. He was an RTE 1 man, with occasional forays into the classical stations.

Maggie was looking at Emily as though Emily held her future in her hands.

'You do a sit-in if you want, Maggie.'

'I can't.'

'You can. You obviously feel strongly about it.'

'I thought you did too.'

'Well, I do . . . look, I've kind of made a promise to myself, Maggie. I'm not taking on other people's problems any more.'

Spoken aloud, this didn't sound half as noble as it did

in her own head. Maggie obviously thought so too.

'That's very convenient,' she said.

Emily felt annoyed again, like people were constantly pricking her with little needles.

'I did the petition,' she said.

'This is just a bigger petition,' Maggie reasoned.

'It's not. This is different. It's taking on something we know nothing about,' Emily argued fiercely.

'It's scary,' Maggie agreed.

'Aren't we scared enough? Aren't we about to have babies?' Emily pleaded. 'Haven't we pre-eclampsia and wheezy lungs?' Not to mention broken marriages.

'I can't do it without you,' Maggie said stubbornly.

Why was Maggie looking at her like she was some kind of leader? A hell-raiser, even? She giggled again.

'I don't know what you find so funny about all this,' Maggie said, miffed.

'You're right. It's not funny at all,' Emily said, sobering. 'Especially when they drag us kicking and screaming from our beds and cart us off in wheelbarrows.'

'They wouldn't do that,' Maggie said confidently. 'Think of the publicity!'

Maggie was speaking like one who had spent most of her life in the trenches.

'And what happens when we have our babies? Are we going to continue to sit in then?'

'Oh, Emily, don't be so negative!' Maggie almost stamped her foot in frustration.

'I'm being realistic. Now go away, Maggie.'

★ ★ ★

Neasa had spent most of the afternoon beautifying herself and preparing the romantic meal. She'd even cooked it this time, instead of opening a jar of Dolmio. She'd bought four bottles of good red wine and put so many candles in the living-room that there was a very real possibility of a house fire. Tonight would work, she resolved fiercely, and made a head start on the wine. Alcohol always added such a nice rosy glow to things.

Gary arrived in from work at half past seven. He'd been working later and later this past while, much to his chagrin.

'Hi, darling,' Neasa said, floating up to him on a cloud of Obsession.

'Those fucking pricks,' Gary raged, storming past her.

Neasa took a moment to regain her balance. 'What's happened now?'

'You'd know if you hadn't skived off this afternoon,' he said sourly.

Neasa decided to let this one pass.

He threw off his coat. 'You know the way we're nearly out of headed notepaper in the office?'

'Oh Gary,' she commiserated. 'Don't tell me they've put you in charge of stationery too?'

Gary's job these days seemed to be less about making sales and more about ordering paper clips and mending photocopiers. He'd even taken to making the coffee.

'Actually, yes,' he admitted. 'But it's not that. I was supposed to get my name on that headed notepaper,

Neasa! As a partner! They said they would change the name of the firm when I was promoted! They promised!'

Neasa told herself that he only sounded childish because he was upset.

'So what's the problem?'

'Well, my surname is O'Reilly, isn't it? They already have an Ewan O'Reilly!'

'Hmmm,' Neasa said. She could see their problem. Crawley Dunne O'Reilly & O'Reilly didn't have a great ring to it.

'I suggested that they put my name first,' Gary said. 'You know, O'Reilly Crawley Dunne & O'Reilly. But bloody Ewan didn't want my name first, said that I was the newcomer and so I should go last! So now *he* wants to go first!'

'So it would still be O'Reilly Crawley Dunne & O'Reilly?' Neasa asked carefully.

'Exactly! But this still wouldn't do him. Oh no!'

'How about Crawley Dunne & O'Reilly Times Two?' Neasa tried to coax him out of his black humour. He was unamused.

'Now Creepy suggests that we leave it the way it is, that we can both share the O'Reilly! I'd like to see *him* sharing his name! And that Daphne one sitting there muttering that they wouldn't have had this problem with Collins.'

Neasa was getting a headache. 'Why don't we have some food? It'll take your mind off it.'

It did not. All through Neasa's superb prawns with

feta and olives, Gary went through every possible per-
mutation. He wrote various combinations down on a
paper napkin while his wild fruit crumble went cold. It
was like an elaborate pick and mix at the sweet section
of the cinema, only minus the fun. Neasa knocked back
red wine and watched silently.

Eventually he looked up. 'I have a solution.'

Thank Christ. 'What?'

'I'll have to change my name.'

He was joking, surely. But he was not.

'Gary, it's your *name*. Your identity. How can you
change it?'

'Deed poll,' he said. 'Now, what would I call myself?'

Neasa watched as he took a fresh napkin and came
up with all kinds of unlikely surnames for himself:
Gray, Greer, Gilmartin, Gunne, Garland. Garland?

'I'd quite like it to start with a G. Alliteration and all
that,' he told Neasa. 'But not something like Glitter,
obviously. That would be silly.'

'Very,' Neasa said thinly, reaching for a fresh bottle of
wine and taking it into the living-room. She would get
very drunk tonight.

Gary was on her heels. 'Gary Gilmartin has a good
ring to it, doesn't it?'

Yes, if he were a porn star. The scented candles dotted
around the room gave off such a strong whiff that
Neasa began to feel sick.

Gary finally realised that he might be banging on a
bit. And Neasa was all dressed up too, he noted rather

sadly. Suspenders and all, he could see the telltale signs under her clingy dress. Sex would be on the agenda later on so. 'Experimental' to boot, if some of the items he'd seen in the fridge were anything to go by. Once, just once, he would like to flake out in front of *Friends*. But she had already opened the bottle of wine.

He bit back a yawn. 'What would you like to talk about, darling? Childhood memories? Deepest insecurities? Hopes and expectations?'

'What would *you* like to talk about?' Neasa asked.

Gary wanted to talk about his new name some more, but this wasn't appropriate he knew. He was also rather worried about the way the radio in his BMW kept switching channels without warning. But this was too lightweight for the third bottle of wine.

Then there was the way Annabel's breasts always seemed to spill out over the top of her bra. Phil reckoned that her bras were deliberately a size too small. But this was yet something else that could not be shared with Neasa. He tried to think of a Deep and Meaningful topic of conversation but couldn't. Fuck it, he just wasn't a Deep and Meaningful type of guy!

Gary wondered when he could become himself with Neasa. Because *nobody* was themselves at the beginning of a relationship. They were always somebody else; mysterious, witty, sexy, and never suffered from flatulence or bad hair days. But with his other girlfriends, Gary had gradually relaxed into himself, and had been able to break wind again. There was no relaxing with

Neasa. It was all a terrible strain and he sometimes wondered whether she was worth it. But of course she was; she was the kind of woman who usually dumped Gary when she found out what he was really like.

She was a catch all right. The other lads in the office looked up to him because they all unofficially knew he was sleeping with her. She never slept with them, and wasn't likely to do so at any time in the future. She always looked terrific, and hadn't put on a single pound in all the time they'd known each other. Some of Gary's past girlfriends had let themselves go disgracefully once the first flush had passed. About the time he started to fart again, now that he thought about it.

Sex, he thought with a sigh, dragging himself to a sitting position on the couch. Sex would keep her happy.

My God, Neasa was thinking. Was it possible that they hadn't a single word to say to each other? How could this have happened? Even with the cross-dresser, the sexist, the chat-room junkie – all of them – she'd always had something to talk to them about right up until the horrible moment of revelation.

With Gary, there was no horrible moment of revelation. Just a slow, merciless disclosure of mildly offensive parts of himself. But nothing that Neasa could really put her finger on. Nothing that couldn't be overlooked in the name of *love*. She was being too perfectionist, she told herself fiercely, that had always been her problem. This time, she must not jump ship. She must rescue the situation. She threw back the last of her wine and turned to him rather desperately.

'Will we have sex? Mad, wild, brilliant sex?'

'I was about to suggest the same myself,' Gary said, opening her bra with one hand. Neasa had always found this extremely sexy. Now she wondered just how many bras he had practised on to become so good.

'I'll just move over . . .'

'No, no, I'm not that heavy, am I?'

'Not at all . . . there we go. Oops! Sorry, did that hurt a lot?'

'I'm fine, honestly. But if you'd take your hair out of my mouth . . .'

'Sure, sorry . . .'

The couch seemed far too small. But they pressed valiantly on anyway, ignoring the fact that there was a perfectly good king-size bed over their heads.

'Come get it, Tiger,' Neasa said huskily. This usually drove Gary wild.

'Miaow,' Gary said, sounding more like a puny kitten than a jungle animal.

Neasa decided to take the initiative, and jumped on him. She sashayed and squirmed and shimmied for all she was worth. It was quite some time before she realised that there was a problem.

'Um, I think I'm more tired than I thought,' Gary muttered.

'Of course, and all that wine doesn't help,' Neasa soothed. 'Do you know what's wrong?'

'What?' Gary asked, slightly alarmed.

'Over-use,' Neasa said, and they both laughed: a funny, forced laugh.

Gary was absolutely mortified. Him! Failing to perform! What the blazes was going on?

Cheeks hot, he struggled out from under Neasa and put the offending article firmly away. He could not look at her.

'You know, maybe I'll go home to my own place. Get a good night's sleep.'

'Not a bad idea,' Neasa said too readily.

Jesus Christ, she was thinking, did he not fancy her any more? Was she not being exciting and innovative enough? But how much more innovative could she get without it becoming illegal?

'Goodnight, sugar.'

'Goodnight, sweet pea.'

They must be using the last of Martha's budget on the heating, because Brenda's Ward was boiling that morning.

'Open a window, Maggie, would you?'

Maggie looked balefully over. 'Do it yourself, you bitch.'

She was sulking.

Emily sighed and threw back the covers. Her belly looked absolutely massive this morning; it was blocking out half the light. And the baby was thrashing about fiercely, making the entire thing lop from side to side violently. It was a struggle to keep her balance as she sat up. Now, how to get down from the bed. The floor looked very far away.

'Get Vera, would you?' she asked Maggie.

'Will not,' Maggie sang.

God, she was in a right old snit this morning. She was knitting with grey wool. A barbed wire fence, now that Emily looked closely. Maggie was such an amateur when it came to sit-ins. They'd cut through that in no time.

Emily tentatively reached down with one toe for the floor, but no joy. She would have to slide down farther. But still there was no floor. She peeked down, saw that the floor was a good hundred metres away, and screamed just before she tumbled off the bed and into the abyss.

'Rise and shine, girls.'

Emily woke sweating, her heart pounding crazily, to see Vera at the end of her bed with the pressure cuff.

'You'd better give me a minute,' she advised Vera. No sense in alerting the emergency caesarean team for nothing.

'Bad dream?' Vera asked sympathetically, making for Maggie instead.

'Nothing I haven't had before.'

But she'd never fallen off a bed until now. A crane, yes. Cliffs and mountains regularly. And she'd once fallen off the roof of the Department of Justice. That had been the night before her final law exams. All her classmates had fallen off the top of the same building, she had later learned; the pavement beneath had been littered with the corpses of nervous law students. It had been a routine fear of failure dream before a big event. The next one they could expect was before their first day at work, they'd reassured themselves. After that, the night before they signed for their first mortgage, and then when they got married, or divorced. Really, it was quite a convenient way of anticipating big events, somebody had argued. He'd wanted to be a barrister.

Emily's fear of failure dreams never quite worked that way. She would get one in the middle of a tedious, boring week, with nothing more stressful than Christmas on the horizon. Or sometimes after Liz or her mother had called around, or when Conor was more withdrawn than usual. But usually when nothing at all was happening and her life was on a steady plateau. When she was plodding along as usual, keeping her head down, and not offending anybody.

The would-be barrister would tell her that she was about to have a baby and her marriage was floundering, and it was a wonder she hadn't fallen off the bed twice.

Well, the baby was going to get out of her one way or the other, and it was a bit late to be worrying about her marriage failing, and what would he have to say to *that*?

But he had been a very intelligent young lad and Emily didn't discount his opinions entirely. What *if* those mid-week dreams had been a premonition? A kind of elbow in the ribs to wake up and look around her?

Or just to stop being afraid.

She was, she decided, going quite mad. Next she would be looking for black cats in the hospital corridors.

Maggie's blood pressure was up.

'Now, what's all this?' Vera said sternly. 'Have we been getting ourselves all riled up?'

'Yes,' Maggie said meekly.

'And you due any day,' Vera scolded her.

'Sorry.' And she looked over at Emily as though it were all her fault.

'I haven't done anything,' Emily clarified. This was quite true. She had absented herself from the ward last night, and any more talk of sit-ins. Nobody had bothered her in the visitors' room, not even her mother, who apparently had been in after hearing some nonsense on a local radio show.

Vera descended on Emily with the pressure cuff.

'That's the best I've seen it in weeks,' she said. 'Any more bleeding?'

'Not a single drop.'

'Mr Chapman will be delighted.' This was said rather tongue-in-cheek. Apparently when Mr Chapman had been told that Emily Collins hadn't arrived as scheduled, he had said some colourful things.

Vera finished making her notes. Maggie was looking avidly on. Vera reached out and smartly pulled the curtain around Emily's bed, shutting Maggie out.

'I believe there's some misunderstanding about Cork,' she said with admirable diplomacy. 'Some of the girls think that there's a sit-in.'

'Apparently so,' Emily agreed. 'Maggie too.'

'Yes, well, Maggie.' Vera left it at that. 'Anyway, I wouldn't worry. It's a silly rumour as far as most people are concerned.' She didn't feel it was necessary to name names. 'I'm only asking, Emily, because they've found you a bed in Cork.'

'That was fast.'

'Indeed. Apparently one just turned up.'

'In an antenatal ward, I take it?'

'Oh, better than that. You've got your own private room.'

'Well, well,' Emily said slowly.

'They've also generously offered to waive whatever extra cost is incurred if your medical health insurance doesn't fully cover a private room.' Vera was looking studiously at her shoes. 'The thing is, they can't hold on to this room for you forever, for obvious reasons.'

'I'd need to go today then.'

'This morning. In fact, Liam and Joe can take you right now.'

'In a luxury ambulance with a free minibar,' Emily said.

'Not quite,' Vera said. 'It's up to you.'

Vera transferred her attention from her shoes to the hem of her uniform.

There was no shame in going to Cork, Emily knew.

And Vera, bless her, would put paid to any more conjecture about sit-ins. And Cork was obviously going to treat her very well.

And really, Emily thought, she probably would have gone if they hadn't tried to buy her off. Or bully her, to be more exact. She felt like they had flicked on her Code Red switch. Up to recently she hadn't even had a Code Red switch, just a little button that made her nod and smile.

'About the baby,' she said. 'Would it be safe here? Would I be safe? Medically speaking?'

Vera didn't look insulted, which was even more to her credit. 'You're certainly safe until the hospital officially closes on Monday week. I honestly don't know what will happen then. It'd be your responsibility to decide after that.'

Emily nodded. 'I wouldn't anticipate all this taking much longer than Monday week anyway.'

Vera showed a careful interest. 'Oh?'

'I don't have a time frame yet, but I'll let you know.'

'And, ah, what would I tell the board? And Cork?' Vera enquired.

'Just that I'm occupying my bed until further notice.'

'Certainly,' Vera said briskly, and left.

Maggie poked her head around the curtain immediately.

'Well?'

'Well what?'

'Well are we sitting in or not?'

'Maggie, I'm just staying for a few days in case anything can be done about this place.'

'Great! I'd better go and tell Dee down in Elizabeth's Ward.'

'Dee?'

'She said she would sit in too. And Laura. And possibly Mary.'

Mother of God. Maggie had been busy last night.

'Obviously, I'll hang in there for as long as I can,' Maggie promised. 'But I've had more pains, Emily. I think today could be the day!'

She scurried off.

Emily contemplated ringing Conor to let him know that she wouldn't be going to Cork just yet, but it was only ten to eight. He wouldn't even be up yet. She'd ring him later on today.

She knew she was making excuses. She just didn't want to tell him about the sit-in. He would think she was being silly and emotional, and letting herself yet again be dragged into things that really had nothing to do with her.

She didn't think he would believe her if she said that, this time, she wasn't.

Conor had got up very early. He'd showered and shaved and put on good clothes. He'd even polished his shoes. He felt like he was going to an interview.

Now he gathered a few things for himself, clothes and toiletries to do him for a couple of days. Billy

Middlemiss had a flat in Cork near the hospital. He was going to be away for a few days and had told Conor he could stay there. He would drive back up for his weekend work in Baccaro's and straight back down again to be by Emily's bedside.

He had to put his things in the huge suitcase, where they rattled around rather morosely, because Emily had his Manchester United bag.

Then he collected the baby bag. They had packed it together, discussing endlessly the number of nappies, Babygros and vests they should take to the hospital, and carefully marking things off in a highlighter pen against a list they'd been given in antenatal classes. This list conflicted in many key areas with the list their baby-book featured. One would sternly warn you to take only the bare necessities, while the other would remind you not to forget a baby blanket. This immediately raised the question of whether the hospital did not provide baby blankets, and if they didn't, did they also not provide baby mattresses, sheets, a cot even? Ridiculous, really, but how were Conor and Emily to know these things? They had argued back and forth, packed and re-packed five times, ooahed and aahed over the tiny Babygros and it had been lovely.

Emily's bag had taken even longer to pack. It wasn't as though they had spare breast pads hanging round the house, or disposable underwear for that matter. Conor had actually thought the disposable underwear was a joke, until Emily had come home triumphantly from Mothercare with two packets of the things. Conor had spent an hour one evening making nametags for the bags: 'Emily Collins' and 'Baby Collins'.

Emily had joked that it was a shame that he didn't have his own bag.

They hadn't quite finished the packing before Emily had been carted off to Martha's. Conor had looked up the list and had got the last few bits in the chemists, including maternity pads.

He unzipped Emily's bag now to put them in. He found a plastic bag on the top marked 'Food'. Mystified, he opened it, and two Mars bars tumbled out, along with crisps, energy drinks, Nutri-grain bars, and those chocolate-covered peanuts he liked.

Didn't she know they would feed her in the hospital?

He consulted the list again. And he saw that she had ticked off in highlighter pen, 'Snacks for your birth partner during labour.'

They were for him. She would not be allowed to eat anything during labour in case of emergency surgery. But she hadn't minded about that, she had thought about him and the fact that he might feel like a bite to eat while she writhed in agony beside him.

'Oh, Emily,' he said.

He did not know if he would be there for the birth. He wanted to, very much, and he felt he had a right to be there. But birth partners were there to support and encourage and whether Emily thought he could give her that was up for grabs. Or whether she wanted him to. She might just want to ring him afterwards and he would traipse in like any other visitor to see his daughter or son.

He sat on the bed with the two bags either side of him and the big suitcase at his feet and he had a pain in his chest.

He would go to Cork and stay until he had worn her down. He'd worked out all his arguments last night; there were so many reasons for staying together, even apart from the baby, and he would give them to her one by one. Emily often caved in to his logic. Probably because she was usually put in the position of looking illogical, he realised now.

But if he could at least persuade her not to make any final decisions about the two of them, to give them a breathing space. He was trying to buy time.

He hadn't got beyond that, really. He knew there was a leap required on his part but he didn't know how to make it. He did not want to pretend that he had mutated overnight, or that he had seen the light. Nobody could do that, except born-again Christians, and Conor didn't believe in God.

But he did believe that the situation was very dangerous right now. Apart from anything else, the baby, when it came, would rightly demand all their time and energy, and there would be nothing left over for anything else. More importantly, the hurtful things that had been said yesterday had opened gaping wounds, and he felt that if he did not move now, immediately, all would be lost.

He picked up the suitcase and bags and went out to the car.

Some of them in Cork thought it was quite funny. A gang of pregnant women holed up in Martha's! What were they doing, holding a couple of breast pads out the window with 'No' written on one, and 'Surrender' on the other?

All the management had to do was threaten to withdraw the epidural. They'd cave in fairly quickly then. Or close the sweet shop on the ground floor. They wouldn't last long without chocolate.

Mind you, it wasn't a bad idea as ideas went. Nothing guaranteed to embarrass the politicians more than the prospect of women dropping babies on the pavement outside. It could set their entire equality drive back a good ten years.

But the general consensus was that nobody would do anything. Let them sit in Martha's. Let them have their babies there. And then just quietly close the place down when they had all gone home.

Secretly, a lot of them in Cork had wanted to give the Health Board a good boot up the arse for years and were quite envious that somebody had finally had the guts to do it. They didn't want Martha's patients in any case; they were already overworked, underpaid and disillusioned. In the meantime, it was certainly entertaining to watch the show, and it passed the time nicely in the canteen.

Mr Chapman did not go anywhere near a communal eating area that morning. He did his usual rounds, delivered two babies, met with his junior doctors and gave no indication at all that he even knew what was going on in Martha's. And if he did, that he didn't care.

He very much cared, because he had been taken for a fool. Last night, Martha's Board of Management had said nothing about a sit-in. They had just insisted that Emily Collins be given an appropriate bed. Mr Chapman had spent an hour reviewing charts to see who could be discharged as quickly as possible. In the end, Duggie Moran had found a couple of patients who were outstaying their welcome and they had been dispatched. Then, a quick reshuffle of beds until a lovely, big private room with a fresh coat of paint had been secured. And then Hannah informs him that it was on the radio that there was a sit-in!

Hannah played the radio a lot these days. It helped to drown out the screaming matches between Mr Chapman and Killian. Mr Chapman had done his level best to show the boy that there were other ways of dealing with this.

'We've decided, Dad,' Killian kept saying. 'We've decided, okay? Will you just stop pushing!'

Mr Chapman had made a big effort to calm down. 'Killian, I understand that for certain people, abortion is the only option. But it isn't for you and Andrea. You have supportive families. We'll help you every step of the way. I promise.'

He was holding out his hand in a way he never had to his son before.

But Killian just shook his head again. 'It's for the best.'

'The best for you, you mean. It's the easy way, Killian, the cop-out!'

Killian had looked at him very coldly. 'This isn't your decision.'

'I'm just trying to stop you doing something you may end up regretting for the rest of your life!'

'You are not. You're just trying to control me, like you try to control everybody!'

Mr Chapman started now as Duggie Moran banged into his office without even knocking on the door.

'Aren't they right bloody bastards? To keep you in the dark like that?'

Mr Chapman sensed that Duggie's sympathy was manufactured. He was loving this, but then again he had always been pathologically jealous of Mr Chapman's standing in the medical community. Duggie Moran knew as well as Mr Chapman that this was a no-win situation. What was Mr Chapman supposed to do? Go up and drag Emily Collins out to his car and drive her down here? Or go up obediently to see her as he had done thus far? Whatever way he moved, it would look like he was taking sides.

They were all watching this one very carefully. And him.

On the face of it, Cork's management was very laid-back about it all. All new patients from Martha's catchment area would still be coming into Cork's system on Monday week as planned. The sit-in was Martha's problem, not theirs, they declared.

And Mr Chapman's, because she was his patient.

'Do you know what I'd do?' Duggie said.

'What would you do, Duggie.'

'I'd go up and induce her on the spot.'

Mr Chapman found jokes of this nature distasteful and very disrespectful. But that was young consultants for you. In it for the money, half of them, he often thought. What happened when you had all the money you could ever need or want? What were you in it for then?

'Either way, I'd check my medical insurance if I were you,' Duggie advised.

What was the point? Mr Chapman already knew that his medical insurance did not cover Acts of God. Or Acts of Emily Collins.

'You've eaten all the caramels,' Karen said crossly to Darren.

'I have not! I always eat the strawberry ones that nobody else likes! And the bloody coffee ones!' Darren was very indignant. 'Tell them, Vera!'

Vera just continued with her notes.

'I like the coffee ones,' Christine interjected.

'Since when?' Darren said a bit spitefully.

The supply of Roses had abruptly dried up as ward after ward in Martha's had closed down. Now you couldn't find a box for love nor money, and tempers could flare quickly and violently over the last few chocolates that nobody had previously wanted.

'You shouldn't be eating them anyway. You're not even supposed to be working today!' Christine returned triumphantly.

This was true. Martha's should have been down to a skeleton staff. But Darren had received a phone call asking him to come and do a day shift on his day off. Vera had been asked to stay on after her night shift was over. It was a mystery.

But not to Vera, who chewed imperceptibly on a caramel. The board of management were avoiding any knee-jerk reaction to the sit-in. Someone very sensible, probably the Health Board's legal team, had advised them not to give the patients any cause for complaint about neglect or coercion. Under no circumstances were emotions to be riled further.

So they laid on extra nursing staff. Extra catering staff too. Mr O'Mara and Mr Dunphy were both on call, and the equipment in Delivery had received an unscheduled service that morning. Even the heating in the place had been turned up, lest the patients might want to complain about the cold. No, Vera thought, there wasn't a hospital in the country safer than St Martha's right now.

Maureen huffed past pushing the lunch trolley,

leaving an unusually delicious aroma in her wake.

'Chicken chasseur,' Christine said, tight-lipped. She had been down in the kitchen earlier. 'They're giving them fecking corn-fed chicken chasseur! And look at the muck we're still getting in the canteen!'

'What, has she demanded special menus?' Karen wanted to know. She wouldn't put anything past Emily Collins any more. And to look at her you'd think butter wouldn't melt in her mouth.

'The food is a management decision, Karen. You know that,' Vera said mildly. If it were up to her, she'd give Emily and Maggie and the whole lot of them caviar and champagne.

'What are they going to do about them?' Darren wanted to know, round-eyed.

'I hope they're not thinking of staying open until they all drop their sprogs,' Christine said, peeved. 'I'm going to Ibiza Monday week.'

'That's the spirit,' Karen said disparagingly.

'They haven't done anything yet,' Vera clarified.

This worried her. There had been no attempt to talk to the women. Apart from laying on extra services, the management was proceeding with its daily business as though the sit-in didn't exist. Indifference was often the death of strikes and protests, Vera knew. Even the local radio station had cooled off a bit, when they couldn't get any juicy quotes from anybody in authority.

The national media had yet to display any interest. There had been so many strikes and protests in the public sector in recent times that it would take something special to make them notice *this* one.

Still, Vera though hurriedly, fair do's to the girls. Fair do's to Emily Collins in particular. At least she tried.

'What are we supposed to be doing exactly?'

'I don't know, do I!' Maggie returned a bit impatiently. 'Sitting in!'

Dee, Mary and Laura had come down to Brenda's Ward, and they were all perched uncomfortably on the end of Maggie's bed.

'Does it mean literally?' Dee wanted to know, trying to stretch out her legs. Maggie's bed wasn't big enough for four pregnant women. And that Laura one was hogging more space than she was entitled to. Just because she was expecting twins!

'We *are* breaking for lunch, I hope,' Laura said. 'I'm starving.'

'I want to go to the loo. Am I allowed?' Mary wanted to know.

'You'll have to ask Emily,' Maggie returned testily. Honestly! All the griping and grousing, and they were only a few hours into the sit-in! Maggie had expected it to be much more exciting and glamorous, which was why she had gone around the rest of the wards with a rallying cry: To Brenda's Ward, everyone! The sit-in starts there! Up the revolution!

But now that they were all there, it was a bit of an anticlimax. At the very least they'd expected some men in suits to come in and threaten them. Maybe even a solicitor or two. Maggie had angled the bed towards the door in anticipation. But nobody came except Vera, who said it was handy to have them all in one place for blood-pressure readings. Mr Dunphy's arrival had caused a bit of excitement. Dee, his patient, was not in her bed where she was supposed to be. But he just said it was good to see her up and about and left. Just like that! Dee had felt very slighted.

'At least they know we mean business,' Maggie said valiantly, trying to rally the troops.

'I suppose,' Dee said doubtfully. 'Oh, scoot over, Laura!'

'It's a waiting game,' Maggie persisted. 'They'll have to do something eventually.'

'Like what?'

'I don't know!' This was Emily's department! Maggie was only second-in-command. It wasn't fair to leave her to field all the questions like this! But Emily was over in her own bed, with that Neasa friend of hers. Chatting away like she hadn't a care in the world – and the sit-in crumbling all around her! (Maggie's pains yesterday had turned out to be indigestion and she was very cross with the world in general.)

'Mick down in Vincent's Ward thought he might join us,' Mary offered.

'Great, we can do with all the support we can get,' Maggie said, relieved.

'But he changed his mind.'

'Oh.'

'Said he wouldn't be comfortable around pregnant women.'

'This isn't a pregnant-women-issue,' Maggie said with a sigh. 'It affects everybody!'

'But we're the only ones sitting in,' Laura pointed out.

'And we need to up the anti,' Maggie decided. If Emily wasn't going to bother her barney, then Maggie would have to.

'What'll we do?' Dee asked.

'Well, we could start refusing food.'

'It's chicken chasseur today.'

There was a small beat.

'We have to think of our babies,' Laura said.

'Oh, we do.'

'Absolutely! We can't be refusing food.'

Maggie thought again. 'In prisons they refuse to wash.'

Dee wasn't enthusiastic. 'Is it fair to do that to the nurses?'

'Not really, I suppose,' Maggie reluctantly conceded. 'Maybe Emily will have some ideas.'

They all looked over at Emily, who was drinking a nice cup of tea and obviously telling Neasa some very amusing story.

Dee, Mary and Laura exchanged little looks. They couldn't quite credit that Emily Collins had started this in the first place. She wasn't a woman to be taken very seriously by the management, in their opinion. No, they wouldn't be at all surprised if this sit-in was a flash in the pan and would all be over by tea. Which was salmon en croûte with new potatoes, according to Maureen.

'She'll think of something,' Maggie repeated strongly, seeing their faces. They were underestimating Emily. In truth, Maggie's faith in Emily was slowly eroding, but she bravely hung on to her loyalty.

In the meantime, she hoped that Emily would finish up with Neasa soon. She was dying to go to the loo too.

'Until someone comes up with an idea, will we have a game of bridge?' Dee suggested.

'Ooh, let's.'

'You see, I had this dream.'

'Really.'

'I fell off the bed.'

'That's very interesting, Emily.' Neasa smiled kindly, much the way she had done for a whole week while her grandmother had rambled on in the hospice. Neasa wondered whether she should buzz for a nurse, or a psychiatrist or something. Poor Emily had tipped over the edge this time.

'It *is* interesting, isn't it?' Emily ruminated.

'And now you want to take the Department of Health to court,' Neasa clarified.

'Not actually the Department of Health,' Emily said. 'Just the regional Health Board.'

'Oh, well, that's all right then,' Neasa said.

'And I suppose Martha's Board of Management. You'd have to include them.'

'Why not? How about the Minister for Health himself?'

'I don't know . . .'

'He might feel left out.'

'You're not taking this seriously.'

'No, I'm not. Because you're fucking bonkers!'

Emily wasn't offended. 'The sit-in isn't going to achieve anything, not really. We have to decide this thing one way or the other.'

'We?' Neasa said incredulously. 'Don't include me in this!'

'Hangover?' Emily asked sympathetically.

'Well, yes, absolutely wicked, but I'm still in possession of all my faculties. Which you are plainly not!'

'You haven't even listened to it all yet.'

'I don't want to!'

'It's quite simple, Neasa. I just want a judicial review of the decision to close.'

Neasa laughed.

'It's just a matter of filing a motion,' Emily insisted.

'Which you want me to do,' Neasa said.

'Well, obviously, I can't,'

'Obviously.'

Emily looked as though it were utterly reasonable that Neasa would take herself off to the High Court and lock horns with the Department of Health and Children.

'Emily, I'm sorely tempted, but I don't happen to have a spare fifty grand sitting in my bank account to pay the costs.'

'Don't be ridiculous,' Emily sniffed. 'We could do it for half that. Less if we're not paying solicitors' costs.'

'No.'

'Oh come on, Neasa! You know you'd love to go to the High Court.'

'Of course I would! I've never been in the High Court! Well, only as an apprentice. But that's not the point.'

'Remember how we always wanted to sit at one of those tables at the front, behind the lads in the white wigs?'

'Stop it, Emily.'

'Leaning over to whisper instructions every now and then?'

'Shut up!' Neasa clamped her hands over her ears. But Emily wouldn't let up.

'And then we'd walk out onto the steps of the Four Courts just in time for the six o'clock news, and say—'

'My client has no comment at this time!' Neasa shouted. 'I remember, okay!'

'So will we do it?'

'No! I don't even care whether the hospital closes or not!'

'That's beside the point. I care enough for both of us.'

Neasa looked at Emily as she reclined in bed, balancing a cup of tea on her big bump, her swollen ankles propped up on a pillow, and she wondered how it was possible for somebody in this condition to look dangerous. But Emily did. Not in a Gary kind of way – she could never hope to look like Jaws in a million years. It was more a quietly determined I-just-might-scratch-you kind of thing.

Maggie waddled past, carrying her own roll of Kittensoft toilet paper.

'Is it all right if I go to the loo?' she asked Emily anxiously. 'I don't want anyone to think I've left the sit-in.'

'Absolutely, take all the time you need,' Emily assured her.

'And can we break for lunch? It's chicken chasseur and the girls are very excited.'

'Eat away.'

'Oh, and Tiernan will be in later to join the sit-in. He'll have to leave, of course, when visiting hours are up, but every little helps.'

'It does,' Emily said. She turned back to Neasa. 'Well, what do you think?'

'I think,' Neasa said sarcastically, looking at Maggie's retreating back, 'that you need all the help you can get.'

'If you don't have anything positive to say, then just go,' Emily said shortly, surprising Neasa. How come Emily could get so fired up about hospitals closing when her relationship was in an even worse state than Neasa's? After last night's fiasco, Neasa had finally realised that there was something dreadfully wrong with her and Gary. Really, any sensible person would finish with him. But she did not want to admit defeat yet – she *couldn't*. This time, it would be like finally conceding that she was a total failure when it came to men. They would time and again let her down and she might as well throw her hat at them all and dedicate herself to her career or something worthy like that. God knows she'd ignored it for long enough.

'I'll do it,' she told Emily grudgingly.

'What?'

'I said I'll do it.'

'You don't have to, Neasa.'

'I do. For my personal growth,' Neasa said rather piously.

'Crawley Dunne & O'Reilly will have a fit.'

'They'll probably fire me.'

'I don't want that to happen.'

'Why not? I do,' Neasa said cheerfully.

'And Gary mightn't like it – him being on the other side, so to speak.'

'He'll be fine,' Neasa said hastily. She had been too embarrassed to tell Emily about Gary's name-change. It made him sound like such an eejit.

'Just so long as you don't fall out over it,' Emily said anxiously.

Neasa gave a rather lean smile. 'No danger of that at all.'

'Maybe you should think about it.'

'Jesus, Emily, I've just agreed! Are you trying to talk me out of it now?'

Emily might look dangerous, but she still had a way to go yet, Neasa thought.

'Does Conor know about this?'

'Sorry?'

'He doesn't then.'

'I don't see what it has to do with him,' Emily said rather defensively.

Neasa had no intention of defending Conor – that pig – but found herself doing it anyway. 'He might feel he has a right to know. And you don't want to make things between you any worse. Or maybe you do, I don't know.'

'I've already tried. His phone is switched off,' Emily protested. This was true, but it sounded very lame. 'Oh, look, we had a huge fight yesterday.'

Neasa nodded wisely, satisfied with this explanation.

Emily did not tell her that they were on the brink this time. And that Emily had not yet decided what to do. Maybe this sit-in was her way of avoiding the issue. But it wasn't going to go away. She knew that. Right now, though, she felt she had nothing to go back to the talks table with. Compromise wasn't the issue. They would each have to offer new parts of themselves and Emily hadn't found hers yet.

The porter in Cork was not well paid. Or at least not well paid enough to listen to gossip. He knew nothing about any sit-in and informed Conor that, according to the computer, Emily Collins should be in Room 2b on the fourth floor.

Conor took the stairs, weighed down by the two bags. He'd also bought a bunch of flowers. Nice ones this time – white roses, Emily's favourite. She'd carried white roses the day they'd married. Oh Lord, would she think the flowers were some sledgehammer attempt on his part to remind her of what they'd once had? He stuffed them into a wastepaper bin on the first floor.

No, words were needed now, not things, he thought, as he rounded the steps onto the second floor. He was going to come clean with her – totally clean. He would tell her about his love for her, that he would die if she left him. She must be left in no doubt about the depth of his feelings for her.

He was running up the steps now, unaware of the bags banging painfully against his ankles. He would tell her about his feelings of insecurity and inadequacy, his fears and anxieties, the whole bloody lot!

His new impulsiveness had come to him in the car, when he'd been rehearsing his logical arguments for them to stay together. And they had sounded so tight-arsed and pompous and dreary – anyone in their right mind would run a mile, screaming for a divorce. So he had thrown the lot out and decided that he would speak from the heart for once in his bloody life. He had nothing to lose and everything to gain.

The third floor now. He barely slowed, taking the

steps to the fourth floor two at a time. He felt that if he paused for breath he might get cold feet and say nothing useful at all. He had to take the risk. He just had to.

Panting and excited, he threw open the door to Room 2b. And that was where the confusion kicked in. The woman in bed was quite insistent that she was not Emily Collins and, indeed, she didn't look anything like her. Her husband strongly backed her up. Conor was ejected from the room, bag and baggage, and trailed down to the nurses' station, deflating rapidly.

In another startling twist, it was revealed to him there that his wife was actually part of a sit-in in Martha's.

'Oh, yes, of course,' Conor said, as though he'd merely forgotten. His face felt very hot. He was as surprised as if they'd informed him that she'd just given birth to triplets. He wanted to ask whether they were sure they had the right Emily Collins, but was too embarrassed.

'Right, well, good luck,' he said inanely, lifting the two bags and feeling more ridiculous than he ever had in his whole life.

'Conor?'

Jesus Christ, he wasn't going to run into one of the neighbours, was he? He was not in the mood.

It was Mr Chapman, looking very belligerent. He peered at Conor over the top of his bifocals.

'This is most unorthodox. Most unorthodox.'

'It is.' Conor looked belligerently back. Even bloody Chapman was in on this.

'As her consultant, I have to strongly advise against this course of action,' Chapman boomed, taking a step forward.

'Really,' Conor said, also taking a step forward. Sure enough, Chapman took a step back. One more step and they would be in a foxtrot.

Chapman looked at Conor's bags. 'What are you doing here anyway?'

'I came to see you,' Conor shot back.

'Ah.' Mr Chapman looked relieved. 'Maybe together we can sort this out.'

Conor didn't want to say anything in case he betrayed his ignorance of the entire situation. He just nodded.

'Is she intending staying in St Martha's until her baby is born do you think?' Mr Chapman wanted to know.

'Your guess is as good as mine,' Conor said honestly.

'Frankly, I'm worried about her,' Mr Chapman said, looking his most serious. 'The stress of this kind of activity isn't ideal for a woman with pre-eclampsia.'

'I don't suppose it is,' Conor said.

Mr Chapman was more relieved. Here at last was a voice of reason. Maybe this entire thing would be over today.

'It's rest she needs. And plenty of it.'

Conor just listened.

'She has to think of her baby,' Mr Chapman went on. '*Your* baby. And really, I can't be responsible for her when that hospital closes,' he finished up, shaking his head regretfully.

Conor looked at him. 'So you want me to talk her out of it?'

Of course Mr Chapman did, but it wasn't nice to hear it put so blatantly. 'Absolutely not. I'm simply urging you to assess the position responsibly.'

Conor looked relieved. 'Oh, that's fine. I thought for a minute there you were washing your hands of her.'

'What? I never said that. No, no, what I meant . . .'

'You'll still be coming up to see her then?'

'Of course I will!'

'That's great,' Conor said sincerely. 'I'll be sure to tell her that.'

Mr Chapman felt the situation had slipped entirely out of his control. Instead of nipping this thing in the bud, he had unwittingly become a party to her madness.

'So when will I tell her you'll be up?' Conor wanted to know.

'I don't know! Soon! I'll ring.' Mr Chapman walked away rather quickly. He felt the nurses at the station looking at him, and imagined that they were laughing behind their hands. And there was Duggie Moran, giving him that falsely sympathetic look again. And he after giving Duggie Moran hundreds of referrals over the years, all the overspill from his packed appointments book! And on top of it all, he had the Board of Management watching his every move over this sit-in business, like he was a junior doctor again.

He had no authority any more, no standing, not even with his own son.

He had to get out of here. He turned on his pager and left.

Conor wondered what to do now. Get his stuff from Billy Middlemiss's flat and go home, he supposed. Cap in hand, all his fine words like ashes in his mouth. He felt angry now for having got so heated and emotional, ready to spill his guts. He felt he had made more of a fool of himself than Emily had.

But wait a minute. Emily! His wife! Staging sit-ins and protests? The most she'd ever done in that field was refuse to cross the picket-line when the Dunnes Stores staff had gone out on strike.

Conor wondered wildly whether she had cleverly disguised an anarchic streak all these years. This wasn't outside the realms of possibility. He had read a biography once of a woman who had been a secret service agent for twenty years and all the while her husband thought she took in ironing. Emily had bought it for him.

But no, Emily was too much of a talker for that. They'd never trust her with sensitive information, knowing that she'd let it slip to the girls down in Milo's after two gin and tonics. And Crawley Dunne & O'Reilly would never give her time off for secret missions.

Conor shook his head, wondering why he was thinking these ludicrous things. It was just that the ground had been taken from under his feet by Emily's latest move. He was strangely hurt too, if he admitted it. He had thought that, like himself, she would be obsessed with the state of their marriage. Instead she was off doing something entirely different, to put it mildly. It was like she was steering away in another direction and leaving him behind, like so much baggage. The reality was that he was superfluous to her life really, and had been for a long time. And he had done it to himself by drawing a line in the sand that he allowed neither of them to cross.

He felt emotion rising in him again. He tried to rationalise it, to control it. But he couldn't this time. He picked up the two bags and went outside and to his mortification he was crying.

'Now, girls, watch carefully. This is how you change a nappy.'

Angela, the midwife, carefully picked up a plastic doll from the table. 'Remember, girls, you have to support the head. If you don't, this is what happens.'

And she let the doll's head flop backwards violently.

'Ooh,' all the women said, wincing painfully.

Angela held up a Pampers and looked at one of the new mothers. 'Now, Marie here has put her baby's nappy on back to front. No, no, Marie, it's all right. It's a mistake many of us make the first time out.'

And indeed Marie's newborn daughter looked perfectly happy in her back-to-front nappy.

'You'll get so used to it that you'll soon be changing nappies in your sleep.' Angela looked around at them leadenly. 'And you think I'm joking.'

Emily and Maggie tittered nervously. They were at the back of St Catherine's Ward along with Dee, Laura and Mary and, strictly speaking, shouldn't have been there at all. It was a class for the first-time mothers who had just given birth in the hospital. Vera had asked them whether they wanted to go along. Time seemed to pass very slowly on this sit-in. She'd assured them that their beds would still be there when they got back. After measured consideration, Emily had decided that they would go, even though they were the only ones there whose babies were still inside them.

'Cotton wool and water, girls, that's all you should use on newborns' bottoms,' Angela lectured. 'Any of those commercial wipes will take the skin off them.'

'Ooooh.' The women all winced again. Angela wasn't pulling any punches.

'I'll never be able to do that,' Maggie whispered, watching as Angela manoeuvred the doll around with speed, flinging its legs in the air, brandishing cotton wool, and finally holding up the doll to show everyone a perfectly applied nappy. It could have gone to a fashion show.

'There was no poo on the doll. I'd like to see her deal with *that*,' Emily whispered back encouragingly. As if Emily herself had ever changed a pooey nappy.

'Now, will we give her a bath?' Angela asked everyone.

'Let's!' the women squealed enthusiastically. Wasn't it marvellous that someone was actually showing them what to do?

While Angela filled a plastic baby bath with water – 'Half-full will do, girls, no sense in drowning the child' – Emily felt some of the other women casting curious glances her way, like she was an oddity in their midst. Here they all were, participating in the most momentous occasion in any woman's life, some would argue, and she was off organising sit-ins. Maybe some of them thought she wasn't maternal, not like them.

And a few of them were undoubtedly thinking that she was using her baby as a bargaining chip with the management.

Emily held her head high. She did not care what they thought of her. Well, of course she did. She was still *Emily* for heaven's sake. She cared very much. But the important thing was not to cave in to it.

Although she was wondering about the wisdom of the whole thing now. Still, most people who instigated a major High Court case would eventually see past the euphoria, she thought reasonably. Especially when they started questioning the cost of it all, the possibility of losing, the unwanted publicity, the wrath of the Health Board . . . Jesus Christ, she was mad!

'It's all right. It'll pass in a minute,' Maggie said soothingly, seeing Emily's face. Emily had had three panic attacks already about the court case, and Maggie had been very sweet about them. 'Look, she's taking the nappy off again!' she said, to take Emily's mind off it all.

'Now, girls, have the bath ready before you take all the baby's clothes off, you don't want it to freeze.' She picked up the doll. 'And remember, girls—'

'Support the head,' they chorused.

'That's it!' Angela was delighted. 'Now. Does anyone want to give the doll a bath?'

Everyone squirmed shyly in their chairs like they were back in Senior Infants. Then they all turned to look at Emily. Bloody hell, did they expect her to take the lead in every situation just because she had instigated the sit-in? She didn't even have a baby yet! She sat firmly on her hands, red-faced.

'Nobody ever looks at me like that,' Maggie said a bit sadly.

'Me neither,' Emily said. Up to now. It was very embarrassing, but it was also rather gratifying. Like she was someone to be reckoned with or something.

'Okay, girls,' Angela said. 'Watch carefully then. First you stick your elbow in the water to test the temperature. Lukewarm, girls, that's all the water should be. You don't want to burn the child alive.'

'Ooooh,' the women said, cringing. Several of them clutched their babies closer to their chests protectively.

'And don't be smothering it in any of those fancy bubble-baths either,' Angela said sternly.

Emily and Maggie looked at each other guiltily. Both of them had filled their bathroom cabinets with bottles of the stuff in bubbly anticipation.

'And a bath once a week or a fortnight is sufficient. There's no need to put yourselves and the baby through the torture every single night.'

That's what Liz maintained. Emily felt a new respect for her. She must ask her more about babies. Ask her properly, that was, not the grudging way she had done so far because she felt it was expected of her, and not really listening to what Liz had to say.

'Don't you wish you could take her home with you?' Maggie said, looking at Angela. 'She knows exactly what to do and I won't have a clue.'

'You will.'

'I won't!' Being around all the newborn babies was getting to Maggie, who was now officially a day overdue. This had not figured in her birth plan at all.

'We'll learn as we go along, Maggie,' Emily said sternly.

Emily herself didn't believe this for a second. How was she to remember all these things when the time came? Already she'd forgotten what Angela had said about the different types of milk formula. And there was that whole complicated business of sterilising bottles to come yet!

She found herself wishing very strongly that Conor were here. He would effortlessly memorise all these details, and calmly regurgitate them back at that crucial moment. Just as Emily was about to pop the baby into a boiling bath, probably. The problem was that you couldn't wing it with babies, and hope that you get it right; one badly sterilised bottle and you've given them a dose of gastroenteritis. How could she live with *that*?

She wanted him here to share the responsibility. It was too terrifying to contemplate being totally account-able for another person's life – a person who couldn't tell you whether they were sick or hungry or whether their nappy was just on back to front. And there were so many things that could go horribly wrong! Really, Emily thought, it was an act of criminal negligence to let women like herself and Maggie and Marie, total amateurs, waltz out of hospitals with defenceless babies. In any civilised society that cared for its young, babies would be brought up by professional midwives until they were about three while their parents did a compulsory MA in child-rearing. Then the child might at least have a fighting chance of reaching adulthood without being killed by gastroenteritis, or being drowned, or starved, or strangled by its own nappy.

When the call came through from Terry Mitton, Senior Counsel, Mandy at reception was totally ill-equipped to deal with it. No barrister had ever rung Crawley Dunne & O'Reilly in living memory. Nobody in the office even knew a barrister, although apparently Phil had met one once while visiting the offices of a proper solicitor. He had talked about nothing else for weeks.

'Hold the line, please!' she sang, before clamping her hand fiercely over the mouthpiece. What was she supposed to do now? 'Here, Gary? Do you know a Terry Mitton, SC?'

Gary stopped in his tracks. 'A senior counsel?'

'Yes,' Mandy whispered.

'He's lying.'

'No, he's not.'

Gary grabbed a copy of the Law Society Directory from Mandy's desk and thumbed through it. And sure enough, Terry Mitton was listed.

'What does he want?' Gary was nervous. Was it possible somebody was taking a negligence case against them?

'He didn't say,' Mandy said. 'Will I put him through to you?'

'Jesus, no!' He went on hurriedly, 'I mean, this is one for the partners.'

'You *are* a partner.'

Fuck. Gary didn't want to get into conversations with barristers. With his inexperience, he would be bound to make a balls of it. And he was already in the bad books with Crawley over the way the filing system had disintegrated into complete chaos. Crawley had actually said to him that it wouldn't have happened if Emily had been here! No, Gary had to avoid any more trouble.

'Phil, will you take a call from a barrister?'

'I will in my shite.'

'But you met one once.'

'I didn't *speak* to him.'

Gary was desperate now. Then Neasa came in from the loo. She'd talk the hind legs off any barrister. He was forced to look her in the eye, which he had been unable to do all morning. 'Neasa,' he muttered, 'would you take a call for me? There's this barrister guy on the phone—'

'Who?'

'Terry Mitton or something.'

'Of course I'll take it.'

'Great.'

'It's for me anyway.'

'What?'

Neasa looked at Mandy in despair. 'Did you not ask him who he wanted to talk to?'

'Um, no. I got such a fright . . .'

'Put him through,' Neasa barked, striding over to her own desk. Mandy, Phil and Gary looked after her in astonishment. What the hell was Neasa doing associating with barristers? More to the point, did the partners know?

Neasa turned her back on them and picked up the phone with admirable coolness.

'Terry. Sorry about that, I got delayed by a cosmetics company.' Well, she'd applied fresh lipstick in the loo. 'Now, what's the situation?'

Terry Mitton went on about making an application to have the initial arguments for a judicial review of the closure heard. That was the first hurdle. If and only if the judge thought they had grounds, then they would get their day in court.

'But first of all, we need to seek an immediate order to stop the hospital closing.'

'Go on,' Neasa murmured. God, he had a lovely voice. Like a big bar of Galaxy chocolate melted in the microwave.

Due to the urgency of the situation, Terry Mitton hoped to be heard in tomorrow's court proceedings. He would be faxing her a draft of his arguments later that day.

'Terrific,' Neasa said, forgetting all about his voice. She had a lovely, buzzy feeling in her tummy with the excitement of it all. Imagine, her involved in court cases and judicial reviews! It was even better than kicking German receptionists' asses. 'You might also mention the petition.'

Terry thought this was a great idea. The voice of the people, nothing like it! Hell, I'm good, Neasa thought. Of course, she had known this all along in a theoretical way. She just hadn't bothered putting it into practice until now. This really had been a great idea of hers, she thought.

'Will I be needed in court tomorrow?' she asked.

She would. Yippee. She must plan tonight what she would wear.

'I need to know for certain whether your client intends to go through with this. If I'm to issue proceedings to the other side,' Terry said.

He meant the Health Board, Martha's Board of Management and all other interested parties.

'Oh, she hasn't changed her mind,' Neasa assured him, hoping this was true. 'I was speaking to her only a second ago.' She'd ring her as soon as she got off the phone.

'Now, about costs,' Terry Mitton said.

'Ah.'

She had been prepared for a rather large sum, and admirably betrayed no shock when informed that it would be twice that.

'Sure, sure,' she said, acting as though he were selling himself cheap. Bloody hell, for that amount he should send a private plane for her in the morning. But it appeared that she would have to make her own way to Dublin.

When she replaced the phone, Gary was standing over her. She'd been acting hurt and confused around him all morning, but she didn't have time for that kind of thing now. There was work to be done.

'Well, Gary?'

'What was that all about?'

'Oh, I can't tell you right now,' Neasa said, very friendly. She would wait until the proceedings were issued before informing the partners that Crawley Dunne & O'Reilly were entered as the official solicitors. They'd lose a lot of face if they tried to weasel out of it. Of course, they might just show Neasa the door. Either outcome was a good one.

This really is the last straw, Gary thought. Now she wouldn't even share legitimate office business with him! And he was her boss, so to speak! He would force it out of her if he weren't so embarrassed about last night. At lunchtime, Dr Purcell had assured him that there was nothing physically wrong with him. The examination had been almost as mortifying, with Dr Purcell poking around down below while Gary looked desperately at the ceiling. Dr Purcell said that these things were most often stress-related and kept on and on about the health of Gary's relationship. Couldn't the man just give him a course of Viagra?

No. He could not. He advised Gary to go and talk to his partner instead. Talk to her? When she wouldn't even discuss work with him?

The more Gary thought about it, the more this non-performance problem was Neasa's fault. She expected everything to be so perfect all the time! Any man would wilt under the weight of her expectations!

Gary badly wanted to finish with Neasa before his self-confidence died altogether. But he couldn't now, not after last night. No, he would have to perform one last time, otherwise she might tell the whole office that it was over between them because of his impotence. Then he'd never get a crack at Annabel, whom he fully intended to hit on next.

'Will you come over tonight?' he asked, wheedling. He'd watch a dirty movie before she came, tank up on a few beers, shag her senseless, and then break it off. The relief, he realised, would be intense.

'I can't,' Neasa said regretfully. She had to do her nails, her bikini-line and polish her shoes for tomorrow. But really, she was afraid that if she went over, he would irritate her so much that she would end up breaking it off. It was inevitable, but she was just putting it off because she didn't want to look at where she was going wrong. 'I'm driving to Dublin early.'

'For what?'

'I can't say,' Neasa said again. 'But the partners' dinner is tomorrow night – we'll be going to that together, won't we?'

'I suppose,' Gary said unenthusiastically. He would have to wait until then. And it would be such a stressful event too, trying to impress Creepy and Ewan and Daphne with his choices from the wine list. It would be a miracle if he were able to get it up afterwards.

Neasa decided that she would give him the boot tomorrow night. She owed it to him to turn up for the dinner – he was counting on it. But that was it.

She felt the familiar crush of disappointment at having failed yet again. What was it about her that seemed to attract nothing but eejits and degenerates? Maybe it was something as simple as her perfume – she'd read a very interesting magazine article once on how human beings are sexually motivated almost entirely by smell. Was it possible that one little spray every morning could account for the shambles that was her romantic life?

She liked this idea – it was so deliciously simple – and thought about it some more. She might even change her entire image, and see what that brought her. Or maybe she was looking in the wrong place for The One. Could it be that he wasn't in Paulstown at all, but alive and well and living in Cork? She must extend her search immediately.

She felt much better now. Really, when you thought about it, she had simply been misguided in a number of key areas such as perfume and location, which were easily rectified. The One would turn up eventually, she had no doubt about it really. And she couldn't wait to be in love again.

The news of the application to put a stay on the closure of Martha's pending court proceedings had two direct impacts: it sent the Health Board into a spin and it got Pauline Ryan into her car during the hours of darkness. It took her half an hour to drive the five miles to Martha's, as she met ten oncoming vehicles and had to pull into the ditch as many times.

Emily sighed and put away her mobile phone as she saw Pauline coming down the corridor. Conor was not home, or at least he was not answering the phone. Neasa had pricked her conscience and she had wanted to tell him about the court case before it hit the local media. But he had been gone for hours and hours now. Despite herself, she was worried. You could set your watch by Conor. Where could he be?

'I hope you're happy with yourself,' Pauline said by way of introduction. She was wearing an extra crucifix today. She must be very upset.

'It's something that had to be done, Mam,' Emily said rather proudly. Her mother must have listened to the six o'clock LKR fm bulletin.

'I don't know how you can lie there and say something like that.' Pauline was aghast. 'And your own marriage in tatters, if what I hear is true!'

'Oh, all true, every word,' Emily said, although she wasn't quite sure what her marriage had to do with any legal action.

'And so you have to drag everybody else down with you?' Pauline demanded.

This was fairly vicious. So much for thinking that Pauline might be a little bit proud of the stand Emily was taking on behalf of the community.

'You can't go through your whole life taking things lying down, Mam.'

'Well!' Pauline looked at her like she had two heads. 'Try telling that to those children!'

'What children?'

'Tommy, Robbie, Mikey, Bobby and Willy! Who did you think I was talking about?'

'You've lost me now, Mam.'

'And they without a father now!'

Dear God. Had Eamon fallen into a cement mixer or something equally fatal?

'What's happened, Mam?' she asked in a weak voice.

'What's happened, says she! She who put Liz up to this whole madness in the first place!'

Had Liz finally lost the rag and *murdered* Eamon?

'Tell me what's happened!' Emily almost shouted.

'She's thrown him out! Oh yes. Just like that. Packed a bag for him and showed him the door!'

Emily was so surprised that her mouth fell open. 'Where's he gone?'

'A brother of his,' Pauline said sourly.

Emily tried to sort through the confusion. 'But . . . why?'

'Money, of course.'

'But she said they were sorting things out. That he was going to see the bank manager.'

'He went to see an auctioneer. He tried to sell the house to refinance the business, told Liz they could live somewhere smaller until things got better.'

Emily realised now that Pauline knew a lot more than she ever chose to let on. She had probably known about Eamon's money problems for ages but hadn't wanted to get involved. Had she also seen the cracks appearing between Emily and Conor, maybe even before they'd seen them themselves? Say nothing, that was another of Pauline's favourite phrases. Say nothing, keep the head down and be grateful for what you have.

'And now she's given him his marching orders. After you filling her head with nonsense!' Pauline said accusingly.

'I did not fill her head with nonsense.'

'Oh? Do you know what she said when I went over? That you told her to pat herself on the back. That she was marvellous!'

'Well, I suppose I did say that . . .'

'That she didn't take enough credit for what she did!'

'Yes, but I meant women in general—'

'And that Eamon Clancy dumped all the responsibility onto her and that if he wanted to bury his head in the sand, then he could do it somewhere else.'

'Now, I did not say that.' Liz had made that deduction herself, and an excellent one it was too.

'And now she has nothing!' Pauline finished up.

'That's ridiculous, Mam. She has self-respect, hasn't she?'

'Self-respect!' Pauline wasn't just a pre-feminist, she was a pre-pre-feminist.

'Mam, you wouldn't want her to stay with someone who couldn't face the music, would you? Come on. That's no life for anyone. Or for those children either.'

'Children! *Children!* And your own with no father and it not even born yet!' Pauline was almost screeching now.

'Keep your voice down, Mam.'

'I will not keep my voice down. Who are you to tell me to keep my voice down, you little pup? And you bandying your business all around Paulstown, like you're someone to look up to! Mistresses and petitions and court cases! Oh, yes, I heard about that too!'

'Stop it, Mam. Now!'

319

Pauline did stop. She put her hand up to her crucifixes uselessly and let it drop again. She was crying, Emily saw. That generally tended to happen when you've spent your whole life toeing the line and the shit still hits the fan. Emily finally had something in common with her mother.

'It'll be all right, Mam.'

'How can it be all right?' Pauline cried. 'Two of you with broken marriages, six grandchildren deprived of good, stable homes.'

'With cowboys and adulterers,' Emily said.

'Nobody would have noticed if you hadn't gone poking your nose in!' Pauline bawled inconsolably. 'I only ever wanted the two of you to be happy.'

'Were you happy? With dad?'

'Don't try that with me, Missy. Who are you now, Dr Anthony Clare?'

'Were you, Mam?'

'Your father was the most inoffensive man God ever put on this earth! You couldn't dislike him!' Pauline shouted, with the air of one who had spent many years desperately trying, but had given up and spent her life with a man she merely liked. Pauline cried harder now at the waste of it all.

Emily let her. She didn't feel particularly good about reducing her mother to tears. But anybody who lived life by a collection of hoary old sayings would some day get a rude awakening.

Pauline eventually looked up, red-eyed.

'I suppose you have it all worked out. You'll get that solicitor's office of yours to file for a divorce and get maintenance for that child, and you'll be as happy as Larry.'

'I thought you wanted me to be happy?'

Pauline just didn't want to believe that people could be happy outside the system. If that was the case, what had she been going to Mass for all these years, and attending the funerals of crusty old feckers that she didn't even know? Her reward was supposed to be at the end of it all, and now here was Emily sitting up and telling her that all her little insurance policies were null and void.

She looked a bit bitter now. 'I hope you can explain yourself to that child inside you.'

'I'll certainly do my best,' Emily said.

Pauline had one more crack. 'He's not a bad man, you know,' she said defiantly. 'Conor. I don't care what you say, he's not a bad man.'

'He certainly isn't,' Emily agreed, peeving Pauline further. 'And I'm not filing for divorce.'

That really took the biscuit, Pauline thought darkly. She goes and smashes everybody else's comfy little world for them, and then goes back to exactly that herself! Talk about the cat that got the cream!

Pauline drove home in the darkness in a rage, forcing three cars, a truck and a tractor to drive up into the ditch.

Ever since LKR's evening news bulletin, the nurses' station outside Brenda's Ward had been a hotbed of intrigue and gossip.

'Go home, Christine,' Vera commanded.

'I will not.'

'And you too, Darren. Your shift finished three hours ago.'

'So did yours,' Darren retaliated.

Nobody would go home. They were all waiting to see what would happen next. Apparently there had been an emergency meeting of the hospital board an hour ago. Someone said that a legal team from the Health Board had shown up too. But nobody told the nurses anything, as usual. They didn't care. Weren't they a mere thirty yards from the centre of all the attention, and she sitting up in bed in Brenda's Ward playing cards? For once, the nurses had got it from the horse's mouth.

'Isn't it delicious,' Christine sighed. 'I've never been part of a court case before.'

'You're not part of it,' Karen said. 'It's Emily Collins' case.'

'It involves the whole hospital,' Vera said diplomatically. 'I think we can all consider ourselves involved.'

This was just like *ER*, Christine thought, Ibiza all but forgotten. Maybe she would be called to give evidence. Wouldn't that be something?

'Right, girls and boys,' Vera commanded. 'Empty your pockets.'

'What?'

'This is going to cost money. And, as we're agreed that we're involved, we should contribute.'

'Oh.' Christine wasn't sure she wanted to be *that* involved. But she stumped up five pounds anyway. Darren only had two pounds fifty on him. Karen wondered if she could get a sub, otherwise her contribution would be a bus ticket and a half-eaten packet of Polos.

'Right, well, thanks anyway,' Vera sighed. She would put in fifty quid herself. It was the very least she could do for Emily Collins – that and bring her extra cups of tea and bonus diuretics. Emily had had her blood pressure read four times in the last hour too, and a thermometer had been popped into her mouth every time she drew breath. Everybody was taking extra good care of their champion. Nothing could be allowed to happen to her. At least not on *their* shift.

'She's being very cool about it all, isn't she?' Darren said, and they all peered in the door of Brenda's Ward at Emily Collins. Maggie and Dee and the rest were perched on the end of Emily's bed. Bridge, again.

'She's that type,' Christine said. 'She's a solicitor. She probably files court cases every morning before breakfast.'

Only Vera could see Emily's fear. It wasn't belligerence or a need for attention or even a huge belief in Martha's that was driving her now, but personal factors that Vera could not even guess at.

Not that Vera was overly concerned. She wouldn't

mind if Emily Collins was in this purely for compensation. Let her have it. The important thing was that this closure would not go unchallenged.

Here came Conor Collins now, walking towards them with two bags. He nodded at them all curtly and went into Brenda's Ward.

'I think he's gorgeous,' Karen offered.

'So do I,' Darren agreed.

'He's after having an affair,' Christine said airily.

'What?'

'Someone was saying it in Milo's. With another opera singer, apparently.'

Vera looked up sharply. 'Since when did we go discussing patients' private business?'

Well, all the time, actually. But the girls and Darren knew when not to cross Vera.

'Now. Everybody who is not on shift is to go home this instant,' Vera ordered. Herself included. She wanted to see whether the national media was picking any of this up.

'Will we go to Dublin tomorrow?' Darren asked impulsively. 'And sit in the High Court?'

'Let's!' squealed Christine.

'We are all down for shifts in the morning. Nobody is going to Dublin,' Vera said sternly.

Conor peered at the piece of toilet paper Emily had handed him.

'What does "posset" mean?'

'Posset?' Emily peered too.

'It sounds like a small animal.'

'Oh, it's nothing to do with animals.' Emily was quite definite about that. She searched through more of the shiny, hard toilet paper upon which she'd made notes at Angela's class. 'Oh, here! It's when a baby pukes up some of its milk. Apparently, that's the baby's way of sorting out an over-full stomach.'

'No Rennies then,' Conor said.

Emily laughed. It sounded a bit incongruous. She stopped. 'Where were you all day, Conor?'

Conor did not tell her he'd been to Cork. He couldn't. 'I just had a few things to do.' He looked at her. 'As indeed you had yourself.'

'Yes,' Emily said. She didn't make any further explanation, just looked at him a bit defiantly.

'You've taken on a lot there,' Conor just said.

'I know, but Neasa will be doing most of the work,' Emily said. She gave a little defensive laugh. 'I just have to pay for it.'

She waited for Conor to say something very practical and very sensible, and therefore very soul-destroying. Reason was anathema to the idealism of sit-ins and court campaigns.

'Well, do what you have to do,' he said. 'You will anyway, whether I agree with you or not.'

'I did try to ring you, Conor,' Emily said, feeling very guilty now.

'After the event. Oh, look, it doesn't matter, Emily.'

He could not let her see just how much it mattered. Instead he went on quickly, 'I'm moving out.'

'Sorry?'

'Out of the house. I'm going to rent out on the Cork Road. It's just two miles from home – obviously I want to be near to you and the baby when you get out of hospital.'

Emily was totally shocked. She had not seen this one coming. Somehow she had thought that it would be her call.

'Why?'

'Why? Because things are wrong, Emily. You're not happy. I'm not happy. What's the point in bringing a child home to that?'

Emily's face felt a bit numb. He had organised all this and she hadn't even made any decisions yet! How could he have swung so quickly from wanting to move on to wanting to move *out*?

'I'm not even in the house – why can't you stay there for the moment?' she asked, hoping it didn't sound too desperate. This was too sudden, too severe.

Conor shook his head impatiently. 'That's just a half-measure. And I'm sick of half-measures.'

'So what are you saying? You're leaving me? It's over?'

'Sorry, I don't think I've made myself clear. I want us to start again, Emily. Independent of the baby. That's why I'm moving out.'

He seemed very definite about this and Emily would

do no more pleading with him to stay. She wondered how or when the tables had turned.

'So what are we going to do, draw up a little roster of times when you'll come by and see the baby?' She sounded a bit brittle.

'I certainly want to do more than just see the baby,' Conor said. 'Just because I won't live there doesn't mean I'm not going to get involved in looking after it.'

'Very noble,' Emily said. 'And what about me? Do I figure in this at all?'

'Well, we'd have to work something out there too. If you want to.'

'You mean, like, we'd meet up for *dates*? Oh, Conor, please!'

'You were the one who said the problems went right back,' he pointed out. 'So maybe we need to do the same.'

'I think you're being very simplistic,' she said. 'We can't make it all candlelight and roses again, Conor, however much we want to! That time has gone!'

'I never mentioned candlelight and roses.'

'But you think it can all be worked out by you running off.'

'I am not running off.'

'You are! Like you always do! Only this time you're actually moving out as well!'

Conor looked a bit tired. 'I don't blame you for thinking that. But that's not what I'm doing, Emily.'

'Really.'

'I'm moving out because before we know it, you'll be home with the baby, and we'll be too tired and stressed to think about anything else, and we'd just find some acceptable way of living together without sorting out anything really because it would just be easier.'

Emily took this as a direct insult. 'You mean I'd find it easier!'

'I might too.'

'But you really meant me. Well, let me tell you, my days of putting up with the second-rate are well and truly over!'

She hoped that this sounded very decisive and dramatic.

'Good,' Conor said. 'That goes for both of us.'

So now he thought *she* was second-rate? It was a wonder he didn't piss off to Australia or somewhere.

'There's a pair of us in it, Emily.'

'No, there is not. I didn't try and solve the problems by having an affair.'

Conor gave a small sigh. 'You see, this is what I mean. You're still angry. I'm still feeling guilty. There're all these feelings going around that are not going to be resolved while the baby possets in the background.'

He had a point and she hated him for it.

'What are we going to do, hire a baby-sitter while we go off and discuss feelings?'

'That's obviously something we'll have to think about.'

'They don't grow on trees, you know!' She flung

herself back in the bed and looked at him belligerently. 'And you're not a bit frightened that once we start living apart, we'll find that we like it better?'

'That's a possibility,' Conor said.

'And it's a risk you're prepared to take?'

'Yes,' he agreed, annoying her further.

She would not let him see her own anxiety. 'Are you sure now that you wouldn't like an open relationship while we're at it?'

'Oh, Emily.'

'Mind you, I don't know where I'd get time for other men, what with trying to keep a newborn alive, having meaningful discussions with you, and finding my waist again. All on my own!'

'You won't be on your own.'

'I will be! You've just said it! You're leaving me to cope on my own!' She blinked a bit fast. 'Look, this is a stupid idea, Conor! I need you back in the house when I come home!'

She had laid herself on the line. Conor said nothing for ages.

'For practical things, Emily. That's all.'

'Yes, for practical things!' She didn't want to get beyond this, she hadn't sorted out her own feelings yet. 'They're legitimate enough when I'm about to have a baby!'

'Okay,' Conor said. 'If that's what you want.'

'It is,' she said, less sure at his sudden capitulation.

'And neither of us will ever know whether we stayed

together for any other reason except practicalities,' he finished.

There had to be a catch of course. Blast him anyway for being one step ahead. Emily tried to fight it, but hadn't she already come to this impasse herself? Whether they loved each other enough at the end of the day?

'Oh, go then!' she said.

He told her that he would be moving out the day after tomorrow. Then he asked when he might come in and see her again. Like he was making a confounded date! Like this whole ridiculous nonsense had already started! Emily had presented him with the back of her head and he had left.

She seethed for ten minutes and then it came to her. Of course! It was so obvious! He was calling her bluff! By declaring that he was moving out, he was hoping to make her all jittery and insecure, fearful that she would actually lose him and that really, everything was fine and she'd only been pulling his leg about being unhappy. It was the oldest trick in the book!

The trouble was, Conor wasn't one for calling anybody's bluff. He couldn't even pull off a simple joke with any aplomb. He always ended up letting the punchline slip halfway through.

He really was going to move out.

Emily felt angry again. How come he had ended up in the driving seat? She'd love to be able to announce she was moving out! She still might! Why not? Why should she sit around the house waiting for a visit from him? With the added confusion of whether he'd come to see her or the baby? She'd be a nervous wreck!

Deep inside was an insidious feeling of relief. She could go home when all this was over and not be hurled into more drama. She would have enough of that, what with sterilising bottles and changing nappies. No, let him move out! She needed her 'space' too!

'What's wrong?' Maggie arrived back from walking the corridors in the hopes of bringing labour on. 'Did they not give us a spot in tomorrow's calendar for the hearing?'

'I'd like to see them try,' Emily spat. 'And it's not a "spot", Maggie, like we were entering a karaoke competition. It's called a listing.'

'So we have one?' Maggie asked doggedly. All her relatives would be asking when they came in later and she had to be sure to give them the latest facts. Apparently, Maggie's Aunt Amy's lodger's best friend worked in RTE. They were trying to get him to give the campaign a plug. He only worked on *The Late Late Christmas Toy Show*, but you never knew.

'Yes, we're listed for tomorrow afternoon, Maggie.'

Maggie hugged herself with excitement and wasn't even put out when Emily declined a game of bridge and said she was having an early night.

The next morning Creepy Crawley was forced to share the lift up to the third floor with two pregnant women.

He coped by pressing himself as far into the corner as he could, and keeping his eyes firmly on his shoes. They were highly polished and perfectly matched his intimidating three-piece suit. The last time he'd worn this suit was two years ago, when he'd gone to visit his wayward nephew in the local garda station over that nasty drunk and disorderly business.

The lift stopped and he elbowed his way out ahead of the pregnant women. The heat and the whiff of antiseptic made him reel, but he bravely headed for St Brenda's Ward. He wished now he'd thought to bring flowers or something. That would have been a good touch. You'd have thought Daphne Dunne would have suggested it, her being a woman. Not that she ever behaved like one. The language out of her this morning! F-ing this and f-ing that! And some B words that Creepy had never even heard before. Ewan seemed to know what she was talking about and had joined in with a few choice words of his own, most of which also seemed to begin with F and B. Oh, and one with a W. Now that Creepy thought about it, that one had been directed at him. It was most unfair. Just because he slobbered all over Neasa Martin didn't mean he had an obligation to know what she was up to all the time. No, that was Gary O'Reilly's department. Or Gary Gilmartin, as he'd taken to calling himself. There was no way *that* would end up on the headed notepaper.

Gary hadn't been invited in to the meeting. Not because of any conflict of interests, what with him apparently dating Neasa. He just never seemed to have anything useful to contribute. He would just join in the f-ing and b-ing because everyone else was doing it.

It was silly anyway, Creepy thought, to go losing the head. Reason was what was needed in this situation. Reason and tact and persuasion. Hence his presence in Martha's this morning.

'Emily! There you are.'

'Oh, hello, Charles.'

He was a bit taken aback. She never called him Charles. It was Mr Crawley to his face, or Creepy behind his back. And she didn't even bother to sit up in the bed.

'Just dropped by to see how you are,' he lied, trying out a big smile.

'Well, you can see for yourself,' Emily said, patting her belly.

Indeed he could. In fact, he had never seen anything like it, except in a documentary about sea lions. But her face looked the same, thankfully. He would be fine if he focused on that.

'And, ah, how long to go now?' he asked jovially. He knew that this was the kind of thing you should ask pregnant women. That, and had she thought of any names for it yet. Then maybe round off the conversation with a little joke about how she would have her hands full. Most of them just wanted you to notice that they were pregnant, Creepy believed, as if it had never happened to anybody else.

'Three weeks, minus a day or two,' Emily said.

'Well, well,' Creepy said meaninglessly. 'I always think Michael is a nice name. Or Jennifer, or Alan for that matter. Something sensible. You don't want to go lumbering it with something trendy like . . .' He couldn't think of any trendy name except from a song which had been playing on the radio on the way in, 'Fatboy Slim.'

'That isn't a name we're considering,' Emily assured him.

'It won't thank you when it gets teased in fourth class.' Creepy said this rather bitterly. Fourth class was a period in his life he would rather forget.

If Creepy got any more transparent he would disappear altogether, Emily thought. She wondered now how she had felt any loyalty towards him or any of the rest of them. But they thrived on people like her, vultures preying on hard-working moles desperate for a word of praise. Dangling partnerships in front her nose like a carrot in front of a donkey.

Emily wondered how she had got into this whole animal-comparison business. It was just that Creepy looked so much like a pig this morning, or a snake in the grass. Possibly he had been genetically modified to combine both.

'I suppose you're here about the hospital closure.'

Her directness momentarily flustered Creepy. This wasn't like Emily at all. Still, he supposed that they had them all on drugs in here. 'It has only come to our attention that we appear to be involved.'

Terry Mitton SC had called this morning to see if Neasa was on her way to Dublin. She was, and Creepy had taken the call instead. Imagine his surprise.

'We don't specialise in litigation, Emily,' he said gravely. 'We're in conveyancing.'

'Right,' Emily said slowly, as though she hadn't spent six years taking two percent on Creepy's behalf. 'So I'm on my own, in other words.'

'No no no no,' Creepy said, when he actually meant yes yes yes yes. 'It's Neasa we have the problem with really. She should have informed us.'

'And instead she's on her way to the High Court right now,' Emily said cheerfully.

Creepy gave an involuntary shudder at the mere mention of the High Court. 'Yes, and frankly, we feel it is not our place,' he said, unsmiling.

Emily looked at him pleasantly enough. 'It's my fault. You see, I didn't think you'd mind representing me, after me working so hard for you all these years.'

Creepy was ready for this. 'Absolutely.'

'With very little reward,' Emily added.

'You *did* get that bonus we credited to everyone's account only last week?' he enquired with a smarmy smile.

'You know what I mean, Charles.' Her expression was flat and unyielding, and Creepy's Joop! deodorant started to experience its first real pressure. Maybe he should have sent Daphne in. Emily's hormones had obviously done something horrible to her, and Creepy was not an expert in this field.

He cleared his throat. 'Funny, we were just review-ing the partnership situation earlier. And I'm delighted to be able to inform you now that you're up for a partnership.'

'I've been up for it before,' Emily said.

'No, I mean you've got it this time. Or, you will in due course once we've ironed out any mis-understandings.'

Emily had to resist the urge to spit on his three-piece suit. Honestly, was the whole world out to compromise, pressure, coerce and generally screw you over? What had happened to all the nice, decent people? Had they become part of the screw-you brigade because that was the only way to protect themselves?

Emily resolved that to become hardboiled was even worse than being a pushover. The prospect of living her life like she was on a survival course was too bleak, always looking over her shoulder for the Creepies of this world. Surely it was possible to be nice and still avoid being screwed?

'If Crawley Dunne & O'Reilly wants to back out, then fine.' She didn't lower herself to refer to the partner-ship. She just let him see from her face exactly what she thought of him, what she'd always thought of him behind that supplicant smile. 'I'll find someone else to represent me. There are plenty of them out there. I'll file for a change of solicitor in the morning. Now, if you don't mind, I'm going for a nap.'

Creepy found himself back on the corridor, scarcely able to credit that he had been dismissed. He should feel triumphant really. After all, he had got what he wanted, which was to be shot of this, with no fuss. And he hadn't even had to admit that there was no partnership. He'd made it up on the spot. Daphne and Ewan would be delighted with the outcome, and they could all go on selling land with gusto.

No, there was absolutely no reason at all to feel a bit, well, sneaky and sly and low.

Which he was, of course – it was just that nobody had had the bottle to point it out to him before. And Emily had always been so nice, too. That's what was so disappointing about this whole thing. Where were all the nice people gone, Creepy wondered?

'Save Martha's!'

'We say NO to closure!'

'Save Martha's!'

'We say NO – mind that bloody placard, Darren, you've snagged my tights – to CLOSURE!'

'Sorry. Save Martha's! We say – oh look, here comes Chapman – NO to CLOSURE!'

The band of protesters outside Martha's, its ranks swollen twenty-fold with news of the court case, stopped to gawk in the window of Mr Chapman's car. He eased indifferently past them as though they were a flock of stray sheep. Then someone actually planted herself in front of his car. Mr Chapman's foot never wavered from the accelerator, and the protestor was forced to dive to one side or else lose a limb.

'Save MARTHA'S!'

'We SAY NO TO CLOSURE!' they screamed after him.

Yes, well, it wasn't up to them, Mr Chapman thought, and a jolly good thing too. He swung into a disabled parking space at the doors of the hospital and sat there for a moment.

He wasn't due to see Emily Collins today. But management had let it be known in their inimitable fashion that his presence was necessary at Martha's. He had coldly asked them whether they believed Mr Dunphy and Mr O'Mara, Martha's consultants, couldn't take proper care of her. On the contrary, they had insisted. But nobody wanted to ruffle any feathers what with the High Court hearing this afternoon. Check her out. Best be on the safe side.

It was as though Emily Collins, by her own actions, had ceased to become a patient for whom medical care was her basic right. She was now a political agenda and medical care would be dispensed accordingly. Plenty of it, it was true, but this was not a situation Mr Chapman was at all comfortable with. It only served to highlight for him how skewed his path had really become.

He had spent the morning arranging to abort his own grandchild. Henry Maher had informed him that his daughter would not be picking a clinic out of a UK phonebook and going over on a cheap flight like she were some little scrubber. Mr Chapman would use his contacts to get her the best doctor, the best clinic. Mr Chapman would also pay all expenses.

He had done it all, even booked the flights. Two return tickets. If this was what Killian wanted, then he would damned well go over with her. He would not shirk *that* responsibility. They would take a week off school, the pair of them, on sick notes which Mr Chapman had also organised.

Hannah had said this morning that he must make the peace with Killian, that the boy was genuinely affected and that he needed their support. Mr Chapman had not even said goodbye to him as he was leaving.

News of the application to keep Martha's temporarily open spilled into the car from the radio. All the Cork radio stations were carrying it. Whether a full judicial review of the hospital closure would be granted would not be known until a later date, the newsreader informed him.

If they got an order to keep Martha's open, they wouldn't be hearing about it on the Cork radio stations. No, they'd be looking at it on the bloody RTE six o'clock news.

Something caught his eye and he looked up. There was Emily Collins in the window above, gesticulating wildly down at Mr Chapman. Good God, what on earth was she doing?

She mouthed something at him, desperately.

'What!' he shouted, as though she could hear him.

She pointed again, face growing more and more pan-icked. Was the woman in labour or something? Then she shut her eyes in resignation just as Mr Chapman was pitched forward in his seat. What the hell . . .?

It took him a moment to realise that he had been rear-ended. Or, more precisely, that someone had backed into his stationary car. The person didn't even notice. He heard a crunching of gears and the offending car moved off smoothly. Behind him, the protesters broke into laughter and a round of applause.

'I'm terribly sorry,' Emily said again. 'It's just that she's not used to driving at night.'

'It isn't night,' Mr Chapman pointed out testily. 'It's three o'clock in the afternoon.'

'She shouldn't really be on the roads any time after lunch,' Emily confided. 'Is there much damage to your car?'

'I haven't looked yet.' He had. The rear fender was dented, and the H on his customised number plate, CHAP, had been damaged. Now it read suspiciously like CLAP. He watched Emily Collins closely now for signs of amusement, but could find none.

Emily felt awful. Pauline hadn't even called by expressly to see her. Oh, no! She'd been dropping Paddy Byrne and Mrs Conlon down to the gates, because they'd wanted to join the protest and neither of them could drive – not that Pauline could either. Pauline had called up to see Emily as an afterthought.

'I'll get her insurance policy number for you.' Emily was anxious to make amends.

'That won't be necessary,' Mr Chapman said stiffly. The last thing on this earth he needed was more legal wranglings with the Collins clan. He would pay for the damage out of his own pocket. And if Emily Collins ever became pregnant again, or if any of her extended family became pregnant, or indeed any friend or remote acquaintance or even a pen pal of hers, Mr Chapman would see to it that his books were full.

He really was decent, Emily thought, not to try and claim for the damage off her poor mother. From the look on his face earlier, she'd thought he might even try and press charges.

'Take it in cash then,' she said.

'Sorry?'

He watched, astounded, as Emily took out her wash-bag, unzipped a little pocket inside and held out a bundle of cash to him.

'There's about two hundred pounds there.'

'I don't want it,' Mr Chapman blurted. Like a lot of rich people, the sight of cold hard cash embarrassed him, even though he gladly took large amounts of it in cheque form.

'It's Mam's anyway,' Emily insisted. 'She gave it to me to buy something for the baby.'

Mr Chapman felt even more embarrassed. Now she was taking the food out of her child's mouth to give to him!

'It's not necessary,' he said again, face hot.

Emily looked at him to make sure he was serious, before putting the money away. 'That's very kind of you.'

'Don't mention it.'

'So long as you're sure,' she said earnestly. 'I was just thinking earlier, there are so many people out there ready to do you over. I just didn't want you thinking that me or my mother is one of those people.'

Mr Chapman had rarely seen an expression of such utter sincerity, and it unnerved him further. And on a solicitor, too.

'Let's get on with the examination, shall we?' he said quickly, before she could make him feel any worse. At least no doctors or interns or nurses or anybody else was looking over his shoulder. He would not countenance it after his spectacular humiliation at Emily Collins' mother's hand. And that porter, Tommy or something, had had the audacity to tell him that he shouldn't have parked in a disabled space in the first place. And now he felt bad about that too!

He cleared his throat loudly. 'Any more bleeding?'

'No.'

'Any pains?'

'Just the usual.'

'Any discharge?'

'No.'

'Anything unusual at all?'

'Well, I have been feeling a bit breathless.'

Not so breathless that she couldn't instruct a solicitor, Mr Chapman thought, feeling a bit feistier now.

'That's usual. The baby is crowding your internal organs due to its size. And also the extra weight you're carrying makes your heart and lungs do more work.'

He reviewed her chart again. Her blood pressure was stable. Her urine had been clear for weeks now. Even the puffiness had gone down. She had colour in her cheeks and the baby was kicking away like a rugby player. Far from this ridiculous campaign increasing her stress levels, he would go so far as to say that she was thriving on it!

'What do you think?' she asked anxiously.

What Mr Chapman thought was that she should be discharged right now. She didn't need to be in hospital. She should be at home, taking it easy and waiting for labour to commence naturally.

He should just walk out to the nurses' station and tell Vera Mooney to send her home.

He was her consultant, wasn't he? He had the authority to do it! And he would stand over his decision, which was medically the right one. Her chart said so. It would back him up every inch of the way. In fact, she could have grounds for complaint if he *didn't* discharge her.

And that would be the end of the sit-in. The rest of them would fall like dominoes. The whole court action might even run out of steam. Get her home in front of the telly and away from the frontline and her cough would soon soften.

Of course, she might refuse to go. But it was one thing to refuse to be transferred to Cork; another thing entirely to refuse to leave a hospital after she had been discharged. Taking up precious resources, beds and money when she didn't need them. Wait until the papers got hold of *that*.

It would be one great weight off Mr Chapman's mind, one way of getting some control back in his life.

She was waiting for his prognosis, her little heart-shaped face anxious and open. Imagine, a woman like her, thirty-seven weeks pregnant, standing up to the might of the Department of Health and Children! How could she hope to win? It was preposterous. Really, he would be doing her a favour in more ways than one.

He wrote the word 'discharge' on the bottom of her chart and signed his name under it. Or at least he tried to. His hand refused to wield the pen. He was afraid that if he persisted, his hand would write something like Homer Simpson, the star of Killian's favourite TV show which blared through the house every evening, setting Mr Chapman's nerves on edge. It had not been on this past week, Mr Chapman suddenly thought.

He fumbled with his pen again, and it slipped from his fingers to the floor.

'Are you feeling all right?' Emily prompted eventually, concerned.

Mr Chapman looked at her with dislike, sick of her concern and her sincerity, sick of her bloody morals, when he had left his behind in some locker room many years ago out of necessity and was now trying to recapture through his son.

In a temper, he picked up the pen and drew a sharp line through the word 'discharge'. Fine! Let her fight the fight if that's what she wanted! Let her see that she was up against a system that was as unyielding as it was archaic! He would like to see what illusions she had left *then*. Oh, they had all been there, every last one of them.

'I'm keeping you in, okay!'

'Um, okay. Is anything wrong?'

'*Wrong?* Ha!' He made an effort to lower his voice. 'No. Nothing wrong. Just for observation.'

'Okay.' She gave him a crooked little smile. 'Although it would have been quite nice to go home.'

Mr Chapman's eyes popped. Honestly! There was no pleasing some people!

'I'll see you Friday,' he said grimly, and stomped out.

She was really starting to like Mr Chapman, Emily decided. He was a stuffy old stick, granted, and she had been dreading what he might say about the sit-in and court case. But he had behaved very professionally about the whole thing. And he had been very sweet about the car business. It just went to show that once you got to know people, they were generally very nice – unless they were Creepy Crawley or Daphne or Ewan or Eamon Clancy or Nurse Christine or Gary or any number of others, of course. No, she was glad now that she had held onto her optimism despite everything.

She reached for her mobile to ring Conor and fill him

in on Chapman's visit. After all his talk of 'starting again', there hadn't been a peep out of him for a whole day. He was probably busy moving the TV and stereo and cappuccino-maker and most of their furniture into his new residence on the Cork Road. Just so long as he left the electric kettle. She would need that to make bottles for the baby, Angela had said. That's if she didn't get the hang of breastfeeding. It had been fairly hammered home in antenatal classes that this was the best for the baby, the implication being that women who didn't at least try were denying their child a higher IQ. But Emily and Neasa and every other person of their generation had been reared on SMA. If you thought about it, the whole Celtic Tiger economy was *built* on SMA. And Soda Stream after that.

'Hello?' Conor said.

'I don't know if I'm going to breastfeed,' Emily informed him loftily.

'Emily?'

'Of course it's Emily. Anyway, have you any objections?' she said in a voice that defied him to have any.

'Well, I hate to point out the obvious, but they're your breasts.'

'I'm glad we agree on something.'

There was a suspicious thud in the background.

'Are you moving the TV?' she asked.

'What? No. I'm in the attic.'

'What are you doing in the attic?'

'Pottering.'

'Nobody potters in the attic.'

'Looking for things, then.'

Emily looked at the phone as though it were his face. 'Conor,' she said, 'my trust in you has taken a severe battering. Now we can talk about starting again all we like, but if you don't make some effort to win my trust back, then you'd better extend your lease on the Cork Road.'

A small silence. 'I'm sorry. You're right. I didn't tell you because, well, it's stupid.'

'Tell me anyway.'

'I'm looking for that music score.'

'What music score?'

'Um, the one I wrote myself.'

'I see.'

'Tried to write. It's not as though I *finished* it or anything. I just thought of it yesterday and . . . well, I decided to look for it. That's all. Anyway, I can't find it, so it doesn't matter.'

'Have you looked in that box over by the water tank?' Emily enquired eventually.

'The box the stereo came in?'

'No, the foot-spa box.'

'I didn't know we had a foot-spa.'

'We don't – oh, look, it doesn't matter. Just try it.'

She heard him picking his way carefully across the attic beams. They'd never got around to laying down a floor. She hoped he wouldn't put his foot through the

347

ceiling of the baby's room. Now she heard him opening the box.

'It's full of birthday cards. My God, Emily, from when you were twelve!'

Emily maintained a dignified silence. Conor kept nothing. He even threw out *The Sunday Times* on a Monday morning, when there was reading in it for the whole week.

'There's my bicycle light!' he marvelled. 'I've been looking for that for years!'

Emily did not know how his bicycle light had ended up in the attic and she wasn't about to get into it now. He said nothing for a minute.

'Conor?' she asked impatiently.

'Sorry, Emily . . .' He seemed very preoccupied.

'What have you found now?'

'Nothing,' he said. 'Anyway, here it is. The music score.'

'I told you,' she said, quietly triumphant. You see, there were advantages to being married to someone like her after all.

She could hear pages turning. He would be wearing his funny I'm-in-music-mode expression. Well, this time she wouldn't be excluded.

'What did you want it for?' she asked.

'I just had this idea that I might, you know, finish it.' He sounded embarrassed again.

Emily thought back to the time when Conor used to compose music. Somehow he never seemed to get anywhere with it. Then the steady job with the orchestra came along and he stopped writing altogether.

'And why don't you?' she asked.

'I don't know . . . I don't even know why I'm digging this stuff out.'

Maggie drifted past with her Kittensoft toilet roll. Emily turned away. Somehow this seemed very intimate.

'I suppose like yourself, I've been doing a lot of thinking about everything really,' Conor eventually said. 'And maybe I was stuck in a rut with the orchestra.'

Mary Murphy popped unbidden into Emily's mind, brandishing her violin victoriously. Emily took the violin, broke it smartly over her knee, and handed it back. Now go away, Mary.

'I thought you liked the orchestra,' she said.

'I did. But maybe I'm tired of playing other people's music.'

She could hear him sitting down. She too lay back on the pillow.

'Finish a piece then,' she said.

'It's not as simple as that, Emily. I mean, I don't know if I can. I don't know if any of it's any good.'

'It is good. It's great.'

'Yeh.' He was brushing her off.

'What, just because I'm not a music buff doesn't mean I can't tell good from bad.'

'Emily, you like Country and Western.'

'You've just never listened to the lyrics,' she said huffily.

'And I've heard your music. I know it's good.'

'When have you heard it?'

She didn't want to tell him about standing outside the living-room door on Saturday mornings while he practised. On some Saturdays he wouldn't practise at all; he would play something she had never heard before, with frequent stops in the middle, and she would know it was his own stuff.

'You're right, Conor. I haven't listened to it because you've never played it for me,' she said instead.

'You never asked,' he said back.

'My mistake.'

'Mine too.'

There was a funny little silence now. Conor eventually cleared his throat.

'All the baby's things are in that box, Emily.'

'What?' She wanted to make him say it, to acknowledge it.

'The first baby's things.' A beat. 'Our first baby.'

'Yes. I wanted to put them away before this baby arrived. There's not much.'

Just a few Babygros bought in the hot excitement of that first pregnancy, a cuddly toy, and pair of tiny white socks that had made her heart feel all funny.

'I didn't want to use them for this baby. It didn't seem fair to it, like it was being forced to carry baggage that had nothing to do with it. But it didn't seem fair to our first baby to put its things away in the attic like so much rubbish, like it never even existed. And it did, Conor.'

She wondered was he holding those things now. She thought he might be.

'I thought it would be better if I were strong,' he said eventually. 'Or at least looked to be strong. I thought it wouldn't be much help if I went to pieces too. It didn't work, did it?'

'No. For either of us.'

'Emily? Are you all right?'

'Yes, fine.' She was probably better than him right now. 'What are you going to do now?'

She was half-hoping that he would say that he would jump in the car and come and see her.

'I don't know. I suppose finish up here and start moving my things out.'

'So you're still moving out.' She felt a bit flat.

'Emily, you're much better at all this stuff than me.' She knew what he meant, not that she would agree with him. She was just farther down the line. 'I don't want to rush in there and get it wrong.'

'Okay. If that's what you want.'

They said goodbye and Emily hung up and she felt less angry, less bewildered than she had in weeks.

The outcome of the court application came via an unusual source.

'I hear on the radio that you won,' Eamon Clancy said, his jolly red face not in the slightest bit jolly today. 'Again.'

'Just the once,' Emily clarified. 'It's only the first stage of a long, drawn-out procedure.'

'You know what I mean.'

'I'm afraid I don't, Eamon.'

He waved a sheet of paper in her face. 'What's the meaning of this?'

'What is it, Eamon?' she asked calmly. A vein throbbed wildly in his forehead and she was afraid it might burst. Still, he was in the right place.

'It's a demand for maintenance!' Eamon shouted.

People seemed to come into this hospital and shout at her a lot, Emily had noticed. Her advanced pregnancy didn't seem to put them off at all. To stop any more hysterics, she whipped the piece of paper from him and perused it.

'It's a demand for maintenance.'

'I know it is. I just said it is!' He looked at her maliciously. 'You've some nerve. But you were always like that. So superior, with your fancy job and your fancy piano-playing husband, looking down on the rest of us, like builders are the scum of the earth or something!' He waited for her to contradict him and was eventually forced to move on. 'And now you're drawing up maintenance demands against me!'

'It's actually Liz who wants the money, Eamon. Not me personally. I just looked after the paperwork. In fact, I didn't even do that, for obvious reasons. I believe Phil in the office handled it in the end.'

'Well, here's what I think of your maintenance demand!' And he tore it in half, something he had obviously been anticipating most of the day.

'Oh stop it,' Emily said, tired of him now. 'How do you think Liz is supposed to feed and clothe those boys?'

'She can do it for less than three hundred and fifty pounds a week!'

'Eamon, those boys go through five packets of corn-flakes a week!'

'Don't talk to me about cornflakes,' Eamon said grimly. 'Don't talk to me about twenty-five litres of milk! Or ten pounds of bananas, two big bags of potatoes, twenty-one yoghurts – but Mikey has decided he likes yoghurts again, so that'll go up to twenty-eight a week now!'

'Twenty-eight yoghurts a week?' Emily was shocked.

'Not to mention the sixty-three nappies a week Willy and Mikey go through between them,' Eamon went on heatedly. 'And the seven night-nappies Bobby still needs. Do you know how much a nappy costs?'

'Ten pence?'

'Ten pence!'

'Um, fifteen, then.'

'Twenty-five pence apiece! That's what a nappy costs, unless you go for those own-brand ones – and to be honest I wouldn't advise you to because they're not as good and you only end up forking out at the other end for detergent to wash soiled clothes.'

'Ah, thanks, I'll bear that in mind.'

'Anyway, don't you be telling me how much it costs

to rear a child, because I know,' he said, hitching up his jeans belligerently. Like most other builders, the waistband periodically slid down to settle somewhere around his knees. Emily wondered whether there was a special store that only builders shopped in.

'Sorry, Eamon, I didn't mean to . . .'

'Don't try and tell me only women *really* know about rearing children!'

'Yes, you've made your point.'

Satisfied that he had, he went on, 'Hasn't the cost of them five fellas been on my mind ever since the business got into trouble? What was I supposed to do? Throw up my hands and say, "Ah well, it didn't work out. Sure we'll have to make do on the dole?" And they roaring and shouting for fuckin' Teletubby videos and trips to McDonald's and I'm supposed to tell them that I can't afford it?' He took a few quick breaths. 'I couldn't tell her – Liz. Jesus Christ, how do you tell your wife that you can't support your family any more?'

Emily felt uncomfortable in the face of his emotion. Eamon, the hard man. 'You're going to have to involve her. Make decisions together.'

'Give up on the business, you mean.'

'That's a matter for the two of you.'

She didn't want to be dispensing advice to Eamon, as though she were a raging success in the marital department herself.

'Can't you talk to her or something?' Eamon asked.

'No. I can't.'

'As her solicitor. You could advise her—'

'No! Do your own dirty work, Eamon!' She moved on swiftly before he got all testy again. 'Anyway, I'm delighted you called around.'

'You are?'

'Yes, I was wondering what kind of a price you could do me to lay an attic floor?'

'What?'

'Our attic floor at home. I'm looking for an estimate.'

Eamon was very taken aback.

'And no cutting corners, Eamon, not like the last time.'

'I didn't cut corners!'

'You didn't level the ground under the patio properly either. Two of the stones are very uneven already.'

Eamon scratched his head. 'They weren't uneven when I laid them.'

'They're uneven now. And I don't want my child going head over heels on its tricycle when I let it out to play.'

'God, no. Of course not,' Eamon said quickly.

'There could be a terrible accident.'

'There could. There could. I'm sorry about that, Emily.'

'Will you have a look at it?'

'Of course I will! Straightaway.'

'No rush,' Emily said generously. 'Any time in the next few days is okay.'

'You can count on it,' Eamon said fervently. 'And I'll bring you in that estimate tomorrow, okay?'

'Just drop it by the house, Eamon,' Emily said hastily. 'Whenever you're doing the patio stones.'

Suddenly he was very suspicious. 'I don't want any handouts, you know. You and Conor throwing me a bit of work out of pity.'

Emily sighed. 'Do you want to do the job or not? Because I can go to Paudie Coyle instead.'

'That cowboy!' Eamon exploded. It appeared that even amongst cowboy builders, Paudie Coyle was in a league of his own. 'He'd skimp on the wood so much that you'd be falling down through the cracks.'

'Kind of like my patio stones then.'

'I said I'd sort that out,' Eamon said, and stomped out.

Emily felt quite proud of herself. At least now he would lay the attic floor on time, and they wouldn't be waiting nine months like they had for the patio. Imagine, after all these years, she had finally learned how to deal with builders.

'Oh my God!' she suddenly squealed.

Maggie looked up from her birth plan, which she had been studying in an effort to work out why she was overdue. 'What? What?'

'I nearly forgot! We got the order to keep Martha's open!'

'Oh my God!' Maggie squealed too, jumping up and down like a lunatic and clapping her hands. Emily was a bit worried that her waters might break.

'Not permanently, Maggie,' she hastily clarified. 'We still have to apply for leave to seek a judicial review, and only then is the real fight on—'

Maggie didn't care. 'We won! We won!' And she went galloping out to the nurses' station to break the news.

Emily watched the rejoicing from her bed. She knew that they all thought it was down to her, and it was in a small way. But she just wasn't the type of person who enjoyed being in the limelight all that much. And really, she thought, there wasn't a damned thing wrong with that either.

Neasa wore a pink, shag-me-now dress to the partners' dinner. But she balanced it out by wearing her hair in a chic, tasteful roll and not a scrap of make-up except for lip-gloss, which she touched up now in the restaurant loo. She didn't bother twisting this way and that in front of the mirror, searching for cellulite or unsightly bulges. She was one of those rare women who loved every single inch of her body. No, given the chance, she often thought modestly, she wouldn't change a single thing about herself. Well, there was the naturally dull brown hair, but why whinge when the supermarkets were stacked high with black dye? And if some part of her happened to displease her some day, she would just go and get it straightened, or pumped up, or sucked out, or cut off. Cosmetic surgery easily tipped the pill as the best thing that ever happened to women in her opinion. And she wouldn't go around spouting that nonsense about how she'd had her boobs or nose done so that she would feel better about herself, and upping her self-esteem. Hell no, forget that PC shit. It was all about sex, and bettering the odds for *more* sex, at the end of the day. Anybody who said otherwise was deluding herself.

Back at the table, Creepy almost did himself an injury in his enthusiasm to hold out her chair for her. On her other side, Ewan O'Reilly placed her napkin on her lap and patted her knees rather slavishly.

Opposite Neasa, Daphne Dunne picked up where she had left off five minutes ago. 'A great win for you, a great win,' she repeated again, her bulbous eyes glazed from champagne.

'For us *all*, Daphne,' Neasa said sincerely. She felt a bit superior because she'd put away twice as much champagne as Daphne and didn't look remotely stupid on it.

'No, credit where credit is due,' Ewan boomed. 'I was just saying earlier that we don't always show our firm's talents to their best advantage. Crawley Dunne & O'Reilly could have a great future in litigation.'

'No, *I* said that, Ewan,' Daphne interjected strongly. 'Why should we be stuck selling marshy land when there are people crying out to be represented in court?'

'You've had some interest then?' Neasa enquired.

'A bit,' Creepy said, guarded.

Regina in the office had told her that the phone had

started to hop the minute the word filtered down about Neasa's triumph. The firm was already considering two substantial actions against insurance companies, a contested will, a red-hot negligence claim and two criminal defences. Not that they would touch the criminal stuff. Criminals generally didn't have the kind of money that Crawley Dunne & O'Reilly would be charging.

'I believe you were on LKR fm, Ewan,' Neasa simpered. 'Talking about Emily's action.'

'Oh! That! Very embarrassing. To be honest, Neasa, I was just winging it.' He had adored every minute of it. They'd had to cut him off in the end due to time constraints.

Neasa smiled around at them all as though she loved them, and then got the boot in. 'I take it we can ask Emily not to file that change of solicitor motion then?'

Daphne, Ewan and Creepy looked at each other as though they had been caught smoking behind the bike shed.

'That was a misunderstanding, Neasa,' Creepy eventually muttered.

'That's not what she told me.'

Daphne shot Creepy a filthy look before planting her two dimpled elbows on the table and pitching forward into Neasa's face. She tried to look confidential.

'We were worried about her taking on something like this when she's so pregnant. That's all.'

Neasa had a great urge to tell them they were right fuckers and that she would rather eat swill out of a trough with a crowd of pigs than dine with them tonight. But she wasn't that drunk, and sometimes there were advantages to be gained by not always shooting her mouth off. She'd learned a lot from Terry Mitton SC this afternoon. In fact, she felt that she had matured quite a bit by the whole experience.

'Emily's very hurt and annoyed,' she said, and this was the truth. 'She refuses to withdraw her application to change solicitors.' This wasn't true at all.

She waited now until she saw them trembling.

'In fact, she's found a solicitor who will do it for nothing just for the publicity.'

This was a total whopper altogether.

'We can do it for nothing,' Daphne eventually said.

'We'll waive all costs,' Ewan butted in quickly.

'She did give us six years of service,' Creepy said. As usual, everything he said to Neasa managed to sound vaguely sexual.

'But there's Terry Mitton's fees. And all the court fees,' Neasa said bluntly.

'They've offered to pay those?' Daphne closed her eyes in pain. That would put a dent in her partner's bonus. A minor dent.

Neasa was about to give a little speech about what a fantastic cause it was, and how the community would respect them for standing up on their behalf, but rightly suspected that this would only weaken her argument with them.

The partners shifted and looked at each other in

anguish. Eventually Ewan spoke.

'I think we can do that. Can we, Daphne?'

'I think so, Ewan. Do you think we can do that, Creepy?'

'Charles. Yes, I think we can. What do you think, Neasa?'

And they all looked at her.

'Let's do it,' she said magnanimously, and they all felt great.

'Oh, look, your glass is empty again, Neasa. I'll order more champagne,' Daphne twittered.

They fussed and fretted and fawned over her, and she let them. It was Emily really who should be basking in the adulation. But in her absence, Neasa might as well enjoy it. And in fairness, she had spared Emily the hassle of selling her newborn to pay the legal fees.

'Now, do tell us all about your day in court,' Daphne insisted.

'Oh, do,' Creepy said, wiping away drool with his napkin.

Neasa proceeded to do so with gusto, giving herself a rather more central role than she'd actually had.

At the far end of the table – at the *unfashionable* end – Gary watched her give forth with a mixture of rage and jealousy. This was his dinner! His inauguration! And he was being upstaged by his own girlfriend!

Not that anybody knew she had come as his partner. He'd even been denied the chance to parade her as his appendage, the only reason he'd wanted her here in the first place. No, she had been personally invited by Creepy and the partners because of her victory in the High Court, and had come under her own steam. Not as anybody's girlfriend. It was enough to make him puke up his wild-mushroom tartlet.

Well, he wouldn't even shag her after this! She didn't deserve it! And let her put around rumours about his lack of libido! He'd have sex with Annabel on the photocopier at the first opportunity and send around copies of the event over the internal email. Then everybody would know how great he was.

The partners boomed with laughter at the top of the table, and Gary's rage and insecurity grew. She had stripped him of everything, he believed, even his masculinity! And now she was coaxing the partners down the road of litigation, when Gary was firmly a conveyancing man. If she had her way, he'd be reduced to making the coffee. Which he already did, he realised with a dull shock.

'Would sir like black pepper?' the waiter asked.

Gary looked up coldly. 'Sir would like black pepper when and only when his steak arrives rare as ordered! Not burnt to a crisp!'

He had meant to sound authoritative and experienced. He just sounded loud and ignorant, and the table fell silent. It was the wrong thing to have done. Again.

'Actually, I don't mind having well-done steak,' Neasa said casually into the void. 'Why don't we just swap plates?'

It was accomplished in ten seconds and everyone nodded in approval at her diplomacy. Gary stared at his plate, disapproval crushing him. And his steak knife and fork had gone with his steak down to Neasa, and he had none. He couldn't bear to draw attention to himself again. He would have to eat his dinner with a spoon, like he was a child.

She had done her best to spare him embarrassment, Neasa thought a bit self-righteously. He might at least have shot her a grateful look. But then again, she wasn't paying much attention to him. And he was staring at his plate, looking very sour and down, and nothing like the love of her life.

She felt guilty, which was most unlike her. She would probably break his heart later when she told him it was all over. He was still in love with her, that much was plain.

But what else was she to do? He was not The One. She couldn't imagine now how she had ever thought he was The One.

Terry Mitton had asked her out. Not blatantly, there was a certain professional code to be observed. He was as gorgeous in the flesh as he'd sounded on the phone. Maybe a bit short at five-foot-nine, but she charitably decided she could overlook that. And so intelligent and cultured, and he filled his white wig wonderfully. He had hinted at lunch. She hadn't said yes, of course. Best not look too keen. But she'd go. It was a little secret she'd been hugging to herself all evening.

Oh goody. Here came more champagne. She must take another trip to the loo first. This pink dress did not look its best on full stomachs or full bladders.

She met Gary coming out of the Men's.

'Enjoying yourself?' she asked kindly. She would be very mature and nice about all this.

'No,' Gary said shortly.

'I know,' Neasa said sympathetically. 'Daphne can really go on when she's drunk, can't she?'

'I wouldn't go pointing any fingers there, Neasa, if I were you.'

Oh dear, he was going to be difficult about this. Still, she must soldier on.

'Maybe we could have a drink together later,' she said. 'At my place.'

'No thanks.'

'We need to talk, Gary.'

He fixed her with a really nasty look and she was a bit surprised. 'Fine,' he said. 'How about nine o'clock in the morning? I'm free then.'

Neasa gave a little laugh. 'Nine is a bit severe.'

'And you'll be struggling with a hangover.'

'I should think we all will after tonight, Gary.'

'But you have more practice than most.'

What was his point here? She started to get a bit annoyed. After she had made the effort to be so civil, too! Still, she reasoned, he could probably see the writing on the wall and was desperately trying to avoid the issue. Well, Neasa was not one for avoidance, no sirree.

'I don't think we're all that suited, Gary,' she said bluntly.

'You've got that right,' Gary said, rather stunning her. 'I don't know what would keep you happy. Fucking Superman.'

He looked very vicious now and Neasa was wary. 'If you feel like that, Gary, maybe we should call it a day.'

Gary stuck his big fleshy face into hers. 'You got there a split second before me, babe.'

Neasa's mouth fell open. 'Don't call me babe!'

'Why not? I can say what the hell I like now you're not like a stone around my neck. Fuck, I feel reborn!'

Neasa looked at this foul-mouthed, sweaty, vicious creature in front of her and it finally hit her. 'My God. You're a creep.'

'I know! I'm a total creep!' Gary cried with relief. 'That's what I've been trying to tell you all along! But would you listen? Oh no! You thought I was Mother Teresa with sex thrown in!'

Neasa felt a bit sick. 'You fooled me.'

'Yeh, well, you fooled me too.'

'I did not!' Neasa was outraged. 'How have I fooled you?'

'Mind you, it took me a long time to see it,' Gary went on slowly. 'Because you do it so well. You don't even see it yourself, do you?'

Neasa felt afraid. 'Go away, Gary.'

'You're a fucking lush, Neasa.'

She laughed very loudly. 'Oh Gary. Take your

wounded male pride and piss off.'

Gary looked at her with a funny expression. 'I'd be delighted to. I'm not looking for true love at the bottom of a bottle.'

You'd have thought Neasa would have come in this morning, Emily thought crossly. Their quick phone conversation yesterday afternoon had covered none of the juicy details of the court appearance. Neasa had rushed off to get ready for the partners' dinner, leaving Emily to find out this morning from the *Examiner* that the application for leave to seek a judicial review of the closure of Martha's had been set for Monday week, due to the urgency of the situation. Still, it was the weekend. Neasa was probably in bed with a hangover and Gary.

'This doesn't happen in John Grisham books,' Maggie said, cross too. Tiernan's relatives had started ringing up in droves to see had she had the baby yet. She felt the pressure mounting on her. And not so much as a twinge.

'Yes, well, this is reality, Maggie,' Emily said tartly.

But there was a bit of a sense of anti-climax in Brenda's Ward, and indeed, across the hospital. The euphoria of the win had gradually worn off, especially when it had sunk in that they really hadn't won anything concrete at all. Martha's would stay open, of course, until this thing was decided. That was something, Emily supposed.

'Does this mean we're not doing a sit-in any more?' Maggie wanted to know.

'What?'

'Well, if the hospital is staying open . . .'

'I don't know, do I?' This constant questioning was getting on her wick.

'You'd have thought they'd have given us a bigger piece in the *Examiner*,' Maggie added, further peeved. They'd got four column inches on page 5. 'They don't capture any of the emotion of the thing!'

'At least we got covered,' Emily said shortly. Maggie expected miracles! Emily wished that Maggie would have her blasted baby and stop driving them all mad.

Maggie rooted in her locker and looked up at Emily accusingly. 'Have you been using my toilet roll again?'

'I have not been using your toilet roll.. I wouldn't dare.'

'That's not fair! Aren't I always letting you use my Sure?'

It was like they were eighteen again and sharing a cramped flat, with all the attendant squabbles and minor irritations. Maggie's toilet habits and the way she picked at her teeth after meals were greatly getting on Emily's nerves. Emily, of course, couldn't see anything about herself at all that might annoy Maggie. Apart from borrowing her deodorant, which was such a minor offence! But that was Maggie for you.

'I'm going for a walk on the corridors,' Emily said loftily.

'Go then! It might improve your mood.'

The corridors were depressingly familiar. Emily looked in vain for a stray wheelchair. She'd had a ride around in one yesterday just for something different.

She walked on fast, edgy and impatient. The baby insistently jabbed at her ribs, and she suddenly felt sick and tired of being pregnant, of carrying this lump around day and night. She looked down balefully at her belly. Oh just come out and be done with it!

The intense desire that the baby would stay safe inside her forever had gone, she realised. There was still that anxiety over the unknown, and the fear that a newborn naturally brings with it, but something had changed. Emily found that she wanted the challenge. She was restless for it.

It wasn't just the baby. Martha's had been a sanctuary of sorts, affording her security and refuge at a time when she had needed it most. But that had changed now too. *She* had changed. There was a great urge in her to take back the reins of her own life.

And she couldn't. Take the court case. Here she was dependent on Neasa to do the job for her, while she waited in vain for her to drip-feed her information!

And Conor was moving out today and there wasn't a damned thing she could do about that either. This enforced separation was rapidly turning into a great disadvantage. It was leading them down the path of action, not discussion.

She felt a great pressure to do something concrete too,

instead of waiting here passively for his next move. But what could she do? Threaten to break her waters?

It was all most unsatisfactory. And here she was, back at bloody Brenda's Ward again! Even the hospital corridors seemed to have shrunk.

'Emily?' Maggie called.

What was she going to accuse Emily of stealing now – her 7UP? It had been flat anyway.

'Come here, quick! Look!' Maggie was pointing out the window.

Emily reluctantly joined her at the window. 'What is it now, Maggie – oh!'

Both of them hung on the windowsill looking down.

'And it's raining and everything, aren't they great?' Maggie cried. 'That'll show the *Examiner!*' Laura was coming out of the loo in the corridor. 'Laura! Come in here and see this!'

Dee followed fast and they all huddled together at the window looking down.

'Who are they, RTE?' Maggie asked, breathless, as the camera crew down below moved a few feet to the left of the entrance, where the nurses and locals walked up and down with their placards.

'I don't think so.'

'It is. That's Charlie Bird!'

'It's not Charlie Bird.'

'It is! I'd know him anywhere!'

'He's under an umbrella. You can't see anything.'

The umbrella moved slightly.

'I told you it wasn't Charlie Bird! It's a woman!'

'Sweet Jesus! It's Marian Finucane!'

'Maggie, would you shut up. It's not Marian Finucane. Marian Finucane is radio.'

'David Davenport then,' Maggie said valiantly, refusing to accept the fact that it wasn't RTE.

Laura had great eyesight and it was she who spotted the letters TV4 on the side of a microphone.

'Oh. Still, isn't it great that we're getting the coverage?'

'Absolutely, even if it *is* in Irish.'

The crew below moved another few feet to the left.

'They're trying to get some of the protesters into the shot,' Maggie said.

'And the sign for St Martha's,' Dee said expertly. They all watched a lot of news on the TV in this place. 'Would you look at that Christine one elbowing her way to the front of the pickets!'

'She's putting on fresh lipstick!'

They all groaned.

'Oh, what's she saying?' Maggie strained to see as the reporter below turned to the camera and her lips began to move.

Laura's expert eyesight again came in handy. 'She's saying that they're going to have to wait until the pissing rain stops.'

'You can make that out, even in Irish?' Maggie was very admiring.

Emily ignored their chatter, peering down. The protesters on the pavement outside, sensing a media presence, had gone rather shy and embarrassed, apart from Christine. There was a lot of giggling and awkward wielding of placards at any rate.

'Save Martha's!' they squeaked, looking at the ground.

'Oh come on! Give it more gas! We say NO to closure,' Emily muttered restlessly. Where was Vera when you needed her? She'd fire them up!

Now the camera crew were packing up and retreating to a car until the downpour passed. It mightn't take much to make them leave altogether, Emily thought grimly.

She turned to the women.

'I think we should go down,' she said.

Predictably, they thought she was mad.

'Why not?'

'Well, um, because we're pregnant?' Laura hazarded. In fairness, she was having twins.

'So what? Does that mean we're incapable of walking up and down for a few minutes?' Emily felt a bit giddy now, like a prisoner about to make a break for freedom. 'Come on, girls. We're the main players here! Why should Christine hog the limelight?'

'Vera would never let us,' Maggie said, worried.

'Vera need never know.'

'I think you're insane,' Dee said bluntly.

'She hasn't been herself today,' Maggie explained to Dee.

'None of us are ourselves!' Emily returned sharply.

'We're like a crowd of battery hens cooped up in an incubation factory!'

'That's a bit harsh,' Laura said.

Emily's frustration spilled over. 'I certainly find it harsh to be stuck in here for weeks on end because somebody put me in a little category labelled "at risk"! Our entire regime revolving around producing safe, healthy babies, like there was nothing more to any of us! And there is!' She belted her dressing gown tightly. 'I'm going down there, and I don't care what Vera or the consultants or the management or anybody else says! Neither do I care whether any of you come with me!'

She told herself afterwards that she certainly *would* have gone on her own, but it was a great relief all the same when Laura blurted, 'Feck it. Wait for me. I haven't had a breath of fresh air in weeks. I feel like I'm going to explode.'

'I don't suppose there's any *law* against it,' Maggie added reluctantly. 'I mean, they can't stop us.'

'Stop us? I'd like to see them try!' Dee said indignantly.

They all wanted to come now, of course.

'Maggie, there's no time for make-up.'

'It's just a bit of powder. I've a big nose. I don't want it accentuated on television. And I might go into labour after all the marching, you never know. I want to look okay.'

Dee and Laura hurried off to change into fresh night-dresses. 'I've egg down this one,' Laura explained. Even Emily succumbed and exchanged her bunny slippers for the sensible navy 'official' ones in her maternity bag.

At last they were ready, and there was a lot of nervous laughter as they hurried down the corridor in a little clump. At the nurses' station, Nurse Karen looked up suspiciously.

Maggie called urgently, 'Susan's gone into labour down in Elizabeth's Ward.'

Karen went scurrying off in the opposite direction, and they all looked at Maggie, greatly impressed by her cleverness.

'There's more to me than babies too,' she said loftily.

At the end of the corridor, they piled into the lift.

'Sorry, you'll have to take the stairs, Laura.'

Laura lumbered off unhappily, supporting the twins with her hands. As the lift descended, they hoped that Tommy-the-porter was on one of his innumerable fag breaks, and wouldn't catch them.

He was, and reception was empty. They slowed down now, less sure as it appeared that nobody was going to stop them at all.

'Are you sure this is a good idea?' Laura ventured.

Emily stepped forward and threw open the front doors of St Martha's.

'It's freezing!' Maggie squealed. Emily didn't find it cold at all. It was crisp and clear and fresh, apart from the diesel fumes from the road and the stench of something unmentionable from Maureen's kitchen, and she lifted her face to it.

'Right. Are we ready?'

Without waiting for a reply, she went. The first step was the hardest. Then she was off, marching right down the middle of the car park. Her nightie was flapping around her ankles, her slippers slapping in puddles, and she was smiling.

'Wait for me!' Maggie was the next to take the plunge, and she scuttled after Emily, puffing asthmatically. Emily looked back to see Dee and Laura bringing up the rear, their bellies swinging in unison.

'Hi, Tommy!' Emily sailed past him. His cigarette fell from his open mouth to the ground.

It started to drizzle slightly again, but Emily didn't care. Her dressing gown fell open and she didn't care about that either. Let people stare. She was only pregnant.

'Emily, you're going too fast for Laura.'

'Oh, sorry.'

On they marched towards the entrance gates. At the picket-line, and she saw somebody notice them, and nudge her friend. More people turned towards them. Emily rounded the bend towards the entrance gates smartly, the women flanking her now. An approaching car was forced to stop, or else drive through them.

'And what are you looking at?' Dee enquired of the driver belligerently as they strode past.

'Isn't this marvellous?' Maggie cried, whooping loudly. She even forgot for a moment that she was overdue.

The chanting at the gates petered out as more people

turned to look. Emily saw with satisfaction the TV team in the car sit up and look out. They'd get out for this one, rain or no rain.

Now they were approaching the entrance gates, and they slowed. There was dead silence as the protesters were confronted by the sight of four pregnant women in their nighties and slippers. The protesters shifted uneasily; had they come to give out to them about the noise?

'Oh, hello, Mrs Conlon,' Emily called.

Her next-door-neighbour peered back suspiciously. 'Emily?'

'How's the kitchen extension coming along?'

'Um, they refused planning permission.'

'That's an awful shame,' Emily lied cheerfully.

Nurses Christine and Darren stepped up quickly.

'Are you looking for Vera?'

'No, no, we're joining the protest.'

Christine and Darren looked at each other blankly. This wasn't allowed. This exact situation wasn't covered in their nurses' handbooks, of course, but they just knew it wasn't allowed.

'Have you checked with any of the doctors?' Christine finally asked, hoping to shift the responsibility onto someone else.

'Oh Christine, are you going to give us your placard or not? You can share with Darren.'

Nurse Yvonne from the now-defunct Jude's Ward muscled forward. 'Here. You can have mine.'

'Thank you,' Emily said.

'And will someone support Laura here?' Yvonne said crisply. 'Just to take some of the weight.'

Old Reggie Dwyer and Yvonne's husband Bill found themselves squiring Laura. She thanked them profusely and their cheeks pinkened with pride. The rest of the protesters weren't quite sure how to respond to the new arrivals. Then the doors of the TV4 car flew open. Everyone turned to look.

'Save MARTHA'S!' a lone voice at the back of the crowd shouted.

That did it. With a shuffle and a squeak, the protest started again with new vigour, bearing Emily, Dee, Laura and Maggie off down the pavement in its midst.

'We say NO to CLOSURE!' Maggie yelled, losing the run of herself altogether.

They marched for twenty minutes before a member of management was sent out to politely inform them that if they wished to continue, then they would have to discharge themselves from the hospital for legal reasons.

Liz looked different.

'Have you done something with your hair?'

'Washed it,' Liz said.

And unless Emily was very much mistaken, Liz was wearing make-up. Just a scraping, mind, but the last time she'd seen Liz made-up was for Willy's christening ages ago.

'Is that a new coat?'

'You're so nosy, Emily! I've had this coat ages, I just never wear it. Beige shows up every speck of dirt, and with that lot . . .'

She jerked her head towards the five boys. Willy was out of his sling and lying on one of the spare beds, while the other four took turns trying to pull him off.

'Are you sure he's . . .?' Emily asked.

'Oh, he loves it,' Liz said.

'We might be on the television this evening,' Emily couldn't help saying. TV4 had captured the whole lot. It had been exhilarating.

'Right,' Liz said with a modicum of interest, and Emily deflated. 'Eamon's coming over this evening to see the boys – I'll be hours getting everything ready. I won't have time to watch the television.'

'He was in here yesterday, you know.'

'I know. Funny how he goes to see you, not me.'

She looked very hard, and Emily could see how Eamon might find it difficult to admit failure to her.

'He says he wants to talk about the maintenance tonight,' Liz said tightly. 'Like I intend to blow it on myself! Like I live the high-life or something!' She jerked her sleeve up to check her watch, and Emily got the whiff of perfume. Perfume?

She looked more closely at Liz and detected an unmistakable air of excitement about her. This, combined with the clothes, the make-up, the perfume, raised her suspicions. Could Liz be up to something daft, like . . . well, Emily didn't want to imagine what.

Liz furtively looked towards the door, as though she were late for a rendezvous or something.

'Emily, I need a huge favour.'

Emily looked at her a bit nervously.

'I need someone to look after the kids for an hour.'

'What?'

'I know. I know. It's not ideal. But Mammy's had palpitations again. Mrs Spencer says she won't take them after the last time – her garden ornaments, remember? I'm really stuck.'

'Can't you ask Eamon?'

'No. I don't want him to know.'

What on earth was she up to?

'Why, Liz?'

'Look, it'd just be for a hour.' This wasn't washing, she saw. 'Oh, you're so niggly, Emily! I'm going for a job interview, okay?'

She looked very defensive. Emily was hugely relieved.

'Where?'

'Just back in the chemist. They're not really looking for anybody at the moment, they said, but they must have *some* work if they're going to interview me.'

'That's great, Liz.'

'It's not, I probably won't get it. I'll be too rusty after all these years.' She looked at her hands, which she'd tried to make presentable with moisturiser and nail polish.

'You couldn't get rusty rearing five boys,' Emily encouraged. 'All the organisation it takes! The hard work! The patience!'

'Well, patience . . .' Liz said doubtfully. 'They have a new computer system in there and all. I won't know how to work it.'

'Ask them to teach you.'

'You make everything sound so simple, Emily.'

'What do you want me to tell you, that you're wasting your time turning up at all?' Emily said loudly. She had that childish urge again to sit on her hands in case she ended up belting Liz. 'Well, by God, if I have to mind that lot for an hour, I'd like you to at least make a *go* of it.'

'So you'll do it?'

'I honestly don't think they'd allow me to look after five children in here, Liz.'

'They needn't know,' Liz pleaded.

'I really think you should ask Eamon. He'd be delighted that you've got an interview.'

'He won't be delighted. He'll just go on about the cost of childcare, and all the tax I'll have to pay, and what happens when the kids are sick – things I haven't even thought about yet because if I start on all that, I won't go at all.'

'He *is* very concerned about the kids, Liz.'

'Oh sure, the kids – but not me,' Liz said rather bitterly. 'He has no idea what it's like to be waiting around for handouts from him, while he plays the big man that we're all dependent upon!' She took out her car keys and closed her handbag with a loud snap. 'Willy has just been changed and fed, so he should be all right. There's books and jigsaws for the boys in the baby-bag, and if all comes to all, there's a big packet of buttons in the side pocket,' She whispered this bit. 'It'll be fine. I've warned them all to be on their best behaviour.'

The five boys looked over at Emily cannily, and she had that horrible feeling a fly must have when it comes up against a spider's web.

'Liz, I . . .' She looked at Liz's nervous, thin, made-up face, and she just nodded. 'Good luck.'

'Thanks.' Liz looked a bit awkward. 'You've been great about everything, Emily. I mean it.'

But lest Emily might get a swelled head, Liz turned away quickly, kissed all the boys anywhere she could reach, and left.

'Well, boys!' Emily said loudly. 'Will we play with a jigsaw puzzle on the bed?'

'I don't want to,' Robbie said at last.

'Of course you do!'

'I don't.'

The little shit. Emily could see disaster looming. 'Buttons,' she said loudly.

There were no buttons in the baby bag. Just a forlorn, empty bag. There was chocolate all over Bobby's face, and he smiled at Emily happily.

Neasa rose early as it happened. She put on the pair of old jeans that she saved for spring-cleaning and redecorating and she went straight downstairs. She had things to do today. The first port of call was the press under the kitchen sink, and a big roll of black bin-liners. Neasa always kept more bin-liners in stock than most people. But most people didn't have nine serious partners in four years and hadn't as much need for bin-liners. She started in the living-room. Into the bin-liner went the copies of Gary's *Law Review* that he had left behind on her coffee table, to be returned to him this morning. These were followed swiftly by two novels, his training shoes, a spare set of car keys, his Ralph Lauren facial moisturiser and a pair of boxer shorts she found behind the sofa. She was nothing if not thorough, and she worked her way around the room with the practised ease of one who had done this many times before.

She briefly hesitated by the CD collection. Had he given her *M People* as a present, or had he bought it for himself?

She couldn't remember, and chucked it into the bin-liner anyway. She always gave the dearly departed the benefit of the doubt. The cross-dresser had actually doubled his CD collection this way. 'It's nice to know that you're not bitter and twisted,' he had muttered, and Neasa had smiled understandingly. Little did he know. She just hadn't wanted to give him an opportunity to go ringing her up about missing possessions, thus dragging the whole miserable thing out a second longer than necessary. Onwards and upwards, that was her motto.

She didn't bat an eyelid as she progressed upstairs to the bedroom, where she efficiently packed up Gary's Hugo Boss underwear, two silk shirts, a pair of pyjamas that he had never actually worn, a five-hundred-pound suit and tie. Oh, and his condoms in case he might want to use one soon. She would strip the bed later and put on a very hot wash.

She sat down on the bed for a minute now, queasy, even though she'd eaten a big fry and taken three painkillers. She'd outdone herself last night. That'd teach her to get drunk on champagne, she thought cheerfully.

Still, it had been a great night. Terrific! Daphne and Ewan and Creepy had hung on her every word. And why not? If she played her cards right, she might be heading up that new litigation division Ewan had talked about over his third brandy. At least she thought it had been his idea. Things had been a bit of a blur at that point.

No, she had no complaints at all this morning. Apart from a hangover, of course, but she would bet that Daphne Dunne was sticking her head down a toilet bowl at this very moment. Gary would probably have ended up accusing *her* of being an alcoholic too had he not left straight after dessert.

'Poor Gary,' she sighed sympathetically. His own worst enemy really. He'd want to watch himself or one of these days someone would take a slander suit against him.

And, honestly, if anyone drank too much it was him – off to the pub at lunchtime three days a week with the lads! Neasa never went to the pub at lunchtime – how was *that* for a so-called alcoholic? Alcoholics went sneaking off to the loo for a quick nip from a flask in their handbags, for heaven's sake! They hid drink in toilet cisterns at home, and they ate Polo mints all the time. They couldn't hold down jobs, they messed up their relationships, and they were usually drunk by eleven in the morning. And, Neasa thought knowledge-ably, they nearly always had some big murky secret in their backgrounds that made them drink their heads off to escape it.

As if Neasa were like that! She did her drinking in public. Quite a bit of it, certainly, but she enjoyed it and there was nothing wrong with it. It certainly didn't affect her work or anything like that. And her past was gloriously free of anything remotely traumatic, apart from her grandmother's death, and she had come to terms with that.

'Oh, stop it,' she told herself brightly. There was no need to go rationalising and reasoning like this, like she had something to worry about. But it was natural to be a bit defensive when someone hurled accusations at you, however groundless.

Her stomach had settled a bit now, and she felt better. The problem with men like Gary was that they were misogynists at heart. They couldn't bear to see women doing as well as them or, God forbid, better. Their answer was to bring them down using any available means. And if they couldn't beat a woman fair and square, then they tried to plant insecurities in the hope that the woman might actually bring herself down!

He was a right pig when you thought about it. And she had been going to return his things to him very civilly, too! Well, not now. The charity shop in Paulstown would be delighted with his Hugo Boss underwear, one careful owner. They'd be delighted with the suit, the CDs, everything. Perhaps not the condoms though. She must take those out before she left. In fact, she might blow them up and hang them from the office ceiling, and tell everybody what a disaster he was in bed. She could plant insecurities too! And hers would actually have some foundations.

She put him from her mind clinically, and started to review her wardrobe. She had her big day in court coming up Monday week, not to mention the date with Terry Mitton. She could feel a shopping trip coming on. She couldn't embark on a new romance in old clothes. And, who knows, this could be The One. She had a feeling about this one.

Ten minutes later, she was in her car with her credit cards. Gary's stuff was in the boot. She would drop it by the charity shop on her way. She would need a big empty boot for all the new clothes she would buy in Cork today.

It was a dreary grey day but she put on sunglasses anyway. Her eyes hurt a bit. She'd take it easy tonight, maybe get a video and a Chinese or something.

The traffic was light in Paulstown. The charity shop was up on the right, past the traffic lights. She slowed and craned her neck to see whether it was open. It was. Good.

'Fuck!'

She didn't see a car coming from the left. She jammed her foot on the brake. So did the driver of the other car, and for a moment it seemed that they had stopped in time. But then Neasa felt the car rock as the other car touched off the passenger door. Terrific. Another hike in her insurance premium.

'Nice driving,' she said sarcastically, jumping out of her car and confronting the other driver, a man. The car had a Dublin registration, she saw. Fucking tourists.

'You broke the lights,' he said, looking a bit shocked.

'What? Don't be ridiculous.'

But he was right. Neasa felt a bit sick as she saw clearly that her light was red. The man had the green light.

'All right, sorry,' she muttered. 'Are you all right?'

'I think so,' he said.

Mortified, Neasa stomped around to the passenger side of her car and threw open the damaged door. She found her licence and insurance details in the glove compartment and thrust them at him.

'Here,' she said, wanting to get this over with as quickly

as possible. 'Obviously I'll pay for all the damage.'

'Shouldn't we wait for the police?' the man wanted to know.

Neasa rolled her eyes. Where did he think he was, Detroit? 'Listen, Frankie Noonan won't appreciate being called out because I jumped a light. Trust me on this one.'

'Oh. Right. It's just that my wife has already called them.'

'Fantastic.'

She was out of the car now, red-faced with anger, telling Neasa what a reckless driver she was. Neasa just stood there defiantly. Garda Frankie Noonan would sort them out. He hated Dubliners, even more than he hated Cork people.

Frankie Noonan didn't come. It was a guy from Mitchelstown. He was young and cocky and Neasa instantly disliked him. He walked dramatically around the two cars as though he were at a murder scene.

'Can you just take the details and let me go?' Neasa said loudly. He probably hadn't had as much excitement in years.

He dutifully stepped up and started to jot down details from her documents into his notebook.

'Headache?' he enquired, looking at her sunglasses.

'A bit,' she replied shortly, snatching back her papers. 'If you need to know anything more, I can be contacted at Crawley Dunne & O'Reilly. Solicitors.' She said this last bit rather loudly.

He was standing very close to her now and she didn't like it. This wasn't the time or the place to be making a pass at her. As if he had a hope.

'Were you drinking last night, madam?'

'Sorry?'

'Last night? Were you drinking?'

'I was out for dinner. I had a few drinks, yes,' she said, very patiently, as though he were a buffoon.

'Quite a few?'

'It was a celebration,' Neasa said tightly. 'Is that against the law, Garda?'

'Not at all,' he said. 'Drink-driving is, though.'

Neasa threw her head back in amazement. 'It's eleven o'clock in the morning! I am perfectly sober.'

'You won't mind doing a breathalyser test for me then.'

'Where's Mammy?'

'I told you a minute ago, Robbie, she'll be back shortly.'

'I'm thirsty,' Tommy announced.

'I'll ask Maureen for a jug of water. How about that?'

Tommy looked at her as though she'd offered him arsenic.

'Would Coke do instead?' Conor asked, miraculously producing a two-litre bottle from a large plastic bag.

The visitors' room experienced a brief lull as the boys guzzled Coke. Emily looked at Conor gratefully. He'd not only brought the emergency supply of buttons she'd requested but also Hula Hoops, Milky Way bars, Coke and apples. They hadn't touched the apples, naturally.

'Isn't it amazing all the same how quickly they can do those jigsaw puzzles?' Conor said. He had a thin sheen of sweat on his upper lip.

'It is. It is. And how they were able to take Bobby's tractor apart. All those screws, too.'

Emily had broken two nails trying to put the thing back together again.

'Still, only fifteen minutes to go now,' Conor said manfully.

Emily nodded optimistically. 'She might even be back earlier.' She looked at him. 'Thanks for staying on with me. I mean it.'

'Of course I was going to stay,' he replied softly, and she smiled. 'You shouldn't have to cope with that lot in your condition.'

Her smile disappeared. 'Oh, so you just stayed out of concern for the baby then.'

'Stop being so high-handed, Emily.' He looked at her. 'Just because you're going to be on the TV tonight.'

He gave her a dry look and she went a bit pink.

'So, have you moved out yet?' She tried to sound cool and unaffected.

'Took the last things over this morning. I've left the place clean and tidy and all,' he added quickly.

'Fine,' Emily said. You'd think he was just a lodger.

'And I've taken the dogs, of course.'

Emily was a bit taken aback. 'You've taken the dogs?'

'Well, yes, you mightn't be home for another month. And anyway, I didn't think you'd want to look after two dogs *and* a newborn.'

'Aren't you great,' she said colourlessly. Now she wouldn't even have the blasted dogs to talk to!

Conor shifted in his chair. 'Emily – don't touch that, Robbie – we've been over this. I thought we decided it was the best thing to do.'

'You decided.'

'You agreed.'

'Because you wanted your "space".'

'I think we both do.'

'People are always going on about "wanting their space". I often wonder what they do with it all,' Emily said sarcastically.

Conor seemed a bit puzzled too. 'Reflect, I suppose.'

'On the shoddy state of their marriages.'

'Something like that,' Conor agreed, smiling a bit.

On the spare armchair where they'd propped him between two cushions, Willy suddenly twisted his head towards them.

'Oh, look at him, Conor. He's all excited for some reason!'

His face was indeed very red. He fixed his gaze on the ceiling rather desperately, and gave a little grunt. The veins under his white skin bulged as he strained hard.

'Oh,' Emily said.

A whiff reached them.

'Yes,' Conor said, sadly.

Willy finished up, gurgled, and turned to look at Emily and Conor expectantly,

'I suppose we should change him,' Emily said eventually.

'We should. We should,' Conor agreed, fresh sweat breaking out on his upper lip.

They looked at each other blankly. Emily wondered if that midwife Angela was in the building.

'It can't be that hard,' she said sternly. 'I'll get the nappies. You lay him down on the floor over there.'

'Um, no problem.'

Emily rummaged in the baby-bag for supplies while Conor approached Willy with great care. After three attempts, he lifted the child off the chair, holding him out awkwardly so that his feet dangled in the air. Willy thought this was great gas.

'Will I support his head?' Emily asked anxiously.

'I think he's got the hang of his own head, but maybe to be on the safe side . . .'

It was with a great sense of achievement that they finally got Willy down flat on the floor. He looked up at them with great confidence.

'We'll have you done in a minute,' Conor reassured him. 'Right, I suppose the first thing is to take off his dungarees.'

This was quite a job given the number of zips, buttons and popper-fasteners. They peeled off the dungarees and found that his top was also popper-fastened

underneath. Once that was pulled up, they were confronted with a vest with more of the things.

'He'd never get through the metal detector at Cork
Airport,' Conor muttered.

Emily undid the last lot and finally he was down to
his nappy. The smell hit them full in the face.

'My God,' Conor said. 'And look, it's leaked out.'

It had too. Angela hadn't said anything about leakages.

'We've plenty of wipes,' Emily said strongly. This was
no time to go to the wall. If the boys over there sensed
any hint of fear at all, they would run riot.

Conor surprised her by bravely reaching for the two
sticky flaps on the sides of the nappy.

'I'm going in now.'

Emily giggled. But when he opened the nappy she
had to turn away.

'How can something so small produce all that?' Conor
said in wonder. He seemed to be enjoying this now.

'Wipe him, quick,' Emily said, handing over a bundle
of the things.

Conor, with calm, methodical swipes, eventually
managed to get him clean. Then he wrapped up the
nappy securely and thrust it into the plastic bag he'd
brought the Coke in.

'I'll dig a big hole when I get home and bury it.'

Willy was delighted to be without his nappy, and he
kicked about enthusiastically.

'He's smiling at you, Conor.'

'I should think so too. You were useless.'

She knew his toughness was only a front. Look at the way he was tickling Willy's foot!

They put on his new nappy and spent ten minutes doing up all the popper-fasteners, zips, buttons and buckles again.

'We're old pros now,' Conor said. 'Ready for anything.'

She felt a great tenderness now as she imagined them with their own baby.

'Why can't it be like this all the time?' she asked suddenly.

'I don't know.'

'What kind of an answer is that?'

Conor looked at her, and it was with genuine curiosity. 'How did you think it *would* be? Marriage?'

'Faithful.' It was out before she could stop it.

'So did I.' He looked more puzzled than sorrowful.

'I expected friendship, the odd bit of passion and romance, companionship, sharing the same ideals with someone.'

'Yes.'

'I also thought it would be intimate and close.'

He nodded.

'So if we both expected the same things, what happened?'

'They're not our God-given right, Emily. They don't automatically come with the wedding package.'

'You mean I'm being unrealistic?'

'No, I don't mean that at all. I suppose it's a question of compromise.'

'So I can have the friendship and the companionship but not the intimacy and closeness?'

'No, I . . .'

'Well, I want those, Conor. I can get companionship and friendship from other people.'

She sounded very hard and unyielding. Conor sat up straighter.

'So you're prepared to give this a go, then?'

'I'm just saying—'

'No, you haven't said anything, Emily! Not a thing about a commitment to me or to our marriage. I'm the one who's been begging and pleading all the way along, for some little bit of reassurance or even the tiniest indication that you love me at all! Instead you draw up lists of requirements and demands, and I always seem to fall short.' He looked at her. 'Maybe I always have.'

Tommy looked over, alert to domestic dispute. He was used to it. When Emily eventually spoke, it was low.

'I'm the one who's had to get used to this affair.'

He looked impatient. 'I know that. But, God Almighty, are we going to have it hanging over our heads for the rest of our lives?'

'It takes time to deal with these things, Conor! We've hardly talked about it, even!'

'My affair?'

'Yes!'

'What's there to say? You want me to keep saying sorry, is that it?'

'No!'

'What then?'

'I don't know . . . if I had an affair, *you'd* want to talk about it!'

'I wouldn't,' he said very definitely. 'I'd want to put it behind us.'

Emily was very annoyed. 'That's very easy for you to say!'

'What is not easy for me is this constant limbo, with no light on the horizon at all. I don't even know if I'm going to be there for the birth of my own baby!'

'This, from someone who's going to be living in a different house when the baby comes home!' Emily hissed back, her anger bubbling to the surface.

'I do not want to live in a house where I'm merely tolerated. If and when I come home, it'll be because you want me there,' Conor said flatly.

'It's not down to me.'

'Oh come on, it is.' He looked at her oddly. 'You've always held the power in our relationship and I'm starting to think that you know it.'

'What? I do not!'

'Stop sitting on the fence then. Say you want me if you do. If you don't, then I'd appreciate it if you'd let me know as soon as possible so that I can get on with things.'

'Shut up! Shut *up*! We're on!'

St Brenda's Ward, packed to the rafters with nurses,

patients, visitors, doctors and Tommy-the-porter, went very quiet. You could have heard a pin drop as the newsreader on the TV looked down at them all sombrely.

'And now we're going to a special report on the increase in petrol prices . . .'

'Oh, Maggie.'

'Sorry, I thought we were going to be on next – how could petrol prices be more important than pregnant women in active protest?'

They obviously were, and everyone turned away from the television to pick up conversations left in mid-thread.

'*Avery*. What kind of a name is that for a child?'

'It won't thank her.'

The doctors were over by the door.

'Said he was out in his vegetable garden when he tripped and fell, and happened to impale himself on a carrot.'

'Was he the same fellow who was in Casualty last year after a similar accident involving a courgette?'

Tommy-the-porter was wondering about his future.

'It's night security work. There's a TV and a toaster and all.'

'God, I'd take it, Tommy.'

Over by Emily's bed, Neasa stuffed grapes into her mouth.

'It's a three-ring circus in here,' she said rather sourly.

'I know, but this is the only television left in the place

395

that actually works. And, naturally, everyone's excited.'

'I suppose,' Neasa said, very unenthusiastic for one who was actually representing the parties in court. She felt Emily looking at her.

'Look, Neasa, it's always hard when these things happen, but you'll bounce back. You always do.'

'I know. I know.' She didn't want the pep talk, but knew that Emily felt she had to say it.

'Just give it a bit of time. And anyway, from what you've said, it's probably for the best.'

'It is, definitely.' She tried to sound bright and normal.

'The office might be a bit difficult, but people forget very quickly, you know. There'll be new gossip in no time and nobody will give you and Gary another thought.'

There certainly would be new gossip, gossip that would eclipse anything that had gone before. Neasa couldn't even think about that right now. It was too awful.

'Neasa . . . you don't think you might be a bit unrealistic in terms of expectations?'

It seemed that Emily was determined to sort her out, she saw. She'd only come in to Martha's at all because she knew Emily would be expecting her.

'Yes, probably.'

'I mean, we'd all love for the honeymoon bit to last forever. It's exciting and great and passionate. But it's false too in a way. You don't really know the other person until it has passed.'

'The voice of experience.' This slipped out before she could stop it.

'Oh, go home and sleep your hangover off,' Emily said testily.

Neasa exploded. 'Jesus Christ! What is *wrong* with everyone! Well, I'm sick of it!'

And she stormed out, just as Maggie squealed again at the television.

'Emily! It's you!'

On the screen, Emily marched right up to the camera, her dressing gown hanging open to reveal her big round belly. And there was Laura, walking on her own despite the efforts of her two chaperones to contain her. Maggie was next, taking those little dainty steps and looking the picture of pretty motherhood. Dee brought up the rear, shooting a belligerent look out at everyone before marching on. They looked magnificent.

'My nose! My nose,' Maggie moaned.

'Nobody's looking at your nose,' Christine snapped. She hadn't been in the shot at all.

The reporter stood in front of the protesters now and did her piece. Nobody was listening. Everyone was busy picking themselves out in the background.

'There's Yvonne!'

'Oh, and look, Tommy!'

Then it was over and back to the studio. Vera started to clap. The whole ward broke into applause.

'Wasn't that fantastic, Emily?' Maggie swooned. Now

she really had one up on Tiernan's relatives. 'Emily? Where's she gone?'

Neasa looked up as Emily entered the visitors' room.

'Why can't you just leave me alone, Emily?'

Emily was hurt, she saw. 'If you want to be alone, why don't you just go home?'

'I'm waiting for a taxi,' Neasa admitted.

'A taxi?'

'Oh, look, my car's in the garage, okay? I had a bit of an accident earlier.'

Emily was all sympathy. 'Why didn't you say! No wonder! Jesus, are you all right?'

'Fine, fine.' She might as well tell her – she'd be asking her to represent her when it went to court anyway. She looked at her hands fiercely. 'I was arrested for drink-driving, Emily.'

She felt Emily sitting down beside her.

'I mean, it was all so stupid! I just had too much last night – I should have known that I might get caught.'

Oh, how she hated this hunched, defensive feeling, this knot of shame in her stomach. And Emily's disapproval hitting her like slaps. As if Emily herself had never got drunk and done something foolish in her life!

'It was a minor accident, Emily.'

'Stop it, Neasa!' Emily flared. 'This is drink-driving causing an accident. You're going to be banned. There's no doubt about that. And you'll be very lucky if you don't get a prison sentence. You know what Judge Morrissey is like about drink-driving.'

'He'll just fine me – anyway, I mightn't even get him.' Neasa was frightened now. 'Will you represent me? Please? I couldn't ask anybody in the office. I just couldn't.' If she still had a job there, that was.

'Yes,' Emily said, without putting her through anything more. Emily stood up to go and her upset with Neasa was clear.

'Emily,' she said after her. 'I would never get into a car knowingly under the influence. Come on, you know that. But nobody thinks they're over the limit the morning after. It doesn't occur to them.'

'I suppose not,' Emily said.

Neasa was relieved. 'I know I had a lucky escape. This'll teach me a lesson.'

'I hope so, Neasa.'

Neasa had that hot feeling in her face again. 'What's that supposed to mean?'

'Just that—'

But Neasa didn't let her finish. 'Jesus Christ! Just because you're pregnant and you haven't had a decent drink in nine months! Are we all supposed to go on the dry with you?'

'I'm not saying that—'

'But you're thinking it! You think I've got a problem with drink, don't you?'

Emily looked at her. 'You told me the truth about Conor when I asked you. So I'm going to tell you the truth. Yes, I think you drink too much.'

'Thank you very much for your truthfulness, Emily.

399

Now, if you don't mind, I'd like to wait for my taxi in peace.'

When she looked up again, Emily was gone. Neasa curled up on the shabby armchair and she was shaking.

Conor didn't come in the next day. Or the next. In fact, he did not come in that whole long week. He was waiting, obviously, for her to make her decision.

It wasn't that she didn't *want* to make that decision. Certainly she didn't appreciate being dealt an ultimatum, but she did not let her minor annoyance cloud the issue. And it wasn't that she did not have feelings for Conor any more. She did, and she admitted this now. In fact, she would very much like this whole thing settled and sorted. Like Conor, she too had felt the impatience and tension building in recent days. Maybe he was right. Maybe it was time to decide this thing once and for all.

But she still couldn't make that decision. Every time she tried to think about it, she was distracted by a nagging, persistent disquiet, a hangover from their row in the visitors' room. It was nothing that she could immediately put her finger on. It seemed silly, and she tried to figure out what it was that was bothering her.

Eventually it came to her. It was Conor saying that she held the power in their marriage and always had. This seemed to Emily to be so utterly off the mark that she couldn't even begin to make sense of it. Her, have power over Conor? The most self-sufficient person she had ever met? A person who gave her reassurance and support only when she begged for it? Now, who held the power *there*?

She could not understand it. And it continued to nag at her.

'The baby's heartbeat is fine,' Mr Chapman announced.

Emily looked down, mildly startled. She was so used to Mr Chapman now that she had completely forgotten that he was somewhere under her nightdress. She had to resist the urge to reach down and pat him affectionately on the head, like he were one of the dogs at home. She really had become very fond of him.

'That's great,' she said.

He straightened up and put away his stethoscope. Emily thought that he looked different. Tired or something. And it was Sunday and everything – you'd have thought he'd have taken the day off.

'And how are you feeling yourself?' he enquired.

'Oh, grand.'

'Good, good. Eating well?'

'Yes.'

'Getting a bit of exercise? A bit of fresh air?' He couldn't resist getting the dig in. It seemed that the whole country had seen the TV piece last week. The pressure on the Health Board and Martha's management had been building all week. The showdown was tomorrow morning in Court No. 3. Duggie Moran and the rest of them had organised someone to phone straightaway from the court with the outcome. Mr Chapman found that he did not actually care.

He really was taking this court thing badly, Emily thought, as he pushed up her nightdress another few inches and began to feel the baby's position with his hands. Emily had on a pair of pink knickers, quite racy really, but the supply of white nun's bloomers with the different coloured trims had rapidly dried up due to the lack of handwashing facilities in the hospital.

'The baby's head is fairly well down in the pelvis,' Mr Chapman intoned.

'When do you think it'll be born?'

'I never give predictions.'

'Oh.'

He proceeded to do so anyway. 'Your due date is not for another ten days. Women often go over on their first child.'

Mr Chapman felt he was acting out a part he had played hundreds, thousands of times before, that of the concerned professional who would facilitate a most momentous occasion in so many women's lives. Women who were at the end of the day strangers to him, and he to them.

Andrea had had her abortion on Friday afternoon. Not that Killian had phoned or anything. Mr Chapman had been reduced to ringing up Patrick Marcus, the contact of his who had carried out the operation. It was only out of concern, for God's sake, but Marcus seemed to think that this was a great invasion of Andrea and

Killian's privacy and had told Mr Chapman in no uncertain terms that it had nothing to do with him and that he had no rights whatsoever to any information. He had then hung up on a stunned Mr Chapman.

'Good luck,' he said to Emily unexpectedly now, and he meant it. But he saw that he had scared her. Consultants were supposed to pretend that luck had absolutely nothing to do with it; that medical science would win out at the end of the day.

'I'll call by Tuesday or Wednesday,' he said more briskly. Why not? He had already worked all weekend, just for something to occupy his mind. And at least she couldn't complain that he was neglecting her.

'Um, thanks,' Emily said to his retreating back. He was being very odd today. She hoped he would be up to it when her big moment arrived. Conor would go mad if he wasn't, and they after paying him a thousand pounds too.

That feeling of disquiet was back again the moment she thought about Conor. She considered picking up the phone and asking him to come in so that they could talk.

But, knowing Conor, he would not even remember the intricacies of their conversation. And if he did, he would tell her she was reading too much into things as usual. He would want to know whether she had decided to move on with him or not.

But they were good at that, weren't they? 'Moving on' without really resolving anything. Pretending that they had sorted things out when they hadn't at all, and off they would walk into the sunset until the next big crisis loomed and the whole thing would fall apart at the seams again. Probably permanently. Because each time they negotiated a crisis, they emerged weaker as a couple, not stronger. And if she picked up the phone to Conor and said 'yes' right now, she was continuing the whole sorry vicious circle.

'Emily?'

'Yes! Oh, sorry, Maggie, what is it?'

Maggie was sitting up in the bed, a mobile phone glued to her ear. 'Auntie Olive is going into the Four Courts tomorrow for the judicial review and she wants to know what the dress code is.'

'It doesn't matter – anything.'

'It doesn't matter, Auntie Olive, anything.' Maggie looked back at Emily again. 'Could you be more precise? She's only seen a courtroom on *Judge Judy* and she doesn't want to make a fool of herself.'

'Tell her trousers and a top.'

'Trousers and a top, Auntie Olive.' Maggie rolled her eyes. 'Would a skirt and a top do, Emily? It would. Great.' She listened for a moment then turned to Emily again. 'She said to tell you that you were fantastic on the telly last week, that it gave her goose bumps.'

It was quite amazing how many people had seen that piece of footage. Cards of support had been arriving in Martha's all week, along with letters and phone messages and even two bouquets of flowers. Oh, and one letter from a woman in the midlands who said they were a right bunch of hussies to be parading themselves in front of cameras in their condition.

'She's taking a whole gang up with her,' Maggie said, having dispatched Auntie Olive. 'She might even make a banner, she said, if she can find markers. Isn't she great?'

'Great,' Emily agreed.

'And there's Laura and Dee after holding on too,' Maggie said. 'You have to take your hat off to them.'

And she burst into tears.

'Maggie,' Emily said softly, used to this, 'I know it's hard going, but you have to hang in there.'

Maggie was now eleven days' overdue. And not a sign in the world of anything stirring, despite four vindaloos.

'I can't stand this, Emily,' she sobbed. 'There's something wrong. Maybe the baby is dead!'

'The baby is not dead. Didn't you hear its heartbeat an hour ago?'

Vera kindly put a stethoscope on Maggie's belly a couple of times a day to reassure her. Everyone was being very nice to Maggie at the moment.

'I'm going to ask to be induced,' Maggie resolved tearfully.

'Maggie . . .'

'I am! You can ask them, you know! You can tell them the mental stress is driving you mad!'

Physically, all was well. Excellent, in fact – Maggie

hadn't had an asthma attack in nine days. The irony of this was something she didn't appreciate right now.

'Maggie, give it another little while.'

'This wasn't supposed to happen, you know,' Maggie said, brittle. 'This wasn't in the plan.'

'Forget the plan, Maggie. Maybe the best thing is to relax right now.'

Maggie smiled bravely. 'You're probably right. It's just that I'm sick of this place. I want to go home.'

'I know. I know.'

'Half of me wouldn't mind if your friend Neasa loses in court tomorrow,' Maggie confided. 'At least Cork would be a change of scenery.'

Neasa had not been in to visit in a week either. She had phoned Emily twice to keep her up to date on the court action. Both calls had been tense and impersonal.

Emily hadn't pushed it. She felt too guilty in any case. Why had she not noticed what was going on with Neasa before now? How had she not seen through the smokescreen of her failed romances? Not that Neasa had propagated her own myth deliberately. Emily felt that she was genuinely stumped by her romantic disasters. But the men were more a symptom than a cause.

Impulsively, she picked up the phone and dialled Neasa's home number. She got the answering machine, even though she sensed that Neasa was nearby, listening. She left a short message anyway, to wish her good luck in court in the morning, and to thank her for doing this.

'Do you want a game of bridge?' Maggie wanted to know. She had not let the dwindling patient numbers in Martha's dampen her enthusiasm for bridge. Desperation had driven her to play a game with herself yesterday.

'No thanks,' Emily said. *She* felt cross now – cross and frustrated and irritated with things in general. And Conor in particular. She would phone him tomorrow, she vowed. She would tell him to come in and they would have a long chat about all the things that were bothering her. And he could stuff his 'decision'! She wasn't ready to make one yet.

Just before eight o'clock, Vera came in. She was on the night shift and was in uniform, but with a pink and yellow party hat on her head. It looked very incongruous.

'The staff are having a bit of a party down in Jude's Ward. Nothing too mad, no drink or anything like that. But we thought we'd like to mark the day.' She looked at Emily hurriedly. 'That's not to say that we're not confident about tomorrow. We are. And if we win, we'll be having another party. With drink.' She held out two more party hats. 'Anyway, the staff were wondering would you join us? And Dee and Laura too, of course.'

Emily shook her head. 'Ah no, Vera, it's a staff thing.' She did not think she would be much company.

'It's not,' Vera said firmly. 'It's a hospital thing.'

'Can we, Emily?' Maggie, as usual, waited for Emily's

permission to do anything. 'There's damn all on the telly.'

'Please,' Vera said. 'Maureen's made bean enchiladas and everything, from a proper recipe book.'

This was their way of saying thanks, Emily knew. She threw back the bed covers and put a smile on her face.

'We'd be delighted to.'

Damn Maureen and her bean enchiladas. Emily tossed and turned much of the night, fighting wind and horrible dreams. Then she would be assailed by interminable periods of wakefulness where she would fret about the court case tomorrow; the baby; Neasa's drinking problem. She even worried a bit about Liz and Eamon, and the five boys. Lest anyone feel left out, she spared her mother a quick thought too, and Mrs Conlon who apparently had launched an appeal against the planning permission refusal.

Maggie's deep and contented snoring filled the ward, and Emily wrapped her pillow around her ears, gritting her teeth. Maggie was fond of saying that nobody else ever complained about her snoring and that Emily was being over-sensitive. So, really it was all Emily's fault. It was funny how people could twist things to shift the blame onto someone else.

Conor jumped into her mind again, accompanied by that growing irritation. The more she thought about his assertion that she held the power in their marriage, the more it seemed like an accusation. Somehow or other she had created an imbalance in their marriage which caused Conor to be so upset that he had gone out and had an affair. That was the bottom line. That was what had been bugging her all week.

No wonder he hadn't wanted to talk about the affair! No wonder he'd hardly said sorry to her at all! He thought it was all her fault in the first place! Oh, he could deny it for all he was worth, but Emily knew.

Were it not a quarter to four in the morning, she would phone him up and demand that he get his sorry ass in here right this moment. She still might!

In the meantime, a mattress spring was digging uncomfortably into her hip. She huffed up onto one elbow, gave the pillow a good belt, shifted over six inches and flopped down violently again.

The force of her landing dislodged more wind and she felt a little ping down below. She expected relief.

It was not wind. She lay there for a moment, quite still, as a warm wetness spread over her thighs, soaking her nightdress. It felt like gallons, but it probably wasn't very much; she had read her books and knew what was happening. When it was over, she carefully got out of bed in the darkness, changed into a fresh nightie and went to find Vera.

'Well, it's earlier than expected,' Vera said.

'A little,' Emily agreed calmly.

'We'd better get you down to Delivery.'

'Sorry?'

'You need to be examined.'

'But I'm not even having any pains. Not proper ones anyway.'

'If your waters have broken at this stage, I'd say you're on the way,' Vera advised. 'The pains will probably start pretty quickly now.'

Emily was shocked, and hadn't the faintest idea why. She only had ten days to go. It was perfectly possible – indeed, highly probable – that she was in labour right now and would have her baby within the next twenty-four hours.

'I'll just get your labour bag,' Vera said, and went off.

Emily stood on her own in the dark corridor, her hands clutching her belly, amniotic fluid dripping down her legs. She calmly told herself that everything was going to be fine. Hell, the moment had finally arrived – she should be enjoying herself!

'Here we go.' Vera was back.

'Thanks,' Emily said cheerfully, and burst into tears.

Vera was very kind. She put an arm around Emily. 'What's wrong?'

'Nothing. Everything.' Emily couldn't explain her upset. She said the first thing that came into her head. 'I thought it was just wind. I ate loads of Maureen's kidney beans at the party.'

'So did we all,' Vera said grimly. The whole hospital had been suffering since. It would nearly make you wish for Maureen's lukewarm shepherd's pies made with cheap mince.

Tommy-the-porter loomed from around the corner,

giving Emily a fright. He was pushing a wheelchair.

'Delivery?' he said.

Emily felt fresh shock and panic rising in her. Maybe it was all those weeks and months of anticipation. When the event was finally happening, she couldn't quite believe it.

'Don't worry,' Vera said. 'I'll come down with you.'

Emily found herself folded into the wheelchair, her labour bag balanced on her knees. She clutched the straps fiercely as Tommy threw his weight behind the wheelchair. They eventually set off on his third attempt.

'Okay?' Vera asked, trotting beside the wheelchair.

'Yes,' Emily lied. She felt quite nauseous now, and Vera was right – the pains were getting noticeably stronger and more regular.

Down the dim corridors of Martha's they trundled, past the kitchen and the smokers' room and the visitors' room. Emily never remembered it being as quiet as this. Doors were dark and wards silent. But most of the hospital was closed. It was all a bit eerie and unsettling, and when Tommy broke into a coughing fit, Emily jumped.

'Are you okay?' she asked.

'Fine,' he said, and stopped to lean against a wall. Emily felt very much a burden, when it was obvious that he needed the wheelchair more than she. But eventually they set off again.

'Will I get one of the girls to ring Conor?' Vera asked casually.

Emily pretended to have a contraction to buy some time.

'Breathe through it,' Vera advised. 'You too, Tommy.'

After much huffing and puffing, Emily felt she had to give an answer. 'Ring him, but tell him there's no rush.'

Vera wasn't sure how to take this. 'The thing with first-time labours is that nobody really knows how long they will last, Emily. You don't want him to miss it, do you?'

'I suppose not,' Emily said reluctantly. She didn't know what she wanted. Someone she trusted, she supposed. Someone she knew. Someone with whom she wasn't extremely angry right now.

Ow. She had a real contraction now, a proper one, and it took her breath away. She hunched over in the wheelchair and she was shocked by the ferocity of it. Something primeval and brutal was happening to her body, something that she could not temper or stop.

When she could breathe again, she looked up at Vera grimly. 'Ring him and tell him to get in now.' By God and if she had to go through this thing for their first-born, then Conor would too. Every inch of the way.

They rounded a corner and the bright lights of Delivery burst out of the darkness. Tommy, seeing a fag-break on the horizon, picked up pace enthusiastically, and they crashed through the double-doors with great noise and fuss.

'Now, Emily, Jessica over there will look after you,' Vera said.

Jessica seemed a most unlikely name for a midwife. She sounded like she should be selling expensive lingerie. Emily had somehow expected all midwives to be called Emer or Maura or something similarly earthy and comforting.

'Hello, Emily,' Jessica said, stepping up. 'Again.'

'Um, yes,' Emily said. This was the same woman who had escorted her from Delivery that very first night.

Jessica looked at her keenly. 'By the way, Martina's doing very well. She had a baby girl. Just in case she didn't get a chance to ring you or anything.'

She was on to Emily all right. But she said it nicely. And Emily was very glad that Martina was okay. She had been thinking of her on and off since that night.

'Good luck, Emily,' Vera said.

'You're not going?'

'You'll be fine. You're with the experts now.'

Emily didn't want experts. She wanted people she knew and trusted. 'Vera,' she blurted. 'I'm afraid.'

'Of course you are,' Vera soothed. 'Every woman is when it comes to giving birth. But don't let the fright rob you of the joy of it all.'

Another savage contraction convulsed Emily. Vera was taking the piss, surely.

Vera waited until the contraction was over, then she patted Emily on the arm and left. Just like that! Oh, cheers!

'Now, Emily,' Jessica said brightly. 'Can you walk?'

Emily, not wanting to make a fuss, hobbled from the

wheelchair, still clutching her labour bag. Jessica tried to take it from her, but Emily held on tighter. People always seemed to be trying to take bags from her. She must be a pickpocket's dream.

'In here,' Jessica said cheerfully, throwing open the door to a labour room.

It was not at all what Emily had expected. She had been given the obligatory guided tour of Cork's labour facilities as part of her antenatal classes. The labour rooms there had been spacious and sensitively lit, with clever, abstract pictures on the walls and sophisticated new beds that went up and down and sideways and possibly inside-out at the mere touch of a button.

Martha's labour rooms boasted harsh fluorescent lights and peeling white-ish paint. The bed was mean and narrow and the medical equipment looked like it was on loan from a museum. The only picture on the wall was a discoloured diagram of what appeared to be the female reproductive system. Surely Martha's obstetricians and midwives already knew what this looked like? Emily felt her confidence dwindle further.

'Now, if you'd just pop up onto the bed,' Jessica said.

Emily was later to reflect that Jessica said 'pop' a lot. It seemed that Jessica had yet to learn that no woman in labour ever popped anywhere. They inched painfully, or they rolled agonisingly. They all *wanted* to pop, but very few of them ever did.

'If you could just let your knees fall apart,' Jessica instructed, pulling on white rubber gloves with much loud snapping. 'This won't hurt a bit,' she said with that rather irritating cheerfulness again.

Emily looked at the ceiling as Jessica did her thing down there. Now she was pulling off the gloves and peering up from between Emily's knees.

'Four!' she chirped.

Four? Four what? Emily's mind went blank. 'Oh, *four*!' She was four centimetres dilated. Already!

'You're doing pretty good,' Jessica sang. 'Keep it up!'

Emily's enthusiasm was dealt a brutal blow as a contraction sneakily pounced.

When it was finally over, she looked at Jessica, uncomprehending.

'It's terrible.'

'I know,' said Jessica, clucking.

'No, no, you don't. I mean it's *really* terrible.'

'You need to relax and breathe over it,' Jessica advised, and Emily wanted to hit her very hard. 'I'm going to ring Mr Chapman,' Jessica added. 'Let him know how you're doing.'

Emily was shocked. 'It's ten past four! I don't want you getting him out of bed!'

But Jessica was gone. It was a relief really to be spared her relentless cheer. Emily was left on the flat of her back looking up at the ceiling again. There was a big crack running across it and one of the bulbs in the fluorescent lights flickered ominously. A part of Emily still couldn't believe that this was happening.

Conor would be here very shortly. He was probably

in the car right now, driving down dark country roads. Would he break the speed limit for this one? She suspected he might. Well, he needn't expect a big warm welcome from *her*.

She wondered was the baby all right. She had not felt it kick or move at all in the past hour. Could it possibly be asleep? In the midst of all this madness?

'Please be all right,' she said, cradling her tummy and crying again, a little bit.

'Emily?' The whisper came from the door. And there was Maggie, in her nightdress and bare feet, peeking in. 'I woke up and you were gone!'

'Maggie!' Thank God – someone nice. 'Come in, stay with me for a bit.'

'I'm not supposed to be down here at all,' Maggie hissed, but skipped in all the same and huddled by the side of Emily's bed, round-eyed. 'Are you all right?'

'I've been better.'

Maggie squeezed her hand. Emily clung on to her, thankful for the support.

'Talk about timing,' said Emily. 'With the court case tomorrow and everything.'

'I know,' Maggie said. 'I don't suppose there's any chance you might be able to hang on . . .?'

'No chance at all.'

'I didn't tell the others you were gone into labour,' Maggie confided. 'I didn't want morale plummeting.'

'I'm going to have to ask you to take over the

campaign, Maggie,' Emily instructed. 'Just until I'm back on my feet.'

Maggie looked delighted at her new position of responsibility. 'I'll do the best I can,' she said bravely.

Emily shifted on the bed uncomfortably. The weight of the baby pressing down on her stomach was making her nauseous.

'Is it awful?' Maggie wanted to know in trepidation.

Emily looked at her worried little face. No sense in giving her a heart attack. 'Easy peasy,' she bluffed.

'Oh good,' Maggie said with relief. 'I knew that Cathy one was exaggerating. No pain threshold, that was her problem.' She reached into her dressing gown pocket. 'I brought you down a damp facecloth. It's not clean, but at least it's cool.'

'Lovely,' Emily said, as Maggie laid it on her forehead. It didn't help at all, but she didn't want to offend her.

Maggie took something else from her dressing gown pocket. 'And here's my birth plan.'

'What?'

'Well, you didn't do one in the end, did you?'

'Um, no.'

'So you can work off mine,' Maggie said generously, spreading the five densely-written pages along the side of the bed. 'Where do you want to start? The foot massage or maybe I could light some aromatherapy candles for you?'

'No candles, thanks anyway, Maggie. We don't want to set the fire alarms off and have to vacate the building.'

'That's true,' Maggie said reluctantly. 'We'll play some music instead. I brought you down the tape Tiernan made especially for me. It's ocean sounds. He managed to get the Atlantic *and* the Irish Sea, isn't he marvellous?'

'Marvellous,' Emily echoed weakly, as she felt another contraction come to life inside her. Surely it hadn't been that long since the last one? But it didn't matter. It was on its way and there was not a damned thing Emily could do about it. She gritted her teeth and cursed the universe.

Maggie was fiddling with an ancient tape machine in the corner. 'Imagine, you're finally going to have your baby, Emily! Isn't it incredible?'

'Yes,' Emily managed, as the pain spread out inexorably from the centre of her, eating her up.

'Have you thought of any names?' Maggie demanded.

'No . . .'

'You're hopeless, Emily! Anyway, never mind, because guess what else I brought down for you?' She reached into her bottomless dressing gown pocket again. 'My baby-name book! Let's start with A, will we? Girls first. Abigail, Adi, Agnes – imagine, *Agnes*! – Ailish, Amanda . . .'

Emily did not hear any more. She was in the throes of the horrible monster now. She tried to relax, to breathe above the pain like Jessica had told her to. And it didn't bloody work. She felt her fingernails sink into the palms of her hands as her whole body felt like it was mangling itself. Surely something was wrong? Surely human beings could not live through this kind of pain? Just when she thought she could not bear it any more, the agony began to subside, slowly. She floated back to planet earth again and her vision cleared. Maggie must be on to B's by now.

Maggie was not. Her eyes were like saucers and her face white as she stared at Emily. 'Golly,' she whispered.

'Sorry,' Emily said, feeling somehow that she had let Maggie down.

'Maybe you're just not relaxing properly,' Maggie ventured.

'I'm trying to.'

'You're not doing your breathing right, either.'

'I am.'

'No – sorry, Emily, but with all due respect you haven't been practising.' Maggie looked quite annoyed now. 'You can't expect to go into these things unprepared, you know.'

Emily wasn't sure where this was coming from. 'Maggie, shut up.'

'I will not shut up! You didn't even do out a birth plan!'

'I didn't want a birth plan.'

'Oh, you didn't *want* one! Of course you didn't. Not like the rest of us mere mortals!'

'*What?*'

A dam inside Maggie seemed to burst, and she looked at Emily with a mixture of anger and resentment. 'We're not all like you, Emily. Able to do it all –

the big lawyer career, the baby, filing court cases and staging sit-ins in our spare time. If anything goes wrong for you, you always have something else to fall back on. I don't!'

All this sounded very insulting. For two pins now she would tell Maggie to fuck off. 'Nobody's stopping you doing other things, Maggie.'

'But that's just it! I don't want to do anything else!' Maggie cried. 'I've never wanted to do anything except have babies.' She looked very defensive. 'Oh, I went to college. I even worked for a while. Went after the promotions and the company car, because you do, don't you? But what was the point? I'm not an achiever; I'm not brave; I can't change the bloody world; not like you.'

This seemed to Emily to be way off the mark. 'I never wanted to change the world either! If you must know, mostly I am terrified and horrified.'

Maggie dismissed this with a flick of her hand. 'And I endured it, you know, those awful dinner parties when people would ask you what you do, and the little embarrassed silence when you tell them you don't have a job. No kids and no job! What is she, lazy, or just stupid? And Wendy over there with three kids and she running Coca-Cola! But I didn't care that they wrote me off. Because I was waiting, you see, for the baby. That was my career, that was my purpose in life—'

'If you'd excuse me for a minute please, Maggie, I'm

about to have a contraction.'

'Oh, sorry, fire ahead.'

Maggie retreated as Emily went into a black hole again. Emily held on to her sanity by focusing on Conor's book *The Pregnant Father*, and how it had warned its readers to be prepared for foul language and mindless accusations during labour. But surely these were supposed to come from *her*?

When the contraction was over she clawed her way back up the bed a bit. Maggie took up immediately where she had left off, looking a little annoyed at the interruption.

'And then it happened, I got pregnant, and everything started to make sense. I thought, here is something that I'm going to be brilliant at. Here, at last, is something that only I can do! And look at me! I can't even go into labour on time!'

'Oh, Maggie.'

'I know,' Maggie said without rancour. 'And look at *you*, ten days early.'

She said this as though she had something to be jealous about! As if Emily were the be-all and end-all! Emily wouldn't feel quite so annoyed if she didn't feel so tired and, well, hungry.

'Get the birth snacks out of my labour bag,' she bluntly told Maggie.

'I'm not hungry.'

'For me, Maggie.'

Maggie was shocked. 'You can't eat! You're in labour!'

'I know, but I'm mad, me,' Emily said loudly.

'No,' Maggie said, firmly.

'I'll have to get them myself then,' Emily said, lunging for her labour bag and extracting a bag of cheese and onion Tayto earmarked for Conor.

Maggie moved with surprising speed and wrestled them from her. 'You might have to have emergency surgery! I'm sorry, but I can't let you eat!'

'Give them back!' Emily was furious now.

'It's for your own good!' Maggie said stubbornly. 'I'd expect you to do the same for me.'

'If you do not give them to me I'll . . . I'll . . . oh, just give them to me!' Honestly! Who would have thought being in labour entailed all this? She'd thought she would only be required to do a bit of puffing and pushing – not defend herself against all kinds of horrible allegations of competence and bravery and taking control of her own life. Maggie had some nerve!

She flung herself back against the pillows and glared at Maggie. 'I'm not what you think I am, you know!'

'Sure, whatever, don't get yourself excited,' Maggie said patronisingly – as though she hadn't started all this in the first place!'

'I mean it, Maggie!'

'Of course you do. Will I wet your facecloth again?'

Emily gave up. Why was she fighting it anyway? Why all the defensiveness? Everything Maggie had accused her of being was, well, *good*. Was it so impossible to believe that everything she had gone through had changed her for the better? She might have a way to go yet, but why not take credit for a damned good start?

'Maybe I will have a damp facecloth after all,' she conceded with dignity.

'Good for you,' Maggie said, contrite now. 'Emily, I'm sorry for having a go at you. It's the last thing you need right now.'

'Your timing could be better.'

'It's all this waiting around for the baby to come,' Maggie confessed miserably. 'I feel sometimes I'm going mad. It's just getting on top of me, that's all.'

'That's okay, Maggie.' Emily could afford to be magnanimous now. Maggie had pointed out some useful facts, after all.

'What's going on here?' Jessica was back, and not pleased to find Maggie in situ, a torn bag of crisps in one hand and a dripping facecloth in the other. 'This is a restricted area.'

Maggie and Emily looked at each other, co-conspirators again.

'I'm Emily's birth partner,' Maggie loftily informed Jessica. 'Until Conor arrives.'

Jessica, despite appearances, was no fool. 'Patients are not allowed to choose other patients as their birth partners. For a variety of reasons.'

'It's my fault,' Emily simpered. 'I asked Maggie to bring me down a tape of ocean sounds.'

'She did,' Maggie lied vigorously.

'Right . . .' Jessica said reluctantly. 'Now, off to bed with you.'

Maggie nipped up to the head of the bed. 'You'll let us know, won't you, Emily? How it goes?'

'Of course I will.'

'Good luck,' Maggie said tearfully, squeezing her hand. 'Oh, and do you mind if I keep these crisps? I'm starving.'

'Out,' Jessica ordered, before hospital management got wind of this.

With Maggie gone, Jessica was back to her buoyant self, and she wasted no time in switching on machines and monitors, and producing a big black belt-like thing. It was an electronic foetal monitor, which she now strapped around Emily's midriff.

'Great,' Jessica sang. 'Now we're all set!'

Emily felt anything but set as another contraction began its vicious, insidious assault on her insides.

'Breathe, Emily,' Jessica reminded her, and did a few enthusiastic puffs to keep her company. 'That's it!'

Emily looked at her with dull eyes. 'Do you ever have a bad day?'

Jessica just made another note on Emily's chart. 'Why are you so angry, Emily?'

Before she could retort, Emily was sucked into the vortex of pain again. When she opened her eyes a little while later, Conor was standing at the end of the bed.

'Hi,' he said.

'Hello,' she said hoarsely.

They regarded each other in silence for a moment; her sweaty and grim-faced, him trying to look calm and collected but wearing mismatched socks. His eyes darted from the monitors and wires and back to her again. He looked pale.

'Where's Jessica?' Emily asked eventually.

'She went to get some ice.'

'Ice?'

'Apparently you wanted some in your birth plan.'

'That's not my birth plan. It's Maggie's . . . oh, it doesn't matter.' Briefly she wondered what Maggie had intended to do with ice. 'You don't have to stand all the way down there, Conor. I'm not going to start biting.'

'I know that. I just didn't want to crowd you.' He reluctantly advanced a few steps and maintained a careful distance at the head of the bed, throwing another look at the monitors and tubes.

'How are you?' he asked.

'I don't know. It's not so bad at the moment, but then again, I'm not having a contraction at the moment.'

'Would you like me to rub your back?' he offered, not sounding all that enthusiastic.

'No. I couldn't bear it, to be honest.' She felt that if anybody touched her now she would scream.

'Okay . . . would it help if I did the breathing with you when the contractions happen?'

'I don't think so,' Emily said, her irritation growing. He was quoting *The Pregnant Father*, chapter and verse.

And he might look a bit more excited about the whole thing! Sneakily, he had worked his way back to the bottom of the bed again.

'Eh, right,' he said. 'Do you want me to talk you through it? You know, give you encouragement—'

'Tell me I'm opening up like a fucking flower?'

He seemed at a loss. 'I don't know what you want me to do, Emily.'

'Have you no imagination, Conor? Have you no idea what I might need?' Here came another contraction. She felt it building up inside her like a small volcano. 'Or maybe you *like* waiting around for my orders, seeing as I'm the one in the saddle in our marriage, apparently.'

The last thing she saw was his confused face before she shut her eyes tight and went to battle with the contraction. It was a tough one, closing around her belly and chest like a vice, squeezing the breath from her lungs. She fancied that it was trying to kill her. Well, it wouldn't. She hung on grimly until it eventually ran out of energy and was forced to subside. Strike one to her.

'Let's go for a walk, will we?' Conor said, when it was finally over. 'Up and down the corridors.'

He had obviously given himself a little pep-talk while she had been in the throes. Get with it, man! At least *look* as though you want to be here!

'I don't want to,' Emily said baldly.

'You did when we talked about this at antenatal

classes. I distinctly remember you telling me that you wanted to walk.'

'You *would* remember that, wouldn't you, Conor? Isn't that just typical of you?'

He ignored this. 'Let's go.'

'I can't! Are you blind? I'm hooked up to that monitor!'

He gave the monitor another wary look as Jessica came back in. 'That thing isn't keeping her alive, is it?'

Jessica laughed heartily. She seemed to find everything hugely amusing. 'Not at all. It's just to keep an eye on the baby – which is doing fine, by the way.'

Conor seemed greatly relieved. 'So you might be able to unhook it? If we were to go for a walk?' He seemed very keen on this walk.

'Of course – we encourage patients to move around during labour,' Jessica chirped. 'Nothing worse than lying on the flat of your back waiting!'

'Absolutely,' Conor agreed heartily.

Emily looked from one to the other and at this moment she was hard pushed to decide whom she hated more.

'I want an epidural,' she informed Jessica.

'Yes, I think we need to look at some form of pain relief,' Jessica agreed. 'I'll tell the anaesthetist. He's down with Laura at the moment.'

'Laura?' Emily was floored. But it was twins: Laura had expected that she wouldn't go to full-term.

'And they've just brought Dee in as well.'

'Dee?' Emily was even more shocked. But Dee was a week overdue. Still, it was a bit disconcerting that the whole campaign appeared to have spontaneously gone into labour.

'And Maggie?' she asked.

'Oh, Maggie's still hanging in there.'

She would be hopping mad.

'Off you go,' Jessica said, throwing open the door to the corridor.

Emily wasn't that happy at being forced off her warm bed. But pride made her climb down all by herself, and take a few cautious steps across the floor. To her relief, she didn't faint and nothing fell out of her.

'Okay?' Conor asked, as she paused for a moment in the corridor to get her bearings. He himself looked a lot better now that he was out of that room.

'Let's go then,' he said briskly. He was definitely back to himself – ordering her about, acting like she needed him to wind her up and point her in the right direction!

'I want to be alone,' she said loftily, walking off ahead of him at a brisk pace.

She passed vases of flowers and dusty religious statues and a photo of a baby with a smiling face. The baby was lovely, and Emily realised with a start that this was what it was all about: the pain, the nausea, the foetal belt, the hormonal madness. It was all just part of the process of her baby being born. It was easy to lose sight of it.

She lost sight of it a moment later as another contraction descended. At its height, she didn't give a hoot whether she gave birth to a monkey; she just wanted it all to be over. Behind her, she thought she saw Conor put out his hand to support her, but she gathered her energy and set off again, leaving him behind.

Time ceased to have any meaning. She measured it by the number of times she passed the photo of the baby . . . twenty, thirty, then she lost count. Doctors and midwives swished by, looking over curiously – her huffing up and down the corridor with Conor trailing three feet behind holding Maggie's damp facecloth. She did not have the energy to care as contraction after contraction overtook her, each one worse than the last. In the middle of one, she thought she heard Dee cry out from a nearby labour room. She didn't have the energy to care about her either. It was every woman for herself in here.

At one point, she registered that the clock over the nurses' station said it was eight am. *Eight?* Could she really have been here nearly four hours? The clock must be wrong.

There was no respite at all between contractions now. Eventually she stopped walking altogether and leaned against a wall, red-faced. She felt like her body was defeating her. She could not see any end in sight; only more and more pain and she wanted to cry again.

Conor was waiting with a glass of iced water. 'Jessica said you could have this.'

'I don't want it,' she said, even though she did.

He put it down without comment. 'Would you like to have a shower? It might pass some time.'

'No.'

'Look, you can try all you like, Emily, but I'm not leaving.'

'What?'

'I am not leaving this place until my baby is born. You can like it or lump it.'

Emily's eyes popped. 'Just a second here, Conor. *I'm* the one in labour!'

'I think we're all well aware of that at this point. But that doesn't mean that I have absolutely nothing to do with it.'

'Your bit is done,' she said childishly.

'So I should bugger off and leave you alone?'

'If you like! If you want to know the truth, you're not much bloody use to me!'

He gritted his teeth defensively. 'You're never happy, are you? On the one hand, I'm supposed to be spilling my guts at every opportunity, confiding every last thought, hope and dream in you. But on the other hand, we don't want me getting *too* emotional, do we? Because I only exist in a supporting role, right? We wouldn't want me robbing you of your moments in the sun!'

'*What?*'

'You don't have a monopoly on feelings, you know. Just because people don't show them doesn't mean they don't have them.'

Emily opened her mouth to retaliate but ended up collapsing against the wall, huffing through a contraction instead. It was another brutal one. Through the mist of pain, she was aware of Conor hovering, his hands half-cupped in case she might topple over and fall. She would love to, and break his leg maybe.

Panting, she flung herself away from the wall and glared at him.

'You're doing it again! I can't believe you're doing it again!'

'What am I doing?'

'Coming up with reasons why you had the affair! First I'm a power freak, and now I don't take account of your hidden emotions!'

'Oh stop it, Emily.'

'No I will not stop it. You're blaming me!'

'I am not blaming you.'

'So why did you do it then, Conor?'

He threw up his hands in exasperation. 'What is the point of going over all this again?'

'*Again*? We've never gone over it! Not once!'

'Because it's history, Emily.'

'History? Like the miscarriage was history?' She ignored his face. 'Things don't become history just because you refuse to deal with them!'

'Fine! So what do you want to know then? Where? When? How many times? Was she any good?'

'Oh, shut up.'

'No! Just tell me what you want to know! If it means

so much to you, I'll tell you the whole sorry saga from the beginning to the end! Right here in the middle of the corridor while you're in labour!'

'I just want to know why!' Emily shouted back. 'Why!'

Jessica was hurrying up the corridor now, looking from Emily to Conor warily.

'Emily? The anaesthetist is waiting to give you your epidural.'

Thank Christ. She could not bear the agony much longer. She turned her back on Conor and hobbled off.

Back in the labour room, the anaesthetist was shifting from foot to foot rather impatiently. He wanted to go home.

They all had to wait while Emily had another contraction. Then Jessica said, 'I'll just do a quick exam first, Emily. If you'll let your knees fall apart again . . .'

The anaesthetist and Conor both looked studiously at the floor. But Emily did not care if she were on MTV.

When Jessica eventually looked up, her face was even more cheerful than usual.

'Eight!' she sang.

'Eight?'

'You're eight centimetres dilated! It must have been all that walking! Isn't it marvellous?' She looked as pleased as if it had all been her own doing.

The anaesthetist deflated totally. Eight centimetres! Someone might have let him know. Without further ado, he turned and left.

'Where's he going?' Emily cried.

'It's too late for the epidural, Emily,' Jessica said.

'It's not. It's not. I want one!'

'It will make things harder and longer for you. Come on, you're doing so well on your own. You're nearly there,' Jessica argued.

'I can't do it . . .'

'You can. We'll help you every step of the way.' She looked at Conor expectantly. 'Won't we?'

Belatedly he nodded. 'Of course.'

'I want Mr Chapman!' Emily wailed. He would get this baby out of her – she had paid him a thousand pounds. He would do what he was told!

'He should be here any minute,' Jessica soothed. 'But I'll give him a buzz on his mobile. In the meantime, let's try some gas again.'

'It doesn't work,' Emily said, rather self-pityingly. She'd already tried it and it had only made her want to vomit.

'Let's try again,' Jessica said firmly, helping Emily into a sitting position, and unhooking the gas mask. 'Actually, Conor, maybe you could help here?'

She held out the gas mask.

He was shocked. 'But I wouldn't know what to do . . .'

'It's quite simple,' Jessica said briskly. 'You're just going to help Emily to breathe through the mask, that's all, when you see a contraction coming. You'll see it on the monitor – the little green line, see?'

He looked at the monitor as though it might self-combust. 'Um, right.'

'Oh, look! Here's one coming now!' Jessica said with a jolly smile, and walked out the door.

There was a nasty little silence in the labour room except for the slight hiss of gas. And on the monitor between Emily and Conor, that little green line started to climb.

Conor couldn't take his eyes off it. Emily saw his Adam's apple bob up and down a few times violently. She saw panic in his face, and . . . fear?

'I'm sorry, Emily,' he blurted suddenly. 'You're right. I'm no use to you here at all.'

'Conor . . .'

'No, no, don't try to make me feel better. This is the moment when you need someone the most, and I'm just not up to it.'

'Conor; please . . .'

'Will I ring Liz? She'd come in.'

'Conor, just give me the bloody mask!'

'Oh, right, sorry.'

The green line on the monitor was nearing its peak now and Emily was engulfed again. Vaguely, she felt the mask press firmly over her nose and mouth, Conor finally springing into action. Then the pain obliterated any other thought. She thought she might have mentally said a Hail Mary at one point – she must remember to tell Pauline that. She would be delighted. But just when she thought it should have

been over, it got worse. She had never known anything like it. Cathy, she screeched silently, I believe
you.

At last it subsided. Slowly. She felt her dry lips fall
away from her teeth again and she opened her eyes
with an effort. The mask lifted from her face.

Beside her, Conor was terrified. His eyes were wide
and wet and his face parchment white. Emily had never
seen him like this before. She was worried.

'Conor? Are you all right? Are the tubes and things
upsetting you?' Her pregnancy books had warned her
to be prepared for all kinds of squeamishness and
fainting from menfolk at this point. It was not a myth.

But Conor just kept staring. 'You're not going to die,
are you?'

Emily knew that this was too serious to give in to any
impulse she might have to laugh. 'I don't think so. I
hope not. I think it's just labour, Conor.'

'You look so sick.'

'I *feel* sick. But they wouldn't have left us in here with
just a gas mask if they thought I was in any danger.' She
tried to lighten the mood, to take the strange look off
his face.

'I'm afraid,' he blurted. 'I'm sorry. I know you don't
need to hear this right now . . . I just wouldn't be able to
cope without you, Emily.'

'Conor, I am not going to die. Can we please stop
talking about me dying?'

But Conor kept looking at her as though she were on

her last breath. 'It's different for you. You'd be able to cope without me.'

'What are you talking about?'

'You always have. You've never really needed me as much as I need you. You've never *loved* me as much as I love you.'

'Conor, that's ridiculous!'

He seemed to think she was being facetious. 'Oh come on, Emily. It's always been like that! From the very first time we met, when you took pity on me—'

'What?'

He spoke very fast as though he were afraid he wouldn't get it out before she expired. 'It's true. And I was so grateful that I pretended to be what you wanted me to be, or what I thought you wanted me to be. But it was never equal between us, the love. Somehow I thought you would catch up with me. But you never did.'

'Gas!' she shouted, as another contraction snuck up on her. It was a nasty one, but she fought back as best she could, anxious for it to be over. She had barely drawn breath again before she turned back to Conor. 'How was I ever supposed to "catch up" when you always run away on me? A relationship isn't going to deepen if you always pull back!'

'I was trying to protect myself, Emily,' he said quietly. 'Hold a bit back. For the day when you finally realised that I wasn't really enough, and you left me.'

Emily's eyes could not get any wider at this point.

And she had thought he possessed no imagination? And all this time he had been indulging in conjecture and speculation and wild fantasies about her leaving him!

'And just in case I didn't get up the gumption to leave by myself, you thought you'd help me along by having an affair?' she asked incredulously.

'I was stupid.'

'Tell me something I don't know!'

He looked at her directly. 'All right. I was lonely.'

Emily felt a tightness in her chest. 'I think that's probably your own fault.'

'I know it was,' he said.

'Go on,' she forced herself to say. Well, she had wanted to know why, hadn't she?

'All right. I could talk to Mary like I couldn't talk to you because I didn't love her and it didn't matter.'

There wasn't a sound out in the corridor now. Even Dee had stopped her screeching.

'What did you talk to her about?' Emily asked.

'Not you. Not us. The miscarriage, a bit.'

'The miscarriage?' This hurt terribly.

'With us . . . you talk and I listen. I always feel you're the more important person in our relationship, so when something *does* happen, you get first dibs on attention.'

Emily felt terribly defensive. 'It's up to you to open your mouth a bit more!'

'I know that! I'm admitting that! But it's on your side too, Emily! You push and prod all right, but only when it's to do with you! Most of the time I feel I can't say anything because I'm supposed to be there for you to fall back on!'

'Rubbish!' Emily hissed.

But he was her plain-clothes garda, wasn't he? The voice of reason when she wanted him to be? And then she expected him to turn around and share with her, but only to a point that suited her. She certainly didn't want a man who went around the house gnashing his teeth, a man with emotional diarrhoea. It was a very fine line to ask anybody to tread.

Naturally, she didn't admit to this immediately. 'So while you were off talking to Mary, I had nobody to talk to!'

'I know. I'm sorry.'

She felt another contraction come to life. Well, she would have her say first. 'If you think *you're* afraid, Conor, I'm terrified! Terrified to ask for the slightest bit of support, frightened to look for anything at all for myself because you'll look at me like I should be on Prozac! It's no bloody wonder I've never been able to stand up for myself!'

Conor did not interrupt.

'I mean, look at you tonight! The very time I need you most, you're faffing around with damp facecloths and gas masks and you're just not going to muck in at all, are you? You're going to stand back and "protect" yourself, because you've got this ridiculous notion in your head about who loves who more!'

It did sound ridiculous, and Conor smiled a bit. Emily would have too, only that out of the corner of her eye, she saw the green line on the monitor rise and rise, and the pain became bad. She hurried on.

'So the upshot is that you're afraid and I'm terrified, is that it?'

'Yes,' he agreed.

'How on earth did we end up like this, Conor?'

'I don't know,' he admitted. 'I'm sorry, Emily.'

'I suppose I'm sorry too.' This sounded a bit too contrite. 'Even though I think you should have said something before!'

But he wasn't going to take this lying down. 'And so should you, if you felt you weren't getting what you wanted! There's no point in giving me those disappointed little looks when I don't know what the hell they mean!'

'You needn't worry on that score! I'm a different woman now, you know!' A woman in labour could get away with this kind of statement, she felt.

'So am I!' Conor retaliated. 'Or a different man at least.' He cast a look at the green line on the monitor. 'Emily, maybe you should have some gas—'

'Are you trying to avoid issues here?' she asked suspiciously, ignoring the pain.

'I am not! It's just that Jessica left me in charge of gas!'

'That decision you wanted me to make, Conor . . .'

'Why don't we leave that for the moment?' he said, looking worriedly again at the monitor.

'I can't make it. Not yet.'

'Yes, yes . . .' The green line merrily raced towards it peak. 'God Almighty, Emily, could we please concentrate on the matter at hand here! Use the gas!'

'You're just not going to stop, are you—' She was cut off mid-stream as the contraction finally hit her full-force. Her mouth fell open and she stared wordlessly, helplessly at Conor.

'Oh Lord,' he said, fumbling about with the gas mask. 'Hang on, Emily, hang on, I'll get this thing on you . . . damn!' He had somehow wrapped the tubing around his leg. He looked at Emily's stricken face, and she saw that fear again, that backing off when things got too tough, and she closed her eyes to him and lay frozen and alone as the contraction attacked.

She started to say a Hail Mary again. It was worth a try.

Then she felt a hand on hers; tight, reassuring. Conor. She opened her eyes briefly to see him close to her, his face comforting, or at least a good impression of it. His voice was low in her ear.

'Don't hit me,' he said, 'but maybe you should try doing your breathing.'

'Can't . . .' she managed.

'You can. You've been doing it all along. Come on. Just try. I'll help you.'

She did try, a little bit, expecting Conor to start puffing in unison. But he didn't. Instead he rubbed her belly, quite vigorously like the midwife had shown them in antenatal classes. She didn't know if it actually helped. But, on the other hand, it didn't hurt.

The contraction was at its peak now and she felt it slipping out of her control.

'Jesus, Conor,' was all she whispered.

He didn't really humour her at all. Instead he said, 'Just remember, Emily, you're eight centimetres. You're nearly there.'

He kept saying that over and over, that she was nearly there and that the baby would soon be born. After a while she started to believe him. It didn't get any easier but somehow it got more bearable. And he never let go of her hand.

That was the way Mr Chapman found them twenty minutes later when he swished in wearing blue scrubs and smelling of canteen coffee.

'Hello,' he said pleasantly.

They looked at him as though he were an intruder. Possibly they didn't recognise him in his scrubs. 'It's Mr Chapman,' he clarified rather sharply. And he after driving up from Cork too! Still, maybe they were annoyed that his predication of the birth date had been wildly off target. That would teach him.

But no, they gave him a cursory greeting before going back to their breathing, both of them very concentrated, very calm really. Mind you, she was huffing much too fast in Mr Chapman's opinion. They were trying to produce a baby here, not run a mini-marathon. He hoped she wouldn't ask to take the placenta home to bury in the back garden. He wouldn't put it past her.

'She's almost ten,' Jessica informed him crisply, after a quick exam.

Of course she was. He wouldn't be here otherwise. Like every other obstetrician, he only showed up for the grand finale.

'Okay, Emily, we're nearly there,' he said with his usual calm authority, snapping on gloves.

Two other midwives joined them now. Mr Chapman liked to think it was because they had heard he was here. It didn't occur to him that they had come for Emily, the woman who was fighting their court case for them in exactly one hour's time.

He had thought of the court case on the drive up. Cork's management would be raging that he had not thought to ring them up and let them know that Emily Collins had gone into labour early. But his first loyalty was, as always, to his patient. And anyway, it was in the hands of the courts now. His job was to deliver her baby safe and sound.

'Excellent,' he said, doing an exam. He felt the baby's head under his fingertips, round and hard, straining to get out. 'I think we can start getting ready to push, Emily. Jessica will tell you when.'

The place was suddenly a flurry of activity. Two midwives helped Emily into the birthing position, slightly hunched over with her chin tucked into her chest, and her hands clamped under her thighs. One of the midwives gave her quiet instructions on how to push – 'One long push down. Keep it going as long as you can, okay?'

Jessica took up residence in front of the monitor, watching and waiting. The fourth midwife was ready to assist Mr Chapman.

'Ready?' Mr Chapman said, throwing a detached smile at Emily and Conor.

They watched him with pale, tired, frightened faces. They looked very young, almost like teenagers, and for a moment he forgot that he heartily disliked the pair of them.

'It'll be all right, you know,' he said, kindly. The midwives looked up in surprise. He was not known for his bedside manner, and he felt a bit embarrassed now.

'Well?' he barked brusquely at them. 'How are we doing?'

'Here comes one now,' Jessica announced, watching the monitor. 'When I tell you, start pushing, Emily, okay?'

On the bed, with her arms locked around her thighs and stringy hair falling in her eyes, Emily tried not to panic. She turned to Conor who was practically on the bed beside her. He was mucking in so much that he was nearly crowding her.

'I'm afraid,' she whispered, as she felt the pain growing steadily stronger. 'I don't think the baby's going to be able to get out down there.'

'He will if he has my driving skills,' Conor reassured her.

'Here we go!' Jessica cried enthusiastically. 'Push now, Emily! PUSHHHH!'

And Emily did. She dug her chin into her chest and gave a long, hoarse shout as she squeezed downwards with all her might. Blood rushed to her head with the strain and she fiercely hoped that nothing up there would burst.

'Don't let up-don't let up-keep going-keep going,' Jessica chanted, her damned enthusiasm strangely infectious now. Emily did as she was told and kept going.

'That's it, Emily! You're doing brilliantly!' Good lord – surely that wasn't Conor shouting like he was at a football match? It was, and she bore down with all her strength one last time.

'All right. Well done. Relax, Emily,' Jessica said. 'Deep breaths.'

Emily fell back onto the pillows, exhausted, feeling that her whole face must be hideously swollen. But it was strange, this feeling of exhilaration and excitement.

Suddenly she was desperate to see this through, to hold her baby in her arms.

'Can you see it yet?' she asked Mr Chapman breathlessly.

'Um, no. It takes a bit more than one push.'

'Oh.'

But she didn't lose heart. When the next contraction came, she attacked it with all her might. The midwives all started braying again and the room rocked to the roar of 'Push!'. She was almost starting to enjoy herself.

It was a different story fifteen minutes later.

'I can't do it any more. I can't.' She was prostrate on the pillows, exhausted, sodden and defeated. Conor had used every last word of encouragement in his vocabulary and even Jessica was starting to repeat herself.

'Here comes another one,' Jessica said. But Emily went at the next contraction only half-heartedly, feeling that she had nothing left to give.

'You might need some help here, Emily,' Mr Chapman informed her, and she froze as she thought she saw him eyeing a large pair of forceps. Surely to God those things wouldn't fit inside her? And if they did, how would he get them back out again with a baby's head stuck between them?

Conor saw her face. His voice was for her only. 'Don't give up now, Emily. After coming all this way. You're on the last leg! Come on. I'll help you. Let me help you.'

'Here we go again,' Jessica announced.

'Are you ready, Emily?' Conor asked. 'Will we give it another go?'

She looked at him. 'Yes.'

'PUSH!' Jessica shouted.

Emily did. She felt she were going to split open with the effort but she kept on pushing, Conor bearing down with her, his hands on her shoulders, his voice in her ear urging her on.

Then, the magic words.

'I have the head,' Mr Chapman murmured.

'Ohmigod!' Emily squealed, beaming insanely at Conor.

'I know. I know. It's fantastic.' He smiled back almost as madly. 'Good luck.'

'Yes,' she said, and she went to work for the last time.

Down below, Mr Chapman didn't feel it necessary to give any running commentary. He had the baby's head in his hands now. Its eyes were scrunched up tight and the little mouth puckered in outrage, all ready to bawl the second it had the breath to do so.

Mr Chapman smiled although he was unaware he was doing so. Almost there. He had a shoulder out now. It was a fine big baby; he would put it at eight pounds or more. And boisterous. All that wriggling! He kept a careful eye on the perineum, but there was no sign of any tear. Good. There would be no need for any stitches at all.

The rest happened very quickly, and the same as it always happened bar the odd few cases. Another push and he had the baby out and he was holding him up to drain away any fluid from the respiratory tract, and he was saying those words, 'It's a boy'. Then he was cutting the cord and Jessica was helping to staple it and the baby, crying, suddenly opened his eyes and looked up at Mr Chapman in that blind way that newborns do. And Mr Chapman involuntarily thought of the grand-child he had been denied, the grandchild he would never deliver and who would never look up at him like that, and he felt bereft.

'Mr Chapman? I need to weigh the baby.'

'Of course.' Mr Chapman blinked and handed over the baby briskly to Jessica. He settled down to wait for the placenta to come out.

He never spoke during this because he wanted to give the parents some privacy as they met their baby for the first time. But he couldn't resist looking up to see Emily Collins bending over her bundle, shocked, exhilarated, uncomprehending. At least she was normal in that respect.

The placenta was taking its time. He checked his watch. Ten-thirty. Two things struck him: the court case would be starting about now, and Killian and Andrea had a ten-thirty flight back from London. He knew, because he had booked it himself. Andrea had insisted on travelling on a Monday morning, as though she were trying to fool people that she was a business-woman or something.

He knew that they would not survive this, Killian and Andrea. He had seen the first traces of blame in her face already. He doubted that Killian had any notion yet.

He found that he felt sympathy for his son, perhaps for the first time. Like most things in Killian's life, the break-up would come from left of centre and take him completely by surprise.

There was nothing Mr Chapman could do. His inter-ference was not wanted, even though he preferred to think of it as protection and guidance. Was this what parenting finally came down to, merely picking up the pieces? Good luck to Emily Collins. She would need it.

The placenta was finally out. He was finished.

'Let's have a look at the little fellow,' he said before he left, as he always did.

Emily Collins looked up at him with shining eyes and held out her baby. Conor Collins hovered protectively. Mr Chapman peered in at the little face and nodded. 'He's lovely. Well done.'

Emily Collins was tearful. 'Mr Chapman – thanks. You were marvellous.'

'My pleasure,' Mr Chapman said politely. He couldn't resist adding, 'And good luck in court today.'

'Um, yes.'

Mr Chapman left, followed by three of the midwives. Jessica pulled a blanket up on Emily.

'Thanks.' Emily smiled hugely at Jessica, her new best friend.

'I'll be back shortly,' Jessica advised. 'Then we'll get you moved down to a post-natal ward.'

Emily and Conor were left alone at last.

'Are you all right?' Conor asked her.

'Yes, yes,' she said impatiently. 'My God, Conor! We have a baby!'

And indeed they had. He was resting on Emily's tummy.

'Is he all right?' Conor ventured. 'Can he breathe, do you think?'

The baby was completely swaddled in a blue blanket, except for his face. His eyes were brown and were squinting against the glare of the fluorescent lights. Apart from that he didn't make a move.

'I think so,' Emily said, doubtful. 'You know, he's not at all how I imagined he would look.'

'Well, you thought he would be a girl, didn't you?' Conor said helpfully.

'So did you!'

'I said I didn't care what it was so long as it was healthy,' he argued. 'I hope he likes the colour yellow.'

'Look at all that hair, Conor.'

'What? Where?'

'Where? On his head!'

'Oh, right. Yes. I didn't think they grew hair until they got out. Still, it suits him, don't you think?'

They just looked and looked at this baby, not sure what to make of him, not sure what to feel at all. Emily, her exhaustion kicking in now, was just glad that he was alive and healthy and normal. And, really, he was beautiful.

'Isn't he?'

'What?' Conor said. He didn't sound himself.

'Beautiful.'

Conor looked down at the baby for a long moment, considering. 'He's all wrinkled,' he said eventually. 'He looks like a little old man.'

'Yes,' Emily agreed. 'My father.'

'I suppose we'll be calling him Robert so.'

'Only if you think he looks like a Robert.'

'He looks like a Robert.'

And it was decided.

Part Three

She saw them the minute she entered the church, huddled together on a seat at the back. Her heart lifted as she went towards them.

'Maggie!'

Maggie looked up, confused for a moment. 'Oh, Emily! Wow, look at your face! It's all gone down!'

'Thank you,' Emily said, not sure at all that this was a compliment. 'And Dee! And Laura! You're great for coming.'

'We wouldn't have missed it.'

It was marvellous to see them all again, and there were hugs and kisses and exclamations all round. They had all meant to meet up ages ago, of course, but between one thing and another . . .

'And you've brought all the babies!' Emily exclaimed. Four car seats were lined up on the pew in front. The babies were all magnificently decked out in Baby Gap and Gymboree. She hadn't seen any of them since they were newborns.

451.

'Look at little Chloe! She's gone huge!' she swooned, leaning in to tickle Maggie's baby under the chin.

'That's actually my Regina,' Dee clarified.

'Of course it is,' Emily said, mortified at having offended two women in the one breath. But Dee said, 'At least you didn't think she was a boy. Most people do.'

And they all guffawed heartily.

'What did you call the twins in the end, Laura?' Emily asked.

'Baby 1 and Baby 2,' Laura sighed. 'We just can't make up our minds.'

'Well, come on then!' Maggie cried. 'Let's see the man of the moment!'

Emily shyly held out her own car seat. Robert was sleeping, a miracle in itself. She'd snatched the soother out of his mouth on the church steps and was glad now. None of the girls' babies had soothers. A lot of parenting books frowned on them.

'Look at him in his little white dress!' Dee said.

'That's actually a christening shawl,' Emily clarified, and they all guffawed again, even more heartily.

'He's gorgeous,' Laura chimed in magnanimously. 'He's the spit of you. The absolute spit.'

'Um, thank you,' Emily said awkwardly. She still found it disconcerting, this need people seemed to have to reassure her that the baby bore some resemblance to either of his parents. They would chop him up into parts, and insist that he had Conor's nose but Emily's eyes. It was like a kind of false flattery – as though either of them had had any control over the matter at all.

'Come on. Sit down, Emily,' Maggie urged.

Out of the corner of her eye, Emily saw Liz, Eamon and the five boys enter and go to the top of the church.

'I shouldn't really . . .'

'Just for a minute,' Maggie insisted. Emily squeezed in beside them, adding her car seat to the cluster on the pew in front. 'Tell us, are you expecting a big crowd?' Maggie wanted to know.

'No,' Emily admitted. 'It's all very last minute what with Conor going away tomorrow.'

'Of course,' Maggie said. 'We were thinking of having Chloe's christening on a Friday – you know, when most people are at work. Tiernan's relatives alone would come to two hundred and forty-three.'

'We're keeping it to a hundred,' Dee confided. 'A nice manageable number.'

Emily and Conor were only having forty people today, but Emily had been up since dawn disinfecting toilets and making interesting sandwiches in the shape of boats. She was exhausted.

There was a funny little silence now. 'Isn't it great that we're all together again?' Maggie heartily declared.

'Great,' the women all echoed.

'And we thought we'd never get out of St Martha's!'

'Well, *you* didn't, Maggie. Imagine, sixteen days overdue! It must have been a record!'

And they all laughed again.

Now that the formalities were over, the women got down to the real business. They huddled in together over the five baby car seats. Emily huddled in too. Wasn't it great to catch up with them all again?

'How is Chloe feeding?' Dee immediately wanted to know.

'Great,' Maggie confided. 'She's on juice and everything now.'

'Juice!' Laura cried. 'Baby 2 won't even drink water. But he's putting on weight really well.'

'Good for him! And how's Robert's cradle-cap, Emily?'

Emily wanted to tell Maggie to keep her voice down. Announcing it to the whole church! 'Fine. I'm massaging it with olive oil.'

'Olive oil?' Dee was disapproving. 'No, no, you need some of that special shampoo, Emily. That'll clear it up in no time.'

'Right,' Emily said, a bit stiff. She'd already tried the shampoo; half of Robert's head had washed away with the suds.

'And how's Regina sleeping for you, Dee?'

'Oh, great. We got eight hours of a stretch out of her last night!'

'Eight hours!' Everyone was very envious.

'Chloe only slept for six,' Maggie said.

'My boys went for five,' Laura said.

Emily said nothing. Robert had never slept for more

than three hours at a stretch since the day he'd been born two months ago. Maybe if he were a better sleeper Emily wouldn't look so much like a washed-out old rag. She wished now that she'd made more of an effort for today. She was wearing a loose-fitting outfit she'd already had in her wardrobe, which she had thought looked perfectly respectable. She just didn't have the energy to traipse down to Cork to scour the outsize shops with Robert in tow. She wished she had now. The girls all looked fantastic, like they were going to a wedding. Maggie's cream trousers still had the shop creases in them. And how come they all looked so *thin*?

On the pew in front, Robert stirred and started a low, lone whinge. Emily looked down at him, willing him to go back to sleep. He cried quite a lot for no apparent reason, usually in the car when she was in the fast lane on the motorway. Or at night, just as she was falling into an exhausted sleep. She would strip him down and look for signs of rashes or stray nappy flaps, but there would be nothing. Up and down they would walk on the landing, him grief-stricken and her guilt-ridden that she did not know what was wrong with him.

'Maybe you should pick him up,' Dee eventually said. Emily's face felt hot at the implication of neglect.

'He sometimes settles on his own,' she said defensively. It was true.

He didn't. His whinge changed into a cry.

'Now, now,' Emily said, furiously rocking the car seat. She was aware of the girls monitoring the situation closely, hoping against hope that Robert didn't wake up their own babies. Laura had started to rock the twins a bit nervously.

More embarrassed, Emily reached down and undid Robert's harness, and scooped him up from the car seat. She took off his little white christening hat and the shawl. He was probably boiling, that was what was bothering him.

'So tell us, Laura, are you breast-feeding the twins?' she asked brightly, bobbing Robert up and down with an air of nonchalance. Shut up now, Robert, she pleaded. After all I do for you, give me a fucking break.

'Oh no,' Laura declared, looking shocked. 'Nobody could manage that. Besides, it gives Mark a chance to get involved.'

No wonder she looked so bloody fresh if the husband was doing all the work.

Robert's face grew redder and redder as he looked at Emily pathetically. She saw Conor's family, seated near the top of the church, turn around with concern, and she teetered between mortification and total sympathy with Robert. Did he have a dirty nappy? A quick sniff told her no. Tell me what's wrong with you, she begged him.

'Poor Robert!' Maggie said, awkwardly. Dee and Laura exchanged looks. Chloe, Regina, Baby 1 and Baby 2 slept on angelically.

Robert's heartfelt wails filled the church now, and everyone looked distressed, apart from Liz's five boys who looked down avidly. Emily craned her neck for Conor. Where the hell was he? She bitterly regretted her airy decision that they should drive to the church separately. After all, they lived separately. Both of them were very careful not to lose sight of that.

'Do you think maybe he's hungry?' Dee ventured, rocking her own silent, gorgeous daughter.

'I fed him an hour ago,' Emily said stiffly.

But, on cue, he started rooting around her chest to find a nipple. He was starving.

'Oh!' Emily said. 'Look at that!'

And indeed they did, the whole damned congregation now, including the priest who had ambled out to prepare the readings. She felt watchful eyes on her as she tried to hitch up her top and open down the flap on her maternity bra without dropping Robert. It was hard enough to do in the solitude of your own home, never mind in front of a bloody audience and God.

What she really wanted to do was go out to the car and feed him there. But the girls would probably think she was acting like breast-feeding was something to be ashamed of. But she just didn't feel competent or confident enough just yet to whip them out wherever she happened to be. And they were her *breasts* at the end of the day, a private part of herself. She didn't feel they had become any less private just because she was breast-feeding.

Robert, sensing a good nosh-up on the way, grew frantic now, clawing at her skin with his little fingers.

She turned away from the watchful eyes and hiked him up under her jumper. For once, he latched on immediately and closed his eyes in bliss. She always liked this bit. It was the one time he made her feel really useful, and she wished that she were alone with him to enjoy it.

'There's a restaurant in Cork that doesn't allow breast-feeding at the table,' Dee announced. 'When I rang to make a booking, I asked.'

'Disgraceful,' Emily muttered.

'Maybe we should boycott it,' Laura declared.

Emily didn't have the energy to boycott anything. How come Maggie, Dee and Laura were coping so well? Did they just have easier babies?

Emily felt guilty now for heaping the blame for her own shortcomings onto Robert, and she hugged him closer. She would try harder. And she would *never* be caught again wearing her dressing gown at three o'clock in the afternoon.

Robert's guzzling sounds filled the church, or so Emily thought anyway, and he was taking twice as long as he usually did. Maggie, Dee and Laura occasionally clucked benignly, and checked every now and again to see how he was doing.

'There! Isn't that better?' Dee said to Robert as he eventually finished up and Emily sat him upright on her knee. Raging, Emily patted his back rather harder than usual, and he gave a huge burp. At the top of the church, Tommy and Robbie broke into loud sniggers.

Eamon roundly clipped them around the ear. Robbie started to cry.

Emily felt fresh sweat break out under her armpits. This day was turning into a disaster.

'I was reading a new report that said formula could well be better for children in the long run,' Dee offered into the silence.

'Is that a fact,' Emily said tightly, regretting even inviting Dee. Inviting any of them! But they had all been so close in Martha's, sisters-in-arms, taking on the world together. Giving birth together. Dee had even had a look at Emily's perineum after the birth to tell her what the damage was. And now look at her – at *all* of them – sitting there prim and superior! It was like they were strangers.

Suddenly, Dee's immaculately made-up face gave a violent twitch. Her eyes screwed up uncontrollably and she started crying. Really crying, sobbing, and a thin keen of despair came from her mouth.

Emily was so taken aback that she just gawked. So did Laura and Maggie. The rest of the congregation pretended not to notice.

'I tried to breast-feed. I wore the nipples off myself,' Dee sobbed. 'After two weeks she was nearly dead with starvation and the district nurse said I had to go on formula.'

Maggie and Laura didn't seem to know what to say. Emily stepped in, strongly. 'You really shouldn't take the breast-feeding thing so seriously, Dee. She looks

459

great on formula. Doesn't she, girls?' She looked hard at Maggie and Laura for a bit of support. She was getting the strong whiff of pretence all around. Well, bugger that. 'Come on. It's hard work,' she declared. 'We all know it's bloody hard work.'

'Thank you, Emily!' Dee cried. 'And everyone expects you to be so fucking happy all the time! Derek coming home from work and wondering why I'm not grinning from ear to ear with joy when all I've talked about for the past three years is having a baby!'

Laura's composure disintegrated even more rapidly. 'And they try to help, don't they? To make the dinner, to pick up some of the filthy laundry off the floor, but that just makes you feel like you've been sitting around on your arse all day long!'

They seemed to have forgotten entirely that they were in a church.

'And the visitors!' Maggie chimed in avidly. 'All Tiernan's bloody sisters who keep telling me to get the baby into a routine. A routine! And there's me sitting on the couch hoping they won't stay long enough for me to offer them coffee, because I haven't made it to the shops for milk because she's puked once and poohed twice before we've even made it to the car and I just don't have the energy left!'

Emily sat back and let them have their say. They were dying to. Honestly! What a crowd of ninnies they all were, herself included, trying to put up a good front, trying to be superwomen!

Dee had stopped crying now, and went on in a low, ashamed voice. 'Sometimes I hate Regina. Sometimes I wish she had never been born. That sounds terrible, doesn't it? If the district nurse knew I was thinking these things, they'd whip her away from me and into care.'

She didn't hate her at all. That was obvious from the way she was cradling her so protectively. Laura and Maggie put their arms around her to comfort her.

'It's just that you can't imagine life going on and on like this,' Emily said sensibly. 'No sleep, no life outside the house, nothing in common with your friends any more who come over to tell you about their nights out and who's shagging who in work. And they coo over her and rock her and tell you how lucky you are. Then they hand her back and go off to join the real world,' she finished up.

Dee and Laura and Maggie looked up, their perfect mascara a bit streaked now. 'You've had those days too?' Maggie asked incredulously. *Emily?* Surely not!

'I've had those *weeks*,' Emily declared.

'Oh thank God, I thought I was a freak,' Dee shouted happily, and the priest on the altar looked down sharply. 'I even thought I might have postnatal depression,' she went on, quieter.

'So did I!' Maggie exclaimed.

'Me too!' Laura added.

By the time the front pews of the church had filled up, the girls were smiling again, and handing around tissues, and promising to phone each other up, day or night, whenever they felt like chucking their babies out the window and opening a bottle of vodka.

'Not that I'd ever do it, not really,' Maggie anxiously clarified, looking around the church as though she expected a district nurse to be eavesdropping, ready to root out dissident mothers.

'Oh, me neither,' Dee agreed very quickly. 'And I didn't mean that thing I said about slipping her Valium.'

'Of course you didn't.'

That peculiar tension, the awkwardness, had disappeared, and Emily felt herself relax for the first time all day. She looked at Maggie and Dee and Laura as they fussed over each other's babies and she loved them all over again.

She put back on Robert's christening hat and the shawl. He gazed up at her intensely, unwaveringly. For all her inadequacies, he seemed to find her irresistible. When she picked him up, he would instinctively cuddle into her. His eyes had started to follow her around the room, and when she spoke, he would look in the direction of her voice.

Nobody had ever loved Emily like that. Not Conor, or Emily's own mother, or anybody else in the world. It made her feel very humble.

It also aroused a fierce feeling of protectiveness in her. Murderous feelings, even.

If anyone even told Robert to feck off, she was

scared that she would pounce on them and strangle the life out of them with her bare hands. It was as if she had turned into one of those primitive creatures in a David Attenborough nature documentary, fighting tooth and nail for the survival of her cub. With minor differences of course; she did her foraging for food at the baby fruit-juice section of the supermarket, and Robert's most predatory enemies would probably be found at the local crèche.

Robert did a little posset now, and Emily admired it before wiping it away.

On the altar, the priest looked at his watch and went off to round up the lone altar boy. The service would be starting soon.

'Listen, I'd better go on up. I'll see you afterwards,' she whispered to the girls now.

'And we should have some news later on this afternoon. You know, about Martha's.'

Maggie, Laura and Dee barely looked up from their babies.

'Oh, yes,' said Maggie, vaguely. Maggie, who had marched up and down in her slippers in the rain; Maggie who had mooted the idea of a hunger strike! Now she was acting as though the battle to save the hospital had been someone else's entirely!

But perhaps Emily felt the same, if she were honest with herself. It all seemed so long ago. They were different people now, with different battles. They were mothers.

Behind her, the church door swung open and she turned around expectantly. But it was only her mother, decked out in a florid two-piece and a hat. Her rosary beads were already wrapped around her knuckles in anticipation of a good praying session. Some things never changed, although Pauline had cut back on the number of Masses she attended a week from five to two. She was still addicted to funerals, though, and rarely missed one.

'A great day, a great day,' she said, delirious at the prospect of welcoming another innocent soul into the Catholic fold. Conor had told her last week that they were considering an ecumenical service just to rile her up.

'I just saw Conor drive up,' she said, looking at Emily with that familiar disappointment.

'Good,' Emily said, wondering if Pauline would be able to contain herself, at least for today.

She wasn't. 'I just don't know what you're thinking of!' she said, shaking her head so violently that her hat slipped down over one ear.

'Yes, thank you, Mammy—'

'Isn't it enough that you have him living in a separate house? Do you have to drive him away to Belgrade too?'

'Belgium. And I'm not driving him anywhere. He wants to go.'

'And that child not nine weeks old yet!'

'Nine weeks and two days actually,' Emily said

proudly. 'Doesn't he look great?'

'Yes,' Pauline was forced to concede. 'But listen, about Conor—'

'You'd better go on up, Mammy. All the best seats are nearly taken.'

This had the desired effect. Pauline set off up the church at a gallop, lest someone usurped her from the position of honour in the front row. Now Liz was on her way down, dragging a red-faced Robbie by his blazer.

'I *told* you to go to the toilet before we came!'

'He can go in the bushes outside,' Emily said, trying to spare Robbie further embarrassment.

'And don't wet your shoes!' Liz warned, sending him off through the doors smartly. But she didn't look that annoyed. In fact, she looked great. Her hair was shiny and well cut, and she was wearing a lovely blue trouser suit that made her look very sophisticated.

'I hope Robert doesn't bring the roof down during the ceremony,' Emily whispered nervously.

'Not at all. And if he does, so what? They're used to it at christenings.'

Liz was being great these days. Emily didn't know whether it was the shared experience of motherhood, or whether it was down to Liz's new job in the chemist, which had given her great confidence.

Either way, Emily was glad for these brief interludes of companionship. Lord knows they didn't last long. This one didn't either.

'Tell us, are you going to keep paying rent on that

house, even when Conor's gone?'

'He *is* coming back eventually, Liz. And he'll be flying home some weekends.'

'I suppose.' Liz looked at her as though the pair of them were quite mad. Maybe we are, Emily thought. But everything had happened so fast. There was no time for dithering or indecision. In the end, it had been Emily who had made up their minds for both of them.

Liz leaned in now, and lowered her voice to a mere whisper. 'I know this isn't the time or place, but Eamon was wondering if you had any news for him.'

'I only filed for bankruptcy on Tuesday, Liz. These things take time.'

'But they won't take the house on us, will they?' Liz betrayed her worry now. 'I've read stories in the papers.'

'They won't take the house on you. But all his equipment and machinery will be seized to pay off the creditors. He probably won't have anything left, Liz. To start again with.'

Liz didn't seem too put out by this. 'No harm. Anyway – between us – he's been offered some work by Paudie Coyle.'

'That cowboy,' Emily murmured.

'Maybe he's a bit economical with his raw materials, but isn't that why he has a thriving business while Eamon's has gone to the wall? Eamon was too generous with his customers; that's what I tell him.'

Emily said nothing. The patio stones lay beautifully

now that Eamon had had another look at them, and you'd hardly notice the four extra ones that had been laid by the hedge at all, and that should have been laid in the first place.

'At least he has something lined up,' she told Liz.

'But he said this morning that he won't take it!' Liz said indignantly. 'Says he's happy at home looking after the boys, says he hasn't spent as much time with them in years!' And she rolled her eyes as though Eamon had lost his marbles.

'Well, I suppose you're earning now,' Emily pointed out.

'I know, I know, and it's good money too. And to be honest it's great to have a bit of freedom from the boys.' But there was something else bothering her.

'If Eamon doesn't mind being at home for a while, then what's the problem, Liz?'

'I don't know . . . I feel a terrible pressure on me sometimes, with them all at home depending on my wage. What if I lose my job? What if my hours are cut? What happens then?'

'You've been there before, Liz, yourself and Eamon would cope.'

'Maybe . . . I never thought I'd say this, but I feel bad now that I was so hard on Eamon. He was carrying the can the same way as I am now.'

'True,' Emily said. 'It's funny how things turn, isn't it?'

Liz looked around impatiently for Robbie, anxious to

get back to her seat before Emily got more philosophical. But she'd always been like that. You could be having a perfectly decent conversation and she'd get all airy-fairy on you.

'I hope I don't do anything wrong up there,' she told Emily nervously.

'Come on, Liz. You've been through it five times before.'

'Not as godmother.'

Christenings had always been a bit of a trial for Liz, because she'd had to go through so many of them, and towards the end had run out of suitable friends and relatives to prevail upon to be godmothers or godfathers. They'd had to resort to a second cousin of Eamon's for Willy last year, and she had turned up in a most unsuitable outfit.

But being on the receiving end of the dreaded request was very different. Liz was totally amazed that Emily had chosen her over all her legal colleagues and fashionable friends. She felt honoured, and had bought a new outfit especially for the occasion, and let Eamon gripe. Anyway, he liked the way she looked these days. He never said anything, of course, but he noticed all right.

'Robbie! Close the door quickly. You're blowing out all the candles! Emily, are you coming up to sit down?'

'In a minute,' Emily said.

She waited until Liz and Robbie went off up the aisle, then she picked up the car seat and went outside in search of Conor.

Honestly, wouldn't you think he'd have made the effort to be early? There was no sign of him, just a lone man walking up the churchyard towards her, tall and lithe. For a moment Emily didn't know who he was. He was wearing a very fashionable grey suit and tie, and a dazzling white shirt. His hair was very short and stylishly gelled and he bounded casually up the church steps two at a time.

'Conor?' She nearly fell over.

'What's wrong?' he asked, seeing her face.

'Um, nothing. You look . . .' She nearly said 'like a ride'. It was quite a shock to discover that she was still in possession of sexual feelings. She'd thought they had come out with her placenta. Even more surprising, it was Conor who had provoked them. Her husband, for God's sake. Surely this wasn't natural?

'You look very dapper,' she said, a bit embarrassed.

'So do you,' he said warmly. She was furious with herself all over again for not buying a new outfit, for slipping up on her diet. He was just being nice.

'I'm not late, am I?' he asked. 'I couldn't get parking.'

Emily looked suitably amazed. 'Most unusual for you.'

'I know. But I'm trying to stop being so predictable.'

'Really.'

'Mind you, I saw your car parked in the priest's spot.'

'Yes, well, I was just being assertive,' she said airily.

They joked quite a bit like this, about each other changing. Emily would sometimes roar at him to put the kettle on for a cup of tea, and tell him she was just making him aware of her needs. Both of them lightly accused the other of avoiding issues when it came to who would change one of Robert's pooey nappies.

These jokes were the only really allusion they made to that long night spent together in the labour ward all those weeks ago. They were both very raw yet, Emily felt, and she had no desire to go poking around again in the murky depths of their marriage. Besides, where would they find the time, what with feeding, bathing, burping, soothing and generally trying to keep Robert alive?

Emily did not think that it was necessary in any case. The admissions made that night, of fear and insecurity and loneliness, were things that surely only needed to be said once in any marriage. What they were dealing with now were the gaps that had been exposed, the struggle to find their feet once again. As themselves, and as a couple.

'How's my man?' Conor said, swooping down to pick up Robert. 'Jesus Christ, Emily, he looks like a girl in that dress.'

'It's not a dress. It's a christening shawl,' she explained patiently.

She watched as Conor tickled, nuzzled, kissed and pretended to drop Robert in a determined effort to make him smile.

'Conor, please, we don't want him to be sick.' But she only said it half-heartedly. She did not want to do anything to discourage this particular change in Conor. She never mentioned it at all, in fact. There were some things that they did not joke about.

She wondered did he even see it himself. He would be ringing the doorbell at nine o'clock every morning, shifting from foot to foot impatiently to be let in. Then he would get dug in straightaway with Robert, hoisting him up on his shoulder and taking him out to see the dogs. As if the child even knew what a dog was! Emily would have to fight hard to get a look-in at all. Then Conor would usually have the bonus of changing a dirty nappy. Conor loved dirty nappies. The whole cleaning process, the disposal of the nappy, the applying of Sudocream, the fresh new nappy, all appealed hugely to his practical side, his sense of enjoyment in a job well done, and he would positively glow as he descended the stairs with a spanking clean Robert.

Emily had not seen this side of Conor before. She would like to think that it was primarily to do with her. But it was Robert, of course. No one, not even Conor, could resist him.

'Is it time to go in?' Conor asked. The openness he'd displayed with Robert was gone now, and that careful, questioning look was back on his face. Maybe she looked at him that way too. It was like they both knew each other's frailties and failings now, and were trying hard not to touch on them.

Instead they delicately felt their way around things, through things, hopefully both moving in the same direction. Last week for instance they had talked tentatively about Conor's family, and Emily's family, and the place of fear and control in the backgrounds. That was how they were working it. It was a long, slow, intricate process, and it was a shame that it was about to be interrupted with this Belgium thing.

'It's five to one,' Emily said, checking her watch. 'I suppose we'd better head in.'

'Neasa's not here yet,' Conor said.

'She can't come, remember?'

'Oh yes, of course,' he said quickly. 'Still, I suppose you'll see her this afternoon anyway.'

The final judgement on the closure of Martha's would be announced today. Emily felt her place should be with Neasa and the rest of the staff in the office who had worked so hard on this case, even if it meant leaving the christening party of Robert halfway through.

'You'll be all right without me, won't you?'

'Stop fussing, Emily.'

Of course she was going to fuss! She'd never left Robert, even for an hour, since the day he'd been born! And in a house where a party would be in full swing?

'I'll manage,' Conor said, seeing her face. 'That's if your mother doesn't attack me.'

'She won't.'

He was unconvinced. 'She probably thinks I'm skipping town and leaving you holding the baby. Literally.'

'She's already accused me of driving you away.'

472

'Which you are,' he said, wearing that jokey face again.

'I am not.' Emily did not smile back. 'We've been over this, Conor.'

'And we both agree that the timing could be better. With Robert. With us.'

'And we both agree that this is an opportunity you won't get again,' Emily pointed out.

'There'll be other chances.'

But they knew that there was no guarantee. It was a fluke that Conor had landed the gig in the first place. Billy Middlemiss had seen the piece of music that Conor had dug out of the attic and had finally completed. Billy had connections in the film industry and Conor had received a call out of the blue on Monday last from the director of a European film just completing shooting in Belgium. The composer originally hired had left due to 'artistic differences' – would Conor be available to write the film score instead? The film was small and independent but a huge toehold into the business. And it was paid. It was also urgent.

'Do you want to do it?' Emily asked baldly. She did not need to remind him that the alternative was playing two nights a week in a smelly, smoky restaurant with no prospects and no hope.

She saw the hunger in his face, the need to strike out on his own, to fulfil some essential part of him. Hadn't she the same needs herself? She only understood now how necessary it was to be utterly selfish before there was any hope of making anybody else happy.

'Yes,' he said finally, but he didn't look excited, or pleased.

'We'll manage,' she said brightly. 'You'll fly back when you can and Robert and I will fly over and it'll be fine. And you'll only be gone a couple of months!'

But it all sounded a bit empty and second-rate, and Emily felt defensive. She was trying to do her best here; to keep everybody happy, even organising the christening at a moment's notice so that he wouldn't miss it! You'd think he'd look a tiny bit grateful that she was encouraging him to do what he needed to do!

'Robert might say his first word and I won't be there to hear it,' Conor hedged.

'Conor, rest assured, he won't be saying his first word for a good year yet.'

'Well, he might forget who I am.'

'How will he forget who you are when he'll be seeing you nearly every weekend?'

It seemed easier somehow to concentrate on Robert. Robert, after all, was a definite in the equation; neither of them was in any doubt about their feelings about him.

It was the 'us' that hung in the air between them. Just as the lack of a definite decision on Emily's part had hung in the air, for the past two months now. The decision had been made, of course. They both knew it, they were both working hard at those changes that needed to be made, even if all they could do at this point was joke about them.

'And when you come back, maybe you'll move back in,' she said quietly.

'Yes,' he said.

No bells rang. No fireworks went off overhead. Emily wondered why it all felt so flat. Like a compromise or something.

'It'll pass very quickly,' she said cheerily. 'You'll be busy and I'll be going back to work before I know it. The time will fly!'

'Yes,' he repeated, giving her another funny, disappointed look.

She felt very defensive again. Would he be any happier if she declared that she couldn't possibly live without him and that he must stay? Why could he not see, as she did, that if the balance in their marriage were to be redressed, they had to start somewhere?

'If you have a better idea, Conor, then I'd like to hear it.'

He hesitated. 'No. I suppose this is the best we can do for the moment.'

'Well, then,' she said. 'Let's go in.'

'I can't believe you didn't bring the baby!' Mandy at reception squealed.

'He just got christened. He's at his own party,' Emily said.

'Oh,' Mandy said, as though this were no excuse.

'Aren't you glad to see me anyway?' Emily enquired.

'I *suppose*,' Mandy said. Emily still looked very fat, she thought. 'Most people have gone to Milo's already to wait for the news. Phil got a new mobile phone just for the occasion!'

'Let's not get too confident, Mandy.'

'Everyone knows we're going to win,' Mandy said breezily, gathering her bag. 'Oh, and when are you coming back to work?'

'Who knows?' Emily said lightly.

Mandy left. Emily walked quietly down the deserted open-plan office for the first time in three months. They'd had a new carpet put down. And the broken photocopier had finally been replaced with a very swanky new one. Someone had put up a rota for coffee-making on the notice board.

She could not believe now that she had worked here for six years. Six years! A tenth of her life, if she croaked it at sixty. And now she felt a total stranger to the place, a misfit almost.

Just how much of a misfit became clear to her when she saw that there was a new nameplate up on the door of her office. It said Gary Gilmartin. Who the hell was he?

She peeked in the door, wondering what changes had been wrought in her little office. But the room was as sterile as she had left it, and even more devoid of personality. Not a single file was out of place, and the desk was bare except for a coffee-making rota.

She forgot about her annoyance now and felt only pity for this poor Gilmartin creature. Crawley Dunne & O'Reilly was leaving its stamp on him just as surely as it had on her. Only she had realised it before it was too late.

Neasa came in from the storeroom at the back. Her arms were laden with items of stationery.

'How did it go?' she asked immediately.

'Okay,' Emily said. 'Robert didn't cry at all. I left Conor in charge of them all back at the house.'

'I'm really sorry I couldn't make it, Emily.'

'I know, Neasa.' Emily checked her watch anxiously. 'I said I'd be back in an hour. Robert might need a feed . . .'

'I hope you're not going to be a pain in the arse about that child,' Neasa complained, hurling a stapler, a puncher and three new packets of floppy disks into a cardboard box on her desk.

'Don't those belong to Crawley Dunne & O'Reilly?' Emily enquired.

'Oh, they won't miss them,' Neasa said. She threw in some headed notepaper too. 'For my references,' she explained.

'I said I'd write you references,' Emily said.

'I know, and thanks, but to be honest I'd prefer to write my own.' Neasa now closed the top on the cardboard box and grabbed a roll of sellotape to tape it all up. She was leaving Crawley Dunne & O'Reilly today for good.

'Are you nervous about the decision?' she asked now.

'A bit. Are you?'

'Bricking it,' she said with her customary baldness. 'I'm kind of glad that I'm not in court when the judgement is handed down.'

She was trying to be brave, Emily saw. Crawley Dunne & O'Reilly had stabbed her in the back.

'They're spineless bastards,' Emily said quietly.

'Well, I wasn't a "suitable representative" for Crawley Dunne & O'Reilly in court,' Neasa said sarcastically. 'They were probably afraid I'd get drunk and make a holy show of them.'

'But to choose Gary to go up instead . . .'

'Emily, I don't care. I am so *over* Gary,' Neasa said plaintively. 'I was over him before I'd even finished with him.'

'True,' Emily said. 'So. Which way do you think it'll go?'

Robert had been one day and three hours old when the courts had handed down the decision that a judicial review would be held of the closure of St Martha's Hospital. Dee, Laura, Maggie and Emily had nearly burst their stitches, those that had them. Then the slow trawl through the courts of the actual judicial review, and now the final moment had arrived. At 3pm in Court No 5 Justice Patrick Leahy would seal their fate.

'I honestly don't know,' Neasa admitted.

Emily felt another nervous twinge in her tummy. 'At least we got this far,' she said stoically.

'Oh, don't give me that shite about how it's not about winning but about taking part,' Neasa said.

She would not understand that to Emily it was in a way. The court action might seem a bit removed from her now, but she had still fought the fight. That would be with her always.

'All set then?' she asked.

'I don't want to go over to the pub at all,' Neasa said gloomily. 'Could we not just wait to hear the news here?'

Gary was on instructions to phone Phil's new mobile phone the minute he left the courtroom.

'It shouldn't take longer than half an hour,' Emily told her.

'Half an hour is about all I'll last on bloody mineral water.'

Emily looked at her. 'How did this morning go?'

'Oh, awful,' Neasa said cheerfully.

'How awful?'

'Cringe-making awful. All these fecking eejits standing up and announcing that they were alcoholics – like none of us knew! Like it was some big surprise to us! And we all at an AA meeting!'

'So it wasn't worth missing my son's christening for?' Emily said lightly.

'I wouldn't miss a tea break for it,' Neasa declared.

She was deliberately making it out to be silly. She could not tell Emily the depth of her upset at being at one of the things in the first place. It was the last stop.

You really were an alcoholic if you turned up at AA meetings.

Maybe it would help her in time. But this morning she had been too embarrassed to do anything except lurk at the back of the room, looking at the door and waiting to see all the desperate, depraved alcoholics arriving in. After half an hour nobody arrived, and it slowly dawned on her that the alcoholics were already present; all those nice, well-dressed and educated men and women who Neasa had somehow presumed were the meeting facilitators. None of them looked any different to her. Or she didn't look any different to them.

'Did you talk to that bastard?' Neasa said, deliberately changing the subject.

Emily knew immediately to whom she was referring: Garda Andrew Mitchell from Mitchelstown, the arresting garda on her drink-driving charge.

'Yes, he's back from his holidays,' Emily confirmed.

'I hope he had a lovely time,' Neasa said insincerely.

'He did, actually, and he apologised for the delay in sending out a copy of your statement. But I have it now, and he'll let us know the results of your blood test as soon as he has them.'

'When do you think it'll get to court?' Neasa asked efficiently.

'Given the courts lists, not a chance before next year, I would say.'

'Next year!'

'It's usual, Neasa. I'm hoping it'll be heard within nine months.'

'Nine months of this hanging over me?'

'I know. I know.'

Neasa stopped her fierce sellotaping of the box. 'I really fucked up this time, didn't I?'

Part of Neasa's decision to move back to Cork City was the fact that she would almost certainly get the mandatory two-year ban for drink-driving, and she needed to be within walking distance of a job, or else near a reliable form of transport. There would be no spur-of-the-moment drives into the country, or trips up to see Emily. Everything would have to be planned and worked out and she would have no freedom at all.

'You still have the car until then,' Emily pointed out.

'I know. The law is gas, isn't it?' Neasa agreed. 'You get arrested for drink-driving but they'll let you merrily drive around for a whole year until it gets to court.'

'Be thankful for small mercies.'

They talked about the probability of her being banned quite a lot. They never talked about the other probability, which was that they might hand down a jail sentence. She might only have dented a bumper, but she had still caused an accident. In those first weeks off drink, when Neasa had literally sweated poisons from her system, she would have wild dreams at night about Mountjoy and porridge and slopping out in the mornings. And having to say to her new co-workers, whoever they might be, 'Cheerio now, I'm just off to do a three-month prison sentence. Keep my seat warm!'

It was just all so wrong. People like Neasa didn't get arrested. They didn't get hauled up before a court, and they certainly didn't go to prison. Their names did not appear in the court reports of the regional newspaper, in the same column as lunatics who had set their neighbours' noisy dog on fire.

'Come on, Neasa,' Emily said sternly, seeing her descent into depression.

'I know. I know. I'll probably laugh about it in two years' time.' She dumped the cardboard box onto the floor. Her desk was now completely bare and she looked at it for a moment. Emily thought that she was getting emotional.

'You're better than this place, Neasa.'

'Of course I bloody am,' Neasa agreed robustly. 'I don't know what I was hanging around here for anyway.' She moved on swiftly before Emily could say 'Gary'. 'Actually, I'm looking forward to setting up all over again in a new place.'

Where nobody knew her or anything about her.

It had been all over the office, of course. That little snitch Phil had been coming out of the chemist the morning it happened and had seen the whole thing. Some of her so-called colleagues had contented themselves with disgusted looks, like she was a mass-murderer or something. Others had confided that they regularly jumped into cars blind drunk but had never had the bad luck to be caught. On balance, Neasa preferred the mass-murderer brigade.

Neasa had never cared about other people's opinions. But that was when people's opinions of her had generally been great.

'Oh, here,' she said, taking a solitary document from her out-tray and holding it out.

'What is it?'

'The blueprint for the new litigation division. Creepy asked me to pass it on to you and get back to him with any comments.'

'What?'

'Didn't he tell you? Honestly! Well, you should be getting a phone call. He wants you to head up the new division, Emily.'

'Does he now,' Emily said slowly, leafing through the introduction. It was full of tight-arsed words and phrases, and everything was broken down into niggly headings and sub-headings. She felt the back of her neck tingle. A migraine.

'Gary's totally pissed off that they didn't ask him,' Neasa confided.

Emily closed the document and threw it back in Neasa's out-tray. There was a silence.

'You're not coming back here, are you?' Neasa said slowly.

'I don't know.'

'Come on, Emily.'

'My maternity leave isn't up for another three weeks, I haven't decided,' Emily insisted.

'If I were you, I wouldn't. They're a right bunch of fuckers.'

'They *did* pay all the court costs for me,' Emily said uncertainly. 'Although if we lose today . . . they might refuse point blank.'

Neasa smiled wolfishly. 'I already got them to sign a letter.'

'What?'

'You can thank me later,' Neasa said airily. 'Anyway, back to you resigning.'

'I haven't resigned yet.' Emily bit the bullet. 'Oh, all right! I've had a couple of people approach me to act for them. You know, after the publicity about the court case and everything. I could do it from home.'

Neasa shook her head, marvelling. 'You'd go into competition against Creepy?'

'It wouldn't be competition,' Emily insisted.

'They're setting up a new litigation division! I would say they'll look on it as a direct assault!'

'So what!' Emily said loudly. 'There's room in this town for both of us!'

It was a relief to say out loud what she had been planning for weeks. Or, half-planning. It was difficult to concentrate on a new career path with Robert puking in the background.

But being here today had only strengthened her

resolve. She could not go back to being a cog in the machine.

'You won't make any money,' Neasa said baldly. 'Not for ages and ages.'

'I know that.'

'Still, I suppose now that Conor is taking Hollywood by storm . . . sorry, *Belgium*.'

Neasa made no effort to conceal her ongoing dislike of Conor. Privately, she thought it was only a matter of time before he strayed again. Oh, once they got a taste for it at all there was no stopping them. Even after her own experiences, Neasa had lost none of her ability to spot glaring great faults in others, including addiction.

'So long as Robert has enough to eat, we'll manage,' Emily said.

'I'd wait until he's on solids before I go making any assumptions,' Neasa said darkly.

Belatedly she realised she was being a tad negative about Emily's new venture. And, really, Emily might do very well, given that half of the southwest now knew her name. Plus there was Emily's marvellous organisa-tional abilities and the wad of start-up cash that must be lying in one of her savings accounts. Emily was a great saver. 'Do you need a partner?' Neasa offered magnanimously. 'I know I said I was moving to Cork, but I'll stay if you need me. We could call ourselves Collins & Martin. Or Martin & Collins, that has a better ring.'

'No, Neasa,' Emily said gently. 'Thanks anyway.'

'Just because I'm a lush doesn't mean I'm not a good solicitor!'

'You're an ex-lush, and yes, you're a marvellous solicitor. But if I'm going to do it, I want to do it on my own.' Emily hoped Neasa would understand. She didn't need the weight of another person's expectations on her. But her reasons were more selfish than anything. And she wasn't going to make any apologies about it.

'You're right. We'd probably end up killing each other anyway,' Neasa said, the idea already forgotten. 'Well, good luck to you.'

'Thanks.'

'Let's go,' Neasa sighed, picking up her cardboard box. 'I don't want that shower of bastards thinking I'm afraid to go into a pub or something.'

She was. She hadn't set foot in a licensed establishment in ten weeks, two days and ten hours. The lunch with Terry Mitton had been in a cheapish café that served no alcohol – Neasa had chosen it. It had been awful. He had been much shorter than he'd looked in his black gown and wig – five-seven at a push. Neasa had thrown back orange juice in the hope that it would loosen her tongue. But she found she had nothing to say, or at least nothing that sounded quite as devastatingly witty or meaningful as it did on red wine. And she couldn't stop noticing the hairs that protruded from his nose, or the way he kept going on and on about how his two properties had doubled in value in a year.

Reality sucked. It was grey and cold and depressing,

and she had no armour any more to protect herself from it. Who could blame her for wanting to dress it up a bit? Was there a single person out there who did not want to escape the daily toil that was work, dreary boyfriends and endless bills? Didn't half the population go to the pub on a Friday night to block it out with a few pints, to loosen up, just to have a good time? That was all she had done.

She had just wanted it to go on.

The boyfriends had gone with the drink. What was the point? She was sure she would eventually become sufficiently comfortable with reality to start dating again. But, by God, The One had better be something special indeed if she had to put up with him stone cold sober.

They stopped down by the front door of Crawley Dunne & O'Reilly. Both of them knew they wouldn't be setting foot in the place again.

'To victory!' Neasa shouted defiantly.

'If we win, I'm going to get pissed,' Emily declared. 'Oh. Sorry, Neasa.'

'Will you miss me?' Neasa suddenly asked, letting two big tears well up in her eyes. Surely she was allowed to be a bit mawkish at a time like this?

'Of course I will.'

'You're only saying that. You won't give me a thought now that you have Robert.'

'Robert only takes up ninety-five percent of my time, Neasa. I'll miss you the other five percent.'

'You won't. You'll be smooching with Conor,' Neasa said jealously.

'I can assure you that Conor and I are not smooching.'

'You can't pull the wool over my eyes – you've kissed and made up, the two of you, haven't you?'

'He's going to move back in when he gets home from Belgium,' Emily admitted.

'So it's all worked out okay in the end,' Neasa said.

'Yes,' Emily said, wondering again why it all sounded so bloody hollow. She was cross now at her own disillusionment. She had got what she wanted, hadn't she? She had dug deep and got to the truth. She had not taken second best. So what if it didn't come with streamers and party hats attached? The important thing was that after all the grief, she had emerged with her relationship intact.

It struck her now how workmanlike all this was. It was the old Emily, putting her head down, doing the hard graft, and expecting the rewards that came with toil. And she knew in a rush that part of her was still stuck back there, for all her new risk-taking and assertion. These she had saved for her career, for High Court cases, for Robert even, who required plenty of assertion and some risk-taking. But not for Conor. Not for her marriage.

Why was she so afraid of making that last leap? Part of it she knew was the aftermath of the affair. Trust was not a cheap commodity. But neither was passion, or impulse, or being in love again.

She thought of that last leap again. Maybe it was finally time to jump.

'Can I use your nappy-changing unit, Conor?'

'Of course you can,' Conor said benevolently.

'I thought I'd change Chloe before we turn the news on,' Maggie confided.

'Very sensible,' Conor said. 'And don't forget to wash your hands!'

'Oh now!' Maggie said, giggling as she disappeared up the stairs with Chloe.

Conor let his big, friendly smile slip. Maggie was the most irritating person he had ever met – bar Pauline, obviously, who was over there in the corner with the priest, talking some kind of shite about the Legion of Mary. Conor had not known the Legion of Mary still existed even. And Laura had just put *Den* 2 on the TV at full blast; *Den* 2, for two-month-old babies! How did Emily manage to surround herself with these kind of people?

Not that Emily was even here. She was in the cosy comfort of Milo's pub while Conor was standing in the midst of curling sandwiches and damp crisps, wailing babies and the smell of vomit. Tommy, Robbie, Mikey and Bobby were playing a very boisterous game of tag, and had knocked over Conor's mother twice. At least all his side had already left. The noise and smell and press of bodies had quickly become too much for them and they had strapped themselves into their big boxy air-conditioned cars with ill-concealed relief.

Conor's impatience wasn't just rudeness. In fact, he had been exceptionally pleasant and chatty all afternoon he felt. Beyond the call of duty, really. Beyond his own capacity for sociability, if you wanted to get down to brass tacks. He was making the effort. If Emily wanted him to walk on hot coals, he would do it. Even if she wanted him to be nice to Maggie . . .

But he just did not want this circus today; not when he should be spending time alone with his wife and child; not when he had a ten o'clock flight in the morning that would take him hundreds and hundreds of miles away.

'Conor! Is it okay if we turn the radio on?' Dee shouted over the TV. 'It's nearly four o'clock, they might have the results on LKR.'

You'd think she was talking about a football match. Conor wondered whether Emily knew the outcome already. He was surprised she had not phoned, especially as Laura, Maggie and Dee were waiting here for the news.

He found that he had a nervous feeling in his belly. He knew it was more than the outcome of the court case.

'Robbie!' Liz screeched out in the hallway, but it was too late. Conor heard the sound of something breaking. He did not particularly want to know what. Instead he picked up Robert, went into the kitchen and closed the door.

Peace, blessed peace.

'Will we make a cup of tea?' he asked Robert.

Conor and Robert often made tea together. It was a little ritual. They would play games around the kitchen as tea bags were sourced, cups put out and the red light on the kettle switched on, to Robert's never-ending fascination.

There were no games today. Conor was not in the mood. Neither was Robert. In fact, the child was looking up at Conor rather despondently, and Conor felt very defensive.

'I don't want to go to Belgium either, okay?' he told Robert strongly. 'It's all your mother's fault!'

Well, it was Emily who was churning out the logic this time, not him. She was the one holding up the pros and cons, refusing to let sentimentality or emotions cloud the decision. Conor found that he could not argue with her reason. Especially as she had just asked him to move back into the house upon his return. Just like that! No conditions, no begrudgery! In reality, Conor was getting everything he wanted, and more – a new career and a second chance at everything he had made a balls of the first time around.

So why wasn't he jumping around the garden?

It was probably the timing thing, he thought. Off to Belgium, when he had already missed out on so much by living in a separate house! Oh, he could kid himself all right – he would arrive here first thing in the morning and don his mantle of doting father, before

becoming the concerned partner to Emily, making her
meals and putting on washes, and engaging in a little
marriage counselling when they were both up to it.
Then he would go back to his house late in the evening,
secure in the knowledge that he had not failed in his
paternal and marital duties, while still managing to
hang on to his bloody pride.

'I'm very sorry,' he told Robert now.

He felt he had let him down very badly. By his
actions, by his affair, he had created a situation where
he absented himself from some of the responsibility of
bringing up his child.

He carried this responsibility around like a great
weight on his shoulders. But he was not daunted by it,
not crushed in the way he was when faced with the
responsibility of marriage. From the day in the labour
ward when Robert had been born, and Conor had
eventually persuaded Emily to hand him over, he had
not been afraid of him. They had regarded each other
with a cool interest, or Conor liked to think anyway,
and he had rather hoarsely promised Robert that he
would look out for him, son. Well, it seemed the right
thing to say at the time, and Robert had looked up at
him with a grave acceptance.

Conor only learned afterwards that newborn babies
couldn't see a thing farther than twenty-five centimetres from their own noses. But it didn't matter because
by then, the pair of them were in cahoots. Conor had
half wanted to keep the relationship on some kind of

professional footing, with him taking care of the nappy changing and laundry loads while Emily did the cooing and kissing. But he had not reckoned on his own spontaneity, a character trait he had always regarded as a bit of a liability and which had always firmly been Emily's department. He had fought it at first and then, three days into his relationship with Robert, had held up the white flag and given in to it gracefully.

He would catch Emily looking at him sometimes when he was unashamedly romping with Robert, like today for instance, and he would remember their conversation in Martha's and he would feel embarrassed all over again.

She knew now. She knew what a small and fearful man he really was; a person with no real courage; a man who had only wanted to half-marry her in case he might have to expose himself. The result was that they had had the good times and the bad times, but none of it had been very good or very bad. It had been a grey way of living, really, antiseptic and passionless.

It could be put down to fear of intimacy, of course, and he was sure now that he suffered from this. But he had made no attempt to overcome it until she had forced him to that night, and that was where his courage had failed him.

But the miracle was that she still seemed to want him. She must love him on some level if she was prepared to work this out. This knowledge made him very conscious of what he had to do, the effort he had to make.

He could not take her faith and let her down all over again. And this time there was Robert to think of too.

He had started to offer small bits of himself; some of his family background, for example, certain episodes in his early career. He used events to reveal himself. He was not able to talk like he had talked in the hospital. Not yet. But he felt they had put their feet on the first rung of the ladder.

And now bloody Belgium in the morning. Still, maybe it would only be a problem if they let it become one. And they would still see each other every weekend, wouldn't they? He even wondered whether it might be a good thing at this point to have a little space between them. Would it be so bad to stop for some reflection?

The kitchen door flew open, startling him. It was Maggie, Chloe under one arm and an unidentified baby under the other.

'The news has just started! Quick!'

'Coming now,' Conor assured her.

But he stood there for a moment, slowly rocking Robert, and he could not hide from the fact that he was doing it again.

Belgium was a safety net for him. An escape route now that things between him and Emily were gradually proceeding to a point where he would have to divulge more of himself, make some emotional commitment once and for all, instead of just talking about it. And he was running for his life.

Lack of courage could perhaps be forgiven once in anybody's life, he decided. But not twice.

He turned and purposefully left.

The smell of garlic and herbs hit Emily the minute she walked in the door. She stood for a moment, bemused. The only time there had been a smell of garlic in the house in the last two months was when Conor got chips and garlic mayonnaise down in Mario's.

There were candles in the living-room. Lighted candles, that is. Emily couldn't even remember the last time they'd put a match to a candle.

The next thing she registered was that the stereo was playing: soft, jazzy stuff, romantic stuff.

The old ghosts came back to ambush Emily and she stood stock still in the middle of the living-room. Mary Murphy rushed into her head, as she did at odd times, no matter how Emily tried to banish her. Sometimes she wondered if she would ever truly go away. Would she be there between them always, like a decomposing body that wouldn't stay buried?

In the kitchen, Conor was turning down the heat on the stove, the baby monitor on the worktop beside him. The lights on it were rising and falling evenly with Robert's breath.

'You're late,' he said to Emily.

'Yes,' she said.

'Drunk?'

'No! Well, maybe a bit. Everybody kept buying drinks

because Neasa was leaving. And she only on water herself.' Emily looked around the tidy kitchen. There was no evidence that a party had taken place here earlier. 'I hope you didn't push people out the door, Conor.'

'I did not! Well, except for your mother, but she never leaves unless she's forced to.'

'I thought Maggie or Dee might have stayed on.' You'd have thought they'd have wanted to hear all the gory details.

'It's been a long day, Emily. And with all the babies . . .'

'I suppose,' she said, secretly glad that he had managed to get rid of everyone. 'How was Robert? Did he miss me?'

'He did.'

'How much? A lot?'

'Desperately,' Conor assured her. 'He's upstairs having a nap.'

Emily was relieved, and felt a bit guilty. But she had a few things to tell Conor. She didn't want to be distracted by Robert or anyone else.

'I'm very sorry, Emily.' Conor got in there first.

'I know.'

'We really thought you'd win.'

'So did I, kind of.'

'Is Neasa upset?'

'Well, we all were, for a while.'

'I know.'

There was an awkward moment where they both

made a kind of sympathetic move towards the other but neither of them went through with it and they both looked at their shoes.

Emily cleared her throat. 'So, um, what did they say on the radio? We couldn't get any sense out of Gary on the phone except that we'd lost. I think he was crying.'

'Just that Martha's would close immediately and that a request for an appeal had been denied.'

'Great,' Emily sighed. 'I couldn't admit it in the pub, but I couldn't bear an appeal.'

'They said that there would be a ruling on costs next week,' Conor added.

'Right.' Crawley Dunne & O'Reilly would be picking up the bill in any case. Upon news of the defeat, Creepy had immediately cancelled the tab at the bar and had left, green-faced, with Daphne and Ewan stumbling in his wake.

'Vera rang,' Conor told her. 'She said she'd call you tomorrow.'

Vera had no doubt been glued to the radio all afternoon as well. At least they'd all hung onto their jobs in Martha's for two months longer than anticipated, even if the hospital had been empty of patients at the end. Open, but empty.

'Do you think I might have a glass of wine or would Robert be pissed when I feed him later?' Emily wondered.

'I think you can chance it,' Conor said, pouring two glasses.

She held hers up in a jokey toast.

'To the campaign.'

'To a great fight,' Conor said quietly.

'Yes. It was worth it.' She took a big gulp of wine. She felt like a chapter in her life had just closed, leaving her with an unusual feeling of satisfaction, despite losing in the end.

She watched as Conor took the lid off a saucepan, threw in a handful of fresh herbs and stirred. It smelled gorgeous.

'Is this a sympathy meal?' she said lightly.

'No. It's just a nice meal. That's all,' he said evenly.

Hmm, Emily thought. Conor seemed a bit off tonight. At least, he wasn't participating in their usual jokey banter. He was stirring that pot very seriously indeed, his brow furrowed.

The thought of Belgium was probably putting him off. Not that there was anything wrong with Belgium per se – didn't they have the most divine chocolate there, wasn't that attraction enough in itself? But the reality of the flight in the morning was probably sinking in with him. She knew he desperately did not want to leave Robert. She hoped that he did not want to leave her as much.

It was time for her to put her cards on the table. She put down her wine and turned to him, already anticipating his relief and happiness.

'Conor,' she said rather dramatically, 'I've decided I'm going to Belgium with you. Robert and I.'

She wasn't prepared for the look of horror on his face. '*What?*'

He must not have understood. She repeated herself more slowly. 'I'm coming with you to Belgium. I've booked a flight ticket and everything.'

'Jesus Christ, Emily!'

'What?'

'I'm not going to Belgium! I rang them this evening and turned the job down!'

Now it was her turn to look appalled. 'Bloody hell, Conor! What did you go and do a stupid thing like that for?'

He looked all huffy now. 'Oh, *stupid!* Just because I decided that I should get my priorities right?'

'I don't believe this . . . why didn't you talk to me first?'

'Why didn't *you* talk to *me*?'

Emily threw up her hands. 'You see? This is just typical of the lack of communication between us!'

'I couldn't agree more!' Conor butted in. 'And now I'm stuck at home with no job and you're flying with Robert to Belgium in the morning!'

'Obviously I won't be using my ticket,' she said stiffly.

'Obviously. Sure haven't we got money to burn?'

Emily began to feel very stupid now, her great act of noble self-sacrifice thrown back in her face. In her head, she had fantasised that he would be overcome by emotion, possibly break down in tears, certainly sweep her into his arms and very probably try to make wild love to her on the kitchen floor (she would tell him that it was too soon, naturally).

But instead he just looked hot and cross and he was muttering something under his breath.

'Pardon?' she asked.

'I said, do you want penne or linguini with this sauce?' he repeated, louder this time.

'You know something, Conor? I really don't care,' she snapped, grabbing her wine and marching into the living-room. Only Conor could talk about pasta shapes at a time like this. How had she ever thought that things between them had changed? Fooling herself! She might as well give up now.

'Emily?' He had followed her in. Probably to ask how long he should boil the fucking penne for.

'Yes, Conor!'

'I'm sorry if I upset you. I wanted it to be a surprise. A nice one, I thought. I'm sorry.'

Emily immediately deflated at his honesty. 'I wanted mine to be a nice surprise too.'

'Yes.'

They looked at each other, awkward now.

'That was a pretty big thing,' she said. 'To give up your job.'

'Not really,' he said.

'Stop being modest.'

He looked at the tea towel in his hands and back up again. 'I just felt I hadn't done enough. I wanted you to know how much I . . . well, you know.'

'Thank you,' she said. 'I suppose I wanted you to know the same.'

There was a little silence; a silence coloured by hope and expectation and optimism. And Emily felt lighter as she turned to him.

'What about the job?' she asked.

'What about it?'

'Can't you ring them and say you want it back?'

'I don't think they'll give it back to me.'

'They would if you begged.'

'I will not lower myself to beg,' Conor said primly.

Emily picked up the phone and thrust it into his hand. 'Beg,' she ordered. 'I'll cook the pasta.'

Amazing Grace

For Ella

Acknowledgements

Thanks to:

All at Poolbeg, especially Paula Campbell, Sarah Conroy and Brona Looby.

Gaye Shortland for her continued editorial guidance, and for working overtime.

Clare Foss of Headline UK for all her editorial input, and to Sherise Hobbs.

Darley Anderson, my agent, and Elizabeth, Julia and all at the agency.

Friends and fellow-writers Ho Wei Sim, Sian Quill, Caroline Williams, Marie Therese Duggan, Bernie Downes and Brian Gallagher.

All the wonderful Irish Girls: Sarah Webb, Tina Reilly, Marisa Mackle, Cauvery Madhaven, Martina Devlin, Jacinta McDevitt, Dawn Cairns, Catherine Dunne, Anne Marie Forrester, Mary Ryan and others whom I have yet to meet over a Chinese takeaway.

Margaret, for always pitching in and giving a hand whenever deadlines loom.

My family in Kilkenny, as always.

Stewart for the ice pops and unwavering support, and Sean for the reality checks.

And a special thanks to Ella, who arrived in the middle of this book. An inspiration!

One

It was a warm bright morning at the end of July when Grace Tynan consulted her map of County Meath. Its shape reminded her of France, and she involuntarily thought of vineyards now, and little street cafés full of locals. And baguettes, brown and warm from the oven. And crepes, perhaps with clotted cream and a little sugar . . . oh, she wished she'd made time for breakfast this morning.

'Anyhow!' she said. She talked to herself quite a bit in the car. Some days they were the only decent conversations she had.

There was a packet of cheesy crisps in the glove compartment and she opened them now. It was a free sample that Ewan had brought home. Free samples were one of the perks of his job. If you could call it a perk – they still had a whole case of Mega Curry Beans to finish up.

Thank God – here came an elderly man on a bike. She rolled down her window and beeped her horn enthusiastically. 'Hello there!'

He hadn't expected this, and his bike wobbled dangerously.

'Sorry,' she said. 'It's just that I'm lost – would you be able to point me in the direction of Hacketts-town?'

He looked at her rather peculiarly, she thought. Perhaps it was a mistake to have flagged down a strange man on a deserted country road. Especially in a flash car with her leather handbag lying on the front seat. She might as well beg to be car-jacked! Really, this was the very last time she would swap with Lisa – if she really was getting a wisdom tooth out, the fifth now by Grace's calculations.

But the man just said, 'If you're *sure* you want to go there, drive on about two miles, take a left at the crossroads and then the next right.' He added heavily, 'Good luck,' before wobbling on.

'Thank you!' She quickly scribbled down what he'd said on the back of an envelope. She had learned over the years never to trust her own memory when it came to directions. It was already burdened enough with the school-run rota, essential items she must buy in the supermarket and nine different pin numbers. Oh, and the damned passports! She must ring Ewan as soon as she could, because he wouldn't remember them either. Head like a sieve, Ewan. It hadn't always been that way. His memory seemed to have got worse over the years as hers had improved, a development that hadn't escaped her in its convenience.

Hackettstown. Twinned with Wart-Hausen. Grace slowly drove past the road sign and up a narrow mean main street, which boasted outlets such as Go West Fashions and Brenda's Unisex Salon (20% off dry-cuts on a Monday). But there was a brightly lit

Spar farther up, and quite a pretty little square with some roses in it – mind you, a group of the town's teenagers seemed to be tearing the heads off them, and threatening each other with what looked to be penknives. They turned dull envious eyes on her silver BMW as it went past.

'Hello there!' She waved a bit nervously at them and drove on.

Bridge Road was out in the suburbs. The driveway of Number 17 was empty and the house looked deserted. Grace parked acceptably and turned off the ignition. The radio, set on some station the boys favoured, was cut off mid *boom-boom*. She had only been listening to it at all because one of the other mothers had told her at the school gates that the whole class was tuning in to explicit songs about sex and drugs. But after weeks of monitoring, Grace had yet to make out a single word in any of the songs. Except perhaps 'yours was yum', once, but she was too embarrassed to report this to the others. Also she wasn't quite sure what it meant. Well, she had her *suspicions*. Then she found that she couldn't get it out of her head: yours was yum, yours was yum! And she a married woman, a mother, and therefore not expected to think about sex. (Why then did she find herself wanting to rush out and buy the entire album?)

Ten to nine. Good. She was early. She closed her eyes and lay back in her seat.

The car was a good place to think – or not to think. Grace could spend the whole day in the car, dreaming, and indeed once had.

Mind you, that had been open to a slight misinterpretation.

'Oh my God, Harry, she's after killing herself!'

'Quick – can you see the hosepipe? There must be a hosepipe from the exhaust!'

'Still, would you blame her? Would you blame *anyone*?'

'Shut up! We need to pull out the hosepipe!'

She'd opened her eyes to find Hilda and Harry Brennan from next door pressed against the windscreen, handkerchiefs clamped over their mouths. At least they'd cared enough to investigate. The boys would have come eventually, she was sure. Hunger would have brought them if nothing else. Would Ewan? Probably. It would depend on how engrossed he was. Well, he did work from home. He couldn't always come running every time a member of the family decided to disappear for ten minutes, as he had said mildly at the time. He had a point, of course – but at the same time, how long *would* she have to be gone before he'd come running? Three days? A week, perhaps? She was being most unfair now, he felt – he would certainly notice if she disappeared for a week. At that juncture the Brennans had made their excuses and left.

Grace had continued to enjoy stolen moments in her car. It wasn't that she was anti-social or unfriendly, but honestly, didn't you get heartily sick of people sometimes?

'Hello there, Grace! Found the place okay?'

A red-faced man of around forty propelled himself out the front door of number seventeen and towards her car. He had a tape measure in his hand, extending out to about ten inches, and he waved it at her excitedly. 'I've got something to show you.'

Grace got out of the car, doing a swift trawl through her short-term memory banks – Fergus? No, Fergus was yesterday. This one must be Frank. After ten years, clients were beginning to look the same she was ashamed to admit.

'Frank – nice to meet you again.' He'd been in the office last week.

But he ignored her outstretched hand now and brandished the measuring tape with a loud snap. 'That fellow from your office measured up the place wrong,' he announced. 'The bathroom is nearly a whole foot wider than what you've put down on the brochure.'

'Is it?'

'Eleven and a quarter inches, to be exact. Look!'

'I'm sorry about that. I don't think it'll make much difference, though.'

She was taking this altogether too calmly for his liking, she could see.

'Some people,' he said, 'bathrooms are their *thing*. Sandy spends about four hours on average in the bathroom every day. That's why she never picks up the phone if you ring – she can't hear it, you see, what with taps running and water gurgling and the ballcock hissing.' He must have seen Grace's startled expression, because he added, 'She's a Pisces, she loves all that.'

'And Sandy is . . .?'

'My fiancée.'

'Oh! I didn't know you were engaged.'

'There's no need to look so surprised,' he said.

'I wasn't—'

'You think nobody would want to marry me? You think I'm not relationship material or something?'

'Not at all,' Grace said, trying desperately not to look at the small pimple on the end of his nose. The more she tried not to look, the more she *looked*, until all she could see was one enormous pimple. Dear God, had it started to throb?

'Anyhow!' she said, whirling around to look at the house. 'You have a very nice place here, Frank.'

More lies. It was a horrible low brown bungalow with nasty net curtains and fake oil lamps over the front door. A small notice had been propped in the glass panel: *No Jehovah's Witnesses Please*.

She retrieved her clipboard from the car and consulted it efficiently. 'I have three couples booked in to view your house this morning. Now, the first pair is due in about ten minutes, so you should really . . .'

He just stood there.

'You might have a little shopping to do . . .?'

He still stood there.

She said gently, 'Or you could just drive around if you don't have anywhere to go.'

His chin jutted up. 'Of course I have somewhere to go! I have any number of places I can go. In fact, I've been invited over by a very good friend of mine – Mrs Carr. That's her house across the road.'

Grace looked over. The house was like something from a fairytale – all turrets, and bits added over the years, higgledy-piggledy. An ancient sign hung over the pink door saying *Lodging House*.

Grace thought it was a shame she wasn't trying to sell it, rather than Frank's brown bungalow. They didn't sell houses outside Dublin as a rule. They had only agreed to take on Frank's house at all because he was related to one of the partners' wives – an accident of marriage, she had been at pains to point out.

Frank was looking across the road in discontent. 'Look at that grass verge out the front!'

Grace did. 'What's wrong with it?'

'Nothing! That's the whole point! Because I had to take out my own lawnmower this morning and mow it. She couldn't be bothered. She never can. But I didn't want people arriving here to view my house thinking that this was some kind of lower class neighbourhood, some shabby do-what-you-like kind of place to live.'

'Well, people do tend to notice their surroundings,' Grace offered, patting his arm. Over the years, she had come to realise that her job wasn't just about selling houses. Depending on the situation, she was often required to provide moral support, relationship counselling, intervention in community disputes, and sometimes just to jolly people along. Lay people didn't realise how multi-layered a career in property was! They thought, rather harshly, that it was all about location and greed and pitting cash-strapped purchasers against each other like it was some kind of blood sport.

'Still, we mustn't lose sight of the bottom line, Grace,' as a young male manager from Head Office had explained to her at a 'training meeting' last month. 'Sales, sales, sales!'

Apparently, she was taking too much time with clients. Gathering unnecessary detail about a property, such as the fact that Paul McCartney's second cousin had once owned it. Or encouraging clients to stay in touch once their properties had been sold, that kind of thing.

'All that might have been fine when you started as a trainee a decade ago, Grace.' He made it sound like a century. 'But with competition what it is, we just can't expect to deliver the same kind of personal service we used to.'

She had looked across at him and, with all the weight of her experience and the maturity of her thirty-four years, had slowly explained to him that these were people's homes they were talking about: places where they had laughed and cried and fought and lived and, in a couple of cases, died (although, she assured him, that this was not something she generally pointed out). Moving house was for some people like ripping a heart from its chest! Surely he could see that it was part of their job to support their clients as well as take their money?

'Absolutely,' he had said, smiling and nodding, before informing her that they would be setting time limits on call-out visits to assess or show clients' homes.

In pure defiance now, Grace gave Frank an encouraging smile. 'Go on.'

'Well, in the end she said I could mow the verge but I wasn't to touch the garden gnomes.'

Grace saw the gnomes now. There were three of them, all grinning widely, their hands wrapped firmly around fishing-rods. Someone had broken off the rods halfway down. The result was unseemly.

'Vandals,' Frank said, his complexion turning a darker hue.

'There's no point in falling out over a garden gnome, is there?' she said soothingly, trying to usher him towards the gate.

'It wasn't the gnomes we fell out over. It was the rosebushes.'

'Pardon?' she said.

'I just gave them a little trim. Well, more than a trim. But honestly, people like her, they let down the whole tone of the place. And I ended up telling her that too. Been wanting to for eleven years!' he finished up stoutly.

Grace had heard of plenty of people who had feuded with the neighbours soon after moving in, but never upon moving out. And after eleven years too! It was a tragedy. Mrs Carr seemed such an interesting person as well; apart from the gnomes, she had two wooden deckchairs parked on the uneven front lawn, and a rickety plastic table, as though she might decide at any moment to flop down with a bottle of wine and say to hell with the world.

'Frank,' she said, with the calmness and authority born of years of family mediation, 'why don't you go over to her and just apologise?'

'She says that she'll never open her door to me again.'

'She would if you bring her a replacement rose-bush.'

9

'She says she's got her husband's shotgun.'

'I'd imagine she was pulling your leg.'

'She showed it to me.'

Grace looked over at the house. 'Are you sure?'

'What, you think I dreamed it all up or something? You think I'm hallucinating?'

'No, I just meant that it might have been a toy or something. My sons have water guns and they look very real—'

'She says she's so mad at me over the rosebushes that she's going to come out and stand on her front lawn and wave the shotgun around when people come to view the house. She says she might even fire a round or two into the sky if the mood takes her. She says that nobody will buy my house when they see they'll have a raving lunatic right opposite.' He paused for breath. 'I wasn't going to tell you, but I suppose you should know.'

'Thank you,' Grace said, faintly.

'So,' he said, 'what do you think we should do?'

The first thing that came into her head was that she did not have time for this. She was booked on a three o'clock flight from Dublin airport to Heathrow, and from there she was flying to Orlando. She was going to Disneyland today – hurrah! Well, tomorrow at any rate. The first night they were staying in a motel somewhere on the outskirts of Florida. She had never stayed in a motel before. The very word conjured up seediness and sex and debauchery, and she found herself strangely excited by it. Perhaps that's what happened when you went to the Isle of Man three summers in a row. Or listened to too many obscene lyrics on the radio.

'Let's call the police,' she declared. This was their area, surely.

Frank's eyes popped behind his thick glasses. 'We're going to have people arriving to view the house at any minute! We can't have police cars parked outside!'

'Maybe we could ask for an unmarked one or something?' Grace wondered aloud, reaching for her mobile phone. Should she dial 999 or just ring the local Garda station directly? But she didn't know the number of the local Garda station and so she'd have all the rigmarole of ringing directory enquiries. If she rang 999 it seemed to be making such a big deal of it. Then again, a gun was a big deal in this country. She would dial 999.

'Look, I know her,' Frank pleaded. 'She likes to huff and puff. It's not as though she'd actually go through with it.'

'We can't just ignore it.'

'Why not?'

'Because she might shoot one of the potential purchasers!' Not to mention her. But Grace was professional above all else.

'Not if we get them to park as near to the house as possible,' Frank said. 'Then kind of encourage them to run to the front door keeping their heads low. Once they're inside, they're safe, and you can show them the house. Then we get them back out to their cars the same way, and tell them to drive off fast.'

'Maybe we could get a booking deposit off them as well before they're shot dead?' Grace enquired coolly.

'Oh, come on! The woman's a nutter! How many nutters have you come across in your profession?' He stared at her rather psychotically. 'If you were to pander to them all, you'd never sell a property! Nobody would ever move house!'

Grace's hand wavered on her phone. It was tempting . . . and, really, he was probably right about Mrs Carr saying that just to frighten him.

'Why don't you just ring your office? They'll know what to do,' Frank suggested.

Grace felt rather patronised. 'We don't actually have a set of guidelines lying around on what to do in the event of threatened shootings, Frank.'

Anyhow, it was after eight thirty; right now all senior staff would be in the meeting that was held on the last Friday of every month to assess performance and set targets. The rest of the crew would be on the road, like herself. Some of them had been showing houses since seven this morning (to facilitate people on their way to work) and would still be showing them at seven tonight (to accommodate people on their way home from work). Grace sometimes thought it was only a matter of time before they went twenty-four hours. And opened a branch in Hacketts-town.

And even if she did phone the office, she would most likely be referred to herself. She had a reputation as being 'a safe pair of hands' (which always managed to sound vaguely insulting). If anyone could deal with shootouts, Grace could, they would declare. She didn't know why. It wasn't as though she encountered violence on a daily basis in the drawing-rooms of the middle classes. This was hardly what you'd call a high-risk job. Not physically, anyway – certainly there were huge risks financially, as she had often explained to Ewan. Look at the asking price for Frank's house, for example! People having to mortgage themselves into old age to pay for it! It was only worth half the money, in her opinion. Three quarters at most. But you couldn't say that to people, of course; increasingly, selling houses made her feel very dishonest.

'Try selling people a chocolate bar that claims to aid weight loss,' Ewan had said gloomily.

'You got the account then?' It would be nice if just once they finished off a conversation about her job before they moved to his. But apparently selling second-hand houses was not as exciting as dreaming up television advertisement campaigns, and there was no use pretending that it was. At least, nobody in Grace's house pretended, and hadn't for years.

'By a whisker,' Ewan had said. 'Right now I'm playing with, "Slimchoc – the Chocolate Bar with Lots of Taste that Sheds your Weight!" '

'And does it?'

'Does it what?'

'Shed weight?'

'Oh, I don't know, I doubt it. We have to talk to the legal people yet. We might have to add, "as part of a calorie controlled diet".'

His gloominess had all but disappeared. It was an act he put on periodically to pretend that he belonged to that greater part of the human race who generally hated and loathed their jobs. But it was no use. The man would literally hop and skip up the stairs to his study on a Monday morning with indecent haste, humming little jingles under his breath, or trying to find a three-syllable word to rhyme with 'bubblegum'. There wasn't one, he'd informed her cheerily, at least nothing that wasn't obscene.

'So, what do you think?' He'd waited keenly for her opinion on his slogan. She had once been very flattered by this, until he had told her that she was a living example of most advertisers' demographic ideal: a white middle-class female in her mid-thirties with a couple of product-hungry children and a successful career to fund luxury goods and impulse-buys. She had taken umbrage; he had said, you're at the top of the food chain, what the hell are you complaining about? She didn't know really. It made her sound so smug, or something.

He added, 'I brought a box of samples home, by the way. Jamie's already had one. He says they taste like washing-up liquid.'

So they would join all the other samples that were piling up in the garage. Despite her nagging, Ewan wouldn't throw them out. In some ways he reminded her of a small boy, hoarding things up. When she emptied out his trousers pockets to take them to the dry-cleaners she didn't find mysterious phone numbers or credit-card receipts for lingerie shops, but elastic bands and half-eaten chocolate products and pencil sharpeners. And a foam cup from the inside of a ladies' padded bra once. That had aroused her interest, until he'd explained that when it was matched with a second bra cup, which his colleague

Mick had in *his* trouser pocket, it formed exactly the right spherical profile for the new Easter Egg campaign they were working on. They couldn't use the Easter Egg itself, of course, which was entirely the wrong shape to sell itself.

She had believed him. Nobody could make that up. Besides, Ewan would have neither the interest nor the organisational capability to have an affair. It wouldn't be because he was so dedicated to Grace, so desperately in love with her. He did love her, she knew that. But sometimes she suspected that he would love any woman who had ended up agreeing to marry him – so long as he was left largely to his own devices, of course, and wasn't interfered with too much. He mightn't like her so much then.

'Oh my God,' Frank squeaked beside her. 'Take cover!'

'What?'

'She's pointing the gun at us!'

Grace swung around towards Mrs Carr's house. One of the side panels of the front bay window was open. Something long and shiny was poking out under the net curtain and directly out across the front lawn at them.

'Are you sure it's a gun?' she asked, trying to buy time.

'What else do you think it is?'

'I don't know . . .'

'Her Hoover maybe?'

'I'm just saying—'

'Don't just stand there chattering, for heaven's sake! Take cover!'

Clare Dowling

Heedless of chivalry, he elbowed past her and dived down behind her car, commandeering the safest spot by the driver's wheel.

Grace stood alone and exposed in the middle of his cobbled drive, staring across at the double barrel poking out of Mrs Carr's front window. Net curtains had never struck her as menacing before now.

'Hello there!' she tried, giving a friendly wave across. She had read somewhere that sometimes it worked if you established a personal relationship with the aggressor. 'Lovely morning!'

The gun malevolently reared out another inch.

Really, when you thought about it, the whole thing was rather cowardly on Mrs Carr's part, Grace decided. If she wasn't going to declare herself openly, then why should Grace demean herself by galloping hysterically to her car? On the other hand, she did have two children at home who needed her (sometimes), and a husband who loved her (he had said so two Christmases ago), and she should give some thought to her own safety. She would, she decided, take cover, but she would do it her way.

So, very casually, very unconcerned, she turned and started to walk away. Not wanting to appear to be making for the car too obviously, she did a little circuit of Frank's front yard, her hands clasped at the small of her back as though she were out enjoying a Sunday afternoon stroll. When a robin chirped nearby, she raised her head towards it and allowed a faint smile to play about her lips.

'What are you doing?' Frank barked. 'Do you want to get your head blown off?'

16

She quickened her step after that, and approached the car at what she hoped was an oblique angle. Then she looked down and pretended that her shoelace had come undone (she was wearing sandals). She *tsk-ed* loudly before bending down as if to tie it. Then she made a crafty and dramatic lunge sideways for the protection of the car, landing on top of Frank.

'Watch it!'

'Sorry.'

She wasn't really. Her heart was pumping fast with unaccustomed adrenaline and her face was strangely hot. She felt like she was in a western, or at least *Hawaii Five-O* – although, on the telly the aggressor tended to be a sinister attractive man rather than a dotty pensioner. She couldn't wait to tell the boys about this. Her, dodging shotguns! Surely they couldn't fail to be impressed?

Although you wouldn't know. Since they'd been about eight she'd had the feeling that they considered her to be mostly background noise. Well, that was probably unfair to them – it was just that she had been hurt about it and still was. In the space of about six months they had changed from her soft-faced twin babies into these semi-grown ups who wanted replica Uzi machine guns for their birthdays, and who spent most of their time beating each other to a pulp. What they did not want any more was her undivided attention and love – she would always remember that heartbreaking moment when Jamie had wriggled out of a kiss, a look of near contempt on his face. It was Ewan they followed around now, Ewan they implored to 'Watch this!' and 'Will you come outside with us? Pleeease?'. Grace would be left waving them off at the doorstep like some kind of benign and detached housekeeper whose sole function was to provide clean socks and hot meals.

Disney had been her idea of getting them all together as a family again, properly. So she'd booked the whole month off work and bought the tickets, cleverly hiding them in homemade fortune cookies which she'd presented one night after dinner.

'A whole month? We'll go mad,' Ewan had declared, looking worried.

'Would this be during school term?' Neil had asked, the younger twin by twenty-two minutes but by far the craftier.

'My ticket is burnt,' Jamie, the other one, had said.

Grace had looked around at them all. They could have changed the car with what this trip would cost. They could have gone to the Maldives, and lay on the peaceful sand for a month, which was what she would have liked, instead of traipsing around the Enchanted bloody Tiki Room in the scorching sun in Florida.

So instead of cajoling and pleading and talking them around, she had dumped the Disney brochures on the coffee table, and let them do what they wanted! They had opened them, of course, and seen the fantastic water rides and the jungle cruises, and they were dying to go then.

A loud, high-pitched call cut through the morning air. 'Frank Gorman! You stay away from my house now, do you hear me?'

Frank visibly shook. 'Jesus Christ. She's going to shoot me.'

'Don't be ridiculous,' Grace said. Lifting her mobile, she rang 999, and inched up a little to peer through the car window and across the road. Some-one had stuck a piece of chewing-gum to the inside of the window. Neil probably. She would murder him.

'Don't provoke her,' Frank warned.

Across the way, the net curtain was pulled back a bit from Mrs Carr's front window. Grace caught a glimpse of lots of white-grey hair piled atop some kind of ruffled dress, or bathrobe. She was reminded of one of the witches from *Macbeth*. The gun was now halfway out the window. It jerked unsteadily before being cocked haphazardly towards the sky.

'Does she drink at all?' Grace asked.

'Like a fish,' Frank confirmed.

Then the net curtain fell back into place, as though Mrs Carr were tired of holding it. Or possibly she had gone to get another drink. The shotgun stayed.

Grace's feet started to ache. Her sandals had three-inch heels which always hurt after about an hour, but what could she do? A certain image had to be pre-sented when selling houses, especially houses in the better parts of town. This accounted for the racks of sophisticated, neutral-coloured suits hanging in her wardrobe at home. The general idea was to comple-ment a property's décor scheme; to blend in, as such. Once she had blended in so well that a client had lost track of her in the same room. There she'd been, standing right by the wall the whole time, while he had turned around in circles muttering, 'Where's that blasted woman gone?'

'Emergency services.' The 999 operator's voice

burst out of her mobile phone.

'Police, please,' Grace said.

A pause, then a man from the police switchboard was on the line, asking her what he could do for her.

'I'm at Number 17, Bridge Road,' she said efficiently. 'And there's a woman across the way who's threatening us with a gun.'

A gun? He sounded alert.

'Yes. A shotgun.'

Was she sure?

'A double-barrel shotgun,' she said for good measure.

She heard the man saying something to another person in the background, and she looked at Frank importantly. This was probably the most exciting thing that had happened to them all month. It certainly was to her.

The man was back on the phone. Was this woman threatening them right now?

'Yes. There was a dispute over a rosebush, you see.'

A rosebush?

'That's correct. Frank mowed down her rosebushes and she got mad.'

Who was Frank?

'Mrs Carr's neighbour.'

Okay, who was Mrs Carr?

'The woman with the gun . . .' Grace could sense she was diluting his interest with unnecessary detail. 'Look, it's all a bit complicated. The fact is that she has a gun and she says she's going to fire a few shots into the air if the mood takes her. She might even do it right now.'

That got his attention again. Was the woman pointing the gun at them at this moment, he wanted to know?

'Yes,' Grace said decisively.

She could actually see the gun?

'Yes, I can actually see the—'

Across the road, the gun abruptly withdrew and the window slammed closed.

After a little pause, she said, 'Would you believe it – it's gone now!'

The policeman paused too. And the woman, he wanted to know?

'She's actually gone too . . . but she was there a second ago. With the gun. I saw it with my own eyes!'

She could feel herself being ticked off at the other end of the phone as a crackpot to be checked out whenever a patrol car had a quiet ten minutes.

'Aren't you going to come down to the scene?' she asked.

He told her he would send a car.

'When?'

Soon. In the meantime, she was to stay exactly where she was. Under no circumstances was she to approach the woman or in any way attempt to communicate with her. That went for that guy Frank too.

'Okay. Thanks for your time!' Grace said. She always ended her phone calls like that. It was a work habit. Even when people took up *her* time, she ended up thanking them.

Frank was fretting. 'I hope this doesn't affect the sale.'

'I'm sure it won't.' To take his mind off it, she said,

21

'So, where are you moving to?' She expected him to say Navan, or Dunboyne maybe.

'New York,' he said.

'Oh!'

'Sandy is American, did I not mention that? Yankee Doodle, I call her! She loves that – cracks up every time. She says I've got a great sense of humour. Anyway, she lives in Brooklyn. She works as a nursery nurse, but just until she has her own kids, she says, then she's going to give up work and be a stay-at-home mom. But at the moment she's just happy doing her job, and taking out her disabled kids' group at the weekends and doing the soup kitchen for the homeless on Tuesday and Thursday nights.'

It was a wonder Sandy got to spend a minute in the bathroom at all, never mind the four hours daily that Frank gave her credit for. But Grace just said, 'Wow! A busy woman.'

'Too busy,' Frank with a frown. 'I tell her, you know. I say, Sandy, you have to think about yourself sometimes. But she doesn't listen. It's no wonder she's been feeling tired lately.'

'When are you moving over?'

'Two weeks' time,' he said. 'I'd have gone sooner only I'm finding it kind of hard to fix up a job over there.'

'What do you do?'

'Birds,' he said.

'Pardon?'

'I'm an ornithologist. I do work with wildlife foundations, zoos, that kind of thing. And I'm compiling a book, *An Introduction to Birds For Beginners*.

Sandy thinks it's a great idea, she says she had no idea until I came along that it was a complete myth that cuckoos went around dropping eggs in other birds' nests the minute their backs were turned. Well, they *do*, of course, but it's much more complicated than that. Sandy says she could listen to me going on about birds all day,' he added.

Grace said, 'I suppose New York . . . well, there would be pigeons, wouldn't there?'

Frank didn't seem too worried about his slim job prospects. 'Sandy says she'll support me for a while.' How she would do this on a nursery nurse's salary, he didn't say. His big red face was all dreamy. 'She's just amazing, do you know that?'

Well, she seemed to like Frank, Grace thought, and that was surely a feat in itself.

Two

Julia Carr was making beans on toast in her kitchen, the shotgun on the worktop beside her. She wasn't in the slightest bit hungry but it was best for the stomach not to be entirely empty. There was a danger of vomiting then, apparently. It had taken three months to store up thirty-six prescription sleeping pills, cajoling and hoodwinking Dr Noonan, and she was not about to waste them.

She was having a little trouble with the tin of beans. It was one of those ones with a ring attached to the lid, which you were supposed to pull to open the tin. She eventually got her finger through and pulled hard. The ring snapped off and came clean away in her hand.

'Bugger.'

This had never happened to her before, wouldn't you know it. Anyhow. A quick inspection of her cupboards revealed that there were no beans left. There was very little of anything, really. Well, it had seemed pointless to stock up on food that would only get thrown out in the end. Besides, pension day wasn't until Tuesday.

So, for her final meal on this earth, she was faced with the choice of a tin of prunes or chickpeas, both of which were out of date. She had decided on the chickpeas (she actually was getting a little peckish now) when she suddenly remembered that they would do a post-mortem on her. She knew this from reading forensic detective novels. What would they think when they discovered a can of out-of-date chickpeas in her stomach, mixed up with the pills? There might be some confusion over what had actually killed her. Possibly they might have to resort to all kinds of costly tests. No, she would already be causing enough trouble to everyone. She would eat nothing.

Now she couldn't stop thinking about food. The image of a fresh white loaf and a nice bit of cheese popped into her head. It was most inappropriate given the circumstances, and she guiltily decided she would leave the kitchen altogether. First she checked that the windows were closed and the taps turned securely off. She had scoured the cooker an hour ago and it gleamed. She'd meant to get around to the kitchen floor – that milk she'd spilled last week was starting to smell – but she was out of mop-heads and a trip to the supermarket would have put the whole thing back by several hours. In the end she'd just had to prioritise, as you do.

And at least the bathroom was clean. Michael would be poking around upstairs, and Gillian, their noses upturned probably. Julia had put out on her bedside locker several copies of *Hustler* magazine left behind by one of her lodgers as a little surprise for them.

The plastic jar of red and yellow pills was laid out on the coffee table. And a jug of water with ice in it, along with a glass. And a photocopy of her will, for everybody's convenience. It didn't look like much now; in fact, it looked a bit thoughtless and mean, as though it had been organised by the public health service.

Maybe she should add a vase of flowers? Or at least put a couple of doilies down on the table to hide the coffee stains. But she didn't know how these things were usually done, except that people sometimes played a piece of music that meant a lot to them. She didn't have any special piece of music like that, except maybe the song playing on the transistor radio the day herself and JJ had gone out on the lake with a picnic to celebrate their fortieth wedding anniversary, and he had kissed her to the strains of 'Boogie Wonderland', which didn't seem all that fitting right now.

She sat down for the last time in JJ's big old red chair. It all seemed very unreal, and she half expected someone to walk through the door and ask her what on earth she thought she was doing, and she would laugh and say, 'You know, I have no idea! I was just being silly for a moment – will we have a cup of tea?' But nobody would come. She had been on her own in this house, save for a few sporadic lodgers, since JJ had died two years ago. Even the cat had run away.

She had continued to function, of course: to eat, to sleep, to open her mouth and have words come out. But there was nothing happening inside. She often thought of herself as one of those accident victims in intensive care units who kept breathing long after what made them human had died.

So, on this rather dramatic note, she slowly placed two pills on her tongue and reached for the glass of water.

Hail Mary, full of grace, The Lord is with—

The phone rang. Bugger and blast anyway. She would just ignore it.

The Lord is with thee, blessed art thou amongst—

But it just kept ringing and ringing until she could bear it no longer and she spat the sleeping pills out into her hand and snatched the phone up.

'Hello!'

'Mammy?'

'Michael?'

He sounded a bit hurt. 'Of course it's Michael.'

She tried not to sound irritated. 'It's just that you usually don't phone at this time.'

'I know, but I'm in the car on my way to a meeting – just thought I'd check on you.'

'There's really no need.' Since JJ died Michael had become a constant fixture on the end of the phone. She had to take it off the hook in the evenings just to watch *Coronation Street*.

'Well, you're on your own now, Mammy,' he pointed out, tactlessly. 'And you know that sometimes you forget to eat.'

'I do not forget to eat.' Sometimes she forgot to wash, certainly, but she didn't mind about that. Old people were expected to be smelly. 'So,' she said, trying to think of something to say. She seemed to have been trying to find things to say to Michael since he'd been a child. 'How's Gillian?'

'Great! She thinks it's not a chest infection now at all.'

'Good.'

'She thinks it might be bronchitis.'

'Wouldn't she be in hospital if it were bronchitis?' Julia enquired. 'Or in bed, at the very least?'

'Apparently with some strains of bronchitis you hardly know you have it at all. She was reading it in her medical books.'

'Well, tell her I hope she gets over it soon. And Susan?'

He sounded gloomy. 'She's not talking to me again.'

'What have you done to her this time?'

'That's just it. I don't know.'

Julia clucked. 'She's thirteen, Michael. It's just the age.'

'Was I like that at thirteen?' he asked eagerly.

'The very same,' she declared, guiltily. Michael hadn't been all that memorable at thirteen. Or at any other age, really. Except that he ate a lot, even back then. 'Anyway, if that's all, Michael, I have a few things to do . . .'

'Right, sure – so we'll see you on Thursday?'

'What?' They'd been over only last weekend. It usually took her a fortnight to recover.

'Your birthday, Mammy.'

Her heart sank. Blast anyway.

'Ha!' he said. 'You thought we'd forgotten, hadn't you?'

'Yes,' she said weakly.

'Not a chance! We're all coming over for the

whole day, have a big party. We have it all planned – Gillian's going to make a cake and everything. Bronchitis permitting, of course,' he added.

'Michael, I really don't want you to go to any trouble—'

'No, no, we insist.' Her lack of enthusiasm must have conveyed itself to him because he said, awkwardly, 'Look, I know you didn't want a fuss for your birthday last year, what with Daddy dying and everything. But he wouldn't have wanted you to go on mourning forever, Mammy.'

The glibness of this, the presumption that her grief could be simply shrugged off once an appropriate time had passed, annoyed her. 'You have no idea what JJ would have wanted.'

'Well, no, of course not, all I'm saying is—'

'JJ liked a party as much as the next person. He threw some wonderful birthday parties for me. He flew me to Paris three years ago, for God's sake!'

There was a hurt silence on the other end of the phone.

'It's . . . I just don't feel ready, Michael.' She suddenly remembered that she would be dead anyway, and that it was immaterial. 'Look, come over if you want,' she said generously.

'Okay,' he said, cheerful again. 'We'll bring masks if Gillian's still infectious.'

She realised now that this was the very last time she would be speaking to him. Her only child. It seemed very important that she say something memorable to him. 'Michael?'

'Yes, Mammy?'

'Just . . . thanks for everything. You've been a very good son.' It sounded stiff and cold, not what she really meant at all. But maybe he was touched because he was silent for a minute. 'Michael?'

'Sorry, Mammy, I just went through a tunnel there – what did you say?'

'Oh, never mind. Go to your meeting.'

She hung up. Now, where had she been? Oh yes, *Hail Mary*. And now she was down two pills as well. Still, hopefully she had enough left to do the trick.

'Oh!' Her hands had started to shake. Look at them, wobbling away! She tried to stop them. But the more she tried, the more they shook, until they were bouncing up and down on her knees as though they were playing an imaginary piano with gusto.

A few deep breaths and everything would be fine. There was no point in getting in a heap about something that she had made a perfectly sound decision on weeks ago. Months ago! Well, she hadn't actually made a decision as such. She wasn't a person who made decisions – they always seemed to be accompanied by such a lot of unnecessary angst and weighing up of pros and cons. Instead she had notions and ideas and impulses, and once in the grip of one, nothing would do her but to pursue it with all her energy and vigour until its conclusion. Take the rockery out the back, for instance; she had been doing the dishes at the sink one morning, staring out the back window, when she observed how little she had to look at. She had not rested until she had placed the very last stone on the top of a wonderful rockery (which was rather lop-sided in truth) with her bare hands. JJ had watched, amused and impressed by her single-mindedness. She'd promptly forgotten about it then, of course, and taken up a home-brewing course.

A couple of months ago – she couldn't remember exactly when – she had woken up one morning and lain there in the bed for an age trying to muster up the energy to present herself to the world for yet another day: to find a dress that was clean, maybe smear a bit of colour onto her lips, rattle around an empty house until it was time to go to bed again. And she just didn't want to do it any more.

Once the thought was there, it was a natural progression to cultivate an insomnia problem, to procure a variety of sleeping pills from Dr Noonan, to update her will and tie up other bits and pieces. That one thought had led her right here to this room, to this table, today. She just had to bring the sequence to its conclusion.

'Stop it!' Her hands would not stop shaking, and she was getting angry with them. Her body was always letting her down, with its litany of aches and pains, its increasing unpredictability; little things designed to irritate her, it seemed, but not serious enough to kill her and save her all this trouble. If it had had any decency, any loyalty to her, it would have died naturally in the weeks after JJ was buried. She had not eaten or slept, she had not even drunk water; she'd downed enough sleeping tablets to fell an ox, and her body just kept on going. Living, even though every fibre of her being had wanted to die. It was a snivelling, cowardly, stupid thing and she would be glad to be rid of it. To be rid of everything.

She managed to tip out more pills onto the table but couldn't hold the glass of water. Her hands were shaking too much. She would just have to go into the kitchen and find a bendy straw with which to kill herself. The indignity of it! She was raging now.

The minute she opened the kitchen door, the smoke hit her. The cooker grill was on fire.

'*Bugger.*'

She'd put two slices of bread on for the beans on toast and had forgotten all about them. Now flames were bursting up through the rings of her immaculately scoured cooker, and threatening to set the curtains alight.

She put the jar of pills down beside the cooker and ran to wet some tea towels. By the time she got back, the jar and her precious pills had melted and were oozing across her worktop in a glorious multicoloured puddle.

The answering machine was on at home.

'Ewan, it's me – can you pick up? Ewan, sorry to disturb you, but can you pick up the phone? It's important.'

Ewan screened calls; otherwise he said he'd get no work done. She'd offered to get a second phone line in, so that he would have his own work number and he wouldn't be bothered by domestic calls. But he had fretted that he would have no excuse for avoiding people if they knew he had his own work line. Sometimes she felt like pointing out that he was inventing advertising slogans, not some ground-breaking vaccine. Oh, when had she become so mean?

More to the point, when had he started screening his own wife?

'Ewan, I know you're there. Pick up the fucking phone.'

'Grace?' He was on the other end, startled.

It just showed how rarely Grace used bad language. She wasn't in favour of it as a rule – not with children around.

'Not tearing you away from Chocslim, I hope?' she said.

'Slimchoc. And I'm not working – we *are* supposed to be going on holidays today.' He was semi-cool in response to her sarcasm, and she was sorry now.

'Are you on your way home?' he asked.

'Not exactly.' She was stretched out on the back seat of her car, out of Frank's earshot and Mrs Carr's line of fire. The leather was getting warm from the sun. If she drew her knees up, she was just about able to curl up like she had as a child on long car journeys, her cheek pressed into the seat and the motion of the car eventually lulling her to sleep. She always liked the part when she woke up and she would look out the window to find herself in a completely different place – a bustling town, or a quiet country road, or even the seaside, if it was summer. That's when her love affair with cars, and sitting in them, had started.

'Grace? Are you still there?'

'Yes – listen, there's been a slight change of plan. Depending on what happens, I may have to meet you at the airport.'

'What? But what about the packing?'

'Do you even want to know why I'm going to be late, Ewan?'

He must have sensed the chill down the phone line because he said hurriedly, 'Yes, of course – why?'

'I'm caught up in a shootout,' she told him.

'Okay,' he said.

Grace counted to three.

Then he said, 'Did you just say a shootout?'

'There's been a dispute with a neighbour. She has a shotgun aimed at us,' she said airily. 'We're waiting for the police.'

'That's quite a bit of drama,' he said, sounding marginally more interested. Or at least fully present. Sometimes when she talked to him he would give every indication that he was absorbed by her words: he would nod and smile and respond at all the right moments. Then she would bring up the topic again a couple of days later and he would look at her blankly and she would know that his mind had been somewhere else the entire time. It wasn't always on work, to his credit. Once he had mentally planned an entire motor route through Germany during a lengthy description of her mother's run-in with a stomach virus.

It had been loveable once, this trait.

'Yes,' she agreed.

'Are you in danger?' He was concerned now, and she felt a little warm glow inside. It was like when she'd burnt her arm quite badly last year and he had spent ages pressing damp facecloths on it before bandaging it all up.

'I don't think so. I'd say her aim isn't too hot. And she's been drinking.'

'All the same – don't do anything to antagonise her,' he ordered. The glow grew warmer. Not that she could ever admit it in front of her girlfriends, but it was so nice to be looked after by a man sometimes. To be fussed over. Bossed. Protected, even.

'I suppose you'd better not tell the boys. In case it might upset them,' she said doubtfully, playing up to him a bit. She even let out a kind of a nervous, jittery breath.

'Do you think?' he said. His macho phase was disappointingly brief, as always.

'I don't know, Ewan – what do *you* think?'

She desperately wanted him to round up the boys with an urgent bellow, and have them gather around the phone while their mother relayed the whole tale in gory detail. She wanted to hear them clamber to ask questions and to express worry about her safety. Then they would all pile in the car and race to the scene.

'You're probably right, I won't say anything to them,' Ewan decided.

Here, Grace thought, was a man who worked in advertising. Here was an expert in consumer psychology, a master at manipulating a highly sophisticated and jaded audience. But in his own house he couldn't pick up a lousy hint?

She knew that it was a childish impulse on her part anyhow. But she'd been like that recently, saving up jokes or funny stories she'd heard on the radio to tell the twins over dinner, and beaming with disproportionate pleasure if she made them laugh. Or pulling minor stunts to impress them, such as showing them on Shrove Tuesday how she could flip pancakes just like that chef on the TV (and had the consistency been a little less runny, she might not have burnt her arm so badly).

She was like some pathetic new kid in the schoolyard, trying to get in with the cool gang. Being children, they could smell a fake a mile off, of course, and the more she tried the less interested they were. It was a vicious circle, with her attempts getting more outlandish. A mere shotgun would probably not be enough now. She might actually have to get herself shot before they'd be sufficiently impressed.

'What do you do when you go off with them?' she asked now.

'What?'

'You and the boys. When you disappear for hours on end?'

'It's hardly "hours", Grace.' He added, 'You didn't happen to tick things off a list, did you? When you were packing?'

She could hear him faffing about in the background with bits of paper.

'Take last night, Ewan,' she said loudly. 'After dinner, you said you were going to take the boys to the park for half an hour. You didn't come home until it was dark.'

'Didn't we?'

She could just see his face, puzzled that she would even have noticed such a thing – such a trivial thing as to where her husband and children had disappeared!

'We were just horsing around, like usual.'

'What does "horsing around" mean, exactly?' She tried not to sound too curious and pathetic. It's just that he never told her. They would all traipse home, red-faced and panting like young bulls, and nobody would think to tell her what they had been doing, or where they had been. She never lowered herself to ask; in fact, she would barely look up as they stormed past to the fridge in case they thought she might be in any way interested.

'We play football, mostly,' Ewan said. 'A bit of basketball. Catch various living creatures down at the river, that kind of thing. Boy scouts' stuff.' He added, 'You'd think as they got older they'd start playing by themselves a bit more.'

'Um,' Grace said. So it wasn't like the three of them spent their time trading secrets or anything. It wasn't as if Jamie and Neil were confiding things in him, revealing bits of their precious selves that they used to whisper to her in the dark, and still did sometimes, when she tucked them into bed at night.

'Why do you want to know?' Ewan said.

'Just wondering.'

A part of them was still hers. They had not taken that from her, and her heart grew less pinched.

The car rocked now as the bonnet suddenly sprang up. Frank. Grace peered out through the front seats. What on earth was he up to?

'This is about that disused mine, isn't it?' Ewan suddenly blurted hotly down the phone.

'What?' Grace said, trying to keep up.

'I didn't know it was a disused mine, okay? It's not

like it had a sign on it saying *Disused Mine* or anything! Actually, it might have, but it was very unclear, ask the boys. But anyway, your mother can say what she likes, Grace, but I would not willingly walk my children into danger for the hell of it!'

'Ewan, I know, okay? Nobody is accusing you of anything.'

Years before the disused-mine incident, Ewan had once taken the twins up to the top of the Papal Cross in the Phoenix Park on a particularly windy day and parked them in their double-buggy without remembering to put the brake on. Only for some quick-footed Japanese tourist, there would have been carnage. If Ewan had thought about it, he would have seen the wisdom in keeping this incident to himself. But he wasn't devious like that, and he was too young to know the way marital arguments and resentments can resonate a decade on. And so he'd confessed when he'd got home and, from that day on, he'd acquired the label of being 'lightweight', as Grace's mother had put it upon hearing the tale. It was a label he had fought against for many years (although fought was perhaps too strong a word. Complained would be a more accurate description. Strongly, at times, to his credit).

Eventually he stopped complaining and accepted it; embraced it even, and made it his own. His reputation amongst friends and family now was that of an amusing scatterbrain – very intelligent though, very creative, which seemed to excuse him somewhat. He'd added other bits and pieces to this myth as time went on: absentmindedness, for example. A poor memory. A preoccupation with career. But he was *marvellous* with the boys, which excused him entirely.

When Grace thought about it, the whole thing suited him down to the ground.

For her part, having lumped him into a box in the first place, she was forced to compensate by going in the other direction. Now she was the organiser in the family, the head bottle-washer as such. If anybody wanted to know where to find something, they asked Grace. Need a dental appointment? Grace will make it. She, who had on her very first date with Ewan been so nervous that she'd mixed up the venue! There she'd sat for an hour in Bewley's café in Westmoreland Street while Ewan was sitting down the road in Bewley's in Grafton Street. It was Ewan who'd eventually had the presence of mind to walk up and check, lest there had been some mistake.

Wasn't it funny how you could grow into the kind of person that you'd never started out as, Grace thought? She remembered again that excited, dreamy girl sitting over a cooling coffee, wearing a black and red striped scarf that Ewan had said made her look like Dennis the Menace. She'd had two tickets in her pocket to a talk by Neil Jordan in the Irish Film Centre on the state of Irish film, and afterwards she and Ewan had sat cross-legged on the floor of his bedsit, passionately arguing back and forth until four in the morning.

And here she was, fifteen years on: a woman who made dental appointments and who blended seamlessly into wallpaper.

'Grace?' On the phone Ewan sounded anxious.

'What's happened, has she started shooting?'

'No, no.'

Frank's head poked out from the side of the bonnet. He waved frantically. He had an oil filter in his hand.

'I have to go,' she said to Ewan. 'You're going to have to finish the packing.'

'Right . . .' he said, mournfully.

'There are some things you might like to remember, such as the passports and stuff.' She desperately wanted to mention the travellers' cheques and the health insurance documents but wouldn't let herself. Perhaps he would mention them. But he didn't, of course. It would never occur to him. Now she would be fretting about the blasted things all morning. Really, weren't there some days when you just did not like yourself?

'Ring me when you know what's happening,' he said.

She hung up, pushed open the car door with her foot, and slid back out onto the cobblestones, anticipating that her oil needed changing or something.

'The first one is here,' Frank hissed instead.

Grace saw a red hatchback drive at a leisurely pace up the road. Her first viewers. What was she supposed to do?

'Get them to drive up as far as they can to the house,' she urged Frank. There was no sense in leaving them down there by the gate like sitting ducks.

'Good idea,' Frank said, a thin sheen of sweat visible on his forehead. Plucking a white handkerchief from his pocket, he draped it over the top of the oil filter. Then he stuck the makeshift flag out from behind the bonnet and waved it around erratically in the direction of the red hatchback.

Nothing happened for a moment as the car occupants obviously conferred. Then the hatchback crawled cautiously up the driveway. Another burst of flag-waving from Frank brought them right up behind Grace's own car, where they stopped.

'Well done,' Grace said to Frank admiringly, and he pinkened a bit.

She scuttled down to the hatchback on her hands and knees and popped up at the driver's side window.

'Hi!' she said.

The occupants jumped. They hadn't seen her until now. Her clipboard was still in her hand and she consulted it.

'Aidan and Amy, isn't it?' It was strange how often prospective buyers' names began with the same letter, Grace had noted. Pat and Pauline. Lisa and Liam. She'd once had a Frances and a Francis. Stranger again was how often people moved to roads that sounded similar to the ones they had just left: from Emmet Road to Elmer Road, for example. Sometimes the house number was even the same. Why was everyone so afraid of change? Increasingly Grace was beginning to think that there was little comfort in the familiar.

'I'm Grace Tynan,' she told them. 'I'll be showing you Frank's house today.' She reached in through the window to shake hands with them. The angle was awkward and she ended up sort of patting them instead.

'I'm sure you're wondering what's going on,' she said.

'Well, yes,' the woman said.

'Anyway!' Grace said – no sense in alarming them – 'why don't you have a look at these and if you have any questions, I'd be delighted to answer them for you.'

She handed in two glossy brochures, surreptitiously taking note of the seat headrests. They were nice big leather ones, plump enough to shield the passengers from Mrs Carr's view. They should be safe enough. 'Back in a minute – oh, and try not to make any sudden movements, okay?'

She scuttled back to her own car where Frank was waiting anxiously.

'Did you mention about the bathroom?'

'No, I did not.'

'Sandy said you should. That's what they do in the States when the brochure is incorrect.'

'Well, we're not in the States now.' She stood up straight and took stock of herself. Her linen skirt was a mess of lines and creases, and her tights were snagged. She brushed herself down as best she could and wondered if she'd remembered to put a lipstick in her handbag.

'What are you doing?' Frank was alarmed.

The front window in the house across the way remained shut tight. There was no other sign of activity. Mrs Carr had probably passed out with drink. And Grace had to get to the airport.

'Back in a minute,' she told Frank, and set off across the cobblestones, her high heels hitting the ground with a sharp click each time. Honestly, she thought, if you wanted something done, you had to do it yourself. If you wanted *anything* done.

Well, maybe one day she just wouldn't bother. She would ignore what had to be done. She would say, hang it, let somebody else do it for a change! And if they didn't do it, she would say hang that too! Who cares! Not her. Because maybe deep down, once you stripped away all the appointment-making and the efficient neutral-coloured suits, maybe she was in fact a sloth.

'Hello? Mrs Carr? Sorry to disturb you, but I wonder could I pop in for a moment to talk to you?'

In the kitchen, Julia swung around, heart hammering. She looked through the open kitchen door and down the gloomy hall. She hadn't heard the doorbell. It must have rung several times, because there was a person pressed up against the frosted glass panels of the front door, hands cupping their eyes as they tried to see in. The cheek of them.

'Who is it?' she called.

'My name is Grace Tynan – I'm Frank's estate agent – Frank Gorman from across the road?'

Why was she speaking like that, as though Julia should really have known these things in the first place? Julia had a vague recollection of a thin woman in a big car and carrying a clipboard. She had reminded her of those career women you see on American television programmes – shiny and kind of brittle, not real at all.

'I'm afraid I'm busy right now!' she answered

44

cheerily. She had just managed to put the cooker flames out, and the kitchen was filled with rancid steam and smoke. The two pieces of bread were charred black lumps when she extracted them with a serving fork and hurled them into the sink, and she realised she would have to clean the cooker all over again, and probably wash the curtains, and she was crying now – furious hot tears at her own incompetence. Far from this being the brave and sensible thing to do (a part of her had even thought it noble), the whole episode had descended into the plot of one of those cheap melodramas JJ used to take her to in the cinema in the fifties, the two of them giggling in the dark at the sheer idiocy of the heroine.

'Mrs Carr?' That blasted woman again, at the front door. 'About the gun . . .'

'Yes, sorry about that. I'll put it away now, you're quite safe.'

'Well, yes, but . . .'

'Goodbye now! Cheerio!'

She shut the kitchen door on the woman. Armed with rubber gloves and a Brillo pad, she threw open the back door to let the smoke out. She found an old wine bottle and made up a solution of bleach and detergent, then went to work on the cooker.

In retrospect perhaps the shotgun had been unnecessary. But those rosebushes had been planted in the spot where JJ used to put a chair out on summer evenings to read his engineering reports. Not that Frank had known this, in fairness. But he had this knack of rubbing her up the wrong way. Had been doing it for eleven long years. Let him sell his house and move to New York to his fancy woman. She for one wouldn't miss him.

When she straightened from the cooker, Grace Tynan was looking in through the back kitchen door.

'Oh, hello again! I hope you don't mind me coming around the back. It's just that you wouldn't open the front door.'

Julia didn't say anything. For the second time that day, the woman had frightened the life out of her.

'Frank is very sorry, Mrs Carr.'

'I doubt that. I've never met a more insensitive man in my life.'

'It's just that he's a little anxious about his house. And then the pressure of getting married . . .'

'Yes, well, I wouldn't be surprised if that fell through. No woman in her right mind would marry that little arse of a man.'

She watched as the estate agent woman's eyes darted involuntarily down to take in the rubber gloves, the smouldering cooker, and the shotgun on the worktop. Half of Julia's long white hair had escaped its clip too, and hung around her face in straggles. She must look like a mad woman. Normally it was not a tag she'd have minded in the slightest. But today it felt just a little close to the bone.

'I burnt some toast,' she said very defensively.

Grace Tynan just nodded sympathetically, and said, 'I'm always doing that. Will I make you some coffee or something?'

Julia was taken aback. Nobody had offered to make her coffee in a long time.

'I only have instant,' she said. Why hadn't she said no?

'Instant is fine! And have you had something to eat?'

'No. The ring-pull broke off the tin of beans,' she said. Honestly – any second now, she would be blubbering!

'Never mind. If you've got a tin opener, I bet I can get this lid off in a jiffy. Now, which drawer do you keep your utensils in?'

And she was off, opening drawers and hunting for tin openers and coffee jars. Julia knew she should get rid of her, like she had Frank that morning. Instead she stood there like a small child, thinking how nice it was to have someone else take responsibility for a change. How comforting it was not to have to cope on your own, even for five minutes.

'And leave that cooker – I'll have a go at it in a minute,' the woman said cheerfully.

Julia found herself nodding in agreement. Wasn't this Grace person marvellous? She'd found a big mug now and Julia watched as she spooned in the coffee.

'Where do you keep the sugar?' she asked Julia.

Julia turned to point to a cabinet. She was turning back to say that she didn't actually take sugar when she saw the woman quickly add another spoon of coffee to the mug. With her other hand, she deftly confiscated the wine bottle of detergent.

It dawned on Julia. 'You think I'm drunk.'

'What? Oh now, I never—'

'Please leave my house,' said Julia.

'Mrs Carr—'

47

'Now.'

'All right, fine. If I could just take that gun . . .'

She reached for it. But Julia was faster. How dare she try and make off with her property?

'Mrs Carr. I'm not going until you give me the gun.'

'No.' Julia gripped the gun tighter between her rubber-gloved fingers. 'I won't disturb your precious house viewings again, if that's what you're worried about.'

The woman stood her ground. 'I'm afraid you might hurt yourself.'

'That's highly unlikely. It hasn't been loaded since 1974.'

'All the same, I'd be worried.'

'Your concern has been noted. Now, if you do not leave my house right now I'm going to call the police.'

They both jumped as the telephone extension on the kitchen wall rang. It rang seven times before Julia eventually reached over and picked it up.

'Hello?'

It was the police. Sergeant Daly, actually. He was wondering whether she would come out and talk to him. And could she please bring the gun?

Baffled, she looked over at Grace Tynan, who didn't seem a bit surprised.

Cornered, Julia put the phone down and turned to look at Grace with chilly contempt. 'Take the gun if it will make you happy.'

She wouldn't please the woman by going over to her; instead she held out the gun, barrel correctly facing the ground, and made her come and get it.

Grace Tynan put out her hand and said, 'Thank you—'

Afterwards there were various theories and explanations as to what exactly happened next. Grace Tynan confessed to the police that it was entirely possible that she had accidentally knocked against the trigger in the handover, even though she didn't think it was all that likely. Sergeant Daly was inclined to blame the rubber gloves – he tried on five different brands during the course of his investigation and he could confirm categorically that they had impeded his sensitivity. Julia Carr argued fiercely that she had never gone anywhere near the trigger, rubber gloves or not. And forensics marvelled that a cartridge that had unwittingly sat in the barrel of a rusty shotgun for nearly thirty years could still deliver such a punch.

Three

'Where did you shoot her?'

'I didn't shoot her! Well, it might have been me, we don't know yet—'

'Where?'

'In the foot, okay? I shot her in the foot!'

'Oh my God,' Ewan moaned on the phone.

Finally she had managed to surprise her own family. Unfortunately it wasn't an occasion to be particularly proud. There wasn't even a peep from the boys. She could sense them in the background, hanging over Ewan's shoulder.

'Where are you now?' he asked.

'Accident & Emergency. They've taken her off to look at her. You know, to see what the damage is.' She didn't go into details. The boys could watch any number of sadistic cartoons but they might not be able to handle the idea of toes hanging by bloodied threads. Well, it was only one toe, and it was more a deep cut than anything else. And it was her little toe as well, as Frank had helpfully pointed out: in fact, she would hardly miss it.

'And, like, is she okay?' Ewan asked.

'No, she's not okay! Would you be okay if you got shot?'

Several people in the crowded waiting-room turned around to have a look. They were all there with sprained ankles, or accompanying toddlers who had swallowed small ornaments – nothing as glamorous as being shot. Was it possible that Grace was some kind of gangster's moll? Despite the oatmeal-coloured suit?

As for Grace, she huddled farther down in her grey plastic chair, the mobile phone pressed to her ear. She had that sick shivery feeling that accompanies accidents. And who would have thought that burnt flesh had such a smell? Like that shoulder of pork they'd overcooked until the blackened skin had curled skywards. At the memory of it, her throat made an odd choking sound.

'Are you all right?' Ewan asked.

'It's the fright of it,' she said. 'I mean, I could have killed her.'

'Come on, Grace.'

'She's an elderly woman, Ewan! Supposing she'd had a heart attack?'

'She didn't.'

'But supposing! Stress can bring it on! Look at Harry.'

Harry Brennan from next door had suffered severe chest pains just after watching the National Lottery programme on television and discovering that he'd won (in the event he'd actually mistaken a nine for a six and hadn't won at all, but the surgeons said it was just as well because they'd found enough fat in his arteries to open a chip shop).

'Why don't you come on home?' Ewan said, and she had that nice warm glow again, that sense of mattering. Wasn't it a pity she couldn't keep on shooting people?

'I can't,' she said. 'I might have to give a statement to the police.'

'Tell them you're going on holidays.'

'I already did, but I got the impression that they thought I was trying to leave the jurisdiction or something.'

For a while back there, she had thought that Sergeant Daly was actually going to accompany her to the hospital and stand beside her the whole time lest she try and pull a fast one. But he had only followed her back over to Frank's house after the ambulance had left to see if she could give him a quick tour of the house while she was there.

'You want a tour?' She wasn't sure she'd heard him right. The blast from the shotgun had left her temporarily deafened, and the last thing she wanted to do was show a property and pretend to be perky. But her professionalism had got the better of her and she had ended up following him around Frank's dark, airless rooms.

'For yourself, is it?' she'd shouted, the buzzing in her ears not letting up.

'No, no, my son Tom has just got engaged ... whirlwind romance ...'

'That's nice,' Grace had said, shaking her head a little. But the buzzing wouldn't stop.

'Yes, met in Birmingham ... name is Charlie,

apparently . . . they want to come back and settle in Ireland . . .'

'Oh! Well, ah, good luck to them!' It was the first gay marriage she'd heard of in this country.

'Tom says Charlie's keen to start a family pretty much straightaway,' Sergeant Daly finished up.

'Kids?'

'Yes. Do you think the study would be suitable for conversion into a playroom?'

'I think it'd be perfect,' Grace had said. Possibly Tom and Charlie were considering surrogacy or something. 'Well, I hope everything goes well for them. And you'll make a great grandfather!'

'I hope so,' he'd said, nearly bursting with pride. 'I'm going to pick them up at the airport now. None of us has met Charlie before – but to be honest, I'm just glad that Tom has found someone.'

Wasn't it marvellous to be so open-minded, so supportive of your children, Grace thought now. It was a lesson to her: to all parents.

'Can you put the boys on the phone? Just for a minute?' she asked Ewan, feeling a sudden rush of tears to the back of her eyes. This whole shooting business was more upsetting than she'd thought. Right now she just wanted to be at home with her children – to wrap her arms around their hard little bodies, to plant kisses on the side of their necks while they squealed, 'Aw, Mum!' and tried to get away.

Neil came on the line first. 'Did you shoot someone?'

'I did,' she said, resisting that schoolyard urge to

sound boastful. She could feel his respect down the phone line.

'Who? A murderer?' he said breathlessly.

'Well, not exactly.'

'What, a robber then?'

'Not as such ... Anyway!' she said, hoping he would drop it.

But he went on doggedly, 'What weapon did he have?'

'Um, he didn't actually have a weapon . . .'

She could sense a hole developing in his admiration. More a crater, actually. 'You shot an unarmed man?' he said eventually.

Oh, for heaven's sake! 'It was an old lady, okay? I shot a defenceless little old lady!' More people turned to have a look. 'But it's not too serious,' she added loudly. 'The pellets hardly got her at all.' Or so she hoped. Still, there hadn't been any great commotion so far. The ambulance hadn't even put its siren on as it had driven off.

'Oh.' Neil's interest had now evaporated entirely. 'Can I have the window seat on the plane?'

She was glad of the change of subject. 'You can have anything you want,' she said indulgently.

'Anything?'

'Within reason.' You constantly had to be on your guard with Neil.

'So I can have the window seat on the plane?'

'You can have the window seat.'

She had thought this was a selfless act on her part (she was a claustrophobic flyer and usually got the window seat) until the phone went muffled at the

Clare Dowling

other end and she heard Neil shouting tauntingly, 'I've got the window seat! I've got the window seat! Mum said so!'

'You little shit!' Jamie.

Grace was powerless as she heard several blows exchanged in the background, along with howls of hurt and outrage. Then Ewan intervening, and a door slamming down the hall. Then the phone being picked up again.

'Hello?'

'Neil! That was very unfair of you!'

'This is Jamie.'

She didn't miss a beat. 'How dare you use language like that!'

'He hit me in the eye,' Jamie protested.

She softened, gave a little cluck. 'Is it bad?'

She extended a good deal of secret sympathy to Jamie. He was the smaller of the twins and had always approached the world with more caution. He'd been slower to smile, to talk, to be toilet-trained. He was afraid of heights and bruised easily, which made him a natural target for other children. Over the years she felt that he had always needed her protection and intervention more, and the two of them would sometimes sneak off from a game of rough and tumble to read a book about mystical fantastical creatures from long ago, or to cook something exotic and colourful in the kitchen, and they would giggle together like they were playing truant from the real world.

'It's not too bad,' he conceded now.

'Tell you what. Neil can have the window seat on

the flight out,' she said. 'And you can have it on the flight back. Okay?' She would make do with an aisle seat.

'I suppose. They have an Astro-Orbitor in Disney,' he added.

'Do they?'

'See you later.'

'Okay – and Jamie?'

She was about to tell him that she loved him; that he was her baby, and that she would see him soon.

'I have to go,' Jamie said. 'One of Dad's ads is on the telly. The cola one – it's brilliant.'

The phone went dead.

'Bye! Thanks for your time!' Grace said loudly, not wanting the other occupants of the waiting-room to know that she had been hung up on by a ten-year-old.

Ewan would ring back in a minute. Well, she didn't know if she would answer the phone! Wouldn't you think that today, of all days, he wouldn't go upstaging her? Wouldn't you think he'd have turned off the television and said, 'Now, lads, this thing is bigger than cola', or something like that? He just didn't think. He never did.

And he wasn't even going to ring back! Her phone lay silently in her hand, and she felt like some teenage girl who had been left waiting all evening for a call from a thoughtless stupid lump of a boy.

Whatever else you do, don't marry him, she found herself imploring the teenage girl. Or, if you insist on marrying him, don't do it at the age of twenty-three, when you have your whole life ahead of you! No, steel yourself against his good looks, his Kawasaki ZR motorbike, the little poems he writes you that always seem to rhyme – even the ones about your first day as a rookie estate agent when you sold a house that wasn't actually up for sale. Oh, he might be great fun, but fun is a poor companion in the supermarket on a Saturday morning with screaming twins trying to vault out of the shopping trolley while he peruses the slogans on tubs of butter (even if he uses quirky accents and ends up making the babies smile). But he'll never phone. He'll never phone you when you want him to.

Her phone rang. It was Ewan. 'Grace? I'm sorry about that. I've just turned off the television.'

There was a little pause, like he was waiting to be patted on the back or something, and she felt even more annoyed. 'Don't do me any favours!'

'I beg your pardon?'

'I said don't turn off the TV on my account.'

'I just have. I told you.'

'Only because you felt you had to. Really, you'd much rather be watching your own ads than listening to me on the phone!'

'That's a terrible thing to say!'

She wasn't going to let him off the hook this time. 'Oh? Any other man would have got into the car and come out to be with me! Any man with feelings!'

There was a little silence, and then he retaliated, 'The packing isn't finished. If I were to come out to you, we'd either miss our flight or have to go with no clothes!'

His rationale, his *excuses*, made her even crosser. 'You didn't even offer! That's the real insult!'

Now he sounded a bit cross too at being on the end

of what he obviously saw as an unprovoked attack. 'You want me to make you an offer I have no hope of keeping? You want an empty gesture or two? Why, I had no idea, you should have said!'

Oh! Just when you thought he was as docile as a lamb!

'You have no feelings,' she informed him loftily. 'Except what you could fit onto the back of a tub of butter.'

'What?' he snapped. 'What's butter got to do with anything?'

'I'm going to hang up now,' she said, haughtily.

'Grace,' he said slowly, 'I know you've had a shock, so I'm putting this down to your nerves, okay?'

Well, he would have to put it down to *something*, wouldn't he? Explain it away. Because surely there couldn't be anything seriously wrong with her, with them. That would be too inconvenient, just when he'd landed the Slimchoc account (apparently Slimchoc biscuits, mini rolls and Wicked Slimchoc Cake were in development). Then he might actually have to do something, to get involved, to dirty his hands. It was much easier to horse around and pretend he was one of the boys, leaving her to deal with the grown-up world of responsibility and emotions.

'Goodbye,' she said.

'Goodbye,' he said back, sounding very annoyed. Well, let him! She was sick of being treated with the kind of benevolent tolerance one would show to the family mutt. She who, single-handed, coordinated the complicated and frequently tiresome operation that was the family unit!

But Disneyland lay ahead. Home of the Astro-Orbitor and the free-spirited holidaymaker! Grace found that she was looking forward to it fiercely. They would be different people out there, she told herself; they would be adventurers, challenging the coyotes in Critter Country, or rafting down the rapids in The Great Outback. She would wear shorts and skimpy tops, and a pair of white strappy sandals that fashion magazines would describe as 'amusing'. She had never bought footwear on the basis of its entertainment value before, and she had walked out of the shop with the kind of giggly, confident feeling that comes after two gin and tonics. She didn't know if she'd have the nerve to wear them, though. It would depend on how the holiday went. It would depend on how liberated she was feeling.

Deep down she knew she was fooling herself. Ewan and the boys and herself would not step off a plane and suddenly turn into people who were more interesting, and nicer and kinder to each other. Worse again: instead of them all being somebody else, they might just be themselves but in a more concentrated form. She could just imagine it: Ewan speaking in rhyming couplets and watching the shopping channels on the TV; the boys clawing lumps out of each other and cursing. And her – what would she be doing? Fussing around the place like some kind of demented mother hen and falling over in her new white sandals. It was enough to make her weep. In fact, she did weep, squeezing out two little tears and allowing herself a sniffle.

'Don't worry. She'll pull through,' the man next to her said, startling her.

'Sorry?'

'That poor woman you shot.'

'Oh, yes. I, ah, certainly hope so,' Grace said with a watery smile.

There was a picture in the Disney brochure of a family on one of the water rides – a couple and their two children in a plastic-looking log canoe, coming off a bend. The man was all testosterone and bravado, his brown face split in a cheesy grin. The two kids in front were laughing and displaying thousands of dollars worth of orthodontics.

But it was the woman Grace looked at the most.

She was perfect. She had that indefinable aura that only very confident people had. Oh, she sickened Grace. You just knew by looking at her that she had never experienced a moment of self-doubt in her life! She had turned out exactly the way she had wanted to all along; everything about her was rounded and complete and full. She just . . . *was*.

In the photo she ignored the man entirely. And the two brats in front. Not for her the desperation of bribing her family with a trip to Disney. No, she was looking straight ahead, her blue eyes frozen on some rosy future that would no doubt be rewarding and comfortable and where nobody would ever dare to take her for granted, while women like Grace struggled and juggled and usually ended up making a balls of things.

Frank bustled up. 'You'd nearly want to have your leg hanging off in here before they'd treat you.'

And, actually, there *was* a man with his leg nearly hanging off over there, but he didn't seem to be getting treated any quicker than the rest of them.

'Well?' Grace asked. 'Did you find her?'

'They said she was in a treatment room and that I was to wait out here.'

'Maybe they're waiting for a special doctor to come. A foot doctor.' She wondered was there such a thing. Guiltily, she stole a glance at her watch: she had to leave in precisely one hour if she was going to make it to the long-term carpark in the airport on time. Surely Mrs Carr would be discharged by then?

But Frank announced, 'They asked me for details of next of kin.'

Grace's throat closed over. 'Next of kin?'

'It's standard procedure,' Frank said, and she relaxed a bit. 'To be honest,' he confided, 'it didn't take very long. Everyone belonging to her is dead, or nearly dead. Between you and me, she doesn't even have that many friends.'

'So there's nobody?'

Frank waved a hand. 'Well, except for Michael, of course. That's her son. And Gillian, her daughter-in-law. I gave them their phone number at reception.'

He consulted his watch now too. 'I suppose I should let Sandy know what's happened. She'll be very disappointed if this holds up the sale. She said to me, "You get your tush over here right now before I find myself another man!"' He added quickly, 'She was only joking. I mean, she's not . . . loose or anything.'

'I didn't think for a moment—'

'She goes to church every Sunday. Sings in the choir

and all. That's if she's not doing a reading.'

Sandy seemed to be putting in an early pitch for canonisation. But Grace just put this thought down to jealousy on her part.

'I suppose this gun business has held up the sale?' Frank said gloomily.

'Well, obviously we had to send the three couples away . . .'

'But you'll reschedule them, right?'

'Of course,' Grace lied. The sight of Mrs Carr being carried out on a stretcher from the house across the road, followed by various members of the elite police force in bulletproof gear and packing heavy-duty firearms, had very likely terminated their interest in Frank's house.

'Mrs Carr. Mrs Julia Carr?' A medical person in green scrubs was standing by the swing doors holding a chart and looking around expectantly.

Grace stood quickly. 'That's us. Frank, you mind the seats.'

She picked her way across outstretched legs and sleeping children. The medical person was gruff and busy and she hadn't seen him around Casualty earlier. She hoped that he didn't know that she was involved in the shooting.

But he said, straight off, 'You're responsible for Mrs Carr?'

Was nothing going to go her way today? 'We don't know that for certain yet,' she said strongly, trying to resist the urge to look shiftily at the floor. But really, whatever had happened to innocent until proven guilty?

The man looked at her impatiently. 'You accompanied her here, though?'

'Well, yes.'

'She's just being prepared for surgery now.'

'What?' She was shocked. It was the word 'surgery'. It always had such an ominous ring.

'There are some pellets quite deeply embedded. And then there are the bones.'

'What bones?'

'The metatarsals. Two of them are going to have to be reconstructed. Or what's left of them anyway.' He gave her another accusing look. Grace squirmed.

'So it's quite serious?' she said.

'An injury is always more serious in someone her age,' he said, the implication being that she should at least have picked on someone younger.

'Thank you for telling me,' she said. 'Maybe I should talk to her surgeon or something?'

'You are,' he said.

'Oh!' Now she had offended the surgeon. This sort of thing would never have happened to the woman in the Disney brochure. The woman in the Disney brochure wouldn't have been here in the first place; the very idea of landing in such a mess would have brought a wry sweet smile to her perfect face.

'How long will she be kept in?' Grace enquired.

'That depends on her recovery, but she seems fairly robust. She should be out in a few days.'

A few days would not make any difference, Grace decided quickly. She would simply arrange to meet Ewan and the boys in Florida. She'd have to forego the motel, but that was a small price to pay for her actions. She owed it to Mrs Carr.

'Okay,' she said.

'She'll be in a wheelchair or on crutches for several weeks, of course – at least until we see how the bones are knitting. And you'll need to bring her up for regular physio and the rest.' Unaware that her face was losing what bloom it still had, he efficiently consulted the chart again. 'You might want to talk to your husband and see what you can work out in terms of support for her at home.'

Ewan? She wasn't sure what he had to do with anything. 'Well, yes, I suppose I could discuss it with him . . .'

'Good,' he said.

There was no doubt now that he knew she had pulled the trigger (allegedly). He was more or less telling her to face up to her responsibilities. And he was right. She would do no more wriggling or squirming to try and get out of it.

'And don't be afraid to rope in other members of the family as well,' he added.

Grace blinked. Her parents mightn't be that easily persuaded from retirement in Co Mayo to look after a complete stranger. And her brother Nick was house-sitting for her and Ewan while they were in Disney, to write his new album, and driving thirty miles to bring Julia Carr bowls of chicken soup would probably not be compatible with his brand of heavy rock.

'Yes,' she said, because she didn't know what else to say.

The surgeon had his hand on the swing doors now.

'You can phone later on to see how your mother-in-law is doing.'

'What? My mother-in-law? She's not—'

But he leaned in, quite friendly now. 'A lot of the elderly people we get in here don't have any family at all, you know. Then we have to send them home alone, weak and in pain. Tragic.' His face hardened. 'If I could get my hands on the person who did this to her . . .'

Her mouth, which had opened in readiness to protest further, slowly closed.

'Anyhow,' he said. 'Goodbye, uh . . .' He checked the chart. 'Gillian.'

And he walked off through the swing doors, taking a good portion of her immediate hopes, dreams and wildest expectations with him.

This is a Public Service Announcement. Please do not leave your baggage unattended at any time in the terminal building or we will have to blow it up.

They didn't actually say they would blow it up, of course, but that's what they meant, Grace knew. Security was tight that day. It was a bonus to have got past the airport police at all, with her snagged tights and reeking of gunpowder.

'Hurry up, Neil! And Jamie – give me that bag, for goodness' sake, or they'll blow it up.'

She snatched up his hand luggage and continued her march down the hall towards Departures. The flight had been called three times already.

Beside her, Ewan gave another low moan and said, 'I just can't believe it.' For almost an hour now he hadn't been able to believe it. 'I mean, why didn't you just *explain*?'

'I tried to! But everything happened so fast! And besides, I didn't want them thinking I was trying to dump the woman or something.'

'So instead you let them think that you were her daughter-in-law?'

'Yes. Which would make you Michael.'

'This isn't funny, Grace.'

'Nobody's laughing.' As if Ewan would have done any better in the situation! He couldn't even bring himself to correct a mistake in a restaurant (once he'd eaten his way through a stuffed calf's heart rather than point out that he'd actually ordered a pizza. Possibly he had been waiting for her to do it for him).

'Neil! Jamie! Stop that *now*.' They had hijacked a luggage trolley. When they got up enough speed, they both jumped onto it and careered wildly down the tiled floor as though they were tobogganing down the Cresta run.

'Maybe we could ring the hospital from here,' Ewan fretted. 'Explain the situation or something. Damn – where did I put the boarding passes . . .?'

'You gave them to me to mind. And what exactly am I going to say to the hospital on the phone, Ewan? That I'm very sorry I shot her but that I'm buggering off to Disneyland for a month?'

'Well, I don't know, do I!' Ewan said. The boys careered into a row of seats now. He winced. 'When do you think you'll be able to fly out?' he asked anxiously.

'I don't know.'

'I mean, a foot thing – it couldn't take that long to get better, could it?'

'She's still in the operating theatre, Ewan.' She didn't mention the physio and the rest. Ewan wasn't someone who dealt very well with large chunks of reality at any one time. Best to split things up and give them to him gradually. Suddenly she was reminded of when she used to sit the twins up in their high chairs and spoon-feed them vegetables she had painstakingly blended to a mush, a little at a time.

Ewan added, 'She has relatives. I don't see why they can't look after her.'

His baleful tone, his lack of sympathy for Mrs Carr, made her so cross that she said loudly, 'Maybe they can! I don't know yet! All I *do* know right now is that three hours ago I shot an old woman, Ewan! An old woman who's having two metatarsals reconstructed in an operating theatre right now because of me!'

Ewan sighed. 'Don't be so dramatic, Grace—'

'So I'm sorry if this disrupts all our plans! I'm sorry if it's all very inconvenient, but if I can't find a bit of compassion in my soul at a time like this – well, then, I'm not much of a person, am I!'

Ewan and the boys exchanged a look, as though she were half-cracked, or pre-menstrual or something. Right now, for two pins, she would walk out of the airport and leave them there! (But she was in charge of the boarding passes, and the drinks for the flight, and two travel board games for the boys, and Ewan's book.)

68

This is the final call for Flight EI102 to London Heathrow. The gates will close in five minutes.

'Jesus,' fussed Ewan. 'After all this, we're going to miss our flight.'

This seemed to Grace to be further recrimination for spoiling everybody's day, and she grimly quickened her place down the terminal building, bags swinging out of her and boarding passes held aloft, like some kind of manic airhostess. Ewan and the boys had to run to keep up.

'Grace. Wait.' He obviously saw that he had upset her in some way (he was quite good at that, even though he usually had no idea how) because he puffed, 'You never know. She could be discharged from the hospital in no time and you'll be on your way out.'

It was the first reference any of them had made to what Grace was missing out on: to her own disappointment. The boys might be excused on the grounds of excitement, but Ewan?

'Maybe,' she said.

They were at the Departures gates now, and she reached into her bag for all the bits and pieces that she had spared everybody else the worry of until now.

'Be good now,' she said automatically to Neil and Jamie. 'And I'll talk to you on the phone, okay?'

'I need a drink,' Jamie said in response.

She handed over a bottle of water. And as she looked at his excited little face – at both her children's faces – she was suddenly overcome with emotion: they were going off without her, on a great journey, and she was being left behind!

Impulsively she hunkered down and threw her arms around them both. 'Goodbye! I'll miss you!'

They squirmed and wriggled and looked around to see was anyone watching the embarrassing display. 'You'll probably see us in a few days,' Neil complained.

Well, yes. The moment had somehow gone, and she let go of them quickly and stood.

Now she handed over all Ewan's things. He blinked and frowned as he tried to find pockets for everything.

'Well, have a good flight,' she said.

'It's the next leg I'm worried about – all the way to America!' he grumbled. 'Did you pack those games for the boys?'

'You just put them in your coat pocket, Ewan.'

'Oh, yes.'

'So! Goodbye then!' She waited for his hug.

This is an announcement for flight EI102 to London Heathrow. The gates are now closed—

'Oh my God!' Ewan grabbed a twin in each hand, and they trampled past Grace towards the gates.

She regained her balance, to see them ducking under ropes and trying to get to the top of the queue.

'Ask those people if you can squeeze in before them, that you're late,' she urged.

They did, and the airport official manning the gates scrutinised the three boarding passes, and quickly waved them through. Thank God.

Grace shifted over a bit so that she could see through the gates to wave goodbye to them. But Ewan and the boys were preparing to empty their pockets at the security scanners. She hoped Neil had remembered to leave the penknife at home that he routinely carried around.

Now the three of them waited in line to go through the metal-detector. And, looking at them, Grace was suddenly shocked to notice that Jamie and Neil reached to Ewan's shoulder. How had she not noticed how tall they'd grown? She must have been looking the other way too when Neil decided that the nice pair of jeans she'd bought him last week would actually be much better as surfer-style shorts, with the help of a pair of scissors. His legs, thin and hairless still, poked out from the fraying ends, but he walked with his feet planted far apart in a good imitation of a macho strut. As for Jamie – her little boy! – was that his *underwear* deliberately pulled up over the waist-band of his jeans?

They were growing up. Shedding their childish loveliness and turning into big, hairy, brutes of men. All underarm sweat and willies. She didn't know if she could bear it.

She saw Ewan turning around.

'Goodbye!' she said, waving.

But he had turned to say something to the boys. The three of them laughed, all buddy-buddy and boys together. The depth of her resentment towards him shook Grace. Perhaps it was because she had done the dogsbody work all these years: the disciplining, the runs to basketball and football and dance classes (which had only lasted two weeks, in fairness). That's not to say Ewan had ignored them – no, he had descended from his perch every evening at six o'clock

71

on the dot, just when she had finished bullying them into doing their homework, and they would run to him like he was their saviour, casting dark looks back at their tormentor.

They got through the metal-detector successfully, and they were now putting everything back into their pockets and collecting their hand luggage. In a minute, they would go through that frosted-glass partition and they would be out of sight.

'Ewan!' She gave another little wave.

But he didn't look back.

'Jamie? Jamie!' He had the best hearing. But no. She dropped her hand, a bit embarrassed. Honestly – they knew she would have waited. Wouldn't you think they'd at least have looked back?

They didn't. Not once. They filled their pockets with all the things she had carefully looked after for them – and they went right on! Through that frosted-glass partition without one of them turning to wave goodbye.

Gone. Without Ewan even saying he would miss her desperately!

Or that he would miss her at all.

The realisation was so upsetting that she stood there, in the middle of the vast tiled floor, long after the flight had closed.

'Are you all right? Do you need help with anything?'

Some nice airport attendant had stopped. Grace felt herself being assessed from her scraggly hair right down to her scuffed shoes as a possible security concern.

'No, thank you, I'm fine,' she said, smiling brightly.

She kept smiling brightly as she retraced her steps all the way back through the terminal building, down the rickety elevator, and into the short-term carpark.

Four

'At least your lot are away in Disney,' her brother Nick said. He was standing in her kitchen. 'Mine are only down the road in Drumcondra – fat chance they'll stay away from me for a whole month. Was I telling you that Janis got on a bus all by herself last week and ended up in Newbridge?'

'You were.'

'The amazing thing is that the bus didn't even go to Newbridge, the police said, so she must have got off and changed connections at some point. I couldn't even tie my own shoelaces at five.' Nick pondered this with amused wonder. 'Have you any more tea bags, Grace?'

'Second press over.'

She'd forgotten how much tea he drank. He didn't seem to have brought any tea bags of his own, despite the mountain of luggage he'd deposited in the hall. No food either, unless you counted a Toffee Crisp. But maybe you had to provide food when you asked people to housesit. Not that they had actually asked him – he'd more or less offered his services. Insisted, in fact, only two days ago, when they'd got all their arrangements in place. Said it would be a mutually beneficial arrangement – he would get to finish his new album and at the same time keep vicious and unscrupulous thieves away. Ewan hadn't been that keen (it was to do with the fact that he worked with advertising jingles as opposed to 'real music', as Nick had once said over a Christmas dinner at which too much wine had been consumed). Still, as Grace had said, Nick was her brother and they should be glad to be able to help him out. And it would be a change from that tiny flat he'd moved into since he and Didi had separated last year.

She just hadn't expected to be in the house when he arrived, that was all. And, watching as he dripped tea all over her lovely clean kitchen floor, she wished she wasn't.

'So! How are Dusty and Lennon?' she asked.

Nick and Didi had named their children after rock legends, which had seemed a great idea when they were babies. Dusty was fourteen now and wanted to change her name by deed poll to Jane.

'Great. Lennon wants to stop going to school,' Nick said, spooning sugar into his tea. Half of it missed the cup and went on the worktop.

'Does he?'

'Can't say I blame him. State propaganda, the lot of it.'

'And what does Didi think?' Grace enquired.

'Didi! She says he has to go, of course. Says that if he drops out now, he'll have no qualifications, no chance of a proper job, his whole future will be ruined, blah-bloody-blah!'

'Well, he is only nine,' Grace offered. You had to be careful on the subject of Didi. Nick could be a bit sensitive.

'Anyway,' he said. 'Didi says she'll probably drop by here with Lennon to discuss it at some point – is that okay, Grace?'

'Fine by me. I just hope you get some work done on your album, that's all.'

'Yeh,' he said, adding milk to his tea. Some of that missed, too.

'How's it coming along, anyway?' she asked.

'What?'

'The new album.'

'We haven't really started,' he said.

'Oh. Okay.' She had thought they were under pressure. 'And look, I don't want to nag, but tell Derek and Vinnie that they're not to block anyone's driveway with their vans, okay?'

Derek and Vinnie were the two other members of Steel Warriors.

'They probably won't be around much anyway.' He didn't quite meet her eyes.

'Why not?' They played lead guitar and drums, for heaven's sake.

'We've decided to change direction,' he announced. 'To be honest, I've been moving away from all that heavy rock stuff for a couple of years now. It's just too immature and loud. You can hardly hear my lyrics.'

'Oh.' Grace always felt backward when Nick started talking about music. It went back to their teenage years when he had roundly scorned her for listening to Duran Duran while he played The Ramones in his bedroom.

Then Nick gave a sigh that seemed to shake the whole kitchen. 'I suppose you're going to find out anyway. Steel Warriors have broken up, okay?'

'What?'

'The record company dropped us last month. So there's no band, no new album, no money, nothing. And Didi says she's sick of scrimping and scrounging and sticking the kids in second-hand clothes. She says that unless I pay six months' arrears in maintenance she's going to take me to court. Isn't that lovely!' He said all this very fast. 'Would you have anything to eat around the place at all? I didn't get a chance to have lunch before I left.'

'I think there's a pizza in the freezer,' Grace said, kind of numb. Steel Warriors, broken up! 'What are you going to do, Nick?'

'A computer course in Clonliffe Road.'

She was more shocked. He bent to rummage in the freezer, his big awkward body hunched over clumsily. He looked like he had been grown specially to jump around an open-air stage in tight leather. He did not look like a computer operator.

'What about the rest of the, uh, warriors?' she ventured.

'Derek's just got a promotion in Dublin Bus – he's in charge of ninety-six double-deckers now. And Vinnie's going to stick with insurance.'

'What a cop-out!' she cried.

'He's got another kid on the way, Grace.'

'Oh. But all the same! A band can't succeed if

everybody isn't giving it a hundred per cent – like you, Nick!'

'Yeh, and maybe I've been the stupid one.'

Grace was appalled. 'Don't ever say that.'

'No? I'm thirty-five years old, Grace! And look at me! A failed band, a failed marriage, three kids who have never even listened to one of my records – they like hip-hop, for God's sake! I've no money, no qualifications, no flat—'

'No flat?'

'Did I not tell you? I kind of fell behind in the rent – is it okay if I stay here until I find something else?'

'Ah . . .'

'Thanks. So you see, it's over, Grace,' he declared solemnly. 'I sold my guitar yesterday and bought computer course books with the money. I'm starting a new life.' There was a little silence. 'You might at least wish me luck.'

'Sorry. It's just hard to take it in, that's all.'

He looked glum too. 'I know.'

'Do you remember the very first gig you played?' she said, after a bit. 'As support in the SFX?' She had been sixteen and she remembered being sick with excitement when her parents had said she could go along.

'God, yeh,' Nick said. 'Derek out of his head on cider. And Vinnie so nervous he couldn't remember how to tune his guitar.'

'But you? You were magnificent!' Grace cried. 'Standing up on the stage like you owned the place! Pointing out the fire exits to the crowd and telling them you'd hurl them out head first if they didn't stop throwing things at you.'

'And they did,' Nick said, excited too. 'We managed to play three whole songs and they loved it! And your friend – what was her name – Fidelma?'

'Philomena.'

'Fainting! Having to be carted up on the stage at the very end in that little white vest! God, that was beautiful.'

'Wasn't it?' Grace said, giving a little clap. They had all walked the streets of Dublin afterwards for hours, too young to get into pubs, too high to go home. Grace had just assumed that this was the start of a global career for Steel Warriors and that she would be a small part of it by virtue of her relationship with Nick – even if she thought their music was, well, awful.

But she hadn't said that, of course. Instead she'd had her hair cut in a kind of rock-chick bob, which had lasted until the release of the Warriors' first single, *Dead Dingo*. It did moderately well. The next single bombed. But she had continued to believe in the cause, in Nick.

'How can you bear to give it up?' she blurted. Steel Warriors was so much a part of him – the very fibre of his being. No matter how hard things got, he was always so sure what he was doing was right. People like that tended to inspire a higher purpose in others. And now he was caving in at the prospect of a job in IT?

'Give what up?' he asked. 'The gigs playing to five people?'

'Stop it. You've played to more than five people.'

'Our record company has dumped us, Grace.'

'So what! Find a new one!'

Why was he being like this? Cynical and hard and washed-up?

'I know it's tough,' she pleaded. 'But surely you should give it one last shot? Don't you owe it to yourself and the guys?'

'What, you mean muster enough energy to record another album so that you can buy fifteen copies of it?'

Grace flushed.

'I saw them in the garage when I was putting in my car. Are you trying to offload them on all your dinner-party friends?'

She met his eyes. 'As a matter of fact, I do give them to some of my friends. I tell them how great you are. How fortunate you are to . . . to have followed your dreams!'

She regretted the ebullience of this statement the minute it was out of her mouth.

Nick laughed again, loudly. 'Anybody can follow their dream if they don't mind being on the dole. But then you wouldn't know about that, would you?'

The nasty little silence was broken by a knock on the back door. Hilda Brennan from next door stuck her head in stiffly.

'I heard voices and I just wanted to check that there weren't wild parties going on or anything. Not that I'm sticking my nose in where it's not wanted.' Her voice was full of hurt and self-righteousness.

'No, it's only me,' Grace said. 'I didn't fly out with the boys after all.'

'What?'

'Her and Ewan have broken up,' Nick explained. This was his type of humour. But Hilda, who was short on humour of any type, took a step forward fiercely.

'What are you talking about?' she barked.

Grace intervened quickly. 'Hilda, this is my brother Nick. Nick, meet my next-door neighbour.'

'Uh, hello,' said Nick.

Hilda just favoured him with a long, distasteful look, and then kind of shook her head at Grace as though to say, '*This* is what you've chosen over us!' Oh no, it hadn't blown over yet, by any means, the rift that Nick had unwittingly caused between the Tynans and their good friends the Brennans next-door two days ago. Harry and Hilda had been most upset when told that they needn't keep an eye on the house while the family was away, as they had done every year for the past decade. Harry had asked Ewan whether they didn't trust them any more around the silver. Hilda had not popped around for coffee yesterday as usual and didn't hang her washing out until after dark. The whole thing had nearly got ugly until Grace had sent Ewan around last night with a bottle of whiskey and big bunch of flowers.

Right now, Hilda wasn't going anywhere. Nick took a step closer to Grace.

But Grace was through baby-sitting men today, and so she picked up her car keys. 'I have a cooker to clean.'

'What?' said Nick.

'See you later,' she said, and walked out.

★ ★ ★

'Look at her. She seems so . . . old. And tiny!'

'Now don't go upsetting yourself, Gillian. She's just after coming through an operation. Anybody would look a bit rough.'

'That could have been me lying there, you know, Michael. With my bronchitis.'

'Yes, well, thank God it was only a too-tight bra-strap in the end.'

'That's still only a theory. The results of the tests haven't come back yet.'

Julia heard the hushed voices from somewhere far away. But she lay very still anyhow. She wasn't quite sure where she was for starters. She could hear a steady *bip bip bip* noise near her ear and thought that perhaps she might be in a spaceship. Or an amusement arcade. But to play the fruit machines surely she should be standing upright?

A different voice now. Childish. Spoilt. 'Dad, can I turn on the television?'

'I told you already. No.'

'But Buffy is on!'

'Susan, your grandmother has just been shot!'

'Yeh, but she's not going to die, is she?'

There was no need to sound so hopeful, Julia thought. The events of the morning came back to her in a rush. Which meant that she was on her side in a hospital bed recovering from a shotgun blast, and not on a spaceship on her way to pill-induced eternity. She tried to open her eyes but her eyelids felt glued together, and there was a nasty, antiseptic taste in her mouth, which was gaping wide open. So was the back of her blue hospital gown, leaving her bloomers on show for the whole world to see. Terrific. She tried to roll over, but she hadn't the energy. In fact, she felt like she would break up into tiny little pieces at any moment – *ping* – which would float off into space, leaving a pleasant nothingness behind.

Hang on – maybe she *was* dying! Maybe this was it. The big exit. Very possibly a sombre phone call had been made to the family: 'I'm afraid the operation on your mother's toe didn't go as well as we'd hoped. Maybe you'd better come in.'

And now they were all gathered around her bed to witness the momentous event, faces grave and hand-kerchiefs at the ready. The hospital Chaplain might even appear towards the end – he had for JJ, surely he'd show up for her? Then they would all go to a warm pub somewhere and tell stories about how great she'd been.

For a brief moment Julia was overcome. Her time had finally arrived. She was *dying*.

'Mammy! Can you hear me? Mammy, it's Michael.'

He couldn't let her die in peace, of course. She was reminded of when he'd been a child – always demanding her attention, always pleading with her to 'see what I can do!' And when she would turn he wouldn't be doing anything at all; he had just wanted her to look at him. Funny little Michael.

'Mammy?' Then he said, 'Here, Gillian, you have a go.'

Chairs scraped back. Then a charm bracelet jangled loudly near Julia's ear and a finger poked in her upper arm. Oh, it was maddening – nobody could die in these circumstances!

'Julia? It's Gillian here.' An expectant pause. Julia lay defiantly still. 'Julia, we're going home for our tea now, but we'll come back in the morning, okay?'

Their tea? She was hardly dying if they were going home to scoff ham sandwiches. She mustn't even be on the critical list!

Failure, twice in one day. She lay there on the bed in dank dark misery, letting the rustle of their departure wash over her: Gillian's handbag snapping, Susan zipping up her coat, car keys jangling.

'Susan, say goodbye to your grandmother.'

'But she can't hear me, Dad.'

'It would still be a nice thing to do.'

Julia was almost touched, but then Gillian chimed in, 'You know, I was reading in one of my medical books that lots of coma victims respond to the voices of their families – imagine!'

'Really,' Michael said, sounding impatient. Well, anybody would, after fifteen years of marriage to a hypochondriac.

'There was this case study of a man who had been in a coma for twelve years – a total vegetable, the poor man. And the very day they were going to switch off the life-support machine, he heard his young grandson's voice, and he woke up just like that and recited the alphabet!'

'I want to say goodbye to her!' Susan squealed now.

How Julia longed to spring up in the bed and give them all an almighty fright. But unfortunately she hadn't the energy and was forced to lie helpless as Susan leaned in over her ear.

'Granny? It's Susan here.' Pause. 'Your granddaughter.' Then, peeved, 'She didn't do anything!'

'We'll try her again in the morning,' Gillian said indulgently.

Everything was quiet for a moment, and Julia thought they had gone.

But then: 'We're going to have to sort something out, Michael.'

'I know.'

'I mean, the Emergency Response Unit was on the way, for heaven's sake!'

'I know, Gillian.'

'And two units of the fire brigade. We'll probably get billed for that.'

'Never mind about that. I just hope they're going to charge that woman who shot her.'

'It was an accident, Michael. It wouldn't have happened at all if your mother hadn't gone bats and started waving a shotgun about.'

'Please don't talk about her like that.'

'I'm just saying. We're going to have to sort something out.'

Then they were gone, and Julia was almost sorry (what could they have meant, 'sort something out'?) and then she drifted off again somewhere that was neither pleasant nor unpleasant.

Rachel, I'm going on my break now. Those two files are for Dr Ryan. Will I bring you back a chocolate muffin?

She surfaced again. She had been dreaming about JJ. He was holding a baby in his arms – Michael, about six months old. And JJ was looking down at him with such love, holding him with such pride.

She tried to hold onto the image of JJ's beloved face, but it grew muzzy and distorted. And why was he wearing lipstick?

'Awake at last!' A nurse was bending over her. There was a chocolate crumb on her uniform.

'Was my family in?' Julia enquired. She wanted to be sure she had not dreamt that too.

'They certainly were! Very concerned about you too,' the nurse said. 'He looks very like you, doesn't he? Your son.'

Julia was a bit taken aback. 'Well, maybe a little around the mouth . . .'

It had never occurred to her that she and Michael were similar in any way, even appearance.

'He's the absolute spit of you,' the nurse declared emphatically.

'Yes, is there any way you can limit their visits?'

'Sorry?'

'You could tell them I need my rest and can't be disturbed,' Julia suggested brightly.

'Um, I'd have to talk to your Ward Sister . . .'

'I'd appreciate it if you would.'

'I'm enquiring about Mrs Carr? Mrs Julia Carr?'

At the other end of the phone the hospital receptionist sang efficiently, 'What ward is she in, please?'

'I don't know. She was going for an operation. Has she had it?'

'Are you a relative?'

Grace hesitated. 'More a concerned bystander.'

Well, there was no point in getting into the whole thing on the phone.

'We can only give out information to relatives.' The voice was firm now.

'Can you at least tell me if I can go in and visit her?'

'If she was due to have an operation then a visit today isn't advisable. Especially if you're not a relative.'

For heaven's sake. 'But all her relatives are dead,' she protested. 'Or nearly dead.'

The person on the other end of the phone wasn't to be swayed. Grace hung up and looked at Frank, shaking her head a little.

'I'll give you Michael's number,' he advised. 'Her son. He'll be able to tell you.'

He bent to rummage in a drawer. Grace had called in to get a spare set of keys to Mrs Carr's house. She was going to spend the evening scouring the blackened cooker and washing the smoke-damaged curtains – it was the very least she could do in the circumstances, she felt. Hopefully Nick and Hilda had struck up a friendship back at the house.

Frank held out the number on a scrap of paper to her, and then said, rather shyly, 'Would you like to see a photo of Sandy?'

'I'd love to,' she said.

She already had a mental image of a plainish woman, large maybe (well, all right, fat), with uneven teeth. And a bleached moustache. Oh, she knew she was being unfair – but, honestly, what else would you picture for Frank? Cindy Crawford?

And so she was quite unprepared for the vision

that stared out at her from a silver photo-frame that Frank handed her.

'That's . . . Sandy?'

'Yes.'

Sandy was blonde, tanned, toned and thin. She had two adorable big bouncy breasts, and a skinny waist, and all her own teeth, and wasn't a day over thirty.

Grace knew now why Sandy took up to four hours in the bathroom. Every strand of her hair was teased and sprayed into submission, her make-up was lavish, and her nails were little round ovals of perfection. Just looking at her made Grace feel tired.

Oddly enough, her right hand was chopped off in the photo, right at the wrist.

'She hasn't . . . the hand thing is a mistake, right?' Best to be up front about any amputations straight away.

'Oh, yes. The photo was taken with an ex-boyfriend, you see. She's resting her hand on his shoulder. She didn't want to upset me, so she just chopped him out.'

It occurred to Grace that the ex must have been quite short – about three foot four, at her estimate – but possibly he had been kneeling at her feet or something. After all, she *was* lovely. And if she could get men to kneel before her, then you had to say fair play to her.

'She's beautiful, Frank.'

'Yes,' Frank said, taking the photo back protectively. 'That's the only photo I have. I keep asking her for more, but she says she gets shy around cameras.'

Sandy appeared to be modest too; if Grace were

that nice-looking, she would have her photo taken all the time, she thought. Not that she was bad-looking. But she just looked ordinary, which surely must be the worst thing to look.

'I know what you're thinking,' Frank said belligerently.

Grace was startled. 'What?'

'I'm aware that I'm no oil painting, okay?'

'Frank—'

'I was voted Student Most Likely to Stay Single at boarding school. Twice. But Sandy says looks don't matter to her. She says she's sick of the kind of guys who try to hit on her all the time. She doesn't go to clubs or bars or the gym any more because of all these muscley, good-looking guys trying to have sex with her.'

It sounded like heaven to Grace, but she just murmured sympathetically, 'Awful.'

Frank continued fervently, 'She says she's never found a meaningful relationship with anyone until she met me, that I am the light in her darkest days, and that we should get down on our knees and thank God that we found each other!'

Grace was a bit taken aback. Sandy sounded a bit, well, over the top. She was obviously very much in love with Frank.

Which was terrific, of course. God knows the romance would wear off soon enough – usually a couple of years into marriage, and was more or less extinct by the arrival of the first child. By the second, it was a prehistoric relic that reared its ancient head only briefly on St Valentine's Day and maybe during a sun holiday in Crete or somewhere, after too much wine in a bar and a walk back along the beach to the Bella Vista family apartments.

She left Frank gazing fervently at his framed photo of Sandy, and went across the road to Mrs Carr's house. She was used to letting herself in to other people's houses when they weren't there, and in no time at all she had familiarised herself with the light switches, and the loose floorboards in the living-room that could trip you up if you weren't careful. Not that she had gone into the room to snoop – that guilty curiosity in seeing how other people lived had passed years ago – just to close the bay window properly. She'd seen from the street that it was open a crack. She pulled up the net curtain energetically and closed the window with a sound bang.

A man was approaching the garden gate from the road, and the window slamming gave him a bit of a start. Reflexively, he jerked away. He was carrying a big heavy backpack, and what seemed to be a bundle of placards, which, in his fright, he swung upwards, knocking the side mirror off her BMW.

They looked at each other through the closed window. Eventually Grace reached forward and opened it again.

'Sorry,' he began, trying to piece the mirror back together again.

'No, *I'm* sorry. Leave that.'

'Your car . . .'

'Banging the window at you like that . . .'

'I didn't mean to . . . the mirror is clean off . . .'

'Don't worry about that, I can get it repaired.'

And they kind of smiled at each other.

'Can I help you?' she asked at last.

'Is this Park View House?' he said. He sounded Australian, or possibly he was from New Zealand. The surfer shorts could have come from either country. And he was more a boy than a man. In his early twenties maybe. Not that Grace was a great judge of these things – the older she got, the less accurate she was about the ages of those younger than herself. Which was fair enough, given the way teenagers callously and wildly overestimated the age of anybody over twenty-five.

'I'm not sure,' Grace was forced to admit. There was no park in evidence. Not that that had ever stopped anybody. She could go on for a whole day about the silly names people gave their houses (La Maison Rouge – for an ex-council house in Crumlin!). Instead, she opened the window a crack more and leaned out to see the number over the front door. 'It's Number 28 anyway. What number are you looking for?'

He consulted a grubby bit of paper. He had very blue eyes. Or possibly they looked bluer because his face was so tanned. 'I don't have a number. Just Park View House. Mrs Julia Carr?'

'Oh! Yes.'

'Nice to meet you.'

'No, no, I'm not actually Mrs Carr. I'm . . .' It was all too complicated, so she just said, 'This is her house.'

He seemed satisfied with this. 'Great. I've just walked all the way from the train station and I thought I was lost.' He smiled at her easily. 'I don't usually get lost.'

She could believe that. Now that he was sure he was in the right place, he opened the garden gate and walked right in. He wore the biggest boots she had ever seen on anybody. Walking boots. He rocked back and forth on them now, confidently, cockily. His blondish hair was in dreadlocks that bobbed about his ears like fat little puppy tails, and an earring glinted in one ear.

'So,' he said. 'Are you going to let me in?'

'I beg your pardon?'

'Into the house.'

Grace kept smiling even as her mind raced to process the implications of this. 'You want to come in?' she clarified.

'Well, yes.' He consulted his bit of paper again. 'Do you want to be paid upfront or something, is that it?'

'No, no, not at all!' she said happily, her confusion turning to a ridiculous determination to battle this thing out. 'Did Mrs Carr say anything about being paid upfront?' Best to throw it back at him.

'She said I could pay when I left.'

'I see,' she said, even though she didn't.

'I did book, you know,' he said. 'I got the number from the local tourist office and I rang her last week.'

Of course! The woman ran some kind of Bed & Breakfast. Grace made sure her expression didn't alter.

'I'm afraid there's a bit of a problem,' she told him. 'Mrs Carr is actually in hospital.'

'Oh.'

'She won't be home for a couple of days.'

'Nothing serious, I hope?' He looked like he meant it.

'A foot thing,' Grace said vaguely. 'The thing is, she won't be in any fit state to look after lodgers. So, obviously . . .'

His face fell. 'Yes. Of course.'

'I'm very sorry about this,' she said. 'Maybe you could try somewhere else?'

'Sure.' He hoisted his backpack further up on his broad shoulders, and shifted the placards from one arm to the other, wincing slightly at the weight. 'I don't suppose there's any chance I could use your phone?'

Grace hesitated. She didn't want to go inviting strangers into a house that wasn't hers.

'My mobile is out of credit, so I'd have to walk all the way back into town to find a payphone. And to be honest, I'm beat.'

He did look tired. And besides, this thing was partially her fault in the first place.

'Come in,' she said. 'I'm sure we can find a phone directory somewhere.'

Inside the front door he took off his boots without any invitation. Grace waited as he lined them up neatly on the mat beside the backpack and the placards, and turned to face her in his stockinged feet. Slightly different social customs obviously prevailed in Australia. Or maybe he belonged to one of those religions that frowned upon footwear indoors.

She kept her own shoes resolutely on and led the way to the living-room. She settled him in the tatty red armchair and presented him with Mrs Carr's cordless phone and a copy of the local directory.

'I really appreciate this,' he told her.

His manners were lovely though. And he had very nice teeth too, even if she longed to take a brush to that hair. Still, the main thing was that he didn't look as though he might make off with Mrs Carr's valuables the minute her back was turned.

She left the kitchen door open all the same when she went back in to attack the cooker with a box of cleaning agents she'd brought from home. It wasn't much use.

The top she feared was blackened forever, but at least the rings still worked. She might even cook her dinner on them this evening, given that Nick seemed to have taken over her entire kitchen. It had taken a great many utensils to prepare a cup of tea at any rate. Already he was irritating her, the way he'd done all through their childhood. How was she going to live with him until she would fly out to Florida? However long that would be. If at all?

It struck her then, all that she was missing: the seedy motel, Critter Country, hot dogs and buttery popcorn – she wouldn't experience any of it. Her new strappy white sandals would remain unpacked, along with the chance to shake off this weird fake person she had somehow become. Instead she was stuck in the midlands looking after a cranky old bag. Happy holidays!

'Excuse me?'

The boy was at the kitchen door. It was an effort to smile. 'Yes?' she said.

'I'm out of luck.'

'They're all booked out?'

'There are only four other B & B's listed in the town,' he told her. 'Three of them are full and Dairy Cottage burned down last month.'

'Good Lord.'

'Some lodger was smoking in bed. Anyhow, thanks for letting me use your phone.'

He had his boots on, she saw. And his backpack was over his shoulders again, and the placards under his arm. They were covered in some kind of protective plastic and she couldn't see what was on them.

'Where are you going to go?' she asked.

He shrugged. 'I'll find somewhere.'

Of course he wouldn't – what was he going to do, bed down in the ashes of Dairy Cottage?

She told herself that he was not her responsibility, but it sounded very weak, given that she had shot his landlady. But what was she supposed to do with him? Take him back to Dublin with her? Nick would have a fit. Ewan too.

And what if Mrs Carr had been counting on the money? Judging by the condition of the house, cash could well be in short supply. Grace felt even guiltier; not only had she put the woman in hospital, but she was jeopardising her meagre source of income too.

She looked at her watch. It was almost six o'clock. 'Would you be able to find somewhere in the morning, do you think?' she asked.

He looked hopeful. 'I'm sure I could.'

She made a decision rapidly. 'All right. One night so. You'll have to fend for yourself for dinner though.'

'All right,' he said. 'And what about breakfast?'

'What about it?'

'Well, if I'm paying for Bed & Breakfast, then I guess I should get breakfast – right?'

He had a point.

'You'll get breakfast,' she said grandly.

'And towels are provided, right? And hot water?'

'Absolutely,' she said. 'I'll sort it out now.'

She set off for the stairs in her new capacity as lodging-house proprietor. She found that she wasn't even surprised, given the way her carefully planned day had turned so spectacularly upside down. In fact, she didn't think she would bat an eyelid if the roof fell in on top of her at that very moment.

'Go right ahead and make yourself at home!' she called back, suddenly inexplicably happy.

He bent down and took his boots off again.

Five

'No, really, you've done the whole thing right,' Natalie declared.

They were eating take-away Chinese in Mrs Carr's kitchen that night. Grace had not wanted to stay in the house all evening on her own with a strange man (his name was Adam). She could have phoned Nick, of course, but that would have entailed all kinds of explanations. And she couldn't very well go home and leave Adam to fend for himself. No, she would stay the night and leave first thing in the morning. Nick wouldn't even miss her and, in the meantime, Natalie had been very willing to come over. Her second baby was due in eight weeks and, as she said herself, it was probably the last time she would get out for a couple of years.

'What exactly have I done right?' Grace enquired.

'Timing,' Natalie said. 'You married young so you didn't have to take the leftovers the rest of us were faced with at thirty.'

'No offence to your Paul,' Grace said.

Natalie was mortified. 'God, no! Paul is great. But you know what I mean. You got in early. Did the whole marriage bit, bought the house, had the babies while you still had the energy. And now they're all grown up leaving you to concentrate on yourself. We were only saying it in the office today, you make us all sick.'

Natalie had a desk opposite Grace, only she was in Rentals and Lettings and she dealt mostly with apartments in the city centre where rents were high and turnover higher. This meant that she always seemed to be renting the same properties over and over again, a situation she often darkly predicted would drive her over the edge.

Grace laughed. 'I never thought of myself as being in such an elevated position before.'

Natalie stuffed a forkful of noodles into her mouth. She had started this pregnancy hopelessly overweight from the last one, but had remained very cheerful about it, to her credit. 'I often think the rest of us were daft,' she said. 'Devoting most of our twenties to that damned company, only to watch the really big promotions go by because we're either off having babies or thinking about it.' She leaned in. 'Imagine – they guessed in Head Office that Orla was pregnant before she knew it herself!'

'That was because Mark went around bragging after the Christmas party,' Grace said.

'The point is that they mentally write us off,' Natalie insisted. 'Look at me! Stuck in Rentals and Lettings for the past four years. The soft job. And you, with your children practically reared and your whole life ahead of you! Oh, it's too much to bear!'

She took the last spring roll without asking.

'Yeh – like I had it all planned or something!' Grace scoffed bravely. 'You think I sat down in my early twenties with a list of Things To Do and ticked them off one by one?'

'Did you?' Natalie cried enviously. 'And there was me getting pissed and backpacking around Europe!'

'Exactly!' Grace said. '*I* envied *you*!'

'You didn't even know me then.'

'I knew people like you! Hundreds of them!' This sounded a bit insulting so she hurried on, 'I was stuck at home rearing twins while you were up to all sorts!'

She had meant travelling and drinking too much, but Natalie's face turned rather dark. 'They're very transitory, you know. The pleasures of your twenties. They don't last. Or at least you hope they don't,' she added.

'It's just the way things worked out,' Grace said, lamely.

The minute the final exams were over, her friends had nearly all scattered to the four winds. They had gone to seek adventure and careers in London, New York, Australia – anywhere but the city where they had spent four years in dingy flats on student grants. And who could blame them? She had been left behind, through her own choice. Things were very serious with Ewan. (Why hadn't she realised that if they were that serious, he would have waited for her to come back? Had she been worried that distance would cool their ardour? Or that experience would shape them into different people?)

Things were different back then, of course. Jobs were scarce and Ewan was one of the lucky ones: a junior copywriter with an advertising agency! A dream job in the dreary late eighties. How could she have demanded that he give it up and go on the dole with her in London, or Los Angeles (where they didn't even have the dole)?

It wasn't that she regretted marrying him, as such. Certainly she did not regret her two beautiful boys. And who was to say she would be any happier if she had waited, like Natalie, and was facing into it all now?

But whatever had happened to that elusive girl in the black and red striped scarf that had made her look a bit dangerous? Was she gone forever, buried under obligations and commitments?

'Maybe I have regrets,' she said loudly, changing her mind. 'Maybe I wish I hadn't married young! Maybe I wish I'd had my twenties to myself!'

'You wouldn't.' Natalie was quite definite about this. 'People are too silly in their twenties, they haven't a jot of sense. This way, you've got the grunt work done and now you can sit back and enjoy it all.'

'Enjoy what?' Grace enquired.

'Having time to yourself.'

'To do what?'

Natalie shrugged: if Grace didn't know that . . .

'Well, obviously, there's my career,' Grace said hastily. She didn't want Natalie to think life was wasted on her altogether.

'Word is they're considering opening a branch out here,' Natalie confided. 'If I were you, I'd signal my interest now.'

Grace smiled weakly. The mere thought of managing a property branch filled her with doom. The only reason she stayed in the job at all was that she liked meeting people.

'Or you could do some courses,' Natalie added. 'I'd love to have the time to do stuff like that. Drama. Or maybe art.'

'Maybe,' Grace said, slowly.

'Look into it anyway,' Natalie advised. 'Now that you've all this time on your hands.'

'Yes,' Grace said. Doing art courses at her age had a kind of an ominous feel to it: anything to take your mind off yourself. Or impending death.

She heard the front door open and close quietly. Adam. He had gone down the town ages ago.

'I'd better go,' Natalie said with a sigh. 'Rosie won't go to sleep unless I'm in the house – remember I was telling you Paul pretended to be a monster the last time I went out for the night? And I have an appointment in the hospital first thing tomorrow. They think the baby might be breach. They're going to try to turn it around or else I'll have to have a section.'

An art course sounded like bliss in comparison, and Grace wondered whether she was being altogether too picky. All things considered, she had a perfectly satisfactory life by any standards. It was ridiculous to suddenly be obsessing about a stripy scarf and a café mix-up that took place nearly fifteen years ago.

'Here, hold the fort for a minute, will you?' she asked Natalie.

She'd left her bag upstairs in one of the spare rooms (she hadn't wanted to tempt anyone – well, all right,

Adam – by leaving it lying around). She took her mobile phone out of it and the scrap of paper with Michael Carr's number on it, and dialled.

She had her little speech all rehearsed; how sorry she was to be the cause of his mother's injury, how she would be prepared to foot any hospital bills – she must remember not to use the word 'foot' – and how she was ringing to enquire after Mrs Carr's health. She hoped this would lead to some kind of discussion about plans for her convalescence, and who would be looking after her. (Well, Grace had her own life to consider too, and the boys would want to know when she might be expected to join them.)

'Hello?' A girl's voice answered, sullen.

'Hello, is that Michael Carr's house?'

'Yeh. I'm Susan. Dad can't come to the phone right now,' she added. 'Mum is having palpitations.'

'Oh!' Grace said, thrown. 'Maybe I should get off the line . . . you might want to ring the emergency services . . .?'

'No, she's coming around now. She thinks the cole-slaw might have been cross-contaminated with shell-fish or something.' She raised her voice. 'Dad! *Phone!*'

Grace's entire speech had gone out of her head now and so she said quickly, 'Look, I just wanted to know how Mrs Carr is? And her foot?'

'She's not going to die,' Susan said.

'Great!' Grace said. She felt more confident now. 'You're probably wondering who I am. You see—'

'Dad says if he gets his hands on the person who did this to her, he'll murder them,' Susan confided in her. 'With his bare hands. But Mum says it was a blessing in disguise, because only for that shotgun today we wouldn't have known how crazy Granny really *was* until it was too late. My friend Kate's Granny lost her marbles and started eating grass and stuff.'

'Really,' Grace managed. 'Anyhow, you see, the gun thing, it was an accident—'

'Dad says he might try and sue or something. He's hopping mad.' Then she shouted, *'Dad!* Are you going to take this call or not?'

Grace said, quickly, 'Actually, there's no need to bother him. I'll just visit Mrs Carr in hospital tomorrow.'

'All right,' Susan said. 'The hours are between two and four in the afternoon. Dad says he might monitor visitors. He doesn't want her getting too tired, you see. Mum says he's carrying on as if Granny's foot had been amputated or something. Dad went *totally* ballistic at that!'

He sounded rather over-protective and the last of Grace's intentions to declare herself died a swift death. She had also wanted to tell Michael Carr about her presence in his mother's house, and that she was putting up a lodger. But he sounded like the type who might not take it in the spirit in which it was intended, and march over straightaway and eject her.

So she held her tongue; and now she really *was* illegally in a stranger's house.

'When is she coming out, do you know?' she asked. 'Your grandmother?'

'Friday, we think,' Susan said.

Three days, then. She and Adam would be long gone from the house. Guiltily, she thought that if she left the place exactly as she had found it – apart from the cleaned-up kitchen, that is – then there might be no need to get into explanations at all. She could slip the B & B money into a drawer or something, as a pleasant little discovery for Mrs Carr somewhere down the line.

'Who did you say you were again?' Susan enquired.

'Oh, nobody,' Grace said, and hung up. She would send a big bunch of flowers to Mrs Carr in hospital tomorrow. She couldn't risk a visit; a conflagration with Michael Carr across his mother's bed might upset the poor woman further. But when would they discuss Mrs Carr's convalescence? And Grace's part in it, if any? Oh Lord. It was getting more complicated by the minute.

There was laughter coming from the kitchen below. She could hear it through the ceiling. Natalie said something in animated tones. More laughter. Curious, she went back downstairs.

Natalie and Adam were eating chips from a wad of newspaper on the middle of the kitchen table, the whole room filled with the delicious smell of grease and vinegar. He was perched on the edge of the table, one brown leg swinging casually back and forth. Grace found that she was a little irritated; she would never walk into a stranger's house and get up on the furniture. But they had such confidence these days, young people. They had been brought up never to experience a moment of self-doubt.

'You're just saying that!' Natalie was round-eyed. Giggly.

'I am not. Scouts' honour,' Adam said. 'Oh, hi, Grace.'

Natalie gave her a look as though she were spoiling the party (in her condition!). Grace wanted to say something witty and unusual, just to show that she could, or else ask to be let in on the topic of conversation, but ended up saying gaily, 'I suppose we'd better organise sheets and towels for you!'

That finished any more light-hearted banter. Natalie and Adam ate up their chips rather sullenly, she thought, while she hovered at the door like some kind of over-zealous dormitory mistress. Natalie made her goodbyes, smiled coyly at Adam, and lumbered off out the door.

'She's very nice, your friend,' Adam said. He would be the sort of man (or boy, Grace couldn't make up her mind which) who would notice attractive women. It wasn't that he was sleazy or lascivious or anything like that; but to him, women were firstly women, whereas to Ewan, women were just other people. If he noticed them at all.

'She is,' she agreed vigorously. She couldn't think of anything else to say, so she just kind of looked towards the door, and Adam, taking what he obviously thought to be a heavy hint, set off for the stairs in front of her, making no more attempts at diversionary conversation.

Well, she just wasn't used to this! Having to make strangers at home in a house that wasn't even hers! In fact, technically both of them were trespassers. And what on earth was she going to cook him for breakfast in the morning?

'You're not a vegetarian or anything, are you?' she asked Adam's back as they ascended the stairs. Although what difference it made, she wasn't sure. Mrs Carr's cupboards were not promising for meat-eaters or any other kind of eaters.

'No,' he said.

She had picked out the largest of the three guests rooms for him. She threw open the door with another cheery, 'Here we go!' He loitered by the bed as she hunted in the chest of drawers. If this were like her room across the hall, there would be sheets and towels in the bottom two drawers.

'They're not fitted, I'm afraid – the sheets. And are two towels enough?'

'Plenty,' he said.

'Great! I've put the immersion on if you want a shower or a bath. And there are spare pillows in that cupboard over there, okay?'

'Yup.' He was looking around, not really paying attention.

She raised her voice. 'There's a fire exit at the bottom of the hall, and I would remind you not to smoke in bed. Look what happened to Dairy Cottage.'

He was sitting on the bed now with his back to her, taking off his socks, not even listening.

She flushed. Really, the day had been long enough without some hippy guy refusing to take proper note of the fire exits! And she was doing him a favour by letting him stay at all!

She flung the sheets, towels and pillowslips onto

the floor at his feet. Now he was paying attention all right.

'You can make the bed up yourself.'

'I hope you're going to bill him for it.'

'It wasn't his fault. Well, not entirely.'

'He broke your side-mirror off. It's a good thing I know a decent garage.'

Frank had officiously appointed himself in charge of her damaged car. She wouldn't be getting it back from the garage until tomorrow. Hence he was giving her a lift down to the Spar to get provisions for breakfast in the morning.

'Who is he anyway?'

'He's Australian.'

'That's it? You let a stranger into my neighbour's house – if Michael got wind of it he'd have a fit – and all you know about him is that he's Australian?'

'And he likes chips,' she added lamely.

'My God! He could be anybody! How do you know he's not got a string of criminal convictions behind him?'

Grace refused to give in to his brand of cynicism. 'Because I just got a feeling off him, okay? Generally, you get a feeling off people. You can sense whether they're good or not.'

'Bah,' Frank said rudely.

'Well, what was your feeling the first time you met Sandy?' she asked.

'What?'

'You must have felt something.'

'I don't think that's any of your business.'

'It is if you're going to criticise my choices in people.'

'I can't remember.'

'You can't remember?'

'No.'

Grace thought about the beautiful Sandy. No man would forget his first glimpse of such perfection. 'Well, did she smile at you? Did you go over and say hello to her? Was it in Ireland? America? Did your eyes meet across a crowded room?'

Frank was getting more hassled. 'You're making fun of me now.'

'Frank! I'm not making fun of you. I'm just curious about the first time you met, that's all.'

'We haven't met, okay? We've never met!'

Grace didn't immediately know what to say.

'I suppose you think that's peculiar. Odd. That's why I don't tell people, you see. People just love to curl their lip knowingly when you say that you've met someone on the Internet. They go, oh, he's a sad loser who can't make any real friends, he has to go on the Internet and exchange meaningless facts with other sad losers. Or else they think you're a weirdo. They hear the word "chatroom" and they think you must be a pervert who only wants to have conversations with other perverts about bondage and fetishes and . . . and animals! Well, Sandy doesn't get off on animals and I don't either!'

Grace still didn't know what to say.

'Sandy says she doesn't care what people think,' Frank said defiantly. 'She says that we must follow our hearts and believe in destiny. We must not let the aura of our love be tarnished by negativity.'

Sandy was beginning to lose the run of herself in terms of purple prose. But Frank seemed to be lapping it up.

He looked at her now, blinking a bit fast. 'Just because you write it down on a computer screen instead of saying it doesn't make it any less real, you know. And sometimes you can say a lot more in a few words that you can in a whole conversation.'

He had a point. God knows she and Ewan had plenty of conversations where there wasn't a thing said.

By the time they pulled up outside the Spar, Grace was feeling rather melancholy. If they sold wine, she would buy a bottle, she decided. Or any liquor, really. She felt like it tonight.

The Spar was cool and empty. Fluorescent lighting bounced off shiny products that promised to satisfy hunger, thirst, and shift stubborn stains. At the counter a girl with greasy hair looked up. With callous speed she registered, assessed and dismissed Grace as non-threatening, and went back to her teen magazine. How Grace longed to tell her that she had pulled the trigger on a shotgun this morning – a real shotgun!

The girl wouldn't care. Grace was almost old enough to be her mother, she realised. In her designer track bottoms and white runners, she looked like a typical middle-class suburban woman out to get a pint of milk for the kids' breakfast in the morning, and a sneaky bottle of wine for herself. No threat in the world.

She picked up a basket, and put in a pot of strawberry jam and some bread. Then to the cooler section, where she got milk and juice and butter. And would eight sausages be enough?

She was perusing a packet of smoked rashers when another customer came in and went to the counter – a man, good-looking. The girl looked up, said hello, and blushed. He said something back; she laughed, went smartly to get his cigarettes. Oh, she was very pleasant now. Grace smiled too, benign and forgotten in the background, and she lifted the waistband of her expensive track bottoms and slipped the packet of smoked rashers down the front of her knickers.

The shock of cold plastic hitting her skin was almost pleasant. Out of her peripheral vision she watched the man hand over money. She snapped her tracksuit waistband back into place over the top of the rashers and pulled her T-shirt down securely. She moved up the aisle a bit and picked up a pot of sour cream as though she had all the time in the world.

'Excuse me,' said the man, stepping past her on his way out.

'Sorry!' Grace said carelessly. He left. The shop girl turned to look down at her. Had she seen something suspicious? For the first time, Grace realised fully what she was doing. Shoplifting. *Stealing*. She was going to try to walk out of here with a packet of cured meat down her knickers: her, Grace Tynan, devoted mother of two and respectable estate agent! Had she gone quite mad?

There was a kind of a humming in her ears now, and everything suddenly seemed brighter, slower, louder – like in a movie. The rashers began to drip.

At the counter, the shop girl closed her teen magazine. Ominously? Grace pretended to dither over the sour cream, buying time. Two hundred and eighty calories per pot! She put it down quickly and bent to pick up some Greek yoghurt instead. Almost as fattening. But the movement had dislodged the rashers. They slipped wetly down an inch, and she clamped her thighs together hard. Mother of God. What was she going to do now?

'Do you need any help?' the shop girl asked. She had a flat, unattractive voice.

'Me? No!' *Divert, divert*, some part of Grace's brain commanded. 'Well, yes, actually. Do you have any low-fat yoghurt?'

That was the kind of thing a thin, middle-class woman like herself would eat. The girl seemed to relax a little. 'We're out. We're waiting for supplies to come in.'

'When?'

The girl frowned. 'Thursday. Maybe Friday.'

'Right! Great! Well, I'll take the Greek yoghurt until then. And the sour cream.'

She smiled brilliantly and chucked in a couple of pots of each. Frank would be in after her in a minute, wondering what was keeping her. But what if further movement dislodged the rashers altogether and they slid down the leg of her pants?

On the other hand, she couldn't remain at the cooler section all night. At some point it would start to look suspicious. She berated herself for not stealing the sausages instead. They were far more compact. Or some biscuits or something. This was what happened when you were an amateur.

Right. Clutching the basket very close at pelvic region to stop any more slippages, and under the watchful stare of the shop girl, she did a kind of sideways shuffle up to the nibbles & dips section. She snatched up a bag of nachos and added it to the basket. Then she pretended that a tin of shoe polish had caught her eye on the next shelf. That got her up another couple of feet. Gradually she worked her way up shelf by shelf to the counter, acquiring some nappies, indigestion remedy, bottled chillies and a tin of dog food on the way. But no wine, dammit. She'd never make it all the way over to the drinks section: it was too risky.

Now came the dangerous bit: getting the basket on the counter without incurring disaster.

'If you could just give me a hand . . . thank you!' She dumped the basket down on the counter, and clamped her hands together fiercely over the rashers.

The shop girl looked at her curiously. 'There's a customer toilet if you want to use it.'

'Oh! No, thanks. I'll, uh, hang on.' Immediately she regretted this. She could have moved the goods to a safer position in the toilet cubicle.

The girl gave her another penetrating stare, and began to take items from the basket and scan them with remarkable speed. Grace looked around casually, pretending to wrack her brain in case she'd forgotten something. She felt a thin trickle of condensation from the packet of rashers slide down her thigh. And another one. Oh God. She was leaking.

Beep. Beep. Beep. The girl packed items into bags as she scanned them. Now she had the sausages in her hand. Was this the point where she would mention the rashers? Grace's heart jolted so hard in her chest that it hurt, and she looked blindly past the girl in the hopes of finding some distraction.

Our Policy is to Prosecute Shoplifters. It was there in bright red letters on a big sign – just beside a CCTV camera, actually, which seemed to be angled right now at Grace's crotch. She thought she would vomit.

Then the girl pounced, her voice deliberate and accusing. 'Was there anything else?'

'What do you mean?' Grace said weakly.

'I mean, is this everything that you want to buy?'

Apart from those rashers down your pants, she might as well have said. Grace just stood there, thighs frozen, mouth open but with nothing coming out. Was this what people risked everything for? This feeling of utter panic and fear? She never would have guessed that shoplifting was so stressful. Or so damp.

She couldn't even claim that the rashers were to feed her starving children – not with a fat purse in her hand. No, in court they would brand her as a wealthy bored housewife, out to get her thrills. The shame of it! Although she wasn't sure which charge was worse – bored housewife, or shoplifter. Ewan would die. They could never go to a dinner party again. And as for the kids! They would be outcasts at basketball, pariahs at school (although she would bet that there were other light-fingered mothers at those staid parents' evenings. Would they seek each other out?). Everyone would try and blame it on stress, of course.

The strain of modern living. They would murmur kindly that she was on medication. Why else would she go stealing rashers from rural Spars? Her, with not a single thing in the world to complain about!

'Is this everything?' the girl repeated, her hand dipping stealthily under the counter; reaching for that little red alarm button Grace knew they always had just beside the till.

She couldn't breathe. She felt everything closing in on her like a vice. The rashers slipped another inch, leaving a trail of frozen flesh in their wake. She bared her teeth at the girl, shook her head, kept shaking it like a dog just out of the sea. The girl's hand moved slowly, inexorably, towards that red button, the hot-line direct to Sergeant Daly's desk—

'Yes! Yes! I have everything I need!' Grace rasped desperately at the very last moment.

Beat.

'Okay,' the girl said, and her hand came back into view, holding a roll of stickers. 'Are you collecting the coupons?'

Suddenly everything snapped back into normal time. The lights seemed to dim and Grace's hearing returned. 'I beg your pardon?'

'For the gift catalogue.'

'No,' Grace said. Was the girl toying with her?

'You're due two coupons,' the girl insisted. 'You can get an electric kettle for fifty. Or a turbo sunbed, but you need five thousand for that.'

Grace allowed herself a cautious breath. 'I'm not collecting them.'

'Do you, um, mind if I have them then?'

116

'Sure. Go ahead,' Grace said.

'Wow – thanks!' The girl smiled – a big, warm, guile-less smile and it transformed her. She couldn't be more helpful now – neatly folding and packing Grace's receipt, and handing over the bags, handles first.

'Thank you,' Grace said.

'No problem. See you again!'

And that was it. Grace made her way to the door, unimpeded by security guards or CCTV cameras. Sergeant Daly's squad car did not roar into the car-park as she stepped out through the glass doors into the cool night air.

'You were ages, I was about to go and look for you,' Frank complained, standing by his car.

'Sorry,' she said.

He took the two bulging plastic bags from her. 'Nappies?'

'Don't ask.'

He went around to the boot of the car, fussing and grumbling. Grace reached down and extracted the rashers. They were streaky bacon, she saw. With two rashers free, ironically.

She wasn't proud of herself. Absolutely not! It was totally the wrong thing to have done. It was mere luck that it hadn't all ended in shame and disaster. The whole thing was a moment of madness that would never, ever happen again.

But she hitched her pants back up with a bit of a swagger, and expertly flicked the packet of rashers through the air and into the car boot. Frank looked up, startled. She jerked a thumb at him and spoke out of the side of her mouth.

'Let's go, cowboy.'

Adam must have gone to bed because the house was in darkness when she made her way up Mrs Carr's uneven front path. It was a lovely warm night, hardly a breeze. She looked up at the sky. Ewan and Jamie and Neil were up there somewhere, half-way to America now. Maybe they were asleep – it was a long flight and they would be tired out from all the excitement.

The seat next to Ewan would be empty. *Her* seat. Was he looking at it right now, missing her and thinking that the holiday wouldn't be the same without her? She liked to believe that maybe he was, and not hunched over a scrap of paper and pencil trying to find words to rhyme with 'weight loss'.

'Grace?'

The word came out of the darkness. She swung around, the shopping bags clashing painfully against her knees.

'Sorry,' Adam said. 'I didn't mean to give you a fright.'

He was sitting on one of Mrs Carr's wooden deck-chairs on the lawn, his bare feet up on the rickety plastic table (he really was taking great liberties with the furniture). He had a bottle of beer in his hand.

'Well, you did,' she said, sounding a bit sharper than she'd intended. But she was tired. She had not expected to arrive back to find her lodger whooping it up on the front lawn. What if the neighbours complained to Mrs Carr when she got out of hospital? Mrs Carr, who knew nothing about Grace entertaining lodgers in her absence?

'Beautiful night, isn't it?' he said.

'Lovely,' she said in a voice that wasn't encouraging.

But he didn't notice. He rocked back in the wooden deckchair, looking at the sky. 'It's winter back home now, but it'd be as warm as this. Kind of makes me homesick.'

'Which part of Australia are you from?' she asked, because she felt she ought to.

'Nowhere,' he said. 'I'm from Tasmania.'

Tasmania. Grace tried to find a point of reference. Dracula country? No, that was Transylvania. But it was famous for something, she knew that.

'Oh, yes – criminals!' she cried.

Adam looked startled.

'Isn't Tasmania where they used to send all the, uh, prisoners in the last century?' she added more sedately.

'That's right.' He smiled nicely. 'Mostly from Ireland, actually. Export the problem, as usual.'

Well! And she only trying to make a little polite conversation! 'If you find Ireland so disagreeable, what are you doing here at all?'

'I came to find my roots,' he replied.

Not another one. Ireland was in severe danger of being strangled by the roots of a hundred million third-generation Irish across the globe.

'That was a joke, by the way,' he said, with a smile that was dazzling. He seemed to have about five rows of perfectly white, even teeth. She was just admiring them when he said suddenly, 'Was he your boyfriend?'

'Sorry?'

'That guy who just dropped you off just now?'

'Frank? Jesus, no!'

'I thought he was a bit square for you, all right,' he said, and Grace found the observation oddly disconcerting.

'He's just . . . just a neighbour.' It was too complicated to go into the whole business at this hour of the night.

'He's got a telescope trained on the house,' he added casually.

'Pardon?'

'Well, not on this house specifically. He kind of rotates it a bit – sometimes he watches the neighbouring houses, especially if someone comes or goes. Sometimes he'll just monitor the traffic. It's behind a net curtain in one of the upstairs rooms, but I can just about make it out. I just thought you should know.'

'He's a bird-watcher,' Grace told him.

Adam took another swig of beer, said bluntly, 'I think he's watching more than birds. If I were you, I'd put black-out curtains on the bathroom window.'

Grace didn't like it: the arrogant dismissal of Frank as some kind of predator. And worse, the portrayal of herself as a sexual victim who had to resort to hiding behind black-out curtains.

'I'll give your suggestion due consideration,' she told him.

He said, 'I can see I've offended you.'

'How could you have offended me? You don't even know me. Or Frank.'

'But I'd like to.'

'Pardon?'

'Get to know you.' He gave another blinding smile. 'Not Frank though.' He swung his feet down from the table, brushed the surface off with his hand. 'Have a beer with me.'

'No, thanks,' she said.

He seemed mildly surprised. 'You don't drink?'

'Oh, I'm always drinking,' she assured him. 'It's just that it's late, I've had a hell of a day, and it's not in my job description to entertain lodgers.' But he didn't look as put out as she had hoped. So she added, for good measure, 'And you probably shouldn't stay out here too late. It can get quite chilly in Ireland at night.'

'Yes, ma'am,' he said, touching two fingers to his forehead in a little salute.

Grace looked across the lawn at him. 'You seem to find me hugely amusing in some way.'

'It's just a while since I've been mothered, that's all.'

She was glad it was dark now; glad that he couldn't see the way her face bloomed bright red. But her years of dealing with all kinds of uncomfortable situations stood to her now, and she gave one of her professional laughs – light and totally unaffected.

'Just making sure you're comfortable, that's all. As Mrs Carr's guest.'

Before he could reply, she contented herself with an extra-cheery, 'Goodnight!' and set off up the path to the house.

It was only after she had put away the groceries and climbed the stairs and got tucked up in the musty single bed across the hall from his room that she

121

remembered that he had not actually said what he was in Ireland for. And she might have denied that Frank was her boyfriend, but she had failed to mention the fact that she was married.

Six

That night Grace dreamed she was making love with a black man.

Well, it wasn't so much 'making love' – so boring – as having wild, dirty, delicious sex. He looked like one of the characters from *EastEnders*, which she found terribly erotic because she'd never met a soap star before, let alone have sex with one.

'I fancy you something rotten, luv,' he told her as they rolled about on the bed. The East End accent was a bit of a turn-off, but she ignored it because he really was very beautiful. And they were doing all the things that she had always wanted to do but hadn't known whether they were legal or not. And his certainly was yum.

Then, without warning, he stood up and started to pull his clothes back on.

'Got to go, pet, I'm due back on the set at three. But will I send in Dirty Den?'

'Ooh, yes, please.'

Grace woke up, and she was in a strange bed, and there was no black man from *EastEnders*. No Dirty Den either; just Mrs Carr's scratchy white sheets and dubious sense of décor.

She flopped over in the bed and looked at the ceiling, wondering about this recent preoccupation of hers with seediness and sex – and how one automatically suggested the other in her head. She hoped she wouldn't want to start buying pornography or something. Ewan would be appalled. Or maybe not. But it was not something he would expect her to add to the *To Buy* list pinned to the fridge. He had boasted once that he had seen such things, though. But that was back when they were young and were expected to watch films like *Working Girls 2*. (The very title sent a small frisson down Grace's spine now – what was *wrong* with her?)

And it wasn't as though her and Ewan's sex life was all that bad. Well, perhaps it lacked a little adventure. Over the years they had settled into the same patterns as every other married couple, apart from the oddballs who were into swinging and all that (and it was debatable whether they were that odd at all, Grace sometimes thought. Maybe they alone understood that monogamy was both unnatural and a waste). Occasionally, on a Saturday night, one or other of them would get drunk and attempt to take things into the realms of the unknown, but the sober one would usually be vaguely embarrassed, and besides, they always seemed to lack some basic food ingredient or piece of equipment, the reminder of which would induce greater embarrassment the next morning.

No, they generally stuck to the tried and tested. Ewan seemed reasonably happy with this – or at least he never complained. She was too, she supposed, although she couldn't imagine another forty years of the same or fifty years, maybe, if medicine continued to progress at the same rate.

Sometimes when she thought in terms of the years and decades stretching out in front of her, she was seized with a kind of panic, an urgency that she couldn't quite explain; it was to do with the decades already behind her, and the feeling that she hadn't done much with them at all.

There was a smell of frying bacon. She hoisted herself up on one elbow and sniffed the air. Sausages too. She was starving.

She found an old dressing gown in one of Mrs Carr's closets and put it on – she was too impatient to dress. The cerise pink colour wasn't all that flattering and the nylon material scratched, but it buttoned up securely from her ankles to the very base of her neck and that seemed quite important. It was one thing to fantasise about being an extra in *Working Girls* 2 but at the same time she was in a strange house with a man who had more or less said he didn't want to be mothered. She was still trying to figure out what that meant.

He was at the cooker when she entered the kitchen, his dreadlocks tied in a ponytail. It looked terrific, all streaky from the sun. He threw a casual look at her, jerked a thumb towards the table.

'Sit down. I'll get you a cup of tea.'

'Thanks.'

He turned his back to fill the kettle. The silence stretched, broken only by the hiss of sausages in the frying pan. Grace, with ten years of conversation-making under her belt, couldn't think of a single thing to say. Adam didn't seem bothered; he just moved easily between cooker and sink, not a tense muscle in his body. Grace vaguely resented him and everyone like him – people who could share a room with others and not be bothered by silence. It was always the ones like her who wilted with embarrassment and who eventually felt obliged to say something, *anything*. She could just imagine herself at seventy, twittering on in dental surgeries and other public places, while the other occupants gave her murderous looks.

Well, today she just wouldn't twitter! She sat and watched as he deftly flipped over a rasher, and he had no idea that it had nestled in her underwear last night, and she gave a little snicker.

He looked up. 'What?'

'Nothing,' she said sunnily. 'So – what's the plan for today?'

He shrugged, gave a wide smile. He smiled a lot, she noted, suggesting an easy-going nature. Somehow she didn't entirely buy it. 'Hang out. Maybe mow the grass for the old lady – Mrs Carr. She probably won't be up to much when she gets out of hospital.'

Grace was taken aback. 'Well, no, but—'

'And something needs to be done about all the loose floorboards in the living-room. They're dangerous, especially for someone who might not be great on her feet.'

'Adam, I thought you were moving on today.'

He shrugged earnestly. 'I've already tried. I phoned around all the guesthouses again this morning. There's nothing.'

'Mrs Carr is back on Friday. The day after tomorrow,' she stressed.

'And I will absolutely be gone by then,' Adam assured her.

'Adam . . .'

'Just one more night. Come on, you're not going to throw me out on the street, are you?'

And he gave her such a winning look that she felt all shivery. And even though she knew she should refuse – it wasn't even her house! – something perverse and probably lustful made her murmur, 'One more night then.'

'Thanks.'

Belatedly she wondered how she was going to explain away a freshly mown lawn and some DIY jobs to Mrs Carr. She could blame them on Frank, she supposed, even though he looked like he wouldn't know one end of a hammer from the other.

Adam laid two plates piled high with greasy fried food on the table. Toast followed, and tea. It all looked divine. She hadn't had a fry in ages; and certainly not one she hadn't cooked herself.

'Eat up,' he said. 'You need to put some meat on those bones.'

When had he been assessing her bone structure? Before or after he had asked about her boyfriends?

'What age are you?' she asked.

'Why?'

'Just wondering.'

'What age do you think I am?'

'I don't like guessing games.'

'Why not?'

'I just don't. They're silly.'

'And you're too old for them, right? Too mature.'

'We're not talking about my age,' she said, regretting ever starting this.

'Just give one guess,' he said.

Oh, for God's sake. 'Twenty-three,' she snapped.

'Wrong.'

'You know something? I don't think I care any more. Pass the butter, please.'

'You're supposed to say, up or down?'

'Butter, please.'

'It's down. I'm less than twenty-three.'

'Right now I would guess you're about *three*.'

He laughed. 'I'm twenty. And I would guess you're about . . . oh, thirty-nine.'

'What?'

'Up or down?'

'Down! Down-down-down!' She was smiling now too.

'I was only joking,' he said. He looked at her seriously, this way and that, and she felt acutely consciously of her shiny, just-out-of-bed face. 'I'd say you're about thirty-three. Maybe thirty-four.'

'And you're right. I'm thirty-four,' she said, still smiling, but a little disappointed that he had not thought that she was younger. Thirty, maybe.

He just reached for more toast, pleased with himself. (He might be confident but he had a lot of work to do on his sensitivity.)

'What are you doing in Ireland anyway?' she asked.

He looked surprised, as though she should have known. '*Full Blast*.'

'*Full Blast*?'

'The music festival?'

'Oh. Right.' It was like Glastonbury – but with the emphasis on rock music. Nick had gone two years ago, and hadn't been seen for nearly a week.

'That's near here, isn't it?' she said.

'Four miles,' Adam confirmed, and Grace immediately wondered whether Frank knew about this. But he must. The festival was in its fifth or sixth year now. Last summer, tens of thousands of people had descended with tents and camper vans and taken over the whole countryside.

'You're a music fan then?' she said, trying not to sound like a maiden aunt. But he had that effect on her: of making her act much older than she was. She wondered whether it was some kind of defence mechanism on her part – he was quite attractive, after all, if you liked that macho sort of thing. And she was a woman whose husband and children were away . . .

She stopped, amused at the train of her thoughts. As if she'd ever have the nerve! (She had once been propositioned by a senior partner at the staff Christmas party years ago. He was sixty if he was a day, and he had been drunk, and he had put his hand on her arm and told her that she was lovely. She had made fun of him to the girls afterwards, of course, and they had all laughed their heads off. But she remembered that word, 'lovely'. It was a dignified word, not like 'gorgeous' or 'sexy', and it was quite the most flattering thing anybody had said to her in years, and she would remember it whenever she and Ewan had a row).

'. . . not that I particularly like Indie music. But I could listen to it,' Adam finished up. 'How about you?'

How about her, what? 'Sorry, I didn't catch that,' she said, hoping to fudge it.

'It doesn't matter,' he said. He didn't like it, the fact that she had not been hanging on his every word. Look at him! He was positively sulking.

Grace didn't dare smile. He was not a boy – man? – used to being ignored by anybody, she guessed, especially not a woman.

He finished up his breakfast rather abruptly and stood. 'Do you know where she keeps her lawnmower?'

'You could try the garden shed.'

'Right.'

And he was gone, his shoulders held a bit stiffly. Grace chewed slowly on a rasher, thinking how much more delicious something was when it was stolen.

Julia was woken from a nap by the snoring. She glared across the ward – that old biddy Ivy from Cork who had bored everyone senseless last night with her daft ramblings about her youth. As though none of the rest of them had ever been young: they just knew better than to go on about it all the time.

'Julia? Are you all right?'

You only had to stir in this place and there was a nurse down on top of you. So much for cuts in the health service.

'Yes, yes, I'm just going to the toilet if that's okay.'

'I'll get you a bedpan.'

'I don't want a bedpan.'

'Now, now.' The nurse clucked in that irritating way they all did, as though they were dealing with overgrown five-year-olds. 'You've had an operation, Julia. You shouldn't be out of bed at all.'

Julia knew she would have to humour her. So she smiled in a kind of half-doddery way and put a hand confidentially on the nurse's arm. 'I know. But I'm too embarrassed to use a bedpan. If you could just help me as far as the toilet . . . you're ever so good . . .'

'You'll need your crutches,' the nurse said indulgently. She got them, tucked a stern hand into Julia's armpit and more or less bore her aloft to the toilet. Once there, the nurse whipped up her nightdress – 'Now!' – deposited her on the toilet bowl – 'Comfy?' – stuffed a lump of toilet paper into her hand – 'There!' – and issued her with instructions to ring for help when she was finished up.

'Certainly,' Julia said, with what dignity she had been left.

'Oh, and some flowers arrived for you,' the nurse said as she left. 'From someone called Grace.'

Grace? Julia turned the name over in her head. She didn't know anybody called Grace. Could it be someone from JJ's side? They always tended to crawl out of the woodwork when there was some misfortune or other.

Sitting up on the toilet like that gave her an opportunity to see her mangled foot for the first time. Not that there was much on view – rolls of white bandages swathed the top half of her foot. A yellowish substance had leaked out in the region of the small toe, but other than that it all looked very innocuous. She couldn't even feel anything. Of course, she was pumped full of morphine. It was starting to wear off a bit now though. She was glad. It made everything very vague and unclear. She had been shot though, she was sure about that. Or was she?

Sitting there on the cold toilet bowl, her bony white knees poking out from under the soiled hospital gown, she suddenly felt weak and small and she wanted to call the nurse, the big bovine nurse who made everything better with a single reassuring 'Now!'

She wanted JJ. Sometimes at night when she woke in the dark the silence was so still and so thick that she could hear her own eyes blink. It was the loneliest sound in the world.

The crutches were stiff and unfamiliar and it took her two attempts to get her forearms through the grey plastic rings properly. But she did. And she managed to open the toilet door without falling over. Hurrah! It was quite cruel really, the way age blasted standards out of the water: now merely staying upright was a cause for celebration.

Michael and Gillian were lying in wait back at the ward. They had obviously got past the Ward Sister.

'Hello!' Julia said, hoping she sounded welcoming. 'Bit early for visiting, isn't it?'

'Naturally we wanted to know how you are, Mammy,' Michael said.

'We brought you some grapes,' Gillian said, wafting past to the locker. Where other women wore perfume, Gillian always smelled of Deep Heat. Already she was looking around surreptitiously for an air-conditioning system, or anything at all that would suggest germ control.

'How's the bronchitis?' Julia enquired. 'Did those test results come back yet?'

Gillian looked at her a bit suspiciously. 'No. But I'm feeling much better.' Her voice was squeaky and breathless. 'More to the point, how are you?'

'Great,' Julia confided. 'I just had a bowel movement and everything.'

Nobody said anything for a moment; then they busied themselves finding chairs and settling down. Michael spilled out over the edges of his. Gillian perched on the seat of hers like an anorexic bird. Julia sometimes imagined the two of them in the conjugal bed together. How did he not crush her to death? Mind you, she was the sort of woman who detested physical activity of any kind so it was highly likely that the risk was minimal. About twice a year, at a generous guess. Poor Michael.

She must stop this. They were her family. The only people left who belonged to her in the whole world. It was nobody's fault that they hadn't a damned thing in common.

'The doctor was around this morning,' she offered conversationally.

'Oh?' Gillian squeaked. Julia wanted to oil her.

'He was one of the doctors who saw JJ when he was brought in.'

'Was he?' Michael said.

'Remembered JJ the minute I mentioned him. Said he had never seen anybody sitting up in the bed like that after a major stroke.'

'Imagine,' Gillian said.

'JJ was even able to tell him the results of the football – can you believe it? But he was always very mentally strong. He broke his leg climbing in the Alps once, Gillian, that's when he was working on that bridge in Switzerland. The pain must have been immense but he never let on to any of them who were bringing him back down.'

'I know. You've told me before,' Gillian murmured.

Julia couldn't remember doing so. But there were so many stories about JJ.

'Listen, Mammy, Gillian and I were talking about it and we'd like to pay for private care for you,' Michael said. He hadn't listened to a word she'd said.

'Why?'

'You'd have your own room, and there's a consultant here, Dr Murphy—'

She was still stung. 'The doctor I have is fine.'

'We just want the best for you, Mammy.'

They had never bothered with health insurance, her and JJ. In fact, JJ hadn't been great with money at all. Spend while you have it, had been his motto. And they had, until there wasn't anything left.

Loyally, she said, 'If the public service was good enough for JJ, then it's good enough for me.'

Gillian said, 'But he died.'

'Gillian!' Michael was appalled.

'What? I'm just stating a fact—'

'Well, don't! It's upsetting Mammy.'

Gillian gave an impatient laugh. 'The man was mortal, believe it or not.'

'Gillian!' He turned to Julia. 'Mammy, I'm very

sorry about Gillian's . . . lack of tact.'

Gillian reddened, then said, stiffly. 'Yes. That *was* tactless of me. Sorry, Julia.'

Ivy across the way loudly broke wind. It added to the pressure-cooker atmosphere, and Michael pitched forward in his chair, cleared his throat, and blurted, 'Look, we've arranged for someone to come around and visit you, Mammy.'

'Who?'

'A kind of a social worker-type person,' Gillian said brightly, although it was obviously an effort.

Julia looked mildly interested. 'But not actually a social worker?'

'No,' said Michael. 'He's more a . . . well, a kind of a . . .'

'A what?'

'A psychiatrist.'

'A *shrink*?'

Gillian gave a little laugh. 'They don't call them shrinks any more, Julia. They're more like friends. In fact, Dr Brady is a friend. He's my own psychiatrist.'

'So he should be able to recognise madness when he sees it then,' Julia said.

Gillian's eyes grew cold.

'Look, I am not bonkers,' Julia added. 'So you can forget about trying to lock me away in a home somewhere.'

Michael looked shocked. 'Mammy! What on earth are you talking about?'

'I heard you yesterday. "Sort something out". I won't be put away.'

'Putting you away in a home is the last thing we'd

135

ever want! Isn't it, Gillian?'

'Yes,' she said, with just the right dollop of doubt.

Michael said, 'Mammy, about Dr Brady. We just want you to have a chat with him, that's all. Maybe there are some things you've been bottling up that you might like to talk about.'

'Like what?'

'I don't know. Maybe there are some issues surrounding Dad's death—'

'I do not have issues surrounding JJ's death.' She was angry now. 'Am I not to be allowed to grieve?'

'Of course you are.'

'Is grieving somehow wrong?'

'No. I'm just saying—'

'Michael.' Gillian turned to Julia and said, very measured, 'Julia, you're in trouble with the guards. It's very serious. You threatened somebody with a shotgun you had no licence to hold.'

'For heaven's sake. It was only Frank. I wouldn't waste a cartridge on him.'

'It's not funny. Michael spoke with the police this morning. He thinks he might have convinced them not to press charges. He said we would get you help. Psychiatric help.'

'Psychiatric help!'

'Yes. It might not sound very nice, but I'm sure you'd rather make smart comments to a psychiatrist than to be hauled up before a court. Am I right?'

She might look as if a gust of wind would carry her away, but she knew where to hit where it hurt all right.

'Fine,' Julia said, dignified. 'Send in the goons.'

★ ★ ★

Sandy had sent a new photo of herself. It had been scanned in and emailed to Frank's computer just that morning and he had printed out five copies immediately.

'What's that on her chest?' Grace enquired.

Frank leaned in to have a look. 'Oh, that's a printer error on my part. I think it was supposed to run across the bottom.'

It was a line of smudged text. *To Frank. With all my love – Kitten.*

'That's a pet name,' he added, boyishly. 'She has one for me too, but I don't think I should tell you. It's a bit rude!'

'In that case, better not,' Grace said hastily. Her breakfast hadn't settled sufficiently.

She studied the photo. Sandy looked as magnificent as ever. Her make-up was perfect and her hair was styled to within an inch of its life. She was wearing a tiny bikini and she smiled out blandly from a beach.

'She took her disabled kids swimming last weekend,' Frank explained. 'She says that's where it was taken.'

There were no disabled kids in the background. Just a couple of blonde, All-America children building a sandcastle. A very good-looking man helped them. In fact, everyone on the beach seemed to be good-looking. Grace couldn't see any fat people, or men with big hairy chests, or women with cellulite.

Then she noticed something else.

'What's that in her hand?'

Frank peered at the photo. 'A towel. Obviously

she's thinking of taking a dip.'

'Frank, it's a tea towel.'

'Is it?'

They both looked at the photo again. It was most definitely a tea towel. It was stripy and with a picture of carrots on the front.

'Maybe she made a mistake,' Frank said. 'It's very easy to pick up the wrong thing from the airing cupboard, especially when you're in a hurry.'

'But she's not actually holding it. It's like it's draped over her hand or something . . .'

There was definitely something odd about it. As if it had been added to the photo afterwards or something. It was her left hand too, Grace realised – the same hand that had been chopped off in the last photo.

'You should ask her about it.'

Frank was dismissive. 'Ask her about a tea towel? Like we have nothing better to talk about!'

There was something in his voice that made her look up from the photo. 'Is something wrong?'

'No, no . . . well, I won't be going over in two weeks' time as planned after all.'

'Oh, Frank!'

He looked very deflated. 'Her sister has just split up from her husband.'

'That's a shame. But, um, what has that got to do with your travel plans?'

'Sandy's flying up to Utah, you see, to be with her sister. But that's Sandy all over. Too kind for her own good, I tell her. But she's already booked time off work and she's going to be flying out the exact day I was due to go over.'

'That's a bit of a coincidence.'

'I know, isn't it? But Sandy says that we'll fix a new date just as soon as her sister is back on track. *Che sera sera*, she says. What will be, will be – that's one of her favourite expressions. She's very philosophical that way.'

He shook his head in admiration.

'Couldn't you go to Utah with her?'

He looked mildly alarmed at being around all that female angst. 'I don't think that would be a very good idea. Anyhow, Sandy has everything all booked. I don't want to go changing arrangements. Especially when she's feeling so tired.'

'She's still feeling tired?' She didn't look tired in the photo. She looked as healthy as a horse.

'She really should go and see a doctor,' he said. 'In fact, I'm going to email her this very minute and suggest it.' He gathered up his precious photo. 'By the way, Sergeant Daly rang.'

On reflex Grace froze. Blast those rashers anyway: would the guilt never leave her?

'Tom and Charlie are over from London, they want to come and see the house.'

She relaxed. 'Great! I'll ring the office and get someone to come out.'

'You wouldn't be showing it to them yourself?' Frank was disappointed.

'You see, I'm actually on holidays . . . '

'It's only across the road.'

'Yes, I know, but Natalie is covering for me. '

'They could call around tomorrow morning. You'll still be here, won't you? Now that you've allowed

139

that Adam fellow to stay another night – not that Mrs Carr knows anything about *that*.'

He *had* to point it out, of course.

'Anyway, Sandy says it's always better if just one person sells your property. That way the focus doesn't get diluted.' He seemed to take it as a given that Grace would be showing his property, because he moved right on to another subject: 'By the way, Sergeant Daly says to keep an eye out for any agitators.'

'What?'

'Apparently they're coming for the festival. Activist types. They might try and book into accommodation, he said.'

'What activist types?'

'Don't know.' Frank left, anxious no doubt to get back to his computer to compose a turgid email. Grace wondered what pet name Sandy had for him. He'd said it was rude. Mr Stiffy, perhaps. But she remembered that they hadn't actually consummated the relationship yet. Then even thinking about Sandy and Frank doing it kind of put her off, and she went upstairs to shower and change.

She got dressed in her clothes from yesterday. She'd washed her underwear out the night before but her socks weren't dry and so when she wandered out into the garden an hour later with two coffees she was barefoot. Adam had finished mowing and the smell was wonderful. It was years since she'd felt grass between her toes (the back garden at home was set in patio, with a barbecue area) and she wandered about amongst overgrown shrubs and a most peculiar-looking pile of stones that resembled a grave, or a lopsided mausoleum. Maybe a beloved pet was buried there – although it would have to have been a very large dog, or possibly a young elephant.

Adam was cutting the hedge at the end of the garden with a pair of clippers.

'I brought you a coffee,' she said.

'Great. I'll just finish this bit.'

She sat down on the lawn and watched him for a while. Well, it was hard not to. He wore a very white T-shirt which rode up every time he clipped at the hedge. Sitting there, drinking coffee and ogling him, she felt a bit like a builder, and had to resist the urge to let out a wolf-whistle.

'So! What do you do in college?' she asked in what she hoped was an interested but detached voice. If he reached over a bit more she might just see his belly button . . .

'How do you know I go to college?'

'Hmm? There's a university sticker on your wallet.'

'Prying?'

'I most certainly was not. It's sitting there on the hall table for anybody to see.'

'Why are you always so defensive?' he asked.

'I am not defensive!' she said, defensively. 'I just don't like people accusing me of being nosey, that's all.'

He wiped an arm across his eyes. The underside of his ponytail was damp. 'If you must know, I dropped out of college.'

'Oh.'

'But the course title was "Business Studies".'

'Was it not a good course?'

'It was a great course. Churned out sixty-four proper little capitalists last year. Just what the world needs, don't you think?'

This somehow seemed to be a dig at her. She felt all defensive again. 'Why did you apply for it then?'

'It was the only course I was offered.' He gave a little laugh, and hacked at a particularly tenuous lump of hedge with the shears. 'I thought college would be interesting,' he mused. 'I thought I'd meet like-minded people. People with opinions and convictions and ideals. Instead I ended up with a bunch of self-centred, label-obsessed assholes who just drank their heads off.' He sounded hurt, nearly. 'What was it like in your day?'

'What, way back thirty years ago?' she said tartly. He smiled. She was getting better at this. 'Probably not much different. We did a lot of drinking, that much I do remember.'

'But did you have any opinions?' he asked.

'On what?'

'On Beirut. World peace. Communism versus capitalism.'

'Maybe . . . I can't really remember,' she said, guiltily thinking about all those nights in the pub spent discussing sex and clothes and the possibility of getting a date with Damien from Applied Physics.

Adam seemed a bit disappointed in her. He turned back to his hedge at any rate. But, honestly, he was so idealistic! She wondered should she tell him that she had been a vegetarian when she was sixteen.

That might impress him. He needn't know that it had only lasted three weeks and that she had caved in sobbing at the feet of a roast chicken one Sunday lunch-time. Oh, when would she grow up and stop trying to impress young boys? Her own, and other people's?

She was so cross with herself that when he said to her, 'What are you doing here anyway, in the middle of nowhere?' in a kind of judgemental tone, she snapped back, 'What business is it of yours?'

'None—'

'None. Exactly.'

He wasn't deterred. 'I just didn't think the country-side would be your thing.'

'What, you think I'm the type who shrivels up and dies once I'm outside a three-mile radius of a shopping centre?'

He looked startled. 'I was just asking a simple question—'

But she was on a roll now. 'You were not! There was an innuendo there! A snideness! Just because you're nineteen—'

'Twenty.'

'Twenty!' A pipsqueak! 'Just because you're twenty you think you know everything. Well, you don't. And you don't know me either so stop acting as if you do!'

He put down his shears slowly, and looked at her. 'Feel better now that you have that off your chest?'

She looked right back. 'It's just that I was prepared to be nice and civil to you, but you just keep niggling away at me and I'm wondering why, that's all.'

He took a gulp of his coffee thoughtfully. 'I don't know, to be honest,' he said. 'I'm inclined to think it's because I want to corrupt you.'

Grace had to bite back a nervous laugh. 'Corrupt me?'

Those very blue eyes of his fixed on her as if across a hot dark nightclub. 'Yeh. I just have this urge. Silly, isn't it? Childish.' He smiled at her. 'But there you go. I can't help myself.' And he took off his white T-shirt altogether. Just like that! He stood there half-naked before her while she picked up the severed head of a daisy and twirled it around in her fingers nonchalantly, as though threats to corrupt her were everyday occurrences.

'Oh, I'm pretty incorruptible,' she said, lightly. Had that come out as a challenge? Dear God.

'So you say.' His hand was resting on the waistband of his shorts now and for a wild moment she thought he was going to take those off too.

'I don't know what you mean,' she said, wondering was he wearing any underwear. But he didn't undress any further. He said, 'Well, you're here on your own in the countryside in a house that doesn't belong to you, and without a change of clothes even. You drive a big swish city car, you left a wedding ring on the wash-hand basin upstairs, and you don't know Mrs Carr any better than I do, do you?'

When he laid it all out like that, it looked terribly incriminating. It must suggest to him that she was running from some dark and dangerous secret at home, or else that she was a flake who periodically broke into other people's houses and started operating B & B's out of them. No wonder he thought that she might be ripe and ready for a little challenge.

She got to her feet quickly. Things were getting dangerous. 'I assure you my reasons for being here are perfectly legitimate,' she said haughtily, adding for good measure, 'At least I don't have Sergeant Daly after me.' Not unless they examined the CCTV footage in the Spar at any rate.

'Who?'

'The local fuzz – is the term known in Tasmania?'

He looked at her a little cagily, she thought. Interesting.

'It is,' he said.

'Apparently there are some activists around the town of Hackettstown. Agitator types with very little else to do.' She let that sink in for a moment, and added dramatically, 'I was told to keep an eye out for them.'

'And are you? Keeping an eye out?'

'It depends on what these agitators are up to. I don't want to get myself into hot water. If you know what I mean.'

He took a step closer. It was a very long time since a half-naked stranger had made any kind of advance on her, and her temperature jumped up a little.

'Risk it,' he said. 'You might like it.'

The air seemed to shimmer over the lawn between them, and Grace could feel her considerable reason and intelligence turn to dust. Then, the ring of a mobile phone in his shorts pocket.

'Hello?'

She watched his whole face crease into the kind of smile she had not seen before. 'Babe. How are you?'

She bent down and picked up the two coffee mugs, smiling a bit. 'Excuse me,' she murmured in his direction, and she went back inside.

Seven

'What do you think I should give Paul for his birth-day?' Natalie asked on the phone that afternoon.

'Sex,' Grace said.

'I beg your pardon?'

'Sorry, sorry, that just slipped out – how about a nice pair of slippers?'

There was a suspicious silence. 'Are you all right, Grace?'

'Fine! Perfect! Here, do you know what the difference is between a lodging house and a B & B? Because I've rung the tourist board and they don't seem to know.'

'I didn't know there *were* lodging houses any more,' Natalie said.

'There are. I'm in one. And I'm confused as to whether I'm supposed to be providing Adam with – ' She almost said sex again, but pulled herself up just in time. ' – with dinner or not.'

Natalie pondered this. 'Have you asked him if he wants dinner?'

'No.' For some reason she hadn't wanted to go back out to Adam in the garden again.

'Ask him,' Natalie said authoritatively. Then she giggled lasciviously. 'I'll ask him for you if you want.'

'Stop it, Natalie.'

'What? He's a bit of a ride—'

Grace said coldly, 'He's my lodger. You shouldn't be talking about him like that.'

Natalie was surprised. 'For God's sake, Grace. I was only joking – I don't know what you're getting in such a huff about.'

Neither did Grace. It was just that those kinds of sentiments sounded vaguely ludicrous when coming from a woman of Natalie's age and circumstances. And Grace was a year older. It would have been different had they been men. Wasn't bloody everything? Still?

She had no more time to ponder inequality because there was so much to do when it came to running a lodging house. There was the laundry for starters. All those towels, and sheets, the duvet covers and the pillowslips – you could spend your whole day washing if you weren't careful! Not to mention all the dusting and hoovering and cleaning. Mrs Carr wasn't too hot on that aspect of things. Grace had opened a couple of presses in the bathroom and closed them again very quickly.

She went upstairs with two clean towels, and went into Adam's room, sure that this feeling of guilty pleasure wasn't normal for a landlady. He had made the bed himself, she was glad to see, and had put away any dirty clothes into his rucksack. The placards were stacked neatly under the bed and she cast a curious look at them as she picked up two used towels from the floor. Then she left, pulling the door quickly closed behind her and running lightly down the stairs, the towels pressed against her chest. She dipped her head and had a quick sniff. They smelled of soap and shampoo, and she felt a bit like a thief.

There was an old radio on the kitchen window and she put it on to a station she liked – *Lite FM*, but she wasn't ashamed – and she loaded the washing machine, turned the oven on, and started to make dough in one of Mrs Carr's wonderful big mixing bowls. She was elbow-deep in sticky bliss and singing lustily along to 'Wake Me Up Before You Go-Go' when her mobile phone rang.

'Hello!'

'Grace? Is that you?' Ewan sounded a bit taken aback by her ebullience, or maybe it was just the distance.

'Of course it's me – is everything all right?' She could never enjoy a conversation until she had ruled out the possibility of accident or injury to either of the boys.

'I suppose – how are you?'

'Great! Well, all right,' she added hastily. Best not to sound too cheerful. 'Wishing I was there, obviously.'

'You sound like you're at a concert.' He sounded a bit peeved.

She hurried to turn down the radio. 'Sorry about that. Where are you?'

'The motel.'

'What's it like?'

She had an image of a grubby double bed with sheets that smelled of sex, and street signs blinking redly through the dirty window: *Adults Only! XXX-citement!!*

'It's got a double power-shower and you can make your own tea and coffee,' he said.

'Oh.' How disappointing. Was every last thing in this world to become standardised? Sanitised? She was suddenly glad she was here in Mrs Carr's shabby, run-down house.

'Did the boys enjoy the flight?'

'I think so, yeh.' He was never one for giving a satisfying blow-by-blow account of things. Didn't he understand that when it came to her children, she would like to know what seats they had, whether he had remembered to give them sweets to suck during take-off, whether they had had the chicken or the fish for their in-flight meal?

'Where are you?' he asked instead.

'Me? In Ireland, Ewan.'

'Yes, but where in Ireland exactly? I just rang home and Nick told me you'd gone missing.'

Damn. She had meant to let her brother know the change in arrangements.

'He's sick with worry,' Ewan added.

Now, that was a bit of an exaggeration. Nick had probably wondered about her once or twice and gone back to his computer books, via the fridge.

'I'm in Mrs Carr's house.'

'What are you doing there?'

'Just tidying up for her and the rest.' She tried to sound very casual. He wouldn't understand at all if she said that she was in fact entertaining a lodger behind Mrs Carr's back.

'How is she anyway? When is she coming home?' he asked.

'Friday.'

'So you've spoken to him then? The son? What's his name – Michael?'

'Well, not exactly . . . I mean, I've rung his house . . .'

'And?'

'And what?'

'And are they going to look after Mrs Carr, Grace?'

'Look, it's all a bit complicated.'

She was trying to think of the best way to explain it but Ewan jumped right in again, rather belligerently. 'What, he's happy for *you* to look after her? Does he even know that you should be in Disneyland with us right now?'

'I didn't mention it, given that I've put his mother in hospital,' she said coolly.

'It was an accident. Surely he can see that? For God's sake, you have two kids, Grace!'

She thought of the airport again, and her hurt. 'So it's not out of concern for me, then, this . . . inquisition? It's for the benefit of the boys? And then maybe you?'

There was a little silence on the phone, then Ewan blustered, 'Don't be ridiculous! I mean, when Nick said you hadn't come home – I was worried. You shouldn't be spending your holidays cleaning a stranger's home, Grace. You should be relaxing.'

She wanted to believe in his concern and so she

said, more muted, 'I know. But I feel it's my duty, Ewan. I mean, there's nothing organised for her yet.'

Ewan backed down even more. 'Well, I suppose in that case ... we can do without you for another day or two.' He even gave a little laugh now. 'Nick was trying to wind me up on the phone – you know, saying when the cat's away and all that.'

'That's just his sense of humour.'

'I know. I said to him, *Grace*, of all people.' And he laughed again.

'What do you mean, "of all people"?' she enquired after a moment.

'What?'

'Just wondering. It sounds a bit derogatory or something.'

'It wasn't meant as derogatory—'

'What did you mean then?'

'I just meant you're too nice, too good – oh, you know what I mean. Just that you wouldn't do something like that, that's all.'

'Sure about that, are you?'

There was another empty little pause now. Then she laughed, and Ewan laughed again too, heartily – great, relieved guffaws rolling across the Atlantic Ocean.

'What's the weather like?' she asked. It was a wifely question and he was further reassured.

'Fabulous. We've already been out to get breakfast – a real America-style breakfast, grits and everything, can you imagine?'

She smiled. 'Did the boys eat them?'

'Every bit. They're really determined to make the

most of this holiday. Even if you can't be here,' he added swiftly.

'I know.'

'We *are* missing you, you know, Grace. It's not the same without you.'

Wasn't it interesting the effect the tiniest bit of uncertainty can sometimes have on people, she reflected? Just the smallest insinuation that things were not entirely as he had left them?

'I miss you too,' she said, wondering if she did.

'Grace, the coach is here – hang on.' His voice grew muffled as he turned away to issue orders. 'Neil – turn off that TV. Jamie? Come out of the bathroom now! What are you doing in there all this time any-way?'

She listened to the background scuffle as they were propelled onwards in their journey and she was sud-denly awash with longing to run out of this dirty old house and jump on a plane to shiny, plastic Florida and eat grits. She didn't belong here, pretending to be in charge of a lodging house and playing word games with a cocky young man just out of his teens.

'I have to go,' Ewan said. There was no time to talk to the kids, just a hurried 'ring you later' from Ewan and then the phone went dead.

Ivy from Cork was crying and carrying on again about people dead so long that only she remembered them any more.

'Poor Ronald!'

'Ronald who, Mammy?' her daughter enquired. You could see her impatience. She had two children climbing up on the end of the bed and probably a car boot full of chilled groceries.

'Ronald Wainwright,' Ivy sobbed.

'From Clonmel? Amy, get down!'

'From Waterford. With the stables.'

'Oh, yes, the show jumper.'

'No! No! He wasn't a show jumper, he never rode a horse in his life!' Ivy was raging, her chalky white fingers shredding a tissue while the children bounced up and down on her bony legs. And the daughter looking at her, bewildered, wondering who was this stranger in the bed.

Julia tried to close her ears to them. She had never felt old until the last two days. She had never even felt elderly. She had, she believed, stopped ageing somewhere around fifty-six. It was such a nice mature age, past those difficult forties, and not afraid any more of anybody or anything.

But here in St Catherine's ward she felt ancient. It was in the very air, which was always too warm, and smelled of old people. She found herself ridiculously upset by the sets of false teeth that sat in glasses on lockers, the pink prosthetic leg lying over there on a chair – all bits and pieces of broken bodies that had to be gathered up and reattached before the simplest of human tasks could be carried out.

More visitors arrived into the ward. Elizabeth across the way was the victim this time.

'What did you have for tea, Granny?'

'Shepherd's pie.'

'That was nice. Did you have a yoghurt or ice cream afterwards?'

'Ice cream.'

'Oh good, you like ice cream. What flavour?'

'What? I can't remember.'

'Was it vanilla? Or maybe strawberry?'

'I don't know! It doesn't matter – why the hell does it matter!'

'All right, Granny, calm down.' To the husband: 'I told you her memory was going.'

For the first time Julia was glad that JJ had gone the way he had. She was grateful now for the suddenness of it, which had been so profoundly shocking at the time: no chance to say goodbye, no chance to say anything at all. She couldn't even remember her last words to him, but they would have been mundane because they had just come in from a walk in the rain and had gone upstairs to change into dry clothes. When he hadn't come down she'd gone back up and had found him on the bedroom floor. He had regained consciousness in the ambulance on the way to the hospital and had spoken to doctors. But she'd stayed behind to get him some clothes and things, not realising the seriousness of it, and Frank had driven her in an hour later. JJ had had the second stroke by then, of course, and was gone.

Which was a blessing really, when you thought about how it could have ended up: bedridden, and at the mercy of your family.

Happy birthday to you, Happy birthday to you, Happy birthday, dear Mammy, Happy birthday to you!

Here they came, Michael bearing a cake aloft, and Gillian and Susan bringing up the rear. The whole ward, of course, turned to have a look, clucking

Clare Dowling

benignly at the spectacle. Several of the nurses clapped. Julia wanted to pull the bedcovers up over her head but instead managed a few gasps of surprise and delight.

'You shouldn't have,' she said, meaning it.

'Speech, speech!' Michael said, as excited as a young boy.

'I'm not one for speeches,' she said, flapping a hand at him.

'Make a wish then,' Susan said.

Julia smiled fondly at her only grandchild. 'And what do you think I should wish for?'

'A battery-powered scooter that every single person in your whole class has,' Susan said, throwing a filthy look at Michael.

'I've told you. They're too expensive,' he said.

'That's a crock of shit,' Susan sighed. 'You're on a hundred grand a year.'

'Susan!' Gillian hissed.

'Anyway!' Julia said, in a very jolly voice. 'Here goes!' She closed her eyes tight, and leaned forward to blow out the candles on the birthday cake. Not that they were lit – it was against hospital fire regulations, Michael explained. But the cake was lovely: a big white frosted affair, with her age marked out by seven pink candles and three blue ones, and a pink ribbon around the whole lot. You had to hand it to Gillian, who had remained in good health long enough to bake it.

She sat down at the end of the bed now, delicate-looking in peach and dabbing occasionally at herself with a tissue that smelled of antiseptic. 'Happy birthday, Julia.'

156

'Thank you, Gillian,' Julia returned, equally civil. 'And to you, Michael, and Susan. You've made it a very special birthday.'

'You haven't had your presents yet,' Michael said, presenting her with several gift-wrapped parcels. Julia made appreciative noises as she opened perfume, a silk scarf, a box of handmade chocolates. Then a silver photo-frame, face cream that one of those supermodels advertised, and a really beautiful gold bracelet.

'This is far too much . . .'

But Michael just beamed at her happily. 'Nonsense. It's your birthday.'

Susan had been getting herself more and more worked up. 'How come she gets all that stuff and you won't buy me a lousy scooter!'

Michael looked embarrassed. 'It's not your birthday, Susan.'

'I didn't get *half* that for my birthday! Did I, Mum?'

'For heaven's sake!' he exploded. 'This is your grandmother's day! Can you not stop thinking about yourself for five minutes?'

Susan's lip was actually quivering. She looked at Michael, very hurt. 'I'm just saying it's not fair.'

'That's enough now,' Gillian murmured. But she too was looking at Michael in a hurt kind of way.

Julia, the cause of this family rift, put on her best dotty-Granny smile, and said, 'You know, I hardly ever wear jewellery – why don't you borrow the bracelet, Susan? On a long-term basis? And take those chocolates too, I only get indigestion. And when are we going to get around to tasting some of Gillian's delicious-looking cake?'

Susan was somewhat appeased. Gillian recognised a sap when she saw it, but was gracious enough to swallow it. Michael, largely oblivious to the politics, jumped to hand around cardboard plates with Winnie-The-Pooh on them – it was all they had in the supermarket, he said – and Barbie drinking cups, and he dished out cake and poured coke for Susan, and non-alcoholic wine for the adults – again, due to hospital regulations.

'To Mammy!' he said, and they all raised their Barbie cups, and Julia smiled under the watchful eyes of Gillian, and thought that she had never missed JJ more than at that moment. But she couldn't say that, because Michael and Gillian and Susan didn't want to hear it. Not now, not two years later, when she really should have bucked up and got on with things and stopped boring everybody with her grief.

So she blinked back her tears and spooned some of Gillian's dry, fat-free, low-sugar frosted cake into her mouth, and said, 'This is absolutely delicious, Gillian.'

Tactless as ever, Michael failed to echo the praise, saying instead, 'Mammy, we have one last present for you.'

She was embarrassed now by his attentions. Surely he had never been this fawning before? Or had she just not noticed? 'I've already had lots of presents.'

'They were just stocking-fillers.' He looked at Gillian, and she gave a tight little smile of acquiescence, and from his pocket he took a small, gift-wrapped box and handed it over, and said very intensely, 'Go on, Mammy. Open it.'

Julia was suddenly aware that there was an 'atmosphere'. Three sets of eyes followed her every move: Michael's, giddy with anticipation; Susan's, unenthusiastic; and Gillian's . . .? She was still smiling but there was something else too. A hint of martyrdom, Julia thought.

She opened the present. 'It's a key,' she said, surprised.

'Yes,' said Michael. He was nearly bursting now.

'You haven't . . . bought me a car?' Julia said, wilting. Please God they weren't going to try and force her to drive – not at her age.

Michael laughed. 'Not a car, Mammy. It's too small to be a car key anyway.'

Julia turned it over in her hands. It was a simple stainless steel key, the kind you would find on any key ring.

'Don't look so worried, Julia,' Gillian said with a little laugh. 'It's not for the front door of a mental institution.'

Oooh. The gloves were coming off.

'Dr Brady declared me sane then?' Julia said. She'd had a session with him yesterday afternoon. He was a very nice man, as it turned out, and a bridge fan. He had a dog called Mopp, and four grandchildren, and he'd been to Crete on his holidays last year. Julia had found out more about him in ten minutes than he'd managed to extract from her over the course of two hours.

'He didn't say a thing about you. Client confidentiality,' Michael assured her. 'But at least we've got the police off your back.'

Julia just snorted.

'Do you not want to know what the key is for?' he asked.

Actually, the whole thing had lost its appeal by now, and she just wanted to go for her afternoon sleep.

'Tell me then.'

'It's a front door key,' Michael said, determined to extract more drama out of it, damn him.

'Whose front door?' she asked.

'Yours. Well, to your new house.'

Her patience ran out and she snapped, 'For heaven's sake, Michael, what are you talking about?'

Michael looked at Gillian, who looked at Susan, and then they all looked back at her.

'We're converting the garage into a granny flat, Mammy,' Michael announced. 'We'd like you to come and live with us!'

'I'm just ringing to enquire about Mrs Carr?'

'Are you a relative?' came the standard reply.

'No, I'm not. And I know you can't give out information to people who aren't relatives, but I only want to know whether she'll be out on Friday?'

'I'm sorry. We can only give out information to relatives.'

'Yes, I know that, but . . . Look, can I speak to her directly on the phone?'

'Her son is in with her right now. Would you like to speak to him?'

'Ah, no, thanks.'

Stymied, Grace hung up and went back to preparing dinner. That's if Adam showed up for it at all. He had disappeared for the whole afternoon. Not that she was keeping *tabs* or anything. Well, all right, she was. She had already been up to his room to check that his belongings were still there. They were, and she was relieved for a number of reasons.

At eight o'clock she stood in the dining-room and looked around. It had seemed a bit too cosy to feed him in the kitchen, so she had dusted off the big dining-table and put on a white linen tablecloth. She had found Mrs Carr's silver cutlery and laid two places opposite each other – well, she was hardly going to eat afterwards, like the hired help. It seemed natural to add a candlestick and a vase of fresh flowers she had picked from the garden.

But now the candlestick looked a bit inappropriate or something. Intimate. It looked like they were on a *date*. She whipped off the candlestick, already regretting the wild mushroom and asparagus risotto simmering away in the kitchen. Didn't asparagus have a reputation as a food of seduction? And what would he make of her dessert meringues, with their stiff white peaks topped by juicy red strawberries? Oh Lord. She should have stuck to spaghetti bolognese. And they would eat in the kitchen.

Too late. She heard the front door opening and closing, followed by a clunk-clunk as he deposited his two big walking boots on the hall tiles.

He entered the dining-room, looked around, stopped in his tracks.

'Hi!' She looked up very casually, hoping to convey to him that she for one dined in splendour every evening of the week, and that he would betray his own lack of class if he mentioned it.

'Why are we eating in here?' he asked immediately.

'Mrs Carr left instructions to serve formal evening meals. She's old-fashioned that way,' she lied. She hoped her tongue wouldn't curl up and turn black, like she often warned the boys would happen.

'Fine by me.' He looked different. Keyed up or something. Excited. She wondered had his afternoon sojourn involved the person he had called 'Babe'. She had a brief vision of slim pale thighs wrapping themselves around him like a pair of frisky boa constrictors.

The thought automatically sent her into motherly mode. 'I hope you're hungry!' she chirped. Raging, she escaped to the kitchen before she started patting him on the head or something.

She would tell him tonight that he must leave in the morning. Mrs Carr would be coming home in any case. She wouldn't even ask him for money. Somehow it would be crass and wrong to charge him for what had seemed like a little holiday. Well, for her anyway. She would go back to Dublin tomorrow with the smell of fresh-cut grass still on her clothes, and flour under her fingernails.

'Can I help?'

'Oh!'

He had come into the kitchen without her noticing. He seemed to be standing very close. But it was only to look over her shoulder at her French onion soup (nothing sexual could be read into French onion soup, could it? Maybe it meant something very suggestive in France. Maybe it was seen as a direct invitation to foreplay over there or something. Sweet Jesus).

'No, thanks,' she said briskly. 'I have everything under control.'

Apart from her hands, which had suddenly become very clumsy. She piled far too much cheese onto the bread floating on top of the soup, but then decided that she didn't care about the calories. She was starving. Everything seemed to taste better in the country; it was like her taste buds had suddenly awoken after a number of years in a perpetual slumber.

'A good cook as well,' Adam said.

'As well as what?' she asked, wondering whether he was flirting with her. It was difficult to tell, given that nobody had flirted with her in years.

He shrugged, the picture of innocence. 'Nothing. Just a figure of speech.'

Back in the dining-room they ate their soup and slices of her homemade bread and watched each other across the table. He had got the sun today. His forehead and forearms seemed even browner. So had she; her own face was sprinkled with freckles. She had examined them in fascination in the bathroom mirror earlier, unable to decide whether they made her look sexy or homely. On balance, she liked them.

'Delicious,' he declared.

'Thank you,' she said demurely

'The soup too.'

Oh! She felt a bit warm, then decided she had misheard. She asked casually, 'Nice afternoon?'

'Yes, thank you,' he said. Whether he had spent it shagging Babe, he wasn't going to say. Instead he put down his spoon with a satisfied sigh, got up from the table and left the room. Just like that! Did he think dinner was over? How could he call her delicious in one breath and then walk off on her the next? So fickle!

She was wondering what to do when he reappeared, holding a bottle of wine.

'For you.'

'Me?'

'Well, us. Thought you might fancy a glass.'

She watched as he opened it and poured two glasses before sitting down opposite her again.

'Let's have a toast,' he said.

'To what?'

'Maybe to Mrs Carr? Seeing as she can't be here in person?' he suggested.

'Yes, of course,' Grace said, guiltily lifting her glass to the woman she had shot and whose house she was merrily entertaining in. Still, she and Adam would be gone tomorrow. When Mrs Carr got back on Friday, she wouldn't know a thing. They still had the matter of her convalescence to discuss, but that would have to wait now until the woman was home.

'And to you,' Adam added.

'Me?' She tried a breathy little laugh. It came out as a kind of nasty smoker's cough.

'For a wonderful meal,' he elaborated.

'You haven't eaten the main course yet, it might be horrible.'

'Don't put yourself down like that – why do you do that?'

She had only been joking; but everything with him was so intense! She tried to imagine a conversation between him and his friends; it would all be terribly serious and earnest and nobody would ever be allowed to crack a joke.

'It's gone a bit dark in here,' he said now.

'I'll turn on a lamp—'

'Why don't we just light that candle up there on the mantelpiece?'

'We could,' she said slowly, trying not to let the situation get away on her. He was pushing it now. After all his 'Babe' talk on the phone, too! What she needed to do was briskly stand, clap her hands and say, 'Now! Dinner! Have you washed your hands?'

But she didn't. She stayed sitting there. She was just curious, she told herself. It would be interesting to see how far he would go. How far she would *let* him. Which wouldn't be very far at all, of course. She was a married woman after all.

Still, she had to remind herself of this when he looked at her over the romantic glow of the candle and said, 'I was thinking earlier. I don't know anything at all about you.'

'What do you want to know?'

'Anything. Everything.'

He fancied her. Most definitely. She might be out of the dating game but she could tell that much.

'I'm not sure I want to tell you,' she said coyly. She was flirting right back! It mightn't be the best flirting in the world, it might lack finesse, but it was still flirting. There wasn't any harm in it. Was there?

Then he said, 'Where do you go to in your head, Grace?'

'Pardon?'

165

'When you're on your own. When you sit in your car and you think nobody is watching you.'

Oh! He had seen her! And she had only got into the car at all this morning to check that the garage guys hadn't left grease all over her seats. (Somehow, here in the country, she didn't feel the same urgent need to lock herself in the car as she did at home – which was a terrible indictment of Ewan and the boys, when she thought about it. She did love them really. She was just sick of them.)

'That's an interesting question,' she said. For someone who just wanted to get into her pants.

'You look like a dreamer, that's all.'

'I think about lots of things,' she told him coolly.

And she would. Mostly she would have detective fantasies, where she would be a cop, modelled exactly on Clarice Starling in *Silence of The Lambs* – the type of heroine who was serious and unsmiling and self-reliant, and who still solved the crime. (Grace was quite particular about her role models. The descriptions 'feisty' or 'sexy' would never apply to her heroines, for example.) She never told anybody about these, obviously – she knew it would look odd for a woman her age to be having far-fetched fantasies which other people had left behind as children.

But why did it all have to end when you became grown-up? It was as though you had to accept your life the way it was and never dream again of being hand-picked by the CIA in the cereal section of the supermarket and whisked away on a secret mission. Anyhow, her fantasies had matured as she had grown older, she felt – at least now they tended to centre on action/adventure, and not meeting a very attractive rich man who wanted to marry her and have children with her. When she daydreamed about romance at all, it tended to veer off very quickly into those lurid porn fantasies again.

Other times, when she sat in the car, she didn't fantasise at all. She thought about the credit-card bill and where they would go on holidays next year. Then it would probably be time to get out of the car and go make the tea.

'I think about private things,' she qualified to Adam, lest he think he could dissect her that easily with his schoolboy questions about what went on in her head. 'Excuse me.'

She left him at the table and went into the kitchen again.

The risotto was done to perfection. She added a pile of parmesan shavings, and took a few deep breaths. She felt all hot and bothered. Not that she couldn't handle the situation or anything. No, no, she was well able for him. The problem was that she shouldn't be enjoying it so much.

But all the same she touched up her hair a bit and made a rather dramatic entrance into the dining-room, the risotto held aloft. Round two!

Adam was gone again. Blast. Deflating rapidly, she was about to go in search of him when she saw him crouched down in the far corner and fiddling with what seemed to be an old gramophone. She hadn't noticed it until now, nor the records piled in a dusty heap on the floor beside it.

'Dinner!' she said.

But he was enthralled. 'Look at this – old 45s.' He examined a couple of records. 'The Everley Brothers – "Bye Bye Love". Pretty good nick too.'

He obviously knew his 50s music. Grace didn't. She needed to get back the mood, so she said, hopefully, 'Risotto?'

'And Buddy Holly! "Peggy Sue",' Adam said. He didn't even look at her.

'With wild mushrooms!' She waved the risotto around a bit, hoping the aroma would reach him. Maybe the way to a man's heart really *was* through his stomach.

'Will we put it on?' he said, holding up the record.

'Oh, I don't think so.'

'Why not?'

'It belongs to Mrs Carr. She mightn't like us poking through her things.'

'We're not poking. We're just playing some music. I don't see how she can object.'

'Maybe after dinner.'

He was putting the record on anyway. 'Come on, Grace, don't get all stuffy on me again. You were doing so well.'

'I beg your pardon?'

'Do you not have music-making equipment in your leafy Dublin suburb?'

'I don't live in a leafy Dublin suburb,' she said, even though she did. How did he know she lived in Dublin anyway? From her car registration plate, probably.

'Peggy Sue' erupted tinnily from the record player.

She gave up and sat down at the table, and nodded her head once or twice to the beat, but felt middle-aged and silly and stopped. She wanted her dinner, she realised.

'Let's dance,' he said.

She started. 'Sorry?'

'Dance. It's when you kind of jiggle about to music.'

'I know what dance is. It's just . . . I don't dance, okay?'

'Why, is there something wrong with your legs?'

She didn't like him any more. 'No—'

'They look pretty good to me.'

With a heavy-lidded look, he grabbed her hand, dragging her up from her cosy, safe chair.

'Please let me go, Adam.'

'That's the first time you've used my name. And I've never heard it sound better, to tell you the truth.'

There was no time to respond: he was flinging her around the place, twisting her arm and twirling her around like a spinning top. There was no time even to feel foolish— one lapse of concentration and she could end up disabled for life.

'I don't know how you listen to this stuff,' she said, as 'Peggy Sue' went into a cheesy second verse. 'Would you not prefer something from your own generation?'

Somehow it was important to keep talking, to poke fun at him. He just gave her a look, and pulled her up very close.

'I have very particular tastes,' he said, looking at her lips. She felt her colour rising, like she was seventeen again and dancing with the best-looking boy in the class at the school disco.

'Can we stop now?' she asked.

'Sorry, is your arthritis playing up?' he enquired, and twirled her away before she had time to reply. She hated him now. She twirled back a little harder than he expected and caught him squarely in the chest, winding him.

'Sorry,' she said insincerely. 'Can we sit down now?'

He let her go immediately. 'Fine. You're obviously not enjoying yourself.'

He had given up. She had played too hard to get. Which was exactly what she had wanted, of course. Absolutely!

They ate dinner and talked about travel, and books, and he declined second helpings of her breast-shaped meringues, and when she went to blow out the candle he didn't stop her, and she felt very flat somehow. Which was ridiculous! She'd had her bit of fun, and he'd had his and it was best just to leave it at that (when had it occurred to her that it might turn into something more?).

He offered to help wash up but she wouldn't let him. She told him that paying guests did not wash their own dishes (she'd changed her mind about making him pay). He offered to make coffee but she wouldn't let him do that either. Eventually he gave up and took the remains of his wine outside to the back garden.

She went upstairs and rang Ewan from Mrs Carr's cordless phone, making a mental note to leave money on the hall table for the call.

'Grace? Is something the matter?' He sounded a bit hassled and very far away.

'No, no. Is something the matter with *you*?'

'No.'

'It's just that you said you'd ring later and you never did.'

'We've just arrived in the park this minute.'

'The park? You mean Disney?'

'Yes. It's unbelievable, we've just seen a huge . . .'

He was drowned out by a roar in the background, like something large passing at speed. She could only imagine what – a giant grinning electronic Mickey Mouse or something.

'Are the boys all right?' she asked, when she could hear him again.

'Having a ball. Do you want to speak to them? Neil, come over here! Neil – Mum's on the phone, she wants to talk to you. *Neil*!'

She moved quickly to smooth over the dawning embarrassment that Neil did not actually want to speak to her on the phone. 'You know, Ewan – why don't I ring when it's evening over there your time? We can all have a proper chat then.'

'All right,' he said. He added, confidentially, 'He can be a bit difficult, you know – Neil. I think it's something we should keep an eye on.'

'Yes,' Grace agreed. She had been keeping an eye on it for years.

'How is she anyway?' he asked. 'Mrs Carr? Is there any news?'

'Well, she's not home yet,' Grace said lamely,

unwilling to recount her fruitless conversations with the hospital.

'But what about Michael? Surely you've spoken to him at this point?'

'Um, we're working something out,' she said, hoping to fudge things.

'All right, great – Neil! So when do you think you'll be flying out? I mean, I'm just asking,' he said quickly, obviously not wanting a repeat of their previous phone conversation. 'I don't want to put you under any pressure or anything – Neil! Excuse me for a moment, Grace.' He was gone, and there were rapid-fire muffled voices in the background, and then Ewan was back. He sounded a little under strain. 'Anyway. Hopefully you'll make it out soon. After all, you're missing your holiday too.'

'Well, it's hardly exciting stuck here,' she agreed. 'I'm just about to go to bed in fact. Curl up with a good book or something.'

She was making it out to be worse than it actually was. She didn't know why. It wasn't as though she had anything to hide.

'Good idea,' he said. 'You know, I was thinking – you should really make the most of these few days. Take time for yourself. Relax, put your feet up. I can just about manage the boys by myself.'

'Good,' she said. He needn't sound so martyred – she did it all year round.

'I mean it. I don't want you thinking they're pining away without you,' he said, and then added insult to injury: 'In fact, it'll probably do you all the world of good to get away from each other.'

'What's that supposed to mean?'

'What? Just that you could do with the break from them.'

'That is not what you said.'

'Grace—'

'Are you hinting that I'm smothering them?'

'Now you're twisting things.' He said this with another little martyred sigh.

'Oh, go back to Mickey Mouse, Ewan.'

There was a little silence, and then he said, 'Why are we arguing like this, Grace? We never do normally.'

'Maybe we should!' she said loudly. 'Maybe it'd be a healthy thing to have a good row every now and again! Shake things up a little before we both die of boredom!' This was a little extreme. But she felt it was called for.

There was a pause. Then he said, 'Can we talk about this later? I'm trying to keep tabs on the boys here.'

Typical man, she thought viciously. Can't do two things at the same time, whereas women routinely did fifteen – and with a jolly smile on their faces.

'Fine,' she said.

'When – tomorrow?' He sounded anxious.

'Soon,' she said again, enigmatically.

If he was not going to stick to definite arrangements about times to phone, then she wouldn't either. She mightn't ring for two whole days! But that would be as long as she would last without word about the boys.

Adam was sitting on an old rug on the grass when

she went out to say goodnight. She shouldn't have gone out at all. It was a silly thing to have done in the mood she was in, and she would reflect on the folly of it afterwards.

He looked up at her as she hovered. 'Everything all right?'

'Fine. Why wouldn't it be?'

He just shrugged. 'Want to sit down?' He moved over on the rug to make room for her.

'I should really go to bed . . .'

He didn't try to dissuade her. She sat anyway. Her shoulder glanced off his and she shifted over quickly.

He was smoking something that he had rolled himself, something pungent. He caught her looking at it.

'You don't mind, do you?'

'Mind? Not at all!' she said, hoping that she sounded blasé and sophisticated. She hadn't smoked weed since her college days. It had been the most rebellious and depraved thing she had ever done and the memory of it now, combined with the two glasses of wine she'd had at dinner, made her reckless.

'Can I have some?'

He looked mildly surprised. 'I didn't know you smoked.'

'Like you said, there are a lot of things you don't know about me,' she said grandly.

'I can roll you one of your own,' he offered.

'No, no, I only want a few . . . puffs.' Was that the right word? Or was it hits? Although she thought 'hits' might be something to do with heroin. She hoped Adam wouldn't realise how hopelessly out of touch she was when it came to drugs. But he just handed over the joint to her. She held it languidly, a bored expression on her face, and tried not to burn her fingers. Finally, when he stopped looking at her, she lifted it quickly. The filter was damp from his mouth. Her own lips seemed to stick fast to the thin cigarette paper and for a moment she thought she would have to ask him to go get a tweezers or a knife or something. But she managed to inhale and extract the thing, choking back a cough. So far so good.

Adam was looking at the sky reflectively. 'It makes you feel very small and insignificant, doesn't it? That great big expanse of sky. We're just pin-pricks down here on earth, of no consequence in the greater scheme of things.'

'Hmmm,' Grace said, her mouth full of smoke. There was a nasty burning sensation in her throat. Probably the drug doing its thing.

'Yet look at us all, scurrying around, busy-busy-busy,' he continued ponderously. 'But what's it all for at the end of the day? What do we all want?'

The joint had obviously worked its magic on him. Grace herself was nowhere near discussing the meaning of life yet, despite two more big drags.

'I couldn't tell you,' she admitted. 'Happiness, maybe?'

'Happiness!' His scorn rang out across the lawn.

'What's wrong with that?'

'The way I see it, you've only got one life and if you can't make a difference to the world in that time, then you might as well forget it.'

'That's aiming rather high, isn't it?'

'When really it's much easier just to get a nice job and a nice car and marry a nice man and to hell with the starving masses?' He looked at her pointedly. She kept her gaze on the sky, took a last big drag of the joint and handed it back.

'That stuff is useless,' she said haughtily.

'What?'

'It just tasted of tobacco.'

'It is tobacco.'

'Whatever stuff you mixed in with it, then. You'd want to change your dealer. I've had a better hit off a cigarette.' To show her sophistication she was going to offer to give him the number of her own drug dealer, but thought this might be going too far. (Besides, he would be very surprised when he got Nick on the end of the phone. Nick would be more surprised at being asked for recreational drugs.)

'This is a cigarette,' he said. Then he smiled. 'What did you think it was, cannabis?'

'Cannabis? Ha! Don't be ridiculous!' she said. Oh God.

He put his arm around her and gave her an affectionate little squeeze, which was nearly more insulting. 'Poor Grace. You're trying so hard, aren't you?'

'What?'

'To break the rules. To be a little crazy. And I'm not helping at all.'

'Don't flatter yourself.' She shrugged his arm off, furious. Was she really so transparent? She felt ridiculous, like some kind of teenage upstart determined to prove her coolness by smoking a joint. 'I think I'll go to bed,' she said.

'Don't,' he said. 'I'll be all lonely on my own.'

She couldn't imagine Adam ever being lonely. He was too self-sufficient, too sure of his purpose in life. She, on the other hand, seemed to have spent most of her adult life just bobbing along in a sea of other people's expectations.

'I'm sure you know more interesting people than me who you could hang out with,' she said.

'I don't know anybody like you,' he said. 'No, no, don't get all puffed up and defensive. I meant it as a compliment.'

'What?' The word wasn't all that familiar to Grace.

'All the girls my age are cynical and hard-boiled, nothing in their heads but the gym and the latest Gucci bag,' he said dismissively. 'But you – you're so . . . you're so . . .'

She waited rather belligerently. Look at him – he couldn't think of a compliment now!

'Kind,' he said eventually. 'Thoughtful. Funny. Beautiful.'

'Beautiful!' She gave a little laugh. She thought that she might be falling in love with him, a little bit.

'You are.' His voice dropped a bit. 'You're amazing.'

The extravagance of this would have been amusing coming from anybody else. But from him, it sounded perfectly natural. Authoritative. Indisputable, even. She was amazing.

Her mouth felt a little dry; she felt his hand drop from her shoulder to rest casually around her waist.

'Why are you so tense? All bunched up,' he murmured.

'Sorry,' she said.

'There's no need to apologise.'

Their ages seemed to have somehow reversed; he was now the worldly, mature one who was complimenting and reassuring her at the end of a dinner date. She was all huddled up on the rug like a nervous virgin, overwhelmed by his attentions and not knowing what to expect next.

She was soon enlightened when he leaned over and kissed her hair. It wasn't her lips, granted. But it was still enough of a shock for her to shy away from him.

'What's wrong, Grace?'

'I'm married,' she said. But her voice carried no great conviction.

'Yes,' he mused. He wasn't taking her marriage seriously either, and that somehow annoyed her. It mightn't be perfect but she had invested eleven years of her life in it, and it was the only one she had.

'And you have a girlfriend,' she pointed out.

'Yes,' he said, not seeming to take this very seriously either.

'She wouldn't mind you canoodling on a lawn with another woman?'

He considered this for a moment, then said, rather coldly she thought, 'My girlfriend is not an issue.'

So, that only left the husband. *Her* husband, she reminded herself. Ewan, for heaven's sake – the father of her two sons! He was probably canoeing down a creek in Critter Country right now, blissfully ignorant of the fact that a Tasmanian devil was kissing his wife's hair.

'All that, it's the real world,' Adam elaborated.

'They're not here. Not now. It's only you and me, Grace.'

'And that's supposed to make it all right?' she asked.

He shrugged, seeming to think she was creating problems where there were none. 'Won't we be back to it all tomorrow?' he said.

And that was it. They didn't attempt to legitimise it any further: there was no more discussion of partners or life in the real world. There was only Mrs Carr's dark garden and the fresh cut lawn and the smell of tobacco on Adam's breath as he kissed her. It was a curiously unpushy kiss, chaste nearly, and it reminded her of when she'd first started dating at seventeen and eighteen, when the kiss at the end of the night was the highlight of the evening in those innocent days. The teenage magazines at the time would devote pages to this kiss; whether to French kiss or not, whether this could lead to pregnancy, how to stop him nicely if the goodnight kiss made him want to 'take things further'.

It did, obviously. Adam was trying to push her back on the rug now. To get into any kind of horizontal position was dangerous; she knew that from experience as well as from magazines. Best to signal in plenty of time that she was putting the brakes on.

'Adam,' she murmured.

'Sorry. Do you not want to . . .?'

'No! I mean yes! I'm sure it would be very . . .' She was glad that he could not see inside her head then; every pornographic fantasy she'd ever had was playing in Technicolor, with him in a starring role.

179

'. . . nice,' she finished chastely. 'It's just that we hardly know each other.'

'I know enough about you,' he said.

She felt the generation gap very strongly. It wasn't that she had been all that prudish at his age. But she suspected attitudes to casual sex were very different now. And she was married, after all.

'I might know you a bit better in the morning,' she said. There was no harm in hedging her bets, was there? And, after all, they would never see each other again after tomorrow . . .

'Till the morning then,' he said, making it sound like a promise.

'Yes,' she said, wondering whether he intended infiltrating her bedroom at dawn. There was no lock on the door either. She could put a chair up against it, she supposed. But she knew that she wouldn't.

She sat on the lawn for ages after he had gone to bed, hugging her knees and looking up at the sky and the stars and what was beyond, and she thought that Adam was wrong about how humbling the enormity of it was, because tonight she didn't feel insignificant at all.

Eight

'You look different,' Frank said rather accusingly the next morning as he stood in the middle of the kitchen.

'How?' she said guiltily.

'I don't know, just . . . different.'

'Probably because I'm wearing Mrs Carr's clothes.' Her own wouldn't stand up to another day's wear and were now spinning around in Mrs Carr's washing machine. If she hung them on the line outside they would be dry in time for her to go back to Dublin this afternoon. In the meantime she had found a kind of shapeless robe-like red garment in the wardrobe that could only be Mrs Carr's from some other era, and had put it on.

'Where's Adam?' Frank enquired now.

'In bed.' His own bed, that was. He had not gate-crashed hers that morning after all. Possibly she had read him wrong. She had lain there naked for an hour just in case, her teeth brushed and her hair fanned out on the pillow becomingly, as though she always woke up like that. She had even rehearsed a token speech about how they ought not to do anything they might

181

regret. In the end she had gone to the bathroom noisily, just in case he was a heavy sleeper. But still he hadn't come. Could it be that he was playing hard to get?

Frank said, 'Could I borrow a cup of flour?'

'Sorry?'

'I'm baking some bread. Sandy says the smell of baking bread is very persuasive. You know, for when you're showing the house to Tom and Charlie.'

'Sandy has worked in real estate, has she?' Grace enquired.

'What?'

'It's just that she seems to be quite the expert when it comes to selling houses.'

Frank sensed criticism. 'Obviously she's interested in how things go for me. We *are* going to be married, you know.'

Grace backed down. 'Yes, of course. And how are preparations coming along? For the big day?'

'Well, she can't decide on a dress.' Frank gave a little sigh, but anyone could see he was delighted. 'She's torn between the Grace Kelly strapless ivory, or the Little Bo-Peep style – that comes with a staff, by the way.'

'And what about sheep?'

'Pardon?'

'Look, never mind about the dress. Have you set a date yet?'

'I'm keen on October. But Sandy thinks the weather will be too bad. And I can see her point – if she's going to shell out all that money on a wedding dress, she doesn't want it to get wet, does she?'

'Golly, no.'

Frank said, 'You don't like Sandy much, do you?'

'I don't know Sandy. '

'Exactly. You don't know her. So please spare me the innuendo.'

'I just hope that she's as committed to this relationship as you are, that's all.'

'Do you know how many times she mailed me last night?'

'Frank—'

'Do you?'

'Of course I don't.'

'Eleven times! And the last time was just to tell me that there was a moth in her bedroom with the most beautiful silky wings, and she asked me to look it up in one of my books to see what it was, and when I mailed back, she was sitting in the dark because she had turned all her apartment lights off in case the moth burned itself! *That's* the kind of person she is – the most decent, honourable, sweet, generous person I've ever met in my life!'

'But you haven't actually met her, Frank.'

Frank's face went even redder. 'I knew you'd bring that up!'

'Did you ask her about the tea towel?'

'As a matter of fact I did.' He was triumphant now. 'She brought along a barbeque to the beach that day for the disabled kids, because some of them don't eat as often as they should, and she bought the food out of her own pocket and she stood over that barbeque for three hours in the heat and the smell while everybody else had a great time dipping in the sea.'

Grace said humbly, 'Oh. I—'

'Then she burnt her hand quite badly but didn't say anything to anybody, just covered it with that tea towel, and smiled for that photo which little Tommy was taking. He's a paraplegic, by the way.'

'Sorry.' Grace wanted to crawl on the floor now. 'She's an example to us all.'

'I won't even mention this to her,' Frank said loftily. 'Not when she's feeling so tired and everything.'

'Has she been to the doctor yet?' Grace tried to sound very concerned to make up for things.

'She's made an appointment. Between you and me, I think she's probably a bit low in iron. She doesn't eat meat, you see. She thinks that animals have as much right to live as we do. Even rats! She has a place in her heart for everything.' He had gone all dreamy-eyed again.

'Incredible,' Grace murmured. 'Any news on her sister?'

'Sandy thinks she's managed to talk her into going to counselling with her husband. So I should soon be able to book my flight.'

'That's great, Frank,' Grace said with feeling. 'I bet you two can't wait to get your hands on each other!'

Frank looked a bit startled. 'Ah . . . uh . . .'

'Unless Sandy wants to . . . wait until you're married?' She probably did too, the sanctimonious little cow.

'You know, I haven't asked her.'

Grace felt bad now. 'Look, Frank, it's none of my business.'

But he went off with his cup of flour, looking rather

preoccupied. Grace took her tea to the kitchen window and looked out at the lawn. Something glinting on the grass caught her eye: Adam's forgotten wine glass from last night. She felt reassured: she hadn't imagined the whole thing. He *had* kissed her. He *had* told her she was amazing. It wasn't some lurid daydream she'd cooked up involving risotto, Peggy Sue and Mrs Carr's young lodger.

'Why are you in such a good mood?' Natalie demanded when she rang Grace's mobile phone a few minutes later.

'Because I'm thoughtful and funny and lovely,' Grace said airily. Adam had said so: she remembered it all, every word.

'Oh, you got it too!' Natalie cried.

'What?'

'Learning To Love The Real You. Lisa was on about it in the office.' Lisa was a self-help junkie.

'A man told me, actually,' Grace boasted.

Natalie sucked in her breath. 'A real man?'

'Very real,' she said, thinking of Adam's chest. She bet it felt as smooth as a baby's bottom.

'For God's sake, who?' Then she sucked in her breath. 'Not Adam?'

Grace gave such a light, incredulous little laugh that she nearly convinced herself. 'Hardly.'

'Who, then?'

'Just somebody.' She had forgotten how persistent Natalie could be and was beginning to regret saying anything at all.

'What else did he say?' Natalie said excitedly.

'That I was beautiful.'

There was a chortle. 'Beautiful!' Then Natalie hurried on, 'I mean, of course you're *attractive*. And you've a very good figure, even after twins.'

'But I'm not beautiful?'

Natalie tried to stop digging. 'You are! You're gorgeous! I just meant that it seems a rather . . . elaborate thing to say, that's all.'

'Yes, isn't it great?' Grace said cheerily, refusing to let the good be taken out of it. Anyway, she didn't care about the beautiful thing (she knew she wasn't really beautiful, but then most people weren't). No, the bit she remembered most of all, the bit that replayed over and over in her head, was him saying that she wasn't like anybody else he knew.

He thought she was different. Special. Unique, even. And she hadn't even had to resort to bragging about the shotgun, or retelling bad jokes she'd heard on the radio. He had not been fooled by the whole public persona of Grace Tynan. She felt that he had seen something in her that nobody had seen for a long time – even herself. And he had liked it – at least enough to try and get her to lie down on the lawn with him.

Right now he was lying in his bed upstairs.

'I think I might be on the verge of doing something silly,' she blurted to Natalie now.

Natalie immediately pounced. 'How silly?'

'I don't know.' If he had come to her room this morning, she might not even be having this conversation. The silliness might be in full swing.

'On a scale of one to ten,' Natalie said, egging her on.

'A nine.'

'A nine!' Natalie was shocked. 'I've only ever done a seven. Remember, when I took off my top at that party?'

'That's only a seven? Mine is a ten then,' Grace said.

'Bloody hell,' Natalie whispered.

'I know. What should I do?'

'How do I know? You haven't even told me what the silliness is!'

'I can't, Natalie.'

There was a very heavy pause, then Natalie said solemnly, 'If this silliness should happen to involve a man who has been telling you you're beautiful, then I would have to strongly advise you against such a course of action, Grace.'

'Yes, I thought you might,' Grace said. It was immaterial anyway. He had not come to her room and tried to make love to her. Not that they were in love. It would be more a question of having sex. Which would be very cold and tawdry (well, morally anyway. In every other way she found it desperately exciting). No, it was just as well it had ended where it had. She could hug his words to her all day – or for the rest of her life if she felt like it – with the assurance that she hadn't really done anything, well, foolish.

'You *are* married, Grace,' Natalie finished up. She made it sound like a government health warning.

'So are you,' Grace said, adding a bit spitefully, 'and up the pole.' She hung up, ran her fingers through her hair and her tongue over her lips, and went upstairs. She knocked on his bedroom door.

'Adam? Breakfast is ready.'

She must say something – just very casually – about being up since dawn. She didn't want him thinking that she had lain in bed for hours waiting for him.

'Adam?'

Possibly he was a very heavy sleeper. Eventually she opened the door just a crack, half hoping to catch a glimpse of his brown body spread across the sheets. Did he sleep naked?

He wasn't there. The bed was empty and neatly made. Far from planning an assault on her bedroom, he had been up and about before she'd even woken up!

She felt a bit foolish now. Imagine having taken a bit of flirting so seriously! And the kiss – had she taken that too seriously too? For all she knew, he might do this kind of thing all the time – seduce landladies on lawns in every port in the world, after first telling them they were amazing. *And* he had a girlfriend! (She had a husband, of course, which was worse – but it didn't stop her feeling slightly bruised and used.)

She wondered where he had gone. To meet the woman otherwise known as Babe? Grace wanted to tear her limb from limb and boil her head in a pressure cooker.

The thoughts of pressure cookers immediately set her mouth watering. And no wonder – she had given over so much time to unrequited romance this morning that she had neglected her stomach entirely! Gathering the red robe around herself in the manner of a Greek Goddess, she set off down the stairs in search of breakfast.

★ ★ ★

Half an hour later she found herself back at the scene of one of her previous crimes: the cooler section of the local Spar. She popped on her dark sunglasses just in case she was recognised, and was trying to decide between a pack of plump sausages and some juicy gammon steaks (would it be too greedy to have both?) when someone said, 'Grace!'

She swung around to find herself face to face with Sergeant Daly.

'I was going to pay for these,' she blurted, wondering whether this was some kind of sting operation.

But Sergeant Daly just chuckled heartily. 'Only the innocent ever look guilty, Grace. I've learned that much in thirty years of law enforcement if nothing else.'

She didn't want to tell him that his thirty years were completely wasted in that case and so she just chuckled back.

'Is this about my statement?' she said. She had gone down to the station yesterday afternoon in between washing towels and putting on the risotto. She'd never had to make a police statement before. It wasn't half as exciting as she'd imagined it would be – they'd even made her tone down the phrases 'pumped a shot' and 'the victim collapsed to the floor, the colour of putty.' 'Just stick to the facts,' they'd said. Honestly, by the time they'd finished with it, it had all read rather like a boring school essay.

'No, no, your statement is perfect,' he said. He

leaned in. 'It was actually the house I wanted to have a word with you about.'

God. You could keep no secrets in a small town. 'I'm leaving today, okay?' she blustered. Could he have her up for breaking and entering? 'And Adam too. And I'll come clean to Mrs Carr. Really, it was all an accident of circumstance.'

Sergeant Daly looked confused. 'I'm talking about Frank's house. You're supposed to be showing it to Tom and Charlie later.'

'Oh! That's right!'

He looked a bit pinched or something, so she said, 'There's no problem, is there? They arrived from Birmingham okay?'

'Yes,' he said.

'Great! And did you meet Charlie?'

'I did,' he said, very heavily. Then he pitched forward over the cooler section and said, very low, 'Do you remember I was asking you about conversions?'

'Yes – turning the study into a playroom. It's simple enough, they wouldn't need planning permission or anything.'

'How about something more radical? Supposing they wanted to convert the whole house into something else?'

'You mean like a crèche, for example?'

He looked over his shoulder furtively, and said out of the side of his mouth, 'A club.'

She was a bit taken aback. 'Eh . . . what kind of a club? I mean, would there be alcohol served?'

'Buckets of it,' he said grimly.

'It's a residential area, I don't think they could,' she

said. 'But all this stuff – isn't it more your area?'

'I wasn't sure, you see,' he whispered. 'And I didn't want to bring it up down at the station. Not in front of the other lads, you know? I'd never live it down.'

'I know,' she said, none the wiser. She felt a great need to put some distance between herself and the law at this point, and so she said, 'Actually, I'd better get going if I'm going to keep my appointment with your Tom. Let's hope they like the house, eh?'

'Um,' he said, very unenthusiastically.

Grace escaped from the Spar, with neither sausages nor gammon steaks, and she was almost light-headed with hunger. So when a shop door opened up the street and the smell of hot coffee and sticky buns wafted out, she elbowed past a couple of pensioners in her haste to catch the door before it closed.

Inside, she went to the counter. 'Coffee, please!' she said to an assistant. 'And one of those scones.'

Now that food was definitely on its way, she could relax enough to look around. The café was full of mid-morning shoppers. She was just looking for an empty table when her eye fell on a red T-shirt with the slogan *Save The World* on it. The wearer was Adam.

She whirled back to the counter, hoping he wouldn't recognise her in the red robe and sunglasses. What if he thought she was following him?

Then she was annoyed with herself. It was a free country, wasn't it? She was as entitled as anybody else to walk into a café and order a coffee! She had nothing to feel guilty about.

So she slowly turned back and had a peek. He was sitting at a window table, drinking a coffee and talking earnestly to someone. Grace was ridiculously relieved that it was not some delicious young hippy girl but another young man wearing scruffy denims and a couple of friendship bracelets, although he didn't look all that friendly to Grace. His mouth barely moved as he spoke.

'The special is cream of carrot soup.'

Grace swung back to the counter. 'Sorry?'

The café assistant held out her coffee. 'The soup.'

'Thanks anyway, but I don't think . . .'

She only wanted cake. But the assistant seemed to take umbrage. 'It's homemade if that's what you're worried about. Minnie made it first thing.'

'Oh! Well, in that case . . . I'd love a bowl.'

The assistant sniffed a bit, knowing a blow-in when she saw one, and went to get a bowl of the soup. Grace snuck another look over her shoulder. Adam and his companion were joined now by a third person: a chunky young woman with long hair pulled into a careless ponytail. She was not Babe either, Grace just instinctively knew. It was in her body language when she squeezed past Adam to take the third stool. Far from displaying any affection or intimacy, she muscled in roughly until she had sufficient room and he had to move over, and Grace admired her for it.

'The main course special is Irish Stew.' The café assistant was back, holding out a steaming bowl of soup. Grace put it onto her tray.

'To be honest, I'm not a stew fan,' she said regretfully. Stew was a food from her childhood; she couldn't remember the last time she'd eaten it. Anyway, it was only eleven o'clock in the morning.

The assistant gave a suit-yourself shrug. 'I'm not either. But that was before I tasted Minnie's.'

'Good, is it?'

'Good?' the assistant barked. 'Do you like meat?'

'Yes, I suppose.'

'Minnie back there doesn't scrimp on meat. Big chunks of the best Irish beef! And carrots from her own back garden – onions too, and those tiny new potatoes. She makes her own stock from scratch from the best bones they save for her over in Morrissey's. Then she marinades the whole lot in a big pot for two days in the yard out the back before cooking it all up.'

Grace suspected that this went against all health regulations, but her mouth was watering like crazy. And she'd had no breakfast after all.

'I suppose it's very fattening?' she said regretfully.

'Lethal,' the assistant said. 'She doesn't even trim the meat.'

'Does she skim the fat off the top?'

'Nope. Says that's what gives it all its flavour.'

'I'll have a bowl,' Grace decided.

'You won't regret it.'

'Not too big though!'

'How about a medium-sized portion?'

'Perfect. And maybe some of that home-made bread?'

'I'll fix you up with two big chunks, and a couple of pats of butter.'

The assistant nodded in satisfaction and went off to get the stew. Grace looked around again at Adam's table. There seemed to be some kind of intense discussion going on. The three of them had their heads so close that Adam's dreadlocks were brushing against the girl's face. She flicked them away – so roughly! – and said something else that seemed to greatly antagonise him. He whispered back fiercely in any case. But she overrode him. She was in charge, Grace guessed. Of what, she didn't know – some kind of clandestine coffee-drinking group? Sergeant Daly was fretting about nothing.

The assistant was back with the stew and Grace eagerly added it to her tray. By the time she reached the check-out, she had been easily persuaded into trying the dessert special of apple crumble with clotted cream, a glass of pressed apple juice and a slice of banana bread, all made fresh this morning by the miraculous Minnie. Grace strained to get a glimpse of her in the back kitchen, but couldn't. Possibly she had collapsed from exhaustion.

'Excuse me . . .' She made her way discreetly towards the nearest empty table, kind of moving backwards. With any luck, Adam wouldn't see her at all and she could eat her lunch in peace and go. But she had forgotten that she was still wearing her black sunglasses, which gave rise to a minor misunderstanding.

'Noel, help that woman – she's blind.'

'No, no, I'm not actually . . .'

'Noel, she's going backwards, turn her around.'

Apparently she was also deaf, and without a sense of direction.

'Really, I'm fine.'

But Noel had been dispatched and he stood in front of her now and firmly took her tray from her.

'Now, let's get you a seat,' he said.

Please God let Adam not notice. But a swift glance his way confirmed that the argument was ongoing. 'That table is fine,' she instructed Noel, pointing to the nearest empty one.

Noel wasn't thrown by her ability to spot an empty table despite her blindness. In any case he ignored her and set off towards the back of the café – and an empty table right next to Adam.

'Noel . . .' she said.

'Let the lady through please,' he told the other diners officiously.

Grace had no choice but to follow him. Everyone drew in their legs sharply and scraped up any handbags that might lie in her way like booby traps. Chairs were hastily pulled in.

'Thank you, thank you,' she murmured, quite enjoying the attention now. Then she guiltily thought that real blind people probably didn't enjoy it at all.

'I can take it from here,' she murmured, choosing the chair with its back to Adam and sliding in discreetly. He didn't even turn his head her way, and she didn't know whether she was insulted or not.

'Okay,' Noel said, patting her on the shoulder. But he was kind. People generally were very kind, she thought, as Noel went back to his table, his back a little less stooped.

She took a surreptitious look over her shoulder.

Adam was close enough for her to reach back and touch. She would very much like to touch him too; the more she thought about it, the more it became a compulsion, until her fingers were positively itching to lunge over and fondle his bottom. She could always claim to the other diners that she was blind and that she'd thought he was a milk jug or something.

Guiltily, she turned her attention to her lunch. The soup was delicious (Minnie wasn't sparing when it came to double-cream either). She polished it off quickly – at this rate she would have her lunch eaten and would be gone before she was spotted at all. Then the occupants of a large table close by upped and left the cafe, and all of a sudden she could hear what Adam and his friends were whispering about.

'I am not selling baked potatoes,' Adam said, low but very definite.

Interesting, she thought.

'It is just a suggestion,' the girl said. She pronounced 'is' like 'iz'. French, Grace thought. 'We could hand out leaflets with every purchase. What do you think, Joey?'

Grace expected Joey must be Italian, or in some way Mediterranean.

'I don't give a balls,' he said.

Irish, then.

She wondered should she mention to Adam later that the Spar had a sign up looking for staff. She remembered seeing it the other night. That way he and his friends wouldn't have to resort to selling fast food if they were running a little short of cash.

But then Adam said, 'You can mess around with baked-potato stands if you want, Martine. They tried that at Oasis last year, and Robbie Williams the year before. And you know what? People were too busy stuffing their faces to listen to the message!'

What message? Grace took a little bite of her stew. It was fantastic.

'All right, cool it,' Joey muttered. But it was obvious whose side he was on. 'We need to come up with something, and fast. We have less than four weeks to go.'

'I say we need to make a big impact,' Adam said. 'Do something a little less conservative. I'm sure Martine would agree with me. If you're not too busy perfecting your culinary skills, that is. Comrade.'

Grace glanced over her shoulder to see Martine give Adam a filthy look. Then she grabbed his packet of tobacco to roll herself a cigarette but, in her belligerence, sent it flying to the floor instead.

It landed at Grace's feet.

'Grace?' Adam had turned around in his seat.

'Mmm? Oh, Adam! Hi.' He was looking a bit shocked. 'Just popped in for an early lunch.' And she went right on eating her stew – she might as well brazen it out at this point. There was a little silence at the table now. Grace turned round again. Martine and Joey were looking rather accusingly at Adam. Grace offered them her most harmless smile. 'Hello there! I'd recommend the stew. It's delicious.'

At this point, Adam was compelled to explain her. 'This is Grace, my, uh, landlady.'

They said nothing, just looked at her. Grace had another spoon of stew and re-crossed her legs under the red robe. She wondered should she take her sunglasses off but decided against it.

'You don't look like a landlady,' Martine said at last, her tongue rolling contemptuously around the vowels.

'I'm just starting out,' Grace confessed. 'In fact, Adam is my very first lodger. We've been muddling along quite nicely, haven't we, Adam?'

Adam looked alarmed, as though she were going to reveal that they had been snogging in the garden last night. She just gave him a rather pointed look, before turning to Martine and Joey.

'I didn't know Adam had friends in Hackettstown?' She deserved an explanation too.

'We're not friends,' Martine spat. Grace wondered where she got the energy to be so aggressive all the time. Then Martine hastily corrected herself. 'I mean, we are, kind of. We hooked up to go to the music festival together.'

Joey wasn't going to explain himself at all, that much was obvious.

'I've seen the posters for it around town. It looks great,' Grace said chattily. 'But aren't you a little early for it?'

By nearly a month, actually. There was another tense silence. Martine glared at Adam for bringing this inquisition down upon them. Joey cleaned under his nails with a penknife.

'I have relatives here,' Martine said finally. 'I'm visiting them before going on to the festival. And Adam is going to see some of the country first.'

'Is he?' Grace said, with great interest. Adam looked at her rather imploringly but she didn't let him off the hook. 'You never mentioned anything at dinner last night.'

He eventually said, 'Didn't I?'

'Maybe you're feeding him too well,' Joey said. His eyes were flat and knowing as he looked at her. 'Or something.'

'Maybe,' she said, with a little laugh.

Martine was oblivious. 'My landlady is the tightest bitch in the whole of Europe,' she complained loudly, uncaring who heard her. 'I haven't had a decent meal in two days.'

'Perhaps she's worried about overheads,' Grace murmured, feeling she should defend one of her own.

'Overheads!' Martine sniffed. 'The shower is set on a timer – you only get five minutes of hot water and then it goes cold!'

'Oh, well, that's not right,' Grace said. There were overheads, and then there was just plain meanness. 'Maybe you should say something to her?'

'Maybe,' Martine said doubtfully. 'I'd move only I can't find anywhere else.'

'Maybe your relatives . . .?' Grace prompted.

She watched as Martine thought furiously for a moment. 'Unfortunately they live in a caravan,' she declared at last.

'Yes, most Irish people do,' Grace murmured into

her stew, earning another suspicious look.

'I don't suppose there's a free place in your house?' Martine asked.

Adam didn't like this. 'Grace only has one guest room.'

That wasn't true. There were three guest rooms in total. But it was immaterial anyway. Grace was leaving today. And so was Adam – so what was he angling for?

'I could sleep on the floor,' Martine said. 'I could go back with Adam later and see the place.'

'It's not Grace's house,' Adam argued, looking to Grace for back-up. For some reason he didn't want Martine going back to the house with him.

She didn't look at him. 'He's right. The owner, Mrs Carr, will be back tomorrow and you can ring her then if you want. Her number's in the book. But she's convalescing and I doubt she'll be up to taking on lodgers.'

She took two large bites of her apple crumble – delicious – and slipped the bit of banana bread into a napkin, which she deftly pocketed. Then she stood and nodded at Martine and Joey. 'Nice to meet you.'

Adam caught up with her at the door. 'Sorry I left without saying goodbye this morning.'

'You don't have to check in with me.'

He looked hurt. The power of it was almost dizzying.

'I didn't think you were the type of woman to play games.'

'Adam, I have to go and show a house. And then I'm leaving for Dublin.'

'Can I see you back at Mrs Carr's before then? Just the two of us?' he said, looking very intense.

'I suppose I can spare a few minutes,' she said rather grandly. She pushed her sunglasses back up on her nose and made an exit.

Nine

'Ivy's dead,' Elizabeth said later that morning.

'Stop that,' Julia snapped. Ivy might have kept them awake half the night again but there was no need for that kind of talk.

'No, I mean she's really dead. A heart attack,' Elizabeth said, her voice quivering. They all looked over at Ivy's empty bed. She'd been scheduled for an early morning x-ray, and they thought that she'd just been held up. 'The nurses say she died about four o'clock. Just like that, they said. Hardly made a sound in the end, for her.' And she started to cry. Julia reached over and covered Elizabeth's bony hand with her own, but it was scant comfort to either of them.

Ivy's bed was stripped and remade by twelve, and a new occupant installed by lunch-time. The speed and efficiency and sheer mundanity of it all was profoundly shocking, and Julia returned her lukewarm fish pie and trifle to the hospital kitchen untouched. She had a brief conversation with the Ward Sister, then she pulled her bag out from her locker and began to pack.

It was a slow process on crutches and she was still

at it when Michael arrived half an hour later.

'Oh, hello, Michael. I'm sorry to drag you away from work. Did the Ward Sister explain?'

He didn't waste any time on pleasantries. 'What, that you've decided to discharge yourself on a whim?'

'I'm sure she didn't say that.'

'You're not due to leave until tomorrow, Mammy!'

'Yes, but I've decided to leave today instead. I just have to sign a form at the desk on the way out. Nobody can keep me here.'

'The Ward Sister has told me it's very unwise. She's not a bit happy—'

'I know, she's already told me. Look, are you going to drive me home or do I have to ring Frank?'

Michael stopped blustering and looked at her with concern. 'Are you all right, Mammy? You look a bit pale.'

'I'm fine.'

'At least let me finish that.' He took the bag from her to finish the packing.

Julia watched from the chair, huddled in a cardigan. For some reason she couldn't seem to get warm and thought that perhaps she had caught a chill.

'Do you want to put your painkillers into your handbag?' he asked.

'No, you keep them for me,' she found herself saying. She, who had hoarded up any pills she could get her hands on in order to kill herself! She could hardly believe it now.

She didn't know what had changed. Perhaps it was her foot, freshly bandaged and resting between her crutches. She had never known disability before, had no idea what it was like to be dependent upon others for even the smallest thing. It tended to make you inclined to hang on to those parts of you which worked properly, and not poison them with pharmaceuticals.

She had also realised that there wasn't a lot of glamour in pain. Even less in dying. Look at poor Ivy.

Or maybe it was this place. In a few short days it had leached away her courage and confidence, bit by bit, like one of its intravenous drips. It was dangerous.

'Hurry, Michael,' she urged.

He insisted on bringing the car around to the front of the hospital. She let herself be installed in the front seat. Before she could stop him, he had put her crutches in the boot. Her feelings of helplessness, of foreboding, grew, and she sat there clutching the straps of her handbag fiercely like you see very old women do.

When she eventually took note of her surroundings half an hour later she saw that they were driving into Michael's housing estate. Big white mock-Tudor houses passed them by.

'I thought we might stop by for a bite of lunch,' Michael said. 'The Ward Sister said you haven't touched a thing today. You have to build up your strength, Mammy.'

'Michael, I just want to go home,' she said. To have normality, or what passed for normality, again.

'I rang ahead. Gillian is cooking a roast for us.'

'Oh.'

'And I thought we might take a look at the garage afterwards.'

Julia turned to him. 'Michael, this is all very sudden. This Granny-flat thing.'

'I know. But like we said, there is absolutely no pressure on you.'

'In that case, don't you think we should talk about it before you go taking measurements?'

'We're not going to be taking measurements. We just wanted you to see the place now that it's all cleared out.'

'You've it all cleared out?'

'We've just thrown out all the junk. It's no big deal.'

She tried to make him see. 'But it is, Michael. Me moving in *is* a very big change for us all. I mean, what does Gillian think?'

He waved his hand. 'If it was her mother, we'd do the same.'

'Her mother is dead, Michael.' He didn't say anything, so she pressed on, 'And what about Susan?'

'What about her?'

'She's thirteen. It mightn't suit her to have a geriatric granny cramping her style.'

'She'll come around in the end. Mammy, I'm just asking you to have a look at the place, okay?'

He seemed intent on railroading everybody with this ridiculous idea of his; Michael, who could never say boo to a goose.

At the house Gillian waved to them from the kitchen window. She was wearing what appeared to be a gas mask.

'Does she wear that to cook?' Julia asked. Possibly

she was allergic to vegetable oil or something. She already had nut, garlic, yeast, fish and dairy allergies. At one point her diet had been right down to dry crackers and olives, until she discovered she was allergic to olives too.

'No, no, she's just been fumigating the garage. After she's finished with the place, you can be sure you'll be the only living creature in it.'

'*If* I move in, Michael. There's been no decision made yet.'

'Oh, I know,' he said.

Gillian came out of the house. Thankfully she had removed the gas mask. 'Julia! Welcome home.'

'This is not my home,' Julia said sharply. Why had people suddenly stopped listening to her?

'I meant it in a general sense,' Gillian said evenly. 'Anyway! I hope you're hungry, lunch is ready.'

But Michael was already setting off eagerly for the garage. 'Come on, Mammy.'

He had forgotten she was on crutches, and she was left to hobble slowly across the grass after him with Gillian at her elbow in case she might trip.

'I was never on crutches,' Gillian said, sounding envious.

'Do you want a go?' Julia offered.

'Lord no!' But you could see she was tempted.

Michael waited in front of the double-garage. 'Ta-da!' he said.

A dense fog of insect spray hung over the place – which didn't resemble a garage in any sense of the word any more. Already partitions had been put in place to divide it into rooms. Fresh wiring hung in clumps from the wall, and a new front door, which presumably her key fitted, rested against a wall waiting to be built in.

'I thought you said you were just at the clearing-out stage?'

'We managed to get a builder at short notice. We didn't want to say anything in case he fell through,' Michael said, his double chin quivering with excitement.

Gillian added, 'Michael sanded down everything yesterday, all ready for the plasterer as soon as they get the front finished. We didn't expect you home today, or we'd have had the front door up and waiting for you!'

The idea that she would want to come and live with them seemed to have become a fully-fledged presumption, and she was angry. 'I didn't ask for this,' she said loudly.

There was a little silence.

'Maybe you just need to think about it for a while,' Gillian suggested.

'I have thought about it. And thank you for the offer, but no. It wouldn't work out.'

Michael and Gillian exchanged a look over her head.

'Mammy, we just don't feel comfortable with you living on your own any more,' Michael began. 'After . . . what happened with the gun.'

'And you'd feel more comfortable with me living in the same house as you? Would you not be afraid that I might come in and mow you all down with an Uzi?'

Gillian gave a nervous little start.

'We're just trying to do the best here for you, Mammy,' Michael said.

'But did I ask you, Michael? To do anything for me?' Suddenly she felt on the edge of tears. Her own son, patronising and talking down to her. Treating her as though she had no mind of her own any more: or at least no mind worth taking any notice of.

Her outrage was as great as her new insignificance.

'Please drive me home now.'

'But lunch—'

'I'm not hungry.'

Now he looked upset. 'Mammy, I can see we've gone about this the wrong way. We just wanted to surprise you, that's all. How about we go inside and sit down and talk about this thing properly?'

'No. I've made up my mind.'

Gillian threw up her hands, said to Michael, 'Oh, let her go if she wants.'

'Gillian—'

'No, Michael! We've bent over backwards for her! Stayed up the whole night working on that place! And she hasn't even bothered to say thank you!'

'Sorry to throw your great act of self-sacrifice back in your face,' Julia said. 'But nobody asked you.'

Gillian was furious now. She looked at Julia, and saw her vulnerabilities immediately; knew exactly what to say to pierce her most. 'Fine. Go back to Hackettstown. Hobble about in that big old house on crutches. I just hope you don't fall down in the middle of the night, that's all, with nobody to help you.'

'Gillian!' Michael said, his face white.

'I have neighbours, you know,' Julia retaliated. She hoped her voice wasn't shaking. 'And friends. Plenty of them! I don't need you and Michael. You've never bothered with me before anyway so I don't know why you're starting now!'

Gillian cut a look at Michael. 'Beats me. I'm not trying to fill the shoes of a dead man.'

'What?'

'Gillian! Enough!'

Michael took a step forward and for a horrible moment Julia thought the whole thing was going to come to blows, but Gillian just turned to her and said, almost triumphantly, 'You'll be back yet.'

She turned on one emaciated heel and walked off.

There was going to be a heat wave. The weatherman had said so on the local radio news at noon. Not that you could believe a word out of the mouths of them usually, but today Grace was inclined to believe they were right. She felt almost giddy as she sat on Frank's manicured grass verge on the side of the road, her bare feet tucked up under her, and her face turned to the midday sun.

A passing car hooted at her. She waved boldly back at it. She had always been brought up to know that waving at cars or trucks or building sites was a cheap thing to do. But it seemed finicky to worry about that now, after kissing a backpacker on the lawn last night.

Her mobile phone beeped. A text message, from Ewan.

Missing you
It's true
Disney is blue
Without You

It wasn't one of his better ones. But it was enough to make her throat tighten with guilt.

Still, Adam was leaving this afternoon. It was just as well. There was no telling what she might do in bare feet and a heat wave (what had he meant, about having a few minutes alone with her before they parted?).

As though to banish any temptation, she read Ewan's poem again, slowly. It was quite sweet, really. And there was another bit at the end; she hadn't scrolled down far enough.

PS Did you pack mosquito repellent?

If that wasn't just typical of him! He'd only wanted to know about the mosquito repellent all along! The love poem was just to soften her up!

Once, when he had forgotten her birthday, to her great hurt and consternation, he had sent a funny poem in the post to her every day for seventeen days until she had eventually caved in, wet-eyed with laughter.

'You see – you love me really,' he had said. Well, yes. But somehow that didn't excuse him any more.

Maybe there were some people who should never have got married at all. She wasn't talking about *herself* – look at her organisational abilities, for heaven's sake! Her sensitivity to the needs of others! Her willingness – her blind eagerness – to mother a whole group of males, whether they were her offspring or not. She was perfect marriage material, she thought gloomily, and she had no one to blame for that except herself. (She could also whip up the lightest batch of scones in the country when the mood took her.)

No, she had meant Ewan. There was a man who, left to his own devices, could actually do very well. There would be no female around to whinge about his absentmindedness, which would grow and mature over the years until it achieved mythical status: 'Oh, Ewan Tynan? Gas man! For the birds!' People in the advertising industry would swap amusing stories about him in the pub. He would win lucrative jobs purely on the strength of having lost his car in an underground carpark two years ago – for surely somebody that kooky must be a genius?

She could see it now: his hair would grow long and he would wear handy non-crease T-shirts with clever slogans on the front. After about two years he would look exactly like Bob Geldof, and he would live in a city-centre apartment that he would never clean and he would develop a short list of easy-to-prepare dishes, such as macaroni cheese and omelettes. Every six months or so he would go on a date with someone from the advertising world: a slim, blonde woman as clever as him, and they would eat Japanese food and then sleep together. But, from what Grace had seen of them, most women in the advertising world were too busy to take on 'challenges', and so would be unavailable when Ewan rang for a second date, and he would be saddened (but only briefly) and he would pour the experience into whatever project he was working on, which would go on to win numerous prestigious awards and he would be happy.

He might miss not having children though. But he could always father a few without ever having to marry anybody, like Picasso or one of those, and he would have the best of all worlds. Wouldn't that just be like him?

She was being very harsh. Deep down she knew that he would be lost without her, aimless and adrift without the anchorage of marriage.

But the point was there was a part of Ewan that would always remain unmarried. Perhaps it was the same with all men. They seemed to have a small, hard core inside themselves that was independent and theirs alone, and that they protected fiercely against emotional demands.

Had Grace been as sensible? Had she heck! The day she'd walked up the aisle, she had willingly let herself be devoured body and soul by the twin institutions of marriage and motherhood. Women had been doing it for centuries, of course. She thought of her predecessors now: all the Beryls and Anastasias and Desdemonas – had they, like Grace, woken up some morning in their mud huts or castles, surrounded by crabby children while their husbands were off inventing wheels or practising with their bows and arrows, and thought, sod this? Had they too lustily eyed up some nubile young stable boy or farmhand with a view to taking something for themselves for a change?

A rental car screeched past her into Frank's driveway, kicking up dust into her face.

'Hello!' a man shouted at her from the driver's side. Tom or Charlie, no doubt. Annoyed, she didn't return the greeting. (Company policy was not to antagonise potential purchasers at least until the booking deposit had been paid. But she wasn't on company time today.)

The man getting out of the driver's seat looked like Sergeant Daly around the chin and the mouth but everything about him was slicker, edgier.

'You must be Tom,' Grace said, going over.

'I was the last time I looked,' he said, and she laughed politely. He jerked a thumb over to the passenger side. 'And this is Charlie. Charlie?' He peered into the car. 'For Pete's sake! There's no need to powder your nose. We're just viewing a house.'

He shook his head in despair for the benefit of Grace.

She smiled politely, anticipating that Charlie must be quite a character. Did he wear full make-up or just the trimmings?

The passenger door was thrown open and a pair of long, tanned legs swung sexily out into the road. A bejewelled hand shot forward to grip Grace's.

'Hello there! I'm Charlie.'

Charlie was a woman, of course. Grace wondered how she had got it so wrong; there was nothing masculine about Charlie from the tip of her unlikely platinum-blonde hair right down to her painted toe-nails peeking boldly from a pair of stiletto sandals. Her top was tight and low-cut, and when Charlie hiked up her bag, the top rode up to reveal a black lace G-string and a diamond belly-button stud. Grace began to understand the peculiar expression on Sergeant Daly's face earlier.

'The heat!' Charlie said dramatically, fanning her heavily made-up face with a copy of the house brochure. 'Tom, where are you going?'

He had wandered off up the driveway, putting his weight down hard every third step or so. Grace wondered whether he had a limp, or a war injury of some kind, and then she realised that he was testing the cobblestones.

'Laid down long, are they?' he asked.

'About five years.'

'Men!' Charlie said to Grace, patting her arm familiarly. 'He likes to know he's getting his money's worth. Us women tend to go more for the feel of a place, don't we?'

The back door of the rental car opened. Grace hadn't noticed a third occupant.

'This is Gavin,' Charlie announced. 'I had him when I was seventeen – didn't I, love?'

Gavin had big brown eyes and a cow's lick. 'She did,' he told Grace.

'He's thirteen now. Thirteen! I'll have to get him to lie about his age soon – won't I, love?' Charlie put an arm around him and squeezed him. He endured it, expressionless.

Grace's arms ached emptily. 'I have two ten-year-olds,' she said.

Charlie nodded and said, 'Ah!'

'Are they here?' Gavin looked around warily.

'No, no, they're in Florida with their dad.'

'Oh.'

'This guy's got a weather dial!' Tom called, seeming to find this very amusing. 'Come and have a look, Gav.'

Gavin trailed over to Tom, his sneakers not quite lifting off the ground.

Charlie looked at Grace sympathetically. 'You must miss them. Your boys.'

'Yes.' Grace blinked a bit.

'It's hard. God knows it's hard,' Charlie sighed. The timbre of her voice was slightly husky and coarse. She had probably spent a lot of money trying to sound more feminine and less like she had spent her youth in a smoky pub, which she probably had. 'But if there's one thing I've learned, it's to try and get on with him. No matter what you think of him, hide it. Bury it. Even if you hate his guts. Even if you want to stab the bastard in the eye!'

'Stab who?'

'Your hubby, of course. Are you still married to him?'

'I think so, yes.'

Charlie clucked. 'Have you considered flying out to Florida?'

'What?'

'I know, I know, maybe everything's too raw yet. But you have to think of those two boys. So you need to talk to him. Establish priorities. Promise each other that no matter how filthy the divorce might get, the boys are kept out of it.' She jerked a thumb towards Gavin. 'I drove over his dad with a jeep.'

'Tom?' Grace was shocked.

'No, no, Tom's not Gavin's dad – I meant Jimmy, my first husband. Well, we never actually got married, it's a long story. But anyway, I had the opportunity one day: there I was, in a four-wheel drive with reinforced fenders, not another sinner around. He was right there in front of me like a sitting duck – it would have looked just like an accident.' She shrugged. 'But he survived, and I got a suspended sentence. Gavin was very upset about it all. And that's when I realised that he needs his father. They'll always need their father. No matter what kind of a slimy shit he is,' she added venomously.

'Well, me and my husband, we're not actually . . .' For some reason she stopped. A simple clarification was all that was needed to put Charlie on the right track. But that would mean claiming Ewan – Ewan who had cunningly wriggled out of the kind of hard work and commitment she had invested in their family unit over the years. If he could do it, so could she.

'We're trying to get through the separation as best we can,' she murmured discreetly instead. She thought of Ewan, maybe on a ghost train or a Big Dipper at this very moment, ignorant of the fact that he had just been dumped by his wife. Maybe he was even composing another love poem to her on his mobile phone . . . Oh Lord. She must stop the lie at once. But Charlie was patting her on the arm again.

'Good on you. And it'll only get better, you know. Once you get rid of him you'll be a different person! I felt that way after all five of mine.'

Grace suddenly found herself a separated mother-of-two with divorce proceedings pending. Still, she would never see Charlie again after today, she reasoned guiltily. And it was only pretend, like her daydreams.

She felt better now. And really, it was quite invigorating to have shrugged off your entire family in one fell swoop. No more nagging or festering resentments! No more endless list-making and people taking her for granted! And she would have the bathroom all to herself in the mornings – unless it was her week to have the boys, of course.

She was getting carried away now. But the white lie somehow added to the sunshine of the day, making her feel bolder. After eleven years, she was a free woman.

'Let's start the viewing!' she cried joyously, producing a set of spare keys and sweeping forward to Frank's front door. Charlie, Tom and Gavin trailed behind her, slightly taken aback. She said, 'If you'd just bear with me while I turn the alarm off . . . not that we get many burglaries around here.'

And she was off, slipping easily into a stream of polished chatter. Had Charlie and Gavin been to Ireland before? They had, but only to Dublin and then it had rained. And what did they think of Hacketts-town so far? Not much, judging by the little look they exchanged.

'Thanks so much for showing us the house at such short notice,' Charlie told Grace.

Tom said, 'It's her job, Charlie.' He smiled at Grace to take the sting out of his words.

'I know that, honey, I'm just saying thanks. Don't forget I know what it's like to have to deal with the public.'

Tom shot an embarrassed look at Grace. 'Yes, well, that's all behind you now,' he said.

'I know,' Charlie said with a pensive little sigh. 'I'm a dancer,' she told Grace.

'Oh?'

'I don't know if you'd classify it as "dancing",' Tom muttered.

'It was dancing. I trained and everything,' Charlie said. She said to Grace, 'His dad doesn't approve.'

'I thought we had agreed we weren't going to tell him,' Tom said to her accusingly.

'I have nothing to be ashamed of, Tom Daly,' Charlie said, flapping a hand at him. But Grace thought her face went a little pink under the heavy powder. She hoped this wouldn't degenerate into a domestic. It happened sometimes.

She ushered them all through the front door. Frank had forgotten to put the lights on, and the place was gloomy and uninviting.

'Here we go!' she said brightly, to compensate. 'This is a very big entrance hall for this type of house – I'm sure you'll agree.' She gestured around in a practised flourish, drawing the eye away from the mud-coloured carpet and towards the nice high ceiling. 'There are tons of things you could do with this space – maybe put in some tall leafy plants, or a telephone unit, or just paint it a nice bright colour and go completely minimal. The good news with minimal is, it hardly costs anything.' It took a moment, as always, but then Tom gave an appreciative little chuckle.

'Minimal,' he explained to Charlie. 'As in nothing—'

'I know what it means, I'm not stupid,' Charlie said.

Grace breezed on. 'What do you think, Gavin?'

'I think it's dark,' he said.

'I agree,' said Charlie.

'We'll paint it a nice bright colour, like she says,' Tom interjected, jerking his head towards Grace.

'My name is Grace,' she said clearly. She didn't feel like blending into the wallpaper today. She was a single mother who had just come through a break-up, after all. She was a survivor! 'Let's move on to the kitchen, will we?'

She threw open the door to Frank's cold, small, bare kitchen. The smell of burnt bread hung in the air. Her smile began to feel brazen and pinned on. 'This is one of the best rooms in the house!' she declared falsely, crossing her fingers behind her back.

Tom inspected the place. 'Look — there's a door out to the back garden so you can put the rubbish out. That's handy, isn't it?'

'Yes,' Charlie said, smiling very courageously indeed for a woman who judged a place by the feel of it.

'The cooker, is it built in?' Tom wanted to know.

'Yes, it comes with the kitchen.' Grace couldn't bear the look on Charlie's face, so she added, 'Unless you wanted to buy a nice new one, of course. That might gizz the place up a bit.'

'No need,' Tom said. 'Charlie doesn't cook anyway. Or at least I'm trying to persuade her not to, eh?'

He winked at Charlie. Her smile looked a bit tight over the cheekbones.

'You don't cook either,' she said.

Go on, girl, Grace thought.

'You know,' Tom finally declared, 'I didn't think much of the place from the outside, but I'm starting to think it has a lot of potential.'

Charlie murmured something incoherent. Gavin was silent.

Grace felt it was her duty to say, 'Absolutely! It just takes imagination, that's all. And a good eye. With a small investment, you could turn this place into a . . .' She was going to say 'palace', but that would have been laughable. Then she was going to downgrade to 'gem' or 'cosy bolthole', but even those would be gross exaggerations. But hadn't nearly every word out of her mouth so far been a half-truth, or an overstatement, or a downright lie?

She stood there in Frank's grim kitchen and, not for the first time recently, she felt so compromised that she had to look at her shoes – her grubby runners, actually, poking out incongruously from under the hem of Mrs Carr's red robe. And they offered her a reprieve: she was not standing here as Grace Tynan MIAVI today, but purely and honestly as herself (if you overlooked the whopping great lie that she and Ewan were separated).

A great wave of righteousness overcame her. There was absolutely no reason why she could not present the facts and let them make up their own minds. Why not? They were adults, weren't they? They didn't need to be patronised or lied to! No, she would no longer be a mere pawn in the great property game; she would stand up for her principles and tell it like it was. Adam would approve utterly.

'Well, let's face it, the place is a total dump,' she said cheerily. 'I wouldn't pay one red penny for it myself. Now – the living-room!'

She swept off down the hall. She heard them whispering behind her.

'Did she say dump?'

'She did not say dump. She said it was . . . divine.'

'Divine? You'd have to be blind to think the place was divine!'

'Are you calling me blind?'

'Yes, well, you're calling me deaf!'

'I really think you're being very negative. We could do this place up, sell it on, make a fortune.'

'I thought we were looking for a "family home"?'

'Jesus Christ! There's no pleasing you, do you know that?'

There was more muffled conversation, then they arrived into the living-room, smiles back in place.

'So!' said Grace.

They waited expectantly for her sales spiel, but she was feeling so full of integrity now that she decided to say nothing. Not a word! She stood there benignly and let them see for themselves the brown patterned carpet, the nasty fake chandelier, the armchair with the sheen of grease on the headrest. Even Tom grew fairly quiet.

'Any questions?' she asked brightly.

'What does that side window look out onto?' Tom asked eventually.

'A brick wall,' she said.

They all laughed and the tension eased.

'No, it really does look on to a brick wall.' She kindly whipped back the heavy net curtain that she had warned Frank on pain of death to keep pulled over. Solid grey concrete looked back at them.

'It's a wall all right,' Tom said eventually.

They all considered it for another moment.

'We'll knock it down,' he added strongly. 'Plant a row of trees instead. Poplars.'

'You could try,' Grace said. 'It's a boundary wall. You'd have a hell of a job with planning permission.'

Well, there was no point in raising false hope. She thought she saw Gavin grin.

Charlie had been getting more and more worked up. 'I don't want my living-room to look out on to a boundary wall.'

'It's only the side window. The main window faces out to the road,' Tom said.

But Charlie wasn't going to back down this time. 'So I get a brick wall on one side and traffic on the other?'

Tom turned to Grace for support. 'Yeh, but the traffic is light here, isn't it? It's the middle of the country, for God's sake!'

'Not for much longer,' Grace said sympathetically. 'They're building a new motorway to Dublin.'

'You're joking.'

'I'm not. The M3. Or is it M4?'

'Yes, well, it couldn't be that near . . .'

'All the same, if I were you I'd check out the plans.' She would too.

'Thank you!' Charlie exploded. 'I'm sorry, Tom. I know how much you were hoping this place would be right. But it's just not.'

Tom threw up his hands. 'What's the matter – too basic for you? Well, don't forget I'm paying.'

Charlie's colour began to rise again. 'I don't mind basic. I do mind bringing up my child beside the M4!'

'As opposed to what? The M11 when you were living with Jimmy? Or the M6 when you shacked up with Phil? I get so confused sometimes.'

Grace stepped forward quickly. She hadn't meant to start any rows with her plain speaking. 'Perhaps the motorway might not be that near. I could check the plans for you myself—'

'It's not just the M4!' Charlie snarled at Tom. 'It's everything! The brown carpet and the poky rooms and the smell! And have you seen the bathroom? That suite is from the 60s!' To Grace: 'You're right – it *is* a dump!'

'Perhaps I've been a bit too honest,' Grace said desperately. 'It has a certain charm, if you were looking for a modest country residence . . .'

'No, no, I appreciate your honesty! Your honesty has *saved* me!' Charlie cried.

'Here we go,' Tom sighed. To Grace: 'Too much confessional TV in the afternoons. Watch TV is about all she's done since she stopped flashing her fanny in bars.'

Charlie shot him another murderous look. 'They were licensed dancing clubs! That's where we met, I'll remind you!' Then, to Grace: 'Only for you, I'd have let myself be talked into buying this kip! Into burying myself down here with a man like that! A man who only feels good when he puts other people down.'

'Oh, really?' Tom said back. 'Why didn't you say so when I was buying that great big rock for your finger last month? In fact, why don't you just give it back?'

It was like the air had been sucked out of the room. Grace watched in horrified fascination as Charlie's face took on the look of a street fighter. Gavin edged closer to Grace as Charlie's impressive bosom swelled further and she planted her balled fists on her hips. She was not a woman to be trifled with in any sense of the word.

'You know something? I'd be glad to,' she said to Tom in slow, measured words. 'I'd be delighted to! Because I'm sick of spending my life living for men. Going from one to the other. Thinking I was nothing unless I had a man on my arm, no matter how pathetic and small-minded and insecure he was! Stupidly letting myself be used and abused and put down by bullies like you!'

She spat this last bit and Tom jerked away. 'Calm down, Charlie.'

She went right on as though he hadn't opened his mouth. 'And I would have gone on doing it! Never getting up the courage to step out on my own, never learning my lesson – until I met a woman like Grace here.'

'Pardon?' Grace said.

Charlie gave her a fervent look. 'A woman who's just broken up with her husband. A woman whose kids are all the way in Florida!'

'Actually, that's not strictly true—'

'A woman who was entitled to stay at home this morning and cry in her bed but she came here to show us a house instead!'

'If I could just clarify one or two points—'

'Look at that woman!' Charlie commanded Tom. He did, meekly. 'A woman who should have been trying to shove this house down our throats! But she didn't! And God knows she could do with the commission – heading for divorce and left without even a decent set of clothes!' All eyes fell on Grace's red robe, and the scuffed runners poking out incriminatingly. 'Does she run mewling to a man to look after her? No!' Charlie was almost weeping now in admiration. 'She stands there, true to herself – which is more than I've ever done. She's an example to us all!'

The only thing missing was a trumpet fanfare to finish it all off. Everyone stood looking at Grace. She felt the weight of expectation and wondered whether she should make a little speech. Or do a cartwheel or something. Eventually she cleared her throat and said, 'Would anyone like to see the hot press?'

Tom looked to Charlie, pleading. 'Will we?'

'No,' she said.

'You know you like hot presses.'

'It's over, Tom. Take your ring and go back to London.'

He wrung his hands in agony as she twisted off the tasteless diamond engagement ring and thrust it out.

'Goodbye.'

'Charlie . . .'

'Beat it, buster!'

He seemed to realise the futility of further argument. He dug car keys from his pocket and without
looking at anybody, walked out, leaving a little frozen
tableau behind him. To underline it, Grace could hear
a clock ticking somewhere.

'Whew!' Charlie said at last. Her voice was shaky.
'Come here, sweetheart.'

She held out her arms for Gavin who walked into
them obediently. He didn't seem all that perturbed by
the drama. Possibly he was no stranger to it.

'I'm very sorry,' Grace said. She felt terribly responsible.

'No, no,' Charlie said. 'It's been coming a long time.
Lately, we just haven't been getting on. So what do I
do? I agree to marry him! Isn't that just so . . . clever.'
She was crying now, great black mascara tears into
Gavin's hair. 'Sorry, honey, sorry.'

'It's all right. I didn't like him anyway,' Gavin said
stoutly. 'Or any of the others,' he added.

Charlie eventually lifted her head and dabbed at
her swollen eyes with a tissue. 'You wouldn't have
the number of a taxi firm, would you?' she asked
Grace. 'I think there's a train leaving the station for
Dublin at three. Maybe they'll let us bring forward
our flights back to Birmingham.'

'I can drive you to the station. It's no trouble.' Grace
was desperate to make amends in any small way she
could.

'Thanks. That would be great.' Charlie gave a
watery smile. 'I thought Tom was my saviour, you

know. Finally I could stop working my ass off in cheap clubs! Finally, I wouldn't have to pay over half my earnings to that shit who owned the place. I thought this was it, no man would ever exploit me again. But Tom just put a different gloss on it.'

'What are you going to do now?' Grace ventured. 'Go back to the club?'

Charlie threw back her great mane of white hair. 'No way! I'm through with that scene. Why should the guys behind the scenes make all the money while we get groped by some fat jerk out front?'

Grace wondered should Gavin be hearing all this. But Charlie was oblivious.

'No, I'm going into management. If you can do it, Grace, I can too!'

The logic of this escaped Grace, but she didn't say anything, because Charlie had started to cry again.

'I really loved him too! The bollocks.'

Grace couldn't send her on her way in that state. 'How about we all go across the road and have a nice cup of tea?'

'I'm sure you've things to do . . .' Charlie protested.

Well, yes, but how could she possibly enjoy a romantic interlude with Adam while a devastated woman cried, watched by her young son? When Grace herself had contributed to the upset? It would take a heart of stone! (Anyhow, they might finish up their tea quickly and be gone.)

'Come on,' she said.

Ten

Nick was sitting on the front doorstep when they walked up Mrs Carr's garden path. 'Gracie!'

She was immediately suspicious. She was only ever 'Gracie' when he needed to borrow something, or when a small loan was required.

'I don't have any money on me, Nick,' she said.

He shot an embarrassed look at Charlie and Gavin. 'I'm not looking for any.'

She was filled with a sudden dread. 'Nick – have you done something to my house? Please tell me there hasn't been a fire or something!'

'Of course there hasn't!' He was in a proper huff now. 'You haven't been home in a couple of days – I came to check on you, that's all!'

She wanted to believe him, even though there was no possibility at all that this was the truth. He might have *intended* to check on her at some point but, like most other things, would never have got around to it unless something else drove him to it. Something more Nick-centred.

Beside her, Charlie loudly hissed, 'Is that him? Your husband?'

'No, no.'

'Her husband's in Florida,' Nick supplied help-fully.

'Yes, it's a shame, isn't it?' Charlie sighed. Nick looked baffled.

'Anyway!' Grace said.

'I've been trying to tell her to keep things amicable,' Charlie told Nick. 'It's hard when they're complete bastards though.'

Nick said, 'What—'

'When all you want to do is stick a ten-inch knife into his gut and twist it until he squeals like a pig. Or rip off his privates with your bare hands and chuck them into a vat of acid!'

Nick reared away in alarm. Charlie started sobbing loudly again.

Grace's remaining hopes of a final rendezvous with Adam were rapidly vanishing, so she said to Nick, 'As you can see, I'm all right. Never better! In fact I'll be home later this afternoon. So . . .' How to put this politely? 'I guess you can go on back to the house and get on with your computer studies. How are they going anyway?'

He shuffled evasively. 'Aren't you going to invite me in for a cup of tea at least?'

'No.'

'No?'

'I can't, Nick. It's not my house.'

Charlie was quick to interject, 'Oh, you should have said. We won't stay either.'

'*You* were invited in for tea?' Nick said to Charlie, wounded.

Grace threw up her hands. 'Right! Fine! Tea for everybody! Why not!'

Oblivious to the look exchanged between Charlie, Nick and Gavin, she led the way into Mrs Carr's house. The three of them sat in silence at the kitchen table looking at the row of porcelain ducks on the wall while she made big cups of tea and found an out-of-date can of coke for Gavin.

'Just the trick,' Charlie said with a sigh.

'Absolutely,' Nick said, adding, 'I haven't had a cup of tea in two days.'

Grace looked at him. 'Why not? I bought more tea bags before I left.'

He looked shifty again. 'I've been trying to cut down, that's all. Apparently too much caffeine—'

'Nick!'

'All right! There, ah, seems to be some kind of problem with the electricity.'

'Oh God.'

'It wasn't my fault! It just went off! And the electricity people said they'd be around but they haven't come yet.'

'Wonderful!' Now she was going home to a house with no power.

Charlie took a packet of Silk Cut from her bag, the extra long ones. 'Want one?' she asked Nick.

'I shouldn't really,' he said, taking one. 'I'm a singer. Well, I *was*.'

As always, that had an impact. Grace gave up any hopes of hurrying them out the door as Charlie and Gavin sat up. Nobody had ever looked at Grace like that. Except Adam.

'I knew it!' Charlie cried. 'Well, not that you were a singer – but I knew your face.'

Nick sat up eagerly. 'Did you?'

'The minute I saw you, I said to myself, there's someone dead famous!'

'She knows all the famous faces from the magazines,' Gavin said proudly. 'She recognised Adam Ant in a petrol station once, didn't you, Mum? Even without his make-up.'

'I wouldn't be that famous,' Nick admitted, adding hurriedly, 'Not in the UK anyway. Although we were quite big over there in the 90s. Well, more 1991 really. When did "Dead Dingos" enter the British charts, Grace?'

'The first week in September,' she said, tempted to add that it had exited the British charts the second week in September.

'I don't think I've heard of it . . .' Charlie ventured.

'It was from our album *Hell and Back*. Kind of along the lines of the Stones. Only more original, if I say so myself.'

The mention of the Stones did the trick. Any lingering doubts as to his rock-legend status were put to rest.

'Do you know Mick Jagger?' Gavin enquired, excited.

'Not that well in person,' Nick said with admirable understatement. 'But I met him at a party once. Lovely guy. Sound.'

'Charlie didn't really like the house. Frank's house,' Grace said quite loudly. Perhaps Charlie would tell Nick about Grace's bravery, and how she was an example to women everywhere. Perhaps Adam would come in just in time to hear it.

'Oh, let's not go there again!' Charlie said with a little laugh. She turned back to Nick eagerly. 'Have you ever played at Wembley?'

Standing by the sink holding the teapot, Grace felt herself fade. Even the silk of her robe seemed to lose some of its shimmer. She was thrown back to their teenage years, where she would hang around in the background while Nick and his friends would jam together, occasionally conferring with her about the base levels or the possibility of light refreshments.

Nick leaned back in his chair, taking a thoughtful drag of his cigarette. 'Wembley, let me think . . .'

'You haven't played Wembley,' she said clearly. 'You've never even been to Wembley. And Mick Jagger had left that party before you'd even arrived.'

She walked out, leaving Nick to bluster about how he'd met Mick at a different party; that it was hard to keep up.

Upstairs, she stripped her bed in the guest room and neatly folded the blankets away. She gathered up the sheets and towels. She would put a wash on downstairs. Then she changed out of Mrs Carr's red silky robe and back into her sensible track bottoms and T-shirt, dry from the washing line outside. In the bathroom she ran her fingers under the cold tap and ruthlessly smoothed down her hair, and found some powder to take the shine off her nose. When she was finished patting and pulling and readjusting in front of the mirror, that feverish look was gone. A neat, tidy woman looked back at her blandly. She could have been anyone.

'Who were you trying to fool anyway?' she asked her reflection. She was a thirty-four-year-old mother with the first sign of wrinkles, and a job in residential property. She could run around in bare feet in a country town for all she was worth, pretending that she was an FBI agent without a tie in the world, but at the end of the day she had a carefully constructed life to go back to: a life that involved too many other people, with too many commitments and too much emotional investment already made, and to stray from it now would surely only lead to heartache. Anyway, it wasn't as though she had anything better lined up.

Adam was waiting outside the bathroom when she emerged.

'There's a whole bunch of strangers sitting in the kitchen,' he complained.

'Yes.'

'Smoking and laughing and drinking beer.'

'I didn't give them any beer.' Nick must have found some. He was like a ferret that way.

Adam looked her up and down. 'Why have you changed back into those clothes?' It was obvious from his face that he didn't like them.

'Because this is the way I dress,' she said evenly.

His eyes were on her face now. Belligerent, nearly. 'Your freckles. They're gone. What's that stuff you have on your cheeks?'

'Make-up. Adam, I was wondering whether you would mind leaving now?'

'What?' He was taken aback.

'I need to tidy up the house before Mrs Carr gets back tomorrow,' she said blandly. 'Most B & Bs require people to be out by eleven. You're way over.'

'Cut the crap, Grace. I thought we had an arrangement.'

'Did we?' Her expression didn't change. 'Well, unfortunately I can't keep it. I need to get back to Dublin.'

He looked at her for a long moment. 'We haven't done anything illegal yet, you know.'

She felt her cheeks explode into colour beneath the powder. 'Of course we haven't! I didn't suggest that for a second! I mean, we only kissed! I don't mean "only" . . .' She took a breath. 'The thing is, kissing is not illegal in this country. It certainly might be in other countries – some cultures aren't that keen on married people having sex with people other than their spouses – but not in Ireland. Morally speaking, that's different; that's where it might get a bit murky. But regarding the law, we're in the clear.'

Adam was looking a bit surprised. 'I was actually talking about me and Martine and Joey.'

'Oh. Oh!'

She felt faint. Imagine! Rabbitting on about them having sex – she had actually said the word sex to him – when all along he had been talking about something else. He must think she was obsessed with him. But he seemed preoccupied with something else – to her relief or chagrin, she wasn't sure which.

'We're just in the planning stages of it,' he clarified.

'Of something . . . illegal?' she said. The word was

so delicious, so suggestive of danger and excitement that she had her 'motel feeling' again. (She was starting to wonder whether it might be time to seek help.)

'Well, yes, probably,' he admitted. 'It's the only way to get the message across. *I* think anyway. As for Martine . . .' His lip curled a bit.

'What message?' Grace whispered.

'You mean you didn't overhear us in the café?'

'No.' She thought of his habit of always taking his shoes off. 'We're not talking religion here, I hope?'

'God, no.' Then he looked worried. 'What, do I look like some kind of Jesus freak?'

'No, no.' Right now he looked good enough to eat. The walk back from town in the heat had given him a kind of a delicious all-over moistness that on other men would just look sweaty. She thought that she would quite like to lick him like an ice cream.

'Go on,' she said.

He moved closer. His breath smelled of coffee and Minnie's apple crumble. 'This is highly sensitive information.'

Illegal *and* highly sensitive. She started to pant a bit now, like a dog, and hoped he wouldn't notice. 'You can trust me,' she managed.

He looked over his shoulder; he obviously felt that this conversation was a little surreal to be having outside Mrs Carr's bathroom. He took her hand – she nearly swooned – and led her across the hallway and into his bedroom. He closed the door behind them a touch dramatically, and for a moment she thought that maybe he was going to kiss her again. In fact, she had just raised her face expectantly, praying her lips hadn't gone all nasty and dry in the heat, when he walked off on her and began to roll a cigarette.

'Want one?'

'Ah, no thanks.'

'You're right too. Wish I'd never started,' he said gloomily.

The situation had lost some of its momentum. Grace began to suspect that she was going to be disappointed at his 'illegal activity'. After all, what could a bunch of backpackers really get up to in terms of badness? Was he going to reveal some kind of a visa scam to her? Or a cunning scheme to defraud Irish Rail?

'Adam, this is nothing to do with... banks or anything, is it?' she asked, hopefully. She might be able to give him a few tips; she already had some experience in thieving under her belt, after all.

He gave a short laugh. 'Ever the capitalist.'

'Shut up,' she said, and went to leave.

'Grace. Wait.' He seemed surprised. 'I'm sorry, okay?'

She turned on him. 'But you're not. You do it all the time – making me out to be some kind of a meaningless person with a meaningless life!' The final insult was to get her into his bedroom and, instead of trying to ravish her, he was rolling cigarettes instead!

'I never said you were meaningless,' he said.

'Selfish, then. Greedy. Just because I don't display my disgust at the world by dropping out of college and bucking the system at every opportunity. Just because I don't go around with a trendy hairstyle sneering at people who sell houses!'

'You sell houses?' From the look on his face you'd think she'd confessed to supplying crack to school-children.

'Yes!' she said, her head high. 'Hundreds of them! Thousands! What, did you think I had a rich husband sitting at home bankrolling me while I amused myself by dabbling in B & Bs?' He obviously had. 'Like everybody else in this world – well, apart from you – I have a job! I earn money! Most of which goes in taxes to pay for other people's pensions, of course. And unemployment benefit, and hospital beds for old people with foot injuries!'

'It was your choice, Grace.'

Was it? She supposed it was. Or, she had no one else to blame at any rate.

'I'm sorry I don't live for my principles, Adam. But I can't afford to.'

'You think I can?' he snapped. 'Oh, go home, Grace.'

'What?'

'Get into that big swanky car out there and go back to your tax-paying life. That's where you were sneaking off to, weren't you? Before I came in and caught you?'

'You didn't "catch" me. I was going to wait for you.'

'Liar. You were probably going to hide over in Frank's house until I'd gone and then you'd have come back and locked up for Mrs Carr.'

She flushed. The thought had occurred to her. 'I was going to leave you a note!' She had been, too.

'A nice-knowing-you note?'

'Well . . .'

'A fuck-off note, you mean.' His customary coolness had evaporated and his tan didn't look as
healthy.

'Oh, Adam,' she said. 'I didn't think there was any
point in . . . well, meeting up again. This way things
are cleaner.'

'Cleaner?'

'I thought—'

'*Cleaner*? What the hell is that supposed to mean?'

'All right, possibly I could have chosen a better
word!' She took a breath. 'Look, what happened last
night was . . .'

'Please don't say it was "nice".' He took such a long
drag of his cigarette that she worried for his lungs.

'We were alone, we'd had wine, it happened. I just
think it's better not to complicate matters further.'

He exhaled and watched her through a thick cloud
of blue smoke. 'Don't want to take the risk of things
getting messy, yeh? A kiss is safe enough, but we
wouldn't want to go rocking the boat, is that it?'

She didn't say anything.

'What's the matter, Grace? Why are you so afraid of
letting your hair down? You think somebody's going
to come along and slap your wrist for enjoying yourself?'

'You're presuming a lot,' she said. 'That I would
want to let my hair down with you in the first
place!'

She had intended that to put him in his box. She
didn't like the way he was making her feel; always
questioning her, pricking her conscience. It was easy

for him. Nothing in the world holding him back except a girlfriend who didn't seem to mind what he got up to.

'Then why are you still here?' he asked.

Silence. Then she heard laughter from the kitchen below. She wondered whether Nick and Charlie could somehow overhear the entire conversation and were chuckling their heads off, much the way Ewan had on the phone the other day: Grace, and a twenty-year-old! Grace, being offered hot sex in a run-down lodging house!

Well, yes, actually, she answered them all rather defiantly. Just because they only saw one side of her didn't mean there wasn't another one! Even if it only had fledging status yet; even if it was some kind of odd mish-mash of amateur grocery thief with career aspirations in either law enforcement or porn film-making. Put like that, she sounded very interesting, she thought. Or she could be.

'Well,' he drawled mockingly. 'Are you staying or are you going?'

'Staying.'

'What?' He was obviously not expecting such decisiveness.

'I said I'm staying. I want to let my hair down.'

'Uh, right . . .'

'To be corrupted.'

'Well, now, let's not take that too literally—'

She pushed him back down on the bed. 'I hope you won't disappoint me.'

He looked nervous. And so well he should.

240

In the car on the way home Julia thought about burst pipes. There was no telling how much damage a burst pipe could do, Frank often warned her. He'd told her of at least one case where the water level had risen so high that the family had practically had to escape in an ark. Julia didn't know a damned thing about burst pipes except that you should always turn the water off at some point. The mains – yes, that was it. Then she realised that she didn't even know where the tap for the mains *was*.

She was being silly. It wasn't even winter yet. There was no need to worry about burst pipes.

Then she thought about birds. Thrushes. One had found its way into the living-room three summers ago when they'd gone away for the weekend. It had flown demented around the room, leaving a bloody trail across her furniture before dying in a corner under a chair. Julia was absolutely sure now that she had left the front bay window open in the living-room the day of the shotgun. What if a bird had found its way in?

Her mind flooded with other things now, frightening things . . . the attic trap door that was loose, and that might bang tonight if there was a breeze; the backyard sensor light that had been broken for ages now and would not snap on to warn her of intruders. And the uneven floorboards in the living-room that she might trip over in the dark, and she would lose her crutches in the fall and she wouldn't be able to reach the phone—

'She didn't mean those things, you know,' said Michael beside her.

Julia gave herself a little shake. 'Pardon?'

'Gillian. She just said them in the heat of the moment.'

People like Gillian never said anything in the heat of the moment. Everything was carefully thought out beforehand and saved up until the appropriate moment. Cold, that's what she was.

'I don't care whether she did or she didn't. I'll cope just fine on my own,' Julia said loudly.

Michael sighed. 'How are you going to be fine? You've just had an operation, for heaven's sake! Naturally we're worried.'

'I'm sorry that I seem to be such a bother to everybody,' she said stiffly.

'Oh, Mammy. It's just that it's time to face the fact that you're not a young woman any more.'

A hearse pulled out in front of them. Brilliant. Julia tried to avert her eyes from the coffin inside. That could have been her in there, had she taken those sleeping pills. She had gone as far as imagining her own post-mortem – it had a certain drama about it – but she had never had the nerve to project herself actually into a coffin. There was something a bit creepy about it. The next stage, after all, was a deep pit, and a lot of hungry worms.

Death. It was everywhere. How could she have wanted it so badly?

'Anyway, here's what I think we should do,' Michael said.

Again Julia dragged her mind back to the matter at hand – which still appeared to be the fact that she was a problem for everybody. 'I'll drop by on the way to work every day, and then again on the way home, okay? And I'll try to get over at lunch-times some days as well – I'll tell Jean I have a meeting or something.'

'I don't want you putting yourself out like that.' She started to feel guilty.

'We'll have to hire someone local to come by and do a bit of housework and cooking during the day. I'll sort that out today after I drop you home.'

'There's no need. If I do want someone, I can hire them myself.'

'But you can't. You're on crutches. How are you even going to get down to the shop to put up a notice? I mean, you don't even drive, Mammy.'

She had that horrible sense of foreboding again, and she wanted him to stop outlining all the things she couldn't do any more, all the dangers that lay in wait for injured elderly women living on their own.

She realised that they were driving down Hacketts-town main street now. In a minute they would be home.

'I don't want a stranger in my house,' she said. She saw the dead bird again, bluebottles swarming over its corpse.

Impatiently, Michael turned down Bridge Road. 'You don't want someone to live with you. You don't want to come and live with me and Gillian. So what *do* you want, Mammy? Because we've all tried to please you but it just won't do!'

She saw her house now. It looked decrepit and old and unloved.

'I didn't ask for anyone to please me,' she said. The

broken shutter on the upstairs bedroom seemed a bit menacing somehow and she was afraid she was going to start crying or something.

Michael swung into her driveway and cut the engine. He turned to her. 'The whole idea of you coming back here today on a pair of crutches is ridiculous! At least stay with us until your foot is healed. Then you can come home.'

'She just wants me to come crawling back, that's all!'

'Stop it, Mammy.'

'Well, I won't come crawling back. Because I have my own plans made!' she ended up saying.

'What plans?' Michael said. She was caught now. 'That guy Frank across the road, you mean? The one you tried to shoot? He's going to come look after you, is he?'

Julia's fists balled helplessly. 'No . . .'

'Who, then?'

She was rescued by a cigarette butt, which landed on the bonnet of the car. It sizzled happily on Michael's paintwork for a moment before dying with a little puff of smoke.

'What the hell?' he said, astonished.

They looked around for the source of this outrage. And they saw that the living-room bay window was wide open.

'Burglars,' Michael said, ashen-faced.

But then a loud burst of laughter rolled out from the windows. Burglars with a sense of humour? Julia held her breath. Somehow she didn't feel in the slightest bit afraid.

There was another sound now. Music.

'They're playing your old gramophone, Mammy!' Michael said. 'The nerve of them!'

'Elvis,' Julia murmured. She was thrown back years, to the parties she and JJ used to hold. 'Heartbreak Hotel'. She hadn't heard it in decades.

Michael said beside her, 'You know, it's more likely that they're squatters than burglars.'

'Yes, shhh, Michael.' She wished they would turn the music up.

Then the front door opened and a rather tartylooking young blonde woman emerged from Julia's house. She was clutching a flagon of cider in one arm. The other arm was wrapped firmly around a tall, lanky fellow in leather trousers and disgracefully long hair. He had a guitar slung over his shoulder.

'Daddy's guitar!' Michael said in horror. 'They've stolen it!'

'I think they're just borrowing it,' Julia said, watching as the pair sauntered across her lawn. The man started to strum the guitar. He wasn't bad. The woman carefully laid herself out on the grass to the best possible advantage.

'Don't you worry, Mammy,' Michael said grimly. 'I'm going to ring the police. They'll get rid of these two in no time.'

But someone else was coming out of the house now: a young boy with floppy hair, who was eating a Snickers bar.

'Gavin!' the woman called over, waving to him.

Michael scuttled down lower in his seat. 'There

could be a whole commune of them in there! Lock your door, Mammy,' he ordered. 'We're driving down to the police station. There's no sense in confronting them ourselves.' But when the leather-clad guy on the lawn lit up a cigarette, Michael couldn't contain himself. He beeped the horn angrily, rolled down his window, and shouted, 'You burned my car, you lout!'

The pair on the lawn looked over laconically.

'Sorry, man.'

Michael's eyes bulged. He beeped again, very angrily, and reached for the ignition key.

'Wait, Michael,' Julia said.

Someone else was coming to the door, obviously alerted by all the commotion. It was a young man, who looked a bit like those rap fellows on MTV with his hair in those dreadlocks, and he was only half-dressed. He looked out at the car.

Then a woman pushed up behind him. She was patting down her hair, and adjusting her clothing, and she looked a bit bright around the eyes. Possibly they were drunk too.

The woman said something to the young man. Then she came out of the house on her own and walked down the path to the car. She shielded her eyes against the sun and peered in very tentatively through Michael's open window.

'Mrs Carr?' she said rather limply. 'I thought you weren't due back until tomorrow.'

Michael was further astounded. So was Julia. 'Don't tell me you . . . *know* this woman?' he said to Julia.

246

'What? I've never seen her before in my . . .'

But she had. As she looked into the woman's eyes she knew exactly where she had seen her before – in her own kitchen, at the other end of a shotgun. Her tormentor! And here she was again, in Julia's house – how had she even got in? – and she was hosting some kind of a wild party behind her back!

It would only take a single word from Julia and the police would descend for a second time in a week on Bridge Road. But the other woman looked back at her, seeming to know Julia's thoughts, and silently begging her not to go through with it. Well, if Julia was going to save Grace Tynan's bacon, then Grace Tynan could bloody well save hers.

'Of course I know her,' she amended to Michael. 'This is Grace. She's the person I was telling you was going to look after me – isn't that right, Grace?'

There was a brief moment in which Grace Tynan and Julia locked eyes and got each other's measure. Then Grace Tynan said to Michael, 'That's right.'

Michael wasn't stupid. 'Are you telling me this was all *arranged*?'

'It was all very last minute,' Grace Tynan lied easily to him, and Julia was very impressed. They would get along just fine.

'So you can go on home now, Michael,' Julia said, energetically throwing open the passenger door. 'And be sure to tell Gillian that I won't be changing my mind.'

Grace Tynan was quickly around to take Julia's arm, to position the crutches, to retrieve her overnight bag from the back seat.

But she wasn't going to get off *that* easily. Julia found her balance, and then leaned over and said in a voice that only Grace could hear, 'You have a lot of explaining to do.'

Eleven

'Do you ever think about it, Grace?' Natalie asked three weeks later.

'What?'

'Having another baby.'

'Me?'

'I don't know what you find so amusing.'

'Sorry. It's just not something on my mind at the moment.' She was stirring a pot on Mrs Carr's stove and looking out the kitchen window at Adam on the lawn, and debating whether or not to tap on the window and ask him to pick her a handful of basil. He would uncurl his long, brown, muscular body and come striding across the grass, with his sexy smile—

'You could easily do it, you know,' Natalie chattered on. 'You're still only thirty-four. And there's Jamie and Neil practically raised – they're no trouble any more. In fact, they could help you with the new baby!'

Suddenly it had become *the* new baby, as though it were already a probability.

'I don't think so.'

'Why not? We could meet up in the afternoons and

go to the zoo and things – it'd stop me going mad,' Natalie begged, rubbing her huge pregnant belly. '*Rosie!*'

Over by the door, two-year-old Rosie was systematically pushing the contents of Natalie's handbag through Mrs Carr's cat flap.

'So I'd be having a baby for you then?' Grace enquired.

'And for Ewan. I'd bet he'd love another baby,' Natalie said.

Ewan had said nothing about babies when he'd rung from Florida last night. In fact, he had complained that he was starved of adult company, so it was pretty certain that he felt little need to procreate any time soon.

Natalie saw that perhaps she had been too optimistic. 'You could talk him around,' she suggested.

'Why would I want to do that?' (She probably could, too.)

Natalie flopped back in her chair crossly. 'You were saying only a few weeks back that you were at a bit of a loss these days! That you were thinking of taking up art classes.'

'You suggested that. Not me. I don't want another baby, Natalie.'

She had never spoken the words out loud; perhaps she hadn't made up her mind until now. It wasn't any big thing; the decision just hung there for a moment then floated away, leaving her with a pleasant, light feeling. Irresponsibility suited her, she was beginning to think.

'Well!' Natalie shrugged as though Grace were

being very selfish. 'I mean, what else are you going to do with yourself?'

'Natalie, Rosie's managed to get her head through the cat flap. We don't want her to be garrotted, do we?' Grace said kindly.

'Oh!' Natalie sprang to the rescue. Just in the nick of time too – the back door burst open and Julia hobbled in on one crutch.

'Two more for dinner, Grace.'

'Oh, Julia!' The numbers were up to fourteen already – most of them were with Adam on the lawn out there. They were having some kind of a strategy meeting, by the looks of it.

'I'll cook if you want,' Julia said airily, and Grace suspected she only offered because she knew full well that it wouldn't be accepted. Judging from her culinary efforts so far, Julia was not a woman who took all that well to a kitchen. Or to any kind of domestication, really.

'Where's your other crutch?' Grace enquired.

Julia shook her head at Natalie. 'Nag, nag, nag! That's all she ever does.'

'I *am* supposed to be looking after you,' Grace pointed out. This included cajoling Julia into keeping her out-patients appointments at the hospital, keeping tabs on her medication, and ordering her into bed for an early night. Looking after two boisterous boys was tame in comparison, and she had told Ewan that when he suggested during one of their phone-calls that she had the lesser of two evils.

'And isn't it time for your exercises?' Grace added.

'Yes, yes, later – Martine is waiting for me.

Cheerio!' Julia poked the back door open again with her crutch and was gone.

A lovely cool breeze drifted in from outside, along with the muffled sounds of a radio they were playing on the lawn.

The Government has yet to decide whether to provide naval support for the controversial shipment of MOX nuclear fuel en route from Japan to Wales and due to enter Irish waters at the weekend ...

'Rosie! Come back here!' Natalie grabbed the child and kicked the back door shut. 'Here, Grace, what really happened with that guy at Frank's house?'

'What about it?'

'Well, him ringing up Head Office to make an official complaint about you.' Her eyes widened. 'You didn't really call his house a dump, did you?'

'Oh, yes,' Grace said cheerfully.

She could feel Natalie's eyes on her back for a long moment, assessing. Well, perhaps the kaftan Julia had lent her was a little big. But the material was lovely and light, and it cleverly concealed the fact that she wasn't wearing any bra (so constricting and sweaty in the summer. She didn't know how she'd ever worn one, really. They weren't natural.).

Natalie hadn't noticed yet, which was surprising. She had already commented on Grace's hair, which she'd said could do with a trim. Good thing she wasn't privy to Grace's armpits, or indeed her legs, nestling cosily against each other under the kaftan now, gloriously unshaven.

'Can you stay for dinner?' Grace asked. 'It's such a nice evening that we're going to eat outside.'

'No,' Natalie said quite definitely, with a little look out towards the back lawn. 'Are all those people actually living here?'

Grace gave a little laugh. 'Lord, no. Just Adam, obviously. And Charlie and young Gavin – they share the third guest room. And Nick stays over quite often, of course, now that he and Charlie have fallen madly in love.' She looked out the back window too at the crowd scattered across the lawn. 'And you've met Martine – and those are her two French colleagues by the shed – and Joey – but they all live in tents out there, we hardly see them at all. Julia doesn't seem to mind. I don't know who the rest of them are, to be honest. But Adam would know them.'

Natalie was giving her That Look again. Well, she'd got a bit of a start when she'd arrived earlier to be confronted by two new-age types squatting on the stairs eating stew, and a skeleton sitting in a wheel-chair wearing a mask of Tony Blair. Grace had explained that the wheelchair belonged to Julia, who had never really needed it in the first place, preferring her crutches. Grace wasn't sure who Tony Blair belonged to; most likely they intended to use him in the demonstration. She had neglected to mention that the skeleton was plastic, now that she thought about it.

Possibly Natalie was thinking about it too, because she suddenly burst out, 'Grace, I'm worried about you!'

'Are you?' Grace was surprised. She had been expecting something along these lines, of course, but not with such force. Surely a kaftan and unshaven legs weren't that remarkable? 'Why?'

'Why? Well, you're not yourself!'

'In what way?' Interested, she looked up from the sauce, which was reducing nicely. Soon it would be time to put on the pasta.

Natalie wasn't going to mince her words. 'Look at you – drifting barefoot around someone else's kitchen like Mother Earth, cooking up a big pot of food for a bunch of weirdos!'

'At least they appreciate it,' Grace said mildly.

'It's not just the cooking thing!'

'What then? My hair, is it?' Grace said helpfully. 'I think it kind of suits me like this. It's softer, don't you think?'

'It's matted. And Grace, you're not even wearing a bra!'

She *had* noticed, of course.

In the garden Adam was picking basil. He had read her mind, bless him. It was quite uncanny sometimes – look at how he had brought her up a cup of tea in bed this morning before she'd even known she wanted one! And just last night, when she'd mentioned after dinner that she had a hankering for something sweet, he had slipped out for half an hour and returned with a big tub of Ben & Jerry's ice cream (double chocolate-chip cookie) from the Spar, and had presented it to her as proudly as a cat laying a dead mouse at her feet.

Nobody had ever tried so hard to woo her. Well, perhaps Ewan had, way back when they were dating – she distinctly remembered him recording a whole tape of love songs off the radio for her, to illustrate how he felt. She wondered now if he had been too mean to buy a compilation album.

She was being unfair, of course. But she found herself doing that a lot – concentrating on all his negative points in order to justify her own behaviour while he was away: the way he made sucking noises through his teeth at mealtimes, for example; his habit of laying his hand on the small of her back, as though he were resting it or something.

And look at the way he had implied for years that she was smothering the boys! All those little sighs, the way he threw his eyes to heaven behind her back whenever she happened to wonder where they were – and they gone five hours! Any responsible parent would worry. But Ewan, with his little looks and throw-away comments, managed to imply that she was a fusspot, one of those over-anxious parents that sometimes featured in his ads on the television, and who always seemed to be the butt of some joke.

Take that ad of his for microwave chips last year! The whole concept had revolved around two children trying to dupe their mother – their hard-working, caring mother – who had made a healthy casserole for tea, but of course they wanted chips. Who walks into the kitchen just then? Dad! He has the brilliant idea of fabricating a phone call to get Mum offside, and the minute her back is turned, the kids and Dad give the casserole to the dog, microwave up three big plates of chips, and snigger amongst themselves as they stuff their faces.

It hadn't occurred to Grace at the time, but it was quite obvious to her now that the whole thing was modelled on her home life. *Their* home life, with Ewan and the boys co-conspirators against boring, fussy Mum. The woman in the ad even looked like Grace! Oh, she had never felt so betrayed in all her life – by her own family! So used, such an object of ridicule! The three of them were probably in some fast-food joint in Florida right now, gorging themselves on double cheeseburgers and laughing to each other at how they had cunningly managed to escape Mum for a whole month. Well, let them! Let them have fat-induced heart attacks for all she cared! She was through being their minder!

Adam suddenly looked up from the herb garden and smiled at her. And it was a smile so full of respect and warmth and liking that she wanted to curl up into a little ball and start to purr or something. He would never refuse one of her healthy casseroles in favour of chips.

When she turned away from the window, Natalie was lying in wait.

'You see? This is exactly what I mean!'

'What?'

'It's like you've gone into some little world of your own! Look at you – you'd prefer to gaze out the window than talk to me!'

'That's not true.' The view was certainly good, though.

'Isn't it? I've told you all about the cutbacks in Head Office, I've asked you about Frank's house – I even told you about Liam shagging the new girl in accounts. And you're acting like you just don't care any more!'

'I'm on my holidays, Natalie – maybe I don't want to talk about work.'

Natalie was not appeased in the slightest. 'You don't want to talk about babies, either. Or what I should do for Paul's fortieth birthday party.'

'I gave some suggestions!'

'Organising a party at Stonehenge?'

'One of the girls out there was saying it's a fabulous experience. And very few overheads either.'

Natalie looked at her as though she had lost her marbles. Grace knew that if she didn't put her mind at rest, she would tell the whole office that Grace was having some kind of a breakdown.

'Look, I've just learned how to relax, Natalie, that's all. To reassess things. To take time out for me. It's not a crime – in fact it's a very healthy thing, you should try it.'

'Oh stop it!' Natalie cried. 'You've done something silly, haven't you!'

'What?'

'Don't look at me like that. You told me on the phone a couple of weeks ago that you were thinking of it!'

'I was only joking you.'

Natalie looked at her very suspiciously. 'Are you having an affair, Grace?'

Grace gave a little laugh. It was very convincing. 'Hardly,' she said.

'What, then?' Natalie cried. 'Is it that gang out there, then? Have you joined them?'

'Who?'

Natalie jerked a thumb towards the lawn. 'The anti-capitalists!'

'They're actually anti-nuclear,' Grace clarified. Although a good few of them were anti-capitalist as well. And vegetarian. Mealtimes could be quite tricky sometimes, trying to keep everyone happy.

Natalie pitched forward in her chair, very serious, and began with the inflammatory words, 'Grace, please don't take offence here.'

'I'll certainly try not to,' Grace assured her.

'I know that sometimes you feel that maybe you married too young. That you didn't experience all the things you could have. And I'm sure all this . . .' She waved a hand rather distastefully at Grace's bare, dirty feet, 'is some kind of delayed reaction to missing out on your youth, but – are you laughing at me?'

'No, no. Please go on.'

'All I'm saying is that there are other ways of rediscovering yourself. Of finding personal fulfilment.'

'Such as art classes?'

Natalie ignored this. 'You don't have to go to extremes, Grace. I'm sure what they're doing is . . . laudable, but at the same time, it'd be a shame if you looked back on this period in your life and had regrets.'

'I certainly intend to regret nothing,' Grace declared.

Natalie looked more alarmed. 'If you can't think of yourself, at least think of the boys! They're at a very impressionable age – you don't want them to be embarrassed to be seen with you, do you?'

'Bit late for that. They're already embarrassed to be seen with me. Up the revolution!'

Rosie clapped her fat hands enthusiastically and gurgled. Natalie flopped back in the chair, bemused and defeated, and Grace hid a smile. She'd only said that last bit to rile her.

But it wasn't fair to tease her like that. Natalie was looking out for her, in her own way. It was strange to think that she herself had thought like that until very recently: so rigidly!

'Look, I'm not joining their campaign, Natalie. I don't have much to do with them at all, if you must know, apart from cook the odd meal. It's too much like hard work.' It was far more enjoyable to lie out on the lawn in the afternoon sunshine with a book on gardening, which Julia was encouraging her to take an interest in. She had planted her very first tomatoes yesterday, and they had celebrated with a bottle of white wine. The revolutionaries had traipsed back from town, hot and tired, to find Grace sprawled in a deckchair asleep, her mouth open catching flies. What use are you to the campaign, Adam had said. None at all, Grace had replied, happily.

'How are Ewan and the boys?' Natalie enquired eventually, obviously striving for a normal topic of conversation.

'Having a whale of a time. They fly back on Sunday.'

'Right. Good.' Then, 'Does he know you're not at home?'

'Sorry?'

'Ewan. He must be wondering what's going on. I mean, you've been here three whole weeks, Grace . . .'

'He is fully aware that I have moved in here temporarily to look after Mrs Carr. And Ewan, I would remind you, is not at home either.'

'No need to be so defensive,' Natalie huffed. 'I was just asking.'

Adam arrived in with the basil, bare-chested and brown from the sun. He looked like an advertisement for milk, or something equally wholesome.

'Hi there, Natalie.' He had remembered her name. But he would, of course.

'Adam,' she said, immediately coy. Honestly! It seemed that good-looking anti-nuclear activists were okay in her book.

'And who's this?' Adam said, bending over Rosie, whose busy fingers immediately tried to grab one of his dreadlocks.

'Rosie,' Natalie said, proud as punch. 'She's two. Say hello to Adam, Rosie!' But Rosie refused. She refused to speak at all, which caused Natalie no end of worry.

'Excuse me,' Grace murmured, taking the basil to the sink. It was better to get out of Adam's vicinity. Especially when she wanted to grab him and crush him to her breasts. *That* would certainly cause a stir in the office.

She stifled a giggle, and there was Natalie looking at her again.

'I was just saying to Grace that she should think about going home,' Natalie said to Adam in a low voice – as though Grace were not there! (She understood now what Julia meant when she said that she had felt invisible since she'd been about sixty.)

'You said nothing of the sort,' she said.

'Well, I was thinking it, I just didn't get around to saying it.' Natalie turned to Adam again. 'Mrs Carr looks absolutely fine to me. Fully recovered.'

'Apart from the metal pins in her foot,' Grace remarked. 'And the crutches.'

'Is there really any need for Grace to hang around here any longer?' Natalie asked Adam. 'Mrs Carr is one thing, but that anti-nuclear lot out there on the lawn . . .'

'I'm actually one of that "lot",' Adam said.

'Oh – yes, of course!' To make up for her slip, Natalie smiled brightly at him. 'So, tell me, what kind of work do you do anyway? Handing out leaflets, that kind of thing?'

'Leaflets certainly form one part of the campaign,' Adam said. His voice was no longer so friendly.

Natalie couldn't take the hint, of course. 'I used to be involved in something like that in college. Do you remember I was telling you, Grace? We had such a laugh!'

'You laughed about nuclear disarmament?' Adam enquired. There was a faint redness on his cheek-bones now. Under her breath Grace started to hum 'I'm in the Mood for Dancing'.

'Ours was more trees really. How to stop the multi-nationals cutting them down to make cornflakes boxes. And paper hand-towels – that was the big one in our day. It took five trees to make a single paper hand-towel or something like that.' Then she frowned. 'But hang on, that seems like an awful lot. Maybe it was one tree made five towels? And a cornflakes box? Oh, I can't remember. Do you do trees as well as the nuclear stuff?'

Grace had the sensation of watching a bluebottle fly into the path of a rolled-up newspaper. But Natalie was such a prattler sometimes! On the other hand, Adam was so terribly idealistic. Grace's natural tendency was to intervene; she had a great urge now to march over and say, 'I will not stand for any fighting in this house today!' and send the two of them to their bedrooms to cool off.

But she wasn't wearing her mother hat in Mrs Carr's house. She wasn't quite sure what hat she was wearing, but it didn't involve solving other people's difference of opinion, and so she reached for the chopping-board instead.

'No, we don't "do trees" as well,' Adam said behind her. 'We're too busy trying to close a nuclear plant less than a hundred miles from your back door. Because if there's an accident or explosion tomorrow morning, and the wind is blowing the wrong way, then there's a significant chance that you'll contract cancer within twenty years, or that little Rosie here will suffer from thyroid problems or leukaemia and will go on to have genetically deformed babies. If she lives that long, that is.'

Dead silence. Grace peeked over her shoulder. Natalie was rather white, and clutching Rosie so hard that the child began to whimper.

'Are you sure you won't stay for dinner, Nat?' she said, kindly. 'There's plenty.'

'I can't,' Natalie said, getting to her feet very quickly. 'If Rosie gets out of her routine at all she's a terror.'

'Okay.' Grace followed her to the kitchen door. 'You'll let me know, won't you? If you have the baby early or anything?'

Alarmed, Natalie said, 'I won't have the baby early – why would you think I'd have the baby early?' Then she looked over her shoulder at Adam, as though suspecting him of putting some kind of hex on her. He smiled back rather nastily.

'I'll see myself out,' she told Grace, and almost ran out of the place.

'That wasn't very nice of you,' Grace remarked when she and Adam were alone.

'She's an idiot.'

'She is not an idiot. She's just not as passionate about nuclear disarmament as you.'

'That's an understatement. "Ooh, I used to dabble in that in college!" ' His mimicry was spot-on. 'I can't stand people like her. Nothing in their lives except their jobs and their husbands and their precocious kids. Too well fed and too well off to care what's happening in the real world.'

Grace said nothing.

'I didn't mean you, of course,' he added hurriedly.

'Good thing I've got a thick skin.'

He was mortified. 'But you haven't! She's the one with a thick skin! You're nothing like her!'

'But I'm exactly like her in lots of ways,' Grace pointed out reasonably. 'In fact, three weeks ago you were very fond of pointing it out.'

'Why do you have to keep bringing that up?'

'I'm not. I'm just saying.'

'I don't point it out now.'

'Why not? I haven't changed. In fact, I'm going back to it all next Sunday.'

Perhaps she shouldn't have mentioned that. They were having such a good time pretending it didn't exist. But Adam just regarded her out of his very blue eyes. Sometimes when she stared into them for long enough she started to sway dreamily on her feet.

'That's just window dressing,' he said.

She was half insulted. 'You're calling my life "window dressing"?'

'It's not the real you. I know the real you.'

'Now that you've stepped in to rescue me. Now that you've corrupted me.'

'Yes,' he said, smiling as proudly as a teacher with a rather slow student. 'You can't fool me, Grace. I've seen your inner core.'

'Oh!'

He could be very intense sometimes. In one way, it was incredibly flattering – nobody had ever bothered with her 'inner core' before. Indeed, she herself hadn't been aware that she'd had one. But now that she did, she felt complicated and interesting and mysterious. Another little gift from Adam.

But sometimes all this made her want to giggle nervously – because surely he couldn't find her all that fantastic? Last week he'd said her brain was the finest instrument he'd encountered in a long time and she actually *had* giggled. All because she had done *The Irish Times* crossword in twelve minutes! He had been very offended and had pointed out that he had met nobody in Ireland who could do it that quickly. That, of course, had made her feel very intelligent indeed, and she had apologised humbly, and started to wonder whether she was wasted as an estate agent. Perhaps she might even go back to college! That would give Ewan a run for his money!

She didn't believe all the things Adam said, of course. But for some reason *he* believed them, and she loved him for it. It was more than flattery. It was a kind of nourishment and, starved, she drank it up.

'What are you thinking about?' he asked. He always liked to know what she was thinking and enquired at least ten times a day.

'Sex,' she admitted honestly.

'You're always thinking about sex.'

'I know. Am I strange?'

'Sometimes I feel like a piece of meat,' he complained.

'All right,' she said. 'I'm thinking about you. Is that better?' And she did think about him quite a lot. Usually in sexual positions. But there was no need to tell him this. He could be overly sensitive, she had discovered.

'Yes,' he said, putting his arms around her. She had to suppress the urge to emit a sort of primitive guttural sound, like those tennis players who gave pent-up grunts every time they hit the ball.

'And what exactly do you think of me?' he enquired.

The urge to grunt passed. 'I was thinking how good you are to me. How well we get on. How nice you feel without any T-shirt on.'

'There you go again. Thinking about sex. I'm trying to have a serious conversation here.'

'Let's not be serious,' she begged. 'I can't be serious about anything any more.' It was true. Since Adam, she felt she was floating along on her own little individual cloud of bliss where, like in fairytale land, there were no bad thoughts or ogres or bills or taxes (or husbands). Or else she felt she was in the throes of a perfect holiday romance, all passion and romance and hot August sun. And it would all come to a natural end before either discovered the other's nasty bathroom habits or gambling addiction.

She did not think she had ever felt such uncomplicated happiness in her life.

'Maybe I want to be serious,' Adam said.

'Do you?'

He looked like he was about to say something, but then he smiled instead. 'There's no need to look so scared, Grace.'

'I'm not.'

'I know what this is about,' he said.

'Yes. You,' she replied. 'And me.'

'You and me,' he repeated, burying his nose in her hair – which hadn't been washed in a week, now that she thought about it. But then again neither had Adam's. Until now Grace had almost forgotten what a human body smelled like when it wasn't coated daily in shampoo and shower gel and perfume. It had a kind of musky, yeasty smell, not at all unpleasant – or at least Adam's wasn't, anyway. She hadn't got close enough to Martine to know what hers smelled like, and didn't intend to. Martine had not washed her hair since Christmas, maintaining that once it was left alone, hair was actually self-cleaning. Hers did not seem to bear out this theory, on appearances at any rate.

Then she forgot about Martine.

'Let's go upstairs,' she said.

'The pigs are back,' Julia hissed.

She was in the garden shed. Through the tiny window she could see a squad car drawing up across the road. Two uniformed police stared out at the crowd of young people sitting on her front lawn.

Martine frowned. 'We don't really call them "pigs", Julia. They don't like it.'

They were so politically correct, these anti-nuclear people. Julia pressed up against the window.

'It's two new ones,' she said excitedly. Usually it was just Sergeant Daly, and rookie Garda Paul O'Toole. They would park under the shade of the elm tree and after a while Julia would bring them out a cup of tea and a plate of fig rolls. They always protested that they were on duty, but she left the tray just the same.

But two *outside* police officers? And after six o'clock?

'Binoculars!' she cried. 'One of them has a pair of binoculars – he's training them on the house!'

Martine didn't even look up. She was obviously used to police harassment and continued to paint a canvas banner with the word MOX, in big red letters. Julia had already ironed on a transfer of a black skull.

'I don't see why they're bothering,' Martine complained. 'We are a peaceful organisation.'

'Until Saturday anyway,' Julia said with relish. She imagined riot police and baton charges and young people chaining themselves to railings singing 'We Shall Overcome'!

'I've told you before,' Martine said with a sigh. 'We are not going to cause trouble at the festival. We're simply making our views on nuclear reactors clear.' She jerked her head contemptuously towards the police car. 'Nothing to justify this – this spying! It's outrageous! It's a violation of our right to protest in a peaceful manner in a democratic society!'

'Yes, yes,' Julia said. Sometimes Martine could go on a bit about her rights. In fact, a lot of them on the lawn out there seemed very aware of their rights, and what they could and could not lawfully do. Which was wonderful, she thought hastily. She would just have preferred a bit more action herself. Like those demonstrations in the sixties: Free love! Ban the Bomb! They knew how to rock the boat back then all right, and to hell with the law.

Privately, she thought the music festivals had been far superior too. Just look at Woodstock, for heaven's sake! That was a proper music festival, with lots of drink and illegal substances and bad food. Not like now, where they had five-star toilets and glossy programmes, and where the catering trucks served noodles, apparently.

There would be mud, though, Martine had promised her. Lots of it. Fifty thousand people squatting on a hill for two days tended to generate a lot of dirt and mud. But apparently they were bringing plastic sheets for the tents, and double-lined sleeping bags. There would be hot food and books to read if things got too boring. One of them was even bringing a coffee-maker!

Anyhow. The important thing was that they were letting her join in. She was a part of it, an important part – not some useless old biddy with a crocked foot who was a nuisance to everybody.

Martine finished with the paintbrush and held up the banner proudly. 'What do you think?'

'Terrific!' Julia said, thinking how much more terrific it would be if they brought along a box of matches and set the thing on fire in the middle of the festival opening act. But apparently there were certain ways of doing things. And any kind of fire was out, she knew without even asking. Apparently so were sharp implements, decaying fruit and hijacking a catering truck. (Back in her day, when an organisation said it was 'peaceful', it didn't actually mean it.)

If she were honest, the banner looked a bit amateurish; not like those wonderful placards Adam had brought over with him. He'd saved them from some previous demonstration, which had obviously been better resourced than this one.

Still, she thought quickly, appearances weren't everything.

There was a knock on the shed door. She pressed herself up against it and hissed, 'Who is it?'

'Mammy?'

She suppressed a sigh and opened the door. Michael squeezed in, blinking owlishly as his eyes adjusted to the gloom.

'I wasn't expecting you today,' she said.

He was dressed in his work suit. 'I thought I'd call in on my way home. And a good thing too! Mammy,

I'm going to have to insist that you come indoors this minute.'

The implication that she was a child up to no good annoyed her. 'I'll come in when we're finished.'

'Where's Grace?' Michael demanded. 'Because she doesn't seem to be anywhere in the house.'

'I have no idea where Grace is. Michael, you're standing on our banner.'

'First she shoots you, then she can't be bothered to look after you properly!'

'Grace looks after me extremely well. She's entitled to an hour off every now and again.'

Stymied, Michael turned to Martine instead. 'She's seventy-three, you know! She's injured! You shouldn't be letting her get involved in all this.'

Martine looked him up and down dismissively. 'It's her own choice. Now, can you leave? You're taking up too much room.'

Michael positively quivered with indignation. 'I will not leave without my mother!'

'Michael—'

'No, Mammy, enough is enough. I didn't say anything in the beginning. I let you get on with it; housing these people, and painting banners, and acting like a hippy. But it's gone too far. There are police cars parked outside, for God's sake!'

'We know,' she said.

'It's time to terminate your involvement with this whole ridiculous – campaign, if you want to call it that.'

Martine curled her lip in a very threatening manner. 'And what is that supposed to mean?'

Michael wasn't used to naked aggression and took a step back. He said to Julia, 'And I don't know why you're saying "we" all the time. You're not part of this madness!'

'But I am, Michael,' she declared proudly, and was rewarded with a nod of solidarity from Martine.

Michael snorted in disbelief. 'You didn't even know what MOX meant before this lot came along! You thought it was something you spread on a bagel!'

'I didn't! That's lox – I know what lox means!' she retaliated. She hoped he wouldn't embarrass her further in front of Martine. But Martine was looking at her watch.

'I'm starving. I'm going to find Grace and see about dinner.'

'Oh yes,' Michael said grimly. 'Nothing like a free dinner. Or a free lunch. Or a free breakfast for that matter!'

Martine took a step forward ominously. But Michael stood his ground.

'I know your game. You think she's a soft touch, do you?' He jerked his head towards Julia. 'Think you'll get free bed and board, and in exchange you can let her dabble?'

'Michael!' Julia's voice cut through the air. 'That is enough.'

With another venomous look, Martine shoved past Michael and out.

'I'll remind you that this is my house, Michael,' Julia said. 'And you'll treat my guests with respect.'

'Guests!'

'Yes, Michael.'

'Mammy, you're making a fool of yourself here.'

Julia picked up Martine's paintbrush and began to daub at the banner. 'What, because I care?'

'About some shipment of nuclear fuel on its way from China?'

'Japan. You don't even know that much.'

'Neither did you until now.'

'So what?' she said loudly. 'Look, why is it so hard for you to believe that I'm doing this because I want to?'

'Because you and Daddy never gave a hoot about environmental issues! Daddy bulldozed that listed building, remember? And you owned a mink coat. I don't ever remember you fretting about the fifty minks that had their necks wrung just so you could look good!'

'In retrospect, it's not something I'm proud of, okay?' Julia said haughtily. 'But people change. Can we just leave it at that?'

'No.' He sucked in his gut officiously. 'I went looking for some information today on Martine and her friends. I got on the Internet, and I rang some of the big anti-nuclear groups, and I combed the telephone directory.'

'Slow day at work then?'

'And guess what? Mammy, they're a mickey-mouse outfit who travel from place to place spreading some daft anti-nuclear message, and relying on the generosity of people like you. Officially, they don't exist.'

'What, because they're not registered in some niggly companies' office? Because they don't have a policy manifesto printed on nice paper? Well, maybe that's because they're too busy trying to save this island from possible nuclear annihilation!'

'They wouldn't save a fly,' Michael said. 'With their homemade banners and their painted tents! They're like a crowd of children let loose with crayons!'

'Shut up, Michael. Just shut up.'

She didn't want him spoiling everything with his probing and questioning and his cynical insinuations that she was being used. For the first time since JJ died her house was full of the sounds of life again. She had a reason for getting out of bed in the morning. And maybe she hadn't known what MOX had meant before now but that was hardly the point. At her very lowest point, Grace and Adam and Martine and Joey – total strangers! – had been sent by some angel of fate to rent rooms in her lodging house.

Not that any of them were actually paying her, of course. But they couldn't be expected to; not when they were dedicated full-time to changing the world! She felt a moral duty to help the cause in whatever way she could, and she didn't care that they weren't part of some established group. Martine said those big earth outfits were all administration, anyway. Paperwork. She didn't want to shuffle papers behind a desk; she wanted to get out there and make a difference.

Michael obviously saw that further argument was hopeless because he said, 'Actually, Mammy, I have another reason for calling around.' He held out a white envelope. 'It's from Gillian.'

The very mention of her name was like a blast of dry ice.

'What is it?' Julia asked, not taking it.

'You know she does some voluntary work with the local tinnitus group?'

Julia looked at him blankly.

'Ringing in the ears. She thought she had it once, but it was just that new kettle we'd bought—'

'Oh yes, I remember.'

'Anyway, she's having a coffee morning tomorrow to raise some funds. She's sent an invitation for you to come along.'

He held out the envelope again.

'She said some very hurtful things to me, Michael.'

'I know. I know that. But she'd already done so much work on the conversion—'

'Without consulting with me first.'

'Yes. That was wrong. The things she said . . . can we not just put it all behind us?'

Gillian could, maybe. It would be a very long time before Julia would forget that day.

'What did she mean, Michael? When she talked about filling JJ's shoes?'

'I have no idea.' His florid face looked uncomfortable.

'Because I don't expect you to, you know – I mean with all this fussing over me, the ringing me up all the time – not that I don't appreciate it,' she added quickly. 'But it's not necessary.'

'Maybe I want to,' he said.

'And that's very kind of you. But I don't want you neglecting your own life. The fact is that JJ's gone, and I'm just going to have to learn to live on my own again. Anyway, I have Grace and Martine and the rest to keep me company now.'

She had meant this to ease the pressure on him, but he looked at her oddly, and said, 'You always know how to make me feel really good, Mammy.'

'What?'

But he was making for the door. 'Can I tell Gillian you'll be along?'

'I don't think so. Not yet anyway,' she added, lest he think she was rejecting the olive branch entirely. Besides, she had her whole day planned tomorrow; they urgently had to come up with a plan to smuggle in the banners and tents to the festival. Security would be on the lookout for them. Adam had suggested hiring a truck and simply driving through the fence with the stuff, which Julia had very much liked. But Martine said things had to be done by the book. How boring!

'She'll take it very badly, you know,' he said.

'I'm sure she'll survive,' Julia said, and put it out of her mind.

Twelve

The waiter wore a shiny black quiff and a pair of blue suede shoes. Not that you could call him a *waiter*, of course – in Walt Disney Land all employees were known as 'cast members'. This one supplemented his uniform with a badge saying 'Elvis', just in case you were a bit slow.

'Hiya doing, kids!' Elvis boomed at Jamie and Neil now.

'Okay,' they mumbled back. They'd just eaten beef burgers containing the meat of a whole cow, or so it seemed, and a mountain of fries, and were slumped bloated and listless on the fake red leather diner seats.

Ewan couldn't blame them. His own colon had packed up about five days ago under the sustained onslaught of fast food. Still, not long to go now. They were flying home on Sunday. Perhaps Grace would cook something homemade for them. In fact, given everything, it was the very least she could do.

'And you, sir?' Elvis said to him, with another dazzling smile.

The relentless cheer was beginning to impinge

upon Ewan's nerves too. But he managed, 'Terrific, thank you.'

'Dessert?' Elvis fired off.

'Oh, I don't think—'

'Sundae? Apple pie and cream? Double-whammy-white-chocolate Mud Pie with Raisin n' Caramel ice cream? Chocolate sauce optional.'

There was so much excess in this country. Ewan found himself offended by it. 'Not for me,' he said. 'Boys?'

'Your foot is touching mine,' Neil said to Jamie accusingly.

'It's not! Your foot is too far over.'

'Tosser!'

'Dad!'

'Now, now, boys,' Ewan murmured, feeling his irritation rise. It was time to leave. To Elvis he said, 'Just the bill, please.'

Not put out in the slightest, Elvis whipped out a docket and put it on the table. 'You be sure to have a nice day now!'

'Certainly,' Ewan said dutifully. This was The Happiest Place on Earth, after all. Any kind of mediocre or off day wasn't allowed. You might just have lost your job, your children and your wife, but it was still mandatory in this place to have a nice day.

Not that any of those things had happened to *him*, of course, Ewan corrected quickly. The Slimchoc account had last week doubled in size (they'd just green-lighted a range of milkshakes – *No Milk!* – according to Ewan's colleague Mick) and he had seen more of his children in the past three weeks than he might have ordinarily wanted. All right, so his wife might have upped and deserted him on what was supposed to have been the holiday of a lifetime and left him in charge of two demanding boys in a weird cartoon town while she tended to some old dear's foot in the leafy countryside, but he hadn't let that little detail spoil anybody's nice day. No sirree, he had carried on regardless. Nobody would be able to point the finger and say that he hadn't pulled his weight on *this* gig.

'So, guys!' he said to Jamie and Neil, feeling unusually superior and high-minded. 'What are we going to do this afternoon?'

Normally he didn't give them any choice. Grace had warned him several times on the phone – in that irritatingly helpful way of hers as though he were suffering from some kind of disability – never to invite any kind of debate because he would only bring trouble down upon himself. 'Just *tell* them, Ewan.' Thinking about it now, Ewan decided that he didn't agree with this rule of parenting at all. It was practically treating the boys as though they were children! All right, so they *were* children. But how were they ever to grow up if they were denied simple choices? Mollycoddled, he thought, that's what they were. (He would never say this out loud.) They never knew what they wanted to do anyway, so there was no harm in giving them a choice.

So it was a bit of a shock when Neil announced, 'We want to go to Tarzan's Tree house.'

Damn anyway. That wasn't what Ewan had in mind at all, so he blurted, 'You can't.' Seeing their faces, he gave a little laugh and said lightly, 'We went to Tarzan's Tree house last week – you'd be bored stiff!'

'We won't,' Neil said, giving him that confrontational look that he'd developed in the last three weeks and which made Ewan slightly nervous. As though Ewan were his enemy or something, the minute he had the temerity to disagree with anything Neil wanted to do! No, it wasn't right, and Ewan would tell Grace about it as soon as they got home.

'Well, you can't go to Tarzan's Tree house because I've got something else planned,' he said loudly, determined to reassert his authority.

'So why did you ask us what we wanted to do in the first place?' Neil enquired, and Ewan began to sweat. He should never have offered them a blasted choice. She had been right.

It was just holiday fatigue, he reassured himself. They'd spent three whole weeks in each other's company. Tensions were bound to be a bit high. And Grace's absence was sorely felt. She was great at kind of gelling everyone together. Sometimes when Ewan looked at his sons he didn't know what to say to them. It was in those odd moments back in the hotel room, in the hour before bedtime for example, when he felt his own lack most keenly. There just wasn't the same intimacy between them all as there would have been had Grace been there too.

Still, they would be home in a little less than a week. Every day on the phone Grace would do a countdown to how many days left before they were back. It would be seven days from today.

It struck him now that Grace hadn't done the countdown in ages. Maybe a week or more.

The boys were waiting for him, so he squared his shoulders and said, 'Today I've arranged for us to go swimming!'

Jamie bolted upright, and said with such vehemence that Ewan was taken aback, 'I don't want to go swimming!'

'But we haven't been swimming at all this holiday. '

Jamie looked across the plastic table at him, face rigid and closed. 'I said I don't want to go swimming, okay?'

Neil had been the confrontational one this holiday. In fact, Jamie had been even quieter than usual, now that Ewan thought about it. Surely to God he wasn't going to start kicking up now? With only a week to go?

'Why?' Ewan said this very nicely in the hopes of getting things back on track.

But Jamie just threw himself back in his seat silently. It was all very odd.

Ewan tried to think of what Grace would have done in this situation. She would have jollied him along. So he said, with a wink, 'Ah, but you haven't been to the guitar-shaped pool!'

'They have a guitar-shaped pool?' At least Neil looked interested now.

'Yes. I've booked diving lessons for you both with Angie-Piranha-Pirelli!'

That impressed them. And so it should. She was costing Ewan twenty-five dollars an hour.

'The piranha bit is her stage name, of course,' he

added hurriedly. He added carelessly, 'She's an ex-Olympic diver.'

Ah-ha! Neil was sitting up straight now, probably already imagining himself on a podium with a gold medal around his neck. Ewan snuck a look at Jamie. Was that the faintest glimmer of interest he saw?

But Jamie just said stubbornly again, 'I'm not going.'

'Oh, for goodness' sake!' But then Ewan took a breath. He must have patience. So he tried again. 'It's all booked and paid for, Jamie.'

'Let Neil go. I'll stay here with you,' Jamie said.

'No.' Ewan would get no time to himself that way. 'You both go or not at all.'

'Hey – so I can't go because *he* won't go?' Neil said. 'That's not fair!'

Ewan said, 'Jamie, what's the problem here?'

'He's a wimp who's afraid of cold water,' Neil said.

'I am not!'

'Or heights or something. Oooooh, Angie, I'm too high up, I'm going to shit myself!'

'Fuck off!'

'Stop it, the two of you!' Ewan gave Neil what he hoped was an intimidating look before turning back to Jamie. 'Are you scared, is that it?'

He tried to sound sympathetic. But, honestly, Grace had him ruined! All that fussing over him since he'd been a baby, like he was delicate or something. And look at him now – no guts about him, not like Neil.

'No.' Jamie slumped down in his seat again, his arms wrapped very tightly over his chest.

Ewan felt his irritation rise again. If he wouldn't

even say what was *wrong* . . . 'Then finish up your drink, eh? Angie said she'd be at the pool at two.'

They shouldn't have eaten all that food before swimming, he belatedly thought. Still, Angie would soon work it off them. She had been frighteningly efficient when he had met her in the hotel lobby last night to arrange a week of lessons. Everything had been 'sure, sir' and 'no problem, sir'. Ewan had liked that; the fact that Angie was prepared to look after any problems.

Neil was on his feet, excited. 'Let's go.'

Ewan said, 'Actually, I'm not coming with you.' He felt guilty, even though there was absolutely no reason why. He had looked after the two of them single-handed for the best part of a month, after all. And they would love the diving lessons. This was his holiday too, and he shouldn't feel bad about taking a couple of afternoons for himself.

But for some reason he hadn't told Grace about the lessons. Well, she'd have gone all silent and judge-mental, wouldn't she? She, who had organised this protracted holiday in the first place and then jumped ship! She didn't know what it had been like for him over here by himself! He hadn't wanted to go on about it too much, he hadn't wanted her to feel bad, and so she didn't know about the night the boys had set the hotel fire alarm off by accident, or the torren-tial rain that had trapped them in the Haunted Man-sion for four hours or the day Jamie had gone missing in a merchandising store. No, he hadn't complained about the crowds or the relentless heat or the peculiar rotting smell in their hotel room or the fact that he hadn't had sex in three weeks! And now he couldn't take a few afternoons off for himself without being accused of being a slack, irresponsible, uncaring parent? It was too much!

His glasses were steaming up. He reminded himself that nobody had actually accused him of anything. It was just his own paranoia, the result of years of being on the receiving end of Grace's 'looks'.

One day he would stand up for himself, he decided. The other option, of course, was to just go on ignoring the looks. That didn't require as much energy.

'I'll see you back here later,' he said. Jamie looked at him over the table, resistance coming from his every pore.

'For goodness' sake, Jamie, Angie will look after you,' he said, as much to reassure himself as Jamie. 'Just try it, okay?'

To stall any further argument he handed over the bag he'd already packed with their swim things. Neil made for the exit without a backwards glance. Jamie eventually slouched after him, his body hunched over a bit. He'd been doing that for a couple of days. Perhaps the child had tummy ache. Ewan wouldn't be surprised, with all the fattening food.

At last he was alone at the plastic-topped table in the vast red diner. He took a breath and, for the first time in days, he felt himself relax. The chrome juke-box was playing 'Stupid Cupid', Elvis was gossiping with Marilyn Monroe at the counter, and Ewan wondered what Grace would have made of it all.

She had been a bit odd on the phone recently, now

that he really thought about it. It wasn't just failing to count down the days; that was just a silly thing. No, it was more a detachment on her part. A feeling of distance or something.

Perhaps he was reading too much into it. The boys didn't seem to have noticed anything; or at least they always came off the phone with big happy smiles on their faces. They hardly ever smiled like that for Ewan, unless he bought them something in one of those damned merchandising stores that were waiting to ambush you around every corner.

Elvis was hovering again. 'Coffee, please,' Ewan said hastily, lest he be pressured again into going for dessert. Everyone around him seemed to be forking in cream-covered concoctions like there was no tomorrow. Almost all of them were obese, or on the way to it.

'One coffee coming up!' Elvis chirped. 'Could I interest you in a chocolate-chip cookie or—'

'No.'

Blessedly alone again, Ewan reached for one of the white paper napkins that had come with the food. It took him a moment to collect himself, to order his thoughts. Then he searched in his pockets until he found the stub of a pencil, which he licked, and then he bent over the napkin and he wrote a few words and then crossed them out, wrote more, and crossed them out too. He no longer heard the music blaring from the jukebox, or Elvis arriving back with his coffee. Finally he turned over the bedraggled napkin, smoothed it out, and started over again: *Eat Your Way Thin*. No, he thought, been done before. *Eat More Lose*

More? Terrible. All the damned sunshine was addling his brain, he thought rather cheerfully.

'Dad?'

It took him a moment to come back to earth and he pushed his grubby glasses up on his nose and looked out of them to see Jamie standing by the table, plucking at his T-shirt, and looking at his feet.

It was an effort to stay calm. 'What are you doing back here, Jamie?'

He wouldn't even answer the question properly; just said, in that plaintive voice again, 'Can I stay here with you?'

Oh, for heaven's sake! After all the trouble Ewan had gone to! And not just over the diving. He'd given them a great three weeks and now he was to be refused an hour to himself because Jamie had decided, seemingly on a whim, that he didn't fancy diving?

And so he snapped, ' No. Go up to the room if you don't want to go diving. That's the choice, okay?'

'I want to talk,' Jamie said now.

More procrastination!

'Too late! You had your chance!' Ewan said.

Jamie walked off very quickly. For a moment Ewan considered going after him. Oh, better that they both cooled off, he decided. He would follow him in a minute.

He picked up his pencil and went back to work.

'Do that again,' she said.

'What?'

'The tongue thing.'

'Grace, I'm getting a bit of a blister here—'

'Five more minutes.'

Oh, good lad. Grace buried her cheek in Mrs Carr's pillow, which smelled musty. Not that she cared. Neither did she care that her toenails needed clipping, or that Adam was making little lapping noises with his tongue. Normally noises like that tended to be vaguely embarrassing. Why else did they always play gushing background music during lovemaking scenes in the movies? It was to cover up any unromantic moist noises or shoulder-joints clicking.

But with Adam, she revelled in it. The more noise the better! Apart from lapping, she actively encouraged sucking, licking, chewing (where appropriate) and the little sticky noise that damp skin makes when unpeeled from other damp skin. Heaven! Or the wet snuffle of a neck being kissed all the way down. Or that delicious—

'You're not even paying attention.' Adam looked up at her, accusingly.

'I am,' she said tenderly.

But now he was unsure. 'What, am I not doing it right?'

'You're doing it just perfectly.'

'Because if you prefer I can—'

'Adam. Just keep going.'

She pushed his head back down. He didn't need any guidance from her in the sex department. They knew it all these days. Some of the things he had proposed, and done, had completely shocked her, and made her own little attempts to spice up her and Ewan's sex life look laughably dull. But honestly, some of them were so rude! Not to mention unnatural. You had to wonder how people discovered them in the first place.

She had tried to appear blasé in the beginning, of course. Bored, even. Except for that time when he had casually suggested that she ask a friend to join them.

'Natalie? For God's sake, she's eight months' pregnant!'

He had been joking. He had laughed at her horror: her, veteran of a thousand porn fantasies (which now seemed as innocent as *The Waltons*). But it was slightly embarrassing that she was so inexperienced compared to him. Surely in this kind of older woman/younger man scenario, she should be teaching him a trick or two? But all she had up her sleeve were a few variations on the missionary position.

Mind you, there were compensations. Men his generation took it completely for granted that her pleasure was as important as his own. Imagine! She thought of the men she'd slept with in the past, and how none of them would dream of putting her before them. Most would only enquire about her satisfaction in the sleepy afterglow of their own, as though remembering their manners. After five minutes' rest, one of them had lifted himself off the pillow with a cheery, 'Now, let's sort you out!'

That had been Ewan, actually. But it had come from good intentions, she'd told herself. It was just that she didn't really know what to tell him. Much less how to show him. Where did you get that kind of confidence at twenty-two?

Ewan had stopped trying to 'sort her out' years ago, and she had stopped asking. Neither of them had noticed her slow metamorphosis from a gauche girl into a fully-fledged, mature, sexually charged woman. No wonder she thought about sex all the time! She was frustrated, and had been for years!

'More!' she commanded, in a magnificently husky voice.

'You bet,' Adam said, filled with admiration. (He liked it when she bossed him around a bit. It was a bit predictable given that she was older than him, but if it kept him happy . . .)

Through sluttish half-closed eyes, she watched him. The deep brown tan of his back ended abruptly at his shorts-line. His little high bottom was very white and somehow vulnerable, and she felt so tender that she reached down and stroked his face.

'What?' he said.

'Nothing,' she said, not wanting to reveal the depth of her feelings to him. He might feel all pressured and run off on her. And he hadn't even finished down there. 'I'm putting on weight,' she said instead.

'Are you?'

So sweet of him to pretend he hadn't noticed.

'Look at my tummy.'

He did. 'Hmm. You might be getting a little Ruben-esque.'

'*Rubenesque*?'

Embarrassed, she pulled the sheet up. They were in his bed. She had spent only those first two nights in her little single bed across the hall.

'Don't,' he said. 'It's cute.'

She took another peek down. There it was – a

solid little white mound of flesh spanning from hip to hip, the kind she hadn't had since she'd been a teenager and had gone on Dr Wright's Revolutionary Combined Foods Diet (he had been wrong).

'I think it suits you,' Adam declared, giving it a little pat. 'You were too thin anyway. Scrawny.'

She felt another big wave of affection. 'I'll miss you.'

He tickled her tummy. 'Ah, but that's assuming that we're going to break up.'

She laughed. 'What are you suggesting? That we stay together?'

He smiled back. 'Why not?'

'I'm too old for you. All my friends would laugh at me if I took up with you.'

'So let's move to Tasmania. None of my friends will laugh at us.'

'That's because you don't have any friends. Except crusties.'

'Crusties are very non-judgemental,' he said. 'So, what do you say?'

'About moving to *Tasmania*?'

'Stop laughing. I'm very patriotic,' he said, wounded.

'What would we live on? Anti-nuclear leaflets?'

'I'd support us.'

'You're a college dropout.'

'I could get a job! Teaching silly tourists how to surf, that kind of thing. We could live in a little hut by the beach.'

'That sounds nice. What would we eat?'

'Fish, of course.'

'And some nuts and wild fruits that I would collect in the forest?'

'You're getting the hang of this,' he said admiringly.

'And I could make all our own clothes from the pelts of wild animals that I would trap and skin!'

'Steady on, Grace.'

She clapped her hands excitedly. 'We'd live off the land, with no mobile phones or filofaxes or cars or anything. We'd be hippies! I always wanted to be a hippy.'

'Did you?'

'Actually, no.' But neither did she want to be the harried hassled thin woman that had first come to Hackettstown. Wasn't it wonderful that people could actually change, she thought sleepily? Heck, she mightn't even be finished changing yet! She might change some more tomorrow! Who knew what she might eventually become? (Although she wouldn't like to get too fat. Curvy was attractive. Obese was not.)

'Grace,' Adam said, after a while.

'Hmm?' she said, lost in visions of herself shopping in outsize stores and having to book two seats when she wanted to fly anywhere.

'I want to talk to you about something.'

'Oh, Adam. Martine doesn't mean those things she says. The two of you are just different, that's all. You're a radical and she's more conservative—'

'She's a fucking fossil.'

'Yes, well, she's running this campaign and there's nothing you can do about that.'

'I wouldn't be so sure. Anyway, I don't want to talk about Martine. I—'

'Sorry to cut you off, Adam.' Something had caught her eye. 'What's that?'

'What?'

'Out the window. No, no, don't sit up!' she hissed.

'How can I look if I don't sit up?'

'Just look!' She pointed. 'There – across the road!'

Being on the first floor, they hadn't bothered to close the curtains. It was still broad daylight outside. And they could quite clearly see the sun glinting off glass in the upstairs bedroom of the house opposite.

Grace squealed and pulled up the sheet to cover her chest. Adam jumped up and shook his fist at the window.

'That little bastard,' he said grimly. 'I told you, didn't I? I told you!'

'Frank? I know you're in there. So you might as well come out now!'

She rang the doorbell again. But still he didn't come. So eventually she took out the office's set of keys and let herself in.

He was hiding in the living-room watching television, and she startled him.

'What are you doing here?' he blustered.

'What were *you* doing, spying on us?' she returned heatedly.

'I was not! I was searching for the Lesser Spotted Woodpecker, a very rare bird in these isles—'

'Balls!'

'Look it up if you don't believe me!' He tossed a reference book at her. 'I was told a pair of them were nesting in Croft's Wood over there. So there I was, going about my legitimate business, and next thing I see two bare bottoms bouncing in front of my nose in broad daylight! Imagine the fright I got!'

Grace fought down a hateful blush. But something told her he was telling the truth. Or partially at least.

'You didn't have to keep looking though, did you?'

'Well, I . . .'

'You could have turned away! That would have been the decent thing to do. You know, I had to stop Adam coming over here. He'd like to give you a good thump.'

'I'd imagine your husband would like to do the same to Adam. Someone should tell him what his wife's been up to while he's been away.'

'And you'd just love to, wouldn't you? That would pay me back nicely for calling your house a dump!'

'My house might have been sold only for that,' Frank said piously.

'Tom and Charlie weren't going to buy your house whether I called it a dump or not.'

'Sandy says that if that had happened in the States, you'd have been fired. And she's right.'

'Yes, well, Sandy is always right. We should know that by now,' Grace muttered.

Frank gave her a look. 'I'm sorry for spying on you, okay? But there's no need to take it out on Sandy! I was only doing it for her in the first place.'

'Sandy told you to go and spy on people making love?' Perhaps there was hope for her after all.

'No, no.' He clammed up.

Grace had a suspicion what was worrying him.

'Frank, is this to do with what we were talking about a while back?'

'I have no idea what you're referring to.'

'Look, every couple is nervous about the first time they make love.'

'Would you like a cup of tea?'

'Sandy won't expect you to be some Lothario with all the right moves.'

Frank sank back into his chair and threw his head back on the greasy headrest with a groan. 'But she's so lovely. Beautiful!'

'Well, yes . . .'

'I'll be too afraid to even touch her. A woman like her, she'll expect perfection, technique, expertise!'

'Maybe not. It sounds like she isn't too active in that department herself. Hasn't she been fighting rakes of them off in the gym?'

'She's had previous boyfriends though. You saw that photo where one of them was chopped out. Greg. *Greg.* I bet he made her happy.'

'We don't know that—'

'I bet he was a hunk with a big lunchbox who knew all the tricks!'

'Calm down, Frank. I'm sure you have a few tricks yourself,' Grace said, rather queasy at the thought. He should have a few more now, after watching herself and Adam at it. Oh God.

'Not really,' he said.

Grace swallowed hard, and battled on. 'Come on now! I'm sure if you think back to your previous . . . experiences, you'll find something to draw on.'

'Hardly,' he said. 'I'm a virgin.'

'Ah! Um!' She nodded sagely, wishing he hadn't confided this in her. She tried not to look surprised or amused in any way and said, in a very jolly way, 'Just think of all the fun you'll have learning!'

Frank looked more miserable. 'I thought if I watched you and Adam I might be able to pass myself off as sophisticated.'

Grace said, mortified, 'Did you see . . . everything?'

'Pretty much.'

She hoped that he hadn't taken any notes. Or drawn diagrams. That would be just like him. 'You know, maybe you should talk to Sandy about this.'

'I can't.'

'She won't mind that you're not experienced.'

'She kind of thinks I am.'

'What do you mean?'

'Well, she was going on and on about Greg! And I just kind of boasted that I'd slept with more women than I actually have.'

'How many more?'

'I told her three.'

'That's not too bad.'

'But then I began to add a couple here and there, and suddenly it was ten, and then twenty, and then it just all got out of control!'

'How many, Frank?'

'Eighty-two.' He rubbed his hand over his eyes. 'I was afraid she'd go off me if she knew I'd never had a girlfriend before. She might think there was something wrong with me.'

'But eighty-two, Frank!'

'I know.'

'You need to tell her the truth.'

'I can't!'

'Why not?'

'She's got enough worries without me adding to them.'

'Her sister?'

'No, no, that's all patched up with the hubby. Do you remember Sandy was feeling tired?'

'Yes.'

'She went to the doctor that time. And he took a whole heap of tests. And something has come back that he's not happy with.'

'What?'

'They won't tell her until they do a second test. The results should be in today. But she doesn't want me worrying. She says I'm just to concentrate on getting my house sold.'

'Does she now.'

'She suggested that maybe you should think about dropping the price a bit.'

Grace was taken aback. 'Sorry?'

'I know it'll affect your commission.'

'I wasn't thinking about my commission.'

'Sandy says we're not attracting much interest.'

'It's August, Frank. Half the country is on holidays.'

'She says that if we cut the price by, say, ten percent, we'll draw in a whole new section of the market.'

Her brain was certainly sharp for someone who wasn't well. But she did have a point. Imagine – a woman living thousands of miles away, who communicated only by computer, a woman who had never even seen Frank's house, could sell it for him.

Grace's job had never seemed so meaningless.

'I'll think about it. And Frank?'

'What?'

'This spying business. I won't say anything to anybody if you won't. Okay?'

Thirteen

The next day Nick and Charlie arrived back from town, red-cheeked and giggly.

'Have you two been drinking?' Grace asked suspiciously. It wasn't unknown, at two o'clock in the afternoon.

'Why do you always think the worst of us, Grace?' Nick complained.

Charlie burst out, 'Oh, I can't keep it to myself a minute longer! Can we tell her, Nick?'

'Go on so.'

'We're engaged, Grace!'

'Engaged?'

'Yeh. Like, we're going to get married,' Nick elaborated helpfully. 'At some point in the future. You know, whenever we can get things organised.'

'We're doing it as soon as we can,' Charlie said firmly. 'Look!'

She held out her hand. A ring with a very small diamond sat on her fourth finger. 'We just picked it in the jewellery shop in Hackettstown – isn't it adorable?'

'It's perfect,' Grace said. 'Well, ah, what can I say! Congratulations!'

'Now, I know what you're thinking,' Charlie told her.

'I don't—'

'I know I said I'd never touch another man with a bargepole. That they were all a crowd of fucking bastards,' she said happily. 'But Nick is different.'

'I am,' Nick said vigorously.

'I knew it the very first time I set eyes on him! I've never felt that way before about any man, have I, sweetheart?' Charlie said over her shoulder. Gavin had trailed in after them.

'Apart from Bob,' he said.

'Well, maybe Bob.'

'And Tony,' he added.

'Oh, yes, Tony! I'd nearly forgotten about him. But we were only engaged for two weeks.'

'You and Nick have only known each other three weeks,' Grace ventured. She didn't want to spoil the moment; but this was Nick they were talking about! Her brother.

'Three weeks, two days, twelve hours and forty-seven minutes!' Charlie said. 'Isn't it marvellous? I always believed in love at first sight,' she confided in Grace. 'Anyway, we'd like you to be matron-of-honour at the wedding – wouldn't we, Nick?'

He nodded. 'Absolutely.'

'Don't forget, you have to divorce Didi first,' Grace said. Now she did really sound like a mean cow.

Charlie gave her a look. 'Kind of like you're divorcing Ewan?'

Touché. Grace flushed. 'I told you. That was a minor misunderstanding.'

'Anyhow, Nick has already been in contact with his solicitor, haven't you, honey? And Gavin's going to be a pageboy, aren't you, darling?'

'I am,' he said proudly. 'Will I fit into the suit I got for the wedding to Tom?'

'We'll get a new one,' Charlie declared. 'We'll get a new everything!'

Nick said, 'Obviously we'll have to look at our budget—'

Charlie gave him a rather steely look. 'This is going to be a proper white wedding, Nick. With printed invitations and a hotel reception and a band playing. I've been engaged six times and this time it's going to work. I'm going to be respectable for the first time in my life!'

'Me too!' Gavin said.

Charlie chucked him under the chin, then said airily to Nick, 'And don't worry about the money. I told you – just look at Johnny Logan.'

Nick cleared his throat loudly, then said to Grace, 'Anyway, keep the news under your hat for the moment. I don't want Didi getting wind of it.'

'Not before she hears she's being divorced anyway,' Charlie said confidentially. 'It wouldn't be fair on her.'

'And what about the kids?' Grace asked Nick.

'I won't tell them for the moment either,' he said. 'Not until things settle a bit.'

'And now, of course, you'll be responsible for Gavin as well,' Charlie reminded him.

'You will,' Gavin said vigorously. 'I can be tough going sometimes, can't I, Mum?'

'You can,' she said fondly.

Nick began to look a bit pressured, Grace thought.

'Things might be a bit clearer when you finish your computer course,' she said diplomatically.

'He's dropped out of that,' Charlie said casually.

'What?'

'The IT industry's bust anyway.' She said to Gavin, 'Come on, let's go upstairs and get my wedding magazines out!'

'She's got ones from 1990 – haven't you, Mum?'

'Before you were even a twinkle in my eye!' she said.

They went off upstairs hand in hand, leaving a little silence behind.

'Go on, then,' Nick said at last.

'What?'

'Say I'm making a big mistake. You know you're dying to.'

'I am not! It's just a surprise, that's all. Especially so soon into things . . .'

'That doesn't matter. I love her.'

'I'm sure you do. '

'Even if she's a bit loud and brassy and not up to your standards of perfection.'

'Nick!'

'But Charlie says we're going to make a great team. She says that under her management we're going to make a packet.'

'Her "management"?'

'She's my new manager – did I not mention it?'

'No.'

'She said you advised her to quit lap dancing and to go into management instead.'

'What? I did not!'

'Well, you said something to her. She doesn't want to be the talent any more. So now *I'm* the talent. We're relaunching me as a solo artist. Steel Warriors, crappy computer courses – that's all in the past now. I've got a genuine star quality, Charlie says, and we have to tap it.'

'I'm glad.'

'I don't need your approval, Grace.'

'I was just wishing you luck, that's all.'

'We don't need luck either. Charlie is going to make us millions!'

Then he bowed his head, and his face was so tortured that for a moment she was frightened.

'What is it, Nick? What's wrong? Is it one of the kids? Are they sick?'

'She wants me to enter the Eurovision,' he blurted.

'What?'

'I know. Imagine! From Steel Warriors to Johnny fucking Logan.' He rubbed his eyes and for a moment Grace thought he was going to cry. 'She wants me to give up rock 'n roll and write ballads. She says that if I win the Eurovision then Scandinavia is my oyster. A number one in Finland could keep us afloat for a year. Sweden, and you're talking a new house.'

Grace didn't really know what to say. To express any kind of enthusiasm would be very false, given that it had been an annual family pastime to mercilessly slag off the Eurovision, from the bad haircuts to the risible lyrics and the naff dance routines. 'Nil point!' she and Nick would roar derisively at the television. How they despised those people: so desperate for success that they would stand up in spangly pink outfits and make fools of themselves in front of a hundred million people.

'I believe the costumes are more stylish now,' she said carefully.

'Yes,' said Nick, after a moment. 'And Celine Dion did very well out of it, Charlie says.'

'Oh, she's right! And Abba! And, um, Bucks Fizz.'

There was a little silence. Three weeks ago Grace might have left it at that. Now she couldn't. 'It's a ridiculous idea, Nick!'

Nick looked relieved, as though she had proved that he was not in fact going mad. 'She's got her heart set on it.'

'It's one thing to give up rock music – the thing you love! But to sell your soul?'

A bit of colour was creeping back into his cheeks now. 'I know! But try telling her that.'

'I will!'

'You will?'

Shit. She hadn't really been serious. So it was a relief when Nick added, 'Thanks anyway, Grace, but it would really have to come from me.'

'Well, then, say it to her!' she cried, remembering that sweat-filled night in the SFX – and Nick, the most alive she had ever seen him. 'You've got to stand up for what you believe in, Nick! Surely there have to be some things in this life that we can't compromise on? I mean, what's the point in it – in any of it – if we end up only half a person?'

She wasn't sure where this was coming from, but

right now she believed it completely. Nick believed her too.

'You know something? You're right! Just because I'm going to marry her doesn't mean I have to sell out! Just because I have an ex-wife and three kids to support—'

'Four now.'

'Four – and nowhere to live and no income doesn't mean I should demean myself!' He ripped off his apron with great drama. 'No, I'm going to tell her straight out that I'll have nothing to do with the Eurovision! I'll tell her right now!'

'Good for you!'

He stopped by the door. 'You know, I never thought you were like this.'

'Like what?'

'I don't know. Cool.'

She gave a little laugh. 'I was always cool. You just never bothered with me. You were too busy with your band.'

'You were our number one groupie,' he said fondly. 'Derek and Mick even thought we should ask you to join the group.'

'Me?'

'Yeh. They said it would broaden our appeal. You were okay-looking back then. Derek said you reminded him of Susie Quattro. That you both looked a bit . . . what was it he said? Dangerous.'

Grace had a flash of déjà vu. Dennis the Menace and Bewleys.

'My red and black striped scarf,' she whispered in wonder. 'He must have seen me wearing it.' It had become an omen now, a thing of great significance in her life.

'No, it was that pair of black leather pants you used to own. Stuck to you like glue. He said they gave him a stiffy every time you wore them.' He frowned. 'I never liked it when he spoke about you like that. I said to him, she's my kid sister for Chrissake, go and throw your leg over someone else.'

'Thank you,' Grace said, faintly.

'Anyway, it didn't work out,' Nick finished up.

'Why?'

'What?'

'Why didn't you ask me to be in the band?'

Nick laughed. 'You? In a band? Didn't figure it'd be part of your life plan. No money, no security. Even at sixteen it wouldn't do!'

'You're probably right,' she said, still smiling.

She didn't tell him that she'd actually had a life plan when she was sixteen, carefully written down on a piece of pink notepaper which she had sellotaped to the underside of her sock drawer. On it was a list of top ten careers. Number one was being a famous actress. That had dropped to number two after she had read a book on fearless women explorers. Under-cover police work or being an international spy, the old reliables, had featured heavily on the list too, along with circus trapeze work (her thighs had been slimmer then), and an untitled one that involved wearing very little clothes and which was probably a career in the sex industry only she hadn't realised it at the time.

Selling property was not on the list. At sixteen,

Grace Tynan had had great hopes and dreams for herself. Back then she could have been anyone she wanted. Maybe she still could.

She picked up the phone.

'I handed in my notice today,' she told Adam sleepily in bed that night. She had a satisfied kind of feeling, as though she had finally done something she had meant to do for ages. Well, technically she still had to put it in writing to the partners – singing, 'I'm not coming back, I'm not coming back', on Natalie's office answering machine would probably not count as official notice.

'Good for you,' he said. 'I finished with my girl-friend today.'

Her eyes sprang open in the dark. 'What?'

'I broke up with her.'

'I'm sorry, Adam.'

'I'm not.'

'Well, the distance . . . it's hard when you're away from each other . . .'

'It has nothing to do with the distance.' She felt him looking at her in the dark. 'Grace, do you not think it's time we stopped all the bullshit? I need to know how you feel about me.'

She lay very still in the bed. Perhaps he would think she had fallen asleep.

No such luck.

'Grace?'

'Yes, yes,' she said.

'We need to talk,' he declared. 'We've needed to talk for a few days now.'

'Have we? It's just that it's a bit late now, and you have lots of, um, campaigning to do tomorrow—'

'Are you putting me off?'

'No. I'm just thinking.'

She wasn't. Or, at least, nothing coherent. How could she rationalise and verbalise feelings that she wasn't even sure of herself? How would she translate those light, airy, effervescent feelings she had whenever she was with him into cold, hard words that might be taken down and used against her?

'Because I think I'm in love with you, Grace,' he declared. He appeared to have no such problem. But he was like that, Adam. With him everything was straight down the line. No nasty blurred edges, just neat black and white, even when it came to emotions. But that was part of his attraction for her.

'How is she?' she asked eventually.

Adam was suspicious. 'Who?'

'Your girlfriend.'

'My girlfriend?'

'Yes.'

'What has she got to do with anything?'

Grace looked at him indignantly 'You've just split up with her! Told her it's over! She's probably nursing a broken heart right now!' Men never thought of these things. The hardest bit for them was the actual act of breaking up. Women knew that the really horrible bit came days, weeks, even months afterwards, when the sight of that special brand of bubble bath in the supermarket was enough to bring you to your knees, sobbing, right there in the middle of the Personal Hygiene section. And as for restaurants!

There were certain eateries that some of Grace's friends still refused to go to, for fear of collapsing with the weight of memories. And this was years afterwards! Trying to organise a girls' night out these days required considerable diplomatic skills, and the very latest copy of the Restaurant Guide.

'Imagine not even knowing how she was taking the whole thing!' she added, getting annoyed now. 'Poor Babe!'

'Who the hell is "Babe"?' Adam said.

Grace was embarrassed. 'Ah, nobody.'

'Look, Amanda will be fine. She has loads of friends and family.'

Amanda. Grace tried out the name in her head. A classy name, of course, for a girl like Babe. Nobody would ever dare call her Mandy, or anything common like that. She wondered what her surname was. Something French, possibly. Or with a double barrel. It certainly wouldn't be Tynan.

'Did you love her?' she asked, almost in love with the girl herself.

Adam hoisted himself up onto one elbow. 'What is this? Why are we talking about my girlfriend – my ex-girlfriend – when we should be talking about us?'

'I was just wondering!'

'Yes, of course I loved her at some point – I wouldn't have been with her for four years otherwise.'

Four years! Babe must have been a childhood sweetheart. Grace could just picture her – a beautiful little girl at the bottom of the street playing with a hula-hoop, her blonde pigtails bouncing, while all the neighbourhood boys looked on longingly from their chopper bikes.

'So what happened?' she asked. This was better than a Mills & Boon.

He looked impatient. 'Nothing happened. Look, it was coming for a while. We were too different, it would never have worked out.'

'How different?'

'Oh, Grace!'

'Does she not believe in anti-nuclear politics or something?' she said doggedly.

'Of course she does – she's extremely active, that's how we met,' he said. 'I meant background. Her family, well, they're pretty well off.'

Filthy rich too! Babe began to take on mythical status in Grace's head, who now had a firm vision of a Miss World type lounging on a yacht, coordinating Save The Whale campaigns from a pink mobile phone. How could Adam be so foolish as to break up with her? For Grace? (Not that Grace was putting herself down or anything, but honestly, if any sane person were given the choice they'd take Amanda. Grace herself would.)

'Is her money such a problem?'

'Money is not what I'm about!' Adam exploded. 'Jesus, if you don't know that much about me!'

She did. The very sight of cold hard cash seemed to greatly offend him. Amanda must have a truly captivating personality if he had been prepared to overlook her millions in the first instance.

'Pretend she doesn't have any. Pretend she's broke!' she suggested brightly.

He gave her a peculiar look. 'Grace, I've just told you I've split up with my girlfriend because of you. I've just told you I'm in love with you. And you're trying to get me back with her?'

Was she? Perhaps she just couldn't believe that he had done such a thing for her: Grace Tynan, thirty-four-year-old mother of two, estate agent. She listened to Lite FM, for God's sake.

'I'm just afraid that you've done something rash,' she said humbly.

'I am well aware of what I've done.' He lifted his head proudly. 'It wasn't easy, but there comes a time when you have to decide what is important to you. *Who* is important. And I've made my decision and I'll stick with it.' He added, 'And now it's up to you.'

To do what? Break up with Ewan? 'Adam . . . all this, it's obviously a bit of a surprise,' she said with admirable understatement.

'I know. But I can't go on like this, Grace. Pretending that we're just having a roll in the hay, a bit of slap and tickle, and that when it's all over we'll go our separate ways as though none of it matters. When it does. To me anyway.'

'I never thought of it as a bit of slap and tickle either,' she said.

'You do! You're always thinking about sex! We're always *having* sex!'

'But that's what people do at the beginning of a relationship,' she protested. Have sex and visit art museums. Didn't he know anything?

'I think we're past the beginning,' he said rather ominously. 'Don't you?'

'I think – I think – I think . . .' she stuttered, desperately trying to buy time. Oh, she would just ask for it. 'I need more time!'

There was a little silence.

'That sounds to me like a bit of a cop-out, Grace.'

'It's not! Look, Adam, I'm having a wonderful time with you. The best! I've never met anyone like you before. I've never *felt* like this before.' She flopped back in the bed. 'I just didn't think past the beginning bit, that's all.'

'Neither did I,' he admitted. 'I didn't ask to fall in love, Grace. I didn't want to break up with my girlfriend. But I did fall in love. And I need to know how you feel.'

There was a great big expectant pause.

'You want to know whether I'll go and live with you in a mud hut on the beach?' She gave a little laugh.

Her levity was not appreciated.

'You know what I mean, Grace. You're going to have to make up your mind.'

It had the horrible feel of an ultimatum, and she looked at him, a bit shocked.

'You mean choose between you and my husband?'

He didn't answer.

'Guess how hot it gets at the centre of a nuclear explosion?'

'A thousand degrees?'

'Wrong! Several millions degrees!' Martine said. 'You'd be vaporised. Kaput! Nothing left but your shadow.'

'I'd take shelter in a bunker,' Julia retaliated as she cracked open her second can of cider (she would dispose carefully of the cans and Grace need never know).

'No good. All the oxygen would be sucked out of the atmosphere and you'd suffocate.'

'I'd drive off in my car then!'

'Forget it. Radioactive rain can fall up to a thousand miles away. You couldn't drive fast enough!'

Julia threw up a hand in defeat. 'We're all sunk then!'

'Exactly!' said Martine, red-faced. 'Which is why we've got to stop all nuclear development, Julia.'

'Let's kidnap the festival lead act and say we're not giving him back until the MOX shipment is stopped,' Julia begged.

'Oh! You've been talking to Adam!'

'He has a point. Maybe we need to be a bit more radical.'

'This is my group!' Martine declared. 'And we'll do things my way. How can we hope to be taken seriously if we go around breaking the law?'

'I suppose,' Julia said, half-heartedly. Martine was far too earnest for her own good sometimes.

'I think he's turning Joey against me too,' Martine said darkly.

'Yes, yes – now, tell me again what kind of internal injuries I might suffer if I was within half a mile of a nuclear blast.' It was quite fascinating.

But Martine was yawning. 'I'm going to bed, Julia. And you should too. I promised Grace I wouldn't keep you up too late.'

'Not everything has to go through Grace,' Julia protested. Still, she didn't say it too loudly; only for Grace, Julia might very well be in Gillian's less-than-tender care right now. And it wasn't as though Grace suffocated her or anything. No, Grace understood boundaries and the value of free time. They had a kind of an unspoken understanding about this free time; it was theirs alone, and no explanations were required on either part.

In that way it was almost a professional relationship, Julia thought, like that between patient and carer. Which suited her just fine.

'Do you need some help up the stairs?' Martine asked.

'No, no. I can manage.' She was still on one crutch, but didn't want Martine to see her as incapacitated; otherwise she might not let her come along on Saturday.

'At least you'll have a bit of peace on Monday,' Martine said.

'Why, what's happening Monday?'

'We're leaving, of course.'

Julia was shocked, but hadn't the faintest idea why. It wasn't as though she'd thought they would stay in her house forever. She just hadn't expected it to be so soon, that was all.

'You'll be exhausted after the festival. Why don't you stay another couple of days?' she said.

'We can't. We're flying to Wales to meet the MOX shipment when it arrives. All the earth groups are going – there's going to be a massive demonstration.' She kissed Julia on the cheek. 'Goodnight, Julia. And thanks for everything.'

It was almost like she was already saying goodbye.

Julia sat there in JJ's old red armchair for a long time after Martine had gone out to her tent at the bottom of the garden. The sheen had gone off the day somehow. And she had that chilly feeling again. But she would have to go out to the shed to put on the heating, out into the dark on her own.

The telephone rang. It sounded very loud in the stillness of the house. Who could be ringing at ten past one?

She picked up the receiver. 'Hello?'

There was no reply.

'Hello?' she said again.

Then, somebody breathing: heavy breathing, loud and coarse and distorted and which seemed to ooze out of the receiver at her malevolently.

She didn't know what to do. So she slammed the phone down and stood looking at it, dry-mouthed. She had an eerie, creepy feeling, like there was some-one in the house with her.

And of course there was. Grace was upstairs asleep in bed. Charlie and young Gavin too, and Adam. Martine was in her tent at the bottom of the garden, for heaven's sake! She had plenty of people around her. Plenty of people to protect her.

But they would be gone on Monday. All of them. Grace too.

There was a peculiar tightness in her throat now that she tried to swallow down but couldn't. The walls seemed to close in on her and she wanted to turn around and leave – to run out of the place fast. She took a breath. It was ridiculous: to be so afraid of her own living-room. Of her own home, for heaven's sake! She would be fine. Fine. She had lived on her own for two years. There was no need to think that she couldn't cope again, even with silly phone calls. They were just cowards, that was all.

But the feeling kept rising in her – panic, coming from the pit of her stomach and roaring up through her like some wild thing out of control, crippling her. She hunched over, and said, 'Grace . . .'

But Grace, asleep upstairs, wouldn't hear that.

Her throat was so closed that she couldn't breathe properly. She lurched over for the support of a chair, knocking the can of cider to the floor. It splashed on her legs but she didn't feel it. She was going to pass out.

'Julia? Julia!'

She felt hands on her shoulders, half lifting and half pulling her across the carpet. Then the support of cushions as she was eased down into a chair.

'Are you all right?' Frank said over her.

'Yes, fine . . . Frank, what are you doing?' His hands were on her head, pushing.

'Your brain needs to be lower than your heart.' He was trying to force her head down between her knees. 'Deep breaths!'

For the second time that evening Julia almost passed out. She managed, 'Frank, you're choking me!'

He let go. And gradually the black dots stopped dancing before her eyes. She felt the tightness in her chest disappear and the strength come back into her legs. She sat up slowly. 'I'm fine now.'

Frank shook his head in disbelief. 'Fine! You're out of your skull on cider.'

'I am not out of my skull on cider.'

'What's this then?' He picked up the incriminating can of cider. 'Wait till I tell Grace!'

'There's no need to tell Grace ... I only had two cans, I'm not drunk, okay?'

He wasn't convinced. 'What then? Your foot?'

'I don't know.' She didn't want to tell him it had been a panic attack, pure and simple. It would sound so feeble and weak. 'Maybe I had some reaction to those new pills.'

'I'll ring Michael.'

'No.'

'He really should know about this. He might want to call a doctor—'

'I said no, Frank.' Her tone stopped him in his tracks. 'Thanks anyway, but I can manage.'

'Hardly.'

To divert him, she said, 'What are you doing here anyway?'

'I was on the Internet late with Sandy and I was just going to bed when I saw your kitchen light still on, and thought I'd come over to check whether you were okay. But the next time I won't bother. Goodnight.'

She was taken aback by his over-reaction. 'Frank, wait. Are you all right?'

'Yes. No.'

'What's wrong?'

He looked a bit pale. 'The results of Sandy's tests came back.'

'Oh, yes?' Grace had mentioned something.

'They're not good.'

'What's wrong with her?'

'The doctors think she has some kind of kidney malfunction.'

'What?'

'They're not sure exactly what yet. It might be viral. Anyhow, the thing is, her system is being flooded with impurities and that's why she's been feeling so tired lately.'

'I'm sorry to hear that, Frank.'

'It's a bit of a shock, all right.'

'Which kidney is it?'

'Both.'

'Both! At the same time?'

'That's why the doctors think it might be an infection of some sort.'

'I'm sure they know what they're doing,' Julia said. 'She'll be back on her feet in no time, you'll see.'

'Yes,' Frank said bravely. 'That's just what I said to her in an email just now. I told her that everything would be just fine.'

The phone rang again. Julia gave a little cry and spun around to look at it.

'Bit late to be ringing anyone,' Frank grumbled.

Julia just stared at it.

'Here, I'll answer it if you want,' Frank said.

But Julia grabbed his arm. 'Don't,' she hissed.

'What?'

'It's her again.'

Frank was mystified. 'Who?'

'I just got a call a minute ago. An obscene call. She's trying to frighten me.'

The phone kept ringing.

'Who, for heaven's sake?'

'Gillian!'

Frank was incredulous. 'What?'

'I wouldn't go to her silly coffee morning. Michael said she'd take it badly. But I didn't think she'd stoop this low.'

'What did she say to you on the phone?'

'Nothing . . . I mean, she didn't *speak*.'

'How do you know it's her then?'

'Because she's malevolent and cowardly and she can't bear it when Michael gives me any little bit of attention at all.'

The phone kept ringing and ringing.

'I'm going to answer it,' Frank declared.

'No! I won't give her the satisfaction—'

'We don't know it's her!'

'I know it's her,' Julia said grimly. 'I've never been surer of anything in my life.'

Frank said, 'Even if it is – which I very much doubt – then maybe a man's voice will scare her off.'

Without further argument he picked it up. 'Hello?'

It was Ewan Tynan, calling from America.

'Oh.' Frank looked at Julia, and asked Ewan, 'Did you just ring a minute ago?'

Ewan told him no. Then he asked to speak to Grace. It was an emergency.

Jamie had grown breasts.

'Ewan, what on earth are you talking about?'

'Breasts, Grace. Two little lumps of things on his chest. With nipples on top. I'm looking at them now!'

319

He sounded vaguely hysterical. Grace had to sit down at the kitchen table. Her heart was still thudding unpleasantly from the fact of a phone call in the middle of the night in the first place.

'Okay, Ewan, let's just take this slowly, all right? Are you sure they're not bruises or something?'

'Bruises?'

'Maybe he knocked against something – oh, look, I'm just trying to get a clearer picture here!'

'They are not bruises,' he said quite definitely.

'An allergy then? Has he eaten anything peculiar over there that might have made him swell up? Those grits?'

'No. Anyway, there's no other part of him swollen. Just his chest.'

It had been a wild hope. 'How long did they take to grow?'

'What?'

'His breasts, Ewan! Did they ... bud over a few days? Or just spring up overnight?'

'I don't know.'

'You don't know! Does everything pass you by, Ewan? Do you observe anything that isn't to do with work?'

'For God's sake, Grace! You expect me to go around all day watching his chest? You wouldn't!'

'I'd have noticed a pair of breasts if I was there!'

'Well, you're not here, are you! I am! I'm the one who has to deal with this, not you! He's been off for a few days, okay? I thought it might have been a damned tummy ache or something! He went around hunched over the whole time – how the hell was I supposed to know he was hiding breasts!'

His voice was perilously high again. Grace didn't think she'd ever heard him so uncollected before. The stress of looking after two boys single-handed must be getting to him. That, and the heat.

She went on in a much nicer voice, 'Would you be able to tell me how big they are? Just roughly.'

There was an uncertain silence. Ewan had never had a great interest in such things. 'Not as big as yours,' he declared eventually.

'I should hope not.' And hers had grown a size too, with all the weight she'd put on.

'They're kind of pert,' he elaborated. 'The way you see on young girls.'

'Ewan!'

'I'm just trying to explain here!' He sounded agonised. She could almost see him forming embarrassed shapes with his hands. 'About as big as that bikini top you bought by mistake last year. What size was that?'

'32A?'

'That's it!'

Oh God. Jamie – with size 32A breasts? Her first training bra had only been 28AA.

'Is he upset?' she said, her heart twisting in sympathy.

'Of course he's upset! He's a boy! And overnight he's grown a pair of tits!'

'Ewan!' There was no need to be crude.

He took a shaky breath. 'Sorry. It's taken us all by surprise. He never said a thing – just refused to go diving. It makes sense now, of course.'

It was the first she'd heard of diving. But then

another thought struck her.

'What about Neil?' she asked in dread. 'He hasn't . . .?'

'Oh, no. Flat as a pancake. I just had a look.'

Thank God. But it would make it worse on Jamie. 'You *are* talking to him about this, aren't you?' she asked.

'What?'

'Supporting him, Ewan.' This seemed an unfortunate choice of words, so she added, 'Reassuring him.'

Ewan said, 'No, Grace, I've put him in a corner and totally ignored him.'

'I didn't mean—'

'Of course I'm talking to him. But it's kind of hard to explain to a boy why he's suddenly grown a couple of puppies like that.'

'Ewan. That is exactly the kind of thing *not* to say.'

'Look, there'll be plenty of time for talking later,' he said impatiently. 'We need action. I'm ringing you to find out what we should do.'

Good question. She felt ridiculously helpless, sitting there on a hard wooden chair in Adam's red *Save The World* T-shirt and precious little else. And shaky, too, after the news – well, obviously it wasn't as bad as a phone call saying Jamie was very sick or something, or badly injured. But it was still unexpected to say the least.

'Well?' said Ewan expectantly, irritating her. Couldn't he take charge for once?

'Let me speak to Jamie,' she said.

'Great,' he said, sounding relieved. 'And while you're sorting him out, I suppose I could look up the phone book and call a doctor.'

Grace plucked nervously at her T-shirt as she waited for the handover to take place. What on earth was she to say to him? That these things happen? That it was perfectly normal? (She could just imagine gym class at school.) No, none of her usual reassurances or guarantees could be applied in this instance.

A voice came on the phone. 'Mum?'

'Jamie?'

He burst into tears. 'I want to come home!'

'Oh, Jamie.' She swallowed back tears of her own. 'Look, I know this is hard. Dad has been telling me all about it.'

'I'm an embarrassment to him,' Jamie said, crying harder.

'You are not!'

'I am. He tries not to look at my chest, and he keeps asking me do I want to have a lie-down, like I'm sick or something! And Neil says they're going to have to cut them off in the hospital.'

'Sweetheart! Nobody is cutting them off.' She was raging with Ewan for not nipping that one in the bud.

Jamie went on, 'Neil says I'll have to get a job in a circus freak show, or on a smutty TV programme – Mum, who's Benny Hill?'

'Nobody, it doesn't matter. Listen, the very next time Neil says something like that, you ring me straightaway, do you hear me? I'll deal with him,' she said grimly.

Her heart was all Jamie's at the moment. Jamie – her delicate little boy! Much better had the whole thing happened to Neil really. He would probably have turned them into assets and made a fortune out of the tabloids.

'Mum, what are we going to do? I can't go back to school the week after next with boobs!'

She made her voice very bright and breezy. 'Don't be silly now. Whatever this thing is, we're going to sort it out. It's probably something very simple, maybe an allergy or something – ' she crossed her fingers behind her back – 'which the doctors will know when they examine you. Okay?'

'Okay,' he said. He had stopped crying.

'I'll just bet that you're not the first boy in the world this has happened to, and you won't be the last.' At last she'd found one of her old reassurances that could apply – surely it must be true, even in the case of renegade breasts?

Jamie appeared to think so. 'I suppose.'

'Now put Dad back on. I'll talk to you tomorrow, all right?'

'Yeh.'

After a long moment Ewan was back on. 'Well done,' he said, sounding quite chirpy now. 'Whatever you said to him really calmed him down.'

'Did you find the number of a doctor?'

'I did.'

'And it mightn't be a bad idea to order in a pizza and rent a film – take his mind off things.'

He must have sensed recrimination in her voice or something, because he said, 'Grace, this isn't exactly easy, you know. The last thing you expect on a Disney holiday is to find that your son has grown a pair of breasts.'

'I know, Ewan.'

They had probably been bouncing merrily under his nose like *Baywatch* extras for days and he hadn't noticed. Although, in fairness, Grace would bet that Jamie had been doing his best to hide them, possibly even strapping them down – all those long sessions in the bathroom! – for how could he confide such a thing to a father and brother whose only thought was the next gung-ho activity? It would be like confessing to periods in a rugby room.

'Right, well, ring me in the morning and tell me what the doctor says,' she instructed Ewan. 'I'll try to find out more this end.'

'Okay,' he said. 'And Grace?'

'What is it, Ewan,' she said impatiently, expecting more excuses and apologies.

'Where were you when the phone rang?'

She sat very still. 'What?'

'Mrs Carr, it seemed she couldn't find you. I thought it was a bit funny, given that it's the middle of the night over there.'

'I was just in the bathroom,' she said, amazed that her voice sounded so normal. 'Call me tomorrow.' She hung up before he could ask anything else.

Fourteen

Even in the midst of all the upset, the sleeplessness, the frantic chats with Natalie's sister-in-law who was a doctor, the phone calls back and forth to the States, Grace could not conceal her sense of triumph; of victory. She hated herself for feeling such things, of course, given the seriousness of the situation, but she couldn't help it: they still needed her. Desperately. Right now she was the only person who would do. Oh, how it made her heart sing! In fact, it was difficult to maintain the required level of gravity at all times.

'Boobs – isn't it awful!' she sang happily to Julia.

Julia looked at her rather peculiarly.

'Poor little mite,' Grace added guiltily.

Of course it was awful – but wasn't every cloud allowed a little silver lining? And if it benefited Grace in this case, was that so awful either? No longer would she be forced to retell bad jokes or perform incredible tricks with foodstuffs in an effort to get their attention. An unexpected twist of fate had brought her boys back to her (well, Jamie anyway. God only knows what it would take for Neil to need her again. The growth of a second willy, perhaps). She felt as if her whole world had shifted on its axis and suddenly come right again.

It was hard to hide her feelings from Ewan, even though she did her best – Jamie was in the throes of a crisis, after all, and now wasn't the time to go chortling loudly to her husband that she was top dog again and he was out, buster! But it was there in her tone, which had acquired a new confidence and authority. 'Put him on to me, will you?' she would instruct Ewan calmly in the days that followed, as though she were an eminent surgeon about to perform a life-saving operation while he was merely the nurse in the background appointed to wipe her brow.

'Grace,' he'd said on the phone yesterday, 'with all due respect, I think I know how to put on a Band-aid.'

'I'm not saying you don't. I'm just reminding you that you need to make sure the area underneath is dry first, that's all. Sometimes you forget,' she said nicely. He did too. (This was nothing to do with Jamie's breasts – Neil had skinned a knee whilst roller-blading. But Grace asserted her new authority in his case too.)

But his protests were token only, and at the end of their conversations he would hand over the phone to Jamie with indecent haste. 'You always know what to say to him, Grace.'

It was flattering. And she *did* know what to say to him. Ewan would only go upsetting him by pointing out other people who were a bit physically odd, as he had yesterday apparently. 'I didn't want him thinking that he was the only one,' he had said in his defence.

Grace had let it pass. She was letting a lot of things

pass because she didn't want Jamie to get caught in the middle of an argument about shortcomings and inadequacies.

Also, she was a bit afraid that if she pushed Ewan too far, he might bring up again the subject of her exact whereabouts that night. Careful questioning of Julia had revealed a couple of worrying details.

'Well, when you weren't in your room or the bathroom, I checked the back garden in case you couldn't sleep and had gone for a walk. You often went missing at night, I told him.'

Grace had felt as though the air had been sucked out of her chest. 'You told . . . Ewan this?'

'Well, it's a cordless phone, Grace. I was just kind of making conversation as I went.' She must have seen something in Grace's face. 'Did I do something wrong?'

'No, no!'

But Julia had been worried, anxious to clarify. 'Remember last week when I lost my crutch in the middle of the night and I couldn't find you anywhere? And the time I woke up and the dressing was too tight and my foot had gone numb . . . I didn't tell Ewan this,' she'd added hastily. 'I'm just saying.'

'Weak bladder. That's always been my problem,' Grace had said limply.

'Yes, of course,' Julia had replied, but her eyes were alert in a way they hadn't been before.

Grace felt she should come clean. This was Julia's house after all; and Grace was supposed to be looking after her, not having it off with one of her lodgers. And now that Julia was suspicious, it wouldn't be fair to ask her to lie on Grace's behalf should the occasion arise again.

'Julia,' she had begun.

'Yes?'

'About Adam.'

'Oh, I know. He's a lovely young man, isn't he? Look at all that wood he cut for me yesterday – and winter months and months away yet! I don't know what I'm going to do when he's gone.' And she had given Grace one of those toothless smiles, as though she were much older and dafter than she actually was. 'Now, I really must go and do my exercises.'

'You haven't done your exercises in days.'

'I'd quit while I was ahead if I were you,' Julia had murmured, and hobbled off on her crutch.

'Testosterone!' Frank pronounced now.

Grace looked up, startled. Frank had got wind of the drama from Julia and was sitting at the kitchen table with a big thick medical book which he had brought over.

'Did you know that boys have eight hundred per-cent more testosterone in their systems as teenagers than they have as toddlers?' he demanded.

'Eight hundred percent!' Grace marvelled. It was along the lines of what the American doctor had mentioned to Ewan.

'It's a fact,' Frank said, jabbing a finger at the book. 'Your two lads are going around right now bursting with it!'

'But they're not teenagers yet.'

'Near enough.' He read some more. 'My God. This testosterone stuff is responsible for all kinds of things!' he said in horrified fascination, as though he didn't possess any himself. 'Aggression! Skin disorders! Poor concentration! Erectile, um, problems.'

'Does it say anything about breasts?'

'I don't see anything here . . .' He turned a page, as though half hoping to see a colour illustration of a pair. 'Oh, there might be something in this. "*Hormonal Imbalance. Can lead to excessive hair growth . . . sleep disorders . . . breasts!*"' he cried. Then he looked a bit embarrassed at his enthusiasm. Probably because he'd never seen a real, live pair in his life.

'What does it say?' Grace said eagerly.

He scanned the book in silence for a moment, then said, 'It's nothing to do with testosterone at all!'

'What? But you just said it was!'

'It's oestrogen that's the culprit. It says here that when the body produces too much testosterone, some of it is converted into the female hormone oestrogen. This can cause swelling of the nipples and breasts!'

She was elated. She would go upstairs and ring Ewan immediately, and tell him about this. He would be very grateful.

'Aren't you marvellous for bringing that book around?' she said.

'Sandy sent it over to me.'

Grace looked at the cover: *The Complete Guide to Illnesses and Disease*.

'How thoughtful of her,' she said.

'She's just trying to keep me in the picture about her condition. I think she'd prefer me to read about it. She's gets a bit embarrassed when she has to answer questions about it and stuff.'

'She has a slight kidney problem, Frank. Not an STD.'

Frank recoiled. 'Look, Sandy is very private that way, okay? She feels very strongly that her body is a temple, and that anything concerning it is a matter for her and her Maker.'

Convenient, Grace thought, but then felt bad. The woman had potentially a serious condition. 'How is she, anyway?'

Frank busily turned to a dog-eared page in the book. 'See all these symptoms? She's marked the ones that she has.'

There were at least twenty symptoms marked. They were highlighted in a rather jazzy pink pen.

' "Dry hair",' Grace read. ' "Dull skin, fatigue..." We've all experienced those at some point. It's called getting older.'

'They're only the minor ones,' Frank said grimly. 'Read on.'

She did. Highlighted in pink were 'extreme thirst', 'chronic fatigue', and 'dangerously low blood pressure'. The accompanying photo was rather alarming: a woman lay supine in a hospital bed hooked up to a battery of machines, and it was arguable from her pallor whether she was alive or dead. It would frighten anyone.

'Frank, is this her way of telling you that it's serious?'

His face crumpled. 'She said she didn't have the heart to come right out with it. Not that there's anything wrong with her heart,' he added quickly. 'But the doctors says she's not responding to standard antibiotic treatment. They've upgraded her condition to serious kidney malfunction.'

'Oh, Frank.'

'Yes, well, the worst things happen to the best people.' It was unclear whether Sandy had said this herself.

'So what's going to happen now?' Grace enquired.

'Well, she's trying some alternative treatments. You know, tea tree oil and stuff.'

'Frank, I don't know if tea tree oil would pack much of a punch against serious kidney malfunction.'

'Obviously you have to have faith. Sandy prays a lot. And she meditates twice a day using powerful words – she repeats, "My kidneys are working just fine!" five times, that kind of thing. You have to remain optimistic about these things, she says.'

'And the doctors? Are they meditating too, or are they actually doing something about it?'

'Of course they're doing something about it!'

'What then? Different drugs? A corrective operation?'

'They don't know yet. But one thing is for sure – she has to go on dialysis straight away.' He looked like he was fighting back tears. 'I feel so helpless. She's over there weak and in pain – the most frightening time of her life! And I'm over here!'

'Go to her then,' Grace said.

'What?'

'Get on a plane. She's your fiancée, Frank.'

'Do you not think I've suggested it? I told her only this morning that she wasn't going to put me off this time! But she said she'd only blame herself if the house sale suffered because I wasn't here to look after it. And anyway, I gather she's in some kind of isolation ward.'

'I didn't realise kidney problems were contagious?'

'They're just taking precautions until they know exactly what's wrong.'

'I'm sure they'd let you in. You *are* engaged.'

He still dithered. 'I don't want her worrying . . .'

Grace said, 'Don't tell her then. Say nothing, just go over. And I'll make sure the house sale goes smoothly from this end. I promise.'

Frank could hardly contain his excitement now. 'If you're sure . . . I'll go and book a flight this minute. Imagine her face when I turn up at her bedside with a big bunch of red roses! Our very first meeting!'

Grace just said, 'I hope she'll be everything you expect, Frank.'

She was rather preoccupied when she met Adam on the stairs a few minutes later.

'Oh! Hi,' she said.

'Hi.'

It had all been a little peculiar since the night before last. His break-up with Amanda and the phone call from Ewan had sent things into a bit of a spin. There had been no time to talk. With the festival tomorrow he was out all hours. And she was on the phone all hours. They hadn't even met at meals.

He asked, 'How's Jamie?'

'Okay, thanks. We think it might be oestrogen excess.'

He nodded furiously. 'I see. Ah, is it treatable?'

'Oh, yes. He'll be fine. Absolutely fine!'

There was a long silence.

'Well!' he said at last, his hands digging deep into his shorts pockets. 'This is certainly embarrassing, isn't it!'

'Adam, I'm sorry,' she began.

'About what?'

'Well, Jamie.'

'It's hardly your fault, Grace. Probably something in the American milk.'

She tried again. 'I meant about me being so ... distracted.'

'Well, I've been pretty busy myself. They're moving the tents and stuff down nearer the festival site this afternoon. In broad daylight! Radical.'

She had never heard him sound this bitter before. Relations must have deteriorated with Martine.

'Adam, can we talk properly?'

His eyes snapped up to meet hers, and the defensive jokey thing was gone. 'About what?'

'You know what.'

'There's no hurry, is there?' he said. 'At least there hasn't been so far. You haven't exactly been seeking me out.'

'This is an emergency,' she pointed out.

'I know,' he agreed. 'Handy, that.'

'Sorry?'

'Well, it's got you out of the whole thing nicely, hasn't it? You don't have to get into all that messy business of trying to let me down gently. Trying to extricate yourself from a little involvement that you had no intention of taking seriously.'

He gave her a look that left her cold. Her Adam! With the perma-grin and the cheeky dreadlocks!

'Come on, be honest here, Grace. It's what you're really feeling, isn't it?'

'It is not!' She took a breath. 'We haven't even had a chance to discuss any of this properly.'

'Because you've been avoiding me.'

'I have not.'

'Why didn't you come to my room last night so?'

'I was tired!' This was partially true. But the look he gave her, so knowing, so cynical, annoyed her. 'Stop sulking. My son is unwell and he needs my attention. I'm sorry if that doesn't suit you. I'm sorry if you feel neglected.'

'Neglected?' he exploded. 'I finished with my girl-friend because of you!'

'I didn't ask you to.'

'You're starting to sound like a defence attorney, Grace.'

She found that she was a bit shaky. 'You're the one who suddenly decided to change the rules, Adam! And I'm supposed to drop everything and everybody for you? Drop my sons because you decided you were in love?'

'I can't help my feelings, Grace.'

'Well I can't help them either!'

There was a horrible little silence.

Grace said, 'I didn't mean it like that . . . but we're not living in fairytale land here, Adam. Whether we like it or not, I am married. I have responsibilities that I can't shake off on a whim.'

'Not on a whim! I'm not asking you to do anything

on a "whim"! If I were asking you to do it, you'd be doing it for me.'

How was she to answer that? Her hesitation must have stung him, because he said, 'I don't know why I'm bothering here. You've already made up your mind, haven't you?'

'No, I haven't.'

'You're already thinking about the trip back to Dublin, aren't you, and how you have to air the house and water the plants and prepare a big welcome home meal for the boys. Busy, busy, busy.'

'Don't be so childish,' she snapped.

'I knew you'd say that sooner or later,' he said conversationally.

'My son needs me,' she said.

'And you just can't bear not to go, Grace, can you? Nothing would stop you swooping in there like super-woman, ready to sort the whole thing out! Get those sleeves rolled up and muck in there until you have your three boys all sorted out to your satisfaction. And if you keep yourself busy enough looking after everybody else, then maybe you'll forget that this ever happened.'

She was not going to listen to this . . . this rubbish. 'Go take your anger out on someone else, Adam. I'm not staying for it.'

'I gathered that much.'

She was halfway to her bedroom when he said, 'Did you care about me at all? Even a little bit?'

She turned around. 'Of course I did. Do.'

'Then come away with me, Grace.'

'Adam—'

'I know, I know. You're not going to abandon your boys, and I'm not asking you to. Stay here then, and I'll come visit you. Come on, we can work it out! We'll rent a cottage for you and the boys, maybe near the sea, and I'll come at weekends when I'm not campaigning. Or I'll only come once a fortnight, or once a month, if that's what you want. We can make this happen, Grace, if you want to.'

She must have looked tempted because he went on, very intense, very low, 'Don't go back there, Grace. Don't go back to that. It's killing you, you know it is.'

'Adam—'

'I love you more than he ever will.'

There was a movement on the stairs and they both turned around. Natalie stood there, red-faced after the hike up the stairs. She had Rosie under one arm and a bag of chocolate doughnuts under the other.

'Hi there!' she tried brightly. 'Say hello to Grace and Adam, Rosie!'

Rosie just stared mutely at them. And Natalie knew there was little point in pretending that she didn't realise what was going on. 'Listen, this is none of my business. I just dropped around for a cup of coffee to try and take your mind off the breast thing. But obviously you're busy. Must go – say goodbye, Rosie!'

Rosie maintained her customary silence.

'Cheerio!' Natalie said, and she puffed off down the stairs, careful to take the doughnuts with her.

Grace and Adam looked at each other.

'That was unfortunate,' Adam said. 'But maybe it's for the best.'

'What?'

'It's make or break time, Grace.'

She was cross at his presumption. 'I'll decide that.'

She left him there and ran down the stairs after Natalie.

'I knew it! I knew you were up to something!'

'Natalie—'

'But with a *boy*, Grace!'

'He's twenty.'

'He's hardly out of short pants.' A thought struck Natalie, and she squealed, 'In fact, he was *wearing* short pants!'

'He was wearing khaki cut-offs.' This sounded vaguely ridiculous even to herself. 'Look, what's bothering you, Natalie – the fact that he's younger or the fact that I'm having an affair?' Had an affair? She didn't know any more.

'My God . . . an affair!' Natalie moaned, mercifully diverted in another direction.

From the back seat of the car, Rosie said clearly, '*Jack and Jill went up the hill.*'

'Oh, good girl!' Natalie said, clapping her hands. 'Did you hear that, Grace? Anyway, listen, have you lost your bloody marbles?'

'I know this is a bit of a surprise to you.'

'I'll say!'

'But really, it's none of your business.'

'What?'

'It's not your concern. Thanks anyway.'

'So I should just butt out and let you make a total mess of your life?'

'I have no intention of making a mess of my life.'

'Grace, you're having an affair. You've given up your job, for God's sake! I don't suppose Ewan knows about that either, does he?'

'No – oh, and listen, about Frank's house.'

'Relax. I sold it.'

Grace was dismayed. 'What?'

'I was just over with Frank to get the okay. He was so excited that he upgraded some airline ticket he was buying to business class. Now stop trying to change the subject. We were talking about Adam!'

'What about him?'

'What are you doing with him, Grace? Experimenting? Enjoying all that "youthful energy"?'

'For heaven's sake, Natalie.'

'What? Well, it's true, isn't it? They have loads of go in them at that age, I hear. You couldn't stop them – at it morning, noon and night!'

'Now you're just being crude.'

Natalie was making it all out to be so cheap and lurid: the older woman desperate for sex, and the young, lithe man only too happy to oblige. Grace could perfectly understand why some women hid their relationships with younger men.

At the same time, it would be very false of her to claim that she wasn't having sex – and enjoying every minute of it.

'It's not just the sex!'

Natalie scoffed. 'What, you're after him for his personality?'

'I think I might be in love with him.'

'You . . .?' Natalie was aghast. 'Please tell me you're joking.'

'*Jack and Jill went up the hill!*' Rosie shouted.

'Yes, lovely, darling.' Natalie twisted in the driver's seat to look at Grace straight on.

'And is he in love with you?'

The way she said it was so doubtful, so insultingly doubtful, that Grace felt compelled to boast, 'Madly. You heard him yourself.'

'Yes, yes. Look, Grace, I don't mean to take the gloss off things, but men that age . . . well, they can say things they don't necessarily mean.'

'Adam does not say things he doesn't mean,' Grace said coldly. Damn her anyway.

'But, Grace, they can get carried away.'

'Does this have a point, Natalie?'

'Look, do you really know what you're doing? I mean, how could this have *happened*?'

Good question. In retrospect she should have weighed up the pros and the cons a bit better before rushing right on in there. She, who could juggle a household budget with one hand tied behind her back! (And do the washing-up.)

'I don't know,' she said honestly. 'I guess it was just one of those impulsive things. I gave in to the heat of the moment.'

'The heat of the moment!' Natalie looked like she would pass out at this point.

And suddenly Grace was sick of it. 'Yes, such things do exist still, you know! Passion, romance, lust – remember those? Just sheer possibilities, Natalie? Or did you leave them behind in the mad rush, just like me?'

Natalie's mouth puckered; how come she was suddenly under attack? 'Don't be excusing your actions, Grace.'

'And don't you be hiding behind your outrage when you'd take it too if it were offered to you on a plate.'

Now Natalie really did look outraged. 'I would not!'

'You'd be crazy not to.'

'Well . . . well . . . supposing Paul found out!'

'Supposing there was no chance that he ever would?'

'Jack and Jill—'

'Shut up, darling! I would never have an affair on Paul!'

'Not even if some gorgeous, charismatic man came along and plucked you from the ironing and the washing-up and told you how beautiful and desirable you were?'

'The ironing?' There was a slight catch in her throat. Rosie's stuff alone was a full-time job.

'Who made you feel special and strong, and like you were the only woman in the whole world?'

'There's no such man!' Natalie shouted jealously.

'There is!' Grace shouted back. 'There is, and I bloody had him, and he makes me feel the best I've ever felt in my whole life, and I'm not a bit sorry!'

This outburst shocked them both, and they flopped back in their respective seats and fanned themselves furiously with road maps and spare nappies. The heat was cruel. Grace took a breath and suddenly she felt like laughing out loud: at the ridiculousness of the situation; at the choice she was facing. As Natalie said, how could she of all people get herself into this mess? And, oh, wasn't it invigorating?

Beside her, Natalie said, 'Where could I find one?'

'What?'

'A boy.'

'You want a boy?'

'Yes. Does Adam have any friends that might be interested in me, do you think?'

'Natalie—'

'After I have the baby, of course. And drop some of this weight – nobody could fancy me the way I am now. Rosie! Eat that banana or put it down.'

Grace said, 'Natalie, you don't want a boy.'

But Natalie pitched forward in her seat, her swollen belly almost crushing the steering wheel, and her face red and upset. 'I do! I bloody do. Why should you have all the fun? You think I don't deserve a boy or something?'

'No, I'm not saying that at all.'

Natalie blurted, 'Paul forgot our wedding anniversary.'

'Oh.'

'I know. Married seven years and he forgets our wedding anniversary. *Two children*, and he forgets our wedding anniversary!' She gave a little high-pitched sob. 'I know it's just a small thing. But it's the sum of the small things, Grace. That's what's so upsetting! That's what wears you down in the end!'

Rosie threw a lump of banana. It hit Natalie

squarely on the back of the head before sliding stickily away. She didn't seem to care. 'Sometimes I look at him, Grace, and I know him so well that I can't stand him. The shape of his ears and the way he answers the phone and the smell of his breath in the morning. Here I am, having another baby with him, and only this morning I wanted to smash his head in with the frying pan.'

Rosie stopped chucking banana and listened with interest.

'Maybe I should have an affair!' Natalie went on. 'Maybe then he might look at me as someone . . . well, as *someone*! Not just the eejit who cooks the dinner and holds down a full-time job and does the crèche run and gives birth to his children. Maybe I *should* start fucking someone else!'

'Fucking!' Rosie said.

Grace didn't quite know what to say. She hadn't meant to go encouraging Natalie. 'I'm not sure you can look on it as a solution to marriage problems . . .'

'Why the hell not? It'd be like taking a course of vitamin pills! Or having colonic irrigation or something. I mean, look at you, Grace! It's done wonders for you!'

'Apart from my matted hair and lack of underwear?' she couldn't resist saying.

'Yes, well,' Natalie said. 'What I meant was that it's softened you up. Changed you for the better. You were always such a control freak.'

A beat, then Grace said, 'A control freak?'

Natalie prattled on, oblivious as usual to any offence she might cause. 'We're always saying it in the office. Look at your desk, for heaven's sake! Never a paperclip out of place. And you do up a work plan for the week, like management tell us to do, and you actually stick to it. To be honest, you make some of us puke,' she confided.

Grace tried to give a little laugh. But she was hurt. Natalie made her sound like such a goody-two shoes. Just because she was conscientious! Just because she was organised.

A working woman with two children *had* to be organised! If she didn't do the organising, then nobody else would bother and then, well, then . . . She tried to think of some dire consequences. Then it just wouldn't get done she supposed, rather lamely. The world wouldn't actually stop turning or anything, now that she thought about it.

Natalie finally twigged that she might have put her foot in it. 'Some of us envy you too, of course,' she added hurriedly. 'And I'm sure the boys appreciate you.'

'Ewan is not a boy,' she said sharply. 'Why does everyone persist in calling him a boy? He's not a boy! He's a grown man, and it's about time everyone started realising that!'

Natalie was rather taken aback. 'I wasn't referring to Ewan. I meant Jamie and Neil.'

Grace was embarrassed now. But she said, 'I knew that! I was just making the point. And what about Jamie and Neil?'

'Nothing,' Natalie said.

'Are you saying I control them too?' Grace said loudly.

345

Natalie blanched. This had all gone horribly wrong. 'I didn't suggest that for a second! All I meant was that you do so much for them – all the dental appointments you make for them and those healthy packed lunches and the way you drive them practically everywhere in case they get snatched by a man with a big bag hiding in a rhododendron—'

'Oh!' said Grace. She had once said this to Jamie, purely as an illustration of the dangers that might lurk should he wander off on his own. She hadn't meant for him to go around repeating it.

'The thing is, you . . . you care!' Natalie finished up, damningly. Then, in a spectacularly bold change of subject, she said sunnily, 'So! Do you think he sees you as a mother figure?'

'Who?'

'Adam.'

'I'm going to thump you, Natalie.'

'What? Do you know if he even has a mother?'

'I've never asked.' She added spitefully, 'We're too busy having sex.'

'Oh!' Natalie said.

Grace opened the car door.

'Hang on!' Natalie said. 'You haven't said what you're going to do!'

'About what?'

'About Adam. Do pay attention,' Natalie said crossly.

'I think he wants me to run away with him.'

'What? Where?' Natalie screeched, and Grace thought that surely all this excitement couldn't be good for someone in her condition.

'I don't know. Tasmania, maybe.'

'Tasmania? But what about Ewan? And the twins?'

'I know,' Grace agreed.

'You couldn't leave him, Grace. Not for a boy.' When no denial was immediately forthcoming, Natalie's jaw dropped another inch. 'Grace!'

'Look, I don't know what I'm going to do about anything.' She stepped out onto the drive and slammed the passenger door.

'But Grace . . .!'

'Bye. Safe home.'

Raging, Natalie was left to manoeuvre her lumpy four-wheel drive with a hungry toddler out into the traffic while Grace drifted off across the lawn, her red kaftan swaying in the breeze.

Fifteen

'I don't believe this!' Gillian exploded. 'She's saying that I've been ringing up and asking her the colour of her knickers?'

'Please don't talk about me like I'm not here,' Julia said calmly.

'Answer the question then!'

'It wasn't about underwear.'

'What then? Maybe I was shouting the word "willy" at you, was that it?'

Michael blanched. 'There's no need for that.'

'Willy, willy, willy!' Gillian chanted.

'Ladies,' Sergeant Daly said sharply. 'There are children present.'

Over by the door, Susan threw her eyes to heaven in despair. 'I know what a willy is. I've seen loads of them.'

'Go outside and wait in the car,' Michael said sharply.

'But Dad—'

'Now.'

She flounced out. Sergeant Daly said, 'Right – let's take this from the beginning, will we?'

Gillian said, 'If I'm going to be accused of making obscene phone calls, then I should at least be told what she allegedly heard!'

'She has a point,' Sergeant Daly said.

'You were doing a breathing thing,' Julia said.

'A breathing thing?'

'Don't pretend you don't know what I'm talking about.'

'I don't.'

'You do! You were doing a kind of heavy muffled breathing.' This sounded a bit lame so she went on, 'It was very threatening. Very intimidating! Frank was there.' She turned to Sergeant Daly. 'Have you asked him?'

'Not yet,' he said.

Gillian, meanwhile, was doing a very good impression of being completely innocent. 'She's bonkers,' she said to Michael. 'She's gone completely bonkers this time.'

Michael, to his credit, didn't entertain her. He just looked anguished that all this had come to pass.

'Let's not bandy about insults here,' Sergeant Daly murmured. Why didn't he just arrest Gillian and be done with it? Instead of standing around talking it over? The law had gone very soft these days, Julia thought darkly. 'Look,' he went on, 'I asked us all to meet here in Julia's house today so that we might try and sort this thing out between us before it all got . . . official.'

'I still want to lodge a complaint,' Julia said defiantly.

'So do I,' Gillian chimed in.

Julia looked at her. 'Sorry?'

'You're not the only one who's upset by this, you know. My name has been blackened by these vicious, hurtful and – and untrue rumours!'

'Try telling that to a court,' Julia said grandly. She wondered whether there would be a jury.

Still Michael said nothing. His eyes must surely be opened now, to what he had married: a spiteful, vengeful woman who had resorted to terrorising a pensioner. Julia was surprised that he hadn't left her.

Sergeant Daly consulted his notebook. 'Have there been any calls since, Julia?'

'No.'

'Just that one?'

'Well, yes.' But one call was all it took to wreck a person's confidence. Especially if you knew they were vulnerable to begin with.

'Right . . .' he said, in a very doubtful voice. Did he think she was making it up or something?

'Why aren't you bringing charges against her?' she demanded. 'She has a motive!'

'And what might that be?' Gillian enquired.

'I didn't come to your coffee morning for deaf old farts!'

Gillian was furious. 'They are not deaf! They have tinnitus.'

'I have a touch of tinnitus,' Sergeant Daly said. 'Damned annoying.'

'I'll give you the number of our support group afterwards,' Gillian offered.

Buttering him up! Oh, she knew how to bend the law all right.

351

'I thought we were here to talk about obscene phone calls?' Julia said loudly.

'We are.' Sergeant Daly closed his notebook with an impatient snap. 'I was hoping this would resolve itself with the minimum of embarrassment, Julia. But I have to tell you – I went to the trouble of checking some phone records. And the call did not come from your daughter-in-law's home phone number on Wednesday night.'

'Are you sure?'

'One hundred percent.'

There was a horrible little silence. 'Could it have been a mobile number?' Julia enquired tentatively.

Michael finally said, 'Gillian was in bed beside me that entire night. Unless she snuck under the duvet to do some heavy breathing at you, you've got the wrong person, Mammy.'

He looked at her very coldly. Like she was the malevolent one here! After all the hurtful things Gillian had said about her tripping and falling down and dying alone! Was it any wonder she had made such a mistake?

'I'm sorry for accusing you in the wrong,' she said to Gillian stiffly. 'I can see that it must have been very . . . hurtful for you. I'm sorry,' she repeated.

Sergeant Daly gave a heavy sigh. 'Right, well, I think we've sorted that out.' Then, completely ignoring Julia, he turned to Gillian and Michael and said, 'I'm very sorry you had to be put through this. I know it's been upsetting for you, but obviously I had to investigate.'

'Of course,' Michael and Gillian murmured.

'And do bear in mind what I was telling you. There are obviously ... outside influences at work here.'

'We know,' Michael and Gillian said grimly. And then they all shook hands!

Julia stood there smarting. There was no mention of her upset. No concern at the fact that she was now terrified of her own phone.

But Sergeant Daly said, 'There was a problem at the central exchange that night. Quite a few people complained of buzzing noises from their phones.'

'I know a buzzing noise from a breathing noise,' Julia said, but she knew she just sounded even more foolish. Worse still, she sounded mistaken. Were her ears playing tricks on her?

'And how do you know the phone call wasn't for you at all?' Sergeant Daly went on. 'It could have been for one of your lodgers! Of which you have quite a few, I hear. Did you ask any of them whether they were expecting a call?'

'No,' Julia whispered, the bottom having just fallen entirely out of her case. It had never occurred to her, so convinced had she been that it was Gillian wreaking retribution.

'No!' Sergeant Daly skewered her with a very long look. 'Consider all investigations into this matter suspended,' he bit out. 'I'll see myself out.'

Julia was left to face Michael and Gillian over the kitchen table.

'I'm sorry,' she said again. And she was. She let her head droop a little to convey this. 'Truly sorry,' she added for good measure.

'So you should be,' Gillian said coldly. She was dressed all in white today. She was obviously going for the pure, innocent look.

'Yes, well, Mammy's apologised, I think we can leave it at that,' Michael said.

'Maybe I could make everybody a cup of tea?' Julia said. She was anxious now to make amends.

'We don't want to put you to any trouble,' Gillian said stiffly. The last time she'd had tea in Julia's house she had kept looking into the milk jug as though she suspected there was something growing inside it. And actually, there had been.

'Beer then?' Julia offered. 'Or Scrumpy Jack – we have plenty of that. And I think there's a bottle of Ouzo lying around somewhere as well that wasn't finished.'

Michael looked worried. 'Mammy, we've been talking to Sergeant Daly. And in the light of that discussion, and what I've seen with my own eyes in recent weeks, we'd like you to reconsider our offer to come and live with us.' He added, 'Despite the phone . . . mix-up.'

'It was hardly a mix-up,' Gillian snapped.

Michael said impatiently, 'Gillian, can we just let this go?'

This was too much for Gillian. 'She falsely accused me, Michael! And now we're begging her to come and live with us again?'

'Gillian, please,' Michael hissed, casting an anxious look at Julia.

'No, really, Michael! It's too much!'

It was only fair that Julia put them out of their

misery once and for all. 'If I could just say something.' She faced them over the kitchen table; her pudgy, unimaginative son and her fractious daughter-in-law (who was covered in little pink blobs of calamine lotion, she saw now. Was it mosquito season or what?). 'Look,' she said to them, 'It's not that I don't appreciate your offer. It's very kind and . . . generous of you, given that I'm probably not the easiest person in the world to live with.' She thought she heard Gillian give a bit of a snort, and acknowledged it with a bow of her head. 'But this is my home. I don't want to leave it. I'm sorry if you've gone to all this trouble converting the garage, but I'm doing quite nicely by myself.'

'Nicely?' Michael said, exploding finally. 'Your lawn out there is over-run by crusties!'

As if to underline his point, there was a high-pitched roar from the garden outside.

Gillian tensed like a startled deer.

'Don't mind that, they're just warming up their vocal chords for the festival tomorrow,' Julia explained kindly.

Michael and Gillian were looking at her with saucer eyes. 'We're worried for your safety,' Michael announced.

'My safety is not in question,' she said.

'Sergeant Daly said there are plans to disrupt that music festival.'

'There are no such plans. We are simply going to make our protest in a peaceful and non-confrontational manner.'

Michael said to Gillian, 'She's talking like a zombie. I told you – they've brain-washed her.'

Julia said impatiently, 'I haven't been brain-washed. I'm going along tomorrow of my own free will.'

'To the . . . festival?'

'Yes. I quite like a bit of a sing-song.'

'This is not funny, Mammy.'

'I know it's not. A shipment of spent nuclear fuel is deadly serious for us all.'

'Well, supposing . . . supposing it rains!'

'I'll be in a tent.'

'A tent!' Michael was quivering in indignation now. 'No, Mammy – I'm sorry, but I simply can't allow you to go. It's totally irresponsible in your condition!'

'You're not responsible for my condition,' Julia said. Why did they persist in treating her like a wayward child?

'Daddy wouldn't have let you go!' Michael blurted.

A little shock of guilt ran through her. It wasn't that JJ would have objected – the notion! It was more that this was the first time she had thought about him the whole day. She felt like she had betrayed him or something.

'Are there any tickets left?' Michael was saying now.

'I've already got my ticket,' Julia told him.

'For us, I mean.'

Julia wasn't sure she'd heard him correctly. 'You . . . want to come to the festival?'

'We don't seriously think we can let you go on your own?'

'I won't be on my own. Grace is coming.' She had no idea whether this was true or not, but it was the only ammunition she had left.

'Grace!' Michael snorted. 'That woman never seems to be around when she's needed.'

Suddenly Julia couldn't bear any more of them, so she said, 'Where did Susan get to?'

'I sent her to the car.'

'Well, she didn't stay there. Isn't that her out on the lawn there with Martine and young Gavin, getting love beads put into her hair?'

'What?' Gillian clattered over to the kitchen window. She moaned, 'Oh, my God! Our little girl . . .'

'They're not permanent or anything.'

But Gillian and Michael were elbowing each other out of the way in their haste to rescue their daughter from the vile influences of zealots. The back door slammed shut after them. The kitchen felt cool and airy again, and Julia inhaled deeply.

Grace's tomato plants were not doing well. For starters, there was no sign of any tomatoes. And the leaves were starting to turn black at the edges, like the lungs of a chain smoker.

She consulted Julia about them after her visitors had gone. 'What can I give them? More plant food?'

'A decent burial,' Julia muttered. 'And for heaven's sake don't give them any more water.' Grace immediately lowered the watering can. 'The roots are rotting – look,' Julia said. 'And that goes for the basil too. Just leave things alone, Grace. Sometimes they do better.'

Grace smarted – how was she supposed to know? She was only a learner when it came to gardening.

And was there no end to the accusations of smothering today?

She picked up the trowel in a bit of a temper. What the hell did Natalie know anyway, about being a mother? Toddlers were so easy! Nothing on their minds except food and sleep and the occasional poo. Just wait till Rosie turned ten and wanted to buy records by bands called Suck. Or until she decided that her left buttock wasn't complete without a tattoo. Then Natalie could turn around and dish out advice. She seemed to think that you could just point them in the right direction and let them off, whilst congratulating yourself for having the courage to 'let them go'! Next thing you knew, you were on the receiving end of irate phone calls from the neighbour two doors up about broken windows and intimidation, or the school checking the truancy records. Or worse again, the hospital emergency room checking whether you had any dental records handy (all right, so this was a bit far-fetched, but not outside the realms of possibility).

No, there was a very fine line between glorious freedom and criminal irresponsibility, and often it was a parent's whole life's work to negotiate it. People didn't realise how difficult parenting was! On the one hand, you didn't want to be so liberal that you ended up with fourteen-year-olds sleeping with each other under your own roof – take Shane O'Leary's mother, who brought up Coco Pops for him and his naked girlfriend every morning before driving the pair of them to school. But on the other hand, you couldn't lock them up (although some of Grace's friends had tried, with moderate success). The thing, of course, was to find the right balance; which was wonderful in concept but usually completely unworkable in practice and you ended up veering towards one or the other end of the spectrum.

Grace was not a Coco Pop Parent and never had been. It wasn't because she didn't *want* to be; wouldn't every parent love to teach their pre-teen five simple recipes, give them a set of house keys and a packet of condoms, before swanning off into the sunset to pick up the threads of their own lives again? Lord knows it must be easier to let the little buggers run wild and free. Wouldn't she just love to do it, and go on the piss for an entire weekend or something!

She dug the trowel hard into the ground again, triumphantly unearthing a lump of rotting basil. 'Take that!' she cried, and hurled it into the hedge. The action felt very symbolic somehow, very right in the light of her soul-searching, and she gleefully attacked the basil again, a little disappointed that it didn't offer more resistance. Perhaps the tomato plants might put up more of a fight.

'Excuse me?'

Grace looked up, red-faced and clutching the head of a severed plant. A girl was standing a cautious distance away, watching her warily.

'Hello there!' Grace said. 'Just doing a little weeding!'

The girl was in her early twenties maybe, with long hair that was neither blonde nor brown but some unremarkable colour in between. She was thin and boyishly flat and wore the standard activist uniform of faded denims and some kind of loose multicoloured shirt. A rucksack was slung over her shoulder.

'If you're looking for Martine, she's out the front, I think,' Grace told her, turning back to the basil.

'I'm not looking for Martine.'

Grace tried to place the accent. South African? It wouldn't surprise Grace. Two activists from Cuba had arrived yesterday.

The girl said, 'Is this where Adam is staying?'

Grace immediately placed the accent now: Tasmanian. She noted the airline luggage ticket on the girl's rucksack, and then she put down her trowel and stood up, heart beating a little fast.

'Amanda, isn't it? I'm Grace. Pleased to meet you.'

She held out her hand. The girl hesitated, obviously confused.

'Adam has told me all about you,' Grace assured her.

'Has he?' Amanda's thin, open face looked painfully hopeful, and all Grace's preconceptions of Babe were banished forever. This girl had never owned a pink mobile phone in her life! (She had money, though. Those runners on her feet cost more than Grace's weekly food bill. Grace had learned designer prices from the boys if nothing else.)

'I shouldn't really have come here, you see,' Amanda said, looking over her shoulder a bit nervously. 'We broke up the day before yesterday.'

Grace had to bite back a sympathetic 'I know', and ended up saying, 'Gosh!' instead, despite the fact that she couldn't ever remember saying the word in her life before.

'He says it's for the best,' Amanda added miserably.

Grace nodded compassionately. The treachery! 'Maybe he spoke in the heat of the moment,' she murmured.

'I don't think so,' Amanda said.

She looked so woebegone and downtrodden that Grace blurted, 'Oh now, come along! You haven't flown all the way to Ireland to show him a face like that!'

Amanda looked slightly startled. But, really, Grace had expected Adam's girlfriend to have a little more bottle.

'Do you think he might want me back?' she asked meekly.

'I don't know, do I?' Grace said a little impatiently. 'I mean, you've hardly talked to him yet! Nothing gets sorted in a quick phone conversation!' She saw from Amanda's face that perhaps she had said too much. 'I mean, I presume all this was in a phone call . . .?'

'It was,' Amanda said, looking a little more alive. 'Not even face to face! A five-minute phone call where he had his little speech all prepared and I didn't get a chance to say hardly anything at all!'

'They're the worst kind of conversations!' Grace cried. 'Especially long distance.'

'Tell me about it!' Amanda agreed.

She really was quite pretty, Grace thought – lovely brown eyes when they looked directly at you, and yet another set of those glorious white even teeth. If you were to describe her in beauty terms, it would have to be 'natural'. A description of Grace right now would probably be 'has let herself go disgracefully'. Oh well.

Amanda said, 'He's got someone else.'

Grace felt a little sick. 'He told you that?'

'Of course he didn't. Gave me all this stuff about how we weren't suited. But you always know these things, don't you?'

Grace thought of Ewan. 'Do you?'

'Oh yes,' Amanda said grimly. 'It's probably one of the girls on the campaign. Some gorgeous girl with long blonde hair and a cute French accent.' She gave a small bitter laugh. 'You probably know her.'

It was with great relief that Grace could state categorically, 'There's only one girl here with a French accent and that's Martine. And I can assure you that Adam is not seeing Martine.' Before she was forced down the road of ticking off the females in the house one by one, until it left only her, she said, 'Are you sure you're not mistaken?'

'I know him,' Amanda said definitely.

'Even if . . . even if he *was* seeing someone else, how do you know it's serious?'

'Well, I don't, I guess,' Amanda said.

She looked less sure now and Grace moved quickly to press home her advantage. 'You know what it's like being away from home! From your family, your friends – all the things that usually keep you grounded. Suddenly you meet someone attractive, they seem to be the answer to all your prayers, and bam! You get involved! And you might like them, you might even genuinely love them, but they're just in your life at a particular time, and they're absolutely right for that time in your life, but then suddenly everything shifts again, and . . .'

'And it's over?' Amanda said hopefully.

'Well, it might be.'

'Thank God.'

'But it might not. Oh, you just don't know what the future holds, do you!' Grace cried, agonised.

Amanda was watching her with a peculiar expression. Dear God, had she let too much slip?

But then Amanda said, 'I wish you'd talk to him.'

'Me?'

'Everything you've just said – it makes perfect sense!'

'Does it?'

'Absolutely! If you knew Adam – he's so passionate and intense, he never does anything in half-measures. And he probably met this girl while she was all needy and insecure – that's how I met him – and he looked on it as a challenge and got involved and now he thinks he's head over heels in love!' She was smiling indulgently now. 'You know, he probably thinks he's going to take this girl home to Tasmania and set up home in a hut on the beach or something – that's his dream, teach tourists how to surf, you know? – but she's probably just a flash in the pan who means nothing to him at all if only he could see it!'

'Hmm,' Grace said.

'That thing you were saying about the future?' Amanda said. 'And what it might hold? Well, you see, I know what it holds for me and Adam!'

A job on the board of one of Daddy's multinationals, Grace thought rather maliciously.

Amanda looked radiant now. 'I just need to tell him.'

So much for lacking in confidence! And really, she wasn't that pretty after all. Flat as a washboard.

'Wouldn't you have to patch up the relationship before you start planning the future?' Grace couldn't help enquiring.

Amanda immediately looked lost and broken again, and Grace felt as though she had deliberately burst a toddler's balloon.

'Say you'll talk to him,' Amanda begged. 'You seem to know him quite well.'

'You could say that,' Grace murmured. 'But really, it's not my place to interfere.'

As if she were going to find Adam with the express purpose of putting herself down! Of talking him into getting back with Amanda! She didn't know whether she wanted him for herself yet or not.

Anyway, she didn't think she could look at him – all that stuff about him liking 'challenges'! Hadn't he said from the start that he wanted to corrupt her? It was almost as though he had looked upon her as some kind of project, much like his anti-nuclear work. He might have ended up falling in love with her, but somehow it took the gloss off things. It took the gloss off him.

Amanda was chewing contemplatively on her lower lip. (What was it with young people, Grace thought? Why couldn't they ever be still? Always worrying at some bit of themselves; poking and prodding and chewing.)

'Maybe you're right,' Amanda declared at last. 'Maybe I should talk to him myself. I might be able to change his mind.'

'Good luck to you,' Grace said, with just the right hint of doubt. Well, she was allowed! 'Here's Julia out now. I'm sure she'll let you have the living-room for a bit, if you want some privacy.' She waved over. 'Julia! Amanda here is looking for Adam.'

She would stay out in the garden with the basil, she decided. She didn't know what she hoped the outcome would be; a passionate reconciliation, or else Adam might identify Grace as the new love of his life. Which obviously had a certain gratification value. But where would that leave poor Amanda?

Immediately Grace berated herself for harbouring such sympathies; surely femmes fatales weren't supposed to worry about the other woman? Perhaps because the other woman in this case was only a girl, and stealing her man off her rather made Grace feel like a big fat bully.

'Adam?' Julia said. 'Oh, he's gone.'

Grace said, 'Sorry?'

'Yes, they needed someone to go on ahead of the main group tomorrow. To set up and things. He left in a bit of a hurry with Joey.'

'What am I going to do now?' Amanda burst into tears.

Grace felt like doing the same. It had been a very emotional day. And, what with Ewan and the boys not arriving home until Sunday, she had half expected another night with Adam.

But her upset wasn't noticed, of course; not with

Amanda spluttering and choking like a walrus beside
her. Then Julia – Grace's friend! – rushed forward to
put an arm around the girl, rudely elbowing Grace
and her pain aside.

'Now, now,' she murmured to Amanda, before
turning to Grace. 'Put on the kettle for a cup of tea,
would you?'

Tea!

'I have to see him! I have to talk to him!' Amanda
sobbed pitifully.

Julia looked at Grace as if to ask what all the
hysteria was about. Grace shrugged – *she* didn't
know.

'This might call for something stronger than tea,'
Julia decided. She led Amanda off across the lawn,
and Grace heard her murmuring, 'Everything's going
to be all right. I have two litres of Strongbow in the
kitchen press.'

Grace was left alone with a handful of rotting basil
and a stomach that felt as though it had just stepped
off a roller-coaster. Oh, why did everything have to
become so complicated? She had been having such a
perfectly lovely time, and now it was all tough questions and hard decisions and soul-searching! She got a
headache just thinking about it.

In fact, she might just sit down and have a rest. She
threw the basil onto the lawn and flopped down into
a deckchair. The fierce sun was adding to her light-
headedness; for a moment there, she thought a young
boy on the road out there was Jamie. The boy wore an
Arsenal T-shirt, just like Jamie's, and had the same
knock-kneed stance – imagine! It was probably

because Jamie was on her mind so much, with the whole boob thing.

Then she sat up a bit in the deckchair. Surely that boy on the road couldn't have the exact same rucksack as Jamie too? With the same football stickers?

But it couldn't be – Jamie was in America, and would be until Sunday. Was she hallucinating in the heat? Worse, was she having some kind of near-death experience? Had all that blasted bending done her heart in?

But it was no hallucination. She saw Ewan now, stepping out of a taxi into the road, and dragging suitcases after him. Then Neil, brown as a berry and wearing a baseball cap backwards.

She was on her feet now, the deckchair knocked backwards, and her fist pressed hard to her chest. She couldn't believe it. They were here. Her children were home.

'*Jamie! Jamie! Neil!*' For some reason she didn't call out Ewan's name.

Then she was galloping across the lawn towards them, her arms outstretched, her heart hungry for them. And they were turning towards her in the road as if in slow motion, and then . . . they were backing away from her. What was going on? Why was Jamie clutching Ewan, like he didn't recognise her or something? Her baby!

She stopped in the middle of the road, hot and cross now. 'For heaven's sake, it's me. Your mother!'

'Mum?' Neil said doubtfully, his eyes wide as he took in this plump, hairy woman in a dirty red kaftan.

'Grace!' Ewan managed. 'You look . . . different.'

'What are you doing here?' she said, still a bit put out that such a glorious reunion had been spoiled by a case of mistaken identity.

'The airline phoned with a cancellation,' Ewan said. 'I asked Nick for the address of this place. We wanted to surprise you.'

'And we did, didn't we!' Jamie said triumphantly, automatically plucking at his T-shirt to hide his breasts.

'Oh, Jamie! Come here!' she said, holding out her arms, and he ran into them, and she hugged him as though she would never let go. She whispered in his ear so that the others wouldn't hear. 'How's your chest?'

'They've gone down a bit,' he whispered back.

'Thank heaven.' Her poor baby! She planted a big kiss on his forehead, and he let her.

She became aware of Ewan hovering.

'You don't mind, do you?' he said, half joking. 'I mean, maybe I should have rung first or something . . .' It kind of hung in the air.

She thought about Adam and Amanda and Julia and the anti-nuclear demonstration at the festival tomorrow, and gave her biggest, sunniest smile. 'Don't be ridiculous! Come on in, everybody!'

Sixteen

'Who brought egg sandwiches?' Frank demanded. 'They're stinking the whole bus out!'

He looked around, very accusatory.

'We didn't. We have tuna and sweetcorn, haven't we, Neil?' Jamie said timidly. He was afraid of Frank. But everyone had to be very nice to him today, apparently.

'Uh-huh,' Neil replied. After the month in Florida, he had acquired a strong American accent.

Julia enquired, 'What did you bring, Charlie?'

'Crisp bread with cottage cheese.' Charlie pulled a face. 'I'm on a diet.'

'You don't need to go on a diet,' Julia protested.

'I do! Here I am, planning a wedding, and I have thighs on me like a turkey, don't I, Nick?'

'Hm? Oh, yeh,' said Nick, who seemed to have acquired an ability to tune out every time he heard the word 'wedding'.

Gavin piped up defensively, 'Well, I think you're gorgeous, Mum.'

'Thank you!' She said to Julia, 'I've worked it out: I only need to lose a pound every six months and I'll be down to my target weight in time.'

'Oh, that's very do-able,' Julia said encouragingly.

'It is.' Charlie smiled very bravely, given that it would be at least four years before Nick's divorce from Didi came through, under Irish law. None of her engagements had lasted beyond eighteen months. But she remained very optimistic, everybody thought.

Young Gavin gave a little look over at Neil and Jamie. They had runners with lights in the soles of them, and didn't have to talk about weddings with their mother.

'Does anybody want a toilet stop before we get on the motorway?' Martine called from the driver's seat.

'No, no!' everyone called, even though several of them actually did. But nobody wanted to upset Frank further by confessing to a perfectly functioning set of kidneys. Not when his fiancée was in a New York hospital at that very moment and listed as 'serious'.

'We'll soon have you there,' Julia said to him encouragingly.

'You're very kind. Everybody has been very kind,' he said.

They were driving him to the airport, as an act of solidarity, before turning back for the festival. He was flying to London, and then on to New York.

'How is she holding up?' Charlie enquired, leaning over to pat his hand.

'All right, under the circumstances. The doctors are still trying to figure out why her right kidney crashed like that.'

It had been a terrible shock. And so sudden! One minute, she had been happily getting dialysis – well, not happily, obviously – and the next, her right kidney had packed up. That was the term written on her chart, she'd said, when she'd spoken to him last night.

Not that they'd actually spoken, of course, because they didn't allow mobile phones in the hospital. But she'd managed to sneakily use hers long enough to get on the Internet, surf some sites on kidney transplants, check the state of her medical insurance, and then compose a long email to him, Frank had said.

'So now she has only the one kidney left?' Charlie said.

'For as long as it holds up. It's getting weaker too.'

Everybody clucked and shook their heads. Of all the bad luck.

'But they're hoping that it'll keep her going long enough so that they can operate. She's top of the list, you know. They're just waiting for a suitable donor.'

'I knew a woman once who had a kidney transplant,' Nick offered. 'It was a terrific success.'

'Obviously not for the poor bugger who owned the kidney in the first place,' Charlie said, after a moment.

They all reflected on this.

'Sandy won't know whose kidney she's getting,' Frank offered, as though this made any difference.

'I'm sure she'll love it anyway,' Julia said.

Charlie patted his hand again. 'It'll be okay, you know.' Then she shouted, 'Martine! Can you get a move on? This poor man has a flight to catch!'

Martine threw a black look over her shoulder. 'I'm going as fast as I can.'

This was perfectly true. The sheer weight of tents,

banners, food supplies for two days, rucksacks and people almost threatened to defeat the ancient mini-bus entirely. But every other vehicle had already been hired, and nobody had a car big enough to fit everybody. Several others had bagged places in other people's cars, including Amanda and Martine's two French colleagues.

It was becoming increasingly apparent that Martine's little band of activists weren't terribly efficient. But their hearts were in the right places, everybody agreed.

'I say that we all have a minute's silence,' Charlie declared. 'For Sandy!'

'For Sandy!' everyone cried, before lapsing into silence.

At the very back of the bus, Grace gave a loud snort.

Beside her, Ewan gave her a look. 'What's wrong?'

'Do you not think it's all a bit coincidental? This whole Sandy business?'

'Not particularly. I'm sure she didn't ask to get sick.'

'And I'm sure it's more than a coincidence that she suddenly needs a double-kidney transplant the very day Frank agrees the sale of his house!'

Charlie looked around disapprovingly. 'Ssssh!'

After a moment, Ewan said, 'This is not like you.'

'What?'

'To be so cynical. Do you not believe in love any more?'

She looked out the window and gave a little laugh. 'Of course I do.' She didn't want to pursue this line of conversation so she said, brightly, 'So! You picked up a great tan!'

And he was wearing his contact lenses for a change, which gave him an unusually alert look. Mostly he preferred to peer vaguely through his rimless glasses. That way people would hand him things, like cups of freshly made coffee, and not bother him with nasty stuff like electricity bills or the fact of his emotional irresponsibility.

'Thanks.'

She said, 'Go on. You can say it.'

'What?'

'That I've got very fat.'

'I wasn't going to say that at all. I mean, look at me.' He patted his own gut, which really hadn't got all that much bigger.

'I'm not going to be offended,' she said.

'In that case, perhaps I can offer you a Slimchoc bar?'

She laughed. But he'd always been able to make her laugh. 'And a packet of razors?'

'I haven't been privy to your underarm hair yet.'

It was the wrong thing to have said, given that she had failed to invite him into her single bed last night. Instead he had slept with the boys on the floor of Adam's vacated room. After the shock of finding his sleek city wife barefoot and hairy in a red kaftan, it was probably his second strong indication that Something Was Wrong.

She felt him looking at her now.

'I hope you don't mind us tagging along today,' he said.

'Gosh, no!' She had said the word 'gosh' again. It was as if her nose had grown five inches.

'Because we don't want to cramp your style or anything,' he added.

Her head whipped around warily. 'What's that supposed to mean?'

He hadn't found a pair of her knickers under Adam's bed last night, had he? But no. Ewan would never recognise a single item of her underwear – even the things he had bought her himself.

'Just, you know, if you're trying to "find" yourself.'

Oooh! How had he known she was even looking? The very same man who had once passed her in the street without recognising her (never mind her underwear)?

She said, slowly, 'I just had this opportunity, Ewan. To do something different. To have experiences I never had before. Maybe you felt the same in Florida.'

'Well, now that you mention it . . .' he said.

She waited, wildly hopeful. Would he confess to watching hours of gay adult TV in the hotel room while the boys were asleep? Or perhaps to snorting a kilo of cocaine? Had he groped Snow White in Disneyland? Could he too have changed?

'Actually, no, I didn't really do anything that different,' he concluded, and she deflated. 'But it's hard when you have to look after children,' he added rather piously. 'You don't get the same opportunities.'

'I know that, Ewan. Believe me.'

'They did miss you, you know, Grace.'

'I missed them too.'

'And what with the whole breast thing . . .'

'Yes.'

'He really needs you, Grace. That's why I kept bugging the airline office for cancellations. I thought, Jamie's in trouble, and the best place for him right now is with his mother,' he declared.

'For God's sake, let's stop this once and for all,' she said sharply, and Ewan looked at her, hurt and surprised. 'This . . . this competition.'

Now he really was confused. 'What? I'm not in any competition!'

'No, you just sit on the sidelines like always. Just admit it, Ewan. It was easier for you to come home early because you knew I would deal with the problem and you wouldn't have to.'

He was cross. 'I did deal with it! Who phoned up doctors and hospitals and health insurers? Who got him started on hormone treatment?'

She sighed. This was pointless. 'You did, Ewan.'

'No, no, hang on here. Apparently I can't cope because I'm hopeless, but the few times I do cope on my own, that won't do either, will it?'

'Don't be ridiculous.'

'You want me to make a balls of things, don't you? You'd love it if we'd arrived home from America half-starved and wearing rags! Nothing would make you feel more superior! Well, I'm sick of it. Sick of always being in the wrong.'

'Then do something about it!' she hissed. 'You've managed to sit in the back seat for ten years now. And I'm sick of that!'

She realised that the chatter in the bus had given way to complete silence. In fact, the bus itself had stopped dead in the middle of the road. Oh Lord. Had Martine decided to eject them? Were the boys crying hysterically at the sight of their parents about to tear the stuffing out of each other?

But nobody was paying them a blind bit of attention. All eyes were riveted to the front of the bus: Julia's son Michael was huffing up the steps, laden with bags, rucksacks, tent equipment and a huge cooler box. He was followed by Gillian, dressed in dazzling white and carrying what appeared to be a fly swat, and, finally, Susan, with an expression of utter boredom on her face. They had obviously got tickets after all. Julia had confided in Grace last night that she hoped they wouldn't.

'Mammy!' he cried now, and they all descended on Julia.

It took them an age to settle themselves, between finding seats, stuffing things into the overhead storage space, taking it all down again because they'd forgotten something, and then pursuing a bluebottle with the fly swat.

'Get it, Michael! They can carry up to fifty different bacteria on their horrible little legs!'

Finally the bluebottle was eliminated and the bus started up again. It passed streams and unremarkable hills and green fields, and Grace looked out the window enviously at the herds of tranquil-looking cows and placid sheep. None of them with a care in the world! Whereas in a few miles she would be at the festival grounds, and Adam would be there, and he would not expect her to turn up with a husband and two kids in tow, and all hell would probably break loose.

Perhaps Ewan sensed something of her inner thoughts, because he said, 'Grace, obviously we have a few things to sort out.'

'Yes,' she said.

'You never know – maybe the month apart was a good thing,' he said optimistically.

'Do you think so?'

'Yes, if it puts things in perspective. Gives us things to work on. I don't suppose there's any harm in giving a marriage a good spring-clean every now and again.'

'Ewan, that's from one of your ads.'

His brow crinkled. 'Is it?'

'The one for lemon-zest floor fluid,' she said dully.

'Oh, yes!' He was delighted at the resonance; pleased that she had remembered. Then he reached over and squeezed her hand. 'The important thing is that we're home now, Grace. Things will get back to normal, you'll see.'

'Maybe,' she said, trying to sound positive.

But too much had happened this summer for her to doff her kaftan and pick up the threads of her old life just like that, even with a few minor improvements. She knew she couldn't go back to being that efficient, oatmeal-suited woman with a good career and a well-turned-out family, because that woman didn't exist any more. She had mutated into a person who was still very fuzzy around the edges: a plumpish woman who was confused and flawed and whose hair needed a good trim.

But she liked her better.

They dropped Frank at Departures.

'You're not coming with me,' he said, alarmed, when Grace got out of the bus too.

'I know that. I just wanted to say goodbye, that's all.'

He was all dressed up in a jacket and tie, like he was going to an interview, and he had a little nick on his chin from shaving. He looked like a country hick on his way to the big city, and her heart constricted.

'Am I all right?' he asked, worried.

'Yes. I just hope that Sandy appreciates how much trouble you've gone to on her behalf.'

'I'm not the one lying in a hospital bed,' he said stoically. 'I'm the lucky one, not her.'

'You know what hospital she's in and all that? And the ward number and everything?' Grace said, hating the doubt in her voice.

'Room 229, Floor Two, Memorial Hospital, New York,' he rattled off. 'She mailed it to me last night.'

'Good,' said Grace. Perhaps this thing might work out after all.

'Mind you, she said that might change at very short notice,' he added.

'And why's that?'

'Medical insurance or something. She may have to downgrade to a different hospital.'

Grace felt a great big sigh work its way up from her toes. 'I see.'

'It's different in America. You have to have insurance or the hospitals won't do a thing for you. Everyone has insurance.'

'Except for Sandy?'

Frank was suddenly very busy checking the tags on his bag. 'You see, she thought her employers were paying it at the nursery school. It was in her employment contract, in black and white. She got a terrible shock when she found out they actually weren't. She'll sue them, of course, once this thing is over.'

'So the only way she'll get those kidneys now is to find the money somewhere?'

'Well, you can't put a price on health, can you? That's what I tell her. You can have all the money in the world but it doesn't matter a damn if you're not well. And you only understand that—'

'What's it going to cost? About a hundred thousand?'

He went right on as if he hadn't heard her. 'You only understand that when someone close to you is sick. When they're near death. That's when you see your priorities in life.'

'Or do you get a discount for two?'

Frank clamped his hands over his ears as though he was a small child. 'Stop it. *Stop it*. She's my fiancée and I'm not going to have you say things against her. Always niggling away, spoiling things! She would never say anything against you, you know, because she's too kind!'

'Frank, sometimes people are not what they seem.'

'How do you know? How do you know *anything*? What gives you the right to go poking your nose into other people's lives and pull apart the people they love? You think you're somehow better than the rest of us? And you sitting on that bus with your husband and your children, and all the time you're sleeping with another man! If I were you I'd get my own life in order before I go commenting on anybody else's.'

'Frank. It's just because I care.'

'You don't care. You pity me. Well, I don't want your pity. Because I've found someone who loves me, all right? And I thought I never would.' He picked up his bags and said to her, 'And she's going to have her operation. Because I'll make sure she has it. I'm going to get on that plane, and I'm going to be by her bedside, and then I'm going to nurse her back to health, and we're going to be happy, okay? We're going to be happy ever after.'

And he turned and walked off into the airport. She watched him until she could see him no longer, and then she went to get back on the bus, hoping that she was wrong.

'Grace! Thank God you're here!' Amanda cried.

Grace didn't know why. Last night at dinner she had been positively rude to the girl – well, they were love rivals after all. But that was before Amanda had started to sob quietly into her soup and Grace had ended up fishing her hair out of it and sending her to bed with a hot-water bottle. And comforting her in the middle of the night when she'd awoken from a horrible dream about Adam bonking another woman

– 'A fat woman, Grace!' – and then this morning coaxing her to eat just a little bit of porridge before making her two ham sandwiches and sending her off to the festival in someone's car.

She might as well just face it: she was Amanda's new best friend.

'What is it, Amanda?' she asked, lifting a lump hammer. She was attempting to put up a tent. On the side of a hill. With a stiff wind at her back.

'He's here!' Amanda announced, bursting with the news.

Grace narrowly missed her foot with the lump hammer. 'Who?' she asked, very vague.

'Adam. There was a sighting of him!' Amanda squealed triumphantly.

'Really?' Now Grace narrowly missed Amanda's head with the lump hammer. She put it down altogether. Probably safer.

'Martine's colleague Francois met John from the UK who said that Gunther had been speaking to Ivan who had just seen Adam!'

'Where?'

'Where what?'

'Where exactly did they see him?'

Amanda looked blank. 'They just said he was here, nothing specific . . .'

'Think, Amanda, think!' Grace rasped, then, at Amanda's rather startled look, said, 'Just, um, curious.'

'You're right! I should have asked!' Amanda was anguished now. 'There are fifty thousand people here, Grace – I'll never find him.'

'Nonsense,' Grace said, looking desperately around at the crowds of young people. Worse still, everybody looked more or less the same: jeans and T-shirt, jeans and cropped top, jeans and . . . well, just jeans. So much for youth being largely a quest for individuality. 'Maybe he's wearing his khaki shorts today,' she said, standing on tiptoe. 'And his red *Save The World* T-shirt.'

Amanda looked at her a bit oddly. 'You seem to know his clothes very well.'

'Me? Yes, well . . .' She felt her face flame guiltily. She must cover. 'I'm a clothes designer.'

'Wow!' Amanda smiled radiantly. 'Do you know any of the Guccis?'

'All of them,' Grace murmured.

'Mummy has dinner with them all the time. Wait till they hear I met you!'

'I try to keep a low profile.'

She was delighted to see Martine marching up the hill to join them.

'Well?' Martine demanded. 'Where is that filthy piece of shit?'

'Sorry?' Amanda said, startled.

'Adam. He and Joey were supposed to have come on ahead to get a good pitch! Instead we end up on the side of a rocky hill, totally away from the action, while he skives off to enjoy the music. After all his radical talk too! The guy is nothing more than an armchair activist.'

Amanda's lip quivered in outrage. 'He is not!'

'Oh? How come he's down by the stage then? Instead of up here with the rest of us?'

'He's down by the stage?' Amanda's head whipped

around. (Admirably, Grace resisted.)

'Yeh, like some fucking groupie,' Martine snarled. 'If he shows his face up here, you can tell him from me to get lost, okay?'

Off she went, back down to her colleagues who were busily putting up their MOX-painted tents and unfurling banners. Someone else opened a box of leaflets. Security would be over in a minute, of course. And maybe even the police. Surely Sergeant Daly would have alerted them to the possible presence of a band of fifty anti-nuclear protestors?

Amanda gave a kind of a half-sob now. 'I'll never find him down by the stage! What am I going to do? I have to see him, Grace! I have to talk to him!'

Her knees buckled rather tragically, and Grace felt a bit impatient. 'Amanda, we're only talking about a man here.'

A very lovely young man, granted, with plenty going for him. Including a good line in making women fall in love with him.

Was she in love with him? She didn't know any more.

'You don't understand a thing!' Amanda cried, which Grace found a trifle irritating, given that she had a good ten years' experience on the unfortunate Amanda. Not that she seemed to have benefited all that much. Well, look at her! Everything solid and respectable and dependable in her life turned on its head, while she toyed with the idea of relocating to a hut in Tasmania.

The whole thing sounded so crazy that she laughed out loud.

'I thought you were nice!' Amanda said, bursting into fresh sobs. 'Instead you're laughing at me!'

'Amanda, I wasn't . . .' Grace looked at her. The girl had flown halfway around the world to find Adam. Now *that* was love. 'Stop all that blubbering and let's find him, will we?'

Amanda was so surprised that her upset shifted down a gear to a kind of a wet snuffle.

'How are we supposed to find him in the middle of fifty thousand people?'

Good question. Grace looked around, her eye coming to rest on a tall metal pole about fifty yards away. Two enormous concert speakers were attached to the top of the pole.

'Follow me,' she ordered Amanda.

Amanda trailed after her, protesting. 'Where are we going?'

'Excuse me . . . thank you . . .' Grace made her way through the crowd. 'If I could just get in there . . .' She shushed away a couple of teenagers who had taken up residence at the bottom of the pole. 'Maintenance,' she told them.

The pole was very tall and slippery-looking, but thankfully there were metal footholds to aid her ascent. She just needed to get onto the first one, which was at shoulder level to deter any would-be climbers.

She turned to Amanda. 'Lend me your shoulder.'

'What?'

'Just do it.'

Amanda's shoulder looked like it wouldn't support a fly, never mind the width and girth of Grace, but it felt surprisingly strong under Grace's hand. Then she put one foot firmly on a rucksack that one of the teenagers had carelessly left behind. Something in the rucksack collapsed with a squishy sound as she applied her full weight to it – it felt like banana sandwiches – but she didn't stop; she hoisted herself up onto the pole and clung to it like a monkey. Now it was simply a question of reaching that first metal foothold. Easy peasy.

'What a marvellous idea!' Amanda squealed. There was a little pause. 'Are you stuck, Grace?'

'No, no! Not at all. Just . . . catching my breath. Ouch! I think I just tore my kaftan.'

Amanda peered up at her. 'Will I give you a push from down here?'

'That won't be necessary.' The pole was too slippery to get any kind of grip on. But people were turning to watch now, and pride and willpower lent her a surge of strength. She managed to pull herself up far enough to get her knee onto the first metal foothold.

'Grace? I'm not sure you should be doing this,' Amanda called. 'Apart from it not being very safe, you might get arrested or something.'

'It wouldn't be the first time I've done something illegal!' Grace shouted back, for the benefit of the onlookers. Someone clapped, and Grace's confidence grew. By now she had both feet firmly on the footholds, and she began to climb. It was much harder than it looked, and she was panting and ready to give up halfway. But she couldn't give up, not with everybody watching. At last she reached the speakers at the top, and grabbed onto the nearer one, praying that it was attached securely. It seemed to be, and now she had a little platform to rest on, and there was a smattering of applause from the crowd below, and she gave them a little wave.

'Grace? Are you all right?' Amanda called.

'Yes, yes.'

She felt very high up, and she could see for miles and miles around; acres of fields, and distant towns, and the thousands and thousands of people below her, milling around like ants. Well, they were more the size of dogs really – she wasn't that far up. And there were wonderful sounds and smells and colours, and the wind was snapping at her hair, and it was as if the whole world was laid out at her feet, just waiting for her, and she laughed out loud again.

'Grace, what on earth are you doing up there?'

She glanced down. Ewan stood beside Amanda, his arms folded over his chest a bit crossly. Neil and Jamie were down there too, looking up at her with interest. They were carrying four cartons of chips.

'She's looking for my boyfriend,' Amanda earnestly explained to them.

'What?'

'Adam. Well, *I'm* looking for him really. But he doesn't know I'm here. He knows Grace very well, though.'

Ewan looked up at her. 'You haven't mentioned any Adam,' he called.

'Haven't I?' The smell of chips wafted up to her. Hmm, delicious. 'It's a very long story, Ewan.'

He squinted up at her in that vague, myopic way of

his that always made her feel tender. 'Come down and tell me about it.'

'I don't think you want to hear it,' she said back.

He said something else, but the wind carried it away.

'Speak up, Ewan, I can't hear you,' she said.

'I said I do want to hear it!' he shouted. More people turned to look at them with interest, and he looked embarrassed, but he went on anyway. 'I want to hear it, Grace. Everything.'

It was a kind of an invitation and she shifted a bit on the speaker.

'Dad, can I climb up too?' Neil wanted to know.

'No. You'd fall and break your neck.'

'Mum hasn't fallen and broken her neck.'

'She might yet. Sorry, Grace. I mean, obviously we hope you won't . . .'

'No, Neil. You can't come up,' Grace said. 'But maybe you could send up the chips?'

Ewan planted his hands on his hips and glared up at her. 'There you go again!'

'What?'

'Butting in!' He saw the boys were looking, sensitive to marital argument. 'Go on over to Nick,' he ordered them.

They did. Amanda shifted from foot to foot, agonised, seeming to sense that this had veered into the personal, but obviously desperately wanting news of Adam.

'Could we have a little privacy here?' Ewan said to her shortly, surprising Grace with his decisiveness.

Amanda reluctantly turned and followed the boys.

Ewan looked up the pole again at Grace belligerently. 'You butted in on my authority with my sons! You're always doing it!'

Grace gave a snort, but the speaker rocked dangerously with the motion and she stopped.

'What authority?' she shouted down. 'You don't have any authority because you don't want to have any! Because that would mean making tough decisions and taking responsibility and just... being there!'

'I spend a lot of time with them! I've just spent the last month with them, for God's sake!'

'Yeh – but you only want the good times, Ewan! The fun times! Where were you when they had chicken pox and bruised egos and when Mr Guppy died?'

'Who the hell is Mr Guppy?'

'Neil's secret friend. The one who held his hand when he felt too shy to leave the house.'

'Neil? *Shy*?'

'Yes. I'd swear he has panic attacks sometimes. But he never lets on.'

'What happened to Mr Guppy?'

'I think he got pulverised in a giant food-processor – look, it doesn't matter. The fact is that you didn't even know about him! Face up to it, Ewan! You've been copping out all their lives.'

A few people in the watching crowd clapped.

'You go, girl!' someone shouted.

Ewan glared around at them.

'Oh, shut up!' he said. 'My wife hasn't been home in a month! She's running around with a bunch of teenagers, she's got dragged into some political cause, and now she's halfway up a pole in the middle of a rock concert! I ask you, who's the mature one here?'

More clapping now, but a louder smattering of boos.

'You would have to belittle it, Ewan!' she shouted down, furious. 'Make it all sound so silly. Well, I'm not the one making up stupid advertising slogans for a living! I'm not the one who invests more of myself in fucking chocolate products than in my own family!'

Silence. Sensing that this had gone beyond mere entertainment, the spectators muttered to themselves and turned away. And after all the shouting up and down the pole, neither Grace nor Ewan seemed to have anything left to say.

'Will you come down, Grace?' he asked at last, quietly.

'I don't think I want to,' she said.

'I know, but the music will start up at any moment and you're sitting on a speaker. You might get a terrible fright and fall.'

'I'll risk it.'

He peered up at her, his hand shielding his eyes from the sun. 'I'm sorry that I seem to have let you down so badly with the boys.'

She gave a sigh. 'It's not just the boys, Ewan. You know that.'

He gave a little nervous laugh. 'Let's not get too dramatic here.'

'Maybe I want a bit of drama,' she announced. 'Maybe I haven't had enough drama! You're in the cut and thrust of the advertising world, Ewan. I show duplexes and the odd semi-detached.' She corrected herself. 'Well, used to. I handed in my notice.'

If he was appalled he didn't show it. 'Did you?'

'I just couldn't bear it any more.'

'So . . . what will you do now, do you think?' He must have thought this was a very loaded question, because he added, 'Work-wise, I mean.'

'I don't know. I can do anything. Or nothing at all.' She thought of Natalie's suggestions of art classes, and she gave a little laugh. 'I might become an artist, maybe.'

He looked confused. 'No offence, but you can't draw a straight line.'

She had meant it as a joke, of course, but had forgotten that Ewan wasn't in on it. A lot had happened to her in the last month – big, important things – that Ewan wasn't in on. Perhaps he would catch up. But she couldn't say it with certainty. That was the problem.

'Are you going to come down?' he asked again.

'In a minute,' she said, hedging. 'Maybe you'd go and make sure that the boys aren't eating my chips.' Even in the midst of a marital crisis, she couldn't stop thinking about food.

'Okay,' he said. He looked up at her for a very long moment, rocking back and forth on his heels, then he gave a kind of jerky little salute and walked off up the hill.

From the top of the pole, Grace could see Julia and Michael and Gillian. Nick and Charlie were going down to queue at one of the catering trucks. There was no sign of Gavin, but Neil and Jamie were stretched out on the grass with their chips, enjoying the sun. Below them, Martine and Amanda and the other anti-nuclear activists had nearly finished setting up their gear, and there was a small sea of tents, banners and flags all bearing one word: MOX.

When she tried to see Ewan in the crowd again, she couldn't.

Instead a red T-shirt caught her eye. She knew it was him even before she saw the T-shirt slogan. Adam. She had forgotten entirely that she had been looking for him.

But she hadn't been, of course. She realised now that Adam was never what she had been looking for. She had just been a bit blinded by the summer sun.

She would have to tell him. Anguished, she wondered how you went about breaking the news to someone that you were not going to live with them in a shack on a beach in a strange country with no income and only fruit and berries for food and abandoning your ten-year-old children to fend for themselves – it was impossible!

But he deserved the benefit of her new insight as soon as possible. It was only fair.

'Adam! Adam!' she shouted, waving her arms hard over her head like someone trying to guide in an out-of-control aircraft.

He looked around suspiciously for a moment.

'Adam! Up here!'

He saw her then, and his expression turned to disbelief. Perhaps he would think that she had flipped over the edge. Perhaps he might decide that, really, she wasn't the one for him at all and that he should extend his search immediately for a suitable candidate to join him in that beach hut.

But he shouted ecstatically, 'Grace! You're here!' and gave such a huge, beatific, loving smile, that her heart sank. Telling him it was over might be harder than she had anticipated. Then he started to push his way through the crowd towards her, the way you would see lovers do in the movies, and she should be swooning at the cinematic turn her life had taken – hadn't she yearned for it? All that was needed was a bit of swelling music in the background and the fantasy would be complete.

But that particular fantasy had gone. She had new fantasies now, fantasies that didn't involve Clarice Starling or small handguns or making videos with titles like *Rita Rides Again*. They didn't involve Adam, either.

She took a deep breath, and then she began to climb back down the pole.

Seventeen

'My God, Michael – did you see that? A cow pat!'

'Brace yourself. There's another one over there.'

'You don't think the cows are . . . still here, do you?'

'Gillian, cows won't hurt you.'

'They can carry TB! And I'm just over a mouth ulcer – my defences are probably down.'

Julia threw her eyes to heaven, and called over, 'Everything all right?'

'Oh, terrific!' Michael called back hastily.

'Couldn't be better!' Gillian chimed in. They were wrestling with a huge red striped tent that stood out like a beacon in the midst of all the other small green ones dotted on the hillside. Already two people had mistaken it for a catering tent and tried to order burgers from Gillian. Someone else had thought it was a public toilet judging by the wet patch on the back of it.

'You don't think it's going to rain, do you?' Gillian asked Julia, plucking at her white trousers doubtfully. She had already acquired a grass stain and two ant bites.

'I don't think so,' Julia said regretfully. A good

thunderstorm might send them home quickly enough. Although knowing them, they had brought umbrellas and waterproof gear: God knows they had brought everything else, including a barbeque, an extensive medical kit, and two folding deckchairs. And they hadn't even opened that third rucksack yet.

Susan emerged from the tent. 'I'm going to the toilet.'

'You can't!' Gillian blurted.

'What?'

'It's just . . .' She looked off down to the bottom of the mucky hill where white prefabs were lined up. Already queues of young people were forming. 'They're probably not that clean.'

'I don't care. I'm bursting.'

'Well, you might get lost!' She looked around nervously. 'There must be at least thirty thousand people here – mustn't there, Julia?'

'More like fifty,' she said.

'Fifty!'

'Stop fussing. I'm going on my own.' Susan flounced off.

'Well . . . well . . . don't touch anything!' Gillian called after her.

Julia gave a little sigh and looked down the hill at Martine and Joey and the rest. They were erecting the MOX tents and some of them were already settling down with banners. There was a great air of excitement and purpose and comradeship. Oh, it wasn't fair that Julia was stuck up here with the lay people, so to speak, away from all the action!

'I hope this isn't going to be too loud for you, Julia,'

Gillian said. She nodded towards the vast stage. 'The first band must be due out soon.'

'Group,' Julia corrected her.

Michael hitched up the band of his Hawaiian shorts over his gut, and adjusted his Red Sox baseball cap. In the midst of the sea of faded denim all around them he looked like something from a cartoon.

'Well!' he said to Julia. 'Here's to a great weekend!'

'You really didn't have to come,' Julia said. 'Grace is here. She would have looked after me.'

'Really. I just saw her up that pole over there,' Gillian said.

'Probably just a . . . temporary aberration,' Michael said. He had never been a fan of Grace's but he was obviously anxious to avoid a renewal of tensions between Julia and Gillian. To her credit, Gillian hadn't mentioned the phone thing once, although there was an odd-looking tightness around her lower face, as though her jaws were wired together. Which they might very well be – she had once contemplated a weight-loss diet that was based on such a thing. But that had been before the discovery of all her allergies and thankfully a diet hadn't been necessary since.

'It's not that we don't trust Grace, Mammy, it's just . . .' He looked around doubtfully at the crowds, the cow pats and the anti-nuclear demonstrators, before rallying. 'Heck, we wanted to come! Didn't we, Gillian? We thought, we've never been to an outdoor concert before – let's live dangerously!'

'Actually, we went to the RTE concert orchestra in the park that time,' Gillian reminded him.

'That's right. And UB40.'

'Oh, yes, they were terrific!' Gillian clapped her hands enthusiastically. ' "Red Red Wine!" ' Then her face clouded over. 'Do you remember we drank some that night? And I came out all in bumps?'

A chant went up from below: *No Mox! No Mox! No Mox!*

Gillian cast a little look down. 'Do you think they'll keep that up all afternoon?'

'I hope so,' Julia said evenly. 'That's why we're here, after all.'

'Of course,' Michael said soothingly. He gave Gillian a look that said, *humour her*.

Julia looked out over the crowd. Pretty soon security would be over to see how they had slipped through the net. But there were no television cameras in evidence. It wouldn't be much of a campaign if it only got reported in the music press. Why didn't someone do something to attract a bit more attention?

She was surprised by the strength of her feeling on the subject. Perhaps some of Martine's zealousness had rubbed off on her.

'Now!' trilled Gillian. 'Who's for a glass of Chardonnay?'

'You came,' Adam kept repeating. 'I didn't think you would, you know. But you came.'

'I did. Adam, we need to talk. There have been some developments—'

'You're here,' he marvelled.

'Yes, I think we've established that much. Is there somewhere we can go to talk?' Preferably out of the vicinity of her husband. 'Adam?'

He was staring at her. 'Sorry. It's just, I've missed you.'

'You only saw me yesterday.' She tried a little laugh. But he didn't laugh back. His blue eyes were kind of starey. Possibly he had been skimping on his sleep.

'I know. But a lot has happened in the last twenty-four hours,' he said, rather hoarsely.

He leaned in and said, 'I have a plan.'

'Adam, please, I don't want to talk about the beach hut any more—'

'I meant the campaign.'

'Oh! Well, Martine would be interested in hearing it, I'm sure. She thinks you're not pulling your weight.'

'Pah!' he spat. 'Amateurs, the lot of them. Doing things by the book. Prissy, fussy little civil servants, that's what they are. No passion! Now, you and me – we understand passion, don't we, Grace?'

'Ah . . . yes! Certainly we do!' she said, humouring him.

'And Julia,' he added. 'She has passion too.'

His eyes were definitely on the burning side. Combined with the dreadlocks and the beginnings of a beard, he had a vague look about him of a young Jesus Christ.

'In fact,' he said, 'I have to go. If the plan is going to work.'

'In a minute,' she said. 'I have something to tell you, Adam.'

'I know,' he said.

'You know?' She'd only just made up her mind herself.

'The very fact that you're here says it all.'

It took her a moment to realise the implications of this.

'No, no, no, I'm not here! Well, of course I'm *here* . . . Adam, I don't know how to say this.'

'Spit it out, Grace. Joey is waiting for me.'

'Right, um . . .'

Over her shoulder she saw Ewan stand up and look around the crowd for her. She ducked.

Adam said, 'Grace, what are you doing?'

'Nothing!' Peering up through cracks in the crowd, she saw Ewan turn to look in the other direction. 'Found it!' She straightened again, holding a muddy size-ten shoe. Possibly the wearer hadn't missed it yet.

Adam moved in on her. 'I know that you feel the same way as me, Grace. You were just in denial. And that's okay. The important thing is that you realised it in the end. The important thing is that we'll be together.'

She clutched the shoe tighter to her chest, like a kind of barrier between them. She looked him straight in the eye. 'Adam. There's no easy way to say this.'

He must have guessed what was on the way, because he started to talk very quickly. 'Then don't say it. Don't speak, don't rationalise, just go with your feelings, Grace. I have, and I know that we're meant to be together.'

It was like he had borrowed the lines from somewhere. A book, maybe. They weren't *his* words, and she suddenly wondered whether he had borrowed the emotion as well. Because there was something very . . . not false, but unreal about all this. It was as if he believed they were both caught up in some big romantic intrigue, and her eschewing her husband and family in favour of him at a crowded rock festival was the natural passionate conclusion to it all. All that was missing was for his T-shirt to be torn strategically at one tanned shoulder, and for her to ditch the smelly shoe.

She saw for the first time how very alike they were, she and Adam: for them both, real life had proved to be disappointing.

'I'm not coming with you to Tasmania, Adam,' she said. 'Neither am I going to sit and wait in a cottage somewhere in Ireland for you to come back when you can manage it.'

He must have realised how unreasonable the request had been in the first place, because he said nothing.

'This summer with you, well, it was perfect. Magical. I'll never forget it.'

'You don't have to forget it,' he said, but it lacked fire.

'Oh, Adam. You must see that it can't go on. Not for either of us, no matter what we might hope or dream might happen. I have two children. You have a cause. Sometimes the two are incompatible, do you not see? Please, let's just leave it like this. Here, now, today. Let's not spoil it at the very end.'

Perhaps he was beginning to see the sense in her words; perhaps they might have had a last hug, and a tear or two, and slipped off their separate ways into the crowd with their store of memories. Perhaps this might have happened had Martine not spotted Adam, and bellowed out across the crowd, 'You lazy pig!'

Adam whirled around belligerently. Grace immediately knew that she had a 'situation' on her hands and that she had better act fast.

'She doesn't mean you!' she said. Ewan and the boys were looking down at the stage, oblivious, she saw. 'No, it's me she's shouting at, and I *am* lazy sometimes, I'll freely admit it—'

But Adam had given Martine the two fingers. This inflamed her further.

'Fuck you!' she shouted, and began to march down towards them.

Then – oh, horror – Amanda turned around to see what all the fuss was about.

'Grace!' she said, waving over.

'Yes, *sssh!*' Grace waved back feebly, still hoping to contain things. But then Amanda spotted Adam beside Grace.

'Adam!' she squealed.

The name 'Adam' seemed to register very strongly with Ewan because he suddenly looked over too, alert to something in the air. 'Grace?' he called.

Grace pretended she didn't hear him, and anyway, there was Martine upon them, poking a finger into Adam's chest.

'You get your ass up there right now!' she ordered, pointing up the hill.

'Shut up, Martine,' he said, his attention riveted to

the hill, and the sight of Amanda joyously skipping down the grass towards him, her ponytail bouncing, just like in the closing sequence of *Little House on the Prairie*. She skilfully dodged tents and festival revellers and catering vans whilst never once taking her eyes off him.

'Adam! Oh, Adam!'

He looked at her like he was seeing a ghost. 'What the hell is she doing here?' he asked nobody in particular.

'She just came.' Grace began to see a way of salvaging all this. 'Imagine! All the way from Tasmania. Just to see you!'

But Adam just looked cross. 'She's a fool then. I told her it was over.'

'At least hear her out!' Grace said desperately. Up on the hill, Ewan was watching them intently. She decided there was no point in pretending she hadn't seen him, so she waved up happily. 'Be up in a minute!' she mouthed.

Martine, ignored, was getting increasingly frustrated. 'I'm giving you one last chance to participate in the campaign, Adam!'

'Who was that?' he asked Grace.

'Who?'

'That man.'

'What man?'

'The man you were waving at.'

'Oh, I have no idea,' she said.

'I'm going to count to three!' Martine warned.

'Count to a hundred if you want.' Adam stared up the hill. 'And those boys, Grace.'

'Boys?'

'Up on the hill. Waving at you.'

'I don't think it's *me* they're waving at . . . Look! Here's Amanda!'

And she was, puffing and wet-eyed at the sight of Adam. But she must have seen something very uninviting in his face because she came to a stop at the bottom of the hill and looked over at him pleadingly.

'Three!' Martine announced. 'Right. That's it. You've had your chance!'

'So?' Adam enquired.

'So I'm officially expelling you from the group.'

'Ooh, you're frightening me now.'

'And you can tell Joey the same too. We can do without your "help".'

'Yeh, I can see you're really shaking the place to its foundations, Martine.' He looked up contemptuously at the small band of protestors.

'We're doing more than you!'

'Don't bet on it.'

She gave him one last look before stomping off back up the hill, almost knocking over the unfortunate Amanda.

'You two should really talk,' Grace said brightly.

But Adam didn't even look at Amanda. His eyes were on Grace, and they weren't particularly warm.

'You should have said in the first place that you'd brought the whole family along.'

'What?'

'Stop it, Grace. The man and the two kids. It would have saved us both a lot of empty words.'

'They weren't empty words . . . look, they just

402

came, Adam. They arrived last night as a surprise.'

'Not too much of a surprise, thankfully,' he said sarcastically. 'We wouldn't want to have been caught in the act, would we?'

Now Ewan was making his way down the hill. Grace had a sick feeling in her stomach.

'Adam, I would have made the same decision whether they had come back or not. It doesn't make any difference that they're here.'

Except for the fact of his wounded pride, of course. Which was not to be underestimated, as she was about to find out.

'Maybe you're getting some kind of a kick out of all this. Me and him here today while you run from one to the other.' He had that rather starey look back in his eyes again, and his hands were jumpy and nervous. She wondered what this plan was that he and Joey had hatched.

'Don't be stupid.'

'Maybe someone should explain to him that his wife was having a little fling while he was away in America.'

Ewan was almost upon them now, his face very watchful.

'Maybe someone should explain to Amanda. But that would just be spiteful, Adam.'

'You're trying to dig yourself out of a hole now, Grace. I have nothing to lose compared to you.'

'It's not about losing. It's about hurting people unnecessarily.'

Ewan must have had the same feeling of impending doom as Amanda, because he stopped beside her at the bottom of the hill, and they watched the drama they didn't quite understand unfold before them, even if they couldn't hear it.

'As far as I'm concerned *I've* been hurt unnecessarily,' Adam told her. 'You used me, Grace. Why should you get away with it?'

'Please don't,' Grace said quietly. 'Not here. Not now.'

Adam turned to Amanda and Ewan and gave a funny sort of a smile.

'Talk to you later,' he told them rather cryptically. It sounded like a warning.

Then he turned and walked off fast into the crowd.

> *Come on, Libby, give it up!*
> *Stop teasing, Libby, get it on*
> *Come on, Libby, give it up!*
> *Let's get it on till the crack of DAWN!*

The deafening din from the stage rolled out over the heads of fifty thousand people and hit them full blast.

Gillian swayed slightly, as though she had been attacked. She said something but nobody could hear her. Michael held on to the armrests of his padded deckchair as though he were in the midst of a particularly turbulent take-off. When the lead singer when on to extol Libby to join in what sounded like group sex – or else rude sex, it was difficult to know – Julia thought Gillian and Michael would pack up their bags and leave altogether. She certainly felt like it – not that she would admit it, of course.

But, to their credit, they stayed put. And, finally, the song was over.

'Not bad!' Michael shouted bravely, as the last strains died down. 'I wonder who's on next?'

Gillian consulted her concert programme. 'Mutilation,' she said, faintly.

'They'll be starting up on the second stage in a minute,' Julia informed them cheerfully.

'They have a second stage?' Michael faltered.

'That way we can move around depending on what acts we'd like to see,' she explained. 'Apparently the hottest gig to catch this year is Plutonium Miss.'

Down the hill, the anti-nuclear protestors began their chant. They did it during every interval between acts.

No Mox! No Mox! No Mox!

'Where's Susan?' Gillian said suddenly.

'The toilet.'

'Michael, that was half an hour ago!'

Immediately it was panic stations all around.

'There are fifty thousand people here!' Michael began to look helplessly around the crowds.

'There's a Meeting Point near the entrance,' Julia suggested. 'Maybe we should try that?'

But Gillian was looking down at the anti-nuclear protestors. 'I'll just bet she's down there. I warned her, you know. I said to her, don't you dare go near any of those smelly people today!'

Unfortunately, just at that moment, there was a lull in the chanting below, and several of the 'smelly' people overheard and looked up at her belligerently.

'Give my daughter back!' Gillian called down, bravely taking a step forward. 'Right now this minute!'

'Who?' Martine asked.

'Susan!' No response. 'Thirteen? Pink top, denim jacket—'

'Oh. Her. We haven't seen her,' Martine tossed back.

Gillian was more determined. 'I saw you yesterday, you know! Putting beads and stuff in her hair. Grooming her, that's what you were doing! You lot, you're worse than those weird religious sects!'

The whole group turned to look at her now, rather startled.

'Found her!' Michael sang into the silence. 'She's in the tent.' Then his face fell. 'Susan!'

Susan was indeed in the tent. Her pink top was unbuttoned and young Gavin was rolling around on her – doing unspeakable things, Gillian would recount later to anyone who would listen. Depraved things. But what would you expect, with a mother like Charlie?

'Sorry about that!' Julia called down to Martine, embarrassed. 'A slight mistake!'

'Ah, yes. Sorry!' Gillian chimed, her normally ashen face bright red. Meanwhile, Michael had pulled young Gavin out of the tent and was shaking him like a terrier with a rat. 'You little shit. That's my daughter you were licking.'

Susan was leisurely buttoning up her top. 'Chill *out*, Daddy.'

'And as for you, miss . . .'

She faced up to him. 'What? Are you going to ground me? Suspend my pocket money? Take away the scooter you never bought me?'

The anti-nuclear protestors attempted to start up their chant again, but half of them were watching the drama up the hill. The chant petered out altogether as Charlie stormed past now, holding three fish suppers and a carton of noodles. Nick trailed after her with three cokes.

'What the hell are you doing to my son?' she demanded of Michael.

Gavin said, embarrassed, 'Mum, leave it.'

'Your darling son was trying to shag my daughter,' Michael informed her. Neil and Jamie, Grace's sons, perked up and listened with interest.

'Michael!' Gillian moaned.

Charlie was outraged. 'Yes, well, if she dressed a little less like a tart . . .'

'Well!' said Gillian. 'If that isn't the kettle calling the pot black!'

'Let him go right now,' Charlie commanded Michael.

'Mum, I said I can handle this,' Gavin protested strongly.

'My pet!' she said. Then she elbowed Nick viciously in the ribs. 'For God's sake, do something.'

'Uh . . .' Nick began reluctantly.

'You are totally ineffectual, do you know that?' she said to him. 'Why is it that I have to do everything around here?'

This was too much for Nick. 'Because I'm only the fucking talent! I just have to look good and entertain the punters, isn't that right? You have no idea how I feel sometimes!'

And he turned on his heel and walked off on her. Just like that!

Red-cheeked, Charlie grabbed Gavin from Michael. 'Come on, baby. Let's go watch the concert from somewhere else.' She marched off with Gavin firmly in the crook of her arm.

'And where do you think you're going?' Michael said to Susan, who was pulling on her denim jacket. 'To get more sex?'

Several nearby males looked over hopefully.

'Michael,' Gillian moaned.

'I'm going because I can't stand it any more,' Susan announced. 'No wonder Granny doesn't want to come and live with us!'

She stalked off, leaving an appalled silence.

Julia said, at last, 'That isn't the reason why I don't want to come and live with you.'

'What reason?' Michael said.

'I don't know,' she admitted. 'Whatever reason Susan meant.'

'Oh. Yes. We know that, don't we, Gillian?'

'Yes, yes,' she said, looking no wiser than the rest of them.

Michael cleared his throat, and rallied. 'Let's fire up the barbeque!'

Julia suppressed a sigh. They just never learned. It was relentless.

Gillian reached for the picnic hamper. 'We brought

some jumbo sausages and all. Would any of your . . . friends like to join in?' She nodded towards Martine and the rest.

'Actually, Gillian, I really think we should leave them alone,' Julia said. Martine had just managed to get everyone going again, and the shouts of *No Mox!* were gradually gathering momentum.

'I want to make it up to them,' Gillian insisted. 'For accusing them in the wrong.'

'I'm sure they've forgotten about it already . . . Gillian, please . . .'

But Gillian was already on her way down to them. She shouted gaily over the chants of *No Mox!*, 'Anybody down there for a spare rib? Or a burger? Homemade this morning!'

Fifty hardened environmentalists stopped their chanting for a second time, lowered their banners and flags yet again, and turned to look up at her in incredulous silence. Well, Julia had tried to warn her . . .

'You brought a *barbeque*?' Martine said at last.

'Just a disposable one.'

'We're in the middle of a political protest here! You can't go lighting up barbeques!'

Gillian swallowed rather nervously. 'Why not?'

'Who is going to take us seriously? Stuffing our faces with burgers?' She spat this last word and Gillian recoiled. 'You stupid woman! Go home!'

'Go home,' someone else echoed.

It was taken up now as a mantra amongst the others, low and pointed. *'Go home – go home – go home!'*

Without another word, Gillian walked back up the hill. She put the jumbo sausages back into the cooler box, and the burgers. Julia felt sorry for her.

'This protest is important to them,' she said to her, kindly. 'They take it very seriously.'

Gillian looked at her. 'Whereas I am an embarrassment to them. A joke. To everyone.'

Julia was taken aback. 'Gillian . . .'

'But especially to you, Julia. We always have been, haven't we, Michael and me? With our boring jobs, and our little illnesses and our stroppy daughter and our attempts to get you to live with us. Oh, please don't protest – you don't hide your feelings very well. But then again, you never intend to, do you? Because that wouldn't be as much fun.' And she started hurling more things into the cooler box with fast, jerky movements.

Michael began, 'Gillian . . .'

But Gillian just flung a hand in the direction of the protestors. 'Go on down to your crusty friends, Julia! They're welcome to you.'

She hurled a tube of sunblock into the cooler box, and the matches for the barbeque, and a couple of glossy magazines she'd brought along to pass the time.

Julia was stricken. She begged Michael, 'Say something – stop her.'

Michael said, 'Gillian, will you calm down—'

But she turned on him, two little red spots of colour high on her cheeks. 'Don't, Michael. *Don't*. I swear to God if you take her side one more time . . .' She hurled her handbag into the cooler and grabbed it up.

She ignored Julia entirely and said to Michael, 'I'm going to find Susan and then hire a taxi or something to take me home. And if you have any sense you'll do the same. Because first she had JJ – Saint JJ, who could do no wrong – and now she has some daft political cause and when that passes, she'll find something else to lavish her attention on. And it won't be you, Michael. It never has been and it never will be, so will you just stop trying! Just . . . stop it.'

Then she turned, the cooler box banging against her legs, and walked off, straight into a cow pat. She didn't even notice.

Julia and Michael looked after her, and it was like everything was frozen for a moment, then Julia tried a breathy little laugh, and began, 'Michael.'

But he wouldn't look at her. All those times he had demanded her full attention, and now he was getting it, and he didn't want it. Julia felt cold under the afternoon sun.

He said, 'You might like to keep the tent for tonight. I'll send someone to collect it tomorrow.'

And he turned and walked off after Gillian.

Nobody had seen Adam.

'What would he be doing up here?' Martine said. 'I kicked him out of the group.'

She looked a bit disheartened. Apart from the unseemly scenes of family drama disrupting the protest, the noise from the stage was so tremendous that their chanting was totally ineffectual. To add insult to injury, security hadn't even bothered to come over to kick them out!

411

'Thanks,' Grace said. She began to make her way down towards the stage. More people were arriving on the hill by the minute. She might as well forget it. She would never find him in this.

'Oh, Nick! Nick, have you seen Adam?'

Nick was sitting on the grass on his own with his lanky arms wrapped around his knees, staring at the stage.

'Huh? No.'

'Are you sure? He must have come this way.' She had a kind of a sick, nervous feeling in her stomach. There had been something very odd about Adam; something reckless. She couldn't think what he might do, but she was sure he was going to do something.

'I haven't seen him, okay?' Nick said.

His voice sounded muffled.

'Are you okay?' she asked.

'Fine.' Then he broke down in long, loud sobs. 'Oh, fuck!'

Grace forgot about Adam and hunched down beside her brother. 'Nick, what's the matter?'

'Listen to it!' he sobbed, poking a finger at the stage. 'Listen to that music!'

Grace did. There were no lyrics. Instead, the bass guitarist's instrument seemed to be possessed, and all she could hear was a relentless *woarr-woarr-woarrrr-neh-neh-neeeeeh*.

'It's so beautiful!' Nick blubbered. He wiped his sleeve roughly over his face. 'That could have been us up there, Grace. Steel Warriors. Me and the lads giving it welly! Derek out of his skull on something. Vinnie strutting around in his string vest. And the noise and the sweat and young girls hurling their underwear at us!'

'That never happened,' Grace reminded him.

'Oh, yeh,' he said. 'We just lived in hope.'

She squeezed his arm. 'You could start again, Nick.'

'No,' he said.

'Come on. Now that you're not entering the Eurovision, you can still follow your dreams.'

'Um,' he muttered.

Grace looked at him suspiciously. 'You haven't told her, have you?'

He pretended ignorance. 'What?'

'About the Eurovision, Nick.'

He flung himself back onto the grass a bit petulantly. 'Charlie can really set her heart on something, you know? I'm starting to realise that much about her.'

'Tell her then. It's not fair to let her get her hopes up.'

'I know, okay?'

'I mean, how far has this thing gone? You haven't entered yet, or anything?'

Nick gave a snort of laughter. 'God no! No, no, I've just jotted down a few lyrics. And Charlie's tinkering about with the overall look, you know? And we've talked to a few backing singers – nothing serious.'

She always knew when he was lying. He was lying now. 'Nick.'

'All right! The song is called "Kissing The Blarney", I'm wearing green and black and my first TV heat is in November, okay? Please don't tell anyone,' he begged.

'Jesus.' Charlie certainly had been busy this past week.

'Not even Ewan. And promise me you won't watch it.'

'But . . .'

'Promise!'

'I promise, okay?'

Now that he'd got it off his chest, he looked a bit more chipper. '*EastEnders* will be on the other channel anyway,' he confided. 'So probably nobody at all will know I've done it.'

'But you'll know.'

'What?'

'It's obvious you don't want to do it, Nick. Look at you, for heaven's sake! You're dying to be up on that stage playing heavy rock!'

'Sometimes we have to do things we don't want to do,' he said bravely. 'And the costume isn't so bad. She decided against the spangles in the end. Says they're too old fashioned. And I agree with her on that one.'

'Nick—'

'She has a good business head, you know,' he said rather defiantly. 'No matter what else you say about her.'

Grace couldn't recall saying anything at all about her.

'Anyway, it's all your fault,' he added in a breath-taking about-turn.

'Sorry?'

'For advising her to go into management in the first place! I have all this pressure on me now to perform!'

'You hardly wanted her to go back dancing in those clubs, did you?'

'No. She still dances sometimes, though.' And he went off dreamily into some private place. Grace didn't particularly want to follow.

'Grace!'

Ewan was hurrying down the hill towards her now, his arm protectively around Amanda. She was in a terrible state. Her face was all blotched from crying, and her nose swollen.

'G-G-Grace,' she began.

'Don't start me off again,' Nick said, sniffing a bit.

Ewan gave Grace a look. 'Thanks a lot. You ran off on us back there!'

'Yes, sorry about that. I had something to do.'

'What exactly did you have to do?'

Amanda was wracked with fresh sobs, and Grace ignored Ewan and put her arms around the girl. 'Now, now.'

'He wouldn't even speak to me!'

'I know, I know.'

'What am I supposed to do now?'

Grace tried to push her down on the grass beside Nick. 'Why don't you have a rest, maybe take a few deep breaths?'

Amanda snapped, 'Stop patronising me.'

She shrugged off Grace's hand and stalked off.

Ewan looked after her sympathetically. 'Poor girl. She's had a terrible shock.'

'But she hasn't. I don't mean to sound cruel, but she

knew before she ever came here that it was over with him!'

Ewan regarded her. 'You seem to know a lot about their relationship.'

'Not really.'

'How come you're so interested?'

'Me? I'm not. I couldn't give a hoot!'

'You seem to know Adam very well too.'

'We lived in the same house for a month, Ewan. You can't live with someone without getting to know them well.'

Although that was debatable. She and Ewan had lived in the same house together for over a decade and he had no idea of most of the things that went on in her head.

'You know something? Adam isn't important to this discussion at all.'

It wasn't that she was trying to wriggle out of the consequences of her own actions. But it would just complicate matters further.

'And what *are* we discussing here? Because I haven't a clue!'

'Us,' she said.

It had been coming all day, of course. All month, really. Actually, thinking about it, she realised it had been coming for a couple of years now.

He was looking at her peculiarly. 'I don't think the middle of a rock festival is the place to be discussing this.'

'Fine. We can go home and discuss it if that's what you want. My position isn't going to change.'

He was angry now. 'Your *position*? And what might

that be? That our marriage doesn't suit you any more?'

'We're not the same people we were when we met fifteen years ago, Ewan.'

'You're absolutely right there. Now we're a married couple who have made a commitment to each other. We're parents of ten-year-old twins.'

It was true. It was also emotional blackmail, and she was angry with him for stooping so low.

'Yes, Ewan. Two boys who have a right to expect more than they're getting right now! And we've a right to expect more of each other.'

'Gee!' he cried. 'I had no idea you were doing it for us as a *family*! You should have said!'

She gave a little sigh. 'Stop it. I know it's not going to be easy. I know people are going to be hurt. And if there was any way at all that . . . but there isn't. Not for me.'

The words were like a cold gust of wind blowing through the very foundations of their marriage. The surrounding crowd gave a little surge forward – a new act had probably come on stage – but Grace and Ewan were frozen, two people standing too far apart to be mistaken for a couple, but with some invisible ties keeping them together.

Then Ewan said, 'Grace, I'm not accusing you here, but if . . . if something had happened while I was away – ' He took a breath. 'If all this was to do with another person, then I wouldn't be angry. Well, I'd try to understand. It can happen to anyone – you think there's something better out there when really it's just short-lived. A flash in the pan, and then you come to your senses and go home to your family where you belong. I could understand that, Grace, if that's what's happened. I could forgive it.'

If she said yes, if she told the truth about her and Adam, then he wouldn't believe a word she'd said about not being happy in their marriage. He would think a young buck had turned her head, and that it was merely a question of turning it back.

He was waiting. She didn't know what to do. Tell him and be honest? Endure his 'forgiveness?' Or shut her mouth and run while she still had the chance?

There was a growing whisper around her that she could no longer ignore.

'Look! Look!'

Everyone was pointing. Grace turned to look too, and at that moment all the lights went out on the stage. The music screeched to a halt. It was as if somebody had pulled the plug on the whole thing.

The rock group on stage looked around, bemused, holding instruments that no longer worked. The lead singer turned to the wings, and said something, obviously along the lines of, 'What the hell is going on?'

Then someone ran on from the wings, and grabbed the microphone from the startled singer's hand, and shoved him away. It was difficult at first to see who it was, because he was wrapped from head to toe in a huge MOX banner.

'Adam!' Martine roared from the top of the hill, startled.

Grace stood on her tip-toes, straining to see. It was Adam all right.

'What's he doing?' Ewan asked

'I don't know,' she said. 'Talk to you later', he had said rather ominously. Was he going to announce to Ewan, to her friends, her *children*, that they'd been having an affair? Surely he wouldn't be so cruel as to hurt them like that just to get back at her?

Suddenly all the lights on the stage came back on. The mike sprang to life. Joey was obviously playing his part.

'Sorry about the interruption, everybody!' Adam roared into the mike. 'But I have something very important to say!'

Then he turned to look directly at her, it seemed. In the midst of thousands of people, was it possible that he had found her? She stood there, mesmerised, as he leaned forward to the mike . . .

'There's a shipment of nuclear fuel on its way from Japan! And we've got to stop it! We've got to take whatever action is necessary – all of us!'

Hoots of approval erupted from some of Martine's gang.

'Stop it! Stop it!' Martine shouted at them, furious. 'He's not engaged in a peaceful protest! We must distance ourselves from this!'

But she was drowned out as the chant went up again: *No Mox! No Mox!*

It spread out across the crowd until hundreds were clapping and chanting, then thousands.

'*No Mox! No Mox!*' Adam roared into the mike, getting everyone even more stirred up. Look at him – he was loving it! It was like he had been born to lead some kind of revolution. Grace found herself clapping along with everybody else.

But then he motioned for quiet, and shouted, 'There's just one more thing!'

Grace swallowed nervously. She cast a little look at Ewan. He was watching the stage very intently too. Looking at him now, knowing it was over between them, she didn't know what she felt: bereft, certainly. But it was a release too.

On stage, Adam said, 'I'd just like to say—'

Here came security at last: four big bruisers of guys bounding onto the stage. The crowd roundly booed them as they set upon Adam. But they couldn't wrestle the mike from him. He managed to get it to his mouth again. 'I'd just like to say—'

'For God's sake! Take him down! Take him down!' Martine roared.

But she was in a minority, and the crowd were really behind him now, screaming NO MOX, NO MOX, and – would you believe it – he managed to get to the mike again, kicking over two amps in the struggle.

'I'd just like to – ' he rasped again.

The mike was finally snatched from him, but not by the inept security guys. There was Amanda on the stage, tiny and determined, and she shouted into the mike for the whole crowd to hear – for the rock group and for Ewan and for Grace and for Adam to hear: *'I'm pregnant!'*

Eighteen

Nick had put on ten pounds, and wouldn't fit into his costume.

'Try holding your breath,' Charlie instructed.

'I can't sing if I'm holding my breath.'

Charlie sighed as though he were being very unreasonable.

'I'm going to let out one of the darts at the waist. That might work,' Grace said, her mouth full of pins.

'He's been comfort-eating like mad,' Charlie confided in her. 'I found him in the fridge at four o'clock this morning making a beetroot and peanut butter sandwich. Maybe I should put a lock on it.'

There was a knock on the door, and one of the television people popped their heads in. 'Ten minutes, Nick.'

He moaned. Charlie said, 'Hurry, Grace!'

'I'm going as quick as I can. It's hard to see with all these ruffles . . .'

The fussy shirt was tucked into a pair of narrow-legged black pants, finished off with a pair of ankle boots. Privately, Grace thought that Nick looked like something from Spandau Ballet. But she couldn't say that, of course – not when Charlie had hand-picked the outfit after looking at nine videotapes of previous Eurovisions. All of them seemed to have been from the 1980s.

'Nick, your nose has gone all shiny again,' Charlie said crossly. She took a big powder brush and swiped at it. 'Try to stop sweating, okay?'

Nick didn't answer. He stood still as a statue in the midst of the flurry, his face white and his pupils dilated and fixed on some distant point.

'Nick? Nick, are you all right?' Charlie said. No reply again. 'Nick, stop it. This is not funny!' She turned to Grace, worried. 'What the hell is wrong with him?'

'Oh, he's always like this before a gig,' Grace said.

'What?'

'It's called stage fright. Usually it passes.'

'*Usually*?'

'Once he escaped through a fire exit, didn't you, Nick?'

'Jesus,' said Charlie.

'But that was in the very early days,' Grace added hurriedly. 'The best thing to do is leave him alone.'

But Charlie said, 'He just needs a little pep talk.' She stepped forward and rapped Nick sharply on the chest with her knuckles. 'Now listen here, buster! You are going to be stepping on that studio stage out there in ten minutes. There are two hundred thousand people tuning in their TVs at this right moment! Our whole *future* depends on your performance tonight!'

Nick gave a kind of a low, animal moan, then gagged as though he were going to projectile vomit.

Charlie took a hasty step back, and obviously decided to change tack.

'How about a cup of tea, sweetie? No? Oh, I know – hash! A little spliff would loosen you up. Tell you what – you wait right here and I'll go score some drugs, okay?'

She hurried out of the dressing-room, waving frantically at a passing member of the television crew.

'Nearly finished,' Grace assured him, deftly sewing up a new dart. They had learned all about darts in class last week: how they were vital in the shape of a garment, but more importantly, in its fall. Of course, they had measured and marked them out properly on the big cutting table, and sewn them up on shiny new Brother sewing machines. Still, this was an emergency.

Nick burst out, 'I can't remember the words to the song! I can't even remember the first line!'

'Of course you can,' Grace said soothingly. 'You won't even have to think about it. The minute you hear the music, you'll be away.'

'Not this time. I can't go out there, Grace.'

He did seem more terrified than usual.

'Nick, it's just the same as all those gigs you used to play with Steel Warriors.'

He looked at her. 'What, in the SFX to an audience of two hundred? Tuam town hall, to fifty people? You heard Charlie – there are going to be two hundred thousand people watching tonight! All hoping and praying that I make a balls of it. It's sick, that's what it is. Sick!'

Each week viewers would telephone in their votes

on the candidates, and each week the one with the lowest number of votes would get eliminated, until eventually a winner was declared and sent forward as the Irish entry to the Eurovision. It was, Nick contended hotly, a particularly tortuous selection procedure, designed solely to appeal to bloodthirsty reality-show junkies. And the beneficiaries of the premium-line telephone charge of course.

'Have you seen the rest of them?' He jerked a thumb towards the other dressing-rooms. 'They're all about twenty, Grace.' The same age as Adam. 'They're wearing leather, and bra-tops, and fucking Bermuda tans. They've all got their own *hair*.' He looked at himself in the dressing-room mirror. 'And look at me. An ageing rocker dressed in a frilly shirt and singing about blarney stones.'

'You're not. The song is good. Whatever else you say, don't put the song down.'

The song had undergone a radical rewrite. He had insisted; had faced Charlie down over it and threatened to walk out if he didn't get his way. Any mention of blarney stones had gone. There was still a strong Dana feel about it but, as Nick had pointed out, people had certain expectations of an Irish Eurovision entry, and he didn't want to disappoint them.

'They'll be watching, you know,' he muttered now.

'Who?'

'Derek and Vinnie.' The other two members of Steel Warriors. 'Vinnie rang me to wish me luck. He could hardly stop laughing.'

'I'm sure that's not true.' She added, 'And even if it were, he's just jealous!'

'They're going to watch it in his house. Derek's bringing popcorn and beer. He mentioned "popcorn" twice, Grace!'

'There are other people watching as well – people who support you,' Grace said. 'There's Didi and the kids out in the studio audience – they're rooting for you!'

'Didi says she wants a fifty per cent cut of any earnings from this,' Nick said. 'Charlie is going mad. And Dusty says she'll be too embarrassed to go to school any more. She says it's the final insult.'

Grace cried valiantly, 'Well . . . well, I'm rooting for you! And Ewan and the kids, and Gavin, and Frank.'

'Frank hasn't even turned up.' Nick was indignant. 'And after getting him a studio ticket and everything! They're in quite big demand, you know,' he added a bit importantly.

'Yes, well, he's a bit down over the whole Sandy business at the moment, Nick.'

Even more so since he'd arrived back from the States, confused and empty-handed, so to speak, only to discover that she had bought sixty-four DVDs on the Internet with his credit card, including *The Greatest Love Songs Ever*. That, he said, had hurt more than anything.

Grace had hoped he would turn up tonight. He was spending too much time brooding by himself, and waiting for the police to ring. Sergeant Daly had tried to tell him that Internet fraud was so endemic that it could take months. Frank had said he didn't care: he couldn't get on with his life until he knew who Sandy really was.

'Where's Charlie?' Nick said nervously now.

'She'll be back in a minute.' Unless she was stoned in a corner somewhere.

'You know the way you hate her?'

'I do not hate her! I never say a word against the woman. Why do you always think I hate her?'

'The thing is, no one's ever believed in me the way she does, Grace. And I know it's only the Eurovision, but I'm terrified of letting her down. If I get eliminated tonight, I won't give a damn for *me*. Well, I might – I've put a good bit of work into this, after all. But it's for Charlie really. Tell me honestly: do you think I'll get through to the next round?'

Grace looked at her long, lanky brother in the Gary Kemp shirt and the drainpipe trousers tucked into cowboy boots and she said, without missing a beat, 'Absolutely! But, you know, I always thought red was more your colour than white . . .'

'I know! I said that to Charlie. White makes my skin look jaundiced.'

'Doesn't Ewan have a red shirt on tonight?'

'Dunno.'

'And you wore your nice new leather trousers in tonight, didn't you?'

Finally the penny began to drop with him. He looked at her, half elated and half terrified. 'She'd murder us.'

'If we're quick enough you'll be on stage before she even knows. Hurry, Nick!'

Julia was watching it on the telly at home in Hacketts-town.

'Good lad!' she shouted, as Nick sang the last note of his song, and then bowed to rapturous applause; well, not as rapturous as it had been for the contestant before him, but she had been wearing a tiny miniskirt, and had simpered and flirted shamelessly with the studio audience. She hadn't had any real talent, not like Nick.

Duncan was on next, the contestant with the stringy beard and unfortunate nose, and Julia turned the volume down.

'Mammy? Do you fancy something to drink?' Michael called from the kitchen.

She perked up. 'Yes, please.' Maybe he had brought some wine, or perhaps even a malt whiskey.

'Tea or cocoa?'

'Oh. Cocoa, I suppose.'

'Coming up. Where do you keep the . . . Ow! Found it. Shit. Spilled it!'

Julia had to suppress a little sigh. No matter how hard she tried, there was something about Michael that would always irritate her.

'Here we go!' He eventually swept in bearing a tray of cocoa and bourbon creams, which he put down on the crowded table top with much huffing and puffing.

'Michael, please don't move the telephone.'

'Sorry . . .'

'I'm expecting a call from Bono.'

Since she'd got shot, she liked to have things within reach. Her foot tended to ache a bit, especially at night, and the doctors said there was a bit of arthritis setting in.

427

And she was getting old. There was no denying that.

'Mammy,' Michael began heavily, and she braced herself. Although recently she had begun to suspect that he liked giving her little lectures. She played her part by letting herself be lectured. 'I wonder whether you're up to all this.'

'I'm just lending a hand, that's all.'

'Stop downplaying it. Bono is ringing you up, for heaven's sake!'

'And Sinead O'Connor,' Julia said proudly. 'She's really very nice, you know. Are you going to come along, Michael?'

He was caught with his mouth full of bourbon cream. 'Me?'

'It's going to be great. Thousands of people marching simultaneously in Dublin and London! And we've got rock stars and actors and politicians marching, and two boy bands – we'll have to separate them, we think – and a couple of game show winners. And Sinead and Bono, of course, if we can persuade them.'

It was going to be the biggest anti-nuclear protest in years. Martine, disillusioned with her solo efforts, had been seduced by one of the big environmental groups in London. She had asked Julia whether she wanted to work from home as a volunteer – 'Stuffing envelopes, that kind of thing.'

Within a week Julia had stuffed as many envelopes as she was going to stuff. She started to mutter about age discrimination and, sure enough, her job was swiftly upgraded to PR assistant for the forthcoming march.

She was surprised by her passion for it. She woke every morning eager to get going for the day, to start phoning Dublin and London and Edinburgh, and winning converts to the cause.

She didn't know what JJ would have made of it all: another of her fads, probably, like the rockery and the rose garden and making home-brew down in the shed. But he'd had a career; that part of him had always been amply fulfilled. He had travelled the world.

She had been left at home on her own with a small child whom she didn't understand half the time. A child who had looked at her blankly when she impulsively suggested that they paint his room the colour of a sunset with a moon rising just over his bed.

He had asked if it would fall on him.

What?

The moon.

It's just a painting, Michael, a fantastical painting.

Oh – can I have something to eat?

She should have had a career too. But it wasn't done in those days. She'd had to wait until now.

She thought now of how close she'd come to missing out on this chapter of her life. She hardly ever thought about her ham-fisted suicide attempt – it was far too embarrassing – except to wonder where her mind had been. With JJ, she supposed – JJ, her most enduring and passionate fad. Well, it was difficult, in the throes of grief, to believe that there might be a new beginning.

'Could you get me their autographs?' Michael asked now.

'Sorry?' She would never be able to tell him – Michael – about that most private and desperate episode of her life. But then that wasn't the sort of thing you told your children.

'The boys bands,' he clarified. 'For Susan. She's into all that.'

'How is she settling into the flat?' Julia enquired. It was no longer referred to as the 'granny flat'.

'Very well. Except that she doesn't want me or Gillian having a set of keys to it. She says it invades her privacy. Gillian says over her dead body.'

Julia was indignant. 'She's absolutely right. Susan is only thirteen. I think you're very brave letting her live in the flat in the first place.'

'It's not as though we had any choice,' Michael said gloomily. 'She threatened to run away with young Gavin if we didn't.'

'They're still an item then?'

'Charlie is coming over for dinner at the weekend. Says she wants to meet us formally.' Michael rolled his eyes. 'Her and Gillian . . . you can imagine.'

Julia cleared her throat. 'How is Gillian anyway?'

'Okay. She's got the hang of the injections now; at least, she doesn't faint any more.'

By a cruel twist of irony, Gillian had snagged herself on barbed wire as she had left the festival grounds that day. A routine blood test had revealed certain abnormalities, nothing to do with the barbed wire. More tests were carried out. And after fifteen years of unfounded concern about her health, of rogue symptoms and false diagnoses, Gillian had succumbed to chronic diabetes.

'They still can't understand it,' Michael said, shaking his head. 'It's usually linked to obesity and sugar consumption in someone her age. But she never *ate* anything.'

'I suppose she has to have regular meals now?'

'Every three hours, to keep her insulin levels up. She carries an alarm clock, you know, just in case she forgets and falls into a coma.'

'Would it be that sudden?'

'Who knows? And she carries two Mars bars in her bag at all times in case she gets stranded in her car during a flood or a hurricane, or there's an extra long queue at the dry-cleaners.' He thought for a moment, then said, 'You know, I haven't seen her this happy in years.'

Julia took a sip of her cocoa and said, 'She doesn't know you're here, does she?'

'Well . . .'

'Michael, I don't want to cause any aggravation between you and Gillian.' Any more than she had already caused, that was.

'You're not.'

'It's not fair to be coming here behind her back.'

He had stayed away for a whole month after the festival. She had wondered whether she would ever see him again when she'd spotted his jeep parked down the road half-hidden behind the big elm tree. It had been empty. She had thought perhaps she had been mistaken when she'd seen him sneaking across her back garden. On tiptoes. Bemused, she had watched as he had climbed up onto her oil tank, looked in, and then stealthily driven off in his jeep again.

The following week he was sneaking across her lawn again, this time with a toolbox. She had gone out to confront him and had found him halfway down one of her manholes.

'Michael, what are you doing?'

'Checking your drains,' he had confessed sheepishly. 'And you need an oil fill too before the winter sets in.'

He had come once a week after that. She didn't know what stories he made up for Gillian. Golf, maybe.

'What do you want me to do, stop coming?' he said stubbornly. 'You're seventy-three, for heaven's sake. You're my mother.'

'That doesn't really matter, Michael.'

'What?'

She said, 'I wouldn't want you to do anything out of obligation. Because obligation is a funny thing. It can tie you down, stop you doing things you want to do. It can make you resentful and neglectful to the very people you should love the most.'

'You're not stopping me doing anything,' he said.

She looked at his round, uncomplicated face and searched for the right words. God, it was hard. Theirs wasn't the kind of relationship where they talked. Or at least about the same things.

'Am I not? Here you are, sitting with an old crock because you feel you have to, when you should be at home with your wife and daughter.'

'Susan's gone with Gavin and Charlie to that telly thing tonight to watch Nick.' He added, 'You should have seen what she went out wearing.'

She tried again. 'Gillian then.'

'It's her diabetic support group tonight. It's the same night as her tinnitus group – isn't that bad luck?'

'Michael, what I'm trying to say is that maybe Gillian was right. Maybe I wasn't the best mother in the world.'

He looked at her. 'Maybe I wasn't the son you wanted either.'

'That is not true.'

'I never could think of anything very interesting to say,' he said, with a little laugh. 'And then when I *did*, Daddy would get in there before me. He had a knack of doing that.' He looked into his cocoa. 'I miss him, you know.'

'Me too.'

'But when he was gone, I thought, you'd need someone. I saw this chance, Mammy. Gillian thinks I'm pathetic,' he added.

'Yes, well, she thinks I'm a cow.' She had to say something smart, because she felt too warm and her eyes were smarting.

'She doesn't. She thinks you're insecure.'

'*Insecure*? I'm seventy-three years of age. I'm as secure as I'll ever be.'

There was a little silence, then Michael said, 'Will we have another cup of cocoa?'

'And then will you promise me you'll go home?'

'Yes,' he said. 'Then I'll go home.'

She watched him pick up the tray, and she said, 'What about Gillian?'

'What about her?'

'She'll hate me even more if you don't tell her you're coming here.'

'She doesn't hate you. She thinks you have a problem with aggression.'

'How can I be aggressive as well as insecure? It doesn't make sense!'

'Apparently it does if you're a passive/aggressive personality.'

'Just get the damned cocoa, Michael.'

'Can we have chocolate?' Neil enquired.

'Have they had chocolate already today?' Grace asked Ewan. It was always best to check. In the beginning, when everybody had grappled to get used to the new living arrangements of weekdays with Grace and weekends with Ewan, some very grave liberties had been taken by Neil when it came to the truth, almost always involving chocolate, McDonalds, and the amount of television watched.

'No,' Ewan confirmed.

Grace reached for her purse.

'If you're sure we can afford it,' Neil added under his breath.

'Poverty is good for the soul,' Grace informed him.

'I'd rather have loads of money than a good soul,' Jamie said gloomily.

'Can you not make her go back to work?' Neil asked Ewan.

'Neil!'

'No, it's okay, Ewan.' She faced the boys. 'You know that I'm studying at the moment. And when I get my qualification, I'll go back to work, okay?'

'No offence, Ma, but you're not going to rake it in making *dresses*.'

'It's not just dresses. It's fashion as a whole. Which includes footwear, hats, ready-to-wear garments, underwear. Look at all the revolutionary brassieres that have been designed recently, for example!'

The boys looked alarmed. 'We'll be a laughing stock,' Neil told Jamie.

Secretly, Grace wanted nothing to do with underwear. This wasn't just because she never wore it any more. It was the texture of the fabric – if you could call it fabric – that put her off. They even had bras with plastic straps now, for heaven's sake! And most modern underwear completely ignored the body's natural shape – how could any normal bottom hope to look good in a G-string? And most padded bras were nothing more than shelves for tired bosoms that deserved a little more comfort.

But, oh, *fabric*. Proper fabric, and the way it could be transformed into a flowing skirt or a beautiful blouse for the fuller woman. And the wonder and versatility of cotton, for example! At night Grace dreamed of bales of the stuff, and linen, and warm vibrant wool, and she would wake up to find herself licking the bedclothes ecstatically.

And to think that she never would have found fabric had it not been for Amanda! That little white lie that had stuck in her head, and matured and blossomed into a concrete idea, and finally into a post-graduate course at The Design Institute.

Natalie was taking all the credit for Grace's new path in life, of course. All because she had gone out and bought a book on further education and presented it to her. 'You'll have to do *something* now that you're an unemployed separated woman, Grace.'

'He's sweating over it. Nick is sweating all over my shirt!' Ewan said, looking up at the television screen in the corner of the room. Grace had hastily engineered a clothes swap between the two men, and Ewan now wore Nick's Gary Kemp ruffled affair – under duress, it should be pointed out. On the television screen, Nick looked splendid in Ewan's red shirt and his own black leather pants.

'Sssh! Here we go!' Grace said.

The presenter sombrely informed them that the telephone votes had been counted, collated, distributed, re-counted, tallied and verified by an independent adjudicator. And he could now confirm that the contestant in the white miniskirt and the flirty smile was the recipient of loads of them.

'Twenty-five thousand votes!' Grace groaned. 'Nick will never beat that!'

'He doesn't have to beat it. So long as he doesn't come last, that's what matters,' Neil said.

'Stop sweating on my shirt,' Ewan told Nick, quietly.

The votes for the beardy guy were now read out – twenty-nine – and he was being roundly rubbished by the presenter – 'You were pretty crap out there, weren't you, Duncan?' – and Grace was on her feet and clapping.

'He was crap! Oh, thank God!'

'Nick won't do worse than twenty-nine,' Neil declared. 'He's through.' And without further ado he and Jamie went off in search of a chocolate-vending machine. Grace still kept on eye on the television. 'Isn't it marvellous?' she said.

Ewan plucked at Nick's white ruffled shirt unhappily. 'Supposing somebody sees me?'

'Nobody's going to see you in here,' she said.

It wasn't like him to be so concerned with his appearance. Especially now that he was slowly but surely morphing into Bob Geldof.

Grace had been right – after a mere three months, Ewan was starting to show all the signs of a scatty genius who lived on his own. His hair stopped artistically just above his shoulder, and he had taken to wearing stubble and a selection of faded denims. Even his speech was more laid-back, and he said 'yah' a lot. All in all, he seemed about ten years younger. Wasn't it sickening?

Grace, of course, had filled out quite a bit more. She now took a fourteen in clothes, a size she found both comfortable and right. She didn't wear kaftans as much any more – very chilly on the legs in winter – and her wardrobe was now full of beautiful silky shirts and loose pants. Her hair had grown longer too, and it was lovely now, and so easy to manage – all she had to do was wash it and leave it alone. For Natalie's sake she got it trimmed every two months but that was about it.

On the television, the twin sisters from the midlands who had sung a cover of 'The Power Of Love' were declared the recipients of over eighteen thousand votes.

'Pah,' Grace said rudely. And then the programme

went to commercial break! 'I don't believe this!'

'It's all part of the plan to build tension,' Ewan, the advertising man, said. He reached up, turned down the volume, and looked at her.

'So!' he said, overly casually.

She wondered whether he was going to ask whether they might try again. He had every day for weeks on end in the beginning. He hadn't asked recently, though.

'Is there something on your mind, Ewan?' she prompted.

'Actually, there is.'

For all his newfound grunge sophistication, his glasses were held together with Sellotape at the bridge, she saw. He had probably sat on them again. A feeling of such fondness came over her that she almost changed her mind.

It would be so easy to get back together. And so wrong. Because one of the first things she would probably end up doing was taking his glasses down to the optician's.

'No!' she blurted. 'I must have said no a hundred times! Honestly, Ewan, I thought we had moved on from this!'

He looked a bit startled. 'I was just going to ask whether I could take the boys on Wednesday evenings.'

'Oh!'

'In addition to the weekends. Look, I can get my solicitor to run it past your solicitor if that's what you'd prefer.'

'No, no. Obviously we'll have to discuss it with the

boys, but I don't have a problem with it . . . Ewan, I thought you were too busy to take them during the week? That you only wanted them at weekends?'

'I never said "only", Grace. You make me sound so heartless!'

'Sorry. It's just with your work and everything . . .'

'Yes, well, I won't be so busy any more. We lost the Slimchoc account.'

'What?'

'Word came through last week.'

'Was it the slogan?' She couldn't really blame them. She hadn't liked it herself.

'The company's gone bust, Grace. I thought you might have seen it in the papers.'

She didn't really buy newspapers much any more. (She had started reading books again, and was in her science fiction phase at the moment, and her fantasies now involved her being captured by a couple of three-fingered Zulites with very large penises.)

'They did some new laboratory research in America,' Ewan went on. 'And they discovered that the fat substitutes in Slimchoc not only did nothing to aid weight loss, but caused abnormal hair growth and stomach distension in male rats. What it does to female rats isn't clear yet, but it's not going to be pretty.'

. 'Oh, Ewan.'

'They've pulled everything – the chocolate bars, the milkshakes, the Wicked Slimchoc Cake. They were going to trial-run the chewing-gum anyway, but decided against it on legal advice.'

'Probably wise.'

'Yes. So it's over. Finished.' He sounded very final and she felt sorry for him.

'Come on, you'll bounce back,' she told him encouragingly.

'You don't understand. I'm glad Slimchoc is gone. I'm delighted!'

'Oh!'

He flicked back a shirt ruffle from his neck and said, 'We've both had a lot to think about in the last three months, Grace. Me especially. And you were right about me not giving the boys a hundred per cent. I wasn't even giving them eighty. So I've decided to cut down on my work. Spend more time with them.' Then he added, very modestly: 'If that's okay with everyone.'

'The boys would love it, I'm sure.' She added, 'Mind you, that means there will be even *less* money.'

'They'll just have to make do,' Ewan said emphatically. 'I don't want money worries to distract you from your course, Grace.'

'Thank you.' She was touched. He had never been so supportive of her career before.

'Imagine! We're both in creative careers now!'

'What? Oh, yes.' He was looking at his watch. Possibly he had left his car on a meter. 'So this Wednesday thing – have we it sorted?'

'Absolutely. I'll tell the boys tonight.'

'It means we'll be seeing each other a bit more too. I don't know how you feel about that.'

It was another loaded question, she felt.

She kept it jokey. 'I'm sure we'll manage. We haven't killed each other so far, have we?'

'Not at all.' He looked out at her from his Sellotaped glasses meaningfully. 'In fact, I don't think we've ever got on better.'

'So we're the classic case of a couple who split up only to discover that we're falling in love all over again? How boring!' she said lightly.

'I never said anything about falling in love.'

She felt a bit foolish now. 'I didn't mean . . . of course we're not . . . '

'Grace, I'm seeing somebody. Obviously I wanted to tell you before anybody else.'

She smiled and nodded enthusiastically. She had no idea why. They had scarcely been separated a wet weekend and there was her husband telling her he was seeing somebody!

'It's not serious,' he added as though by way of compensation. 'I mean, we've only just started going out.'

She kept smiling as she wondered what he expected her to say. That she was glad for him? At the same time, it seemed a bit rich to feel so hurt, given that she had been seeing somebody *during* their marriage. But still, three months seemed a bit, well, indecent.

'What's her name?' she asked. Not that it mattered. Anyhow, she already knew that she would be called Sophie or Clio, and that she would work in advertising, and that she and Ewan had been out twice, probably three times, for sushi, and that they had probably slept together. (Had he initiated things by licking her neck the way he always had with Grace, or had Sophie said crossly, 'Oh stop it!', as Grace had

441

wanted to many times, and made him put on a leather collar and bark like a dog?) She tittered.

'Anna,' he said, looking a bit hurt. 'She's a hairdresser, she does films and stuff.' He added, a bit bashfully, 'She says she won't rest until she gives mine a good trim.'

Poor, poor Anna. Grace felt a flash of sympathy for the woman who would gradually, without even realising it, start to organise Ewan's life for him. Eventually she would be making his medical appointments and getting him two pairs of glasses for the price of one.

'I wish you and Anna the very best of luck,' Grace said, with the fervent sincerity of one who had narrowly escaped.

'Thanks, Grace!' He was delighted with himself now – at least there would be no unpleasantness with the ex-wife. He even went so far as to enquire jokily, 'And how about yourself? Any sign of a bit of romance on the horizon at all?'

It was like Adam had never happened; like he had never had a suspicion in the world that his wife was cheating on him with a twenty-year-old.

'Oh, no,' she said, smiling nicely. 'What with the boys and the course and everything, I don't have time.'

'I'm sure,' he said, nodding sagely. 'Still, you never know what's around the corner!'

He obviously harboured no mixed feelings at all about his wife starting to date again. Grace saw again, very clearly, how little of him had ever really belonged to her, and to their marriage. And for the first time in three months, she was completely sure that she had done the right thing.

For herself, in any case, and very probably Ewan, who had that unmistakable excitement about him of being back on the market again. It was Neil and Jamie she worried about.

Sometimes she thought it would have been better had they been very young, and had no memories of being part of a conventional family. Or older, in their teens maybe, with a better grasp of the difficulties of relationships. Ten seemed to be the very worst age, halfway between childhood and adolescence, and she didn't know how to make it easier on them.

'Night nappies,' Natalie had declared.

'What?'

'They've probably started wetting the bed again, have they? Lots of children going through a separation do.'

'Not at ten, Natalie.'

They seemed okay, at least on the surface. But it *must* affect them, how could it not? It was so hard to know. And if there was one thing she had learned out of this whole experience, it was that she knew absolutely nothing at all.

Except that Ewan had a date tonight. He was wearing the aftershave she had given him for his birthday last year. The idiot.

'Are you meeting her tonight? Anna?'

He tried to be casual. 'As a matter of fact, I am.' But he was fidgeting, looking at his watch, then at the TV screen. 'It's just . . . my shirt. I've got a table booked for nine. Anna's not keen on eating too late.'

It wasn't like him to be so sensitive.

'You'd better run then,' Grace said.

'Yes . . .' He plucked at the Spandau Ballet shirt, agonised.

Grace said, rather spitefully, 'I suppose it'll be a kind of a test. If she really likes you, she'll overlook it.'

Now he was even more worried, and he hardly said goodbye as he left.

He was back within ten seconds, looking sheepish. 'Hi, I think I might have . . . '

'Yes. Your car keys,' Grace said crisply, handing them over and roundly closing the door on him. She might still pick up after him occasionally but, by God, she didn't have to pretend any more that it was love.

When the door burst open a minute or so later she thought it was him back again, to look for change for the parking meter perhaps. But it was Nick, fresh off the stage, and jerky with adrenaline.

'Well?' he demanded. 'What did you think?'

Grace stared back guiltily. Imagine – she had been so engrossed in Ewan's revelations that she didn't even know how many votes he had scored! And she couldn't tell anything from his face; that peculiar stare could mean it had gone either way.

'I saw your performance,' she said, hedging her bets. She added strongly, just in case he *had* been eliminated, 'And you were great. You have absolutely nothing to be ashamed of.'

He exploded, 'Ashamed? I was fan-fucking-tastic, man! They loved me! They wanted me! I would have won only for your woman flashing her legs at the cameras. The lighting guy said a girl at the back fainted during my encore – chew on that, Vinnie!'

And he ripped off Ewan's sodden red shirt and flung it to the floor, then spat on it for good measure.

Charlie danced into the dressing room, hooting and whooping. 'Second place! What do you think of that, Grace?'

'Brilliant!' Grace said, just glad that she knew.

'Hey,' Nick said to Charlie. 'Maybe tonight. But there are no second places. *There are no second places*. We're going all the way to the Eurovision, baby!'

And he grabbed her, swung her around, and gave her a long hot kiss. Grace studied the ceiling.

'Nick!' Charlie said, when she eventually broke free. 'Are you serious?'

'Course I am! What do you think I was doing out there? Scratching my balls?'

'Well, no, it's just, I felt I was pushing you . . .'

'I need to be pushed. No kidding. Sometimes I need to be pushed, don't I, Grace?'

'I—'

'But sometimes I feel I'm pushing you too hard.'

'Push me harder. Push me all the way. Oh, baby, you smell good.'

'Listen to me. I want you to be happy too. I don't want to make you do something you don't want to do—'

'They loved me out there, didn't they?'

'They adored you. But are you sure you won't miss rock music too much? Will he, Grace?'

'I—'

'Rock music? What the hell is that? A load of old

noise! I never thought I'd say it about the Eurovision, but I got respect out there tonight, man. I got artistic *gratification*. I've never played to a sober audience before – the hairs stood up on the back of my neck,' he said fervently. 'In fact, they're still standing. Mmmm, come here, baby.'

'Nick . . .'

'I love your bottom.'

At that point Grace gave up and left.

Nineteen

Her full name was Sandy Elizabeth Roth. Aka Jennifer O'Carroll. Aka Pavlova Martinez. Aka Marie Trudeau. The search had finally led to a semi-detached on the outskirts of Ballybunion.

'She was in Kerry all the time?' Grace said, eyes wide. She had only just recovered from the Eurovision last week.

Frank said nothing. He sat on the edge of his sofa, hunched over, his eyes fixed on the brown carpet.

Julia answered for him. 'In a manner of speaking.'

'And have they arrested her?'

'Yes, this morning, Sergeant Daly said,' Julia told her confidentially. 'I thought I'd better ring you to come over.'

She was loving all the excitement, Grace could see; not to mention the fact that she had all the inside information, and Grace didn't. Look at the way she was patting Frank's arm!

'So what's her real name?' Grace asked.

He looked harder at the floor, his cheek muscles bunching furiously.

'Frank,' she said. 'There's nothing to be embarrassed about.'

'Isn't there?'

'Of course not!' Grace reiterated strongly. 'You have done absolutely nothing wrong here. Except perhaps trust too much. She's the one who's taken advantage of you! Exploited your love and stolen your money!'

'Steady on,' Julia murmured.

Grace tempered herself. 'I'm just saying that if anyone should feel bad, it's her.'

'*Him*,' Frank whispered.

'Pardon?'

'Mr Liam Hughes. Sandy is a man.'

There was a moment of dead air, and then Grace finally said, 'Well . . . well . . . I might have known!'

Julia looked at her askance, eyebrows arched. Oh shut up, Grace mouthed back at her.

'Imagine,' Frank moaned. 'All this time, I was engaged to a man!'

Julia stood. 'I think this calls for a drink,' she declared, and set off for the kitchen.

Alone with Frank, Grace put her arm around him. 'Oh, Frank!'

'What's worse,' he said, 'is that he was cheating on me!'

She eventually coaxed it out of him. At the time of his arrest, Liam Hughes was conducting at least eleven Internet romances through his various aliases. He selected his targets carefully, and his modus operandi was the same: after a number of months of grooming, he would encourage and agree to a marriage proposal, get the victim to put his house on the market with a view to moving to the States, and then at the point of sale a serious illness would suddenly strike which almost always required an expensive transplant. The double-kidney transplant was his favourite, but in the past he'd gone for a heart transplant, heart-and-lung, lung only, and once a complete brain transplant.

'But the police believe that may have been a cry for help,' Frank said. 'They said nobody could have been so stupid as to buy that one.'

'Well . . .'

'But we were. The lot of us.'

'You're not stupid. We all want to believe in people, Frank.'

'Everybody could see it a mile off except for me! *You* saw it! Well, didn't you?'

'Yes, but I'm naturally cynical, it doesn't mean—'

'The fact that she never seemed to be able to come to the phone. Her sister having a bust-up with her husband the very week I was due to go over . . . God, when I think of the lies she wrote! *He* wrote, *he* – I can't seem to get that into my head. The stuff about disabled kids, and singing at church, and wanting to be a stay-at-home mom. All that shit about fate and destiny and how we were so lucky to have found each other.' He took a breath. 'And all the time he was laughing his head off at me in Kerry!'

'I'm sure he wasn't.'

'Thinking how hilarious it was to wind up some sad old fart at the other end of the country! Cracking up every time he opened one of my emails to him!'

'Frank, stop.'

'You know, I think the police are wrong. I don't think he was in it for the money at all. I think he just got a kick out of making middle-aged men fall in love with a Perry's hot-dog girl!'

'What?'

'Oh – I didn't show you, did I?' From his pocket he took a folded A4 sheet. He spread it out, handed it to her and looked away.

It was a copy of the photo Sandy had sent to him of her on the beach, supposedly on her day-drip for paraplegic children. Only in this copy there was no tea towel covering her hand, which quite clearly held a nine-inch hot dog. There was a caption underneath: *I love Perry's Hot Dogs*!

'Oh, Sandy,' Grace said with a sigh, looking at the hot dog. Still, it could have been worse.

'That's actually an obscure model called Carole Wall. Liam Hughes just lifted the ads from American magazines, knowing full well the chances of me spotting them were slim. And he was right.' He gave a bitter laugh.

'So what happens now?' she ventured.

'Nothing.'

'But the money she's – he's – stolen from you, the DVDs . . .'

'Gone.'

'Surely that can't be it? What are the police going to do?'

'They can't do a thing unless I want to prosecute.'

'And do you?'

'What, stand up in some court and have the intimate details of my emails read out to a crowd of strangers? Try to explain how I could possibly believe that a woman like Sandy – had she existed – could have fallen in love with a man like me? No thanks. I've made enough of a fool of myself.'

He tore up the photo of Sandy on the beach and threw it into the bin. There was a very long silence.

Grace ventured, 'At least you still have your house.'

'At least I still have my house,' he repeated bravely. 'At least nothing was signed before I found out.'

'And your car.'

'He was never after my car.'

'I know, but I'm just saying. And your friends. Me, and Julia, and Nick.' She had meant this to be reassuring, but the little roll call just sounded short and sad. She thought of something else. 'And your health!'

'Oh, shut up, Grace.'

'Yes, sorry.'

He sighed and said, 'Deep down I knew it. Knew it couldn't be true. Grace, don't even say it, okay? Let's just be honest for a minute: I'm a middle-aged man with a strange job and no friends, and who hasn't had a date since – oh, it doesn't matter. The Sandys of this world don't go for men like me unless there's something in it for them. In her case a couple of kidneys.'

'And I think it says a lot about you that you were prepared to give them to her!' Grace said strongly.

'They're fictional. The kidneys.'

'It doesn't matter. She didn't pick just anybody, you

451

know. She only went for generous guys.'

'Is that supposed to be a compliment? And she is a he.'

'And guys that were easy to talk to. Well, she had to, if she was writing up to eleven emails a day!'

'Guys that were gullible, you mean.'

'Frank, if she was only trying to rip you off then she could have done it in less than eleven emails a day.'

'She had nothing better to do.'

'That's a lot of stuff to say to someone you despise or pity or just want to make fun of. A lot of personal stuff, *beautiful* stuff – do you remember the moth? And how she turned off all her lights so that it wouldn't burn itself? And she described what its wings looked like and you took out your books and looked up what it was?'

'She also described how her kidneys had shrivelled up like a couple of old prunes,' he said, but she could see he was affected. 'And she is a he.'

'So what, Frank. So what! Maybe you were both pretending to be things you weren't.'

'I never pretended!'

'So how come she thought you'd slept with eighty-two women?'

'Oh. Yes.'

'But it doesn't mean you didn't get on. It doesn't mean she didn't like you. Love you even, in her own way.'

Was this pushing it a bit far? She held her breath.

'She is a he,' Frank eventually said. He sounded a bit more robust. 'How many times do I have to keep telling you?'

Julia came in with a tray of drinks then, and her timing was so perfect that Grace knew she had been waiting inside the kitchen door. And she was glad that they had each other, Frank and Julia, their houses just right across the road. Because Lord knows nobody could *live* with either of them.

'I made them doubles,' Julia announced.

'I'll just go and clean up.' Frank gave a bit of a sniff and set off for the bathroom.

'Your limp seems to have improved,' Grace couldn't resist saying to Julia, as she deftly handed out drinks, pulled up the coffee table, and settled the bottle within top-up reach.

Julia gave her a look. 'Well, it's a while since you've seen me. But I know that you're busy with your own life . . .' She gave a little sigh, ever the drama queen.

'So are you,' Grace retaliated. 'Any time I ring, your phone is engaged!'

'That's because of the march. You *are* coming, aren't you?'

'Of course I am.'

'So is Michael. And maybe Gillian.' Julia lowered her voice. 'We're in the middle of peace negotiations. Michael is the broker.'

'That's great, Julia.'

'I have a list of things to apologise for, apparently. Don't hold your breath.' She took a big swig of her whiskey, and then said, 'I was talking to Martine today. Adam's case is in court next week. He's flying back for it.'

At the mention of his name, Grace tensed, her eyes flying to Julia's. 'Is he?'

But Julia was studying her glass. 'Martine wanted to come over for it – she says she feels half-responsible, seeing as he was part of her group – but the people she works for now have said no. They don't want to be associated with a lawless element, they said.'

'I suppose.' Grace didn't know how she felt.

'He should be given a medal in my opinion. Not many people stand up for what they believe in, and to hell with the consequences!' Then Julia reined herself in. 'Still. We must do things by the book these days.'

'Yes.'

Julia added, 'Anyway, I just thought you'd like to know. Seeing as we all shared a house together for a month.'

'Yes. Thank you, Julia.'

A week later Grace was driving back through County Meath.

She hadn't been meaning to go at all. She'd had no intention of it. She'd been sitting over a leisurely breakfast that morning, with her day all planned out. She'd had a lunch date arranged with Natalie, for goodness' sake. And she had suddenly wondered whether she would regret not going. She already had so many regrets in her life that she couldn't bear another one, so on the spur of the moment she had cancelled all her plans and jumped into the car.

Natalie hadn't been a bit impressed, of course.

'But *why*?'

'I don't know. Maybe I want to say goodbye to him.'

'So send him a postcard. You don't have to go and see him.'

'Nat, I can't explain it, okay? It's just been going around in my head like some kind of . . . oh, I don't know what.'

'A festering sore?' Natalie had jumped in.

'Well, no, it's not as big as that . . .'

'A nagging toothache then.'

'It's not really anything painful—'

'A niggling itch?'

'That's it exactly.' Anything for the sake of peace.

'If you want my opinion, I think you're making a big mistake,' Natalie had declared.

'Everything I've done recently has been a mistake according to you.'

'That's not true. Although I think that house-swap idea with those people in Spain *is* a big mistake.'

'It's not decided yet, it was just something Frank saw on the Internet . . .'

'And we all know his track record with the Internet.'

'I'm just toying with it, okay?'

'Grace, there are some things you don't toy with. And going to see Adam is one of them.'

'I'd like to know how he is.'

'What makes you think he would want to see you, anyway? You dumped him, his girlfriend is pregnant, and as far as he's concerned you're history!'

A bit stung, Grace had said, 'You don't know that – maybe it's a festering sore with him as well!'

'Maybe he has the sense to leave things alone. Oh – you said it was only a niggling itch!' She had said, very sternly, 'Are you still in love with him?'

'Oh, Natalie.'

'Not even a little bit?'

'No! I wasn't ever in love with him in the first place. Not properly in love anyway.'

'Really.'

Natalie would never understand, and Grace had long ago given up trying to explain it to her.

Natalie had finished off with, 'You're not going to start running after young lads now, are you, Grace? Now that you and Ewan have split up?'

'I don't know what I might run after. I'll have to see what takes my fancy.'

'Because you won't be popular, you know. A lot of our friends have teenage boys.'

'Adam was not a teenager. And you wanted a boy too, if I remember correctly.'

'Oh! I was pregnant! That was my hormones speaking! And I don't *ever* want you to mention that to Paul, okay?' And she had rung off quickly with some excuse about having to give Paul Jnr his bottle.

Grace saw a signpost for Trim now, and she had an odd kind of feeling: anticipation or something. Which was ridiculous! She had a whole new life now. Well, it wasn't quite there yet, it was still in the making – which was probably the fun part, like assembling a complicated toy which, when finished, didn't seem all that great given the amount of work that had gone into it. But it was still hers, and she was enjoying it.

And she began to wonder whether Natalie was right – what sense was there in stirring everything up again? Getting everyone all agitated and worked up over something that was all in the past anyhow?

But that was the thing: it wasn't.

It began to rain just as she reached the outskirts of Trim. By the time she had found the courthouse and parked, it was pouring. She pulled on her raincoat, hunted for her rather decrepit black umbrella and got out.

She felt nervous as she approached the courthouse entrance. A woman about the same age was going in too.

Grace nodded to her. 'Filthy day!'

'Mine's up for handling stolen goods,' the woman said, without being asked. 'What about yours?'

'Well, he's not actually my . . . we *were* . . . Disturbing the peace and damage to property.'

'What, like a pub? A shop front?'

'A microphone and two amps.'

The woman gave this some consideration and then declared, 'He'll get off with a fine.'

Grace was delighted. 'Do you think?'

'And maybe some community service.'

'That might be difficult. He's from Tasmania.'

'Well, that's even better!'

'Is it?'

'Justice Murphy, he generally doesn't go too hard on foreigners. You'll be fine, love.' She patted Grace's arm and disappeared into the building.

Grace huddled outside for a moment under her umbrella, reconsidering her entrance. What if he were standing in the dock, for instance, when she barged in? (Would he have to stand in the dock for damaging a couple of amps? She didn't even know that.) What if the sight of her threw him so much that he blurted 'Guilty!' when really he'd meant the opposite? What if, at the sight of *him*, she was so overcome with sudden emotion – or worst still, lust – that she jumped on him and started to drag his clothes off? Or her own? Mind you, she didn't think she would; she was confident that she had sufficiently detached herself from that period in her life – from him – to do anything silly.

Still, better to wait outside, she decided. That would make it more casual. She would catch him on his way out, and they could exchange a few civilised words on the pavement, like two acquaintances pausing for a brief, concluding chat, before continuing on their respective journeys. Yes, that was the effect she wanted exactly.

The problem was, it was lashing rain. And it was coming in at an angle too, and Grace was getting wet from mid-thigh down. Her hair was blowing into rats' tails as well, which was certainly *not* the effect she wanted.

'Shoot!' Now the umbrella refused to stay up, and kept collapsing on her head ('shoot' didn't express her feelings adequately at all, but she'd picked it up from Neil, who still spoke in an American dialect, and it was better than cursing and swearing on the step of a courthouse).

The pub across the road was rather aptly called The Crooked Penny, and Grace waited for a break in the rain and ran for it. She struggled in the door, ignoring the curious stares of the few mid-morning male drinkers, and shook herself like a wet hen. Hoping her mascara wasn't dripping, she went to the bar.

The barman was already reaching for the jug of filter coffee in anticipation. The presumption annoyed Grace, and she plonked herself down on a bar stool, and said, loudly, 'A gin and tonic, please.' Less loudly, she added, 'And a packet of those bacon fries.'

She was munching and sipping away and hoping the rain would soon let up when, out of the corner of her eye, she saw a man in a suit approach her. Honestly – a young mother couldn't have a couple of drinks in peace on a Tuesday morning in a tavern without some man thinking she was fair game! There was no real equality yet, she thought darkly.

She stared haughtily ahead, trying to think of some scathing put-down. She could say that she'd seen better-looking specimens crawling out of a sewer on a Saturday night. Or she could comment loudly on the bad smell (Natalie's favourite – old fashioned but effective, she maintained – not that she'd had cause to use it in recent years). Some of the younger girls in work had had some really nasty ones involving genital size and odour and Grace tried to remember them now. Oh, yes—

'Grace?'

The man in the suit was Adam. Any scathing put-downs about his manhood died in her throat.

'Adam?' she said, uncertainly.

No wonder she hadn't immediately recognised him: apart from the ill-fitting grey suit, which he wore over a white shirt that was too big around the neck, he was close-shaven and rather pale. Instead of his familiar big walking boots, he wore a pair of black leather shoes scrubbed so shiny that Grace could see her own startled expression in them.

'And your hair!' she cried indignantly. 'What have they done to it?'

It was gelled and combed and darker than she remembered. It was *short*.

'I had no choice,' he said, and Grace thought he sounded very tortured. What on earth could have happened to him? Instead of a free spirit, he looked like a double-glazing salesman!

Suddenly, it all came together in Grace's head with perfect clarity – of course! Amanda's pregnancy! Her family had shunned her, cast her heartlessly out into the world, and he had been forced to trade in his ideals for a nine to five job to support them both. It was very likely that he *was* a double-glazing salesman!

'Oh, Adam!' Her heart swelled with pity. She half expected him to whip out a glossy brochure.

He looked at her rather oddly. 'It'll grow back, Grace.'

'Sorry?'

'My hair. I did it for Judge Murphy. I haven't been in yet, but apparently he doesn't like long-haired louts.'

Grace felt presumptuous, at best. 'All this . . . it's for the court?'

'Of course. The suit, the shirt, the tie – it's all borrowed.'

'Really, there's no need to—'

'The shoes belong to my brother.' He gave her another look. 'You didn't think I was going to show up in court wearing shorts and a T-shirt?'

'Of course not,' she murmured, unwilling to offer her theory about PVC windows and sliding patio doors (he would hardly have been trying to flog them in Ireland, anyhow. Mind you, everything was gone global these days, in her defence. They sold fresh fish from the Mediterranean by post now). Still, anxious to make up for her speculation, she said, 'He likes foreigners, though. Judge Murphy.'

He looked a bit more cheerful. 'Do you reckon?'

'I have it on very good authority,' she said. 'I was over at the courthouse just now. That's why I came. To . . . wish you well.'

'Thanks, Grace.' He half smiled, then drummed his fingers nervously on the counter. 'I just hope I don't get a prison sentence. I can't go to prison – not with . . . well, not with everything.'

'I know,' she said, even though she didn't. Did he mean Amanda and the baby? Or the next big anti-nuclear demonstration? She felt she couldn't ask – things weren't like that between them any more. In fact, it was all a bit more awkward than she'd antici-pated. She found herself searching for a neutral topic of conversation – dear God, what did you say to a young man you'd spent a month bonking? – and was about to make some clumsy excuse and leave when Adam said, 'Do you mind if I sit down?'

'Um, not at all.'

He joined her on a barstool. 'It's just that these

shoes are a size too small and, to be honest, they hurt like hell.'

Both of them looked down at the shoes. Along with being mean in size, the leather looked particularly tough and unyielding.

'I suppose you could take them off,' Grace suggested eventually, veteran of hundreds of pairs of uncomfortable shoes.

'In a pub?'

'Why not? Nobody's looking.'

And indeed they weren't. The other male drinkers in the pub had lost all interest now that someone else had apparently got in ahead of them with Grace. And a slip of a lad too!

Adam slipped off the shoes surreptitiously. And almost immediately he seemed to relax, to become more himself, as though deep down he were a creature of nature that would resist any attempt by fashion, or the courts system, to rein him in.

Some of the tension in the air had gone with the shoes, and she was glad. They looked at each other for a little moment, and Adam said, 'Thanks for coming today. It's good to see you.'

'You too.'

'How are the boys?'

'Great.'

'And Jamie's . . . you know?'

'Nearly gone, thank God. He still won't go anywhere without wearing a baggy jumper though.' She looked at him. 'And how are you?'

He gave a jumpy grin. 'Apart from a court appearance in half an hour?'

'It'll go okay,' Grace assured him. 'You're still in touch with Martine, I gather?'

He gave a bit of a snort. 'She rings me occasionally – she gets bored sitting on her ass at a swanky desk all day long. Selling out to the establishment didn't turn out to be everything she'd thought.'

Still as radical as ever. And he hadn't mentioned Amanda yet. Another theory began to form in Grace's head, and not a particularly attractive one: was it possible that Adam had decided that early fatherhood didn't suit him? Had he told the hapless Amanda to sling her hook, that he was off to save the world?

'Why are you looking at me like that?' Adam asked.

'Oh, I wasn't—'

'You were!' He was indignant. 'Like I did something rotten on you!' He shot her a glance. 'You were the one who dumped me, if I remember correctly.'

There. It was out in the open. But he said it without any great heat, and she didn't know whether she was relieved or miffed. Then she was amused by her own vanity.

'I suppose I did,' she agreed.

Adam played with a beer mat. 'And how's Ewan?'

'Pretty good. I think.'

He stopped playing with the beer mat and looked up.

'Ewan and I have split up, Adam.'

'What?'

'Amicably, I think is the term. We're sorting out the conditions of the separation at the moment. I initiated it, by the way.' She drew herself up on her bar stool, tossed back her hair over the ankle-length wool

463

cardigan she'd knitted herself (she'd got a bit carried away) and went on, 'And I've gone back to college – I'm doing design. I was top of the class at the end of the first term. And I'm writing a science fiction book. Well, I just started it on Friday, but I've got five pages written already, and Natalie thinks it's really good. And I'm probably going to be summering in Spain, if a time-share thing works out.' She was going to mention too that she had collected more Computers For Schools tokens than any other mother, but that would just sound like boasting.

Adam said nothing for a moment, just watched her with that old expression of affection mixed in with mockery.

'Are you laughing at me?' she said. She decided that she didn't care anyway.

'Not at all. I'm just thinking that I can't top that.'

'It's an age thing,' she said sweetly. 'You'll get there eventually.'

Any further banter was cut short when the door of the ladies' toilet opened, and Amanda emerged.

'Grace!' she squealed joyously. She hurried up and swatted Adam on the arm. 'You never said she was coming today!'

'I didn't know,' Adam said.

'I didn't know myself, really,' Grace confirmed.

Any further speculation as to Amanda's position in Adam's life was laid to rest when she put her arm around him tenderly and patted her belly.

'I spend most of my time in the loo,' she said confidentially to Grace. 'It's the baby. It's on my bladder, you see.'

Grace dutifully had a look. Underneath a multi-coloured hippy smock-top, Amanda's pregnancy was a small, hard, neat bump, no bigger than a honeydew melon – in fact, Grace was half convinced it *was* a honeydew melon until Amanda took her hand without invitation and placed it on her belly.

'There! That's you two introduced!' she giggled, and Grace had that old familiar urge to slap her very hard.

'Congratulations,' she said instead, retrieving her hand. 'I'm delighted for you.'

'We are too,' Adam said evenly.

'Well, *eventually*,' Amanda said tartly, giving Adam a little look. 'It's taken a little while to get used to it,' she told Grace.

'Of course it has,' Grace said. 'I remember when I was pregnant with the twins. I didn't know what to expect. Suddenly everything is different, *you're* different, you're going to become a parent, and you start worrying to yourself that you haven't the first clue about anything!'

'That's it exactly!' Amanda cried. 'I knew you'd understand, Grace.'

'We've got books and stuff,' Adam interjected strongly. 'We're not going to make a complete mess of it.'

'Of course not,' Amanda said. 'It's just probably not a good idea for us to go on that campaign in Chile next month. Supposing my waters break?' She added to Grace, 'He thinks I can just squat down and give birth in some bush hospital.'

'As opposed to a private suite in the hospital your

465

father is on the board of?' Adam shot back.

Amanda sighed. 'He just *offered*. We don't have to take him up on it.'

'And we won't.' Adam looked steely. 'No child of mine will be born with a silver spoon in its mouth!'

Amanda looked to Grace again in despair. 'We're not talking about silver spoons. It's just that Daddy feels offended that we won't accept any help.'

Grace made a diplomatic 'um' kind of sound, and watched the squabbling from some detached place in her head. And she suddenly saw how right they were for each other, Adam and Amanda. Adam needed someone to bring him down to earth every now and again, and Amanda was just the woman for the job. But she had spirit too, in her own way.

Grace finished up her gin and tonic and snuck a glance at her watch. If she hurried, she could still make her lunch date with Natalie. And there was a lecture this afternoon in college on period costumes that she would really love to catch.

She suddenly felt a great urge to leave the pub now, to get on with things. That feeling of anticipation that she'd had all morning wasn't anything to do with Adam at all, she realised. Or anybody else, for that matter. It was entirely to do with her.

Amanda and Adam were still arguing. 'Daddy does kind of have a point, Adam, about us not having any jobs, or anywhere to live, or even a nappy to put on the baby when it's born.'

'Ellsworth will have a nappy,' Adam declared.

There was a little silence. 'Ellsworth?' Amanda ventured.

Adam shrugged, a bit embarrassed. 'I thought that's what we might call the baby. It means "lover of the land".'

Amanda's bossiness dissolved into dreamy adoration. 'Oh, Adam. I think it's beautiful.'

'Yeh?' Then he looked at Grace. 'What do you think?'

Grace thought that the child wouldn't thank either of them when it got to school age – look at poor Dusty – but that was something they would have to learn. Grace had finished giving out advice a while ago.

'I think that it's none of my business,' she said lightly. She slid off her bar stool and reached for her umbrella.

'You can't go yet!' Amanda said. 'We haven't caught up properly at all!'

'I know. But I'm in a rush.' She leaned over and sort of patted Amanda (a hug would be going too far). 'Good luck with the baby.'

'Thanks, Grace. We'll let you know any news, won't we, Adam?'

'Just tell Martine,' Grace said. 'She'll pass it on.'

Adam walked her to the door. 'Are you sure you won't stay for a drink?'

'No. I'd better be getting back.'

'All right,' he said. 'I'm glad you came, Grace.'

'Me too.'

She turned to face him at the door. He seemed awkward and inexperienced in a way that she had never seen before.

'Maybe we can meet up again sometime?' he said. 'You know, when I'm back in Ireland . . .'

'Adam.' She smiled at him affectionately. 'Let's just say goodbye, will we?'

'I suppose.' He put out his hand to shake hers. 'Goodbye, Grace.'

'Oh, Adam.' She brushed his hand aside and leaned in and kissed him on the cheek warmly. Then she turned and left the pub.

It was still pouring outside. She lifted her umbrella.

'Blast!'

It refused to yield to persuasion. She tried again. This time it went up halfway before two spokes snapped and reared malevolently through the black plastic. She huddled under it and made a dash across the road to her car, trying to dodge puddles on the way. Eventually she stopped trying to dodge them, and she began to jump from one to the other. She lifted the broken umbrella high over her head, and she did a little pirouette.

Too Good To Be True

Sheila O'Flanagan

Can love at first sight last a lifetime?

Air-traffic controller Carey Browne is used to handling unpredictable situations. So when Ben Russell, a man she's known all of five minutes, proposes, she calmly deals with the matter – and accepts, much to the horror of her family and friends.

Has the woman gone completely mad?

Despite their disapproval, and the icy reception from Ben's sister, Freya, Carey is determined to make the marriage work. She knows she's found her soulmate. If only everyone would leave them alone.

But it seems that Ben hasn't been entirely honest about his past, and Carey soon starts to wonder whether she's made a dreadful mistake. After all, something so perfect must be too good to be true . . . mustn't it?

Praise for Sheila O'Flanagan's bestsellers

'A must-read' *Woman's Own*

'The Sheila O'Flanagan guarantee is a pretty powerful one' *Irish Independent*

'Witty and touching' *Family Circle*

'The appeal is obvious . . . a romantic, feel-good factor, they're funny and she doesn't shy away from emotional issues' *Irish Post*

'Highly readable' *Daily Express*

0 7553 2380 7

headline

Nadia Knows Best

Jill Mansell

When Nadia Kinsella meets Jay Tiernan, she's tempted, of course she is. Stranded together in a remote Cotswold pub while a snowstorm rages outside . . . let's face it, who would ever know?

But Nadia's already met The One. She and Laurie have been together for years – they're practically childhood sweet-hearts and she still gets butterflies in her stomach at the sight of him. Okay, so maybe she doesn't see that much of him these days, but that's not Laurie's fault. She can't betray him.

Besides, when you belong to a family like the Kinsellas – bewitchingly glamorous grandmother Miriam, feckless mother Leonie, stop-at-nothing sister Clare – well, someone has to exercise a bit of self-control, don't they? I mean, you wouldn't want to do something that you might later regret . . .

Acclaim for Jill Mansell's novels:

'Fast, furious and fabulous fun. To read it is to devour it' *Company*

'Slick, sexy, funny stories' *Daily Telegraph*

'A sure-fire bestseller from the queen of chicklit' *Heat*

'An exciting read about love, friendship and sweet revenge – fabulously fun' *Home & Life*

'A jaunty summer read' *Daily Mail*

'Riotous' *New Woman*

'A romantic romp full of larger than life characters' *Daily Express*

0 7472 6488 0

headline

The Sweetest Taboo

Carole Matthews

Falling in love is never easy.

Sadie Nelson ought to know – she's got two men to choose from and neither one is hassle-free.

First there's Gil McGann, a Hollywood producer who's flown her from a grey day in London to sun-soaked LA in order to win her heart. He has more to offer Sadie than she could ever have imagined . . .

Then there's gorgeous actor Tavis Jones, whose sense of fun makes Sadie feel immediately at home. But can they ever be more than just good friends?

The longer she leaves it, the harder it gets, and Sadie's about to discover that in LA anything can happen . . .

'A cracking book that'll keep you guessing right to the last page' *More* magazine

'Classic boy-meets-girl chick fic' *Daily Mirror*

'Feel good chick lit . . . with plenty of hilarious scenarios along the way' *OK!* magazine

'A fabulous read' *Glasgow Evening Times*

0 7472 6770 7

headline

Now you can buy any of these other bestselling
Headline books from your bookshop or
direct from the publisher.

FREE P&P AND UK DELIVERY
(Overseas and Ireland £3.50 per book)

A Married Man	Catherine Alliott	£6.99
Olivia's Luck	Catherine Alliott	£6.99
Cuban Heels	Emily Barr	£6.99
Amazing Grace	Clare Dowling	£6.99
Pure Fiction	Julie Highmore	£6.99
Azur Like It	Wendy Holden	£6.99
Falling For You	Jill Mansell	£6.99
Nadia Knows Best	Jill Mansell	£6.99
A Compromising Position	Carole Matthews	£6.99
The Sweetest Taboo	Carole Matthews	£6.99
Right on Time	Pauline McLynn	£6.99
Too Good To be True	Sheila O'Flanagan	£6.99
Dreaming of A Stranger	Sheila O'Flanagan	£6.99

TO ORDER SIMPLY CALL THIS NUMBER

01235 400 414

or visit our website: www.madaboutbooks.com

Prices and availability subject to change without notice.